Vengeance

Susan Lewis is the bestselling author of twenty-eight novels. She is also the author of *Just One More Day* and *One Day at a Time*, the moving memoirs of her childhood in Bristol. She lives in Gloucestershire. Her website address is www.susanlewis.com

Acclaim for Susan Lewis

'One of the best around' *Independent on Sunday*

'Spellbinding! ... you just keep turning the pages, with the atmosphere growing more and more intense as the story leads to its dramatic climax' *Daily Mail*

'Mystery and romance *par excellence*' *Sun*

'... tale of conspiracy and steamy passion will keep you intrigued until the final page' *Bella*

'A multi-faceted tearjerker' *heat*

'Erotic and exciting' *Sunday Times*

'We use the term "a good read" far too lightly: it should be reserved for books like this' ...his'

'Susan L ... ons

Also by Susan Lewis

A Class Apart
Dance While You Can
Stolen Beginnings
Darkest Longings
Obsession
Summer Madness
Last Resort
Wildfire
Chasing Dreams
Taking Chances
Cruel Venus
Strange Allure
Silent Truths
Wicked Beauty
Intimate Strangers
The Hornbeam Tree
The Mill House
A French Affair
Missing
Out of the Shadows
Lost Innocence
The Choice
Forgotten
Stolen
No Turning Back
Losing You
No Child of Mine

Just One More Day, A Memoir
One Day at a Time, A Memoir

SUSAN LEWIS

Vengeance

arrow books

Published by Arrow Books 2007

8 10 9

First published in Great Britain in 1994 by William Heinemann
First published in paperback in 1994 by Mandarin Paperbacks
Arrow Books
Random House, 20 Vauxhall Bridge Road,
London SW1V 2SA

www.randomhouse.co.uk

Addresses for companies within The Random House Group Limited can be found at: www.randomhouse.co.uk/offices.htm

The Random House Group Limited Reg. No. 954009

A CIP catalogue record for this book
is available from the British Library

ISBN 9780099514725

The Random House Group Limited supports The Forest Stewardship Council® (FSC®), the leading international forest-certification organisation. Our books carrying the FSC label are printed on FSC®-certified paper. FSC is the only forest-certification scheme supported by the leading environmental organisations, including Greenpeace. Our paper procurement policy can be found at www.randomhouse.co.uk/environment

Printed and bound in Great Britain by Clays Ltd, St Ives plc

For an absent friend

Acknowledgements

I should like to express my thanks to all those who helped me in New Orleans, especially Carrie Jo Martina at the Richelieu Hotel, Little Joe Catalanotto of Independent Studios, Danny, whose guidance and friendship was greatly appreciated, Sargeant Wayne H. Cooper of the New Orleans Police Department and Dr Paul Wagner of Honey Island.

On a personal as well as professional level I thank my editor, Helen Fraser, for her invaluable support.

My love and thanks go also to my cousin Karen Shields and to my friends Lesley Morgan, Bridget Anderson, Barbara Thorn, Pat Cockram and, of course, Denise Hastie who were with me throughout the writing of this book and so much more. Most especially of all though, I should like to thank Carl and Brenda Clump, they know why.

Vengeance is mine, said the Lord; but why wait for the Almighty when He had given her the power to seek it for herself. So vengeance would be hers. She would use the mightiest of her weapons, she would expose the temptress and watch her squirm in the spotlight of degradation and contempt until she was spurned by those she loved, ridiculed and scorned by those she knew, and damned by all. She would pay for taking that which was not hers, she would learn, slowly and painfully, that she would never have that which she wanted: love, friendship, trust. For her there would be nothing, not even death. There would be only a living hell, an interminable journey of suffering and a timeless reaping of her own iniquity.

Dermott Campbell lifted his head and looked into the expressionless eyes observing him. For a brief moment a mean relish flickered in his own revealing the pleasure he took in having the power to carry out the destruction he had just outlined. Then his lips, strangely effeminate in a face that was otherwise so masculine, curved tremulously at the corners, showing the discomfort he felt under her scrutiny.

'Kirsten's on her way back,' he said squinting, as though creasing his eyes could disguise the nervous tic in his temple. 'She'll be arriving tomorrow.'

The woman seated opposite him casually crossed one leg over the other and nodded, barely perceptibly.

It was hard for Campbell not to squirm. His hand moved to the slim file he'd placed on the table between them. As he opened it his heart was thudding with revulsion at what he was about to do. For a moment he almost panicked and only by sheer effort of will did he manage to calm himself. But maybe he could hold off, maybe he could get the co-operation he needed without ever revealing the contents of the file. To destroy one life was enough, was, in these circumstances, about all he could stomach.

'You know her,' he said, pressing the file closed. 'You can help me. You know her secrets, you know her past. You've studied her . . .' He stopped at the look of confusion that came into her eyes. 'OK, perhaps studied isn't quite the right word,' he said. 'It's my employer who has studied her, diligently, for the past five years. That's how your name has come up. You know as much about her as anyone is ever likely to know. You knew her back then, can you help me.'

'And why in the world would I do that?'

'Because if you don't, I'm finished.'

Campbell flinched at the look of astonishment and amusement. 'But you've been washed-up for a long time, Dermott,' she said smoothly. 'No one dances to your tune any more. Least of all me.' She laughed. 'Oh, sure, the column still goes under your name, but everyone knows you no longer write it. Your glory days are long gone, Dermott.'

'I'm making a come-back,' he said, feeling as foolish as he sounded.

She nodded as though interested, but the smile of derision remained on her lips. 'And Kirsten Meredith is your target?' she said. 'Tell me, what's she ever done to you?'

Campbell's head jerked to one side in annoyance. 'Look,' he said, failing to conceal his impatience, 'in this life it's dog eat dog. And if destroying Kirsten Meredith is the only means by which I can get back on top, then so be it.'

'And *you* want *me* to help you?' The pedantic reply came with such contemptuous incredulity that Campbell actually blushed.

'You've got to help me,' he said, his voice barely audible.

'*Got* to?'

Campbell nodded. 'Dyllis had given me this,' he said, pushing the file across the desk.

He was slightly appeased to see a slight crack opening

in the implacable composure at the mention of Dyllis Fisher. As the undisputed baroness of Fleet Street and empirical ruler of banks, underwriters, heavy industry, big businesses and political campaigns, the power Dyllis Fisher wielded was awesome. 'I have been instructed,' he continued as his companion scanned the contents of the file, 'to make this public if you refuse.'

He waited, his hands clenched together so tightly it hurt. Once, and only once before she had finished did she raise her eyes to his. Those strangely youthful and alluring eyes that haunted him almost to the point of madness.

At last she replaced the file on the table. 'You'd do this to me, you'd do it to Kirsten, and all to save yourself?' she said, her tone so scathing that Campbell felt as nauseated by the wave of self-disgust as she'd intended. 'I don't intend to do anything to you,' he answered. 'That,' he said, prodding the file, 'will never be made public . . .'

'Just so long as I dish the dirt on Kirsten Meredith?'

He stared at her. 'There's big money in this,' he said. 'Dyllis is a generous woman when she wants to be.'

'And my fee is thirty pieces of silver? What's yours? Oh, I'm forgetting, your come-back.'

Once again Campbell coloured. He lifted his glasses from the table and put them on, as if by doing so he could shield himself from the panic rising in her eyes – a panic her manner so far belied.

A sudden brittle laugh erupted from her throat and though it surprised him he knew it was an indication that she was as afraid to say no as he had been. So she should be, for neither of them had what it would take to stand up against Dyllis Fisher, particularly not her.

Agitation brought her sharply to her feet. Campbell

watched her as she paced the room. Should he tell her that he despised himself far more than she ever could for what he was prepared to do? Would it make a difference? Such a fatuous question. 'All I'm asking,' he said, 'is that you tell me whatever you know about her. The facts can always be embellished and I will take sole responsibility for that.'

'You do realize,' she said, 'that any scandal you fabricate about Kirsten will almost inevitably involve other innocent parties?'

Campbell had been waiting for that, but the cruel truth of her words stung him nevertheless.

'Are you going to feel good about putting your best friend's life under the microscope?' she challenged. 'Do you want the whole world to know what he did to Kirsten?'

'There are ways and ways of telling a story,' he defended himself lamely.

'I can't help you,' she said with sudden bravado. 'I'm just not going to be a part of it. She's suffered enough . . .'

'And you care more about that than you do your own mother?' he said, looking at the file.

'Yes.'

Shit, he groaned inwardly. *She means it.*

She was eyeing him now with all the distaste he felt at himself. But to hell with it. This was no time to entangle himself in a web of spineless chivalry – and what did it matter if a few reputations were damaged, a few raw nerves exposed. God knew, he'd trampled over enough lives in his heyday and had never thought twice about it.

He forced himself to meet the burning, yet still uneasy, gaze of the woman he loved. It was time now, he knew, to play his trump card. Did he have the courage for it? Could he really take the envelope containing the most damning evidence of all which he had secreted in his pocket and confront her with it? Dear God in heaven, was he really capable of this kind of blackmail?

A few minutes later, still trembling with the effect of watching her break the seal, Campbell pressed his fingers to his tired eyes as he heard her say, in a voice so strained that he too could feel the tightness choking him:

'Until now I had always believed that everyone, you included, had at least one shred of decency in them.' She threw the envelope back across the table as though anything that had been touched by him was foully contaminated.

'We're not talking decency,' he replied dully, unable to meet her eyes, 'we're talking survival.'

'And you seriously think that any of us are going to survive this?'

'Some might.'

'Then I hope to God it's not you.'

– 1 –

'Honestly, I'm not interested,' Jane said.

'What do you mean, you're not interested! He's got heaps of money, oodles of charm, a flashy car . . . What is it he drives, Laurence?' Pippa asked, turning to her husband.

'God knows,' Laurence murmured, not taking his eyes from the morning paper as he sipped his coffee.

'Well, it's a smart one,' Pippa said forcefully. 'And he dresses rather snazzily, you've got to admit that.'

'I've only seen him once,' Jane giggled, the colour in her normally pallid cheeks deepening, 'and he didn't notice me at all. So please, Pippa, don't say anything to him,' and in an attempt to end this embarrassing conversation Jane too picked up a newspaper.

'Mm,' Pippa grunted, 'I suppose he is a bit full of himself, men like that often take some time to notice anyone else. But we could work on it.'

Jane reached across the breakfast table to Tom, Pippa and Laurence's three-year-old son, trying to extract a soggy piece of toast from his hand. For a moment or two Pippa watched her, a vague and unpalatable feeling of irritation injecting itself into the otherwise genuine fondness she felt for the girl. Pippa wasn't too sure why, but for some reason she felt almost as responsible for Jane and her welfare as she did for Tom's. And feeling responsible wasn't something Pippa particularly enjoyed. Laurence was much better at it.

Still, there wasn't a bad bone to be found in Jane's scrawny little body, which, to Pippa's mind, made her about as dull as it made her irritating. But as Tom quite simply adored her, almost as much as Jane did Tom, Pippa considered herself extremely fortunate in having such a perfect nanny.

Catching Pippa watching her Jane gave one of her annoyingly self-conscious giggles. Pippa bit down hard on her irritation. Jane had been with them for over three years now and still Pippa hadn't managed to break her of that infuriating habit. Still, Pippa reminded herself, she mustn't concentrate on Jane's shortcomings, in fact why should she concentrate on Jane at all when she had so much else to think about.

Realizing she was temporarily off the hook Jane picked up her tea and turned another page of the newspaper. She loved breakfast time when the whole family, and she counted herself as one of the family now, sat down together in the basement kitchen of their Kensington home, idling away the first half hour of the day where the mouthwatering smells of toast and freshly ground coffee filled the cluttered room. As usual the radio was playing, though this morning it could barely be heard above the frantic chattering of the birds coming through the open french windows and Tom's cheerful little conversation with his imaginary friend. Despite having spent all his short life in England, Tom had almost as pronounced an American accent as his father's and at times as colourful a vocabulary, which only a few moments ago he had been reprimanded for.

'Laurence! You must know someone we could invite along for Jane,' Pippa suddenly declared, coming out of her reverie. 'What about that researcher of yours? He's single, isn't he?'

'Oh, Pippa, stop it, please!' Jane groaned. 'I don't want to meet anyone, honestly.'

'But a girl's got to have some fun,' Pippa protested. 'It's not normal to shut yourself away like you do with only Tom for company.'

Jane smiled as Tom's huge blue eyes gazed up at her waiting to see what she would say. 'What are we going to do with Mummy?' she said to him. 'How do we get her to take no for an answer?'

'If I were you, Jane,' Laurence said, leaning back in his chair and reaching out to stroke the back of Pippa's neck, 'I'd just tell her to mind her own business.'

Jane watched as Pippa turned to Laurence. She could no longer see Pippa's face, but she could see Laurence's as he gazed into Pippa's eyes, and for just a second or two Jane felt like an intruder. She turned to Tom who was now wheeling his toy train around his breakfast dish while mashing an eggshell with a spoon.

She started to clean him up half-listening to Pippa and Laurence as Pippa cleared the table then weaved her way through Tom's toys to the sink while discussing her schedule for that week. Laurence stood up, waited for Jane to finish with Tom then swung him up into his arms. Jane smiled as she watched them, loving the way Tom responded to his father. He adored Laurence and was never happier than when he was with him. Pippa could, and often did, go away for days on end, but Tom was never so fretful at her absence as he was at Laurence's. Which, in it's way, was a good thing since Pippa, as a freelance editor with authors dotted around all over Europe, was away a good deal more often than her film-producer husband, who, unless in production, worked mainly from home. In fact, probably because she saw so much of him, there were times when Jane wondered if she didn't know Laurence better than Pippa did. She guessed she knew more about him, at least so far as his professional life went, since he conducted so many meetings at home. Jane also knew when Laurence was being subjected to the over-zealous attentions of an actress, or make-up artist or female journalist, for it frequently fell to her to ward them off. As far as she knew Laurence had never been unfaithful to Pippa, but Jane could hardly blame these women for trying, since Laurence, with his unruly mass of black hair, piercing blue eyes and devastating smile was quite simply the most handsome man Jane had ever set eyes on. And, at six feet three inches tall, with the hard, muscular body of an athlete and the self-mocking humour of someone at odds with his looks, he was, in Jane's book, just about perfect in every way.

Fortunately for Jane she was over her crush on him now, but it had taken some time – almost two years in fact. Now, at last, she could look at him and no longer suffer those stomach-wrenching surges of adoration and, of course, disloyalty. But even worse had been the horribly deep-rooted humiliation. She'd known throughout that miserable time that a man like Laurence McAllister would never be interested in someone like her, would probably not even notice her existence were it not for the fact that she was his son's nanny, but sadly that knowledge had done nothing to quell her feelings. Neither had the fact that he was so much older than her, almost the same age as her father.

But at last the pain was over. Jane could never be too sure exactly when it was that her feelings had changed, that the unbearably exquisite ache in her heart had ceased to be there and the churning knots in her stomach at last unfurled. All she knew was that one day, about a year ago now, she had suddenly realized that she was looking at him and feeling only a very genuine affection, unencumbered by the pain of longing. It had surprised her, delighted her and in a way disappointed her, for the buzz of excitement she'd always experienced when in the same room as him had died leaving her feeling as drab, perhaps even drabber than she had felt before. But that didn't really matter too much, she'd told herself brightly, as long as she had Tom, this perfect child whose mischief and tempers were as like his father's as his thick, glossy black curls and heart-stoppingly blue eyes, she would have all she needed. And who could say, perhaps before much longer he would have a little brother or sister she could dote on too.

Now, as Laurence rested Tom in the crook of his arm and he and Pippa started to discuss their plans for that day, Jane returned to the newspaper, helping herself to another slice of toast. She was on the point of biting into it when she suddenly stopped. It was the strangest thing. She couldn't explain it, all she knew was that this wasn't the first time something like this had happened to her, and in its way it was quite frightening. To be able to look at someone and to know that that person was going to play an important, if not vital role, in her life was as bizarre as it was inexplicable. And even odder was the fact that the person she was looking at now was Kirsten Meredith, a woman she had never met, nor, so far as she could tell, was she ever likely to meet.

'Oh, old Dermott's not laying into her again, is he?' Pippa said, coming to read over Jane's shoulder as Laurence wandered out of the kitchen. 'What's he saying this time? No, I'm not sure I want to know. By the way, did you give Laurence the message that he'd called yesterday?'

'Yes,' Jane said, turning up her nose.

Pippa laughed. It wasn't very often that Jane took a dislike to someone, but she certainly had to Dermott Campbell, who, to Jane's dismay, had been an all too regular visitor at South Edwardes Square these past couple of years.

As Pippa turned away Jane discreetly pushed the newspaper into the side drawer of the table. She would read it later when there was no one around.

A few minutes later the telephone rang and Jane reached out to answer it. 'Oh, hello, Mrs McAllister,' she said. 'Yes, Tom's right here. No we didn't have anything special planned today . . .' She turned to Tom. 'Are you going to speak to Granny?' she asked.

'Granny Mac!' Tom whooped and shot across the room to take the phone.

The way Tom referred to Laurence's extremely elegant, rather snobbish American mother as Granny Mac, never failed to amuse Jane for it was difficult to imagine anyone who looked less like a Granny, but that Thea McAllister and her grandson were devoted to each other was beyond question. In fact, Don McAllister, Laurence's Scottish father, had retired early from the diplomatic service, leaving his post in Washington DC – where Laurence had spent most of his childhood until going to University at Oxford – to move back to London, so that he and his wife could be near their grandson.

As Tom chattered on with his grandmother and Laurence strolled back into the kitchen Jane became aware of Pippa's mounting tension. She knew that Pippa disliked Thea McAllister and though Jane liked Thea herself, she could understand why Pippa didn't. Thea was an overbearing woman who was possessive enough of her son and grandson to make any wife and mother uncomfortable, but in Pippa's case there was more than mere discomfort. She'd only recently confided to Jane that the 'damned woman' made her feel so ridiculously guilty.

'And it's not as though I've got anything to feel guilty about,' Pippa had grumbled. 'But whenever she looks at me I feel like she's accusing me of something.'

Jane would never dream of saying so, but she too thought that Thea's manner towards Pippa held a certain, well yes, a certain sort of reproach, but then she guessed that was fairly typical in a mother-in-law and didn't really set too much store by it.

'So,' Pippa said now as she stacked the breakfast things into the dishwasher, 'we still haven't resolved the problem of who we are going to invite to the party for you next Saturday.'

'Oh hell, you're not back on that are you?' Laurence groaned. 'Give the girl a break, why don't you?'

'Well maybe if you were to come up with some suggestions . . .' Pippa snapped.

'I'm off,' Laurence said, 'some of us have work to do.'

'When don't you have work to do?' Pippa remarked sourly, but Laurence didn't answer, he simply left the kitchen and ran upstairs to his study.

To Jane's relief Pippa didn't pursue the subject of finding an escort, instead she turned her attention to Tom, who had finished speaking to his grandmother and was trying to reach up to the TV set to turn it on.

'You'll pull the damned thing on to your head one of these days,' Pippa barked, smacking his hands away.

Tom looked up at her, hugging his hands to his chest.

'And don't look at me like that,' Pippa said irritably. 'I've told you a thousand times, you watch too much TV and I'm not having it. Now tidy up these blasted toys before someone breaks their neck.'

As Pippa turned away Tom dropped forlornly to his knees his bottom lip starting to tremble as he fought back his tears. Quietly Jane set about helping him reload his toy box while Pippa continued to slam about the kitchen. They were all well used to these sudden mood swings of Pippa's, which usually preceded a spell away from home – and Pippa was flying to Italy the next day and would be gone until the end of the week. For all her protestations that she had nothing to feel guilty about, she obviously did feel guilty about the amount of time she spent away from Tom and because he made her feel guilty he annoyed her. Though not half so much as Laurence seemed to lately, Jane reflected, and felt her heart sink as Pippa suddenly rounded on her, her violet eyes flashing and her pretty mouth tight with anger.

'How dare that bastard speak to me like that!' she said. 'Anyone would think that he was the only one around here who's got a career. Oh, but I'm forgetting, aren't I, his is the only one that matters. Mine's just a little indulgence, nothing to be taken seriously, well I'm going to tell him just where he gets off patronizing me,' and pushing Tom out of her way she stormed up the stairs.

Picking Tom up Jane carried him out to the garden and settled him in his swing hoping they were far enough out of earshot for him not to hear the inevitable row that was brewing. It would be over almost as soon as it had begun, Jane was sure of that, for Laurence had a way of handling Pippa that, as much as it infuriated her, Pippa could never resist. And as Jane envisaged Laurence's startled face when his indignant wife crashed into his study she smiled fondly to herself and swung Tom up in the air.

'For Christ's sake, Pippa, just listen to yourself, will you?' Laurence sighed, throwing a pen down on his desk and turning in his chair. 'You're over-reacting and you know it!'

'Oh am I? Well as it so happens I think I've got something to over-react about. You speak to me as though I'm a complete imbecile and right in front of Jane too! Then you walk out of the kitchen like Mr

Important Producer Himself and to hell with everyone else, then you've got the fucking audacity to tell me I should have knocked before I came in here. This is my home as well, in case you'd forgotten.'

'All? I said was the door was shut because I didn't want to be disturbed. I still don't want to be . . .'

'Well tough fucking luck! I'm here now and you're going to bloody well apologize to me for the way you spoke to me just now.'

Laurence shrugged, still not too sure what it was he'd said. 'OK, I apologize,' he grinned. 'Happy now?'

'There you go again!' Pippa seethed, throwing up her hands in exasperation. 'I'm not a fucking child . . .'

'Then why don't you stop behaving like one.'

'Perhaps I would if you started behaving like a husband!'

Laurence's face tightened. He knew what she was going to say next, but she sure as hell wasn't going to get any encouragement from him. Besides, they'd been over and over this these past six months and right now he had other, more immediate things he needed to deal with.

'It's still the same, is it?' she said, waspishly. 'You're too busy to spend a little time with your wife and son. You just want to be locked away in here, undisturbed! Well, pardon me for interrupting you, but like it or not we're going to damn well have this out.'

'Pippa, why don't you just go pack your suitcases and check your flight reservations.'

He ducked as the book flew across the room and slammed against the wall behind him.

'Don't do that again,' he said quietly.

'I want your attention, God damn you! I want you to look at me, to listen to me . . .'

'I've listened, Pippa. I've listened and understood. You don't want that we go and live in the States. So we stay here.'

'We stay here because I've got a career too,' she yelled. 'What the hell would I do in fucking Hollywood? I hate the place, all those phoney people . . .'

'I said, we stay here.'

'And now you're punishing me for it. You lock yourself away in here and don't come out from morning till midnight. Well I can't stand it, do you hear me? I can't put up with it any more!'

'Pippa, I'm in here because I need to work. Because getting a movie off the ground in this country is next to impossible. I don't have to remind you what happened the last time and one failure is already one too many. I can't afford for that to happen again. Now will you just quit thinking about yourself for once and leave me in peace?'

'I don't suppose for one minute you'd throw Tom out if he walked in here, would you? On no, not your precious son. It's only his mother you can't tolerate . . .'

'Because his mother should know better. And being jealous of your own son isn't healthy, Pippa.'

'How can I help being jealous of him when all he has to do is bat his eyelids and you're all over him. What do I have to do, Laurence? What do I do to get your attention? Does Alison have this problem? Do you ignore her, too? Of course you do, but she still comes back for more, doesn't she? They all do, don't they, Laurence? We all want you and there's not enough of you to go round. So who's the one to suffer? Not your son, no, never him! Not your goddamned mother either. And certainly not your mistress. Do you listen to her when she needs to talk, or do you just fuck her? Do you do

– 17 –

it here, in this room, when I'm not around? No, I'll bet you don't, your darling Thomas might walk in and that would never do, would it? Do you think of me when you're with her, Laurence? Do you think of her when you're with me? Or are you just thinking about your precious movies the whole time, because that's what you really get off on, isn't it? Just to think of those endless reels of celluloid gives you a hard on like no woman ever can . . .'

Laurence sat watching her, saddened by the way she was working herself to such a frenzy, but knowing there was nothing he could do to stop her – not yet anyway. She had to get it off her chest and any minute now she would start contradicting herself, get herself into complete confusion and then she would cry.

This wasn't the first time she'd accused him of having an affair with Alison Fortescue, the production designer he always worked with, and though he guessed she knew it wasn't true, lately, he'd had an uncomfortable feeling that she almost wished it were. But he wasn't. He loved Pippa every bit as much now as he did when they'd married, five years ago, but he, like her, was aware that recently they had started to drift apart. He didn't want that to happen. Despite their occasional difficulties and Pippa's unreasonable tantrums, they were good together, they always had been, right from the start, which was why he had taken no longer than three months to propose to her. Pippa had had everything he was looking for in a woman then and still did. Perhaps, he told himself now as he watched the tears start from her eyes, he should make more of an effort to understand her and it could be that she was right, that he did patronize her, but she sure as hell made it difficult not to sometimes.

Getting to his feet he walked across the room and

closed the door. Then, taking her by the shoulders, he pressed her up against the wall and looked down into her face. Christ, there were times when she felt so frail in his hands, so vulnerable that he was afraid he would crush the very life from her were he to give full vent to his feelings. Of course that was nonsense, but even so it had taken him a long time to get used to the fact that such a slight and delicate body could handle the overriding passions of his own. How many times over the years had he secretly searched her tender pale skin for the bruises he was sure he must have inflicted during the heightened moments of their love-making? And even now he could still sometimes be surprised by the flawlessness of the smooth milky flesh that covered such fragile bones when his ruthless masculinity had ceased its demands for fulfilment.

As she gazed up at him her eyes were angry and bewildered and, he realized with a sudden and painful jolt to his heart, strangely lonely.

He lowered his head and as their lips touched his hand went behind her and brought her body hard against his.

'It's not true, is it?' she whispered. 'About Alison, I mean.'

'You know it's not,' he said softly.

'Kiss me again, Laurence. Hold me close.'

He gathered her tightly in his arms and pushed his tongue deep into her mouth. They kissed for a long time feeling their desire building to a pitch where one of them would break away and begin the ritual of love-making. This time Pippa was the first and Laurence's head fell on to his arms against the wall as she slid down his body, unzipping him as she went. He looked down as she lifted his semi-erect penis from his jeans then groaned as she took him into her mouth. She pushed his jeans to his knees, inserted her fingers between his legs, raked her nails over his buttocks and thighs and tightened the grip with her mouth.

She knew he loved this and would have brought him to climax had he not reached down for her and pulling her to her feet buried his tongue in her mouth. She whimpered softly as he lifted her short skirt to her waist and pressed himself to her.

After a while she whispered, 'Pull my knickers down.'

He heard the catch in her voice and kissed her hard. It turned her on to say it, which in its turn excited him too. He eased her panties to mid-thigh, the way he knew she liked it, then slid his fingers into the wispy thatch of blonde hair between her legs.

'I love you,' he murmured.

She pulled back to look at his face, but as he opened his eyes she caught him to her again. 'Take me now,' she moaned. 'Put it inside me. Deep inside me.'

As she stepped out of her knickers he cupped his hands under her buttocks and lifted her. Her legs circled his waist and pushing her hard against the wall he penetrated her. For a fleeting moment he was aware of her frailty again, but he pushed it from his mind. It was true that he felt less urgency with Pippa, that there wasn't, nor ever had been, the overpowering intoxication of being totally submerged in a sea of femininity, but in its place was a deep and unparalleled love the like of which no amount of lust could ever destroy.

But equally true was the fact that making love to her was no solution to their problems. He knew that Pippa would never forgive him if he made her move to the States, but if they stayed in England his career would undoubtedly continue to suffer and maybe die altogether.

The following morning Laurence cancelled Pippa's taxi and drove her to the airport himself. Tom went along too, though Laurence wondered after a while whether it had been such a good idea to bring him. Pippa was as jittery as she always was before going away and no matter how much Laurence tried to persuade her that they would be fine for a couple of days without her he could see that nothing was going to assuage the guilt. Their parting, when it came, was much more tender than usual and for a moment Laurence actually thought that Pippa was going to back out.

'I don't want to leave you,' she said, her eyes brimming with tears. 'I know it's silly, but I don't.' She looked up at him then and Laurence knew what she was going to say even before she said it.

He shook his head. 'I can't do it, honey,' he said softly. 'I can't ask you to give it up. That has to be your decision and yours alone.'

'I know,' she said, attempting a smile. 'Oh God, Laurence, why do you have to be so reasonable?'

'I guess I'm just that sort of guy,' he grinned. 'Now, do I get a kiss?'

She leaned forward awkwardly as Tom was clinging to her – unlike his father he was more than ready to ask her not to go. But both Pippa and Laurence knew that within minutes of Pippa handing him over to his father he would be filled with excitement at the prospect of having Laurence to himself for a few days.

'Do you have any idea just how much it makes my heart ache to look at you two together?' Pippa smiled

wistfully as she put Tom down and watched him automatically reach up for his father's hand.

'Sure I do,' Laurence answered. 'It kind of gets to
me too, when I see him with you.'

'I don't deserve you.'

'I guess you don't at that.'

'Am I really so hateful?'

'Yeah, I reckon you are.'

'Don't let me destroy us, Laurence.'

'You think I'm gonna do that?'

'I love you.'

'Yeah, I know. I love you too. We'll get through this,
honey, we'll find a way, you'll see.'

As he watched her walk through to the departure
lounge Laurence's face was inscrutable, though deep
down inside he was hurting. He was hurting because she
was hurting. He sighed. Women were strange creatures,
almost alien at times. Just how did a guy handle it when
the woman he loved was unable to take a decision herself,
when she longed for her husband to make it for her,
and yet would deeply resent him for doing it? Somebody
answer him that for God's sake, because he sure as hell
couldn't answer it himself.

He turned to the news-stand intending to pick up a
paper before heading back into London. It was almost
midday and most of the morning editions had sold out,
but there was one tabloid left which he would have
bought had it not had a picture of Kirsten Meredith in
the top left-hand corner. Immediately Laurence's jaw
tightened. She was one woman he sure as hell didn't
want to read about, didn't even want to think about and
scooping Tom up into his arms he started out to the car
park.

— 2 —

It was just before midnight. The wind was picking up again, swelling through the narrow streets of Chelsea in a gentle roar. The rain will soon follow, Kirsten was thinking absently to herself as she looked out of the window, but maybe tomorrow, if only for an hour, the sun might shine. How she missed the sunshine.

She was sitting alone in a pasta bar on the Fulham Road waiting for a take-away and huddled into the large raincoat that had belonged to Paul. By anyone's standards she was a beautiful woman. With her wide, slanting green eyes, impossibly sensuous mouth, delicately flared nostrils and rich, olivey skin she was a sublime mix of the exotic and erotic. Yet when she laughed there was such a freshness, perhaps even a naivety about her, that it never failed to affect those she was with. It never seemed to matter how she dressed for the tantalizing fullness of her figure and the superb contours of her long, shapely legs were all but impossible to disguise; and despite the fact that right now a paisley silk scarf was wound tightly round her abundant coppery curls defiant tendrils had escaped their imprisonment to rest gently against the flawless skin of her forehead and neck.

Following the quick glance through the window Kirsten had once again bowed her head to look down at her loosely knitted fingers on the table in front of her. There were several reasons why she kept her head lowered when in public these days, and one of them was to conceal her lovely face. Though it was a face that any other woman would have been proud of, for Kirsten it, perhaps more than anything else, was the cause of the terrible and seemingly endless pain locked so deep inside her that sometimes she wondered if it was only that which held her together now.

A wave of choking misery threatened to overwhelm her. It would be the easiest thing in the world to join hands with self-pity, to allow herself to be led to that longed for sanctuary of oblivion, to a self-inflicted end to the pain. So many times during these past weeks she had come close to giving in, to surrendering herself to the beckoning arms of release, but she hadn't. She didn't know why she was resisting it, for there was nothing here for her now, so wouldn't it be better to put an end to this intolerable, interminable farce she called her life?

Abruptly she swallowed hard and squeezing her hands tightly she forced her head up. Sometimes it was so hard to remember that she had nothing to be ashamed of, that the whole world was wrong about her and that she had every right to hold her head high. But being the victim of a campaign so powerful and so unjust did that to a person. You started to forget your own innocence, sometimes you even reached the point of believing all the lies yourself.

Dear God, she sighed inwardly, how has this happened to me? So alone at thirty-six. No friends, no job, no anything. Maybe she could endure that if only Dermott Campbell would leave her alone. But she knew already that Campbell's campaign had hardly begun. Day after day he printed stories about her. Stories with little foundation and no mercy. And to Kirsten's dismay the other newspapers had immediately picked up on those stories, adding, of course, their own scurrilous embellishments.

She'd been a fool to come back, she should have known that Dyllis would use the might of her great newspaper empire to wreak her revenge.

Kirsten felt tears welling in her eyes at the injustice of it all. Right now all she wanted was to be able to run back to Paul, to have him make her feel safe and secure the way he had over the past five years. But there was no going back now, those wonderful days on the Côte d'Azur were over.

She and Paul Fisher hadn't had many friends on the Riviera, but they'd been happy with each other, even though Paul had tried many times to make Kirsten return to England and live a normal life. It was true that there were times when she'd wanted to, but her feelings for Paul had kept her at his side – she just couldn't bring herself to walk out on him when he loved her so much.

No one understood that, because no one wanted to. All they saw was that their darling Paul Fisher – the great Shakespearean actor, the great movie actor too – had, in his old age, been bewitched by the Kirstie Doll, as the media had taken to calling her, whose only ambition in life was to take him for every penny he had.

When they'd first gone to France Paul had done everything he could to shield them both from the press, but it hadn't been easy. The scandal was as titillating as any rag could wish for – at the age of seventy-six Paul Fisher gives up stage, screen and wife to run off with a thirty-year-old TV producer. Not that the press ever referred to her as a producer, in fact they'd only just stopped short of calling her a whore. No one had been interested in the truth then, no more than they were now. What did it matter to them that she, Kirsten Meredith, had, for the first time in her life, found someone who truly cared for her, who had made her feel as though she mattered and wanted to do all he could to repair the damage of her early life? More to the point what did they know of Paul's marriage? Of how for over twenty years he had been subjected to his wife's megalomania, had been forced every day to show his gratitude for what she had done for him. She wanted nothing more from him than the glory of being married to a man who was so adored, respected and revered by all. But Kirsten had made him happy in those last years and to her he had been everything, friend, brother, father and, yes, lover.

And now he was dead.

Kirsten felt the familiar tightening in her throat. God, how she missed him, and dear God how she longed to talk to him now, to ask him how she should handle this. It had come as no surprise that he had remembered her in his will, he'd talked about it often enough, but Kirsten had been unprepared for the fact that he had left his entire fortune in trust for her until the end of her life, at which time the staggering sum was to be split between his own three children and any that Kirsten might have. Not a single sou had gone to Dyllis, who for the past month had been giving the performance of her life as the grieving widow.

Dyllis, very cleverly, had decided not to contest the will – that may not have won her much sympathy when the whole world knew that she was richer than Croesus. Neither had she seen fit to make public the fact that her children were, in truth, beneficiaries. Instead, via the press, she had told Kirsten to keep the money and that she herself would see that Paul's children were taken care of. And if she, Kirsten could live with her conscience, having wheedled herself into an old man's will during his years of senility, then really, what could Dyllis say?

Not surprisingly, the press went to town with this, and since, according to the press, Kirsten had no conscience, every columnist without exception was currently urging Dyllis to rethink the situation and get her children's rightful inheritance out of the money-grabbing Kirstie Doll.

What a manipulative and cunning woman Dyllis Fisher was. She had the world on her side, and no one had even thought to question her claims that Paul was senile – which of course Dyllis knew was nonsense and was also why she wasn't contesting the will. She knew she'd never win on those grounds, and there simply weren't any others. Paul had made his decision, and they all, including Kirsten, had to live by it. He had probably never dreamed of the pain it would cause her.

Suddenly Kirsten realized that she had been waiting an interminably long time for her pasta. She looked over at the counter and at the same moment the lights dimmed in the restaurant.

'Excuse me,' she said to one of the waiters. 'I still haven't had my take-away.'

'I'm afraid it's too late for take-aways,' he answered avoiding her eyes. 'The chef finished an hour ago.'

'But I saw you serve someone long after I'd . . .' Kirsten started to protest, but her voice trailed off. She understood perfectly. The waiter had recognized her and hadn't even bothered to put her order through.

Saying no more Kirsten got to her feet and walked out on to the Fulham Road. It didn't matter about the food, she had no appetite anyway, but what did matter was the continued and horrible snubbing she suffered every time she ventured from the house. Dimly she wondered if Dyllis actually knew just how successful her vendetta was proving.

The cinema was just turning out, but thankfully the rain had come so most faces in the crowd were shielded by umbrellas. Nevertheless Kirsten lowered her head as she hurried by heading for the house Paul had also left her, in Elm Park Gardens.

It was a wonderful house, much bigger than it seemed from the outside, yet every bit as cosy as the cottage-like exterior promised. There was no front garden to speak of, just a few paving slabs and no fence or gates. At the back however, was a beautiful and immaculately kept oval lawn with a little fountain in the middle and trees all around the high brick walls to keep it from being overlooked. Inside, the house was a little like a maze with hidden rooms on haphazard landings with low doorways and wooden floors strewn with ageing oriental rugs and any number of antiques and paintings.

Locking the front door behind her Kirsten went into the sitting room, by far the largest room of the house, yet somehow the snuggest. She loved this room with its pretty marble fireplace, deep armchairs, kelim-covered sofa and soft lighting. The endless rows of books made her think of Paul and feel closer to him. How he had loved books. But then so did she, and how much reading she had done these past few weeks. It had been her only escape.

She flopped down on the sofa, unravelling the scarf from her hair and shaking out her shoulder length curls.

'I should cry,' she said aloud to herself. 'I should let it all out and stop bottling it up this way. There's nothing to be afraid of or ashamed of in grieving for someone you love.'

But the tears wouldn't come and she knew that it was because she dare not let go, if she did she might never stop.

She curled up in a ball, resting her head on the cushions and hugging herself tightly. Even if she could sleep she still wouldn't have gone to bed. Lying there alone without the comfort and warmth of Paul's body beside her was the hardest of all to bear.

To her dismay, when the papers arrived the next morning she found a photograph of herself leaving the pasta bar. She hadn't been aware of the photographer, but that was no surprise. They followed her everywhere these days and she rarely, if ever, saw them. The accompanying story was predictably by Dermott Campbell. It was as cruel as ever, pointing out her loneliness and the fact that even the friends she had had before she went to France had deserted her. She wondered if that were true. Had everyone really deserted her? She hadn't tried contacting anyone since her return, but then who was there to contact? There never really had been anyone she could call a friend – except Paul. And, of course, Helena. There had always been a companion though, a companion as constant, as unrelenting and as cruel as Dyllis Fisher's revenge. Loneliness was her companion. It had been with her for so much of her life that it was sometimes hard for her to remember a time when that dull ache wasn't circling her heart waiting to steal into the precious moments of happiness and stifle them. Throughout the years she had known Paul though, which were ten in all since they had been friends long before they had become lovers, there had been no ache. With Paul's help she had conquered her fear of people, of herself even, and had allowed herself to believe in happiness. She was already a successful woman by the time he came into her life, but it was he who had taught her how to enjoy her success, and most importantly of all how to trust in those who had already put their trust in her. He had made her understand and eventually believe that no one wanted to hurt her and in time that tightly knotted fear inside her had started to unravel, so slowly at first that she had thought it would never let go. But it had and she would never forget the years that had followed when she had led a normal, happy, and almost totally fulfilled life. There had only been one thing missing, but eventually, she had found that too. And then she had really known what true happiness was.

But all that was five years ago now, and Paul had been there to pick up the pieces, the way he always was, when it had all gone so disastrously wrong. And typically of him he had been filled with remorse that he had been the one to introduce her to the man who had, in the end, broken her heart. It was then that Paul had taken her to France and she had decided to devote herself to him and him alone.

Now the ache of loneliness was with her again. It had returned with Paul's death and seemed more oppressive, more suffocating than ever. And through it she could once again hear the laughing voice of her beloved father on that last morning when she had waved him off to work.

Ever since Kirsten could remember her father had been the centre of her world. It was to him she had run when she'd fallen and hurt herself, and to him she would turn for praise when she'd tried so especially hard at school. Always his twinkling eyes were there, watching her, loving her and making her feel the most special person in the world. At night she would curl up in his lap and listen as he read her stories and in the morning he would always be there ready to lift her into his arms for a kiss before going off to work. She had been his little princess and he had been her father, the king.

Kirsten had virtually no recollection of her mother during those times even though her mother had been there, for her tiny six-year-old world was filled by her father.

And then one day he wasn't there anymore.

She remembered her mother telling her that he was dead, that he'd been killed in a road accident, but Kirsten didn't understand dead. She didn't realize that it meant he was never coming back, so day after day she had sat outside on the doorstep waiting for him. She'd begged her mother to tell him she was sorry, that whatever she had done wrong she would never do it again if only he would come home. But he never came and Kirsten's mother had never really tried to explain death to the little girl. So in the end Kirsten, in her own quiet way, had managed to convince herself that her Daddy just didn't love her anymore because she was a wicked, wicked girl.

All those bitter and desperate feelings of bewilderment, rejection and failure Kirsten had relived during the first two years she was in France. They had been coaxed out of her by the analyst she was seeing following her breakdown and as always Paul had been there to see her through it. Just as he had when Kirsten had allowed the analyst to make her face the years that had followed the death of her father and all that had happened. The way her mother had continued to neglect her, and the terrible years of bullying she had faced at school when the other girls had teased and tormented her. And then there was the music teacher, Mr Phillpott, who had taken such delight in pulling down her knickers and spanking her bottom for crimes she didn't even know she'd committed. There had been so much, too much already for one little life.

But there was worse to come. Much worse. And it had started with the rape. It had happened when she was still only thirteen years old, when two boys from the lower-sixth had chased her into the buttercup field near her home and repeatedly forced themselves on her.

Now, as Kirsten sat there in her Chelsea home, so far from the nightmare of her teenage years, that thirteen-year-old child seemed like a stranger, someone with whom it was impossible to identify, nevertheless it was that stranger who had mapped her life, who had created a security so false and so tragic that even to think of her now could almost move Kirsten to tears.

She'd known the two boys who had raped her, at least she'd known their names; Danny Fairbrother, the school heart-throb, and his friend Christopher Ball, but in the months, years to follow, she came to know them a whole lot better, for Danny, in the moments following the rape, had suddenly realized the immensity of the crime he had committed. She was a minor and he was seventeen. Christopher, on realizing it too, had run away, but Danny, as afraid and agitated as he was, had stayed to make sure she was all right. And it was because he had shown her that kindness that Kirsten had agreed to keep silent. Not only that, she had agreed to meet him again the following day.

Kirsten was so grateful and so elated by Danny's friendship that she was happy to let him do whatever he wanted. If she didn't she knew he wouldn't come any more and she just couldn't bear to go back to the loneliness she had known before he had come into her life. Then Danny introduced her to a couple of his friends, then a couple more and a couple more. And as the number of Danny's friends increased so the faces became blurred by the choking fog of confusion and pain closing in on her heart. But just so long as Danny kept coming, was kind to her and made her feel special was really all that mattered.

Looking back now it was a miracle that she hadn't got pregnant sooner, but it hadn't happened until she was fifteen. And it was the day she had found out that she was pregnant that she also found out that Danny had a girlfriend. A real girlfriend whom he took to dances, let ride on his motorbike and took home to meet his parents.

For the next month Kirsten knew such misery and desolation it even surpassed the fear of her pregnancy. Day after day she watched and prayed that Danny would call for her again. At weekends she even walked through the rain down to the hay barn where they went when the weather was bad in the vain hope that he might be there. Of course he never was, and she'd stopped going there with the other boys now too. Most of them were begging her to see them, were promising her anything, even engagement rings, if she'd just give them one more quick tumble. Always she refused, until one Sunday when Christopher Ball turned up for the third time that day and Kirsten's mother insisted that she put the poor boy out of his misery and go for a walk with him. Naturally they went to the hay barn, but instead of taking off her jeans when they got inside, to Christopher's annoyance Kirsten plumped down on the straw and started to cry. So it was to Christopher Ball that Kirsten finally confided her pregnancy.

He was horrified. She watched him backing away from her, swearing he'd deny ever touching her if she so much as mentioned his name. All the hurt, the anguish and fear she had bottled up inside suddenly erupted in a storm of such unmitigated anger as she threw herself at him that all she knew was that she wanted to kill him.

'For God's sake, Kirsten, calm down!' Christopher shouted, grabbing her arms to stop her hitting him. 'How can you tell anybody that Danny's the father when you've let half the bloody sixth form into your knickers?'

'No! No!' she cried, throwing herself at him again. 'I only did it for him. You know that, you *all* knew that. And now you're all going to leave me . . .'

'But what the hell else can we do?' Christopher protested. 'That kid could be anyone's . . .'

'No! Not anyone's! It's mine! Do you hear me! This baby is mine and I'm going to keep it. No one is going to take this baby away from me . . .'

'Kirsten!' he yelled. 'No one's saying they're going to take it away. Now for fuck's sake calm down . . .'

But Kirsten wasn't listening. The pain was unleashed, out of control and was going to make itself heard. And all the bitterness and betrayal she felt seemed to have no end.

It was only when Christopher yelled at her that she was going to harm the baby if she didn't stop that her temper finally started to abate. Her baby! The one human being in the world she could love and who would love her. Soon there would be something in her life that no one could take away – it would be hers, all hers, and she would protect it with her life. So what if Danny was seeing Catherine Watts, would go out in public with her, something he had never done with Kirsten? She had her baby now, her very own baby. She had someone to love.

Smiling sadly to herself Kirsten put down the book she was holding and got up to go and make herself some tea. It was all such a long time ago now, such a very long time, and it was where it should have ended, but it hadn't. How many years had she punished herself for going through with the abortion? How many men had she allowed to abuse her body in order to carry out that punishment? She'd lost count now. The analyst had said that she'd done it in order to get pregnant again, but she wasn't sure that was true. Perhaps it was in part, but she had always used contraception, just as, when she had finally come to understand the power of her body, she had gone on sleeping with men, but now to get what she wanted. For years, right up until she'd met Paul, she had been nothing better than a whore. And very soon now Dermott Campbell was going to find out about that, and make public the whole grisly business.

But she would survive it, she would have to. Please God, just don't let Campbell ever find out about Laurence; don't let him get hold of what they had shared and twist and soil it with his lies, the way he was doing with what she had known with Paul. For what she had had with Laurence McAllister, the man who Paul himself had so proudly introduced her to, the man who she had loved so much that no amount of words could express it, was the man who in the end had broken her completely. And that was something she would never want to be made public, and something that even now she didn't know if she could ever truly put behind her . . .

— 3 —

'Kirstie! Kirstie, is that you?'

Kirsten looked at the receiver then put it back to her ear. 'Hello?' she said cautiously.

'Kirstie! It's me! Helena! Shit, I've had one hell of a time trying to get hold of you. Why haven't you called me?'

'I thought you were in Hollywood,' Kirsten answered, wondering whether or not she should believe her ears.

'I was, it didn't work out, so I'm back. Looks like we're both back.'

'I don't believe it!' Kirsten suddenly started to laugh. 'I was just thinking about you. God, Helena, tell me I'm not imagining this call.'

'I'm right here, honey. Now, you gonna give me your address so I can come over and see you? We got one hell of a lot of catching up to do so we'd best get started. You are free I take it?'

'You bet your sweet Louisiana bum I'm free. Just get here as soon as you can, I can hardly wait to see you.'

Half an hour later Helena was sitting the other side of the kitchen table sipping the champagne Kirsten had cracked open to celebrate. Her wild, frizzy black hair, coffee coloured skin, startlingly large brown eyes and generous mouth were so familiar and such a welcome sight that Kirsten could almost have wept with joy. Instead she laughed at the way Helena was so openly assessing her with all the frankness Kirsten remembered so well.

'*Sheeit*, Kirstie!' Helena exclaimed, grinning widely. 'You just get more gorgeous by the year. Can't you do the decent thing and start to age, like the rest of us?'

'I'll do my best,' Kirsten laughed. 'But you're looking pretty terrific yourself. Something in Hollywood must have agreed with you.'

'A plastic surgeon. He agreed I needed lifts and tucks and all that rubbish, so I went for it. Didn't get me any work though. In fact I've been resting, as they say, ever since the soap folded.'

'No!' Kirsten gasped. 'But that's over four years now. Surely you've done something in all that time.'

'Nothing worth mentioning. So I'm here hoping that my favourite producer might have a l'il ol' role for her li'l ol' friend. Anything doing?'

'Give me a chance,' Kirsten laughed. 'I've only been back in the country a month, and it can't have escaped your notice that I'm not exactly the flavour of the month.'

'No, you sure aren't,' Helena agreed. 'Would I be right in thinking that Dyllis Fisher is behind Campbell's campaign?'

'You would.'

'God, that man's such a prick! Words escape me for her at the moment, but never fear I'll think of some. Still, I'll have a word with Campbell if you like, see if I can persuade him to back off.'

'You mean you know him?'

'Unfortunately. He had the hots for me once, well, he has the hots for anything in a skirt. But I'm telling you, honey, I'm not that desperate – not yet anyway. To tell the truth I feel insulted that he could actually believe

I'd be interested in a creep like him. Still, it's the story of my life, as you well know. Why can't I ever pull the gorgeous ones like Laurence McAllister, is what I want to know? Incidentally, I just got to ask, what the hell happened between you two in the end, you never did tell me. You just skipped off to France with Paul Fisher and we never heard from you again. So, come on, dish the dirt. What did the bastard do?'

'Nothing really,' Kirsten smiled, looking down at her glass. 'It was me. I kind of went into self-destruct.'

'And good old Paul was there to help put you back together. Well, let's thank God for him anyway. Did you two ever get it together in the end?'

Kirsten nodded. 'We did. Eventually.'

'I knew it!' Helena cried, clapping her hands with glee. 'Paul Fisher was in love with you from the day he met you, though why the hell he didn't do anything about it then beats me. Still, if anyone ever deserved his roll in the hay it was him.'

'I'm glad he's not here to hear you put it like that,' Kirsten grimaced. 'He spent a long time getting me over the way I always used myself to, amongst other things, reward people.'

Helena looked suitably chastened. 'I guess you really did have your problems back then, didn't you? There you were, just about the most successful woman in television, at least certainly the youngest to be so successful, churning out one hit show after another after another, looking for all the world like you'd really got it together and all the time you were so badly screwed up. Tell me you're all right now. Tell me you got yourself sorted.'

'I'm sorted,' Kirsten smiled.

'With Paul's help, I'll bet. That man is a candidate

for sainthood. I guess you really miss him, don't you?' she added softly.

'Yes. But he'd be the first to tell me that life has to go on, which it does. I don't think it's going to be easy though. Getting Dermott Campbell off my back could be a start. Will you speak to him?'

'Sure I will. But I've got to tell you, Kirstie, I don't really hold out much hope. Not when Dyllis Fisher is pulling the strings. She is one powerful lady.' She looked thoughtful for a moment, then lifting her eyes back to Kirsten's she said, 'Look, I've been reading all that stuff, and well, did it ever occur to you that someone is giving Campbell his information? I mean a lot of what he's writing is based on the truth. For sure there are a hell of a lot of lies, but . . .'

'Yes, it had occurred to me,' Kirsten answered, 'but I just can't think who it would be. Can you?'

Helena shook her head. 'I mean, I guess you made plenty of enemies back when you came in to revive the soap, with all the people you fired'n'all, but that was years ago now. I can't believe anyone would hold a grudge for that long, I mean things like that happen in this business, everyone knows that. Still, we can't rule it out. Has anyone from back then been in touch with you at all?'

Kirsten shook her head. 'You're the only one.'

Helena looked surprised. 'Not even Anita Browne? You were pretty friendly with her for a while.'

'Never so friendly as I was with you, and no, I haven't heard from her in years. Whatever happened to her, do you know?'

Helena shrugged. 'Haven't got the faintest. Or, hang on, didn't she meet some Australian cowboy or something and emigrate?'

'No idea. The last I heard of her she was doing rep in Manchester. But that has to be at least seven years ago.'

'Mmm, well I'd be careful about who does try to get in touch over the next few weeks, if I were you.'

'Have you ever met anyone more careful about people than me?' Kirsten grinned.

Helena laughed. 'No, I don't guess I have,' she said, over-emphasising her Louisiana drawl. 'But you have been known to make mistakes.'

'Oh yes, I've made plenty of them,' Kirsten chuckled, 'and one of them was not keeping in touch with you. So come on, let's have it, what have you really been up to all these years?'

Like most actresses Helena didn't need much encouragement to talk about herself, which she did, quite happily, for the next hour, by which time Kirsten was aching from laughing so hard.

'But I have to tell you,' Helena said, 'none of it was so much fun as we had back in the old days. Shit, the things we got up to. Do you remember the time when old what's-his-name, the head of drama, ordered you to fire me? Me! The star!'

'Yes, I remember it only too well,' Kirsten said dryly. 'And I should never have told you, going into his office the way you did and throwing his coffee over his head. You really were lucky not to be fired then.'

'But you saved me,' Helena grinned.

'Only just. I really had to stick my neck out . . .'

'*Your neck*!' Helena cried.

'Well, all right, a bit more than that,' Kirsten conceded, 'but I'd only just taken over at the time, I didn't have anything else to bargain with.'

'So you really did screw him just to keep me on the series?'

'You know I did. And stop reminding me of the way I was then . . . We all know I screwed my way to the top . . .'

'Yeah, but no one ever denied that you were a damned good producer. Even so, you sure were hot to trot. Yeah, I know, I know, it was because of all the problems you had in your past, but Paul sure sorted that out when he came along, didn't he? Do you remember the day you met him, at the garden party? You hogged him all afternoon when the whole world was dying to speak to the great man . . .'

Kirsten smiled nostalgically. 'God, yes, I remember that,' she said. 'I'd never felt so important in my life. There I was, twenty-five years old, the producer of a dying soap opera . . .'

'Which you very successfully revived . . .'

'. . . which I revived. And there I was chatting away with the great Paul Fisher as though I'd known him all my life. God, that seems such a long time ago now.'

'Do you ever wonder what might have happened to you if he hadn't come along?'

'I shudder to think. I mean, I might have continued to produce, but I don't think I'd ever have been able to have a relationship with anyone. Not the way I was. God, I was such a mess. But even Paul didn't stop me hankering for a baby. I asked him once if I could have his.'

'I remember. It was why you and I went off on that hilarious skiing trip and I ended up breaking a leg. He'd thrown you out of his flat for trying to seduce him after he'd told you no a thousand times.'

Kirsten winced and laughed. 'He told me I was

embarrassing us both, then threw my clothes at me . . . God that was awful. I hadn't slept with a man in three years by that time, I had no confidence at all, at least none to speak of, if anything I was terrified of any kind of involvement with anyone, and then to have Paul react like that . . .'

'But he was right. He was too old, he was married to someone else and you were just starting out on your career. About, if I remember rightly, to go off and produce that Hamish Fullerton drama. Real big time.'

Kirsten nodded. 'Paul was always right. Do you know, he cried when I went back to apologize. He was so upset by the way he had treated me. He just wanted me to meet the right man, was what he said . . .'

'Which you did. Eventually.'

'Well, I thought I did. In fact I was so sure of it I even wrote to my mother to tell her. It was the first time I'd contacted her in years.'

'What did she say?'

'Nothing. She didn't even bother to write back. Still, that's not surprising, we never did get on, and after she forced me to go through with that abortion I swore I'd never speak to her again. Which I haven't really, from that day to this. How's your mother, by the way?'

'The same.'

Kirsten nodded. 'And your love life?'

'About as barren as barren can get. It's not easy meeting anyone when you're my age . . . I'll be forty-two next week, you know, and that's not a good age when you want a husband and baby and have a penchant for seventeen year olds. The two don't go hand in hand somehow.'

'I didn't know you wanted children,' Kirsten laughed.

'I don't. Well, I do. Oh, what the hell do I know. I

wish though, that just for once in my life I could fall in love and have someone fall in love with me . . . I've never really had any relationships to speak of, at least nothing like you had with Laurence.'

'Yes, well,' Kirsten said, her smile fading slightly, 'that didn't exactly work out, did it?'

'But why?' Helena said, shaking her head incredulously. 'I just don't get it. Come on, what happened back then?'

Kirsten gave a wry smile as her head tilted to one side. 'He met Pippa,' she answered simply.

Helena shook her head. 'No. I'm not buying it,' she said. 'That guy was so crazy for you he'd never have looked at another woman.'

'But he did. He met Pippa, fell in love and they got married. End of story.'

Helena was about to protest again, but stopped herself. There was no point in trying to get anything out of Kirsten until she was ready to tell. 'And how do you feel now?' she said softly. 'Do you still care for him?'

Kirsten looked down at the champagne glass she had cupped between her hands. 'I don't know,' she answered. 'It's hard to say when I haven't seen him for so long.'

Again Helena was shaking her head as though she still couldn't believe, even after all this time, that Kirsten and Laurence had parted. 'I remember the night you met him,' she said. 'I was there for that too.'

'We were always there for each other in those days,' Kirsten smiled.

'It was the night you won the BAFTA award, wasn't it? For that Hamish Fullerton series. And Laurence won one too, if I remember rightly. God, what a night that was for you two. A BAFTA each and love at first sight. I'll never forget the look on Paul's face when he introduced the two of you. God, talk about the proud father. Come to that I'll never forget the look on Laurence's face. He could hardly believe his eyes. You sure did look gorgeous that night, but then you always do. Did you sleep together that night, by the way, I can't remember now.'

'Oh yes,' Kirsten smiled. 'We slept together all right. It was the first time in my life a man had ever actually made love to me. It was also the night he told me he loved me.' She laughed. 'He couldn't believe he'd said it. Neither could I, come to that. It was so absurd it really made us laugh, but he swore it was true. He said he thought that things like that only ever happened in the movies.'

'For most of us it does,' Helena remarked. 'How long were you together in the end? A year, was it?'

'Just about,' Kirsten answered, her voice taking on a soft, dreamy quality as her eyes moved to the middle distance. 'God, we had some crazy times. I'd never been that happy, I could hardly believe it was happening, but at the same time nothing in my life had ever seemed so real. He used to call me up in the middle of the day just to remind me he loved me. I've still got most of the little presents he gave me . . . Do you know, he taught me things about myself I didn't even know, well my body actually.'

Helena, her chin resting on her hand, smiled wistfully. 'Mmm, I remember you telling me at the time. God, I was so jealous. I mean, happy for you, but he was so damned gorgeous everyone had the hots for him. And when you used to tell me what he was like in the sack, it just about blew my mind. Well, I guess it did yours too.'

'It certainly did. I'll always remember the day we

were flying back from a weekend in Rome. We were sitting on the plane and suddenly I wanted him so much I just couldn't wait. We did it right there in our seats. Fortunately we were the only ones in the first-class cabin and the stewardess, who must have known what was going on, turned a blind eye. But, it was like that with us, the whole time we were together, we just couldn't seem to get enough of each other.'

'You're right there. You were damned near inseparable. You never used to dance with anyone but each other at parties, always sat together at dinners, Christ, I bet you two even went to the john together. And tell me about the presents! I recall teasing him once about all the flowers he sent you, you know what he said? "Helena, I love that woman so much there aren't enough flowers in the world or enough words in the dictionary to express it".'

'He said that?' Kirsten smiled, feeling her throat tighten.

'Yep. So, come on, what the hell went wrong?'

Kirsten shrugged and sighed. 'Me. I went wrong. I thought I was over all those problems in the past, but suddenly, one day, there they were staring me right in the face again. I just couldn't believe he would continue to love me the way he did.' Her eyes drew focus as she came back to the present. 'And I was right,' she smiled. 'He didn't.'

'But something must have happened. I mean, he couldn't have stopped loving you,' Helena clicked her fingers, 'just like that.'

'No, he didn't. I forced him to. God, it was an awful time. I just couldn't stop myself hurting him. I was so convinced he was going to leave me, I was so insecure and afraid he just didn't know what to do. He got so desperate at one point he asked Paul to speak to me, but I wouldn't even listen to Paul. Of course, I've been through enough analysis now to know that it all stemmed from the death of my father, and not believing that someone I loved would stay with me, but none of us realized that then. Well, I think Paul did, but like I said, I wasn't prepared to listen.'

'It's still hard for me to believe that Laurence didn't stand by you. I mean if Paul knew what was going on he must have told Laurence.'

'He probably did, but then Laurence met Pippa and the rest is history.'

'Except that you're still not over him, are you?' Helena asked gently.

'As I said earlier, it's hard to say when I haven't seen him for so long.'

Helena's nerve ends were starting to prickle. She knew she'd be going right out on a limb to suggest what she was about to, but hell, why not give it a shot? After all, it could be the answer. 'There's a party at his house this weekend,' she said. 'As it so happens I've been invited. Why don't you come along too?'

Kirsten's eyes widened in amazement. 'You've got to be joking!' she cried, horribly aware of the sudden sickening dip in her stomach. 'Go to Laurence's house! Helena, you're out of your mind.'

'Well, it's one way of finding out how you feel about him,' Helena said, still not really sure whether it was a good idea or not. 'And look at it this way, everybody who's anybody will be there. Think of all the contacts you could make, contacts you're going to need if you want to get started again – I take it you are intending to start again?'

'Of course I am. But right now Laurence McAllister

is just about the last person in the world I want to see. And I'll most definitely be the last person he'll want to see.'

'But why would he feel that way when so . . .'

'He just would,' Kirsten interrupted.

'Well you're going to run into him sooner or later.'

'Then let's make it later, shall we? Besides, with Paul so recently dead I'm really not up for . . .'

'Oh come on, Kirstie! You and I both know that Paul would be furious to hear you using him as an excuse not to face the world. And OK, it's a tough world, tougher for you than most right now, but that's all the more reason to get out there and show them what you're made of.'

A quick anger sparked in Kirsten's eyes as she met Helena's. 'You're forcing me to tell you things I don't want to tell anyone,' she snapped, 'but this much I will tell you, perhaps then you'll drop the subject. When Laurence and I split up I had a total breakdown. I was such a mess that for the first six months I was in France I was confined to a hospital bed. I had nurses on duty twenty-four hours a day to stop me trying to kill myself, I put Paul through the kind of hell no one ever deserves to go through and it was all because of Laurence McAllister. Because of what he made me do to myself and to him. So please, Helena, don't try to make me see him again, not yet anyway. I'm still not ready for it and I don't know that I ever will be.'

Helena's luminous eyes were filled with remorse as she looked back at Kirsten. 'I'm sorry,' she whispered. 'I had no idea it had got that bad.'

As the anger faded from Kirsten's eyes she reached across the table for Helena's hand. 'I'm sorry too,' she said. 'I shouldn't have told you like that. But it's not something I particularly enjoy talking about.'

'Does Laurence know?' Helena asked. 'I mean about the breakdown?'

Kirsten smiled. 'He more or less witnessed it, at least the start of it, though whether he realized it was a breakdown, I don't know. All he wanted was to get me out of his life, but I just couldn't let him go. I'd rather not repeat the things I did at the time, just suffice it to say that I told him I'd get him back one day even if I had to kill Pippa to do it.'

Helena giggled. 'You said that? How theatrical! Did you mean it?'

'At the time, yes. I'd have done anything to get him back.' She gave a sardonic grin. 'Though I don't think Pippa's untimely despatch would have enhanced my chances much, do you?'

'Not much, no,' Helena laughed. Then the humour was gone and she sighed deeply. 'God it's such a shame things turned out that way, Kirstie,' she said.

'Mmm, well, it's in the past now. He has a new life and I have one to create. So, shall we change the subject?'

'Sure. I know, what are you doing for dinner tonight? My treat, if you're free.'

'Are you kidding?' Kirsten laughed. 'I'm always free these days, and my treat — after all I'm a wealthy woman . . .'

'You sure are,' Helena said smiling at her fondly.

'Oh no, you're not going to get all mushy on me, are you?' Kirsten cried throwing up her hands in horror.

'Hell, I nearly did for a moment there,' Helena said, feigning astonishment at herself and making them both laugh. 'It's a shame about the party,' she said, 'but there'll be others and we were always so good at parties, weren't we?'

'Outrageous, is what I'd call it,' Kirsten grinned. 'And sure, there'll be others.' An impish light suddenly shot to Kirsten's eyes. 'Mind you,' she said, 'it could almost be worth going to his just to see the look on his face. God, can you imagine! He'll probably think I've come to pop off Pippa. What's she like, by the way? Do you know her?'

'Not very well,' Helena shrugged. 'She seems an OK sort of person, I guess.'

'And she and Laurence? Are they happy?'

'Oh, now that's one hell of a question. What sort of answer are you looking for?'

'How about the truth?'

'OK, well, let's put it this way. Some would say that they're very close, and others would say that they're welded at the hip. So I guess that must mean they're happy.'

'That's good,' Kirsten said, feeling the warmth seep from her smile. Then clapping her hands together she said, 'So, where shall we go for dinner?'

'How about San Lorenzo's where we always used to go?'

They left the restaurant just before midnight having discussed just about everything under the sun – dredging up yet more outrageous deeds from the past, throwing out crazy ideas for their futures – but still they weren't done. They returned to Kirsten's house where they opened more champagne and talked and laughed into the early hours of the morning. It was somewhere around three o'clock by the time they finally staggered up the stairs together. Helena crashed out in one of the guest bedrooms and Kirsten picked her way through the maze of packing cases yet to be sorted and flopped down on the bed she had shared with Paul during their brief visits to London.

To her surprise, after all the champagne she had consumed, she couldn't sleep. Her mind was racing, going round and round in circles and always coming back to the point when she and Laurence had finally broken up. She fought it, tried every trick she knew of blotting it from her mind, but for some reason tonight it was impossible. And in the end, so exhausted by her efforts, she stopped trying and for the first time in years allowed herself to go back to that terrible time, for the way it had finally ended simply couldn't have been worse.

What she had told Helena was true; Laurence had met Pippa, but there was more to it than that, much, much more, and Kirsten knew she would never forget the events leading up to what she had done in the end.

It had started the night she saw Laurence and Pippa together. By that time Laurence had already tried several times to end their relationship, but Kirsten had never dreamt that it was because he had met someone else. Why should she think that when despite all the problems they were having they were still, albeit rarely, sleeping together.

At first, when she'd seen him with Pippa, she was so shocked she could feel nothing. But the pain, when it hit her, was so bad it seemed to empty her whole body. It filled her, it took her over so completely that nothing else in her functioned. She waited for him to call, day after day after day, until in the end she called him. He came to see her and the minute he walked in the door and stood in the middle of the room in which they had shared so much she knew that any tiny hope she might have cherished that they could try again was already dead.

'I'm sorry,' he said simply. 'I'm sorry you had to find out like that.'

For a long time Kirsten had just looked at him. She could hardly believe that it was possible for something to hurt so much. 'How long have you been seeing her?' she whispered, her voice coming from the very core of her pain.

'A few weeks.'

Something inside her was screaming. Her hands came up as though to ward off a blow. Laurence reached out to steady her, but Kirsten tore herself away. 'So you've been seeing her, sleeping with her, while you've been sleeping with me?' she said.

Laurence turned away.

Kirsten's world started to spin. She reached for the chair beside her and closed her eyes trying to steady herself, but the pain, the betrayal, was coming over her in a relentless tide. Suddenly she was six years old again, waving her father off to work. He'd never come back, she'd waited and waited, but he'd never come back for his princess. And now Laurence was going to leave her too. This time it really was over.

Somehow she held herself together, forced what little courage she had left to summon her dignity. She lifted her head and found Laurence still looking at her. 'What's her name?' she asked.

She had never seen him look so distraught in his life. 'Pippa,' he said quietly.

'Why didn't you call, Laurence? After you saw me, why didn't you ring me?'

'I didn't know what to say,' he answered, dashing a hand through his hair. 'Christ, Kirstie, I tried with us,

God knows how much I tried, but you just wouldn't let it happen.'

'I will now,' she said. 'I promise you, Laurence, I'll let it happen now. If you'll just say you'll try again.'

'It's too late, Kirstie. You've killed it. Can't you see that?'

'But you love me. You always said that you loved me.'

He shook his head and her blood turned to ice. 'Maybe I did love you,' he said. 'I don't know anymore. You got me so confused I just didn't know what I was doing.'

'But you knew what you were saying,' she persisted. 'And you said you loved me. I believed you, Laurence . . .'

'No! That's just it, you didn't believe me.'

'But I do now.'

'Kirsten, for Christ's sake! I don't love you now. Can't you see that. There's no point in believing it . . .'

'But you do love me, Laurence. You do.'

'No!'

For a long time there was silence until Kirsten said, 'Do you love her?'

'Don't ask me that.'

'I'm asking you.'

'Kirsten, just leave it, will you?'

'I need to know.'

'Why? For God's sake what good will it do you?'

'A lot, if you said no.'

'Well I'm not going to say no. I'm not going to say it because I don't want you thinking that there can be anything between us now. We're finished, Kirsten. I'm sorry, the last thing in the world I wanted was to hurt you . . .'

'Then why are you doing it?'

'Because you're fucking well making me. All you've done for weeks now is make me hurt you and I can't take any more. I thought I loved you, Kirsten, but I was wrong. There! I've said it. I was wrong. I didn't love you, I just thought I did. And I'm sorry.'

'I'll do anything, Laurence, anything you say, if you'll just give me another chance.'

'I don't want you to do anything, goddammit!'

'I'll go to see a psychiatrist, get myself sorted out,' she pleaded. 'If I do that will you change your mind?'

'No! It's over!' His anguish was so apparent that Kirsten could no longer bear to look at him. 'Oh, Kirstie,' he groaned, as she covered her face with her hands. 'You're just making this harder on yourself. I'm going to go now and I'm going to call Paul and ask him to come round. He's the only one who can help you now. It's beyond me, Kirstie. I can't do any more.'

As he started to turn away Kirsten caught his arm. 'Just tell me, Laurence, do you love her? I have to know . . .'

'But why?'

'I just have to. Please, Laurence, tell me.'

He sighed. 'Yes, Kirstie,' he said, 'I do love her. And I guess I'd better tell you now before you find out any other way, I'm gonna ask her to marry me.'

Kirsten rolled over and pushed her face into the pillow. God it still hurt so much. All these years later and the ache was as heavy in her heart as it had been then. But nothing, nothing in the world could ever hurt as much as what she had done to punish him. Even now she could hardly believe she had done it, but as much as it had hurt him it was she who had paid the price. It was why her breakdown had been so severe.

Now that Paul was dead only she and Laurence knew

what she had done and, please God, that was the way it would stay.

When Pippa returned three days later to Laurence's surprise and delight she brought Zaccheo Marigliano with her. The Italian author, whose huge frame and booming laughter seemed to fill the entire house was a man for whom Laurence had any amount of time. Some years ago Laurence had had one of Zaccheo's books adapted for the screen – it had turned into a cult movie still earning them both royalties from all over the world. Ever since, they had been firm friends and though Zaccheo's insatiable interest in everything and everyone could be exhausting for some, for Laurence it presented an intellectual challenge he found as stimulating as he did satisfying.

'Surprise, my friend!' Zaccheo roared the moment he saw Laurence come out of his study. 'It has been too long, I have missed you. I leave my Tuscan retreat to see if the rust has set into the brain after this long English winter of yours.' His laughter reverberated down the hall as he clapped his arms about Laurence and hugged him.

'Wacky Zacky!' Tom whooped and beetling past his father he ran into Zaccheo's arms squealing with delight as Zaccheo tumbled him upside down and tickled his bare belly with his beard.

Gifts seemed to spring from Zaccheo's every pocket with the same ease as profundities flowed from his pen until finally he settled Tom on his shoulders and wrapping an arm around both Pippa and Laurence he led them into the sitting room.

'But my, it's good to be home,' he sighed, flopping on to the sofa and tipping Tom into his lap.

'Would you like some tea, Zaccheo?' Jane asked.

'Tea! What is this tea?' he demanded. 'Bring me whisky, woman, then come sit on my knee and make an old man happy.' He laughed long and loud at that since he was not yet forty though knew he looked fifty and revelled in the easy conquests he still made.

Flushing with pleasure, as she usually did at the way Zaccheo flirted with her, Jane crossed the room to the drinks cabinet and poured a generous helping of Scotch into a glass then took both the bottle and glass to Zaccheo. Though it was still just the middle of the afternoon Laurence and Pippa took a gin and tonic each and at Zaccheo's insistence Jane and Tom sat down with them.

As Zaccheo's mellifluous voice rumbled on for once Laurence's attention wasn't wholly on what the big man was saying. He was watching Pippa whose vivid violet eyes were bright with laughter and he could see how the lovely alabaster face had, these past few days, relinquished the lines of anxiety and confusion that had troubled it before she had gone. She seemed so relaxed and, at least for the moment, at peace with herself, leaving Laurence in no doubt as to how much she loved her work. It always revived her which was why he knew he could never take her away from it.

Catching him watching her Pippa smiled and seeing the intimacy in her eyes Laurence felt a tightening in his heart. He badly wanted to hold her right now, to have just a few moments alone with her so that he could tell her that come what may he was going to squeeze some money out of these damned Brits in order to make his next movie. He wanted her to know that they didn't need to go to Hollywood, they could stay right here where she was happy and where he could continue to see her eyes shine that way and feel the pull of love each time she looked at him. He was going to make it work for them, somehow, and he wanted to tell her. But there would be time enough for that later.

He started to laugh then as he realized Zaccheo was taking over the plans for next Saturday's party. The guest list which had started life with no more than twenty people on it was already up to over fifty and Zaccheo was still reeling off names. Caught up in the spirit of it Pippa was excitedly adding to them, having, Laurence guessed, completely forgotten that it was supposed to be a party for Jane.

Laurence glanced over at Jane wondering if she minded. Probably not, he decided, if anything, knowing Jane, she would be only too happy to be relieved of the starring role. However it didn't seem that she was going to get away with it that lightly for Tom suddenly piped up with,

'Guess what, Zacky, Granny's cook is making a huge cake for Jane.'

'Oh Tom!' Pippa groaned. 'That was supposed to be a surprise.'

Tom's eyes rounded as he put a hand over his mouth and looked up at Jane.

'You're hopeless at keeping secrets,' Jane told him, tickling him.

'I'm not!' Tom protested. 'Daddy told me a secret and I kept that.'

'And what was Daddy's secret?' Zaccheo asked, winking at Laurence.

'That he's going to take Mummy away for a weekend,' Tom declared proudly.

Everyone laughed as Laurence hoisted Tom on to his

lap and shook him. 'You fell for it, big guy,' he said, planting a kiss on his son's head, then feeling Pippa's eyes on him he looked across to where she was sitting on the sofa beside Zaccheo.

'Do you have a problem with that?' Laurence asked her.

Pippa glanced uncomfortably at Zaccheo then back to Laurence.

Laurence grinned. 'Well for sure we're not going to go while we have a guest,' he said.

Pippa looked instantly relieved and came to perch on the arm of his chair. 'But we will go,' she said, leaning over and kissing him. 'Soon.'

It was brief, so brief in fact that it barely had time to register, but an awkward silence followed. Zaccheo instantly plunged into it. 'So it's going to be your birthday, Jane!' he boomed. 'Twenty-one. Ah, to be twenty-one again. Now let me see, what was I doing when I was this young? Why for sure!' he cried, slapping a hand on his thigh, 'I was a-drinking the whisky and a-loving the women and a-fighting a war.'

'You were never in the war,' Pippa laughed.

'My whole life is one long war,' he bellowed mournfully. 'But we must not be talking of me, we must plan this party for Jane. Who would you like to invite, *bellezza mia*? Name any man in the world whether he be movie star, a politician or great writer like me, for I, Zaccheo Marigliano shall produce your heart's desire.'

'Yes, come on, Jane,' Pippa enthused, highly entertained by the shy devotion glittering in Jane's eyes as she looked at Zaccheo. 'Zaccheo knows everyone, so who really gets you going?'

'I don't know,' Jane giggled, blushing right to the roots of her hair. 'I can't think of anyone.' They all waited. Jane shrugged, looked at them all in turn then threw out her hands helplessly. 'I'm happy just to let you do the organizing,' she declared.

'But you've got to choose someone,' Pippa insisted.

'I know! Phillip Schofield!' Tom cried, naming his current TV favourite, then looked bemused at the way everyone exploded into laughter. 'You said you liked him,' he said accusingly to Jane.

'I do,' she chuckled, 'but I think Mummy had someone a little grander than that in mind. I know,' she suddenly said, 'I'll invite Tom. He can be my partner for the evening.'

'Oh Jane!' Pippa wailed. 'He's going to be here anyway.'

'And someone has to keep the little rascal out of mischief, don't they?' she said winking at Tom.

'What do you do with her?' Pippa sighed, going to sit back on the sofa. 'Incidently, did you invite your parents?'

Jane nodded. 'I'm afraid they can't make it though, they've got some function on that night at Daddy's school.'

'On your twenty-first!' Pippa cried. 'Surely they can miss some stuffy old function for that.'

'They're taking me out to dinner during the week,' Jane assured her. 'Besides, they're not really the partying types, and they'd be a bit uncomfortable amongst so many people.'

Pippa let it go at that, though Jane didn't miss the way she and Laurence exchanged glances. Jane read their unspoken communication only too well, they had been expecting her parents to back out, mainly because Frank and Amy Cottle always did when Pippa and Laurence invited them over. In fact, Pippa and Laurence had only ever met Jane's father for Amy Cottle had never been to the Kensington house. Jane had explained, not long after she'd first started with the McAllisters, that her mother was very shy and would be so overwhelmed by this wonderful house that Jane felt it better not to insist she came. Only on one other occasion had Jane discussed her mother with Pippa, which was the only time in the three years Pippa had known her that Jane had shown anything even approaching rancour. It had been so out of character that Pippa had tried to bring her mother into the conversation again at a later date, but Jane was completely closed on the subject. 'I really don't want to talk about her,' she had said. 'In fact, if I could, I'd like to forget that she even exists, but I don't suppose I'll ever be able to do that.'

Pippa had been so surprised at what, coming from Jane, were such strong words, she had broached the matter with Laurence, wondering if they should try to get to the bottom of it. At first Laurence was unsure, but after giving it some thought he'd decided that Jane's personal life was her own affair. Not everyone got along with their parents, he'd said, reminding her of her fractious relationship with her own mother, 'besides which, there's not one of us who doesn't have something in our pasts we don't much want to share with anyone else.'

That had been a mistake if ever he'd made one, for Jane's problem had been instantly forgotten as Pippa had wanted to know exactly what it was that he didn't want to share with her . . .

Dermott Campbell was riding high. Everyone said so, including him – probably too often, but people were as used to his immodesty as they were his vulgarity. The

Kirstie Doll campaign was proving such a success that, single-handedly, he had succeeded in upping his paper's circulation by almost twenty per cent in less than a month. Dyllis was almost as pleased with that as she was the damage being caused to the Doll's reputation. Campbell smirked at that – in truth there really wasn't much of her reputation left to destroy now.

He'd run his last few articles as a 'Teach Yourself, by Kirsten Meredith', series. There was Teach Yourself how to Exploit Your Beauty; Teach Yourself Social Mountaineering! Teach Yourself How to Inherit; and Teach Yourself How to Use a Guy. That one had really got the papers flying off the stands. Sadly, Campbell's source, the woman he had fancied himself in love with a month or so ago, hadn't known Kirsten's tricks of the trade, but with the help of *The Joy of Sex* they had been easy enough to concoct. And, added to his scathing wit, was, of course, the fact that the Kirstie Doll was so fucking gorgeous everyone was buying the papers just to look at her. Shit, was she an easy target!

So, everything was moving along as smoothly as a train – trouble was every now and again it dropped him off at a station he didn't much want to be at. Meaning, that for the most part he was getting carried along by the sheer momentum of the campaign. But in quiet moments he was doing some reflecting he wasn't too comfortable with, which left him with the uneasy feeling that at the journey's end, when that train was moving full pelt towards the buffers, he, Dermott Campbell, was going to be the only one on board.

However, he – and his source whom he hadn't heard from for a fortnight – were beginning to run out of material. Dyllis wasn't too bothered at this stage, after all the general public could only take so much and the signs were that their sympathy was beginning to veer in Kirsten's direction. No, they'd relaunch the campaign once the Kirstie Doll started to venture from the house.

At that moment Campbell was standing in front of his copy-strewn desk gazing absently at the photographs of Kirsten and Helena Johnson that had been taken as they were leaving San Lorenzo's. There was nothing he could write about that. Nothing at all. But the picture of Kirsten was pretty good, in fact, laughing the way she was made her look so goddamned beautiful that if he weren't who he was he might just find himself falling for her. His eyes moved to Helena Johnson. Now that was someone he had already fallen for, at least he thought he had . . .

Wearily he sank back into his chair, wishing the damned phones around him would stop ringing and for just five minutes everyone would stop yelling. He didn't want to admit how much all this was getting to him but right now he had to admit that playing the role of Mr Big Shit wasn't anywhere near as pleasurable this time round. Maybe he'd gone soft in his old age. Maybe once a man passed forty his cutting edge became blunted by sentiment.

Pushing his fingers into his hair he rested his elbows on the desk and ignored the phones. Sometimes, at least recently, he had felt as though he was playing out his life on a stage with himself, his real self, as the sole member of the audience. His acting wasn't bad, he'd give himself credit for that, for weren't the people fawning around him again, clamouring to get into his column, wheedling their way into his esteem, laughing uproariously at his unfunny jokes just so's he'd write something flattering about them? God, they disgusted him at times.

But without them he'd be nothing and he sure as hell didn't want to be that again.

So, there was nothing else for it, but to pull up the curtain and get out there and continue with his sublime impersonation of a man who sneered at the world and just didn't give a fuck . . .

'Hey, Dermott! You going to pick up that phone?' someone yelled.

'Yeah, yeah,' Campbell answered, reaching across for it.

'Hello,' the voice at the other end said, 'is that you, Dermott?'

On hearing the woman he just couldn't work out his feelings for Campbell's back straightened. 'Yeah, it's me,' he said.

'Good. Are you ready? I've got something for you.'

'I'm ready.'

'She was at San Lorenzo's . . .'

'Christ, tell me something I don't already know, will you?'

'OK. But you're not going to like it.'

'Try me.'

It didn't take long in the telling, but by the time she had finished the blood had drained from Campbell's face. She was right, he didn't like it. He didn't like it one bit, for what she had just told him was the very thing he'd been dreading. Of course he'd known it was going to come sooner or later, but he'd been banking on it being later, by that time he might have worked out a way to handle it. For a moment or two he toyed with the idea of keeping the information from Dyllis. But if he did his source would only wonder why he hadn't gone public with what he knew, and who could say, unlikely as it might seem, she might, out of panic for her own skin, actually go to Dyllis herself – and that was a risk he couldn't afford to take.

So now the fun really starts, he said despondently to himself, looking down at the photographs. Then he chuckled, a dry, humourless sound that in no way cheered him even though he could see the comical side of his thoughts . . . He didn't need make-up for his role, neither did he need direction, he didn't even need any rehearsals – all it would take was a few stiff gins and he could go out there and play the part of a complete fucking asshole. And that shouldn't be difficult, God knows he'd done it enough times before.

– 4 –

'I just can't believe I allowed you to talk me into this,' Kirsten said, as Helena walked in through the front door, clad in so much jewellery and sequins she glittered like a Christmas tree.

'Me!' Helena cried. 'It was your idea.'

'I know, but I've got to blame someone. In fact, I think I've changed my mind. Let's stay here.'

'Not on your life. I've been looking forward to this. Anyway, what was it that made you change your mind?'

'Some kind of mental aberration. Plus the fact that you're right, I have to face him sometime, so why not get it over with?'

'That's my girl,' Helena grinned. 'And I'll be right there with you.'

– 63 –

'You'd better be. I'll just pop upstairs and get into my party frock, help yourself to wine, there's some in the fridge.'

Ten minutes later, her fingers shaking so hard she could do nothing more than fumble with her earrings, Kirsten walked into the kitchen.

'My God, you look fantastic!' Helena declared when she saw the creamy white off-the-shoulder dress clinging to Kirsten's perfect figure and which showed off her flawless olive skin in a way that made even Helena's heart skip a beat. 'In fact altogether too fantastic if you ask me,' Helena decided. 'Those many assets shouldn't be allowed on just one woman, they should be shared out a bit. Pull that skirt up and let me check the thighs for cellulite, it might make me feel a bit better. On second thoughts don't, 'cos I just know you're not going to have any.'

'And neither do you,' Kirsten laughed shakily. Dear God, she really was nervous.

'No, you're right. Solid as a rock these thighs,' Helena said, slapping them. 'Comes from clamping them round young boys' heads. Nevertheless, looking like that I should send you back upstairs to change, but I can't be bothered to wait. So come on, your carriage awaits.'

'You don't think I've overdone it a bit, do you?' Kirsten said as they got into the taxi.

'It wouldn't matter what you wore, Kirsten, you'd still steal the show. But rest assured in that dress you'll knock Laurence McAllister right off his feet.'

'What do you mean?' Kirsten said in a taut voice.

'Well that's why you're wearing it, isn't it?' Helena teased. 'To get him eating his heart out for what he gave up?'

'Is that what you seriously think?' Kirsten demanded, dismayed by how transparent she was.

Helena laughed. 'Come on, lighten up,' she said. 'It's just the right sort of dress for tonight. Knock 'em dead, why not! You got it, you flaunt it!'

Kirsten wasn't at all sure she was happy with that answer either, but she should have expected no less coming from Helena. 'Listen,' she said, 'are you sure you checked this with Pippa? I mean, I would have thought I was the last person she'd . . .'

'I checked it,' Helena said firmly. 'Now stop worrying and relax.'

'What did she say?' Kirsten asked.

'She said that she reckons the press are giving you a real tough time, which they are, and that you haven't done anything to deserve it, which you haven't. She says she'd be real glad to have you at her party and that I should tell you that there'll be lots of people there you should meet.'

'Does Laurence know?' Kirsten asked, feeling so sick all of a sudden that she considered asking the driver to stop.

'Who knows? Who cares? Well, yeah, sure, Pippa's bound to have told him. Besides, he's just one man, Kirstie. There's gonna be heaps of others there, you know, like writers, those people a gal like you can't function without, and you got to get started some time. Now, *stop worrying and relax*.'

The party was in full swing by the time they arrived. Kirsten's nerves were by now in such a state that her teeth were chattering. She had to be insane, she just had to be, because no one in their right mind would even consider doing what she was now. What the hell was he going to say when he saw her, but presumably he had already worked that out, because presumably Pippa *had* told him she was coming. Which, she told herself by way of comfort, must mean that he had gone some way at least to forgiving her for what she had done . . .

As they started to press their way down the hall Kirsten was suffering from the horrible feeling that she was losing touch with herself. But perhaps it was the noise and the heady cocktail of pungent drinks and perfumed bodies making her feel that way. Or more likely, she realized, it was the fact that she was actually in Laurence McAllister's house! This huge Victorian mansion with its high ceilings, black and white chequered floor and awesomely grand rooms belonged to him – and his wife of course. She could almost have been in a dream for it was exactly how she had imagined it would be, and coming face to face with the reality of it was as dizzying as the madness that had made her come here.

Suddenly she found herself smiling, for the voice booming from the room they were heading towards she would have known anywhere. Zaccheo Marigliano! And wasn't he doing his favourite old party trick of impersonating Pavarotti while playing the piano badly? He'd done it so often when visiting Paul's house in the South of France.

'God, he's so animal!' Helena purred, as they came to a stop at the threshold of the room which was overflowing with guests.

Kirsten turned to her in surprise. 'Who, Zaccheo? I thought you liked them in short trousers.'

'Not quite, darling,' Helena laughed. 'Seventeen's the youngest I've had, I think twenty-three is the oldest, but for Marigliano I could be persuaded to make an exception.'

Laughing Kirsten turned to look about her. There were several faces she recognized, but for the moment she didn't quite have the courage to approach any of them. And no one, she thought sadly, looked as though they were going to acknowledge her. Several faces were turned in her direction, and she felt herself smiling awkwardly as her hand tightened on her bag. It took several seconds, perhaps even as long as a minute, for the silence to spread through the entire room, but to Kirsten, as she realized what was happening, it felt like eternity.

The sea of hostile faces suddenly started to swim before her as her heart pummelled her chest so hard her whole body seemed to vibrate with it. She was on the point of turning and running when Helena's hand gripped her arm savagely.

'It's all right,' she murmured. 'I'm right here with you. You can do this, Kirstie.' Then in a voice brimming with laughter she cried, 'Hi, everyone. We've arrived, so *let's party!*' and she started wiggling outrageously towards the man nearest her.

As the hustle and bustle started up again Kirsten stood frozen in the doorway. She had read their expressions only too well – how did she, the Kirstie Doll who had duped their beloved Paul Fisher, the man whose memory she had defiled – have the nerve to show her face in public?

She could see people snickering behind their hands and suddenly, dressed as she was, she felt like the whore they intended her to feel. Somehow she managed to take a step towards Helena. 'You're wrong, Helena,' she said. 'I can't do it. I'm leaving.'

'The hell you are,' Helena hissed back. 'They've got

over the initial shock now, so come on, show 'em what you're made of.'

'They're reading that every day in Campbell's column,' Kirsten reminded her angrily. 'They don't want me here, and I don't want to be here, so I'm going.'

'Kirsten! Oh, Kirsten, how lovely to see you. I'm so glad you could come.'

Kirsten turned to see a petite blonde woman wearing skin tight blue leggings and matching overshirt pushing a path towards her. Kirsten had only ever seen Pippa once before in her life, the day she had found out about her and Laurence, but she would have known her anywhere. She was, however, a good deal more attractive than Kirsten remembered.

'I'm Pippa McAllister,' Pippa said, taking Kirsten's hand and smiling up into her face. Kirsten was looking for the tell-tale glint of hostility, perhaps even triumph, in her eyes, but there was none. 'Laurence is around somewhere,' Pippa went on chattily. 'Probably down in the kitchen sorting out the drinks. And you don't have one! What can I get you? I think we have just about everything.'

'Well, actually I was just about to . . .'

'Champagne!' Helena chipped in from where she was bopping around beside them. 'She adores champagne.'

'Who doesn't?' Pippa laughed. 'I'll get one of the waiters to go down and get you some. Now there's someone over here I've just been dying to introduce you to,' and before Kirsten could object she was being led across the room towards a tall, slightly overweight, middle-aged man, with dusty-coloured hair, a swarthy complexion and whose half-glasses were perched pompously on the end of his nose while he waved around a huge fat cigar.

The instant Kirsten saw him she tried to pull away from Pippa. 'No,' she said, 'I don't think . . .'

'Dermott,' Pippa cried, 'just look who I have here.' She turned to Kirsten and spoke softly so that Campbell couldn't hear. 'Give it your best, Kirsten, he deserves it after what he's been doing to you,' and she was gone.

How Kirsten managed to stop herself running after Pippa she never knew, but with a supreme effort of will she made herself turn to face Campbell. His quirkily handsome face was pinched with, Kirsten thought, something like discomfort, but the arrogance was so pronounced it masked it well.

'Well, this is a surprise,' he said, glancing at the woman next to him in the hope she was listening. She was. So too were several others.

The last thing Kirsten wanted was a scene, which she could see, was exactly what Campbell was hoping for. Well she'd be damned if she was going to give him the satisfaction, so after sweeping him from head to foot with her piercing green eyes she treated him to the sweetest smile she could muster and said, 'I've frequently wondered what I would do on coming face to face with you and now I find that strangely you inspire nothing in me whatsoever, except perhaps a modicum of pity.' In the brief moment before she turned away she saw the surprise on his face, and, just as she hoped, the outrage. But clearly he recovered quickly for, as she started to walk away, she heard him sneer,

'The bitch has got one hell of an ass, what do you say? She could hump it over my dick any time. Hey, Kirstie Doll,' he called after her, 'come on, it's got to be my turn!' and he roared with laughter.

Kirsten kept going. Burning with embarrassment and rage she walked out of the nearest door along a deserted hall and smack bang into someone coming the other way.

'Excuse me,' she mumbled, trying to get past him.

'Don't mention it,' he answered. Then, 'Hey, Kirsten. It is you, isn't it? It's me, David Gill. Remember me?'

'Oh, David, yes. How are you?' she said, taking the hand he was holding out.

'Great. Just great. Thanks to you.'

'To me?'

'Well you were the one who gave me my break all those years ago, weren't you? I'm writing the big stuff now, you know? Nine o'clock slots and all that. Still jobbing, obviously, haven't got an original thought in my head. But I earn a buck or two. How about you? What are you doing with yourself these days?'

'Not very much,' Kirsten answered.

'No, well, I guess it's a bit soon after Paul. I was really sorry to hear he had died. He was a great guy. Well, you don't need me to tell you that, do you? And by the way, all that crap they're writing about you in the press, well, here's one guy who's on your side.'

'That's nice to know,' Kirsten smiled.

'If I could,' he said, 'I'd stand up and speak out for you. Well, a lot of us would, but you know how it is. The Fisher woman's got a lot of clout and I sure as hell don't want the poison flowing through Campbell's pen about me. Not that anyone'd be interested to read about me, I suppose, but they'd find some way to finish me. Still, if there's anything else I can do . . .'

'It's OK,' Kirsten assured him. 'I'll survive.'

From the look on Gill's face she could see how much he doubted that. But it was nice of him to bother saying it, not many would have, and when he suggested they go and get a drink she went with him.

As they walked into the kitchen she found herself scanning the room nervously for Laurence. Hadn't Pippa said he would probably be down here? But there was no sign of him and Kirsten smiled wryly to herself at the relief she felt. She'd have just this one drink then see if she couldn't get away without actually running into him.

In no time at all David had dragged her into a group who were discussing Laurence's next movie project. All of them, without exception it seemed, thought he was mad to have taken on Ruby Collins as the screenwriter – whoever the hell she was.

'Dermott knows her,' a woman beside Kirsten remarked. 'I think he might have been the one who introduced them. Anyway, she's a Yank. Perhaps Laurence thinks she'll give him a foot into Hollywood.'

'But no one in Hollywood knows who she is. I'm telling you, she'll crucify him. Have you met the woman?'

'No.'

'She's a dipso. Can't function without gin. Now tell me, who the hell in their right mind is going to take on a writer like that when there's so much at stake? She's got no credentials, no talent by all accounts and no, absolutely no, finesse, darlings.'

'Perhaps Laurence knows something the rest of you don't,' Kirsten heard herself say.

The man who had spoken arched his eyebrows haughtily in her direction then continued as if she hadn't spoken, turning his back slightly as though to ease her out of the group.

'I told him,' he continued, 'I said, Laurence, you're committing professional suicide taking on a project like that with an unknown writer. But you know what Laurence is.'

'I'd have thought he'd have been only too willing to take your advice, Baz, after his last disaster,' a woman with purple hair chipped in. 'He can't afford another or he'll be finished.'

'What's his next movie about then?' a rather dowdy middle-aged woman enquired. She had to be the wife of one of these pumped up know-it-alls, Kirsten reckoned. Someone who was only ever wheeled out for occasions, and the fewer the better.

'Oh, some woman who lived during the last century, went to New Orleans, became a prostitute then got herself hanged or murdered, I can't remember which,' the pompous man answered. 'Pretty banal stuff, if you ask me. And period! He's out of his mind. He'll never get the finance. I told him, Laurence, I said . . .'

Kirsten stopped listening. How many conversations like this had she endured in her life, and how she detested them. Everyone thought they knew better than the producer and everyone thought the producer was mad. Of course, should the film prove a success they'd find a way of sharing in, if not taking all of, the credit.

As she turned away her eye was caught by the childish drawings pinned to the refrigerator. Instantly her heart froze. God, she would never forget the terrible setback she had suffered when she had first found out that Laurence had a son. But that was all behind her now, she reminded herself taking a deep breath and forcing herself to move on. Just please God don't let me come face to face with the child tonight.

She was on the point of leaving the kitchen when she heard someone say, 'Hello there.'

Kirsten turned round. 'Hello,' she said, wondering if she knew the woman standing at her elbow.

'Molly Forsyth,' the woman said. 'And you're Kirsten Meredith.'

For some reason Kirsten didn't like the look of this woman. There was something shifty in her eyes and her thin, heavily lipsticked mouth was, to Kirsten's mind, spiteful.

'I have to tell you,' Molly said 'that I heard what Dermott Campbell said about you just now. Quite vulgar, I thought, though I imagine you've heard a lot worse.'

Kirsten simply stared at her, wondering why some people enjoyed being nasty to people they didn't even know. Then, to her dismay, she realized that those behind her had stopped talking and were now listening to Molly Forsyth.

'I have to tell you that I told Campbell he'd be insane to hump you over his dick, as he so eloquently put it,' Molly continued, 'after all, there's no knowing what he might catch, is there?'

As the blood rushed to Kirsten's cheeks she heard someone behind her snigger. Her luminous green eyes were still holding Molly's showing nothing of what she was feeling inside, but for a fleeting instant it was as though she was a child again, surrounded by mocking, sneering faces who wanted to hurt her in any way they could. She almost felt herself begin to take a step back, but somehow managed to stop herself. 'Do you feel better now?' she heard herself ask. 'Are you glad you've got that off your chest, or is there more?'

Molly pulled down the corners of her mouth and raised her eyebrows as she glanced round at the others. 'Just one question,' she said sweetly, turning back to Kirsten. 'While you're here wallowing in all that cream you juiced out of Fisher do you feel at all guilty about the fact that it was you who gave him AIDS?'

It was all Kirsten could do to stop herself gasping. This was the first time she'd heard that rumour and for one blinding instant she wanted to hit that supercilious face so hard she'd knock it right into next week.

Instead she took a deep breath. 'As you already know Paul died of a heart attack,' she replied. 'But if it makes you happy to insult someone as profoundly as you just have me, and to soil Paul's memory into the bargain, then I can only say that right now you must be ecstatic. Now, if you'll excuse me.'

She brushed past Molly Forsyth, but not before hearing David Gill say, 'What's she ever done to you, Molly?'

'Obviously not what she's done to you, lovey,' Molly answered with lightning wit and everyone laughed.

Kirsten would have left then and nothing and no one would have stood in her way, except Zaccheo Marigliano. When she saw his beaming face heading towards her as she walked into the sitting room to tell Helena she was leaving Kirsten instantly felt tears burn the backs of her eyes. Zaccheo's felt like the first friendly face she'd seen and right now, feeling as she did, one kind word was highly likely to bring the tears flooding.

'I'm not going to say anything about Paul,' he whispered in her ear as he swept her into his arms and held her tight. 'It's not the time and I can see you are suffering. But no matter what they say about you or do to you, Kirstie, I am your friend. Remember that. Zaccheo, he loves all the women, but you I love most of all.'

'Don't or I really shall cry,' Kirsten sniffed, turning her head away so that no one in the room could see the way her eyes had filled with tears.

'But these beautiful cheeks are made for the kisses of

a lover, not the tiny droplets of pain,' Zaccheo's voice rumbled in her ear, and then he gave a protracted, ostentatiously romantic sigh, which made Kirsten laugh.

'By the way, thanks for going to the funeral,' she said, 'I know Paul would have appreciated it. And thanks for taking my flowers. She sent them back, I'm afraid.'

'I know. But he knows you loved him, that's all that matters.'

'You're right.' She took a breath and forced herself to smile brightly. 'So, what brings you to England, Signor Marigliano?'

'Pippa McAllister. She is my editor. And Laurence, of course, he is my friend. I stay here with them until the end of the week. Maybe I come to see you before I go?'

'I'd like that.'

Zaccheo moved to one side then to let someone pass and as Kirsten looked across the room she saw Helena dancing with Dermott Campbell. He was holding her extremely close, too close for such fast music, Kirsten thought, but Helena didn't appear to be objecting. Kirsten was momentarily disturbed by that, she'd thought that Helena found the man repulsive. But, as Helena lifted her head, Kirsten smiled at the conspiratorial wink she received. Obviously Helena was over there doing her stuff in getting Campbell to back off.

Kirsten was already half turned back to Zaccheo when suddenly the smile froze on her lips; it was as though a giant vice had taken hold of her heart. Zaccheo was still speaking though she had no idea what he was saying, all she knew was that she was looking straight into Laurence McAllister's eyes. He was standing at the other side of the room, just in front of the bay window, but for the moment, as though by some extraordinary preordination a space had opened in the crowd between them. Kirsten felt she might be swaying, that her entire body might be dissolving. Not even for a moment had she forgotten how incredibly handsome he was, how compelling his eyes, nor how physical his presence, but neither for a moment had she expected that seeing him again would affect her so profoundly. Suddenly the blood was beginning to pound through her ears and her chest felt so tight she was unable to breathe. So many memories were passing before her eyes, so much love, so much passion and so many promises. This man had once been her whole life, she had loved him so much and even now, looking at him she felt as though he was still hers. They had meant so much to each other, how could they be apart?

And then it was as though a smothering fog was being lifted from her senses and she realized how insane she had been to think she could handle this. She felt herself start to falter, as though a dam in her mind had broken and everything she had suppressed for so long was rushing at her. It might have been only yesterday that he had told her he didn't want her. She could almost hear herself begging him to stay, pleading with him to love her, to give her another chance.

This can't be happening, she told herself vehemently. It just can't. She was over him, she had to be because there was simply no way there could ever be anything between them now. She was just in some kind of shock and in a few minutes she'd be herself again. The new self. The woman who could hold her head high and know that she had been through hell for this man and come out the other side. The woman who had spent the last five years learning how to come to terms with her past so that she could at last deal with all that life threw at her and survive.

Yes, that's all it was, shock, she decided with relief, and how ridiculous she was to have allowed herself to be taken in by it. She found herself smiling over at him then, a shaky calm spreading its soothing warmth through her. He smiled too, then turned his attention back to the man he was talking to.

Kirsten guessed that very soon now he'd come over to say hello. She experienced a childish sort of excitement at the prospect, felt herself start to tingle even, which almost made her laugh and for one breathtaking moment she felt almost deliriously happy.

She carried on chatting with Zaccheo, though thankfully they were continually interrupted for Kirsten's powers of concentration were eluding her. Unable to stop herself she kept glancing in Laurence's direction and though their eyes didn't meet again, she was certain that he was watching her too. Then Helena came to join them and when Kirsten looked up again Laurence had disappeared.

Excusing herself Kirsten went off to the bathroom, but as she walked out of the door, still looking back over her shoulder and laughing at something Zaccheo was saying, she collided with someone coming the other way. Before she could do anything to stop it there was Campari and soda all over the front of her dress.

'Oh no! I'm sorry!' the girl gasped. 'Oh, heavens, what can I do? Your dress, your lovely dress! I'm just so sorry, I didn't see you . . . .'

'It's all right,' Kirsten said, irritated but at the same time slightly amused by the girl who was clearly mortified at what she had done. 'I'm sure it'll come off.'

'But please, let me . . .' the girl stopped suddenly as

she looked up into Kirsten's face. Kirsten was momentarily startled by the expression in the girl's eyes. Was it fear? Shock? In a way it was like recognition. And then Kirsten remembered, that of course the girl would recognize her, who wouldn't these days? And, by the look of the girl she was quite simply horrified at having come face to face with the infamous Kirsten Meredith. And now that she had, and had ruined an extremely expensive dress into the bargain, what was the infamous Kirstie Doll going to do? Beat her? Scream at her? Humiliate her in front of all these people?

'Really, it's all right,' Kirsten smiled, closing the door behind her so that they were alone in the hall. 'Please, don't worry about it. I'll send it to the cleaners, I'm sure they'll be able to sort it out.'

The girl was obviously still shaken, couldn't quite bring herself to believe that there were no disastrous consequences to be faced for a simple accident, so Kirsten tried again.

'Please don't look at me like that,' she said kindly, 'you're making me feel like an ogre. I told you, the cleaners will sort it out . . .'

'But what about now?' the girl said, the uncertainty at last starting to retreat from her eyes. 'I mean, it's all over you. Please, come upstairs and let me see if I can sponge some of it out.'

'But there's a bathroom right here,' Kirsten said.

'I know, but everyone's using it. I've got my own, at the top of the house. I'm Jane, by the way, Tom's nanny. And I really am so very sorry.'

'Please, just forget it,' Kirsten told her. 'I'll just go and . . .' she broke off as they heard raised voices coming from a room to one side of them. The door was slightly ajar so both Jane and Kirsten could hear every word that was being said.

'I don't care, Pippa, I don't want her in the house. I don't know what the hell got into you, inviting her here, but I want her out. And I want her out now!'

'Laurence, for God's sake, be reasonable. How can I just walk up to her and tell her she's got to go?'

'If you don't then I damned well will,' he raged.

'But she's a friend of Zaccheo's.'

'Zaccheo isn't the host at this party, I am. And I don't want Kirsten Meredith in my house . . .'

'I don't see why you're getting so het up over this. It was all such a long time ago. She's probably changed . . .'

'Women like her never change. Now you heard what I said . . .'

'Oh come on, can't you at least be generous enough to give her the benefit of the doubt? Everyone's giving her such a hard time . . .'

'Pippa, I'm not arguing about this. Now just get her out of here!'

A door slammed in the distance and Kirsten and Jane turned to face one another. Kirsten's face was ashen, Jane's was hot with embarrassment.

'Come on,' Jane said rapidly pulling herself together, and before Kirsten could object Jane was sweeping her up the stairs.

'No, no,' Kirsten protested as they reached the first landing. 'Let me go. Please, I have to leave . . .'

'But, you can't go anywhere with that stain all over you,' Jane said, her shoulders hunching as she giggled nervously. 'Come on, we'll go to my flat.' She looked into Kirsten's face and her grey eyes shone with sympathy as she saw the very real distress in Kirsten's. 'Oh dear, I'm sorry you had to hear that,' Jane murmured. 'It was awful. I'm sure he didn't mean it . . .'

'Just let me go, please,' Kirsten mumbled. 'It would be better . . . If he finds out you've helped me . . .'

'He won't find out,' Jane assured her and wondered whether Kirsten realized how hard she was shaking. So hard in fact it was doubtful she'd even make it up the stairs.

But Kirsten did know, which was why she had no choice then but to go with Jane, for the idea of disgracing herself by collapsing on the stairs was too terrible even to contemplate.

By the time they reached Jane's flat Kirsten was hardly able to stand. 'It's all right,' she gasped, as they went in through the door. 'I'll be fine in a minute. I just need to sit down.'

Holding her by the shoulders Jane led her to a small sofa and gently eased her into it. 'Is there anything I can do, something I can get you?' Jane asked, her pale, freckled face taut with concern. 'You look dreadful.'

'No, no really. I'll be fine. It's not the first time I've had an attack like this. It'll pass, I promise.' But even as Kirsten spoke a welter of huge, dry, racking sobs started to tear through her body. Oh, dear God, not in three years had she had an attack like this, three years! And now here she was right back at the beginning. Vulnerable and frightened and wanting him with the same desperation she had then. But it was an illusion, she tried to tell herself. Just a bad dream come back to haunt her. If she took deep breaths, held herself straight and squeezed her hands tightly, the way she had then, it would go away. Those three years would resurface and come to stand between her and all the hurt.

But it was no good. The indignity, the self-loathing,

the desperate humiliation was coming over her in wave after relentless wave. To think that she could have been so stupid as to have come here, to have expected that he might even be pleased to see her filled her with such an excruciating shame it seemed to seep into her every pore.

It was some time before she was aware that Jane was holding her and smoothing her hair, or that she was clutching Jane in a way she only ever had Paul. 'It's all right,' Jane was whispering, 'let it all out. Just cry, I won't let you go.'

Embarrassed Kirsten pulled away and started to fumble in her bag for a handkerchief. 'I'm sorry,' she said shakily. 'I guess things just got the better of me, but that's no excuse to have made such an exhibition of myself.'

Jane dropped to her knees in front of Kirsten and took Kirsten's hands. 'You didn't make an exhibition of yourself,' she said softly. 'Anyone would have been hurt to hear themselves spoken about that way, and with everything else that is happening to you . . .' She trailed off and shrugged self-consciously, but still she held on to Kirsten's eyes, looking searchingly into them as though it was the most important thing in the world that she should somehow reach Kirsten.

Ordinarily so reticent with strangers Kirsten found herself looking back and wondering what it was in this girl that had not only made her cling to her the way she had a few moments ago, but was now encouraging her to draw down her barriers and let her in. It was bewildering, but it was undeniable. This girl, this almost waiflike child, who she'd known for less than half an hour, really did seem to care. She really did seem to mind about the vicious lies being told about a woman whom the rest of the world wanted only to spurn. Why should that be, Kirsten wondered. What did Jane want from her? Slowly she started to shake her head and as she did Jane smiled and squeezed her hands. There was something in Jane's eyes then that seemed to reach deep down inside Kirsten as though to touch her very heart.

'I've never experienced a death so close to me, the way you have recently,' Jane said, 'so I can't say I know how you're feeling. But if you were as close to Mr Fisher as I heard Zaccheo telling Pippa you were then all I can say is that I am truly, truly sorry for what you must be going through. I just wish that there was something I could do to help.'

Kirsten's heart had tightened with every word Jane uttered. It was as though Paul were speaking to her, as if somehow through this girl he was gently reminding her that it was all right to trust someone. That not everyone wanted to hurt her, and those who did only could if she, Kirsten, allowed them to. 'Oh, Jane,' Kirsten laughed through her tears. 'You have helped. You've helped very much. But if Laurence finds out that you've brought me up here . . .'

'I told you, he won't find out.' A mischievous twinkle shot to Jane's eyes. 'Besides,' she went on, 'he and Pippa are forever trying to drum into me that this is *my* flat where I can entertain *my* friends, throw parties, have orgies or do whatever *I* like.'

Kirsten chuckled and using her fingers wiped away her tears. 'So how many orgies have you had?' she asked.

'I have to confess not many,' Jane sighed forlornly. 'In fact, none. Nor parties either. Though tonight was supposed to be a party for me. I'm twenty-one today.'

'You are? Well, happy birthday. How does it feel being twenty-one?'

Jane shrugged. 'OK.'

'And where are all your friends? There didn't seem to be many people your age downstairs.'

'That,' Jane said, moving into a sitting position and hugging her knees, 'is because I don't really have any friends. I had one once, but she moved to Canada.'

'But a girl your age should have lots of friends,' Kirsten protested. 'And parties. I'm not too sure about the orgies though,' she added with a smile.

'No,' Jane laughed, 'me neither. I don't think I'm quite, well, worldly enough for that sort of thing.'

'Have you ever had a boyfriend?'

'No.'

'Not even at school?'

'Uh-huh,' Jane said, shaking her head. 'I was too shy or too plain, probably both. Anyway, it didn't really matter because I didn't want one.'

'And now?'

'No, not really. I expect I might one day, but who knows?' Suddenly she looked at Kirsten from the corner of her eye. 'I'll tell you a secret,' she said, 'if you swear you'll never tell anyone else.'

'I swear,' Kirsten said, crossing her hands over her heart.

'I had a raging mad crush on Laurence for *two* years. Can you imagine? *Two* whole years. It was the first crush of my life, in fact the only one. It was agony.'

'I think I can imagine,' Kirsten smiled. 'And now?'

'Oh, I'm over it now.'

'But you still don't have any friends your own age? Why's that?'

'I suppose it's because I don't go out much,' Jane answered, tucking her fine brown hair behind her ears. 'In fact, all in all, you could say that I have a pretty dull life really – at least compared to most people. But I love it. Well, I love Tom, actually.'

'Laurence's son? But don't you want any children of your own?'

'Oh yes, I'd love some. How about you? Would you like children?'

Kirsten felt her face turn numb. 'Yes,' she answered. 'I'd like them very much.'

There was a short silence then during which they could hear the distant sounds of the party going on downstairs. Kirsten cast her eyes around the little sitting room, noticing that amongst all the cuddly toys and dog-eared paperbacks there were only photographs of Pippa and Laurence – and Tom. She returned her eyes to Jane's.

'You really are very beautiful,' Jane said, shyly.

Kirsten laughed. 'I suppose I should thank you for that, but I promise you it feels like a curse sometimes. Tell me, Jane, where do your parents live?'

'South East London.'

'Are they here tonight?'

Jane shook her head. 'No.'

'Do you have any brothers or sisters?'

'God, no,' Jane laughed. 'My mother never wanted any children in the first place, though I don't suppose she'll ever admit it. My father wanted a son, he'll admit that all right. In fact when I was growing up you'd have thought I was a boy from the way he treated me. He wanted me to go on to be a great scientist – or at the very least a science master like he is.' She pulled a face. 'Can you think of anything more boring? They hate me being a nanny, they think I'm wasting my talent, but as far as I'm aware I don't have any particular talent so I don't know what they're going on about.'

'Perhaps your talent is with children.'

'Perhaps.'

'Don't you ever get lonely?' Kirsten asked.

'Yes, but I'm used to it. I was a lonely child.'

'Mm, me too.'

Jane looked at her in astonishment. 'I can't imagine anyone like you could ever be lonely,' she said, then remembering Paul she hastily added, 'At least not for long.'

Kirsten sighed. 'If you only knew the half of it, Jane.'

'If you want to talk I have the time,' Jane assured her, then her cheeks flushed at the presumptuousness of her remark.

Kirsten smiled. 'Perhaps another time,' she said. 'I don't want to spoil your birthday, and besides, it looks like this stain has dried in so there's no point trying to wash it off now. Maybe I'd better just go home and like I said, send it to the cleaners in the morning.'

'You will let me pay for it though, won't you?'

'Certainly not,' Kirsten said, standing up. 'It was an accident and accidents happen.'

'Then at least let me lend you something of mine to go home in. I mean you can't go out like that. It looks like someone's tried to murder you.'

'Oh Jane,' Kirsten laughed. 'I'd never fit into anything of yours, you're so tiny.'

'I'm sure I'll be able to find something,' Jane said eagerly. 'It won't be quite as glamorous as the dress you're wearing,' she said, looking back over her shoulder as she walked into her bedroom. 'In fact it won't be anything like it at all.'

In the end they managed to fix Kirsten up with a long flared skirt and a baggy sweater to conceal the unfastened waistband.

'Well, you look a bit like Cinderella after the ball,' Jane remarked when Kirsten was dressed, 'but it'll do.'

Kirsten was watching her closely, fascinated by the sudden spurts of humour and frankness that struggled through the inherent self-consciousness. 'I guess I'd better post them back to you,' Kirsten said, her eyes still dancing at Jane's observation. 'After what we heard down there in the hall tonight I don't think it'd be a very good idea for me to show up again.'

Jane shook her head sadly. 'I really am sorry you heard that,' she said.

'Don't worry, I've heard a lot worse.' Kirsten sighed. 'Actually the truth is I needed to cry, I'm just sorry you were the one who had to bear the brunt.'

'I'd rather you weren't sorry,' Jane said, her young face imbued with feeling. 'I'm glad I was there.'

'Yes, I'm glad too,' Kirsten said touching her cheek.

'Do you feel all right now?'

'Yes. Just fine.'

'I've got an idea,' Jane said suddenly as they started out of the room. 'You must say no if you want to, and I won't be in the least offended if you do, but what about if I come to pick up my clothes? I have the afternoon off on Wednesday, I could come then. But no, you'll be busy, of course you will. Perhaps you're right, you'd . . .'

'I won't be busy,' Kirsten stopped her, 'and I'd love you to come. Shall we say around three? Or why don't you come for lunch if you're not doing anything? I'll introduce you to Helena as well. I think you'll like her. We're both a bit old for you, I suppose, but what the hell? If you don't mind . . .'

Jane's homely little face was beaming. 'I'd love to

come,' she said, but when Kirsten's face suddenly fell she added, 'is there a problem?'

'Not really. Or at least there could be. Laurence. Honestly, Jane, he'd be furious if he thought you were coming to see me . . .'

'It's my life,' Jane said defiantly. 'I can see whomsoever I please. And I really would like to see you again. I've enjoyed talking to you.'

'I've enjoyed it too,' Kirsten smiled.

'If you like,' Jane said as they reached the door, 'you can go down the fire escape.'

The absurdity of it appealed to Kirsten, making her laugh. 'Why not?' she said. 'I don't really want to run the risk of bumping into Laurence again, so would you mind searching out Helena for me? Explain what happened and tell her I'll call her, OK?'

'See you on Wednesday then,' Jane said as Kirsten stepped out on to the fire escape.

'About one,' Kirsten smiled. 'And happy birthday.'

By the time Kirsten arrived home her mind was racing. She knew she wouldn't sleep and neither did she want to. She had so much to do and was eager to get started. Feeling the way she still did about Laurence was one thing, but sitting around moping about it was quite another. She had to get herself back in motion, get her career back on its feet, and the only way to do that was to start right now. And going into her study she sat down at her desk and pulled out the file filled with the ideas she and Paul had discussed during those wonderfully balmy evenings in the South of France.

— 5 —

Pippa moaned sleepily and snuggled deeper into the bed as Laurence's hand came round and cupped her breast. After a while, as he lazily teased her nipples, a smile stole across her lips. She loved to be woken this way and gave a gentle sigh of contentment as Laurence moulded his body behind hers and pressed himself against her.

'Mmm,' she murmured returning the pressure when she felt the hardness of him against the small of her back. His hand was softly caressing her stomach now, his long fingers spanning the width of her hips. She pushed her head back into his shoulder, raising her chin as he kissed her neck.

'Good morning,' he whispered when she turned her mouth to his. He gave her a long and deeply erotic kiss, lowering his fingers as her legs parted.

'I'll give you two hours to stop doing that,' she murmured as he began stroking her. 'Oh God,' she moaned when a few minutes later she felt the tip of his penis start to push into her. She raised her arms over her head, reaching behind her to touch his face. He was taking a very long, sensual time to enter her, but he couldn't reach full penetration with her in this position. Pippa moved herself forwards, half rolling on to her stomach as Laurence lifted her hips. Then suddenly the door flew open.

'Daddy! Daddy! Wake up, Daddy! Play Humpty Dumpty!'

'I don't believe it,' Pippa groaned, pushing her face into the pillow. 'I just don't fucking believe it.'

'Not now, soldier,' Laurence laughed.

'But Daddy, it's eight o'clock and you said you would,' Tom protested.

'Eight o'clock?' Laurence repeated frowning.

'You said if I came in at eight o'clock we could play Humpty Dumpty and Jane says it's eight o'clock.'

Laurence glanced at the bedside clock. 'It's seven-thirty, Tom,' he said.

'Just tell him to go,' Pippa muttered angrily.

'Jane said it was eight o'clock,' Tom said stubbornly, his eager little face starting to lose its smile. He hated to be sent away and sensed that he was about to be.

Laurence reached out to pick up his watch. Tom was right, it was eight o'clock, something was obviously wrong with the radio alarm.

'You promised,' Tom said.

'Sure I did,' Laurence winked, feeling his heart tighten as he looked into his son's forlorn face, and disentangling himself from Pippa he rolled on to his back, checking that he was still covered to the waist, and swung Tom up in the air. 'And a man has to stick by his promises, isn't that right?'

'Humpty Dumpty?' Tom cried his face beaming with joy.

'Laurence, for God's sake.' Pippa seethed as Laurence settled Tom on to his raised knees. 'Just tell him that you don't want to play and send him back to the bloody nursery.'

Tom looked wide-eyed in his mother's direction, his

tiny brow furrowed, his eyes almost afraid. Pippa just looked at him, as though challenging him to defy her.

'Let him stay,' Laurence said, lifting Tom up and kissing him.

'You spoil him,' Pippa grumbled as Laurence resettled Tom on his knees, but Laurence wasn't listening.

'Humpty Dumpty sat on a wall,' he and Tom chorused, 'Humpty Dumpty had a great . . . *fall*!' On the last word Laurence opened his legs and let Tom fall through. Laughing with delight Tom scrambled back up and Laurence began again.

Pippa kept her silence throughout three more falls, then, 'Has Jane given you your breakfast yet, Tom?' she snapped.

Tom shook his head.

'Then tell her I said you can have some flaky chocolate with your cornflakes.'

'Oh, yes!' Tom cried, waving triumphant fists in the air, and leaping from the bed he ran from the room yelling for Jane.

'I guess we ought to be getting up,' Laurence said still laughing as he watched Tom go.

'That wasn't the idea,' Pippa said, cuddling up to him.

'Sorry, I've got a meeting at nine,' Laurence told her and flipping back the covers he got out of bed.

'For Christ's sake! Is it too much to ask for some precious minutes of your time?'

'No more than it is to ask for precious minutes of yours,' Laurence countered, heading towards the bathroom.

'And just what the hell is that supposed to mean?'

'Work it out for yourself,' he answered and closed the bathroom door behind him.

He was already showered and half way through shaving when the door opened and Pippa sauntered in. 'Are you sulking because I haven't let you have sex for the past week?' she asked.

Briefly he met her gaze in the mirror. 'No. If I were sulking I wouldn't have woken you up the way I did,' he answered.

'So what's changed your mind now?'

'I told you, I've got a meeting.'

Pippa eyed him angrily.

'Hey come on,' he laughed. 'You're making too much of this. I told you last night I had a meeting this morning . . .'

'But I notice that Tom doesn't get deprived of his share of your time,' she said petulantly.

'Pippa, for heaven's sake, do we have to go through this every time? He's just a kid. He doesn't understand about meetings. Now pass me the towel, will you?'

'All right,' she said as she flipped the towel over his shoulder, 'I'm sorry about the way I neglected you last week . . .'

'I told you, it's not a problem.'

'But obviously it is, so I'm apologizing. It's just that I can't make love when Zaccheo is in the house. He puts me all on edge – I can't concentrate on anything. But he's gone now and I want to fuck!'

'Then you're gonna have to wait,' Laurence grinned.

'God you can be so damned infuriating at times,' Pippa seethed and flounced out of the bathroom slamming the door behind her.

When Laurence returned to the bedroom some five minutes later it was to find Pippa doing her exercises. As he dressed he watched her, slightly less amused now than he had been for he could sense her smouldering resentment. He could do without this right now, today was going to be difficult enough as it was.

'What are your plans for today?' he asked making an effort to diffuse the situation, but Pippa wasn't playing ball. She simply continued bending and stretching as though there was no one else in the room.

Rolling his eyes Laurence slipped his feet into his brogues, fastened his watch strap and started out of the room.

'I've worked out what it is now,' Pippa snapped. 'You're still pissed off with me because I invited Kirsten Meredith here last Saturday.'

'Pippa,' he said, pronouncing her name with deliberation as he turned back, 'I'm not pissed at you at all, but you sure as hell are at me. So come on, let's have it, what's really eating you?'

'Are you sure you have the time?' she asked sarcastically.

Laurence sighed heavily. 'As a matter of fact I don't right now.'

'Then book me in will you?'

'OK, I've just about had it,' he yelled. 'You wanna talk, we talk right now,' and slamming the door he came back to sit on the edge of the bed.

'Go to your meeting,' Pippa cried. 'Just go. We'll sort this out later.'

As he left the room Laurence didn't see the tears glittering in Pippa's eyes – if he had he wouldn't have left. Pippa knew that, which was why she had told him to go. She hadn't really wanted to get him off to a bad start for the day, she knew how important this meeting was to him, though for the life of her she couldn't remember if he'd told her what it was.

Still smarting with guilt she peeled off her leotard,

– 92 –

took a quick shower then went downstairs to join Jane and Tom in the breakfast room. She hadn't heard the front door close and half hoped Laurence was still there, but he wasn't.

'I take it you heard us shouting?' she said to Jane as she poured herself some coffee.

'I'm afraid so,' Jane smiled awkwardly.

'Did Tom?'

Jane nodded.

Pippa looked down at her son who was sitting on the floor at Jane's feet engrossed in winding up a clockwork toy. 'It's your fault,' she suddenly snapped at him. 'You take up all Daddy's time and if you hadn't come into the bedroom like that this morning Daddy and I wouldn't have had an argument.'

Tom's wide eyes were filling with tears as he looked up at his mother. Pippa glared back, but as his face started to crumple Jane scooped him up in her arms.

'Sssh, sssh,' she soothed as he buried his face in her shoulder, quiet sobs jerking his little body.

'Oh God,' Pippa groaned dashing a hand through her already dishevelled hair. 'I'm sorry, Tom. Tom, Mummy's sorry. I shouldn't have said that. It wasn't your fault at all, it was all mine. Are you going to give Mummy a kiss now, show that we're friends?'

Tom lifted his head to look at her, his soft cheeks were flushed with colour, his deep blue eyes steeped in apprehension.

'I'm sorry, darling,' Pippa said again. 'Come to Mummy and show me what a big boy you are by accepting my apology.'

Still Tom just looked at her, but after a while he twisted in Jane's arms and leaned towards Pippa.

'I love you,' Pippa said, smoothing his tousled curls

and kissing him. 'Mummy loves you so much, and I'm such a silly Mummy to get so angry, aren't I?'

She didn't hold him for long though before handing him back to Jane and going to sit at the table. 'Oh God, what a mess,' she sighed angrily and buried her face in her hands.

'Tom, would you do something for me, please?' Jane asked.

Tom nodded.

'Would you go upstairs and get your pyjamas, they need washing.' She put him down and watched as he reluctantly left the room. He was being sent away, he knew it, and Jane knew how much it troubled him. But it was clear that Pippa wanted to talk and it was probably better that Tom didn't hear. She waited until she knew he was no longer in earshot then went to sit down too.

'Laurence is so bloody hung up on this next movie,' Pippa said, starting right in with what was on her mind. She was so used by now to having Jane as her sounding board that she simply took it for granted that Jane would want to listen.

'He eats, sleeps and breathes the damned thing,' Pippa went on. 'It's coming between us, I know it is and I just don't know how to stop it. Christ, we don't even make love any more.'

Jane's mouth twitched with an uncertain smile. 'I thought that was because Zaccheo was around,' she said, gently reminding Pippa that they'd been down this road just the day before.

'I thought it was,' Pippa answered, 'but I'm not so sure now. The thing is I'm always so ready to blame myself for everything that I tend to forget that it might just be Laurence who's at fault.' She lifted her head then and looked Jane straight in the eye. 'Tell me honestly, Jane, do you think he's having an affair?'

Jane's eyes widened. 'No, not at all,' she answered.

'Well I do,' Pippa declared irritably, 'and if I could only find out who with I could do something about it.'

'Have you *asked* him if there's anyone else?' Jane said, helping herself to a triangle of cold toast and starting to fiddle with it.

'Of course I have, and he denies it. Well he would, wouldn't he? But what about Kirsten Meredith, don't you think he over-reacted a bit when he found out she was here?'

Jane drew back her head in surprise. 'You surely don't think he's having an affair with her, do you?'

'No. At least not yet he isn't. But give him time.'

Jane spent the next few moments mulling this over in her mind. 'Would I be right in thinking,' she said carefully, 'that Kirsten and Laurence knew each other before?'

Pippa gave a snort of derision. 'Oh yes, they knew each other all right. He was the great love of her life, or so she made out. She even threatened to kill me if he didn't give me up and go back to her . . .'

Jane's astonishment showed. 'Gosh,' she said, looking down at her toast. Then returning her eyes to Pippa's she said, 'So what made you invite her here on Saturday night?'

'To test him, of course. To see if he really was over her.'

'You mean you thought he might not be?' Jane said incredulously.

'Well do you think he is, behaving like that?'

'I don't really know,' Jane said somewhat at a loss. 'I mean on the face of it I'd say he definitely was.'

'Well you're right,' Pippa cut in, her exasperation with herself suddenly deflating her irritation. 'He is over her. He has been for years and I'm just being a pain in the ass. Laurence wouldn't go near Kirsten Meredith again if she was the last woman on earth. But if you ask me she'd have him back tomorrow. I mean, why else would she have come on Saturday?'

'I don't know,' Jane said, which was true, but she felt decidedly uncomfortable all of a sudden. She was silent for a while, but in the end realized that she really couldn't, or perhaps shouldn't, hold back on Pippa. 'There's something I think I should tell you,' she began tentatively. 'Kirsten Meredith overheard what Laurence said about her on Saturday, you know, when he was telling you to get her out of the house. She was pretty upset, I know because I was with her when she overheard it. I'd spilt a drink all over her dress, you see, and was about to take her upstairs to clean up when we heard you and Laurence in the study. Anyway, I did take her upstairs in the end and she borrowed some of my clothes to go home in. I went round to collect them on Wednesday.'

Pippa was staring at her. 'You mean you've actually talked to Kirsten Meredith! Actually been to her house?'

Jane nodded then to her amazement Pippa suddenly started to laugh.

'What's so funny?' Jane asked.

'What's so funny is that if Kirsten Meredith thinks she's going to get back with Laurence through you she's got to be out of her mind. He'd see through that quicker than he could see through glass and if there's one thing Laurence can't stand it's scheming women.'

Neither of them spoke for a while then, but Jane watched Pippa as the thoughts raced round in her mind.

Finally Pippa smiled. 'So Kirsten was upset was she?' she said.

'Well, yes, she was a bit. I mean, I suppose anyone would be hearing themselves spoken about like that,' Jane answered. She didn't know quite why she should feel the need to defend Kirsten, or why she should choose to be loyal to her, but for some reason she knew she was going to withhold the true extent of Kirsten's distress.

'Yes, I suppose you're right,' Pippa sighed. 'And I'm just being a cow. I don't have anything against the woman really, why should I, he married me, didn't he? And in actual fact I do feel genuinely sorry for what the press are doing to her. If I thought it would do any good I'd speak to Dermott myself and try to get him to stop, but you know Dermott, once he's got his teeth into something there's no stopping him. And my guess is Dyllis Fisher is paying him a whole whack of bonuses to keep him at it. Oh Jane, if you could see your face,' she laughed. 'You really don't like poor old Dermott, do you?'

'I just think it's a horrible way of earning a living,' Jane said, 'riding high on someone else's misery. I never have been able to work out why Laurence has him as a friend.'

'They've done each other some favours in the past,' Pippa chuckled. 'Well, you know that. And once you get on the right side of Dermott he's not so bad, you know. He's really fond of Laurence.'

'And of you,' Jane said.

'Because we helped him out at a time when he was down on his luck. Still he's really making a comeback now. He should be grateful to Kirsten in fact, he might still be in the wilderness if it weren't for her. Anyway, those two don't really concern me right now. What does is Laurence. Do you know who this meeting of his is with today?'

Jane shook her head.

'Then I'll just have to look in his diary and find out, won't I. Oh, get that will you,' she added as the telephone started to ring.

Jane reached over to the kitchen counter and lifted the receiver. As soon as she heard the voice at the other end she stiffened. 'Speak of the devil,' she said, holding the receiver out to Pippa.

Pippa looked at her questioningly.

'Dermott Campbell,' Jane grimaced.

It was half an hour or so later that Pippa wandered into Laurence's study and found Jane standing at the desk. 'Oh, I didn't know you were in here,' she said, clearly surprised. 'Were you looking for something?'

'Just these,' Jane smiled, holding up two carriages from Tom's train set that Laurence had been repairing.

'I'm on my spying mission,' Pippa confessed. 'Where's his diary?'

'Just here,' Jane answered, pulling a large leather-bound book out from underneath a script. They both knew Laurence's diary well since both of them frequently acted as his secretary.

'OK, let's see,' Pippa said starting to flick over the pages. 'Here we are, Thursday . . . Oh shit, no!'

'What is it?' Jane said, leaning across to take a look herself.

'You mean *who* is it?'

'Then who?'

'Ruby bloody Collins, that's who.'

'The writer?'

'The writer. Oh shit and fuck and all the other vile

words I can't think of right now! I was just deciding to cook dinner tonight, candles, good wine and all the rest of it to try and make up for this morning, but he's bound to come back in a foul mood after seeing her.'

'What does that say there?' Jane said, still looking at the diary. 'The pencilled in name.'

Pippa turned back and Jane lifted her eyes to her face as she felt Pippa tense. 'Alison Fortescue,' Pippa muttered. 'Does this mean he's seeing her today, too?'

Jane wasn't quite able to meet Pippa's gaze then for she knew that Laurence had called Alison before leaving the house, and she also knew that Alison had been the cause of many bitter arguments between Laurence and Pippa. 'It's only in pencil,' she pointed out feebly.

'I'm not fooled by that Jane, and neither are you,' Pippa retorted. 'It's Alison bloody Fortescue he's having an affair with and you know it as well as I do. No, there's no point in denying it, Jane, you've known for some time and haven't wanted to tell me. I'm right, aren't I?'

'No!' Jane cried. 'I don't know anything. Honestly Pippa, I don't know how you can think these things. You're accusing Laurence of so many affairs it's almost as though . . . well, I don't know, as though you're trying to push him into one.'

Pippa recognized the accusation instantly. 'Is that what he's been saying to you?' she raged.

'No, no,' Jane said. 'But I've heard him saying it to you, and I'm beginning to think he might have a point.'

'Oh really!' Pippa responded scathingly. 'Well let me tell you something, Jane. *Never* underestimate how clever, nor how bloody devious Laurence can be. Because I can assure you that he's more than capable of turning a very real affair into my paranoia and sending me to the loony bin into the bargain. He damned nearly put Kirsten Meredith there five years ago!'

For a moment Jane seemed too astounded to answer. 'Laurence would never do something like that,' she said eventually.

'Oh, wouldn't he? Then try asking your friend Kirsten, see what she has to say.'

'Well, he'd never do it intentionally,' Jane said feebly.

'Oh, wouldn't he?'

Jane was already drawing breath to say no, when suddenly a vision of the way Kirsten had been on Saturday night flashed through her mind.

'I see, not so sure of yourself now,' Pippa said smugly. 'The trouble with you Jane is that just like every other woman on this damned planet you think the sun shines out of Laurence's backside. Well believe you me it doesn't. My darling husband has plenty to hide, make no mistake about that. And he's a past master when it comes to deception.'

'I'm not convinced he's having an affair with Alison,' Jane said quietly.

'I don't suppose you'd say he was having an affair with Ruby Collins either, would you?' Pippa smirked.

Jane's mouth and eyes formed three circles of astonished disbelief.

'Sit down Jane,' Pippa smiled maliciously, 'I'm going to tell you all there is to tell about Ruby Collins. Let's see how quick you are to rush to Laurence's defence then.'

'Aw, come on, honey, let's take a break now, I've had about as much as I can take for one sitting.'

Through the fading sunlight still seeping across the room Laurence eyed Ruby Collins with candid annoyance. 'We've got to get this sorted,' he snapped, 'but if you can't hack the course I'm gonna remind you that there are plenty out there who can.'

Ruby's porous face with its faded make-up, watery blue eyes and flabby jowls was turned in Lawrence's direction, though he could see that her mind was elsewhere.

'Did you hear what I said, Ruby?' he barked.

'Sure, I heard you, honey,' she drawled, 'but you know and I know that you're not gonna give this script to anyone else so quit threatening me, son.'

Laurence's face tightened and seeing it Ruby leaned across from the sofa to where he was sitting on a chair covered in cat fur and patted his hand.

Laurence pulled his hand away, but deciding to give her a minute or two to ruminate, in the slim hope that she might be fishing around for something approaching a solution to the problem that had just coughed itself up, he cast his eyes about the sitting room of her Richmond flat.

It was neat enough, with the exception of the overflowing ashtrays and cluttered desk in the corner, but he wouldn't want to vouch for the cleanliness beneath the surface. The pictures hanging on the walls, however, were surprisingly tasteful, given that the way she dressed and made herself up was so gaudy. Across the mantelpiece were photographs of her in her earlier years when she had paraded the catwalks and been heralded as one of the most beautiful girls of her generation. But the gin and cigarettes had put paid to that, aging her beyond her years and making her look closer to seventy than sixty.

As Laurence turned back to look at her he could read the dilemma going on in her mind only too well. She wanted a drink and she wanted one real bad. But she didn't want to admit it. For a moment he was tempted to give in and tell her to go ahead, but they'd never get through today if she hit the bottle.

He knew only too well what had led to her drink problem, for her career was as chequered as her drunken diatribes were long. She'd insisted on recounting her life history to him, *ad infinitum*, during the first weeks they'd started working together, and that he himself had played a role in it had made the listening even more excruciating. But, thank God, she seemed to have run out of steam on that topic now. Regrettably he couldn't say the same with regard to the subject of Pippa. The two of them had despised each other on sight, and by the look of her, Ruby was cooking up something savoury to throw at him on the subject of his wife right now.

'All right,' he said sharply, making her jump, 'let's try this scene again.' He didn't care how much she'd suffered in the past, she had no damned business criticizing his private life and goddammit he wasn't going to tolerate it. 'If we cut the dialogue from the top of page forty-four to half way down,' he continued, 'where the second set of stage directions begins . . .'

'Laurence, we need that dialogue,' Ruby interrupted with a supercilious smile.

'Why? It's overwritten, it's tacky and . . .' he poised his pencil over the page, 'it's cut.' He drew a thick line through the closely typed lines and turned over. 'Now let's take the end of the scene . . .'

'I need a drink,' Ruby said, starting to heave herself to her feet.

'You touch that bottle and I'm out of here,' Laurence warned.

For a moment or two Ruby looked torn. Which did

she want most, that Laurence should stay, or a fix? Laurence watched her, his eyes a steely blend of daring and distaste. In the end Ruby flopped back into her seat. 'You sure as hell are ticked about something today,' she complained. 'You've been at me ever since you walked in this morning.'

'Let's get back to it, Ruby,' he said. 'Now, the end of the scene as it stands is terrific, but the lead into it is unshootable, so we've got to rethink it.'

'What do you mean, unshootable? Nothing's unshootable.'

Ignoring her Laurence went on. 'I think we should bring the dialogue at the top of scene forty-eight, with some adjustments, forward to here . . .'

'Nah, I don't agree.'

'Why?'

'I just don't.'

'Then give me a reason.'

'The dialogue works where it is. I don't want it in this scene.'

'That's not a good enough reason. Now look, if we put it here . . .'

'Are you listening to me, son? It works where it is.'

'Will you just hear me out?'

'What for? We're never gonna agree. What we need is a director. He'd tell you I was right.'

'No director worth a dime is going to touch a screen-play in this state!' Laurence shouted.

'If it's so bad then what are you doing here?' she snapped back.

Laurence bit down hard on a scathing response, getting into a fight with her now was going to get them nowhere. 'Look,' he said, 'this screenplay *will* work, and we are gonna make it work, but somewhere along the line you've got to give.'

'You know my terms. You come here and stay with me while I write it, I'll . . .'

'Drop it, Ruby.'

'Those are my terms.'

'I said, drop it.'

'OK. How about you stay for some dinner and we discuss it?'

'No!'

'How about I promise not to drink? Would that make you happy?'

'Very. But I'm not staying, so quit hassling me.' He looked at his watch and groaned inwardly. They'd been at it for over eight hours now and he wasn't sure how much more he could take. For two pins he'd throw the script down and walk out of here. But he wasn't going to do that, not when, in her better moments, she exhibited a real talent. He knew everyone thought he was crazy for taking her on, for even considering going ahead with a period piece, but this story had something and once they got to grips with it they were going to come up with one hell of a movie. So there was no point dwelling on the pleasure that walking out on her would give him for it would only be fleeting. Besides, she was only difficult this way when he was; at other times she could be as compliant and innovative as she could be outrageous and amusing and if the truth be told he had a real fondness for her.

'That silly bitch of a wife of yours been needling you again?' she drawled, the bracelets around her wrists clanging together as she lifted a hand to pat her untidy red hair.

'It's you who's needling me, Ruby, so can we get on with it?'

'I don't know why you put up with her,' Ruby commented, as though he hadn't spoken. 'She didn't grow up yet. It's like you got two kids in that house.'

'My family is my affair,' Laurence said tightly.

'Is that right? Well bully for you, is all I can say.'

Laurence slammed down his script. 'Pour yourself a drink, Ruby.'

Her eyes darted suspiciously to his. 'Why? You going some place?'

'No.'

'So what's with the "pour yourself a drink?" '

'Just do it!'

While Ruby went off in search of a fresh bottle of gin Laurence walked over to her cluttered desk, moved aside several days' worth of cigarette butts and a stale sandwich and picked up the telephone. He'd wanted to be home in time to see Tom before he went to bed, but that wasn't going to be possible now.

'Hi, Jane,' he said when he heard her voice at the other end. 'Is Tom in bed yet?'

'Just going.'

'Put him on, will you?'

He waited a few seconds until Tom's chirpy voice came down the line. They talked for a while and Laurence felt his tension start to ebb as his son recounted his day then asked when he was coming home.

'I'm gonna be late tonight, soldier,' Laurence said. 'But I'll be there in the morning.'

'For Humpty Dumpty?'

'If that's what you want,' Laurence laughed. 'You gonna put Mummy on now?'

'OK. 'Night-night, Daddy.'

'Good night, son.'

'Hi.' Pippa's gentle voice came through the receiver a second or two later. 'How's it going?'

'Badly.'

'You're still there, at Ruby's?'

'Still here.'

'What time will you be home?'

'Difficult to say. I'm gonna hang on in for a while, see if the gin softens her up a bit.'

'What about dinner?'

'I'll grab a sandwich when I get home. Anyway, how are you doing? How's your day been?'

'Pretty good. I've got myself a new client, an author who's just been poached from Hoddards by Strachans. Strachans have asked me to take her on.'

'Great.'

There was a pause before Pippa said, 'Darling, I'm sorry about this morning.'

'I'm sorry too. I've been thinking about you all day. I shouldn't have gone off leaving things the way they were.'

'I love you.'

'I love you too.'

'Shall I wait up?'

Again Laurence looked at his watch. He was tempted to tell her no, but he sorely wanted to see her tonight. 'I won't be back until around midnight at this rate,' he said.

'That's all right.'

'We gonna finish what we started this morning?' he said lowering his voice.

'That was the general idea,' Pippa answered and he could hear the smile in her voice.

When he rang off he turned to see Ruby standing in

the doorway, a bottle in one hand a glass in the other. 'Can I fix you one?' she offered, the unmistakable note of seduction in her voice.

'No, thank you,' he said stiffly.

'Suit yourself,' she shrugged and sauntered back to the couch, her tight fitting canary-yellow suit making even stranger movements than her no longer willowy body. 'So,' she said, as she sat down, 'you reckon a drop of the juice is going to soften the old bird up, is that right?'

'I see you've added eavesdropping to your list of unattractive habits,' Laurence retorted.

Ruby chuckled. 'My, are you a touchy boy. Come on, sit down, let's see what's to be done here.'

Laurence eyed her. He'd have liked to think that it was simply the gin that was persuading her to be reasonable, but he knew better. For sure that would be a part of it, but she'd obviously heard him telling Pippa how late he'd be and now that she was confident she was going to have him to herself for the evening she'd decided to mellow.

They continued on for another hour during which, to his relief, Ruby really got down to it. He couldn't deny it, when she was good she was damned good, a natural in fact, especially with dialogue, he just wished her moments of eloquence weren't so erratic. But she was right when she said they needed a director. Trouble was, the guy Laurence wanted for the project was tied up in Hollywood and though there were any number of others he could choose from he hadn't managed to come up with anyone he felt totally suited.

Feeling her eyes on him as he jotted down some changes in stage direction he looked up. She was smiling, quite happily, but her eyes had that tell-tale glassy look about them.

'You know,' she sighed, 'I just can't get over what a real handsome boy you are. Why don't you come sit here,' she said, patting the cushion, 'let me get a better look at you.'

Laurence sighed. 'OK, let's call it a day,' he said reaching for his briefcase.

'Oh don't go,' Ruby slurred, her blurry eyes blinking up at him. 'We were getting along . . .'

'Just fine,' he interrupted. 'But if you're going to start in on that then we're going nowhere.'

Ruby attempted to stagger to her feet, but Laurence pushed her back again, picked up the bottle on the table beside her and stuck it into her hand. 'Good night, Ruby,' he said starting for the door.

'I love you, Laurence,' she called after him.

When he was outside he took several lungfuls of fresh air before getting into his car. He glanced up at the window of Ruby's apartment and saw her staring down at him, but as she started to heave the window open he turned away.

He was on the point of closing the car door when he heard her yell. 'Dump the stupid bitch! Get her out from around your neck! You don't need her, I'm telling you.'

Laurence simply closed the door, turned on the ignition and drove off into the night. The first thing he'd do when he returned home was take a shower, he decided. It was the way he often felt when leaving Ruby's, but unfortunately no soap in the world could wash away the way she sometimes made him feel inside. Just thank God he had Pippa to go home to, and Tom of course, and recalling the way Pippa had sounded on the telephone earlier he pressed down harder on the accelerator.

It wasn't until he reached Hammersmith that he remembered he was supposed to have called Alison back some time during the day. Well, she wouldn't worry too much that he hadn't, she'd fit him into her schedule somewhere over the next few days, the way she usually did.

He sighed wearily as a wave of guilt washed over him. He didn't rate those who took others for granted too highly, and that was just what he was doing with Alison. She'd probably worked her butt off during the day to be ready for him when he called and now he was going to repay her by not even bothering to pick up the phone.

Well that was easily remedied, he told himself, swinging the car across the three lanes of traffic and veering off towards the Hammersmith roundabout. Pippa wasn't expecting him until much later so he'd pop round and see Alison now.

'So what do you think?' Alison said, some twenty minutes later as she handed him a cup of coffee. Her wild yellow hair was sticking out around her face like the petals of a sunflower, and with the splashes of green velvet plastered strategically over the transparent mesh of her figure-hugging mini-dress and the clumsy, brown Doctor Marten boots she looked about ready for the Chelsea Flower Show. 'Have I got your imagination piqued?' she asked.

'You sure have,' Laurence grinned turning back to the model. 'Truth is though that I'm still not convinced about any of the London scenes.'

'What! You mean my talents haven't caused poetry to flow from your every orifice?' Alison cried, clasping her hands to her heart.

Laurence smiled. 'Not poetry, no. But you've given me an idea. Or at least confirmed one I had a few days ago.'

'Oh Christ, you're going to pay me with your body!' Alison gasped. 'I knew it. I just knew I'd get into your knickers some day . . .'

'My pocket, more like,' Laurence laughed. 'I'm going to pay for you to go to New Orleans with Ruby and do some research there. I've got this theory that if we can get that end of things standing up then the London end will just fall into place.'

'Sounds reasonable,' Alison said, being serious for a moment. 'But what about you? Don't you want to take a look at the place?'

'Sure. I'm off to LA the week after next to speak to some distributors. Maybe I can catch up with you in New Orleans when I've finished."

'I'd be grateful if you did. Handling Ruby Collins on my own isn't my idea of fun. Anyway, now you've brought up New Orleans I'll give you what I've done so far. No, I know you didn't ask me to, but I thought I would anyway. I've had to do it all from books and it's only rough, but you'll be able to see which way I'm thinking, 'cos to my mind the murder scene and the hanging scenes are fucking dull the way they stand. Visually they can be a dream, but we've got to have the right action, right dialogue. Darren,' she said, turning to her boyfriend who was sitting behind them at his drawing board, 'have you still got that stuff I gave you to look at? The stuff for New Orleans?'

'Right here,' he said, reaching over to the next drawing board and picking up a sheaf of sketches and handing them to Laurence. 'Got yourself a director yet?' he asked.

'Not yet,' Laurence answered. 'To be truthful, Darren, we can't afford one right now, but I guess with the right guy on board the finance might be a lot easier to raise.'

'Still no luck on that front?' Darren said.

'Uh-uh,' Lawrence answered shaking his head. 'But I got a few irons in the fire.' He flicked through the sketches for several minutes, then said to Alison, 'I'll take these with me if I can and call you in a couple of days to sort out the New Orleans trip. Simon Howard's just come on board to help with the research, he'll go with you too. I'll get him to organize the flights. Contact Ruby in the meantime will you, get her to give you the rewrites we discussed today.'

When he at last arrived home Pippa was already in bed, though sitting up reading a manuscript, with a plate of sandwiches one side of her and a bottle of wine the other.

'Hi,' she said, putting aside the manuscript as he came to sit on the edge of the bed.

'You look busy.'

'Nothing that can't wait. You look tired.'

'Battered, I think is the word. Got a kiss for your old man?'

Pippa leaned forward, put her arms around his neck and brought his mouth to hers. 'That feel better?' she said a while later.

'Much,' he murmured, then she laughed and pulled away as he scratched the stubble of his beard over her cheek.

'Hungry?' she asked.

'Starving. I'll just take a shower,' he yawned, 'then fix myself something to eat. Those sandwiches look good.'

'There's a proper dinner downstairs,' Pippa told him

as she started to get out of bed. 'I'll pop it in the microwave for you.'

'Come here,' Laurence said, reaching for her as she passed.

For some time he simply held her loosely about the waist, gazing down into her almost childlike face.

'What is it?' she asked, smiling up at him.

'Just that I'm sorry about this morning,' he said gruffly. 'And that I love you.'

'Do you?'

'Very much.'

'So where did you go after Ruby's this evening?' she asked benignly.

Immediately Laurence frowned. 'What do you mean?'

'I mean that Ruby called here about an hour ago wanting to speak to you.'

'Shit!' Laurence groaned.

'I take it you were at Alison's.'

'I was. But Pip, if you're gonna start in on that . . .'

'Sssh,' she said, putting her fingers over his lips. 'You're tired, you're hungry and the last thing you need right now is a jealous wife, am I right?'

'You got nothing to be jealous of.'

'I know. I guess I just can't believe my luck sometimes that I should be married to someone as wonderful as you.'

'You're pretty wonderful yourself, you know.' As he spoke his lips were brushing against hers and then he kissed her deeply, pulling her against him and pushing his tongue into her mouth. She could be downright impossible sometimes, and her unpredictable moods coupled with her jealousy nearly drove him to distraction, but when he was holding her like this he loved her so much he felt it filling his entire body.

Fifteen minutes later, somewhat revived by his shower Laurence was sitting on the bed eating the meal Pippa had brought up for him. She was sitting opposite him alternately feeding and kissing him.

'Oh, by the way,' she said, popping the last forkful of risotto into his mouth, 'Dermott rang this morning wanting to know if you were free to play cricket on Sunday.'

'I'll give him a call,' he said, taking the plate from her and putting it on the floor beside the bed.

'He's having lunch with Helena Johnson tomorrow,' Pippa said as Laurence pulled her into his arms so that she was lying with her head on his shoulder.

'Helena who?'

'Johnson. You know, the actress. That friend of Kirsten Meredith's. Apparently she's going to spill more beans about Kirsten.'

'I wouldn't call that a friend,' Laurence yawned.

'No, I guess not,' Pippa said thoughtfully, as he hugged her and kissed the top of her head. 'Laurence?' she said a few minutes later.

'Mmm?'

'I want to talk to you about Jane.'

'What about her?'

'I think she's becoming a little too attached to Tom.'

'You have a problem with that?'

'No, not exactly. But it's not normal, is it? I mean, she doesn't have any friends her own age, in fact she doesn't have any friends at all as far as I can make out. Her whole life is wrapped up in this family. She hardly ever sees her parents . . .'

'What are you really getting at here?' Laurence interrupted, turning slightly so he could hold her closer, but Pippa pulled away.

'I'm not sure you're going to like this,' she said, 'but well, I've been thinking, and I'm not sure whether or not we should let her go.'

'You mean fire her?' Laurence said incredulously.

'You don't have to put it like that,' Pippa said uncomfortably. 'But to be honest she gets on my nerves a bit. All that giggling and stuff. I don't want Tom picking that up. And she's so immature at times. She needs to grow up and she's not doing it around here.'

Laurence rested his head on his hand and thought about that for a moment. 'You know,' he said, 'she gets a lot of pleasure out of looking after Tom, well all of us I guess, and she'd be real hurt if she thought you wanted her out. And we'd be hard put to find anyone else who's as dedicated as she is.'

'Mmm, I suppose you're right,' Pippa said, lying back in his arms. In truth she didn't really want to let Jane go, for having her around made life so much easier. But she wasn't at all sure about this friendship she'd struck up with Kirsten Meredith. Still, it was probably just a one-off thing, that visit Jane had made to Kirsten's house, and nothing at all to worry about. She wondered how Laurence would feel if he knew about it. Knowing how he felt about Kirsten he probably would fire Jane. Or would he? There were things in the past, things that had happened between Kirsten and Laurence, that Pippa believed still held them together even though Laurence would never admit it. But she'd stopped being jealous of Kirsten a long time ago and now was no time to start it up again. No, now definitely wasn't the time when she had so many plans of her own. Plans, she thought, not without irony, that had been made because of Kirsten Meredith, when Kirsten was still in France. Pippa had never yet had the courage to carry them

through, but now that Kirsten was back . . . . She'd just
have to see how Laurence continued to handle Kirsten's
return, maybe then the decisions would be easier to
make.

— 6 —

Dermott Campbell was sitting at a corner table in Bibendum, one of London's chicest restaurants. As he sipped
his gin and tonic and scanned the menu he was vaguely
aware of the nerves clawing away at his appetite and not
for the first time he glanced at his watch. She was ten
minutes late.

The last time he'd seen her had been at the McAllister's party, ten days ago, when he had got the hots for
her all over again. She was like a witch, in appearance
as well as in spirit. She seemed to have woven some
kind of spell over him which had completely annihilated
any interest he might have in other women. And, given
the mood he was in right now, not even knowing that
she had a penchant for the young boys did anything to
lessen his hopes. He was going to have that woman if it
was the last thing he ever did. In fact, that very afternoon
he was going to take her to his bed and fuck her so hard
she'd think yesterday was tomorrow and next year was
last week.

He winced. Actually, what he was really going to do,
was listen to what Helena had to tell him, thank her,
then get up from the table and leave, because today

wasn't the day even to consider trying to embark on anything else – not when the outcome was going to be a betrayal of both their best friends.

Shit, Campbell groaned inwardly as his head started to throb. For two pins he'd just get up and walk out of here before she showed. But he couldn't do that, not now, if he did Dyllis would just give the assignment to someone else and there would be nothing Campbell could do to protect Laurence from the kind of publicity he sure as hell wouldn't want. But one way or another Laurence was going to get it, because even if nothing came of this meeting today, Campbell already knew what was going to be in his column tomorrow – Dyllis herself had already written it.

Why the hell did it have to be Laurence that the Kirstie Doll had been involved with, Campbell seethed. Why couldn't it have been someone he didn't know, that way he wouldn't be having to go through this. But it was Laurence, and what Dyllis wanted to know was exactly what was behind their break up. And in a way Campbell could understand that, after all, whatever it was had resulted in the break up of Dyllis's marriage.

But to be fishing around in Laurence's past like this was almost enough to make Campbell wish himself back on the scrap-heap. Laurence had always stood by him and this was how he was repaying him – by drinking gin to find the courage to betray him. No, he was protecting Laurence, he had to keep reminding himself of that, but it gave him small comfort.

'Mr Campbell?'

Feigning nonchalance as his stomach clenched with nerves Campbell reluctantly tore himself from his perusal of the menu and looked up at the waiter.

'Your guest has arrived, *Monsieur*,' the waiter smiled.

Campbell started to smile too, but as the waiter stepped to one side the shock jammed his tongue to the back of his throat. He started to splutter, loosened his tie, tried to get up and failed.

'Another drink for Mr Campbell please,' Kirsten smiled at the waiter as she sat down. 'A mineral water for me.'

The waiter left and Kirsten turned to face Campbell. 'What the fuck . . .?' he hissed, making to get up.

'Please sit down, Mr Campbell,' Kirsten interrupted smoothly. She held his eyes, her own so steely and intense that Campbell found himself slumping back into his chair stupefied.

Kirsten smiled and as she did her eyes softened. 'I apologize for the subterfuge,' she said affably, 'but under the circumstances I felt it necessary.' Inside she was triumphant. Just as she'd hoped, the shock of seeing her had thrown him totally, she was starting out with the edge.

She waited patiently as his panicked eyes darted about the restaurant, knowing exactly what was going through his mind. The last thing in the world he would want was to be seen dining in public with Kirsten Meredith, for, were they to be recognized it could do untold harm to his credibility. Which was why Kirsten had chosen to dress the way she had, in an exquisitely cut black linen suit with a matching wide-brimmed straw hat, both of which were guaranteed to turn heads. It was unlikely that any of Campbell's colleagues would be amongst the other diners though, which was a little disappointing, but if Helena had asked him to meet her in any of the journalists well-known haunts it would have seemed mightily suspicious when she was promising to reveal all about Kirsten Meredith.

'OK,' Kirsten said at last, placing her purse on the table and folding her hands over it. 'I will come straight to the point. What will it take to stop this vendetta against me?'

Campbell's eyes were livid as they regarded her across the table. He had never taken well to being tricked, even though he was a master of trickery himself, but he had to hand it to her, she had really out-trumped him. And she was one daunting woman dressed like that, and her seemingly intractable confidence was pretty impressive too. But he had regained at least some of his composure by now and was already planning how he could make this work for him. And work it better, because if Dyllis got to find out about this, which she would, she'd be expecting . . . Well, he didn't know what she'd be expecting, but he'd better come up with something. Trouble was, having prepared himself for Helena Johnson, he was in the wrong persona. He was going to have to switch, fast. He took a large mouthful of gin, and as he did the implications of her question suddenly hit him. God, he had her! He had her right in the palm of his hand already and she didn't even know it. But he'd take it slowly, build up to it one step at a time, and still she wouldn't know, not until the papers hit the stands. 'What's the problem?' he asked. 'Don't much like having everyone know what you're really like?'

'But you don't have the first idea of what I'm really like,' Kirsten answered pleasantly. 'In fact, all you know is what you have manufactured yourself, and what other people have told you. Incidentally, how can you be sure, when you're waving a nice fat cheque in front of them, that what they are telling you is the truth?'

'If it's not, sue.'

'Believe you me, Mr Campbell, I have considered it. And if it comes to it, I will.'

Campbell wasn't fazed. 'You want to air your dirty linen in public then that's fine by me,' he said. 'It's all good copy.'

'And that's all that matters, is it? You don't mind at all about what you're doing to my life, of how much damage you're causing with your lies. But it would seem that attacking my reputation isn't enough. I am fully aware of who is blocking all my approaches to various television companies recently. It would seem that Mrs Fisher is out to destroy me completely. Am I right?'

You're dead right, Campbell was thinking to himself as he looked directly into her eyes. Jesus Christ, was she one beautiful woman! Perhaps he wasn't too sure how he felt about Helena Johnson after all. Still, now wasn't the time to think about that, he had a job to do. 'Tell me,' he said, avoiding the question, 'did you think of the damage you were doing Dyllis Fisher when you ran off with her husband of forty-five years?'

Kirsten looked up at the waiter as he placed her mineral water on the table and thanked him. After taking a sip she turned back to Campbell. 'Have you asked yourself why it is that Paul should have wanted to run off in the first place, Mr Campbell? Or why it is that Mrs Fisher is not contesting the will? Oh, I know what you've printed in your column, but there's a lot of money at stake here, and you know it. So why, do you think, is she letting it go so easily?'

The quality of that dark, husky voice was as mesmerizing as her eyes. 'Because,' he answered, clearing his throat, 'she doesn't want her husband's name, or more particularly his senility, dragged through the courts.'

'Paul wasn't senile, Mr Campbell. He died with all

his faculties intact. But if you don't want to believe me then I suggest you talk to his doctor.'

'For all I know you're giving the guy a cut.'

Deciding to ignore such a contemptible remark, Kirsten simply smiled. 'Dyllis Fisher isn't contesting the will, Mr Campbell,' she said, 'because she doesn't want people to know the real truth of her marriage. Which they would if I decided to speak out.'

'Is that some kind of a threat?' Campbell challenged, hooking an arm over the back of his chair. God, she was fascinating.

'No, just a fact.'

Campbell laughed mirthlessly. 'No, I'm not buying it,' he said. 'If Dyllis Fisher had anything to fear from you she'd never have taken you on so publicly.'

'Dyllis Fisher is relying totally on my discretion because she knows she can. I would never do anything that would in any way discredit Paul's name or his memory, both of which would become subject to the distortions of the press if I decided to tell my side of the story. In other words, Mr Campbell, I did, and still do, care far more for Paul than I do my own reputation, which you have to agree is more than can be said for Dyllis Fisher with her accusations of senility . . .'

Campbell was shaking his head. 'Nice try, but we both know why you're not taking Dyllis on and it's got sweet f.a. to do with preserving an old man's name. You're keeping quiet for one reason and one reason only, because you don't want any more sordid little secrets dug out of that shady past of yours.'

Kirsten could see by the look on his face that he hoped he'd hit a raw nerve. He had, but she wasn't going to give him any satisfaction by showing it. 'You're right, Mr Campbell,' she said evenly, 'I have no desire to see any details of my life, sordid or otherwise, spread across the newspapers. And you're right again when you intimate that Mrs Fisher has a great deal more power than I do. She can, and will I imagine, try her very best to see that I never work again. I assume she would deem that as some kind of victory, though quite what she stands to gain from such a victory escapes me. But it is because she is so determined to ruin me that I am appealing to you now, and not to her. When I returned to England it was to try to pick up my life and start again. This would have been difficult under any circumstances, given the length of my absence, but with this vendetta going on it is impossible. So, I want to ask you to leave me alone.'

Outwardly, Campbell was regarding her expectantly, as though waiting for her to continue, but his inner-eye could see the return of those destitute years looming. God, she was really getting to him. 'Look,' he heard himself saying, 'if you're trying to elicit my support here you might as well forget it, 'cos even if I gave it it wouldn't do you any good. If you want to call this to a halt it's Dyllis you should be talking to.'

'But you and I both know that she'd never agree to see me.'

He cocked an eyebrow. 'So you're asking me to mediate?'

Kirsten nodded. 'In a way.'

'But Kirsten, you've got nothing to bargain with. That woman wants you dead.'

'That doesn't mean that you have to help her.'

'It does. Believe me.'

'But why?'

'It's a long story. But let me tell you this, you're better off with me handling this than you are anyone else.'

– 121 –

'Oh, do me a favour!' Kirsten cried. 'With all the lies you've . . .'

'Laurence is a friend of mine,' he interrupted, craning his neck to look at something across the restaurant. His eyes came back to hers.

Kirsten was very still. The mention of Laurence's name was so unexpected she simply didn't know what to say.

Campbell, almost as shocked as she was at what he'd just confided regarded her with cool, inscrutable eyes, but inside he was reeling. Shit! Holy Christ! He knew he was a sucker for a pretty face, but this was unbeliev- able. This woman, he knew for a fact, was still in love with Laurence. She'd befriended his nanny, she'd gone to his party – she was after breaking up his goddamned marriage and he was sitting here like some love-lorn teenager gazing into her eyes and practically telling her he would help her! And right now Dyllis Fisher herself was sitting over in the corner watching his every move.

He was about to speak when Kirsten, picking up her purse, said, 'I can see that I've been wasting my time.'

'I don't see what that's got to do with anything,' he said, startling her as much with his non-sequitur as the way he had suddenly raised his voice. 'But I'll tell you what does. What does is the fact that you're not looking to get your career back on the line at all. What you're looking for is the next marriage to bust up.' His voice lowered as he pushed his face towards her. 'But like I said, Laurence McAllister is a friend of mine, a very close friend, and so's his wife. So you keep away from them, do you hear me?' He drew back and once again raised his voice. 'You keep right away or I personally am going to blast you so fucking hard you'll wish you'd never been born. Are you receiving me?'

Kirsten was stunned. The outburst had been so sudden and so vicious she had no idea where it had come from.

'And as for making an appeal to my better nature,' he went on before she could speak. 'Don't bother because I haven't got one. But I'll tell you what, I'll take what you're offering to get me off this vendetta – but before I do I'll be wanting to see the results of a few tests, 'cos from all I've been hearing about you you've been round the block a few too many times . . .'

He got no further. Kirsten's movement was so swift that no one else in the restaurant could have seen it, even Campbell didn't know it was coming until Dyllis Fisher's face, together with the huge stained-glass windows, tilted before his eyes and a wash of gin and tonic splashed across his neck. And by the time he realized what had happened Kirsten had already left the restaurant.

'You did what?' Helena shrieked, gripping her sides with laughter. 'Oh, tell me again! Tell me again!'

'I tipped him backwards off his chair,' Kirsten answered with only the ghost of a smile.

'Oh, what I wouldn't have given to see his face,' Helena gasped. 'So what happened then?'

'I walked out. I could see I was wasting my time so there was no point in staying.'

'I'm sorry,' Helena said, dabbing her eyes, 'but I did try to warn you. Dermott Campbell just doesn't have a better side to his nature.'

'Yes, well that's as may be,' Kirsten said, 'but the real point here is that I've achieved nothing.'

'That's not true,' a voice behind them said.

Helena started. She'd forgotten Jane was there. She turned and watched Jane as she carried a tray of coffee to the table.

Jane looked at them sheepishly, clearly embarrassed by her moment of indignation. 'You had the guts to go out there and confront him,' she said awkwardly. 'I'd say that was an achievement.'

From the look on Kirsten's face it was obvious she didn't agree. 'But to what end?' she said. 'If anything he's just going to renew his attack on me now.' She shuddered. 'I dread to think what he's going to write in tomorrow's paper.'

Even Helena sobered at that for there was no denying that Campbell would go to town on what had taken place at the restaurant that day. 'You haven't actually told us yet what he said that made you bash him,' she reminded Kirsten.

Before she could stop herself Kirsten had glanced at Jane, which in itself was answer enough for Helena.

Jane looked from one to the other of them, then realizing that Kirsten didn't want to elaborate in front of her she sprang to her feet, almost knocking over her chair. 'Um, uh, I think I'll just go to the loo,' she said and hurried off.

Helena waited until she heard the lock of the downstairs bathroom click before turning to Kirsten. 'What's she doing here?' she whispered.

Kirsten grinned. 'She brought round a pyjama case she made for me.'

'A what?' Helena cried, screwing up her nose and

laughing. 'She's got a real crush on you, you know that, don't you?'

Kirsten nodded. 'She's kind of sweet though, don't you think?'

Helena shrugged. 'She's OK. Not much of a looker though, is she?'

'Sssh, she'll hear you,' Kirsten said, turning to look over her shoulder.

Helena waved a dismissive hand in the direction of the bathroom, then clearly discarding all thoughts of Jane she said, 'Do I take it Campbell said something about Laurence?'

'He did. He accused me of trying to break up his marriage.'

'*What!*' Helena hissed. 'But how on earth does he know about you and Laurence?'

'He could have found out any number of ways, but I imagine Dyllis Fisher told . . .' she broke off as the bathroom door opened and Jane's anxious face peeped round the corner.

'It's all right,' Kirsten laughed. 'You can come out.'

As Jane came back into the kitchen she looked so painfully uncomfortable that, as she passed, Kirsten took her hand and squeezed it. 'Dermott Campbell said something about Laurence,' she told her causing Helena's eyes to fly open.

'Are you sure this is wise?' Helena said, casting a quick look at Jane.

'Jane was there when Laurence told Pippa to throw me out,' Kirsten reminded her. 'So I would imagine,' she added, turning to Jane, 'that Jane has managed to deduce for herself that Laurence and I . . . knew each other . . .'

'But she works for the man,' Helena protested.

'I'm fully aware of that,' Kirsten smiled.

Jane was watching them. 'I won't say anything,' she assured them, suddenly realizing they were both looking at her. 'Honestly, I wouldn't dream of it.'

'I know you wouldn't,' Kirsten said.

Helena almost burst out laughing then at the look of near devotion Kirsten received. She was about to speak when Jane said, 'Actually, I did work it out for myself, but Pippa told me anyway.'

Kirsten's eyes darted to Helena's whose surprise was as evident as her own. 'And exactly what did Pippa say?' Helena asked.

Jane's pallid little face was filling with colour. 'Just that Kirsten and Laurence had known each other five years ago and that Kirsten took it pretty hard when they broke up,' she said.

'But how did you and Pippa come to be talking about Kirsten in the first place?' Helena asked, voicing the question she knew was in Kirsten's mind.

'Umm, I can't really remember,' Jane said turning fearful eyes to Kirsten. 'I hope you don't mind,' she went on, 'but I told Pippa that I'd been to see you. I felt I had to.'

'No, it's all right,' Kirsten said. 'What did she say?'

'That she had no right to choose my friends,' Jane lied.

'What about Laurence?' Helena asked. 'Does he know that you've been coming here?'

'Not unless Pippa's told him.'

The three of them sat in silence for a moment staring down at their coffee cups. Then Helena and Kirsten looked up as Jane got to her feet. 'I think I'd better be going now,' she said. 'I've got to pick Tom up from his grandparents.'

Kirsten saw her to the door, then strolling thoughtfully back down the hall she said, 'Do you think Pippa would have told him Jane's coming here?'

'God knows,' Helena answered. 'Would it bother you if she had?'

'I'm not sure. Yes, I suppose it would.'

'Then why keep inviting her? I mean, if he doesn't know already he's bound to find out some time.'

'Actually, I don't invite her. She just calls up and asks if she can come.'

Helena's brows knitted together as she concentrated on her thoughts. Then raising curious eyes to Kirsten's, she said, 'You don't suppose that Dermott Campbell's somehow found out she's coming here? I mean, if he has, it could well be the grounds for his accusation. After all, you've only got to look at Jane to wonder why someone like you would have her as a friend if not to get closer to Laurence?'

'Oh God,' Kirsten groaned. 'I hadn't thought of that. But how would he have found out?'

'Well I wouldn't imagine that Jane had told him. Pippa might have, however.'

'Oh, I wish this would all just go away,' Kirsten groaned, burying her face in her hands. 'All I want is to be able to get on with my life.'

'Then I'd start by telling Jane not to come here any more.'

'I can't do that,' Kirsten sighed. 'At least I could I suppose. But I feel sorry for her. Don't you?'

'Not particularly.'

Kirsten laughed. 'I didn't think you would, somehow.'

'Actually, I don't have any feelings about the girl one way or the other, all that concerns me is how your friendship with her is going to be construed, because the last thing you need right now is more bad press.'

'Mmm. You're right.' She let her mind drift back over the conversation she'd had with Campbell, then pursing her lips, she said, 'You know, Campbell didn't say so in so many words, in fact it's probably just my own paranoia making me think it, but I reckon what he's really after is the reason why Laurence and I broke up.'

Helena frowned. 'But why would that be of any interest to anyone all these years later?'

'Because,' Kirsten answered, measuring Helena with her eyes, 'Dyllis believes that I did something back then that I'd give my entire fortune, my entire life, never to be made public.'

Helena's bright eyes darkened with interest. 'And did you?' she said.

'Yes.'

'Are you going to tell me what it was?'

After long moments of deliberation Kirsten shook her head.

'Is it so terrible?'

'For me, yes. Less so for Laurence, but I don't imagine he'd ever want it made public, either.'

'Oh God, I'm dying of curiosity here,' Helena wailed. 'Did Paul know?'

'Of course he did. It was partly the reason he left Dyllis. Oh, he had plans to retire to the South of France without her, but when I . . . did what I did, he brought them forward and went then. Still,' she said with a sudden briskness, 'as Campbell pointed out, Laurence is a friend of his, so we'll just have to hope that he's loyal enough a friend to keep Laurence's name out of things. And without Laurence's name the story won't really stand up. No, what concerns me right at this moment is what to do about Jane.'

'Just dump her,' Helena said, pouring fresh coffee into her cup.

'You can be so cruel sometimes,' Kirsten laughed.

'Well, she's not exactly going to leave a gaping hole in your life, is she?'

'No, but . . .'

'. . . you'll leave one in hers,' Helena finished.

'I wasn't going to say that. What I was going to say is before I tell her she can't come here any more I want to try and find out for sure if it's Pippa who's been giving Dermott Campbell his information. Jane might not know of course, but I'll bet she could find out.'

'I'll bet she could too. The way that girl blends into the background is damned spooky, if you ask me.'

'But in this instance it's something of a gift.'

'Mmm. You know,' Helena said thoughtfully, after a pause, 'I don't really see how it can be Pippa, not when so much of the early stuff Campbell wrote happened long before you knew Laurence.'

'But Laurence knows about it, I told him. He might have told Pippa.'

'OK. And if it is her, what are you going to do?'

'I'm not sure. Maybe it'll mean speaking to Laurence. That is, if he'll speak to me, which I doubt.'

'Well, I guess you'll have to cross that bridge when you come to it. But would I be right if I said that your suspicions of Pippa let me off the hook?'

'You?' Kirsten laughed.

'Yeah, me. Oh, come on, don't tell me it never crossed your mind. I mean, who knows you – and your past – better than I do?'

'No one, I suppose. But truthfully, it never even occurred to me that you'd be behind it all.'

'So you trust me implicitly?'

'Of course.'

'Then for God's sake tell me what happened back then!'

— 7 —

Everyone was unnervingly silent. The only sound was that of the sombre news from Bosnia issuing from the radio and the delicate clatter of cups as they were lifted or replaced in their saucers.

Laurence, Pippa and Jane were all half-hidden behind the newspapers Campbell had just handed them; Tom, lying on a beanbag and sucking his thumb, was watching a muted cartoon on the TV.

The article they were all engrossed in was a long one, written mainly by Campbell, but edited by Dyllis Fisher. Over a week had gone by since Campbell had seen Kirsten at Bibendum and in all that time he had been doing battle with Dyllis to try and stop Laurence's name going to print. He'd succeeded, this time, but even so the innuendo wasn't going to be lost on Laurence. Which was why Campbell had judged it wiser to bring the paper round himself so that he could – at least in some way – attempt to defend himself when Laurence got sight of it.

'For Christ's sake, Dermott, this is a bit strong, isn't it?' Laurence said, glancing up at him.

'Did she really offer to go to bed with you to get you to stop writing about her?' Pippa asked, obviously having reached the same point as Laurence.

'More or less,' Campbell answered, running a finger under his collar as he recalled the moment it had dawned on him how he could misconstrue Kirsten's question, 'What will it take to stop this vendetta?'

Laurence eyed him sceptically, before returning to the paper.

Several more minutes ticked by. Campbell was watching Laurence's face, bracing himself. For a moment his eyes drifted over to Jane, but they shot quickly back to Laurence as he said, 'And just what the hell is this?'

Jane's head came up and to her astonishment she found he was looking at her.

'Just what the hell is going on here?' he demanded, looking from Jane to Campbell and back again. 'Would you like to explain this?' he said, turning back to the paper and reading aloud. " . . . adopted a new ploy in befriending nannies to get close to the children before striking at the heart of the family . . . "

'It means,' Pippa said prosaically, 'that Jane and Kirsten have become friends.'

Laurence's expression was thunderous as he turned back to Jane. Jane's face had visibly paled.

'I thought Pippa might already have told you,' she said lamely, then started as Laurence suddenly slammed down the newspaper and scooping Tom into his arms walked out of the room.

'Sorry,' Pippa said to Jane. 'I would have told him if I'd thought it was important, I just didn't think it was.'

'Then you're a fool, Pippa,' Campbell told her. 'Never underestimate what lengths women like Kirsten Meredith will go to to get what they want.'

'Actually, I didn't,' Pippa answered. 'I jumped to the same conclusion as you, but unlike you, Dermott, I knew what Laurence's response would be. Anyway, how did you find out that she and Jane were friends?'

'Let's just say a little bird told me,' Campbell answered.

The door opened and Laurence came back into the room without Tom. 'OK, Dermot,' he said, 'just what the fuck is all this about, bringing my family into your slander campaign?'

'Actually, it was my way of trying to warn you,' Campbell said, feeling a slight constriction in his throat as he lit a cigar.

'There are telephones, Dermott. If you wanted to warn me . . . For Christ's sake, do you have to smoke that thing at the breakfast table!'

'Sorry,' Campbell crushed his cigar into a saucer. 'I think you'd better read on,' he said miserably.

A few minutes later Pippa looked at him incredulously. 'She actually *admitted* to wanting Laurence back?' she gasped.

'Not in so many words, no,' Campbell confessed. 'But if you'd seen her face when I put it to her . . . Well, she physically attacked me for even suggesting she might have you in her sights,' he added to Laurence. 'Now if that isn't a case of the lady doth protest too much . . .'

'I don't suppose it occured to you,' Laurence remarked, 'that you might just have deserved a thump for the way you've treated her since she was back in England?'

'Funny that she chose to do it over you though, don't you think?' Campbell countered.

'What I think is that you pushed her too far,' Laurence retorted. 'And you're coming pretty close to it with me, printing stuff like this.'

'There's no mention of your name,' Campbell pointed out.

'Come off it, Dermott, anyone with half a brain can work out who you're talking about. And I don't want my name even associated with hers. You know that, so why the hell are you doing it?'

Campbell looked at Pippa, then at Jane. 'Can I speak with you alone a moment?' he said to Laurence.

Laurence turned to Pippa. She nodded.

'Look, it's Dyllis,' Campbell said, as Laurence closed the study door behind them. 'You know she's out to get the Kirstie Doll in any way she can.'

'Then let her. But tell her to keep the hell out of my life.'

'I'm doing my best,' Campbell said. 'Believe you me, she was all for printing your name and to be frank with you I don't think I'll be able to stop her next time.'

'Next time?' Laurence said tightly.

Campbell sighed. 'All I'm saying is that Dyllis is delving deep. You and Kirsten split, Paul runs off to France with Kirsten. And something happened then . . .' he trailed off as the blood drained from Laurence's face. He'd never seen him so angry.

'If you print one word of that, Dermott, then I swear you'll never set foot through my door again.'

'I don't even know what it was,' Campbell protested.

Laurence stared at him. 'But Dyllis is trying to find out?' he said.

'Yes!'

'Shit!' Laurence seethed. He was thinking fast. 'Only Kirsten, Pippa and I know,' he said. 'She'll never find out.'

'OK. Keep it that way. It's not a story than can easily . . .' he stopped, horrified at what he was about to say.

Laurence eyed him with disbelief. 'You're lying,' he said, a sudden and dangerous edge to his voice. 'You know what happened. How the hell did you find out? Kirsten would never have told you . . . Shit! Dermott, tell me it wasn't Pippa. For God's sake tell me . . .'

'It *wasn't* Pippa,' Campbell said forcefully. 'I swear it, Laurence. Pippa never breathed a word.'

'Then who was it?'

'Oh come on, Laurence,' Campbell said in a pained voice. 'You know a journalist never reveals his sources.'

Laurence turned and walked over to the window. 'So what are you going to do?' he said, staring sightlessly out at the rain spattered street.

'Nothing.'

'Christ, you just can't print a story like . . .'

'I said, nothing,' Campbell repeated, then sinking into the nearest chair he dropped his head in his hands. 'I guess I understand why you hate her so much now,' he said.

Laurence nodded absently. His mind was elsewhere, trying, but afraid, to light on that terrible week that had, in the end, killed it all. She thought he didn't know how much she had suffered for what she'd done, but he did; Paul had told him. But Jesus Christ, did she have any idea how much he had suffered too? Even now he still couldn't believe she had done that to him, much less herself. He wondered if he could ever forgive her. 'You've got to know enough about her by now to know that if you go to print on this you'll break her,' he said quietly.

'I know,' Campbell said. 'But like I said, it's not an easy story to tell . . . .'

'Dyllis will find a way,' Laurence said, turning back. 'But she still doesn't know what happened. And she'll never find out through me.'

'What about the person who told you?'

Campbell shook his head. 'I can't give any guarantees on that, but I don't honestly think there's a problem there.'

'Isn't there anything you can do to get Dyllis to back off?' Laurence asked.

Dismally Campbell shook his head. 'I've got no sway with the woman,' he answered. 'I doubt anyone has in this instance. She's out to destroy Kirsten in every way possible. Not even with all that money Kirsten's got is she going to be able to work again. I know for a fact she's considered financing herself, but no one will work with her. Dyllis will see to that. And as far as Kirsten's private life goes Dyllis has got me over a barrel. Either I write it or I'm out. And it's better that I do it than some hack you don't even know. At least this way I can temper it a bit . . . .'

'But from what I've read, from what you've said here, it sounds to me like you're gunning for Kirsten yourself.'

'In a way, yes, in a way, no. I don't want to see her coming between you and Pip. I meant it earlier when I said I was trying to warn you. The Kirstie Doll is still in love with you. She wants you back and making friends with your nanny is just the start of it. Dyllis knows that and Dyllis is going to do all she can to prevent it. So am I.'

Laurence laughed without humour. 'Pippa and I don't

need your help, Dermott. Sure, we have our problems, but it'll take a damn sight more than Kirsten Meredith to bust us apart.'

'That's what I want to hear,' Campbell said. 'But the Kirstie Doll, well, she's one hell of a lady. I can see why you were so crazy for her . . . Hell, I almost found myself falling for her . . .'

Laurence laughed and pushed himself away from the window ledge. 'That kind of misery you can well do without, my friend.'

When Campbell had gone, Pippa and Laurence sat in the kitchen reading through the article again, until Pippa looked up to find Laurence grinning at her.

'And what's so funny?' she asked.

'Campbell. I sure as hell would have liked to be there when Kirsten clocked him one.'

Pippa giggled. 'Me too.'

'Come here,' Laurence said, pushing the paper away and sliding his chair back from the table.

Pippa went to him and as she settled into his lap he wrapped her in his arms. 'You're not worried about any of this, are you?' he said.

'Should I be?'

'You know the answer to that,' he murmured sliding a hand under her sweater and gently caressing her breasts.

Pippa sighed contentedly and rested her head back on his shoulder. 'Are you still sure you don't want me to come to the States with you at the end of the week?' she said after a while.

'I do want you to come,' he answered, 'but I thought you were going to Zaccheo's.'

'I could always cancel.'

Laurence laughed. 'Zaccheo would never forgive me for taking you away from him.'

'What about him taking me away from you? Doesn't that bother you?'

'Put like that it does,' he said, squeezing her.

'I'll miss you.'

'I'll miss you, too.'

Suddenly, for no apparent reason, Pippa's eyes filled with tears, but with her head where it was Laurence didn't see. 'What time did you get back last night?' she said after a while. 'It must have been late because I didn't hear you come in.'

'Almost three,' Laurence answered. 'Ruby's come up with some pretty amazing stuff, believe it or not. She was on a roll last night, I didn't want to do anything to . . . Mmmm,' he groaned as Pippa turned his mouth to hers and pushed her tongue deep inside.

'What was that for?' he asked as she pulled away.

'For being you.'

'Then how about,' he murmured slipping his other hand inside her sweater, 'I get another. For being me.' He smiled then as she turned to sit astride him pressing her groin to his. 'I kind of reckon you're after something, Mrs McAllister,' he grinned.

'I could be,' she said, running her fingers around his neck and up into his hair.

Thank God, he was thinking to himself, as she started to suck gently on his lips while pushing herself harder against him, that her jealousy, which had been threatening to run out of control these past few weeks, seemed to have disappeared altogether, and even Campbell's warning that Kirsten was aiming to come between them didn't seem to have fazed her. Laurence was profoundly glad of it, for having Kirsten back in London was, for him, too close for comfort. The year they had spent together still lived all too vividly in his mind and though he would never admit it to anyone, he knew that despite what had happened at the end he had loved Kirsten in a way he would never love any other woman. What they had shared together came only once in a lifetime, but what he had with Pippa was something he would *never* give up the way he had given up on Kirsten. In a way he was grateful to Kirsten for she had, in coming back, reminded him just how much Pippa meant to him. For a while though, it had scared the hell out of him to find that he couldn't make love to Pippa. Mercifully it hadn't lasted as the past week had proved and his love for Pippa had deepened immeasurably for the way she had handled what she must have guessed was a real problem for him. And that was why Kirsten would never be able to come between them, for Pippa's unspoken support, loyalty and love was the very mainstay of his life.

'Hey, where are you going?' he said as Pippa drew herself up from his lap.

'To lock the door,' she smiled over her shoulder. 'OK, I know you've got a meeting at the bank . . .'

'It can wait,' Laurence said wryly, knowing it couldn't but he wanted her so much right now it would just have to.

She came back and stood beside him, looking down at the bulge in his jeans.

'Take off your clothes,' he whispered as he started to lower his zip. 'Take them all off and come sit right here.'

As he spoke Pippa's eyes fluttered closed showing him how turned on she was. She loved to be naked while he was still dressed.

Seconds later she was astride him again, slowly lowering herself on to him while looking deep into his eyes. He held her about the hips one thumb gently massaging her between the legs.

'What was she like in bed?' Pippa murmured.

Laurence frowned. 'What?'

Pippa's head fell back and she groaned ecstatically as he reached full penetration. 'Kirsten,' she said. 'What was she like in bed?'

'Oh Christ, Pippa! You sure as hell pick your moments.'

'Was it as good as this?' Pippa asked, bringing her head back up and gyrating her hips as she pushed her tongue into his mouth. 'Do you ever think of her while you're fucking me?'

'Quit talking,' he said lifting her with him as he stood up.

'You're thinking about her right now, aren't you?' Pippa said, smiling up at him as he laid her across the table. 'Do you want to fuck her again, Laurence? Do you want to push it right into her the way you're pushing it into me? Oh God, Laurence,' she suddenly gasped as he pushed her knees wide and thrust into her. 'Fuck me, fuck me hard. Are you thinking of her now? Can you see her? Do you want to screw her this way? She's beautiful, isn't she, Laurence? So beautiful you can't get her out of your mind. Pretend I'm her, Laurence. Fuck me as though I was her.'

Laurence's eyes were closed. He wouldn't listen, he couldn't, but the turbulence in her voice was driving him crazy. He pounded into her, holding her tiny waist as her legs circled him, locking him to her.

'Can you feel her, Laurence? Can you see her? Did she ever fuck you like this? Oh my God!' she cried as suddenly he started to hammer into her harder than he ever had before. 'Is this what you did to her?' she gasped breathlessly. 'Are you with her now?'

He pulled back, rammed himself into her, pulled back

and did it again. She sobbed for more and yet more, begging him never to stop. Then suddenly the semen was spurting from him. He ground into her feeling the strength start to seep from his legs. But still it came and still he pushed into her.

'Oh Christ!' he seethed as he felt her start to come too. 'Jesus Christ!' and snatching her up from the table he pressed his mouth hard against hers. 'I love you. Dear God, I love you.'

'Oh Laurence, I can't stop,' she sobbed, clinging to him. 'I just can't stop. Hold me. Please, hold me.'

His arms tightened around her as her whole body vibrated with the force of her orgasm, but his legs felt so weak he knew he couldn't stand much longer. Scooping her up he carried her back to the chair and sat down. Their arms were still entwined, their bodies joined and they stayed that way for a long time, just holding each other and waiting for the steady rythmn of their hearts to return.

At last Pippa lifted her head. 'Are you angry with me?' she whispered.

Laurence's face was grim, though he couldn't say for sure whether he was angry or not. But what he did know was that as much as he wanted that he and Pippa should have another child he hoped to God she hadn't conceived then. The very last thing in the world he wanted was for Pippa to carry a child that had been conceived while in his head he had been making love to Kirsten Meredith.

It had been dark for hours. So dark, so very, very dark, that her eyes couldn't adjust. She lay silently and still, her shallow breathing not even disturbing the covers.

She could almost be dead, she mused to herself. Lying here in the inky black silence was like lying in the swallowed cavern of a grave.

After a while she moved. Reaching out a hand she pressed the switch beside her bed. A dim, greyish glow spread a circle over the floor. As she lifted herself up her distorted shadow loomed large across the wall. It stalked her as she moved to the door. She turned the key, locking herself in. Securing her tomb.

Very gently she eased open a drawer and lifted out the book. Such a precious book. Bound in leather, embossed in gold. As she folded back the cover a rush of air sucked at the first, transparent page. She pulled it back. A smile hovered on her lips, tears stung at her eyes.

Using her fingers she began to trace the outline of the photograph, as though reading brail. She closed her eyes as though to sink the memory of the face into the very depths of her mind. After a while she could hear the voice, the longed for voice, murmuring words of comfort, of love. Pulling her elbows to her sides she felt strong, caring arms go around her. Very slowly, like a flower coming to bloom, a warm, cherished glow spread through her heart.

After a while she opened her eyes. The face was still there, gazing up at her in the misty light.

Suddenly she closed the book. She didn't want to look at it anymore.

She tiptoed across the room and peered into the cot. Flushed, tender cheeks lying on a pillow of lace. A tiny fist clenched. Soft, downy head turned to one side. The warmth and smell of new human life. How God had blessed her with this one, unexpected happiness.

– 8 –

It was no wonder that so many artists chose to live in this wonderful place, Kirsten was thinking dreamily to herself, as she stood on the bougainvillea-covered terrace of Zaccheo's Tuscan home and looked out on the endless rows of olive groves sloping gently into the valley far below. The light was incredible, so soft and mysterious as it shimmered on the silvery green leaves and cast spectacular cloud shadows over the slumbering mountains. She inhaled deeply, reaching high above her head as though to open her entire body to the bracing, early morning air and thought of the last time she had stood on the terrace of this magnificent hillside villa. She smiled, relishing the memory, and looked to the sky as though turning her face to the voice which now existed only in her mind.

Hearing the gentle clatter of a tea-tray she turned to see Mañuella coming on to the terrace with her breakfast. The table was already set, but only for one – Zaccheo was in Rome and Kirsten wasn't too sure when he'd be back.

He'd called her two days before to invite her here, saying he felt she should get out of England for a while, at least until things had calmed down. How he had learned about Dermott Campbell's latest attack, Kirsten wasn't sure. Maybe he had got hold of an English newspaper, or it could be that Pippa McAllister had told him. Whichever, it didn't matter, for he was right, she had needed to get away to somewhere where she could concentrate on how she was going to bring her ideas to fruition. Dyllis might be doing all she could to destroy Kirsten's attempts at a comeback, but Kirsten was simply not going to allow herself to be beaten.

A few months, perhaps even a few weeks from now, Paul's death and her inheritance would be old news. No one would want to read about it any more, other events would be under the spotlight and by that time she should be ready to make what she hoped, given the project she had in mind, would be quite a comeback. Meanwhile, no one in the world knew where she was with the exception of Helena and Zaccheo

She chuckled quietly to herself as she sat down at the delicate wrought-iron table and filled her cup with piping hot tea. Helena had been incensed at her coming here, had accused her of running away and had demanded to know how they could possibly work together on Kirsten's ideas when Kirsten was so far away. It had been hard for Kirsten to stop herself laughing outright, for she knew only too well that Helena was piqued because she hadn't been invited too. Zaccheo's reputation as an expert lover was too much for Helena to resist, she was simply dying to find out for herself if it were true, but though Kirsten was sympathetic, for she herself was not impervious to Zaccheo's charm, she had explained that Zaccheo was going to be in Rome and that she was looking forward to spending some time alone.

For no apparent reason, as she bit into a succulent pastry, Jane suddenly came into her mind and with the thought came a pang of guilt. Laurence had delivered an ultimatum – either Jane stopped visiting Kirsten or Jane was fired. Hiding her own pain at the harshness of

Laurence's response, Kirsten had told Jane during their brief telephone conversation that it would be for the best. Saying goodbye to Jane though was more of a wrench than Kirsten wanted to admit, for she couldn't deny that she had come to see Jane as a link to Laurence and it was a link that, as much as she despised herself for it, she just didn't want to break. But she had and now, as she smiled grimly to herself, she realized she was going to miss Jane, for despite all that giggling and sometimes annoying self-consciousness she was often quite relaxing to be with, so undemanding and easy to talk to.

Kirsten spent the next few days ambling through the hills with her tape recorder or sitting amongst the ornamental palms around the swimming pool transcribing plots and breakdowns on to the portable typewriter she'd found in Zaccheo's study. The flow of ideas was like a bubbling stream, hitting obstacles, but never long deterred from its purpose. It was so exhilarating to find that she still had the ability to take a simple concept and turn it into something dramatically powerful. Not that there was anything simple about the ideas she was working on now, but her confidence was riding high.

It was early in the evening on the fifth day of her visit that she finally plucked up the courage to take a swim. The clear blue water looked so utterly irresistible that even the knowledge that the spring sunshine wouldn't have warmed it much could no longer deter her. She hadn't thought to bring a swimsuit with her, but didn't see that as a problem since Mañuella wouldn't return to the villa for at least another hour and she'd waved Raimondo the gardener off home a few minutes ago.

As she stepped up to the edge of the pool she could

feel the thrill of the balmy air curling itself around her naked skin. Strangely it felt like a lifetime ago that she had last done this, when she and Paul had swum together each evening before going to sit on the veranda looking down over Cannes and out on to the magnificent expanse of the Mediterranean sea.

Feeling as though his eyes were on her now she poised herself ready to dive. The shock of the cold water when it came was breathtaking, but she swam on down the pool, somersaulted a turn and swam back again. She'd done several lengths by the time her body had become acclimatized and her breathing was steady again, then rolling on to her back she floated lazily across the surface gazing up at the rosy sky. It was like being in paradise, she laughed to herself, as she turned again and, using long languorous strokes, began several more laps of the pool. A few minutes later she was again drifting aimlessly on her back, listening to the distant sounds of the valley when she heard a stirring in the bushes nearby. Her eyes came open and she looked across to the vast stone wall from the where the noise had come just in time to see a lizard scuttle back into the undergrowth. She relaxed, letting her arms drift from her sides as she gently moved her legs and was just deciding to do a few more lengths before going to take a shower when she heard someone say,

'Twas not for the want of beauty he rested his eyes on the nymph, but for the want of mortality and the satiation of his dreams.'

Kirsten could feel herself smiling even before he had finished. 'Good evening, Zaccheo,' she said still looking up at the sky. 'As you can see, I wasn't exactly expecting you.'

She heard him chuckle then rolled over to look up at

where he was standing on the veranda. His arms were resting on the lobelia covered wall, his dark eyes were sparkling.

'If you were a gentleman,' she said, 'you'd turn your back while I climbed out of here.'

Zaccheo's grin widened. 'I am a gentleman, Kirsten, *bellezza mia*, but I am not a fool.'

Kirsten tried and failed to suppress a smile, then tossing back her hair she hauled herself up over the steps and having no choice but to walk towards him, for she had left her clothes on the veranda, she put her shoulders back and stalked through the garden never taking her eyes from his as though challenging him to lower his gaze to her body. He watched her, every step of the way, until she was standing beside him waiting for him to hand her the towel he was holding. Still their eyes were locked, then Kirsten felt her smile widening as his body started to tremble and his deep resonant laughter seemed to erupt from his very depths. His head fell back as he roared his amusement and laughing too, Kirsten snatched the towel from him and wrapped herself in it.

'You thought I wouldn't have the courage, didn't you?' she said, somewhat surprised herself that she did.

'I hoped you would,' he answered still chuckling as he ran his fingers over her face. 'You are such a pleasure for my eyes, such an indulgence for my mind. Will you take an aperitif now? Or will you shower first?'

'I think,' Kirsten said, 'that I will take an aperitif.'

'Then it will be my pleasure to serve you.'

As Kirsten sank into a cushioned wicker chair she watched his enormous body move almost lithely into the sitting room. She wasn't too sure why she had chosen to take the aperitif before the shower since the cool night air was prickling her skin, but there had been something in those few moments that had made her want to remain here, unclad beneath the towel and, perhaps, still in his eyes.

When he came back he handed her a cocktail she had never tasted before and sat down on a chair facing her. Kirsten eyed him, waiting for him to speak.

'So,' he said at last, 'you are enjoying your stay here?' She nodded, a tiny smile hovering about her lips.

'This is good,' he said, putting his head to one side as he regarded her intently.

'It was kind of you to invite me,' she said softly.

'You needed to come.'

There was an ambiguity in his words which, coupled with the sleepy, knowing look in his eyes, sent a quick thrill through her veins. It was so rare that she allowed herself to flirt this way, but with Zaccheo it was almost impossible not to. Though Paul had always been there before, watching them in silent amusement, like a father indulging his children.

'What brought you back from Rome so soon?' she asked.

The look in his eyes was answer enough and again Kirsten felt her pulses leap. She found herself looking at his immense hand holding the delicate glass, the jet black hair that curled over his arms, the gentle rise of his massive chest as he breathed. After a while she returned her gaze to his patrician face, the heavy beard that almost disguised the fullness of his mouth, the large nose and deep, sardonic eyes. She could see the moisture on his lips, almost feel the tension mounting through his body and felt herself so drawn to him it was as though the shadows stealing across the veranda were merging them into one. Her chest tightened as he stood up and moved behind her, resting his hands on the back of the chair. Neither of them moved or spoke as together they looked out at the burning orange sky watching the sun sink imperiously into the horizon.

Not until it had disappeared fully did he touch her, so softly that were it not for the electrifying tremor that went through her Kirsten might not have known it.

'You are cold,' he said as she shivered. He walked across the terrace to pick up a fresh towel. When he came back he lifted her hands and pulled her to her feet. As she stood the towel covering her fell away and Kirsten made no attempt to retrieve it. She knew she was going too far, that the harmless flirtation had some time ago taken on a new momentum, but his magnetism was too strong to resist. She wanted to be naked under his gaze, to feel the cooling breath of night air whisper over her skin like the caress of his fingers. But soon she would stop, any moment now she would laugh and so would he, and that strange remoteness she was feeling from the exquisite tingling of her body would be at an end.

She bowed her head, watching the indolent movements of the towel as he began to wipe the tiny droplets of water still glistening on her shoulders. Her breasts were aching to be touched and when at last he brushed the velvety fabric over their fullness she felt lightheadedness wash over her. She thought she might be swaying or trembling, but aside from the burning heat spreading through her body she was still. It was as if his hands allowed her no freedom for either movement or thought.

He moved beside her, resting one arm loosely about her shoulders as he lowered the towel from her breasts to her abdomen, caressing her tenderly with its softness until he was dabbing gently at the pearls of water clinging to her pubic hair. Then the hand resting on her shoulder came up under her chin and lifted her face to his. He looked long into her eyes his other hand now motionless, yet still touching the join of her legs. It was as though she was floating away from herself, watching herself surrender to a desire she had no power to break.

As his mouth covered hers Kirsten felt a sob shudder through her. She felt the towel slip from his fingers and pool at her feet. Then, as with one hand he massaged her neck, with the other he cupped one magnificent breast and lightly squeezed the achingly distended nipple.

Slowly he drew her to him, lifting his head to gaze into her eyes as his hands dropped to her waist and his fingers fanned over her hips. Coasting further into a daze of overpowering longing Kirsten allowed him to push her gently back into the chair and her heart started to pound as he once again lifted the towel and parting her knees began to stroke her inner-thighs.

Desire throbbed heavily through her body. Her head fell back against the chair, her eyes were closed and all she could hear were the tiny moans escaping her lips. The voice of caution was now no more than a remnant of a distant echo and as he pulled her forward, resting her buttocks on the very edge of the seat before lifting her legs and opening them wide, Kirsten knew that she was going to yield to him completely.

As his tongue flickered against her she gave a startled sob of pure ecstasy. Her head rolled from side to side, her fingers snaked through his hair and as he sucked her with his lips and probed her with his tongue she could feel herself rising on a soaring tide of impossible sensation. With his thumbs he pulled her wider apart and took that most sensitive part of her full into his mouth.

Kirsten gasped, and as her head fell forward she opened her eyes and looked down to where his mass of inky black hair was resting between her thighs.

It came at her from nowhere with such ferocity and such lightning speed and clarity there was nothing she could do to stop it. Her entire body seemed to jar with the impact as the shock lashed through her. The last man to do this to her was the only man ever to have done it, and he too had black hair, he too had an expertly questing mouth and a dazzling sorcery in his finger tips. And it was him she was seeing now. It was for his body that her own was trembling, for his heat she was yearning, wanting to feel it pressing so deep inside her until she could take no more.

As though she had been struck Kirsten pulled back, knocking Zaccheo off balance as she curled her long legs into the chair. 'I'm sorry,' she gasped as Zaccheo looked up at her in astonishment. 'Zaccheo, I'm sorry, I just can't do it.'

His face darkened with fury, but as he made to get up Kirsten sprang from the chair and ran into the house.

When she reached her room she closed the door behind her and stood against it, panting for breath. But just being away from Zaccheo, by removing herself from the intoxicating ambience of a Tuscan night and the potency of his Italian charm, had restored some semblance of order to her mind.

As she walked to the bed and picked up a robe her lovely face was tight with anger. Not in five years had she allowed herself to relive the full intensity of the passion she had shared with Laurence, never had she dwelled, not even for a moment, on the image of their entwined bodies, the eroticism of their games, the indescribable beauty of his nudity. It had all, every bit of it, been banished from her mind's eye until those moments with Zaccheo had tricked her so cruelly.

She stalked furiously to the bathroom, snapped on the shower and stood under the giant rose letting the scalding water pummel her body. She was going to deal with this, she told herself vehemently. Like the love she still felt for him, the desire was going to be conquered too. How could she have been so stupid as not to have realized before that the two were inseparable? It was a brutal reflection of how stupefyingly naive she could be. Thirty-six years old, she seethed as she savagely soaped her legs, and still she didn't know how to deal with the treachery of her own mind.

But she would deal with it, and what was more she knew exactly how she was going to begin. And stepping out of the shower she picked up a towel, stalked into the bedroom and opened up the wardrobe. Half an hour later, her hair still damp, her skin lightly perfumed and clad in a dress that clung to every curve of her body she turned to look at herself in the mirror. Just one glance was enough to see that she wore no underwear and as she looked deep into her own eyes it was almost as though she could see reflected in their depths the erotic images of Zaccheo's vast body joining with hers . . .

Laurence had been in Los Angeles for just three days and was already exhausted by so many meetings, but he knew that his energy would never give out, he felt so alive in this place. The superficiality and bullshit amused him as much as it infuriated him, but he could play the game just as well as anyone else – and right now he was loving the game.

He was staying in the Hollywood Hills with a British director he knew from way back and even Victor's negativity over the story of Moyna O'Malley hadn't managed to get to Laurence. Victor had said just about the same as everyone else. 'It's period, Laurence, no one wants to touch period these days.' And, 'You've got to get some heavyweight names on board, your own just won't carry it this time.' Or, which was more to the point the way things stood, 'You don't have a strong enough story there. OK, the ingredients aren't so bad, but it needs a real workover.'

For sure, Laurence knew all that, but the way Ruby had been shaping up these past couple of weeks filled him with optimism. She was even, according to Alison, coming up with some pretty amazing stuff down there in New Orleans. He'd be joining them in a couple of days and by then, if today's conference at Universal was anything to go by, he'd have some encouraging news for them.

It had been his second meeting in the Black Tower in as many days, though he and Bill Cohen had spoken frequently on the phone during the weeks prior to Laurence's arrival. Bill was an old friend, but Laurence had known better than to trade on that. He'd had to give Bill something that would knock his hat off or future access to the big man would prove a damned sight more difficult than it already was. But the seemingly endless hours spent with Ruby, coupled with Alison's inspired settings and his own tireless efforts had in the end paid off. OK, Bill's hat hadn't actually been knocked off, but it had certainly tilted. And Bill was no time waster. The reason he'd called the conference at Universal that day was so that the other executives could hear direct from Laurence what they'd be putting their money into. Not that they were even considering financing the movie, but they were open to distributing it if he could pull it off. And once he had a distributor Laurence knew that the money would just fall into place.

'Well, if the look on your face is anything to go by,' Victor said as Laurence let himself into the air-conditioned oak-beamed kitchen, 'I'd say you've managed to pull it off.'

'Getting there,' Laurence grinned. 'But you know what this town's like, the ship never sails on schedule. Any beer in the fridge?'

'Help yourself,' Victor said already turning his attention back to the script he was working on.

Not wanting to disturb Victor any further Laurence wandered out on to the deck and gazed absently down at the swimming pool on the terrace below. He'd give it an hour or so before calling Pippa, he didn't want her to hear the enthusiasm for Hollywood in his voice, it would only unnerve her, but he sure as hell wanted her to share in the celebrations if Universal came up trumps. If they did then perhaps he would ask her to fly out here, 'cos he sure was missing her. Those last few days they'd spent together before he'd come out here had been like the first days of their honeymoon.

He sighed contentedly as he relaxed in a chair. God he loved it here, looking out on to the densely wooded hills, marvelling at the breath-taking sunset and listening to the haunting cries of the coyotes. Even enclosed in a garden like this he had such a sense of space.

Pippa understood completely the way he felt about LA which was why she never minded him coming over here. He was always in a better mood when he returned home, though there were times when she worried that one day he would go and never come back. But that would never happen, for as much as he loved his own country the way he missed Pippa when he was away from her was enough to get him on a plane back to Heathrow at the earliest opportunity.

'Any calls?' he asked looking up as Victor came to join him.

'Mmm,' Victor answered, an upraised beer bottle in his mouth. 'Ruby in New Orleans. Some guy from London, Campbell I think he said his name was, and someone from Fox. I've written it all down next to the phone.'

'Thanks,' Laurence said, lifting his own bottle to his lips. 'How you doing with that script of yours?'

'Getting there,' Victor quipped, 'but I could use your help.'

'You could?' Laurence said, his surprise showing.

'I've got an idea on how to shoot a particular scene and reckon it's going to cost a fortune. Maybe you could tell me just what kind of a fortune before I wade in and make a fool of myself.'

'I'll give it a shot,' Laurence answered. 'Want me to take a look now?'

'No, it can wait. I wanted to talk to you about who's going to direct your Moyna O'Malley story – if you pull it off.'

Laurence's eyebrows arched. 'Don't tell me you're offering?'

Victor laughed. 'Not me, no. I'm pretty tied up here for the next year or so. But I wanted to suggest someone to you. His name's Willie Henderson. Ever heard of him?'

Laurence shook his head.

'He's English. Lives in London. His father's something big in the City, got some sort of title as well I believe. Anyway, more to the point, if the grapevine is to be relied upon the old man came up with the finance for the one feature Willie has done. Before that he did mainly TV and a couple of commercials I think. Anyway, the boy's got real talent – and contacts.'

'Boy?'

'He's late twenties. Still needs some guidance, but I think he's worth a try. I've got his movie on cassette in the house, you can take a look for yourself. It's my opinion he's really going places.'

'But I thought you were advocating big names here?'

'I am. And by all means get them if you can. But it's all dependent on the kind of money you raise and what I'm saying is, if you don't get what you're hoping for then think about Willie. He'll cost you a fraction of what one of the named boys will, he'll do a bloody good job providing you hold his hand and he might just be able to point you in the direction of potential backers.'

'I'll take a look at what he's done,' Laurence said, turning to look back indoors as the telephone started to ring.

Victor went inside to answer and a few seconds later called out for Laurence. 'It's Cohen,' he hissed as he passed the receiver to Laurence.

Laurence's eyes widened. He hadn't expected to hear from Bill Cohen for several days, maybe even weeks yet. Three minutes later he rang off and went back outside in search of Victor. 'You got any champagne in that ice-box of yours?' he asked.

Victor stared at him in profound astonishment. 'Are you telling me . . .?'

Laurence was laughing and nodding. Then shrugging he said, 'Sure there are a few conditions to be met, more meetings to be got through, guarantees and the like to be delivered, but Cohen reckons we can prepare the ship to sail.'

'Then to hell with the ice-box,' Victor cried. 'We're out of here and celebrating tonight, my friend. Fuck me! Three days in Hollywood with a project that stinks worse than Lucifer's breath and you got yourself a distribution deal! What are you, some kind of magician?'

Laughing, Laurence headed back inside the house. 'Before we go anywhere I'm gonna call Pippa.' He glanced at his watch. It was still early in the morning over there, but not so early that she would mind being woken.

'Hello, darling,' her sleepy voice came across the line a few minutes later. 'How are you?'

'Just fine,' Laurence answered softly. 'Did I wake you?'

'No. I was just lying here, thinking.'

'You were? What about?'

'You and me and Tom.'

Though he smiled Laurence was aware that his heart had suddenly tightened with something like anxiety. 'Are you all right, honey?' he murmured. 'You sound kind of low.'

Pippa sighed. 'Yes, I suppose I am a bit.'

'Do you want to tell me about it?'

There was a long silence, so long that if he hadn't been able to hear her breathing Laurence might have thought they'd been cut off. Then quite suddenly he remembered a time, some four years or so ago now, when Pippa used to lie in bed of a morning, thinking and crying and unable to find the energy to get up. And the reason for it was that she had been three months pregnant with Tom. A surge of almost overwhelming joy overtook him. He wanted nothing more than they should have another child and if Pippa was three months down the line then that meant she would have conceived long before that morning in the kitchen.

'Laurence?' she whispered.

'Mmm?'

'Do you love Tom?'

For a moment Laurence was perplexed. 'You know I do, sweetheart. What makes you ask?' Then suddenly, 'Dear God, Pippa, he's all right, isn't he? Nothing's happened to him?'

'No, he's fine.'

'Then what made you ask?' Laurence said his heart still pounding from the sudden onslaught of terror.

'I don't know really. I suppose I wanted to hear you say it. Do you love him more than anything else in the world? More than me?'

'Oh, darling, there's no contest. I love you both more than anything else in the world.'

'Do you, Laurence? Do you really?'

'You know I do.'

'But what if I died, Laurence . . . I mean if I got sick and was going to die, what would you do then?'

Laurence could feel himself frowning as the reality of her words closed around his heart. 'Pippa, what are you saying?' he breathed. 'What are you trying to tell me?'

'Nothing,' she said listlessly. 'I just wondered, that was all.'

'Pippa, have you been to see a doctor? Has he told you something?'

'No,' she said. 'I'm all right. I was just wondering what you would do if I wasn't here any more. Do you think you would marry again?'

With a supreme effort Laurence forced himself to

remain calm. For sure the last time she hadn't thought about dying, but she'd been pretty maudlin for a while.

'You didn't answer my question,' she said.

Not at all sure how he should handle this Laurence said, 'I don't know, honey. It's not something I've ever thought about.'

'I'd want you to,' she told him. 'I mean I'd want you to be happy, darling, you know that don't you?'

'It's you who makes me happy.'

'Oh Laurence, you're making me cry.'

'Pip, honey,' he said gently, 'do you think you could be pregnant?'

She laughed softly through her tears. 'No. I'm having my period.'

'Do you think it's that making you feel so low?' he suggested.

'It could be,' but there was no conviction in her voice and once again Laurence found himself trying to stave off the panic. He was certain she was holding back on him about something and if she wasn't being straight with him about seeing the doctor, if she had found out there was something wrong with her then he knew she wouldn't tell him over the phone.

'I'm coming home,' he said. 'I'll get the next flight out . . .'

'No, don't do that. Oh darling, I've frightened you. I'm sorry. There's nothing wrong with me, honestly. I'm just being silly.'

'Nevertheless, I'm coming home.'

'No, Laurence, please. I'm fine, and besides I'm going to Italy tomorrow. Now tell me all that's been happening to you out there.'

Hardly thinking about what he was saying Laurence told her about the call from Cohen, but, despite her very real delight for him and the way she was starting to sound much more herself, he was still worried.

'Are you sure you don't want me to come home?' he said just before they rang off.

'No. Like I said, I'm going over to Italy tomorrow.'

'Then how about when we both get back we take that weekend we've been promising ourselves?'

'With or without Tom?'

'Whichever you prefer.'

Pippa laughed. 'Tom always wants to be with his daddy,' she said.

– 9 –

'Well, are you one dark horse!' Helena cried into the telephone. 'I thought you said Zaccheo was in Rome.'

'He came back,' Kirsten answered prosaically, though Helena could hear the smile in her voice.

'You're not kidding!' Helena laughed. 'And just what have the two of you been up to since? No, don't bother to tell me, I already know.'

'What do you mean? He only answered the phone so how can you . . .'

'Kirstie! There are photographs all over the centre pages of Campbell's rag this morning of you cavorting nude in a swimming pool while Zaccheo stands by and watches.'

'What!' Kirsten gasped. 'How the hell did . . .? Who told him I was here?'

'Search me,' Helena shrugged, as she hunted around for an ashtray, 'but he's found out somehow. And I gotta tell you that apart from a strategically placed fig-leaf to satisfy the censors there's nothing left to the imagination. You look sensational!'

'I don't believe it!' Kirsten cried. 'Jesus Christ, no one was supposed to know I was here. What's he written?'

'It's not good I'm afraid. Do you really want to know?'

'Yes. No! Oh God, who told him where I was, that's what I want to know.'

'Jane?' Helena suggested taking another puff of her cigarette as she stared casually down at the busy Crouch End High Street below her flat.

'Don't be ridiculous,' Kirsten snapped.

'Well she's the only other person who knew, that is assuming that neither you nor Zaccheo called Campbell.'

'Very droll,' Kirsten said tightly. 'But it wouldn't have been Jane.'

'Why not?'

'Because unless you told her where I was going . . .'

'*Me*! It was you who told her.'

'I did no such thing.'

'Sorry, but you did. Well, actually it was me you were talking to, but Jane was there. See what I mean about that girl, she's got a metaphysical state that makes you forget she's in the room. Anyway, it was just a thought. My reckoning is that it was Pippa. It might even have been Jane who told Pippa, but it was more likely Zaccheo. She's his editor and she's a friend of Campbell's.'

'I'll ask him,' Kirsten said. 'But I don't think it was Zaccheo, as far as I know he hasn't spoken to anyone since he got back. So try calling Jane to see if she did mention anything to Pippa. I want to find out once and for all who's giving Campbell his information.'

'All right,' Helena said, without much enthusiasm. 'Anyway the main reason I'm ringing is to ask if I can stay over at your place tonight. Melissa Andrews is holding some teenage garden party this afternoon for her pimply faced daughter and I said I'd lend some moral support. And, as they live just around the corner from you, I thought I could get smashed and crash out at yours.'

'Be my guest,' Kirsten answered.

'Thanks. Now, what I really want to know is just exactly what is going on over there with you and Signor Marigliano?'

'Not now,' Kirsten said, lowering her voice as Zaccheo came into the room.'

'Ah! He's there I take it. Well just answer me yes or no. Are you screwing him?'

'Mind your own business.'

'Yes or no?'

'Now I am, yes.'

'Now you are?' Helena repeated mulling it over. 'Obviously there's something behind that. Well, you can tell me when you get home. So, what's he like? Does he live up to his reputation?'

'Mmm.'

'Is it serious?'

Helena was aware that Kirsten had turned slightly from the phone, probably to look at Zaccheo she thought as Kirsten said, 'Mmm, I reckon it could be.'

Helena toyed with the idea of telling her what was in the papers that morning then, but decided not to. Kirsten would find out soon enough, so why burst her bubble now? It sure was going to upset her once she found out though. THE FOX CIRCLES THE COOP, was the headline, and after giving the general low down on Zaccheo's literary successes, not to mention his wealth, Campbell had gone on to point out that he was a close friend of 'one of the Kirstie Doll's old flames, whose nanny, as disclosed in an earlier column, has already been enticed into the Meredith web. So it still remains to be seen just what the Kirstie Doll is planning over there in Italy.' He was turning Kirsten's life into a regular soap opera and as far as Helena could tell the nation was glued. She had to confess that even she found it compelling reading, and when the stories were accompanied by pictures of Kirsten in the altogether she could understand why Campbell's rag was boasting yet a further increase in sales. If Kirsten wasn't quite so gorgeous no one would be interested, but as it was she had become the woman everyone loved to hate. Or mock, as the newspaper reviewers had on the early morning chat-show Helena had just been watching.

'Well,' Helena said, 'I guess I'm just going to have to wait for the real lowdown, but whatever it is, babe, enjoy it!'

'I will,' Kirsten smiled, and promising to call again in a few days Helena rang off.

Much later in the day, having read Campbell's column so many times now she virtually knew it by heart, Helena was leaning against the door jamb of Melissa Andrews' Edwardian house nursing a very large vodka and feeling so thoroughly wretched as she contemplated her life that she couldn't even work up the energy to find a nice young boy to help take her mind off things. Hearing a screech coming from the garden she looked up, tried to focus on the heaving mass of nubile young bodies, and promptly wondered if she was going to be sick. Being fat and over-forty when you fancied men who were fat and over-forty was bad enough, but when you fancied the hell out of fresh-faced youths with skinny hips, barely developed muscles and inexperienced cocks it was pure torture. God, what she could teach them if she could just get her hands on them, but there was nothing doing – at least not while Melissa was around. She'd have a fit if she thought Helena was planning to corrupt the sons of her bourgeois friends.

But it wasn't fair, Helena grumbled to herself as she downed the vodka in one go. There was Kirsten over there in Italy getting her brains humped out by the only man fat and over-forty Helena could conceive of screwing and here was she standing in a doorway like a frustrated old spinster who's only chance of fulfilment that day was to go home and masturbate.

But that wasn't true, she reminded herself miserably. There was somewhere else she could go, someone else she could turn to, and the more she had to drink the more tempted she was to give in.

She reached for the vodka again, downed another large one then poured yet more into her glass. She could hardly believe this was happening to her, but it was, and had been for some time now. Drunk or sober she was lusting for a man whom the very sight of had always made her stomach churn. Well, maybe that was a bit strong, but she'd always loathed the man. Until recently.

Was it because she suspected he was falling for Kirsten, she asked herself dismally. Or was it because she had got so desperate now she was prepared to do anything to ease the loneliness in her life?

A faint smile started to hover over her lips. What would he say if she called him now and asked him to meet her at Kirsten's? Christ, what was she thinking of? How could she even consider inviting Dermott Campbell to Kirsten's house? Would he come, she

– 163 –

wondered. She wouldn't know unless she asked, and why the hell should Kirsten have all the fun? She'd get a real kick out of running rings round Campbell and she was more than curious to know what he was like in the sack . . .

An hour later Helena looked across Kirsten's sitting room at Campbell, sitting there in the fading light, and felt her earlier defiance start to recede as all the alcohol she had consumed turned her mood morose. She noticed the way his eyes looked kind of vulnerable without his glasses. There were deep lines on his brow, more pronounced because he was frowning and his mouth looked somehow smaller in the strange shadow his nose cast over it. He wasn't a handsome man, not really, but when he smiled . . .

She lowered her eyes to his hands. His elbows were resting on his knees, his fingers were locked together. They were short and stubby, there was hair on the backs of them. He'd obviously come out in a rush because he'd forgotten to fasten his cuffs. He didn't have any socks on either. Who looked after him, she wondered. It sure didn't look as though he took much care of himself. Not the way he looked right now, anyhow. In fact, his whole demeanour suggested that he was just about as fed up and depressed by life as she was. Or was she just imagining that because it was how she wanted him to feel? But now she came to look a little closer she could see that his hands were shaking. Probably he'd been drinking too. Did he do it for the same reasons as her, to blot out the loneliness? He'd got here pretty quickly after she'd called him. Was it because he was keen to see her? No, he'd come because he thought she was going to tell him something about Kirsten. A surge of resentment suddenly lodged in her throat. Kirsten, always Kirsten.

'You fancy her, don't you?' Helena challenged quietly.
'Who?'

'Kirsten. Who else?'

For a moment or two he eyed her steadily, then dropped his head into his hands. His fingers spread through his hair. 'I don't know,' he said at last. 'Sometimes I think I do . . .' He raised his head and Helena felt strangely touched by the way his hair was sticking up. 'Why did you ask me over here?' he asked.

'I'm not sure. Maybe I just wanted to talk.'

He half smiled, half laughed. 'To me? I thought I'd have been the last person . . .'

'So did I.'

Campbell got to his feet and stuffing his hands into his trouser pockets he walked over to the fireplace. He had no idea what was happening here, whether it was the dwindling light that had masked the contempt he was so used to seeing in her eyes, or whether it was the alcohol that was lending a sporadic gentleness to her voice. But what he did know was that he was on foreign ground in more ways that one.

'It was the party,' she said.

He looked at her and felt for a moment as though he was swaying. Her normally bright, almost startling eyes were steeped in confusion, the smooth plains of her face seemed pinched by an emotion he wasn't too sure he recognized.

'The McAllister's party,' she went on. 'You did something . . . Or maybe you said something, I don't know. But it got to me.'

'Got to you in what way?' he said hoarsely.

For a long time she just looked at him, then her head

fell back and she closed her eyes. 'Oh God, I don't know what I'm talking about,' she murmured.

'You've seen me since then,' he said.

'I know.'

'Look, Helena, you've got to know . . . I mean, it must be obvious to you . . .' His voice trailed off and shaking his head he gazed down at the empty hearth.

'What must be obvious to me?' she said her eyes still closed.

'Nothing,' he whispered. How could he tell her when he might be reading this all wrong? She'd never wanted him before, couldn't stand him near her . . .

By the time Helena spoke again night had shrouded the room and the only light was from a streetlamp outside. 'Talk to me, Dermott,' she said. 'Tell me how you really feel about Kirsten.'

He turned and moved slowly back to the sofa. 'Helena,' he said when he was sitting, 'you're looking at someone who's so mixed up that right now I don't know how I feel about anything.'

Helena smiled then let her eyes drift to the Provençal landscape hanging above the marquetry cabinet. 'Kirsten slept with someone once just to secure my job,' she said. 'That's how good a friend she is to me.' Her eyes returned to his. 'I'll sleep with you, Dermott, to stop you doing what you are to her.'

He rubbed a hand over his unshaven chin and swallowed hard. 'I don't want you to do that,' he said.

Helena's heart turned over. She was only using Kirsten as an excuse. 'Why? Because you'd rather sleep with her?'

As his eyes came up to hers he smiled, sadly. 'No. Because it wouldn't do any good. You know it's not me who's driving this vendetta.'

'Does it bother you that she's still in love with Laurence?'

'If she is then what's she doing over there with Zaccheo?'

Helena laughed. 'I thought you had the answer to that. Finding another way of getting close to Laurence.'

'Laurence's marriage is sound. She won't get him back.'

Helena shrugged. 'You're the one who wrote the story. But maybe you're right, she won't get him back, but do you really think you stand a chance?'

'It's not her I want, Helena.'

It was Helena's turn to stand up. She crossed the room, switched on a lamp then drew the curtains. 'Then who is it you want?' she heard herself say.

She was standing behind him so neither could see the other's face. 'You know it's you,' he said huskily.

'But you said just now . . .'

'I don't want you under those circumstances,' he growled.

'The real truth is, Dermott, you don't know what you do want. Tell me, why haven't you gone to print on the real reason Kirsten and Laurence broke up?'

Campbell turned to look at her. Helena averted her eyes and walked over to switch on another lamp.

'Are you holding back on it to protect her?' she demanded.

'In part. Helena, look, can you just tell me what's going on here? I mean, it's like you're sounding jealous or something.'

'Is it?' she snapped and suddenly, to his amazement, she started to cry.

'Helena,' he said going to her and trying to put his arms around her.

She shrugged him away. 'Just tell me when you're going to print it, Dermott. Stop keeping me in suspense this way.'

'I'm not going to print it,' he said.

'But why?'

'Because I can't.'

'Because you've fallen for her.'

'No. Because if I even mention it to Dyllis she'll print Laurence's name too. Now listen to me. Listen!' he said, catching her arm as she made to move away again. 'You've got no reason to be jealous of her. Not where I'm concerned. She's a beautiful woman, a man can be forgiven for losing his head . . . Helena, listen!'

'Just tell me who told you about the break up, Dermott! I know I told you everything else, but I didn't tell you that. So who was it?'

'You know I can't tell you.'

'But she'll think it's me. If you print it, she'll think I told you . . .'

'Look, come and sit down,' he said, putting an arm around her and leading her to the sofa.

'Oh God!' Helena sobbed as he pulled her head onto his shoulder. 'What's going on here? You're a bastard! A loathsome, despicable bastard who's blackmailing me into betraying my best friend . . . I should hate you. I do hate you.'

She lifted her head and as her huge, watery eyes stared back at him he wondered how the hell he could get so mixed up about his feelings when all he had to do was look at her to know that she was the only one he wanted. He lifted a hand and smoothed a tear from her cheek. 'Tell Kirsten what you've done,' he said. 'Don't let her find out from someone else.'

It was a long time before Helena answered and when

she did it was with a slow, uncertain shake of her head. 'I can't,' she whispered. 'I don't want to lose her as a friend.'

Campbell sighed and as she sank back against his chest he wrapped her in his arms. Surely she understood that he got no pleasure out of what he was doing. He was just a pawn in Dyllis's game. Were it up to him the things Helena had done would stay locked in the past. So too would the secrets of Laurence's life. His jaw tensed with a quick anger. That they should all of them be caught up in this deadly combat between two women, have their own lives abused and trampled over the way they were for the sake of an old woman's pride was so fucking unjust it defied words. He knew that if there were any way of doing it he'd go right in for the kill and get Kirsten out of their lives now. He wouldn't lose much sleep over that, a woman as beautiful as her would always find a way of surviving. But Dyllis was pulling the strings not him. Shit, what he wouldn't give to get himself out of that fucking megalomaniac's clutches and leave her to fester in her sick delusions of supremacy.

As Helena stirred in his arms his anger faded. It was hard for him to think of anything else for long when he was holding her this way and wanting so very badly to kiss her. 'I guess we just go on the way we were then?' he said.

Helena nodded, then her breath caught in her throat as his hand came under her chin and he lifted her mouth to his.

'Can you handle it?' he said when finally she pulled away.

'What us, or the deceit?'

'I guess they're one and the same thing.'

She shrugged. 'I'm an actress, aren't I?'

'Oh shit,' he groaned. 'Tell me you're not acting now.'

Taking his hand she raised it to her lips and kissed each finger in turn. 'No, I'm not acting,' she smiled.

Campbell left Kirsten's at seven the following evening. At one minute past seven there was a knock on the door. 'Jane!' Helena gasped, almost reeling. She glanced quickly down the street to see if Campbell was still anywhere in sight. 'What are you doing here?' she asked.

'I came to see Kirsten,' Jane answered.

'She's in Italy.'

'I thought she might be back.'

'No, no. Um, you'd better come in.'

As they walked through to the kitchen Helena tightened the belt of her dressing gown still reeling at the narrowness of the escape. Christ, if it had been any closer Jane and Campbell would have met on the doorstep! 'Can I get you something?' she said to Jane. 'Coffee? Tea?'

'No, nothing, thank you.'

Helena looked at her, not quite sure what to say.

Jane shrugged, but as she tried to smile her mouth quivered and to Helena's amazement she dissolved into tears.

'What's up?' Helena said, trying not to be shocked at how awful the girl looked with her face screwed up that way.

'Nothing, nothing,' Jane cried and fled to the bathroom.

For a while Helena stared at the door trying to swallow her exasperation at having to deal with an emotional kid when she had so much else to think about right now. Like her feelings for Campbell and what had happened between them. It was incredible and had she not experienced it herself she'd never have believed it was possible. They had spent an entire night wrapped in each others arms and neither one of them had made any attempt to make love. She wasn't too sure why, especially when that had been her motive for getting him over here, but if the truth be told she wouldn't have changed what did happen for the world for it had been so long since a man had held her that way – in fact she couldn't remember ever having been held that way. Kirsten, it seemed, was the only one round here who experienced that sort of thing.

The thought of Kirsten brought a stab of dismay to her heart. The guilt she felt at the way she was betraying the closest friend she had ever had was indescribable. Just about every damning story Campbell had written so far had been based on information she, Helena, had provided. In an effort to save her own skin, to avoid the scandal of her own past, she had given Campbell all he wanted to know about Kirsten's. But she hadn't stopped with the past, for amongst all the minutiae of Kirsten's day to day life she, Helena, had been the one to tell Campbell that Kirsten had befriended Laurence's nanny and it was she who had disclosed the fact that Kirsten was in Italy now staying with Zaccheo Marigliano – someone else with a close connection to the McAllister family. But Helena hadn't told Campbell what lay behind Kirsten and Laurence's break up. She had no idea who had and it almost frightened her to think that there was someone else out there who was either betraying Kirsten as mercilessly as she was or who was as determined as Dyllis Fisher was to wreak some kind of vengeance on Kirsten. Helena knew that the odds of Kirsten getting her life back together now were stacked so heavily against her as to make it virtually impossible. Dyllis was already proving that she more than had the means, as well as the contacts, to annihilate Kirsten's career, and Campbell's determination that Kirsten would never come between Laurence and Pippa was unshakable. But there was always Zaccheo, Helena reminded herself. A quick flare of jealousy burned in her throat. For Kirsten there was always someone. Dyllis had ordered Campbell to do all he could to destroy whatever there was between Zaccheo and Kirsten but Helena couldn't see Zaccheo being too swayed by what was written in the press, particularly not the British press.

She started as the lock on the bathroom door snapped open. Jane had been gone so long she'd forgotten she was there.

'Are you all right?' Helena said as Jane came into the kitchen.

'I think so,' Jane sniffed, dabbing at her nose with a wad of toilet paper.

'Do you want to talk about it?' Helena offered, hoping the answer would be no.

Jane's bottom lip was sucked under her teeth as she half-sobbed. Her normally lifeless eyes were glittering brightly as they darted about the kitchen, then to Helena's surprise she walked over to the draining board and picking up a cloth started to dry the dishes. Helena watched her, vaguely amused by the fact that she seemed unaware of what she was doing. 'I took Tom to Laurence's parents today,' Jane said, putting the cloth back down again.

'Did you? That was nice.'

Jane looked at her. 'I took him there because Pippa asked me to,' she said.

'Oh.'

'Tom and I often go there.'

'That's nice,' Helena said again, feeling a growing urge to shake the girl.

'It's just that . . .' Jane's eyes filled with tears. 'Well, I know Pippa wanted me and Tom out of the way while she was packing . . . Tom's still with his grandparents, he's staying the night. I am too. Laurence's parents are so nice to me. They always make me really welcome . . .'

'Oh. Well, I'm sure they do. Uh, are you sure you won't have a coffee?'

'No, no thanks. I went back home again just now. Pippa was already gone.' Helena could see the effort going into her holding back yet more tears and silently she was willing her to succeed. 'I knew she was going.'

The words were out before Helena could stop them. 'I imagine the fact that she was packing put you on to her,' she quipped.

Jane's eyes came up to hers. 'You don't understand,' she said. 'Pippa wasn't just packing for a trip, she was packing because . . .' Her voice was so strangled over her final words that Helena wasn't too sure she'd heard right.

'What did you say?' she said.

Jane swallowed hard. 'Pippa's left Laurence,' she whispered.

Helena blinked.

'Oh, what shall I do? What am I going to do?' Jane sobbed covering her face with her hands.

'Well, I don't see that there's much you can do,' Helena said. 'I mean, it's up to them really, isn't it?'

'But if I'd got there sooner I might have been able to stop her.'

'Surely that's up to Laurence.'

'But Laurence doesn't know!' Jane cried. 'He's in America and he's not due home until the end of next week and I don't know whether I should ring him and tell him or just wait until he comes back. I was hoping Kirsten could tell me what to do.'

Helena wasn't too sure how much Jane knew about Kirsten's feelings for Laurence so, deciding not to voice her opinion on what she thought of Jane coming to Kirsten for such advice, she said, 'Look, are you sure Laurence doesn't know? I mean, she can't have just gone off without saying a word.'

'She's left him a note.'

'Oh, I see. Do you know where she's gone?' Helena asked, more out of curiosity than concern.

Jane nodded. 'She's gone, or at least tomorrow she's going, to Italy. She's staying with her mother tonight.'

'Italy?' Helena said stupidly.

Again Jane nodded. 'Pippa's left Laurence for Zaccheo.'

'But Kirsten's with Zaccheo,' Helena said, feeling her head starting to spin. The implications of all this would have been hard to handle at the best of times, but with a hangover . . . 'does Kirsten know Pippa's on her way?' she said.

'I don't know.'

'Well, I think we'd better find out, don't you?' But when Helena made the connection to Zaccheo's villa there was no reply.

The early morning mist was suspended over the valley, the dew glinted like tiny stars on the vivid green leaves and the air was so fresh and exhilarating as it wafted in through the open bedroom window that it had roused Kirsten long before Zaccheo reached for her.

She adored these wonderful late spring mornings and

couldn't think of anywhere in the world she would rather be than half-lying, half-sitting here in this tapestry-strewn bedroom gazing dreamily out of the windows. Her eyes fluttered as Zaccheo's hand slipped across her stomach. She lay very still, pretending she was still sleeping, but as he leaned over her her lips started to twitch with a smile.

'*Buon giorno, mia cara*,' he murmured as her eyes opened and after kissing her lightly on the mouth he drew himself up taking the warm, linen sheets with him. Immediately Kirsten's nipples puckered as the cool air touched them, but she merely lifted her hands behind her head and lay back, allowing Zaccheo to look at her and feeling the thrill of his eyes as they moved sensuously over her body. Sometimes their intensity was as palpable as a caress.

She looked up to the ceiling as his hands slipped gently between her thighs and parted them. Their mirrored reflections moved languorously above them and she watched as he lowered his head to kiss the dark thatch of hair his fingers were already parting. As tall and as full-figured as she was, beside the immensity of him she seemed almost frail. His muscled arms were as erotically powerful as his skilfully probing fingers, his vast chest was as hard as his thighs. His waistline had turned to fat, yet there was something deeply sensual about so much flesh.

For five days now they had slept, walked, talked and made love. And the more she came to know him the more she was coming to care for him. His mind was so intellectual and challenging that that alone was enough to make Kirsten's pulses race. When he laughed the deep resonance of it seemed to vibrate through her body

- 175 -

and so often she would find herself reaching for him, wanting to feel his hardness filling her.

Getting him to forgive her for the way she had so unceremoniously pushed him away that first night had been easier than she'd expected. He had returned from Rome to be with her, he'd said, he'd wanted to show her all that he had harboured in his heart for her for so long. So of course he forgave her, and his gentleness had calmed her fears, his loving hands had smoothed away the memories and his brutal thrusts had bound her to him and him alone. It was as if he had understood what had happened to her that night and now wanted to show her that she was right to shut out the past, she must let it go, for here, with him, there was a new beginning, a future filled with hope and attainable dreams.

Kirsten sighed and shivered and pressed her head hard into the pillows as his tongue seemed to draw her every nerve end to the point it touched. She groaned her disappointment when he lifted his head, but as he moved over her, covering her body with his, her arms opened to embrace him. His hardness penetrated her and she looked up again to the mirror, watching the calculated thrust of hips. Her long legs encircled his waist and as she lowered her eyes she found him studying her. She smiled then closed her eyes, for sometimes to watch him as he made love, as he judged and manipulated his every move for the sole purpose of her pleasure, was almost unnerving. It was as though his sublime expertise somehow detached him from the body he used with the delicacy and ferocity of the player of a finely tuned instrument.

The telephone suddenly pierced through the sensuous silence. Kirsten moaned irritably, letting her legs drop back to the bed as Zaccheo reached for it. Yet even as he listened to the voice at the other end he was holding her to him, pushing into her even deeper.

'It's for you,' he said resting the receiver on her shoulder, but as he raised himself on his arms and looked down to where their bodies were joined Kirsten fumbled the receiver back into place.

Zaccheo laughed and when Kirsten's eyes found his she too started to smile. Then the laughter was gone and he was clutching her hips, pounding into her so hard that she could only cling to him and whimper with the sheer power of the sensations coursing through her.

Deftly he rolled on to his back, taking her with him, and as she rode him, meeting every mighty thrust of his hips, he clasped and kneaded her breasts in his bear-like paws.

Again the telephone rang. Zaccheo reached out for it, slowing his pace, but never quite stopping as he listened. Kirsten rested against his knees, her head falling back as his thumb pushed its way between her legs. She looked down at him, saw him smile as he increased the pressure of his thumb, then without uttering a word he replaced the receiver.

The restraints he could put on his own orgasm were incredible, holding back always until he knew she was ready. And as the shuddering tide started to simmer within her he jerked her forward so that she almost lost him, but not quite. Then with long, determined and rapaciously savage strokes he took them both over the edge into oblivion.

Several minutes later, his heart still pounding in his chest, he started to snore gently. Smiling, Kirsten pulled herself up and looked down at his sleeping face. Kissing him softly on the lips she eased herself carefully from him and went off to the bathroom.

Later that day they were going to drive to Siena where he would walk her through each chapter of his latest book. It was something Kirsten had been looking forward to ever since he'd first suggested it. She loved Italy and to be shown one of its most beautiful towns through the eyes of Zaccheo Marigliano she knew was going to be one of the most precious experiences of her life.

She had more or less decided to stay in Tuscany for another two weeks, by which time she knew she would have to return to England if only because she needed to visit the libraries to carry out her own research. Despite the all too frequent distraction of Zaccheo, her own projects were progressing, one in particular, which she was quite excited to show Helena. There was a great part in it for her, and perhaps between them they could decide on who would be best to write it.

In fact the idea of going back to England didn't fill her with as many misgivings as she might have expected. Whatever Dermott Campbell had written about her recently, or whatever he chose to write in the future, didn't bother her any more than it seemed to have bothered Zaccheo. As far as they were concerned their lives were their own affair and what anyone else chose to think was simply of no consequence. And England was going to be so much more tolerable when she knew that most weekends she would be flying over here to be with Zaccheo.

'Ouch!' she laughed as Zaccheo came into the bathroom and slapped her bottom.

'Time to be going, *cara*,' he said, reaching into the still steamy shower and turning it on.

'Already?' Kirsten said, rubbing cream into her arms. 'I thought we weren't leaving until lunch-time.'

'Ah!' he sighed, turning back to her, his face a burlesque of sorrow. 'You misunderstand me, *cara*. It is time for you to be going, not I.'

'I'm sorry?' Kirsten said, stopping what she was doing.

He shrugged. 'My editor, Pippa, she is arriving today. It is better that you are not here when she comes.'

Kirsten could feel the muscles freezing in her face. 'But what difference does it make whether I'm here or not?' she said.

'It is better that you leave,' Zaccheo answered. 'Raimondo will drive you to the airport,' and turning into the shower he closed the door.

Dumb-founded Kirsten stood staring at his enormous bulk through the steam-plastered door. For the moment both her mind and body seemed locked in paralysis, but as the shock slowly permeated her senses she felt herself start to shake with fury.

She wrenched open the shower door, forced a hand past Zaccheo and snapped off the water. 'What the hell do you mean, it's better that I go?' she seethed. 'What am I, some kind of dog to be dismissed when its master becomes bored? You invited me here for as long as I wanted to be here . . .'

'*Cara, cara*,' he sighed, turning to face her. 'You make such a drama of this when it is nothing.'

'Nothing!' she yelled. 'Five days and five nights of unadulterated passion and you call it nothing!'

'But what did you expect, *la mia volpe furba*? That I would change my will?'

As though she had been struck Kirsten reeled back. She hadn't read Campbell's column so had no idea that in calling her his wily fox Zaccheo was referring to that, but that he had called her it at all was almost as injurious as his remark about the will. 'I don't believe you said that,' she gasped. 'I don't believe you could think that of me. I came here . . .'

'You came here, *cara*, because you believed that one way or the other it would benefit you. My fortune or Laurence McAllister. Perhaps both. But you are going to use neither his wife, nor my fortune to get what you want.'

'But you invited me . . .'

'Of course. Always I have wanted to make love to you. You know that. You are a beautiful woman, what man would not want to make love to you? And you, *mia bella*, are a Venus. You make love as though you were the goddess herself, but as you see, it is not so easy to outfox Zaccheo Marigliano. I have eyes that see right through to your heart, and your heart, Kirsten Meredith, is greedy for material prizes.' He lifted an eyebrow. 'Maybe it is greedier still for Laurence McAllister.'

Laurence was standing beside the bed staring sightlessly down at Pippa's note. Despite her protests that she was all right he had cancelled his flight to New Orleans and come straight back to London. And now, God help him, he wished he hadn't for had he known he was coming back to this then he might never have come back at all. But maybe he had known, maybe in truth it was the fear of this that had driven his need to see her to the point of desperation. But how could he have known when in his heart he had truly believed that she loved him.

Yet strangely, he thought distantly to himself, it all

seemed to fit into place now. Her accusing him of having affairs was because of the guilt she was suffering at her own affair. He winced at the sudden bolt of jealousy that lurched through his gut as in his mind's eye he saw her in Zaccheo's arms. Jesus Christ, all this time she'd wanted him to fall for someone else, because it would have made it easier for her to leave him. The fact that she was always so irritable with Tom was only because she'd resented him for making her feel so bad about her imminent desertion. How long had she been planning this? How long had she been lying to him?

He leaned against the dressing table and stared down at the faint rings in the dust left by the things she had taken. Why was it only now that he was understanding all that she had done for him? Had he truly been so ignorant of the fact that it was only because of her that he had been able to handle all that happened with Kirsten? To shut it out and pretend it had never happened.

Sinking down onto the stool he buried his face in his hands. Kirsten! Kirsten! Kirsten! He should have known that something like this would happen as soon as she came back. For weeks now it had been as though he was facing an eclipse of his own emotions and his love and need for Pippa was blinding him still to the bitter deceit of his life. Except now, and perhaps only now, he realized, there was no deceit. He loved Pippa, truly loved her.

The shock of her going made him nauseous. Did Tom know yet that she was gone? For sure he'd know she was on a trip, but had anyone told him that Mummy wasn't coming back? A surge of protective love wrapped itself around his heart and without thinking what he was doing, he took himself to Tom's room and sat down on the bed beside him.

His throat started to tighten. Where in the hell were they going to be without her? What life was there for these two guys without the woman they loved? He gazed down at the innocent, childish face and felt the defencelessness of those tender limbs and the untroubled joy of the tiny heart pierce through him like a knife. He could almost feel Tom's delight when he woke to see his Daddy watching over him. They always had had a closeness that some said was unusual for a father and son of Tom's age, and now Laurence couldn't help wondering if Pippa had deliberately pushed them together knowing that in the end they would need and console each other when she had gone.

Unable to stop himself Laurence lifted Tom into his arms and held him tightly. Drowsily Tom pushed his arms around Laurence's neck and settled his head on his shoulder. Laurence smoothed his hair, kissed him softly on the cheek and only just resisted the urge to squeeze him with the full force of his love. Pippa, he was crying inside, Dear God, Pippa, please let this be some kind of joke. Please let me open my eyes and find you sitting there, laughing at me . . .

A few minutes later he heard Jane come into the room. He kept his head averted, not wanting her to see the tears on his cheeks.

'Dermott Campbell's on the phone,' Jane said quietly.

'Tell him I'll call him back,' Laurence answered gruffly. But as Jane was turning to leave he remembered that Dermott had tried to get hold of him in the States. 'No,' he said, 'I'll take it.'

Gently he handed Tom over to Jane and went into his bedroom to take the call.

'At last!' Campbell's voice boomed down the line making Laurence wince. 'I've been trying to get hold of you for days. I just heard you were back so I called to tell you the latest.'

'And what's that?' Laurence asked dully.

'I guess you didn't see my column at the weekend,' Campbell said. 'No, well, I don't suppose you would have jet-setting around the world the way you do. Incidently, how did it go over there in LA? Anything doing?'

'It was OK,' Laurence answered. He took a deep breath. 'Look, Dermott, do you think we can get to the point here?'

'Sure. The point is, my friend, that the Kirstie Doll is over there in Italy getting laid by none other than Zaccheo Marigliano! And you don't need me to tell you who Marigliano's editor is. And who is Marigliano's editor married to? Are you following me, Laurence? Kirsten Meredith is trying new tactics. She's got your nanny, she's getting your best friend, next thing you know she's going to be pally, pally with your wife. So at the risk of telling you I told you so . . .'

All the time Campbell had been talking Laurence had felt a burning rage running through his veins and suddenly it erupted. 'For your fucking information, Dermott,' he seethed, 'my wife is out there getting laid by Zaccheo Marigliano herself. So get your fucking facts straight. And get the fucking hell off my back about Kirsten Meredith or . . .'

'What!' Campbell gasped. 'What did you say? Did I hear you right? Pippa's out there . . .'

'You heard me.'

'You mean . . .? Are you telling me you two . . .? Shit, Laurence! What the hell's going on here? I thought you two . . .?'

'Yeah, well you thought wrong. Seems we both did.'

'Oh, Christ, Laurence, I don't know what to say. I

mean, are you sure you've got this right, 'cos I'm telling you the Kirstie Doll's out there too.'

'I couldn't give a fucking damn where Kirsten Meredith is,' Laurence raged. 'My wife's walked out on me, she's shacking up with my best friend, as you call him . . .'

'I'm coming round there,' Campbell interrupted.

'Don't. I got to have some time to think this through . . .'

'You can think about it later. Right now you need to get drunk.'

'That's the last thing I need. I got a son here, remember. He needs me right now.'

'He's got a nanny!'

'He's about to lose his mother, for Christ's sake! And I've got to do something to stop that happening. So stay where you are, Dermott. I'll call you when I'm ready.'

He slammed down the phone and was about to turn away from the bed when his eye was caught by the note he had dropped there. He picked it up, crushing it in his fist. It wasn't over yet. Oh no, it was a long way from over. The debilitating shock and anger would wear off soon enough, but he knew that even before that he was going to do everything it was humanly possible to do to get his wife back. He had to because he just couldn't bear life without her.

Like the captive of a painting she sat immobile in her frame of solid darkness. Though her hands didn't move the silky smoothness of the photograph was cool beneath her fingertips. Little pools of light glimmered happily on the surface lending an almost ethereal quality to the beautifully expressive eyes. The warmth from her skin seemed to seep into the gloss bringing the beloved face to life. She could almost hear the laughter bubbling from the parted lips, feel the joy reflecting itself in her heart. She smiled, dreamily, but then, as her eyes closed, instead of seeing the wondrous images of the past a shadow of fear darkened her thoughts.

Things were changing. So much was happening. Nothing was in her control. What would become of her baby? And as though sensing her distress the baby started to cry. The sound of its wails echoed through her ears, gently at first then louder and still louder, until it was as though her mind was being lashed by the cruel shards of a punishment undeserved. She bunched her fists at the sides of her face. She had to go to it, she had to. But she couldn't. . . .

– 10 –

'So what do you think?' Kirsten said, bunching her thick hair behind her head as she looked up from the stack of papers scattered across the table. 'I say Zeus and the Titanesses is perfect for the opening programme.'

'I like the story of Persephone better,' Helena said.

'No.' Kirsten was shaking her head as she picked up a slice of cold pizza. 'It's a great story, but it's not powerful enough to launch with.'

'OK. You know best,' Helena yawned. 'But at the risk of repeating myself, Kirstie, I reckon you're over-reaching . . .'

'I know what you think, but why not aim high?'

'But this,' Helena laughed, sweeping her hand over the table, 'is mammoth. I mean, nothing like it's ever been done before – putting modern day interpretations on to Greek myths. Who are you going to get to write it, to start with?'

'I've a few names in mind,' Kirsten answered dismissively, 'and I've started the script for the Titanesses myself. I'll let you read it when I'm happier with it.' She bit into the pizza. 'Now, let's go on to Artemis and Orion. The way I see it . . .'

'Kirstie! It's nearly midnight, for God's sake, can't we take a break?'

'But Artemis and Orion is a terrific story. According to one version, the one I'm going to use, she ends up killing him . . .'

'I know, and if you don't stop I'm going to end up killing you. We've been at this all day, all week! Isn't there any light relief to be had around here?'

'Not when light relief to you means discussing the break up of Laurence's marriage,' Kirsten said, putting the slice of pizza down as her appetite vanished.

'But all this work,' Helena protested, 'can't you see, it's you running away from things?'

'No! It's me getting my life back in order.'

'And how the hell are you going to raise the colossal sums you'll need when you've got Dyllis blasting all your arrows before they even reach the target?'

'Had we not just been discussing Artemis I'd have said that was a poor metaphor,' Kirsten remarked. 'But as we were it'll suffice.'

'Kirsten! Listen to me. You might be able to convince the rest of the world that Laurence and Pippa's break up means nothing to you, but . . .'

'Helena, I don't want to discuss it. Besides which,

you heard what Jane said earlier, he's going over to Italy tomorrow to try to get her back. He'll probably succeed so . . .'

'But what if he doesn't?'

'I don't know,' Kirsten cried.

'But you're still in love with the man!'

'OK, but after what just happened with Zaccheo – I take it you are aware of the fact that this is the second time in my life I've lost a man to Pippa McAllister?'

'Yes,' Helena answered. 'I expect you'd like to kill her again now, wouldn't you?' she grinned.

'Believe you me, for a while there I could have been tempted. But I'll just have to content myself with never testing the waters of romance again – and especially not with Laurence. Rejection hurts, Helena. It not only hurts it can cause a lot of damage, lasting damage.'

'I know that. But . . .'

'Back to Artemis and Orion,' Kirsten interrupted. 'I reckon you'd be perfect for the part of Artemis and John Callway for Orion.'

'I thought you had me earmarked for one of the Titanesses?'

'I have, but what's to stop you taking on both roles?'

'Only that they're never going to happen.'

'Why are you being so negative?' Kirsten almost shouted.

'Because you're not going to be able to do this, Kirsten! You're not! Do you hear me?'

'Then what the hell do you want me to do? Persuade myself that Laurence and I can make a go of it, when you and I both know that that's even less likely than me getting this series off the ground.'

'Oh God, I don't know what I want you to do,' Helena

sighed, pushing her fingers into the mass of frizzy black hair.

'Go to bed, Helena. Go to bed and try to get up in a better mood tomorrow.'

'And what about Jane? What kind of mood do you think she's going to be in tomorrow?'

'Helena, please, don't do this,' Kirsten said, trying to ignore the sinking feeling in her heart. 'I had no choice but to remind Jane that she's only going to get herself into more trouble with Laurence if she goes behind his back the way she suggested. I did it for her own good.'

'She was pretty upset though. I felt kind of sorry for her.'

'Don't you think I did? But while Campbell's writing all his stuff about me being responsible for the problems in Laurence's marriage I don't see what else I could have done. You must have noticed how nutty she is about him. Why else do you think she's taken his break up with Pippa so hard? Because Laurence is hurting and she just can't bear to see it. She practically worships the man and she just hasn't got what it takes to stand up to his temper. And believe you me, if she keeps coming here and he finds out he'll fire her.'

'Mmm, I guess you're right. But she's pretty nuts about you too.'

'She'll get over it.'

'OK, have it your way, I'm off to bed. And don't work too late.'

When Helena had gone upstairs Kirsten walked over to the kettle and filled it. She was so tired she felt she could sleep for a week, yet she knew that the second her head touched the pillow she would come wide awake again.

She sighed heavily. It really was hard work having

Helena around right now. Not that she didn't want her there, being alone at this time would probably only make matters worse, but she wished Helena would stop trying to make her confront things she just wanted to forget. But no amount of coaxing on Helena's part was going to get her to confess to how frightened she was really feeling, for once she gave into the fear she knew there was every chance she would be right back to where she was five years ago when she and Laurence had split up, and she really didn't think she could come through it a second time.

But Paul's death, Laurence's hatred, Dyllis's campaign, Zaccheo's rejection – it was all starting to get to her now in a way she recognized only too well. It was too late to stop the terrible feelings of insecurity, they were with her already, maybe they had never really left her, but it wasn't something she wanted to show the world. What she wanted, perhaps more than anything else, was that Laurence would get back with Pippa, because the idea of him being free was something Kirsten knew she would be unable to handle.

Pippa was curled into one corner of the huge leather sofa in Zaccheo's drawing room, hugging her knees to her chest as though to protect herself. Laurence was standing at the centre of the room, his face as thunderous as the gathering storm outside, his very appearance a reflection of the pain she had caused him. There was no mistaking the fact that between them she and Zaccheo had shattered his life and Pippa knew that Zaccheo would feel every bit as bad about that as she did.

Earlier Laurence had asked her how long it had been going on between her and Zaccheo, and not wanting to lie to him any more Pippa had told him. Almost two years. She had seen the way her betrayal had cut into him, could read his thoughts as clearly as if he had spoken them. He had trusted her, believed in her love as he had always believed in her fidelity. It was as though she had torn out the very roots of his life, leaving him disoriented, confused and yes, devastated. Her heart weighed heavily in her. She felt she might drown in remorse, yet she knew that no matter what he said, no matter how much he was suffering she wouldn't go back to him. She was where she wanted to be, where she had always, for the past two years, known she would eventually come. It had simply been a matter of choosing the right time.

Laurence had walked to the window and was now staring out at the rain spattered garden. His whole demeanour was one of barely restrained anger, but Pippa knew he was fighting it. She longed to go to him, to lend him the comfort of her arms, but knew that would be the wrong thing to do. He had to get used to the fact that she would no longer be there for him, that his troubles were his own and that whatever the future held he must face it alone.

'What about Tom?' he said, his gruffness piercing the silence.

The pain seared Pippa's heart. 'What about him?' she whispered.

Laurence spun round. 'What about him?' he seethed. 'He's your son, for Christ's sake! Your own flesh and blood.'

'He's yours too,' she said simply. And when Laurence only glared at her, she added, 'He's more yours than mine. He always was,' but the tears had already started in her eyes.

– 190 –

'Pip, please,' he implored, 'you love him as much as I do, so if only for his sake let's try again.'

Pippa buried her face in her knees, but Laurence saw the barely perceptible shake of her head.

'I don't understand it!' he cried, slamming his fist into the wall. 'I thought we really had something you and I. I thought you were happy, as happy as I was. For God's sake, why didn't you tell me if you weren't?'

'I was,' Pippa choked. 'I loved you, Laurence. I still do, but just not in the way I love . . .' her voice trailed off and Laurence's eyes closed as a wave of jealousy swept through him.

'But what about before I went to the States? Shit, Pippa, I thought we'd recaptured everything then. We were so close, so . . .'

'No!' she cried. 'No, we weren't. Don't you understand what happened then? Didn't it once occur to you that it was the only time in our married life you had ever made love to me that way? That all these years I've known that you've been holding back on me, that all the time you've been crying out for her! That day proved it, Laurence. I always knew it, but that day showed me that what you and I had was never the same as what you'd had with her. And you still crave it, Laurence. You want her every bit as much now as you ever did. It's like you're saving yourself for her. You've always said you can never forgive her, but don't you understand, Laurence, you long to forgive her. So why don't you let . . .'

'No!' he roared and Pippa cowered away as he stormed towards her. 'You're not blaming me for this, Pippa! I'm not going to let you, do you hear me? What I had with Kirsten is over, in the past. You're the only woman I want, you always will be.' In his fury he hadn't realized that Pippa hadn't even mentioned Kirsten's name, but Pippa did and she gave a sad smile as she looked up at him. 'You've got to understand,' he raged on, 'that the only reason I ever held back was to protect you. You're so damned fragile, so precious to me, I didn't want to hurt you . . .' Suddenly he laughed bitterly as he thought of Zaccheo. 'God, what a fool I am!' he spat. 'What a fucking mess I've made of everything.'

'Face the truth, Laurence,' Pippa said softly. 'For God's sake accept it and stop torturing yourself this way.' She jumped as Laurence grabbed her arm and twisted it away from her body.

'You're still doing it!' he yelled. 'You're still trying to convince me – or is it yourself – that I'm in love with someone else just so's you can ease your own guilt. Well it's not going to work, Pippa. I love you, I've always loved you and nothing you or anyone else says is going to change that. You're the mother of my son – ' His voice suddenly caught in his throat and he turned abruptly away. To think of Tom now was too much to bear. Yet at the same time he yearned to see that beloved little face, to hold him in his arms and let him know that nothing, just nothing in the whole damned world would ever part them.

'I left him with you because I know you'll be a much better father than I ever could be a mother,' Pippa said. 'But please don't think that it hasn't hurt me to do it. I love him, Laurence, believe me, I love him as much as any mother can love her child. But I'm just not up to it. I can't give him what he needs. Don't ask me why, I just can't. So I did what I thought was best for him, what I *know* to be best for him. He's your son, Laurence. He loves you and we both know that if he were given the choice he would rather be with you.'

Laurence's smile was vicious. 'And it would have nothing to do with the fact that he'd get in the way over here, I suppose? That Zaccheo wouldn't want a three-year-old cramping his life?'

'It's true,' Pippa said calmly, 'it would be difficult to have Tom here. But if I thought it was best for him, I'd have brought him.'

'Over my dead body,' Laurence snarled.

Pippa turned her face away, looking at but not seeing the garish painting that covered the chimney breast. All the time they had been arguing the sky outside had been darkening and now there was very little light in the room. She wanted this to be over, she wanted him to go, but even as she thought it she felt devastated by the knowledge that it would then be over – forever – between them. Nothing in her life would ever be as difficult as this, but her conviction that she was right to have left him was absolute.

Laurence's voice suddenly punctured the silence. 'Doesn't it bother you to know that he's been sleeping with Kirsten?' he snapped.

'Probably as much as it bothers you,' she shot back.

'Then I take it you couldn't give a fuck,' he shouted, his inner frustration manifesting itself in the tightness of his jaw and the clenching of his fists.

'You're wrong,' she said, forcing herself to remain calm. It hadn't escaped her that for the second time in her life she was committing herself to a man who had loved Kirsten Meredith. Except, she reminded herself, Zaccheo hadn't loved Kirsten. He'd merely used her to while away the time until she, Pippa, arrived. 'I do care,' she went on. 'But I can handle it. And shall I tell you why? Because Zaccheo hasn't lied to me about it. He's told me everything that happened between them, exactly what his feelings are for her, which is more than you've ever done, Laurence. More, I think, than you are capable of doing.'

Laurence's temper exploded and before he could stop himself he had grabbed her up from the sofa and was shaking her so hard he felt he might crush the tiny bones under his fingers. 'You fool!' he groaned. 'You bloody fool! You're destroying us, you're destroying everything we ever had because of some goddamned illusion. She's gone, do you hear me? Gone from my life, gone from my mind. I don't have to talk about her, I don't have to tell you anything about her, because there's nothing to tell. Everything I have, everything I do, everything I am is for you. I don't feel the need to sleep with anyone else because I have all I want in you. Can Zaccheo tell you the same? Can you seriously believe he'll remain faithful to you? You know his reputation, for Christ's sake! Do you think that's going to change? Do you think you're so special you can –'

'Yes, Laurence,' Zaccheo said, 'she is that special.'

Laurence swung round. As he did so Pippa wrenched herself free and staggered back against the sofa. Suddenly she cried out as Laurence advanced on Zaccheo. She ran after him, throwing herself between them at the very instant Laurence's fist flew through the air. It connected with the side of her head and she slumped to the floor.

Horrified, both Zaccheo and Laurence stared down at her for one moment frozen with shock. Laurence was the first to stoop, lifting her shoulders, cradling her head and frantically whispering her name.

Pippa's eyes blinked open. It was clear that the force of the blow had dazed her, but as she fought to focus on Laurence's face he felt as though his heart was being torn in two. Her expression, in those fleeting seconds before her eyes hunted around for Zaccheo, was one of profound regret and sad understanding.

'Pip, I'm sorry,' he said helplessly. 'Oh God, I'm so sorry.'

'It's all right,' she murmured, reaching a hand out to Zaccheo who was kneeling the other side of her. And, as she weakly strained towards him, Laurence's loss and grief expanded through his entire body.

Letting her go he eased himself back to his feet and stood staring down at them. Zaccheo was holding her now, engulfing her with his immensity. He was murmuring to her in Italian and as Pippa's fragile hand came up to stroke the wiry hair of his face Laurence had never felt more of an intruder in his life. He took a step back, hardly able to believe that it was his own wife he was watching turn to another man for comfort. His mind recoiled from the reality that their sudden togetherness showed him. This was how it would be from now on. It was this man, no more than a stranger now, who would hold his wife, who would love her and cherish her. It was to him she would turn for the love and laughter in her life. In his arms she would seek her happiness, and it would be for his heart that she would care.

His sense of defeat was almost crippling, but somehow Laurence managed to turn away, to walk across the room towards the door. Once again Tom's face flashed before his eyes and as the overpowering need for his son engulfed him he felt the tears welling in his eyes. Somehow he would deal with this, somehow he would manage to hold himself together, but what about Tom? How was he ever going to explain to a three-year-old child that his Mummy had gone and was never coming back?

That his Mummy just didn't love him enough to stay? But of course he would never tell Tom that.

He was already half out the door when he heard Pippa say his name. He turned back to see Zaccheo helping her to her feet.

'Laurence, I'm sorry,' she whispered.

Laurence lowered his eyes and was about to walk on when she spoke again.

'I know right now you'll find this very hard to hear but one day you'll thank me for this.'

A grim smile crossed Laurence's mouth. 'No, Pippa,' he said, 'you're wrong. I'll never do that.'

'You will. And so too will Kirsten.'

Laurence's eyes looked right into hers as he answered. 'You're wrong about that too,' he said. 'And maybe one day you'll know just how wrong.'

— 11 —

'What on earth are you doing here?' Campbell choked, fumbling his cup back into the saucer and spilling the coffee.

'I might well ask you the same question,' Helena responded looking pointedly at Campbell's companion.

'This is one of my regular haunts,' he said, trying and failing to master his unease.

'Is that right?' Helena was still looking at Ruby.

'Oh, uh, this is Ruby Collins,' Campbell said, belatedly getting to his feet. 'Ruby, Helena Johnson.'

Helena and Ruby exchanged sugary smiles. Helena wasn't entirely sure where she'd heard the name Ruby Collins before, but it would come to her.

'Won't you join us?' Campbell offered.

Helena's thick brows arched as she regarded him. This was the first time they'd seen each other since the night they'd spent at Kirsten's and Helena had been trying desperately hard not to mind that he hadn't called. But the truth was she did mind and seeing him sitting here with this woman was bothering her a whole lot more. Her eyes flickered towards Ruby. She looked a bit old for Campbell, but there was a certain sort of glamour about her even if it was, to Helena's mind, seedy. She glanced at her watch. 'Well, actually I'm meeting someone,' she said, but the instant she sensed Ruby's relief she added, 'I'm a bit early though.' Which, thank God, was true for of all the people to run into when she was having a clandestine coffee with Jane, Dermott Campbell had to be about the most unfortunate. Still, should Jane arrive early she'd make up some excuse because nothing was going to tear her away from this little tête-à-tête now.

'What'll you have?' Campbell asked as he pulled out a chair for Helena to sit down.

'Espresso, thanks.' She looked at Ruby again, whose eyes were narrowed as she peered back through a cloud of cigarette smoke. 'I hope you don't object to me joining you, Ruby,' Helena said sweetly.

'Joining me to what?' Ruby retorted, her pencilled brows loftily raised.

Helena blinked.

Campbell laughed.

Helena looked at him. 'Oh, I'm sorry,' she said, 'was

that a joke?' and throwing back her head she laughed too.

Ruby watched her, a supercilious smile curving her heavily lipsticked mouth.

Campbell cleared his throat. 'So, Helena,' he said, 'how are you?'

'Pretty good,' she answered. 'Actually I was just thinking about you the other day – wondering if you'd managed to get it up yet,' she added spitefully.

She had the satisfaction of seeing Campbell colour before Ruby said, 'I guess you have your answer now.'

'Yeah,' Helena said, sweeping Ruby with her eyes, 'I guess I do.' She turned to Campbell. 'I had no idea you were into Help the Aged.'

Campbell squirmed.

Ruby laughed. 'Tut, tut,' she said, shaking her head, 'not very subtle.'

Helena's teeth clenched. Ruby was right, she'd allowed her claws out too far. Shit! she suddenly thought to herself, what am I doing? It's only Dermott Campbell and who the hell is he anyway?

'So what do you do with yourself, Helena?' Ruby drawled.

'I'm an actress,' Helena replied. 'And a pretty good one, actually,' she added shooting a meaningful look at Campbell. 'And you, Ruby? What do you do?'

'Ruby's writing the screenplay for Laurence's next movie,' Campbell chipped in.

'Oh, is that right?' Helena said, suddenly wanting to kick herself for getting on the wrong side of this dragon. 'How's it going?'

'Pretty good, from my point of view,' Ruby answered.

'Not so good from Laurence's,' Campbell added.

Helena looked at him, waiting for him to elaborate.

'Do you know Laurence, Helena?' Ruby enquired, grinding out her cigarette.

'I used to.'

Ruby's head tilted to one side as she put a fresh cigarette between her lips.

'Ruby and I were just discussing how best to help Laurence over this bad time,' Campbell said.

Helena's big eyes flashed her surprise. 'From what I remember of Laurence,' she said, 'I wouldn't have thought he'd much appreciate – '

'Laurence doesn't always know what's good for him,' Ruby interrupted, with such a condescending smile Helena would have liked to punch it.

'And you do? Know what's good for him?' Helena said.

Again that nauseating smile. 'I do,' Ruby confirmed.

Helena was tempted to ask by what right Ruby gave herself such delusions of grandeur, but wasn't too sure she wanted to get into it.

'Ruby and Laurence go back a long way,' Campbell provided. 'She knows him pretty well. You've seen him over a few bad times, isn't that right, Ruby?'

'One or two,' she nodded. 'He was much younger then, of course. Well, weren't we all?' she laughed.

'I expect you were quite a looker in those days,' Helena said, unable to stop herself.

'You're right. I was.'

'So,' Campbell rushed in, 'who are you meeting, Helena?'

'Just a friend. Someone else who knows Laurence, actually.'

'Oh?' Ruby's interest was evident.

Assuming Helena meant Kirsten Campbell waded in again, for he was only too aware of Ruby's feelings towards the woman who, as Ruby put it, damned near broke Laurence's heart. 'Actually, I think it's about time we got on over there and met Willie Henderson, don't you, Ruby?' he said.

'Willie Henderson? The director?' Helena enquired.

'That's him. Laurence has just hired him.'

Helena looked confused. It was none of her business, but she was going to ask anyway. 'So what are *you* meeting him for?' she asked Campbell.

To her surprise Campbell looked decidedly uncomfortable.

'Dermott,' Ruby answered, 'is about to become second producer on our movie, isn't that right, honey?'

'Well . . .' Campbell shrugged.

'But you've never produced anything in your life,' Helena objected, trying not to laugh.

'There's always a first time,' Campbell said, obviously wishing he was somewhere else.

'Laurence has said we need someone else,' Ruby smiled, 'especially now that Tom no longer has a mother. His time's pretty taken up with the boy, so I said we should give Dermott a try.'

'And Laurence has agreed?' Helena said incredulously.

'Not in so many words,' Campbell admitted. 'It's still under discussion. But there's no harm in meeting the director.' He glanced uneasily at Ruby. 'The script needs a bit of a workover . . .'

'And you reckon you're the one to do it?'

'No. The director's doing that. But that's why I'm going to this meeting, so I can listen in, find out what's what. How these things are done.'

'And what about your column?'

'Well . . .'

'He wants to give it up,' Ruby answered for him. 'And

so he should. Having to go about the place pretending he's some vulgar individual who actually enjoys prying into other people's affairs when he's so obviously a sensitive, caring human being!'

Helena's eyes grew so big that Campbell couldn't bear to look. 'Excuse me,' she said to Ruby, 'assuming that we are talking about the same person here, how does being sensitive and caring qualify him to produce?'

'We'll let Laurence be the judge of that, shall we?' Ruby smiled, picking up her bag and getting to her feet. 'It was a pleasure meeting you, Helena.'

'The pleasure,' Helena said, 'was all mine.'

Ruby walked to the door, Campbell, holding back to put money on the table, said, 'Don't mock it, Helena. It could be a new start – and just the one I'm looking for.'

'Then I wish you luck,' she said, looking across the café towards Ruby who had reached the door.

'It's not what you think,' Campbell said.

'Isn't it?'

'Can I call you?'

'I've got nothing to tell you about Kirsten.'

He seemed hurt by the response. 'How is she?' he asked.

'How do you think? Thanks to your employer she can't even get herself arrested.'

Campbell looked at her steadily. 'I've missed you,' he said.

'Me? Or Kirsten?'

'*You*. I'll call you,' and with that he was gone.

It was some ten minutes or so later that Jane arrived, by which time Helena had worked herself to quite a pitch of excitement. This jealousy she had of Kirsten made her feel so damned guilty that she was constantly thinking of ways to try and make it up to her. Now, after what Campbell had unwittingly thrown in her lap, she was pretty certain that she had, well, the answer to everything. And the one person who could help her get things on the road happened to be Jane.

'Hello,' Jane said, shrugging her shoulders awkwardly as she reached the table. 'Sorry I'm a bit late.'

'It doesn't matter,' Helena told her, practically shoving her into a chair. 'What would you like to drink? Bring us two glasses of wine,' she said to the waiter. 'So what have you been doing with yourself, Jane?'

'Well, actually, not as much as you might think,' Jane answered. 'Now that Pippa's not there any more I thought I'd have more to do, but Laurence seems to want to do it all himself. He hardly ever lets Tom out of his sight, they even sleep together now.'

'Really,' Helena said, shaking her head sadly. 'I guess it must be real tough for him. How's he bearing up?'

'It's difficult to say,' Jane answered. 'He's really bad tempered. Not with me or Tom, but with everyone else. He's never really bad tempered with us. He told me yesterday what a great job I was doing. I don't expect I am, but it was nice of him to say so, don't you think?'

'Very,' Helena agreed. 'And I'm sure you are. In fact, I expect you're a godsend to him right now.'

Jane virtually glowed. It was so easy to get through to this girl, Helena was thinking, just a few kind words that made her feel appreciated and she was practically eating out of your hand.

'How's Kirsten?' Jane asked, her smile wavering.

'Not as good as she would like everyone to think,' Helena said mournfully.

Concern leapt instantly to Jane's eyes. 'What's the matter with her?' she asked.

'She can't get any work, and, well,' she shrugged, 'you know how these things are.'

Jane sucked in her bottom lip.

Helena smiled. 'You're really fond of her, aren't you?' she said.

Jane nodded.

'She is of you too.'

'Is she?' Jane said, her eagerness to hear more showing. 'I mean, I thought she might be, well, I hoped she might be. Did she say that to you? That she was fond of me?'

Helena nodded. 'In fact, I think she quite misses you and the little chats you used to have.'

'I miss her too. She was always really nice to me.'

'I guess you understand though why she had to ask you to stop coming?'

Jane nodded miserably.

'It was you she was thinking of. She didn't want you to lose your job because of her.' She sighed. 'All this has been pretty hard on her, you know. Losing Paul, not being able to get any work, and what with the way she still feels about Laurence . . .' She cast a sidelong glance at Jane. 'You do know how she feels about Laurence?' she said.

Jane shrugged, clearly embarrassed. 'Well, I suppose I sort of did. I mean, it was in the papers and everything, but Kirsten never really told me herself.'

'No, well, she doesn't like talking about it much and I guess with you working for Laurence and all . . .' She took a sip of her wine and decided that now was the time to start coming to the point. 'How's his movie coming along, by the way?' she said casually.

'Um, OK, I think. He doesn't tell me very much

about it, but I know he's managed to raise some of the money he needs.'

'He has?' Helena said, genuinely surprised – this couldn't be going better. 'Well, good for him. It's probably just the boost he needs right now.'

'Yes, he did seem quite pleased about it. At least at first he did. Ruby, that's the writer, she keeps accusing him of losing interest lately though, but he's got such a lot to think about and her getting on to him like that just makes him angry.'

'Poor Laurence,' Helena sighed. 'But like I said, thank God he's got you. Coping with a three year old, getting a movie up and running, it can't be easy. But you need your respite too, Janey.'

Jane almost jumped at the unfamiliar sound of her name being used so affectionately. And, just as Helena had hoped, a flickering warmth started in her eyes.

'We all need our respite,' Helena went on. 'I guess Laurence sees his work as his ... He's lucky to have it, it's been so long since I worked I can hardly remember what it was like.'

'I remember seeing you in that soap opera,' Jane said softly. 'You were really good.'

'Thanks,' Helena smiled. 'But it feels like a lifetime ago now. What I wouldn't give to be back in front of a camera.' Suddenly her eyes opened wide. 'Do you know, I've just had an idea,' she declared. 'I mean, I'm going out on a limb a bit, and I've got no right to ask, but, well, I don't suppose there's any way you'd be able to get hold of a copy of this Moyna O'Malley script for me, is there?'

Jane looked at her uncertainly. 'Well,' she said, 'there are always lots of them hanging around the house ...'

'What I was thinking is that there might be a part in it for me. But no, no, I can't ask you to go behind Laurence's back like that. Forget it, it was wrong of me to ask.'

'It would be quite easy to pick one up,' Jane said. 'And I don't mind doing it, honestly, I don't.'

'Well, only if you're sure.'

'Yes, I'm sure,' and Jane's pleasure at being able to do something for someone was so touching that Helena had to fight hard to stave off the guilt.

'Do you think you could get it to me soon?' Helena asked. 'I mean, I don't want to waste any time, they're probably already talking about casting, so I'll need to get in quick.'

'I could bring it tomorrow,' Jane said.

'You could? Oh, Janey, that's fantastic. We'll meet here, shall we? At the same time. And I'll tell you what, I'll have a little chat with Kirsten tonight, see if I can't get her to change her mind and let you come visit once in a while. I'm sure she'll say yes, because like I said, she really misses you. We both do.'

Fifteen minutes later Helena was boarding the tube heading for Sloane Square. Exploiting Jane's weaknesses wasn't making her feel any too good for she knew that were Jane not such an innocent she'd very likely have come clean and confessed to what she was really about. But it would have been too much for Jane. Deception on that level wouldn't feature in Jane's repertoire of vices – come to think of it Jane probably didn't even know what a vice was. Still, if Helena managed to pull this off it would all come good in the end, everyone would get what they wanted and everyone would be happy. Including Jane. She pulled a face. God knows what Dermott Campbell would say if he knew what she was up to, but to hell with him! If he was screwing that old witch then he could go flush himself down the nearest john. OK, he said he wasn't, but Helena wasn't buying it. He'd looked too damned shifty. And even if he did call her, there was always the question, why hadn't he picked up the phone before? And the answer to that was; where women were concerned Dermott Campbell was always crazy about the one he was with.

'You did *what!*' Laurence exploded, rounding on Ruby.

'She thumped him,' Campbell repeated.

'I don't believe it!' Laurence cried, dashing a hand through his already dishevelled hair. 'I just don't fucking believe it.' Was the whole world going crazy, or was it just him? He'd had a blazing row with Pippa on the phone not half an hour ago. Tom had overheard and was upstairs crying. His mother was on to him to go live there. Jane was going about the place like she was scared half out her wits, he hadn't had a full night's sleep since God only knew when, and now this! He turned, his brilliant blue eyes boring into Ruby's. 'What the hell got into you?' he seethed. 'How much had you had?'

'I didn't like what he was saying,' Ruby answered, avoiding the question.

'I don't like what you say most of the time,' Laurence shouted, 'particularly when you're pissed, but I sure as hell don't resort to thumping you. But believe you me, Ruby, right now you're pushing me damned close. I take it you do realize that it's mainly down to Willie that we've managed to get what finance we have. If he pulls out then we're right back at the beginning. So you better just get your ass round there and apologize.'

'Aw, come on, honey . . .'

'Get round there and apologize!' Laurence roared.

When Ruby, still slightly the worse for all the gin she had consumed, had taken herself off Campbell walked quietly across the sitting room and opened the drinks cabinet.

'Put that away!' Laurence barked.

Campbell did as he was told.

Several minutes ticked by. It was evident that Laurence was trying to get himself back in control and as Campbell watched him he noticed how tired he looked, almost to the point of exhaustion. He'd lost weight too and the lines around his eyes had visibly deepened these past few weeks. Campbell knew he was on the point of throwing in the towel and letting this movie sink, but somehow Campbell had to stop him doing that. Not only for Laurence's sake, but his own too. Like he'd told Helena this movie could be a new start for him, one that meant he could tell Dyllis Fisher where to go, before she told him. There was no more to print about Kirsten, the public had had enough, and he, Campbell, wasn't party to the tactics Dyllis was using to halt Kirsten's career. In other words, Dyllis Fisher didn't need him any more and he, Campbell, was reaching out for this life-line in the hope that it would hook him to safety before he fell back into the gutter.

Indeed, Campbell was quite excited about the idea of becoming involved in a major movie, so excited in fact that he'd spent the best part of two weeks with Ruby picking her brains about the script. And if that wasn't dedication to the cause then nothing was, for two weeks with Ruby Collins was tantamount to a life sentence – or even a death sentence, because the chances of coming out in one piece weren't good. The way she came on to him when she was drunk was as embarrassing as it was life-threatening, and the nightly tussles between the sheets were something he couldn't even bring himself to think about. But if screwing Ruby was what it took to get himself on to this movie then screw her he would, for despite their all too frequent contretemps Campbell knew that Ruby held a lot of sway with Laurence. And, during her sober moments, Campbell could see why. She went at what she did with a passion that left him reeling and a talent that could make his hair stand on end with awe. She just needed a little guidance now and then, something that brought her back from the crazy tangents she went off on and Laurence had decided that the director should now take that on.

'Willie had some pretty good suggestions,' Campbell said tentatively as Laurence flopped into an armchair.

'Yeah?'

'Yeah. Well, I thought so. Obviously Ruby didn't, but . . .'

'Why the hell did she do that?' Laurence demanded, his handsome face once again tightening with anger.

'Because Willie disagreed with something that was your idea.'

'So fucking what? He's got the right. He's the director, godammit! What is it with that woman?'

'She reckons we've all got to go easy on you,' Campbell sighed.

'I'm not a fucking invalid,' Laurence raged, suddenly on his feet again. 'I liked her better when she was arguing with me, at least we managed to get somewhere.' He slammed a fist on the table and lowered his head as he tried to swallow his frustration. 'Shit,' he growled. 'I don't know why I ever agreed to do this fucking movie.'

'Because it's good,' Campbell said. 'Or it will be . . .'

'Cut the bullshit, Dermott! It's bad enough with her at it all the time without you starting up. And what the hell's with this crazy notion of you coming on board? You've got no experience!'

'Hey, come on. I'm on your side,' Campbell cried. 'If you'd just listen to what I have to say you might – '

'I don't want to hear it.'

'Laurence, for God's sake, what are you going to do, throw it all away because it's taking up too much self-pity time?'

Laurence's eyes were smouldering with fury as he glared back. 'You're way out of line, Dermott,' he said dangerously. 'Way out of line. You want to work on this movie then quit interfering in my private life.'

'OK, OK,' Campbell said, holding up his hands defensively, though somewhat cheered by what had sounded something like an acceptance of his role on the movie. 'So, what do you say we get down to some work?' he suggested.

'Not now.'

'But – '

'I said, not now,' and before Campbell could protest further Laurence slammed out of the room.

He took the stairs two at a time. He was going to the nursery to be with his son and right now Dermott Campbell, Ruby Collins and the whole goddamned movie could go straight to fucking hell.

'I'm up here,' Kirsten called out, hearing the front
door open and close behind Helena. She listened for a
moment, then smiling to herself as Helena started up
the stairs she relaxed back in the warm, scented water
and turned a page of the album she was holding.

'Where the hell are you?' Helena grumbled from the
bedroom.

'In here,' Kirsten laughed, the foamy water swishing
up the sides of the bath as she made herself more
comfortable. 'How did it go?' she asked as Helena
wandered into the huge creamy white bathroom with its
gold accessories and plonked herself down in the feathery cushions of a hand-painted rocking chair.

'Don't ask,' Helena pouted as she regarded herself
critically in the long, Grecian mirror. 'God knows why
my agent put me up for it, they were looking for a
sylph-like blonde with legs up to her armpits and eyes
as big as her tits. Now tell me, do I look like a bimbo
or do I just act like one? Still, I guess after I got onto
him last week he did it to try and keep me sweet.
Asshole!'

Kirsten chuckled and turned another page. 'Life isn't
looking too good for us lately, is it?' she said. 'No work,
no love lives . . .'

'At least you've got money,' Helena said grudgingly.
'Anyway, what are you doing inviting me up here like
that. I could have been anyone.'

'I should be so lucky,' Kirsten murmured. 'It was the rust-bucket. I heard it coughing all the way from the King's Road. So, what are we going to do to cheer ourselves up?'

'Looks like you're already doing it,' Helena remarked as Kirsten lifted a foot to turn on the hot-water tap. 'God, you should see yourself. You look like Venus herself wallowing away there.'

Kirsten screwed up her nose as she recalled the way Zaccheo had likened her to Venus. Not a memory she wished to dwell upon.

'What's that you're looking at?' Helena asked.

'Pictures of Paul and me in the South of France,' Kirsten answered, passing over the album. 'I was reminding myself of happier days.'

'Seems we had the same idea,' Helena said, scanning the pages. 'I was poring over old photos myself last night. This is a really good one of Paul here,' she said, turning the book for Kirsten to see.

'Mmm, I thought so too,' Kirsten smiled fondly. 'I think I might get it put into a frame. So, what were you looking at photos of?'

'Old flames, mainly. Though they all burnt out so quickly they weren't really much more than one-night stands.' Helena's normally lively face looked so dejected that Kirsten threw a sponge at her to try and make her laugh.

'Come on, what's really bothering you?' Kirsten said, when Helena picked the sponge up and tossed it back into the water. 'You haven't been yourself for a couple of weeks now.'

'Well, actually I met someone, a little while ago now, and I really thought we might get it together.' She sighed despondently. 'Seems I was wrong.'

'You never said,' Kirsten remarked. 'Who is he?'

'No one. No one important, anyway. I guess desperation just got ahold of me for a while . . .' She handed Kirsten a towel as she stood up. 'I was thinking that I wanted to be a wife and a mother and all that crap,' she went on, automatically sucking in her stomach when she saw how flat Kirsten's was. 'Well, I do want all that. Or I want to be an actress, I don't mind which, 'cos I'm past thinking I can have both, like some women. I'd be grateful for anything . . .'

'Oh come on, it's not as bad as all that,' Kirsten said, wrapping her hair in the towel and reaching out for another.

'Isn't it? Try looking at it from where I'm sitting.'

Kirsten lifted a foot on to the side of the bath as she towelled her legs. 'You know I'd give you a job if I could only get something moving,' she said. 'And I will, eventually. But we won't get on to the subject of Dyllis Fisher again.' Nevertheless her hands started to move more quickly as she dried herself and she pulled the comb viciously through her hair as she recalled the indescribable frustration of the past weeks. 'Still,' she said as she wandered out of the bathroom and into the bedroom, 'at least Dermott Campbell seems to be leaving me alone these days.'

Helena watched her as she started to coat her exquisitely full breasts in an expensive oil. Not for the first time she found herself thinking of Kirsten as one of nature's perfections. And standing there as she was now in a pool of early evening sunshine that made her rich, smooth skin glisten like honey she was so beautiful it could almost take your breath away. But if nature had been at its most benevolent when handing out gifts to Kirsten, fate was at its most malevolent. She hadn't yet told Kirsten that Campbell was working on Laurence's movie, though in truth there wasn't much to tell. From what she'd heard Laurence seemed to have lost interest these past weeks and it was only Dermott and Ruby who were toiling on. As far as Helena could make out even the director wasn't getting involved in Dermott and Ruby's meetings, so quite what they thought they were achieving was anyone's guess. Campbell hadn't called Helena either, which was part of the reason she was feeling so depressed. It was unbelievable that she should be feeling this way about him, of all people, but it just went to show how desperate she really was. Still, she had no confidence that the movie was going to be made, at least not as things stood and it pleased her no end to think that Campbell was going to fall flat on his face. But on the other hand there was the most fantastic part in it for her . . .

'Ah, there you are,' Kirsten said, as Helena followed her into the bedroom. 'I thought you'd fallen asleep in there.'

'It's life that's fallen asleep,' Helena answered gloomily. 'We've just got to come up with a way to wake it up.'

'And there was me thinking you'd already done that,' Kirsten said, a mischievous light shining in her eyes.

Helena looked at her curiously.

Still smiling as she hooked the straps of a black lacy body up over her shoulders Kirsten turned to her bedside table and picked up a script. 'You left this behind last time you were here,' she said, handing it to Helena.

Helena's eyes moved from the ornate lettering of *Moyna O'Malley* back to Kirsten's face. The script had been at Kirsten's for days and this was the first time Kirsten had mentioned it. As a result Helena's spirits started to lift with the vague hope that maybe all was not lost.

Kirsten was watching her, her tongue planted in her cheek, her eyebrows raised. 'I take it Jane managed to get hold of a copy for you,' she said.

Helena grinned sheepishly. 'Desperate times call for desperate measures,' she said. 'And before you start getting on to me about using Jane that way she was willing to do it.'

Kirsten laughed. 'Jane is willing to do anything for anyone as you well know. Still, at least she didn't get caught and I can hardly blame you for trying. She called earlier, by the way, I've invited her to come to the cinema with us.'

'I'll bet she peed her pants with gratitude,' Helena remarked. 'So, did you read it?' she asked, flopping down on the bed and folding her hands behind her head.

'I did. So what's stopping you going for the part of Marie Laveau? And please don't say it's out of some kind of loyalty to me.'

'I only wish it were,' Helena sighed. 'No, it's Laurence who's stopping me.'

'Laurence? You mean you've spoken to him?' The warmth was rapidly seeping from Kirsten's smile.

Helena shook her head. 'I don't think anyone's spoken to him, not in ages. Except Jane, of course. Apparently he just wants to spend time with Tom and to hell with the world.'

'I see.' Kirsten's heart was churning. To think that he had taken his break up with Pippa so hard wasn't easy to deal with. She threw the script on the bed beside Helena then sat down at the dressing table and picked up a pot of Dior moisturiser.

'What did you think of it?' Helena asked, watching

the circular motions of Kirsten's fingers as she smoothed the cream into her face.

Kirsten shrugged. 'It's OK,' she answered. 'If it were mine I'd approach it from a whole different angle, but I guess Laurence knows what he's doing.'

'That's just it, he's not doing anything,' Helena complained. 'I hear on the grapevine that he's taking on an associate producer or co-producer, or something.'

'What he needs is a director.'

'He's got one. Willie Henderson. But if you ask me the whole thing's falling about their ears.' She hesitated, but only for a second. 'What they need is your kind of talent to get this thing in shape.'

Kirsten turned until she was facing Helena. 'I've got to hand it to you, Helena,' she said, shaking her head incredulously, 'you nearly had me fooled for a minute there.'

'What? What are you talking about?'

'Honestly,' Kirsten laughed, 'you're so transparent. You left that script there deliberately for me to pick up, didn't you? You want me on that movie so's you can play the part of Marie Laveau.'

'Sure I do, I don't deny it. But you've got to admit it's a great opportunity for you too. I'll bet Laurence is one of the few guys in this town that won't be railroaded by Dyllis Fisher. And he's already got most of the finance, courtesy of the director, so she can't get to him that way either. So, why don't you pick up the phone and call him?'

'*What?* Are you out of your mind!' Kirsten cried, so amazed that Helena could even suggest it that she couldn't help laughing.

'Go on. Nothing ventured and all that. What have you got to lose?'

'What have I got to lose! Helena, I can't believe . . . What on earth's got into you?'

'Just begin by calling him up and telling him how sorry you are about him and Pippa,' Helena said, undaunted.

'And why the hell should I do that?'

'So that you two can bury the hatchet and get on with your lives.'

'Have you been drinking?'

'What?'

'Well it's the only explanation I can think of for you coming up with such a hare-brained idea.'

'It's a brilliant idea and you know it. You'd give your eye-teeth to work on a feature – well, wouldn't we all? And here's the opportunity staring you, *us*, right in the face.'

'My God, you really are serious,' Kirsten murmured, feeling as though she might be sick.

'Sure I am. He needs another producer, you need a job. You're still in love with him and I'll stake my life on the fact that he's still in love with you.'

'*Helena*! For God's sake! This isn't about anyone's feelings and the last thing I'm going to let you do is try to convince me of his. Not when we both know – '

'We know nothing! Neither of us. So why don't you find out. The field is clear now . . .'

'Have you got any idea what this conversation is doing to me?' Kirsten said, her dark eyes flashing with temper. 'Now just stop it.'

'Why? OK, you're scared. I understand that, I would be too in your shoes. But you've got to give this a go, Kirstie. And look at this,' she said, picking up the script and flicking through the pages, 'notes all over it. So tell me now that you're not interested.'

'I make notes out of habit,' Kirsten said irritably, turning back to the mirror. 'Now, where's Jane? If she doesn't get here soon we'll miss the start of the film.'

'She'll be here,' Helena answered. 'Now getting back to Laurence . . .'

'Let it drop, Helena. I don't want to discuss it any further.'

Since the doorbell rang at that moment Helena had little choice but to do as Kirsten said. Still, it was enough for now just to have floated the idea – though she'd gone in so heavily she was probably in danger of sinking it. Good old Jane and her timely arrivals! But if Kirsten thought she'd heard the end of this she was very much mistaken. And grinning happily to herself Helena tripped off down the stairs to answer the door. It looked like life's little retreat into slumberland was coming to an end. Sure, it might just be yawning right now, but if Helena had anything to do with it, it was going to be alive and kicking within the space of a week.

And that was just where she was wrong for it wasn't going to take anything near so long as a week, in fact to her unutterable amazement, it was standing right there on the doorstep the minute she opened the door.

Kirsten's hands froze on the buttons of her dress. 'Helena,' she said, turning to face her, 'if this is one of your jokes . . .'

'I swear it!' Helena whispered. 'He's downstairs, in the sitting room.'

Kirsten's face paled even further as her heart rose to her throat. 'What does he want?' she asked.

'I don't know. He just said he wanted to speak to you.'

'Oh my God! Oh my God!' Kirsten mumbled a frenzy

of nerves surfacing through the shock. 'What am I going to do? What shall I say?'

'Well I guess you'd better find out why he's here.'

'Didn't he say anything? Didn't he give you a clue as to what it's about?'

'Not a word. But my reckoning is that he's come to his senses at last and realized, just like I did, that what his movie – and his life – needs is you.'

'Helena, stop it!' Kirsten cried, holding out her hands as though to ward off the words. 'Just stop.' But it was too late, her hopes were soaring, her heart was crying out for it to be true. 'Oh my God,' she spluttered, 'I don't think I can face him.'

'Of course you can. You have to. Now come on, get yourself together, it's only Laurence McAllister.'

'Don't say his name!' Kirsten gasped, pressing her hands to her cheeks. She closed her eyes, forced herself to take long, deep breaths and at last a smile, together with a trace of colour, returned to her face. 'You're right,' she said, 'it's only Laurence McAllister.'

'That's my girl,' Helena said, pushing her to the top of the stairs. 'Now off you go, give it your best, you'll have him eating out of your hand in no time . . .'

'Don't talk like that,' Kirsten muttered over her shoulder. She took three steps down then turned back to Helena. 'I can't do it! I feel sick!' she whispered.

'Of course you can,' Helena said turning her round. 'Come on now, poise and dignity.'

Kirsten was still repeating the two words silently to herself as she walked into the sitting room, her heart struggling with such a turmoil of emotions she was finding it difficult to breathe. And even though she knew he'd be there the shock of actually seeing him rooted her to the spot.

Laurence was standing with his back to the door looking down at a photograph on the table of Kirsten and Paul. Hearing her come in he turned to face her and for one unguarded moment his heart seemed to tighten in his chest. Even with her hair wet and pulled back that way and without a scrap of make-up on her face she was still the most beautiful woman he had ever set eyes on.

Kirsten's voice was trapped beneath the knot constricting her throat. She tried to smile but her face was frozen. His presence in her house was overwhelming. His deep, penetrating blue eyes were watching her, holding her as firmly as he had once held her in his arms. Neither of them moved yet some remote and intangible part of herself was responding as though he was touching her, folding her against him, taking her and binding her to the very depths of his soul. No one but him had ever had this effect on her, for no one had ever been so much a part of her.

'Can I get you a drink?' she said, her voice as steady as the rays of sunlight slanting across the room.

He shook his head and as he lifted a hand to his face and rubbed it harshly over his chin, Kirsten felt a shiver of memory go through her. It wasn't only the familiarity of the gesture it was the sight of his fingers, so long, so well manicured, yet so undeniably masculine.

'Would you like to sit down?' she offered, a slight catch in her voice.

Again he shook his head and then, as he removed his hand from his face, she saw the anger that had tightened his mouth.

'I've come here,' he began, 'because I want to know exactly what you said to Zaccheo to persuade him to break up my marriage.'

Kirsten blinked. Her astonishment was so profound that for a moment she wasn't too sure she understood the question. 'What I said to Zaccheo?' she repeated.

'We both know,' he went on, a very real edge to his voice now, 'that you were over there in the days leading up to Pippa leaving me – '

'Hang on, hang on,' Kirsten interrupted holding out a hand. 'Let me get this straight. You are accusing me of influencing Zaccheo to break up your marriage. Is that what you're saying?'

'That's exactly what I'm saying. I don't know how you did it, but I want to know . . .'

'Laurence, you're wrong,' Kirsten said anger deepening her voice. 'I had no idea Pippa and Zaccheo – '

'Don't lie!' Laurence growled. 'You were behind it, you did something while you were over there and I want to know what it was.'

'For God's sake, Laurence! What the hell do you *think* I did?'

'I don't know,' he seethed, exhaustion and grief almost dulling the bitterness in his eyes. 'That's why I'm here. I want my wife back, my son wants his mother back and you are going to tell me what it was you did to make Zaccheo persuade her to leave us. It's the only way I can think of to get her to come home, to undo whatever it was you – '

'I didn't do anything!' Kirsten cried. 'Whatever was going wrong in your marriage was going wrong long before Pippa left you.'

'And just what the hell do you know about my marriage?' he thundered.

'Nothing. But no wife who's perfectly happy with her husband just walks out and leaves him for another man who, according to you, didn't even want her until I told him he did.'

'She'd known Zaccheo for over three years, it's too much of a coincidence that she should run off with him at the very point you arrive back on the scene. Now I don't know how you did it Kirsten, but what I do know is why. And let me tell you here and now there will never be anything between us again. Do you hear me? Never!'

The pain of his words was searing her, but outrage surpassed it. 'You flatter yourself, Laurence!' she cried. 'I've never said or done anything since I arrived back in England to give you the impression I wanted you back.

'You turned up at my fucking house, at a party to which you weren't even invited!' he roared. 'You go over there to Italy and before I know it my wife's left me. So what's it all about if it's not – '

'What it's all about is your own damned conceit, your paranoia and your refusal to accept that your wife could love another man. It had nothing to do with me, Laurence. *Nothing!* You want her back, you do all you can to get her back, I'm certainly not going to stop you. But don't come here . . .'

'It was because of you that she left!' he yelled. 'She told me that. So what was it you said to Zaccheo?'

'Laurence, will you just listen to yourself! What do you think I am, some kind of god? I don't have that sort of power and if you were thinking rationally . . .'

'It was because of you!' he raged. 'She left me because of you. But we're finished, Kirsten! We were finished the day you killed that baby!'

The shock was so brutal it took her breath away. She stared back at him, her face had turned horribly pale. 'You're not making any sense, Laurence,' she said quietly. 'It was Zaccheo she left you for – it had nothing to do with me . . . Nothing to do with . . .'

'Go on, say it! It had nothing to do with the way you murdered my child – or the way you told me!'

'Laurence, don't,' she said, starting to shake. 'It's in the past now . . .'

'And so are you! You're not a part of my life anymore, so quit right now thinking you can be. I have a wife. I love her and I'm going to get her back. Now I want to know what it was you said to her, or to Zaccheo, to convince her that I'd never gotten over you.'

'I've never spoken to Pippa – or to Zaccheo – about you in my life,' Kirsten murmured. Her eyes were darting around the room as though searching for something that might return the strength she could feel deserting her. His cruelty was worse than anything she had suffered these past months, his hatred was crushing her. 'Did it ever occur to you,' she said, 'that Pippa might just have been using me as an excuse?'

'Don't try to get out of this, Kirsten. I came here for answers and damn it, you're going to give them to me.'

'Laurence, you're blinding yourself,' she said. 'If Pippa loved you then nothing I said, or did, could have persuaded her to leave you. I'm sorry, I'm truly sorry that you're having to go through this . . .'

'Not half so sorry as I am that you ever set foot back in this country,' he seethed.

Kirsten flinched. She was on the point of asking him to leave when the door opened and Helena walked in.

'I can't take any more of this,' she declared, slamming the door behind her. 'For Christ's sake, aren't either of you listening to what the other's saying?'

'Helena, please.' Kirsten interrupted, but Helena was already rounding on Laurence.

'What the hell is it with you? Don't you think she's suffered enough? And tell me, just what do you stand to gain by trying to convince her you hate her?'

'Jesus Christ!' Laurence exploded, a scornful laugh in his voice. 'I wanted her out of my life five years ago and I want her out of my life now . . .'

'Then would you mind telling me what the hell you're doing here? I don't recall her inviting you.'

'And I don't recall asking your opinion, so butt out of this.'

'The hell I will. If you think I'm just going to stand by and let you bully her . . .'

'Helena! I can fight my own battles,' Kirsten interjected.

'Yeah, you sure can do that,' Laurence sneered. 'History proves it. But this is one battle you're not going to win, Kirsten. I don't want you back, I've never wanted you back . . .'

And I don't remember ever asking you to come back!' Kirsten screamed. 'Now just get out of here. Go somewhere else and sort out your marriage!'

'Will you two just stop it!' Helena raged. 'You're getting hysterical over things that . . .'

'Helena! Will you just *butt out of this*!' Laurence roared.

'No! Pippa's gone, Laurence! Face it! She left you because she loves another man, *Ipso facto* it's time to move on. Blaming Kirsten for what happened five years ago is going to get you nowhere because you're every bit as much to blame yourself!'

'Me!' Laurence cried incredulously.

'Yes you! You pushed her into doing what she did and now you can't forgive her. Well it's high time you did. Maybe then you two guys could get on with the real business here and get that goddamned movie of yours made.'

Laurence was so stunned by the sudden change of topic that he could only look at Helena as if she were some kind of lunatic. Then, with a very dangerous light burning in his eyes, he turned to Kirsten.

'So that's what it's all about,' he said. 'You can't get any work so you thought you'd bust up my marriage and come work with me. Well you got to be one crazy lady if you think I'd let you within . . .'

'I told you five minutes ago to get out of here!' Kirsten yelled. 'And you, Helena, give him back his goddamned script and – '

'My what!' Laurence roared. 'Are you telling me you've got a copy of *my* script?'

'Oh shit!' Helena murmured. 'No, *I've* got a copy of your script!' she said aloud. 'Kirsten read it . . .'

'And it stinks!' Kirsten shouted. 'So don't flatter yourself that I want anything to do with it, because as far as I'm concerned, Laurence McAllister, both you and it can go and rot in your fucking paranoia.'

His face taut with rage Laurence started for the door.

'Hold it, hold it!' Helena cried making yet another attempt to calm things down. 'Let's just try to get to the bottom of this, shall we? I mean, why you really came here. What is it you want from Kirsten?'

Shaking Helena's hand from his arm Laurence turned back to Kirsten. 'She knows that already,' he said. 'I want her to speak to my wife and undo whatever it was she did. I want her to tell Pippa that I'm not in love with her . . .'

'Not in love with who? Kirsten or Pippa?'

'Kirsten! Who the hell do you think?'

'But how can Kirsten know whether or not you're in

love with her – only you know that. So surely it's up to you to persuade Pippa . . .'

'Don't you think I've tried?'

'OK. Well maybe it's time you tried convincing yourself.'

Laurence stared at her with such profound hostility that Helena almost laughed.

'All right, all right, I've got it now,' she said. 'That's what you're doing here, isn't it? You're here to do just that, convince yourself . . .'

'Helena,' he said dangerously, 'I don't need convincing. After what she did . . .'

'What did she do, Laurence? What was it she did that was so bad?'

Laurence's eyes moved back to Kirsten and seeing the pain on her face his heart churned. 'She knows what she did,' he growled, pushing aside the hurt.

Kirsten turned away, but he grabbed her roughly by the arm and turned her back. 'Why?' he shouted. 'Why did you do it?'

'Laurence,' Helena said quietly, 'If you need to deal with it yourself don't do it this way.'

Laurence's eyes didn't move from Kirsten's face and when finally she brought herself to look back at him she could see his anguish, confusion and pain. 'I can't ever forgive you, you know that don't you?' he said.

'I know,' she whispered. 'It's why I can't ever forgive myself.'

Seconds later the door closed behind him leaving Kirsten and Helena facing each other in the sudden stillness of the room.

'I need a drink,' Helena said turning to the cabinet.

Kirsten lifted a hand to her mouth to stifle a sob. 'I'm sorry,' she whispered. 'I need a bit of time to get myself

together. But at least you can see now why I couldn't
have called him about the film. I couldn't have called
him about anything.'

Helena sighed heavily. 'I had no idea he was so bitter
about it all,' she said. 'I thought, after all this time . . .'

'I know,' Kirsten smiled. 'But maybe it's a measure
of how much he did love me that it could have hurt him
so much.'

'Yeah, well I wouldn't argue with that.'

– 13 –

Laurence woke with a start, the hammering of his heart
and almost stifling breathlessness veering him away from
the dizzying height of the dream. He was covered in
sweat, his entire body was rigid with the force of his
desire. Something was digging into his side and as he
reached down to remove Tom's foot he heard himself
groan at the excruciating ache in his loins.

He stared into the darkness, looking at but not seeing
the light through the curtains that cast strange patterns
across his eyes. The sheets clung damply to his limbs,
the humid night air was suffocating.

He'd lost count now of how many nights he had
woken this way, so submerged in the power of his body's
need, so racked with guilt at the way he had treated her.
He should never have spoken to her that way. He should
never have spoken to her at all. But he had and now, so

many weeks later, his arrogance and cruelty still tore at his mind, just as regret dragged at his heart.

He would never go back to her, he knew that as surely as he knew that Pippa would never come back to him. What he and Kirsten had had was in the past, that chapter of his life was nothing more than a memory that from time to time, like all memories, came back to haunt him.

He turned and pulled Tom gently against him, brushing his lips over the tender, sleep-flushed cheek that pressed against his. There was no room in his heart now for anyone but this child, his son who he loved so much it hurt.

He closed his eyes and swallowed hard on the pain and guilt that rose in his throat. He didn't love her anymore, he could never love her now, but even as he thought it he could see her eyes as she'd looked up at him and told him why she could never forgive herself. Because he couldn't forgive her. Goddammit, why had she said that? Didn't she realize that it just made him hate her all the more? He pressed the heel of his hand to his forehead. Dear God, what was happening here? Why was it that he just couldn't let go?

It had all happened such a long time ago, but he knew he would never forget that time, not as long as he lived. And even now, as he lay there in the darkness, he could feel the past embracing him, pulling him into the tortuous memories he'd tried so hard to forget.

He had been going to go back to her – he had been going to end it with Pippa and go back to her. He'd made the decision even before she'd called him. It had nothing to do with the baby, he was going back because he loved her so much he couldn't live without her.

He'd been on the point of calling her himself when the telephone had rung.

'Laurence,' she'd said. 'Laurence, it's me,' and just to hear her voice, as exhausted as it was, had filled his heart so full that for a moment he'd been unable to speak.

'How are you?' he said.

For a long time there was only silence. Then in a voice so soft he barely heard her, she said, 'I'm going to have a baby.' And then she started to cry. 'I feel so alone without you, Laurence,' she sobbed. 'Why can't I make myself believe you love someone else?'

'Kirsten, Kirstie, listen . . .' he said.

'You always wanted a baby so much,' she went on. 'You always said that, that you wanted us to have a baby. You wanted to be a father, but I'm the wrong mother, aren't I?'

'No! Kirstie, listen to me . . .'

'Do you still want to be a father, Laurence?'

'Yes. Oh God! Look, stay right where you are, I'm coming round.'

He'd gone straight over only to find she wasn't at home. He went to Paul's, but Paul didn't know where she was either. For three days the two of them had looked for her. Knowing how unbalanced she was, they were both frantic with worry, but no one had seen her and no one had heard from her.

She turned up on the fourth day. She was standing at the window of her apartment when he walked in, using the keys he'd never returned. He made instantly to go to her, but there was something about her that stopped him.

'I was about to call you,' she smiled.

'Where have you been?' he asked. 'We've been looking for you everywhere.'

Her eyes were glittering in a way that sent a curl of alarm through him. 'Were you worried about your baby, Laurence?' she said. 'The baby with the wrong mother? Well you don't need to worry anymore. It's safe now. It's with Jesus.'

He felt the colour drain from his face even as the derangement contorted hers.

'I killed it, Laurence,' she laughed. 'I killed your baby. I had it scraped from my womb so that I have nothing left of you. I killed it. I killed my baby and you made me do it.'

She'd said so much more, but most of it was lost to him now. All he really remembered was how she had gloated at hurting him so much. Killing the baby was her revenge. She'd lost her mind, he'd known that at the time, just like he'd known that if ever she'd needed his help it was then, but he'd felt such bitterness, such frustration and anger that he'd wanted only to get as far away from her as he could. So he'd turned his back on her, returned to the calmness of his new life with Pippa and left Paul to pick up the pieces.

Now, as Tom stirred sleepily in his arms, Laurence could feel the tears on his cheeks. He knew, because he'd known for a long time now, that it was himself he couldn't forgive, not Kirsten, it was just that he hadn't been able to bring himself to face it. All these years he'd hated her for killing a baby that she had wanted even more than he had, but he hated himself more for being the cause of her doing that to herself. He knew her past, he knew how powerless she was to control the hatred of herself that was brought on by rejection. He'd known too what the first abortion had done to her, but instead of being there for her he had turned and walked away.

Through Paul he had learned of the depth of her suffering and the more she had suffered the more he had hated her. She had filled his life with a guilt so consuming that there had been times he had thought it would destroy him. For years he had blamed her for a crime of which they were as guilty as each other. But they hadn't been the only ones to pay the price, Dyllis Fisher had lost her husband and because of that Kirsten was still paying. She had nothing in her life now except the inheritance Paul had left her, whereas he, Laurence had his son and his work.

Lifting himself carefully from the bed he went downstairs and poured himself a drink. He'd hurt her so badly back then and now he was doing it again. Her life was a mess and the last thing she needed was him throwing his pain and resentment in her face the way he had. He still wasn't sure what had driven him to going round there like that, or what he'd really hoped to achieve by confronting her. She'd asked him for nothing, had made no attempt to contact him, yet he'd stormed in there like some kind of mad man and accused her of trying to push her way back into his life. He grimaced. He'd made a prize fool of himself, but feeling a fool was nothing compared to the way he had probably left her feeling. What he wouldn't give to be able to turn back the clock. But that was something totally beyond his power, so what he must look at now was that which was in his power; in other words what he was going to do to repair *all* the damage he had done.

Of course he knew the answer, he'd known it for some time, in fact ever since Helena had pointed it out to him, but putting his own neck on the line by helping

Kirsten to stand up to Dyllis Fisher was going to bring him the kind of problems that would cause one hell of a lot more than sleepless nights. But he owed her and if he didn't do something to help her now then his damned guilt was only going to get worse.

The big question though, was would she let him help her? Suddenly he laughed. He knew her so well he could almost hear her response when he offered. As vulnerable and insecure as he knew she was, pride alone would make her refuse him. But he would persevere, he'd make her come work with him on a strictly platonic, totally professional basis. He'd have to make that clear, because he didn't want her thinking that he might still be in love with her. He wasn't, nor was he ever likely to be, not now. Still, it was something they'd have to discuss, and not for one minute did he think that being around each other all the time was going to be easy, especially not when he was having these damned erotic dreams about her. But those he could handle, what he couldn't was the guilt. So with any luck working together, achieving something together, might just prove to be the way that both of them could exorcise all the ghosts of the past.

– 14 –

'Laurence! Are you listening to me? Are you receiving me loud and clear? Good, because I don't want any misunderstandings over what I'm about to say. I'm not a charity case, and neither am I desperate, so we might just as well end this call right now.'

'If you come to work for me I think we'd better get a few things straight,' he said.

'Didn't you hear me, Laurence? I'm not coming to work for you. I know your ego is finding that difficult to accept, but try.'

'Kirsten!'

'Don't shout at me, Laurence, I don't have a hearing problem.'

'I know I'm not handling this too well, but look, I really am sorry about all the things I said . . .'

'Forget it. It's not the first time you hurt me, but it'll be the last,' and for the fifth time that day she slammed down the receiver and turned to Helena.

'That's three days he's been calling now,' Helena remarked, 'and I'm gonna say it again, you're going to blow it if you keep that up.'

'Impossible,' Kirsten answered. Then clapping a hand over her mouth she said, 'Oh, sorry, did I forget to tell you? I don't want the job, I'm just enjoying myself making him suffer.'

'What do you mean you don't want the job?' Helena cried. 'You're hardly in a position to turn it down.'

'You're beginning to sound like him,' Kirsten commented.

'Kirstie! He obviously really wants you on that film and as far as I can see, that puts you at an advantage. And let me remind you again, this is a feature we're talking about. Big time.'

Laughing Kirsten flopped on to the sofa and stretched out her legs. 'All right, I'll come clean,' she said. 'I will do it, I just think Laurence and I have a few things to iron out before I say yes. Like professionalism. I can't have him speaking to me or treating me any way he likes just because we were once lovers.'

'And what about that side of things?' Helena asked carefully. 'Do you think you can handle it?'

'I won't know until I try. It's not going to be easy, that's for sure.'

'Maybe not for him either.'

Kirsten moved restlessly. 'Let's not discuss that,' she said. 'The most important thing is that I get that script up together. I looked at it again this afternoon, it's a pretty good story, but it needs quite a workover. I wonder what Ruby Collins is like?'

Helena didn't feel that now was the time to relate Jane's story of how Ruby Collins had whacked the director. Kirsten would find out soon enough what Ruby was like. What interested Helena right now was how Dermott Campbell was going to take it when he found out he'd been replaced by Kirsten Meredith.

'Incidentally,' Kirsten said, starting to jot yet more notes on to the script, 'you'll be happy to hear that I called Jane this morning. She's coming over later if she can get away.' She looked up. 'You know, I was thinking, maybe we could try to do something about getting a little romance into her life.'

'You've got enough to think about without playing cupid for Jane,' Helena laughed, getting up to go and look out of the window as someone knocked on the door.

'You're right,' Kirsten grimaced. 'Like preparing myself for more bad publicity once Dermott Campbell finds out I'm working with Laurence. Come to think of it I wonder if Laurence has thought about that?'

'Now's your chance to find out,' Helena said, letting the curtain fall back into place.

'No, I don't want to discuss any of this with Jane,' Kirsten said.

'It's not Jane,' Helena grinned. 'It's the man himself. And bearing gifts from what I could see.'

Kirsten's heart did such an almighty somersault that whatever she'd been about to say never materialized.

'Well, do I let him in or don't I?' Helena laughed.

'I don't know. Let me think!' Kirsten was suddenly so agitated she didn't know whether to stand, to sit, to lie down or to scream. 'Oh, for God's sake let him in,' she cried when he jammed his finger on the doorbell and kept it there.

As they slipped into their chairs in a dimly lit corner of the restaurant and a waiter handed them the menus Kirsten was so nervous she knew she'd never be able to eat. However, she was going to try because tonight was the first test as to whether or not she could be around him and keep her feelings in check. If she couldn't she would have to turn him down, but she wasn't going to allow herself to think about it too much for she knew that the enormity of what was happening would almost certainly overwhelm her if she dwelled on it.

'OK,' Laurence said, putting the menu down. 'Did you choose yet?'

'I'll have the liver,' Kirsten answered, folding away her menu.

'But I don't like liver,' Laurence objected.

'Well it's not you who has to eat it,' Kirsten declared. Then seeing the way his eyes were dancing she started to smile. Whenever they'd gone to dinner in the past she'd invariably ended up eating his food, leaving him with whatever she'd ordered. 'It's OK, I'll eat it myself,' she said coolly.

'Good. So, where do you want to start? We can go back over the past, say all the things . . .'

'No, I don't want to do that,' Kirsten interrupted. 'Let's just leave it where it is, shall we?'

Laurence looked at her for some time. 'OK,' he said at last. 'But any time you feel you . . .'

'No, honestly, I don't think it'll serve any purpose. We're colleagues now, not lovers, let's operate on that level, shall we?'

He nodded his head slowly. 'Sure,' he said, glancing up as the waiter passed him the wine list. 'Red or white?' he said to Kirsten.

'White.'

'But you're having liver.'

'I know.'

'So you want red wine.'

'Why did you ask me what colour I want if you're going to make up my mind for me?'

'I'm not, I'm just saying . . .'

'Look, if it makes you happy I'll have red.'

'No. You want white, you have white,' and he ordered a 1979 white burgundy.

That done he sat back in his chair and surveyed her. At least that's what Kirsten thought he was doing until she realized that he was lost in thought.

'Shall I begin by telling you what ideas I've had for the opening scenes?' she said watching his eyes come back into focus.

He shook his head. 'No. I'll begin by admitting that I've brought you here under false pretences.'

Kirsten frowned. 'I'm sorry,' she said, her heart starting to thud. 'I don't understand. I thought you wanted me on the film.'

'I did,' he answered and Kirsten's heart plummetted

at his use of the past tense. 'I'm afraid,' he went on, 'there isn't going to be a film.'

'What?' She waited as Laurence tasted the wine then nodded for the waiter to pour. 'Then what's all this about?' she said when the waiter had gone.

Laurence sighed heavily. 'I'm not sure,' he said. 'I've been mulling it over in my mind all day and I reckon I've come up with a solution, but – '

'Laurence! Has Dyllis Fisher been on to you? I mean, how did she find out?'

'No, she hasn't been on to me,' he interrupted. 'But I guess she soon will be, unless . . .'

'Unless what? Laurence, will you please tell me what's going on.'

'Willie Henderson, the director, pulled out today. He's also pulled out the money.'

'But why? Did he give a reason?'

Laurence nodded. Then with a wry smile he said, 'I guess I'd better come clean here, 'cos if what I've got in mind is going to work you'll need to know what you're up against.'

'A producer who's getting on my nerves is enough to be going on with,' Kirsten remarked.

Laurence grinned, but it quickly faded. 'Willie pulled out because he can't work with Ruby, the writer,' he said. 'You've read the script, you know she's got what it takes, especially when it comes to dialogue, but I'm not going to lie to you, the lady's got a few problems.'

'Show me a writer who hasn't,' Kirsten remarked.

'Well Ruby tries to solve hers in a bottle,' Laurence said. 'I know, show you a writer who doesn't. Trouble is, when Ruby gets drunk she's hopeless. When she's sober she's terrific, well maybe that's putting it a bit strong, she's not an easy lady to handle, but well, like I said, you've seen her work so you know she's capable of coming up with the goods. I haven't known her not deliver yet, though there are times when it has to be dragged out of her. And, like a lot of writers, she's pretty touchy when it comes to other people putting in their ideas. Which brings me back to Willie. Unfortunately the two of them never did see eye to eye and yesterday, they had an almighty row and she slapped his face not for the first time.'

'Really?' Kirsten said, feeling the beginnings of a grin.

'Yeah, well, I guess under any other circumstances it would be funny,' Laurence said smoothly. 'But as it stands we're right back at the beginning, with a distribution deal providing we can raise the finance. And you and I both know we're not going to be able to do that while Dyllis Fisher is . . .'

'Then I'll pull out,' Kirsten broke in. 'I don't want you to lose this because of me.'

'I've had a better idea,' Laurence said. 'Now I want you to hear me out because it's pretty crazy, but I think – no, I know – it can work. But most of it depends on you.'

Kirsten eyed him steadily. 'Go on,' she said.

'I want us to go into partnership for this movie,' he said. 'McAllister and Meredith, Meredith and McAllister, whichever way you want to play it. In other words, we form a production company and raise the finance ourselves.'

Kirsten blinked. 'Do you mean personally?' she said.

He nodded.

'But we've got to be talking about over ten million sterling here.'

'Eight. By using what capital I have, cashing in

investments and mortgaging the house I can put in close to four. I have no idea what your inheritance was . . .'

'My inheritance is in trust,' Kirsten interrupted. 'But I can always borrow against the income,' she added, vaguely aware that her head was starting to spin.

'Can you raise as much as four million?'

'I don't know – until I try.'

'Then you will try?'

'On the condition we dedicate the film to Paul's memory,' she answered, knowing that she was fast losing touch with reality.

'I don't have a problem with that,' Laurence smiled.

They sat quietly then, toying with their food when it came and mulling things over in their minds. Kirsten could barely get herself to think straight. This was such a monumental step they were considering taking, not to mention risk, that for her at least, it was somewhere in never-never-land. In fact she could hardly believe that the conversation had been so simple when what it entailed was so staggeringly complicated. But perhaps even more bewildering was this sudden about turn in Laurence. Having declared he never wanted her in his life again it seemed he was now prepared to tie her to him almost as effectively as if he were marrying her. She was about to speak when Laurence interrupted her.

'There's something else,' he said.

'I haven't quite got used to the first bit yet,' she said.

'I know, but I want you to consider the package I am proposing as a whole.'

'I'm listening. I'm not sure I'm believing, but I'm listening.'

'I don't want you to produce the movie, I want you to direct it.'

Kirsten's fork clanged against her plate. 'Laurence, is this some kind of a joke?' she declared. 'I've never directed anything in my life, and you know it!' But despite her protest, despite the fact that he really might be playing with her, his words had already sent a tingle of excitement buzzing through her veins.

'But you and I both know that you've always wanted to direct,' he said, smiling at the way her eyes were giving her away.

'But this is a feature film, Laurence. I've never even worked with 35mm, let alone directed it.'

'I'm aware of that.'

'. . . plus the fact I've been off the scene for five years . . .'

'I know that too. But I still reckon you can do it.'

'No,' she said, shaking her head. 'No, we have to get someone who knows what they're doing.'

'Will you stop eating my food,' Laurence complained. 'I told you, I don't like liver.'

Kirsten looked at him, nonplussed. He nodded for her to look down at his plate and only then did she realize that she'd started to reach across the table and fork up his lamb. She put her fork down and reached for her wine.

'We can discuss this as much as you like, right now,' Laurence went on, 'but if you'd like to take some time to think it over before we enter into negotiations . . .'

'But the crews, the budget, the cast, it's all so much bigger than anything I've ever worked with,' she protested.

'Sure. But that doesn't mean you can't handle it. And I'll be right there.'

'Then why don't you direct it?'

'Because you could do it a lot better than I could. We both know you've got a real talent when it comes to the creative side of things, so why not use it where it really counts and take the credit for it?'

'Oh God,' Kirsten said, taking another gulp at her wine. He was right, this was something she had always dreamed of, but only to him and to Paul had she ever confided it. But nothing was this easy, nothing! But what was she thinking of? It wouldn't be easy, it would be a damned nightmare – and she'd love every minute of it. And like he said, he'd be there, holding her hand every step of the way . . . Her head came up.

'We'd fight,' she declared. 'We'd never see eye to eye.'

'You were prepared to take the risk if we produced together,' he reminded her.

'But this is different. I'd want to shoot it my way and I know what you're like, Laurence. You'd undermine me in front of the crew.'

'The hell I would,' he declared. 'And since when have you not been able to stand up for yourself?'

'In a professional capacity? Never.'

'Exactly. And that's what this is, a completely professional relationship.'

'Partnership,' she corrected.

'Does that mean you'll do it?'

'I want to give it some more thought.'

'OK. But should you agree I don't want to go public until you've arranged the loan with the bank. Get it signed and sealed first then Dyllis won't have anyone to lean on to turn you down. And if she pressures them to call in the loan we'll sue.'

'We will?'

'We will.'

Kirsten looked down at her barely touched food, still not too sure whether she was going to wake up any second and find herself back in Elm Park Gardens. 'Laurence,' she said, lifting her eyes back to his, 'why are you doing this? I mean . . . Does it have something to do with the past? Are you . . .'

'Everything about us is to do with the past, Kirstie,' he said softly. 'But as of now we're going to change that.'

As she looked back at him in the flickering glow of the candlelight her heart was so full that for a moment she was afraid to speak. 'OK, then,' she said, picking up her glass. 'Let's drink to us and to a great future as partners.'

'I guess that must mean you've done that thinking you mentioned,' Laurence teased, then promptly winced as she kicked him.

'Get a good night's sleep,' he said when he dropped her at her house later. 'You're going to need it because it's going to be one rough road from here-on-in.'

But just how rough neither of them could ever have begun to imagine.

'Dermott!' Helena cried as she opened the door.

He pushed past her and stormed into her cluttered studio. His sparse sandy hair was a mess, his oddly handsome face virtually quivering with rage. 'I want you to know,' he seethed spinning round to look at her, 'that as of now the real battle begins!'

Immediately Helena drew an imaginary pistol from her hip and shot him. 'I reckon I just won,' she grinned.

Campbell slapped her hand down, obviously not in the least bit amused.

'OK, what are you talking about?' she said.

'You know damned well what I'm talking about,' he seethed, 'and I just can't believe you could be that fucking stupid!'

'It had nothing to do with me!' she protested. 'It was Laurence's idea . . .'

'Put there by you! No, don't bother denying it, he told me himself. When he fired me. And who got him to fire me? Kirsten fucking Meredith, that's who.' He clamped his stubby fingers to his hair. 'Shit, Helena, are you out of your mind pulling a stunt like that?'

Helena's jaw was clenched. 'Are you?' she said. 'Screwing Ruby Collins!'

'You did it out of jealousy?' he roared, incredulously. 'What the fuck's going on in that head of yours? With what I know about Kirsten Meredith . . .'

'You'll never be able to print that story!' Helena shouted, half-laughing with contempt. 'Especially not now she and Laurence are working together. Can't you see, that means he's forgiven her – and even if he hadn't, just what was there to say . . .?'

'Oh believe you me, there was plenty. And never, never underestimate Dyllis Fisher. If she got her teeth into that story she'd wipe the fucking floor with Kirsten Meredith.'

'And you and I both know that if one word of that ever hits the papers Laurence will throw lawsuits at you faster than you can blink.'

'And what about you, Helena? Do you think they'd have you on that film if they knew it was you who'd told me?'

Helena's eyes rounded with fear and amazement. 'I never breathed a word . . .'

'Can you prove that?'

She stared at him. He stared back and for several moments they eyed each other with such resentment that the air between them seemed to burn with it. Campbell was the first to look away.

'Shit!' he cried, slamming his hand down on the table. 'If you knew what I'd been through to get myself on that movie . . .'

'Don't come here looking for sympathy. You said you'd call me! Did the phone ever ring? Did it hell!'

'Helena, you seem to be missing the point here! The point is that if Laurence knew the truth about *you* he'd never let you within a mile of that set. He couldn't afford the publicity.'

He reeled back as her hand lashed across his face.

'Don't ever do that again!' he said, a dangerous edge to his voice.

'Then don't come here threatening me! Now just what is the real issue here, Dermott? Because from where I'm sitting it's you, bleeding with jealousy that Kirsten Meredith got what you wanted – and more.'

'And you helped her! Jesus Christ, how could you do that?'

'I did it because I owed her. I did it because I wanted the part . . .'

'*I'd* have given you the part.'

'Get real, Dermott. You'd never have had that much clout.'

His dark eyes flashed. 'If I were you I'd look out for my back, Helena, because with Kirsten Meredith on board there are going to be plenty of long knives heading towards that set . . .'

'You do anything to disrupt that movie and you can kiss goodbye to any friendship you might have had with Laurence.'

'Laurence has already shown me where his loyalties lie.'

Helena laughed nastily. 'The same place as mine?'

Campbell's eyes bored into hers. 'And just where *do* yours lie, Helena?' he said.

'You already have the answer to that.'

'Are you sure? Do you want to take some time to think about that?'

'I already told you once,' she warned him, 'don't come here threatening me.'

He watched her, his heart churning with emotions. He didn't want to do this to her, but if he couldn't have that movie then neither could she. They were all against him now, closing ranks and shutting him out like he just didn't matter. Well that was just where they were wrong, he did matter, and by the time he was through, with Dyllis Fisher on his side he was going to do a whole lot more than matter . . .

– 15 –

Everything seemed to be happening with lightning speed. Neither Kirsten nor Laurence had wasted any time in contacting their banks, their lawyers and accountants and at the offices they had taken in Windmill Street just five weeks after their dinner, pre-production and recruitment was going ahead in earnest. In fact already there was barely room for everyone in the six-room suite on the fourth floor of an old Victorian building.

The place was in sore need of a lick of paint, but now that schedule boards, cast and crew lists, first draft graphics, photographs, telephone lists and a thousand other things were finding their way onto the walls the peeling paint was barely noticeable. Production managers, accountants, line-producers, production secretaries and location managers had all moved into the two larger offices; the casting directors and assistants were just along the hall in what had probably once been a very grand bedroom; the unit publicist and her team were next to casting, and at the end of the hall was Kirsten and Laurence's office, which adjoined a small attic type enclave that had been converted into a screening room and was also the room where they would receive the satellite link-ups with New Orleans in order to audition the American cast. Their personal assistants were in the hall itself along with four spare desks for the costume and make-up designers, stunt-arrangers and film crew to use when they needed to. The drive and excitement was such that no one found time to complain about the lack of space, but if they needed more those who could simply worked from home or took themselves off to Alison's design offices which she had leased just around the corner in Colville Place.

Kirsten's time was split mainly between Ruby, Alison, and Jake, the director of photography. Jake, with his boyish good looks and incorrigible eye for the ladies, was someone with whom Laurence had worked in the past – as indeed were most of the team – and it was only with Jake that Kirsten had so far managed to build up a rapport.

However, quite unexpectedly, Kirsten managed a

breakthrough with Ruby. It came about when she was at Ruby's flat one afternoon and happened to open a photograph album lying on the coffee table. When Ruby came into the room, toting a tray of coffee and biscuits, Kirsten hurriedly closed the album, apologizing for the intrusion. But Ruby simply set down her tray and opened the album again. Her pride in the way she had looked in her earlier years was so evident and brought about such a change in her as she gazed wistfully down at the undeniable beauty of the face that had once been hers that Kirsten was moved to ask about her life on the catwalks. Perfectly sober Ruby waxed lyrical for the entire afternoon, each photograph having its own story to tell, each memory softening the harsh lines that pinched Ruby's mouth. The sun had long since set by the time Ruby closed the album, they had done no work that day – at least not on the script, but Kirsten knew that it had been one of the most valuable days they had passed so far. She had found Ruby's Achilles' heel and it was one she could make work for them both. She even, much to Ruby's delight, accepted a gin and tonic and stayed drinking with Ruby until the early hours of the morning.

This wasn't to say that Ruby became in any way pliable after that, but at least the script debates that followed were no longer filled with the bitter resentment and jealousy Kirsten had encountered before. In fact, Kirsten was coming to enjoy her exchanges with Ruby for when Ruby was sober her mind was so acute, her ideas so innovative that it not only kept Kirsten on her toes, but served to engender a respect for Ruby that Kirsten hadn't at all thought to find. She only wished that she herself could get the same respect from the ever-expanding production team.

It wasn't that everyone was set against her, but those who really mattered were dishearteningly influenced by the things Dermott Campbell was writing in his column. Laurence rarely commented on it, but Kirsten knew that Campbell's accusations that she had managed to bewitch Laurence into giving her a position for which she was in no way qualified, irritated him as much as it did her. In fact, Kirsten wasn't too sure if it was that that made Laurence so moody with her. Or was it, she worried constantly, that Laurence was now regretting the rashness of persuading her to take on something that everyone else was convinced was totally beyond her.

But no matter what anyone thought Kirsten knew she was going to succeed. The fact that Alison and her art directors, the line-producers and production managers always took their queries or problems to Laurence when they should have been coming to her was something she was just going to have to suffer until such time as she had proved herself. Laurence invariably re-routed them to her, but the lack of co-operation she sometimes came up against was as wearing as it was infuriating. She didn't want to discuss it with Laurence because she didn't want him to think she couldn't cope. Besides, if she couldn't hack it here in the office, then what chance was she going to stand once they were out in the field? Just thank God for Jake, who was not only fully aware of what was going on, but flatly refused to tolerate it from his crew. And the support of the camera crew once they were out there was going to be as necessary as film in the camera.

There was one other person who was proving a god-send and that was Vicky, Kirsten's personal assistant. She was the only member of the team Kirsten had hired herself and in her own inimitable fashion had managed to organize Kirsten's busy schedule. Vicky, just like Jake, succeeded in keeping Kirsten's spirits buoyant during times when she just wanted to throw up her hands and scream or fall to her knees and weep. In fact Vicky, who was as pretty and lighthearted as she was efficient, had worked for Kirsten on the drama that had won Kirsten a BAFTA, so even if no one else had known Kirsten at her best at least Vicky had. But even if the others had known Kirsten then, there was no getting away from the fact that Kirsten's success had been in TV and that held sway with no one. Stripes had to be earned in the world of features or they were no stripes at all and that, even more than Campbell's attacks, was what really lay at the root of the problem.

Still, it wasn't all bad, she reminded herself when she tucked herself up in bed at night. She couldn't have wished for a greater challenge and neither would she have dared to hope that her own confidence would turn out to be her greatest ally. Things were beginning to take shape, the re-working of the script was exciting everyone and the casting, by now almost complete, was terrific. There was only one part on which she and Laurence couldn't see eye to eye and that was the one of Moyna O'Malley herself. Laurence wanted Anna Sage, who was, to Kirsten's mind, too young for the part and far too pretty. She had the talent to carry it off, Kirsten would concede that, it was just that she looked wrong. They'd tested her and though the wigs, make-up and costume had undoubtedly helped, she still hadn't quite worked for Kirsten. Laurence had ended up storming out of the screening room, not uttering a word, but obviously furious at her stubbornness.

In fact the tension between Kirsten and Laurence was growing by the day and Kirsten knew that it wasn't only professional disagreements that were causing it. It was the proximity they shared that seemed to be creating the real difficulties. Their office, at the back of the building, gave them a privacy they both needed to work – which was of course precisely what they did. But all too often the need to sit closer together, or to lean over the other's shoulder as something was being explained, would create an atmosphere of such acute awareness of the other that it required a superhuman effort on Kirsten's part to keep cool. To her annoyance he seemed to sense her tension and though it could all too easily make him irritable with her it could also, though rarely, bring a teasing lilt to his voice and a softness to his eyes that was in its way so intimate and so compelling it was as though he was stealing into her with all the potency of a lover.

Kirsten smiled sleepily to herself as she turned over, hugging the pillow. It was inevitable that part of her was now daring to hope that eventually they would get back together. She was exhilarated by the unsteady beats of her heart when she watched him taking charge, when she felt his presence as though he was touching her, when she heard his laughter and felt herself almost melt at the incredible intensity of his blue eyes, yet in a way she was terrified. For, as intransigent as her confidence might appear to others, she knew how reliant it was on Laurence for its strength. That in itself told her that it had been a mistake to take this on, but it was too late now to back out, not that she would have dreamt of doing so, it was just that her nervousness that he might do something that would hurt her emotionally was hard to shake. She knew she was in danger of becoming paranoid, but Anna Sage's resemblance to Pippa was as unsettling as Laurence's determination to cast her. And

Anna's obvious attraction to Laurence on the few occasions she and Laurence had met with her irked Kirsten in a way that only added to her unease. Laurence couldn't be ignorant of the likeness though he'd never mentioned it, not even when a couple of weeks ago Dermott Campbell had run with the headline 'Kirstie Doll snubs wife look-alike.' Kirsten knew that Laurence hadn't spoken to Campbell himself, he'd instructed the publicists to handle the situation; then he personally had got on the phone to Anna to laughingly tell her not to believe everything she read in the papers and had invited her to lunch to – as he put it – explain the situation. Exactly what explanation he'd given Kirsten had no idea, and neither would she ask.

She sighed heavily as she reminded herself that Laurence strongly objected to relationships on the set. It was small comfort. So too was the flirtation she had started up with Jake. She couldn't deny that she enjoyed the attention, almost as much as she did the sour looks it provoked from Laurence, but in truth she was doing herself no favours and she knew it. Everyone on the movie had read enough about her in the press to know that she'd slept her way to the top once, so as far as they were concerned she was doing it again. What they made of her relationship with Laurence she had no idea, but her friendship with Jake had reached Campbell's ears and so too had the fact that Jean-Paul, the quirkily handsome Frenchman who was playing the part of Moyna's lover and conspirator in crime, had flown into London the previous day and spent the evening with Kirsten. If only, Kirsten thought to herself, she could get her hands on whoever it was who was giving Campbell his information she'd . . . Well, she didn't know what she'd do, but whatever it was it wouldn't be pleasant.

Wearily she reached into the darkness for the telephone as it started to ring. It was just before one in the morning she noticed on the bedside clock as she said hello.

No one answered.

'Hello,' she said again, feeling her nerve ends start to prickle. Had she not been half asleep the unease might have reached her sooner for this wasn't the first time her telephone had rung at this hour bringing an anonymous presence into the privacy of her darkened room. 'Hello,' she repeated.

Still there was only silence. But someone was there, she could hear them breathing.

'Hello, who is this?' Kirsten said, her heart starting to thud as she sat up and flicked on the light.

More silence, but as she listened Kirsten thought she could make out the distant tinkling sound of music. She pressed the receiver closer to her ear. It was a gentle, comforting sound, like a musical mobile used to lull a baby to sleep.

'Hello,' she said again. 'Hello.'

The line clicked and the whine of the dialling tone replaced the silence.

A week later Kirsten was on a flight back from Dublin giving an interview to a freelance reporter who was doing a piece for *Screen International* and whose only chance of fitting herself into Kirsten's schedule was to accompany her on this flight.

'So,' Kirsten was saying, 'Rochette isn't there, he's out trying to find food. Moyna is asleep on a makeshift bed and doesn't realize until the man starts to attack her that it isn't Rochette who's come in. She struggles, but to no avail. The man leaves and when Rochette returns he finds Moyna dead.'

'Dead?' the reporter gasped.

'Yes. She's been strangled,' Kirsten said matter of factly. 'Rochette is hunted down. He stands trial for Moyna's murder and is once again sentenced to hang.'

'So does he hang?'

'Yes.'

'You mean the bad guys are going to win?'

Kirsten grinned. 'You'll have to watch the film and find out, won't you?' she said, looking at Jake who was trying very hard not to laugh, and gathering up her things she prepared to disembark.

'I thought for one minute there you were going to leave her up the garden path,' Jake remarked as they left the aircraft and the reporter was whisked away by a publicity assistant.

'Now would I do something like that?' Kirsten said, all innocence. 'Poor thing she'd never find her way back. Anyway, what I want to know is why *I* had to tell her the story when the publicist should already have given her a press handout. Telling it cold like that never works.'

'So young Lisa's in for a bollocking, is she?' Jake grinned, his brown eyes dancing.

'Don't mock me,' Kirsten warned. 'I'll get around to sounding off one of these days, believe me.'

'Here, let me carry that,' Jake interrupted, as Kirsten moved her heavy bag from one shoulder to the other.

'It's OK, I can manage,' she said, but he'd already taken it from her. 'Ah, such chivalry,' she laughed. 'You wouldn't have done that if I were a man.'

'There are a lot of things I wouldn't do if you were

a man,' Jake responded, 'and before you get on your high horse I apologize for the sexist remark, it's just that you bring out the macho beast in me.'

'Well, just so long as the macho beast remembers to be a Director of Photography when the time is called for . . .'

'He will. But I don't suppose he can take a beautiful woman to dinner tonight, can he, and forget for a while that he's really a DP and you're really a director.'

Kirsten laughed. 'OK, why not? These past three days have been pretty gruelling racing around the Irish countryside, I guess we could all do with some relaxation.'

'I wasn't planning to take the whole unit,' Jake objected.

'And I wasn't planning for them to come.'

'Kirsten,' David said, catching up with them, 'could we go over the Walk On list again on the way into London?'

'Yes, of course,' Kirsten said readily. She didn't mind how many times they went over it as long as he discussed it with her and not Laurence.

'Hey, what do you mean, on the way into London?' Jake suddenly cried. 'My need is greater, more pressing and since I'm more senior I get to drive her.'

'Jake, for heaven's sake,' Kirsten said, glancing uncomfortably at David as the three of them were swallowed up in the crowd of people waiting.

'Actually, I get to drive her.'

Kirsten spun round and found herself face to face with Laurence. 'Laurence!' she gasped. 'Where did you come from? I didn't know . . . You didn't say you . . .'

'I'll take that,' Laurence said, taking Kirsten's bag

from Jake and without uttering another word he turned and started out of the terminal.

'If he weren't the producer I'd smack him one for the way he always cramps my style,' Jake muttered.

Kirsten laughed uneasily. 'Looks like we'll have to take a rain-check on dinner,' she said, her eyes still on Laurence.

'I'll keep you to that,' Jake said, but Kirsten wasn't listening. She'd have liked to think that Laurence's foul temper was because he'd seen her clowning around with Jake, but she knew instinctively that it was nothing so trivial. In fact if it had brought him out here to the airport to meet her she could only conclude that it must be pretty serious.

'Just quit hassling me for what this is about,' Laurence said, hitting the indicator and pulling from the slip road on to the M4, 'and tell me about Ireland. Did you settle on Killua Castle?'

'Yes,' Kirsten answered, 'and I'll give you a full report as soon as you've explained why you came to the airport.'

'Did David work out yet how many days you're going to need at the castle?' Laurence asked, pressing his foot harder on to the accelerator and steering his black Mercedes into the fast lane.

'Twelve, I think he said – four of those will be night shoots. And before you ask I'm going over the Walk On list with him again and the total is somewhere around one-fifty. Now, will you please tell me exactly why you're in such a vile mood.'

'It can wait till we reach the office,' he said with a finality that made Kirsten want to scream.

'Laurence,' she said through gritted teeth. 'I am not

a child and I deeply resent you turning up like this and behaving as though . . .'

'I wanted to be sure you didn't pick up a newspaper before I had a chance to stop you,' he said, flashing someone in front for them to pull over.

Kirsten paled as she turned to look at him. 'What do you mean?' she said. 'What's happened?'

'You can read it for yourself once we get to the office, then I'll be asking *you* for some explanations,' he said keeping his eyes straight ahead.

'Is it . . .? Does it have something to do . . .?'

'With the movie, yes. With you personally, no,' he interrupted.

'For God's sake, Laurence, stop doing this!' she cried. 'I'm not in the mood for guessing games.'

'Then stop trying and talk to me about Ireland.'

Some forty minutes later they walked into the office. It was past six o'clock, but there were still people around. Laurence stopped to speak to one of the accountants while Kirsten went on ahead to their office hoping to find a newspaper, but what she found instead was something she was totally unprepared for.

For several seconds she merely stood in the doorway watching the little boy who was happily tapping away on a computer keyboard. With his black curly hair, thick dark lashes and deep blue eyes he was so like Laurence there couldn't, even for a moment, be any mistaking who he was and for one horrible moment, as her heart contracted painfully, Kirsten wanted to run. But it wasn't only that he was such a beautiful child that was causing her to back away from him, it was the fact that she was only now realizing that Laurence had very likely been keeping him away from her deliberately. He was prepared to work with her, to flirt with her even, to support her and encourage her, but she could see now what a distance in reality he had kept from her. His son was the very core of his life and not once had he ever discussed him with Kirsten, nor had he mentioned Tom to anyone in front of her.

She was about to slip away quietly when Tom looked up from the keyboard. For an instant he seemed frightened, as though he had been caught doing something wrong.

Kirsten smiled shakily.

Tom continued to look at her.

'Hello,' she said softly.

His eyes grew wider.

'Are you Tom?' she said, her heart pounding in her ears.

He nodded, uncertainly. 'This is my Daddy's,' he said pointing to the keyboard.

Again Kirsten smiled, but had to bite her lips to stop them from trembling. 'Does Daddy know you're here?' she said.

'I came on the bus with Jane,' he answered.

'And where's Jane now?'

'She's gone to the toilet. Can I ring someone up?' he asked, trying to reach the telephone.

'Please,' Jane corrected him, coming in behind Kirsten.

'Please?' Tom repeated, looking at Kirsten.

Kirsten nodded and walked forward handing him the receiver. 'Who are you going to call?' she asked.

'My Mummy.'

Again Kirsten's smile wavered. 'Hello Jane,' she said turning to her. 'How are you?'

'Oh, I'm fine,' Jane said, shrugging as awkwardly as ever. 'How are you?'

'Yes, good, thank you,' Kirsten mumbled. 'Look, I'm sorry I haven't returned your calls, things have been so hectic around here.'

'Oh, that's all right,' Jane said hastily. 'I understand. Tom, this is the lady I told you about. Do you remember? Did you tell him your name?' she asked Kirsten.

Kirsten shook her head and turned back to look at Tom.

'This is Kirsten,' Jane said. 'I told you we might meet her today, didn't I? And we've got a present for her, haven't we?'

'Is it your birthday?' Tom said to Kirsten, the telephone pressed to his ear.

'No,' Kirsten smiled.

'It's my birthday soon. I'm going to be four.'

'Here you are Tom, would you like to give this to Kirsten?' Jane said, taking a package from her bag. Dimly Kirsten was aware of the difference in Jane's voice as she spoke to Tom. She seemed so much more confident with him than she ever did with adults.

'Can I have a present too?' Tom said, turning back to Jane once he'd handed the packet over.

Jane laughed. 'You've already had a present today,' she reminded him. 'We went for a ride on the bus.'

'Oh yes,' he said dolefully. His eyes returned to Kirsten's. 'Can I open your present?'

'Please,' Jane chided. 'And no, it's not for you . . .'

Tom's bottom lip jutted forward.

Kirsten was on the point of handing it over when Tom's eyes suddenly lit up and he was out of the chair like a shot leaving the telephone dangling. 'Daddy!' he shouted.

Laurence swept him up in his arms, turned him upside down then raised him up to kiss him. 'What are

you doing here?' he laughed into Tom's up-turned face.
'I thought you were going to Granny's.'

'I went on a bus,' Tom told him.

'Did you now?' Laurence said, swinging him round
so that he was sitting in the crook of his arm. 'Was it
good?'

'Yes. Kirsten's got a present.'

'She has?' Laurence frowned, turning to look at
Kirsten.

'Jane brought it, but I helped to make it, didn't I
Jane?'

Kirsten hardly knew what they were saying, all she
could feel were Laurence's eyes on hers, as she somehow
kept the smile on her face.

'Jane,' Laurence said, 'take Tom out into the production office, will you?'

Tom started to protest, but Laurence assured him
there were lots of treats in store out there and setting
him down he stood aside as Jane led the way out then
closed the door behind them.

'Are you OK?' he said to Kirsten.

'Yeah, yes, I'm fine,' she answered.

'You don't look it.'

'Well, I suppose it was just . . . Well, the shock . . .
He's so like you . . .' tears were burning so painfully in
her eyes and her heart was so filled with emotion she
could barely speak.

'Hey, come on,' Laurence said, putting his arm round
her shoulder. 'I know what's happening . . .'

'No, don't, please,' Kirsten said, trying to, pull herself
away.

'Kirstie . . .'

'Oh God, Laurence, I didn't know it would hurt so
much,' she sobbed.

'I know,' he whispered. 'I've been trying to think of the right way for you to meet him. I knew it wouldn't be easy for you . . .'

'He's wonderful,' Kirsten said her voice muffled by his shoulder, her senses drowning in the belovedly familiar smell of him.

'Yeah, well I kind of like him,' Laurence smiled pushing her back so he could look at her.

'Oh God, what an idiot I'm making of myself,' Kirsten groaned, pulling away.

'Hey, listen,' Laurence said, catching her hand. 'I understand how you're feeling. And I told you, any time you want to talk about it . . .'

'No amount of talking is ever going to change what I did.'

'Kirstie, you've got to let it go, stop hurting yourself.'

'I've tried,' she said, 'but it's not easy. And seeing Tom . . . Oh God, what am I saying? I'm sorry, I'll be all right in a minute.'

Laurence dropped her hand, but he was aware of how the need to say more was almost choking him. Worse though was the feel of her still burning through his body. Sure he wanted her, he'd never deny that, but he didn't love her and it would be wrong of him to give her any hope in that direction when they had so much at stake here. He wished to God Jane hadn't brought Tom even though he knew that Kirsten would have had to meet him sooner or later, he'd just wanted it to be later. Having her around his son was going to be difficult to handle, for him as well as for her, and he sure didn't want Kirsten getting attached to Tom when it was only going to end up hurting her all the more.

Abruptly he turned and walked out of the door. He'd give her a while to collect herself while he got someone to drive Jane and Tom home. They had a pressing matter to discuss tonight, but as mad as he was about it he knew already he was going to go easier on her than he might have done if Tom hadn't shown up.

Fifteen minutes later Kirsten and Laurence were sitting at their desks with the door closed. Kirsten had by now finished reading the article about Helena in that morning's paper and was looking at Laurence waiting for him to comment.

'Did you know?' he asked.

Kirsten nodded.

'Then don't you think you should have told me?'

'I would have if I'd thought this was going to happen,' she answered.

'You realize that we'll have to pay her off and re-cast.'

'But why? It all happened such a long time ago.'

'The story's right here in today's paper,' he reminded her. 'And how's it going to look once we come to shoot the scenes in New Orleans, scenes that involve boys the same age, when we've got someone notorious for her affairs with boys playing the part?'

Kirsten knew he was right, she also knew she didn't have much of an argument to put up in Helena's defence except to say that Marie Laveau was a voodoo priestess not a paedophile. The fact that young boys were being procured from the school and that Helena was going to take part in those scenes was enough. With a weary irony Kirsten recalled how she had once slept with the head of drama in order to safeguard Helena's job – that wasn't going to work this time, Laurence would never be so easily coerced. But even if he could be it would have to be someone else who did the coercing, for never had he seemed more unapproachable than he did now. It was strange how those few moments of intimacy had brought down the barrier between them, and yet he now seemed to resent her for breaking down in front of him. And right now she was so tired and so confused all she wanted was to go home.

'I can't help wondering why this story should have broken now?' she said.

'The cast list was published yesterday. With your agreement to Anna Sage I saw no reason to hold it back.'

'So it would seem that Campbell has been waiting in the wings. I mean, he couldn't have got that story together overnight.'

'No.'

'So it's not just me he's out to destroy it would seem, it's Helena too.'

'It would seem that way.'

'But you're prepared to put up with what he writes about me? Why not this?'

'This is different.'

'So, we give in to him and fire Helena?'

'Kirsten, Helena Johnson went into a boy's boarding school to research the role of a schoolmistress for a BBC play. While she was there, under total trust of the school authorities, she seduced, corrupted it says here, a fifteen-year-old pupil. Not once, not even twice, but repeatedly. She got that boy so mixed up and so crazy for her that when the authorities found out they expelled him and he hanged himself. Now tell me, how in God's name can you defend that when we're going to have her working with boys the same age?'

'I'm not trying to defend it, I'm just asking you to help her put her past behind her, the way you have with me.'

'I am not a charity, Kirsten.'

'And neither are you perfect, you supercilious bastard.

Don't you think she's paid for that? How many nights do you think she's lain awake thinking about that boy and dying inside for what he did to himself? Do you honestly think she intended that to happen?'

'She was a grown woman. He was just a boy. But even if that were supportable, which it's not, what about her mother? For God's sake, Kirstie, the woman's still in prison for terrorizing people with voodoo curses. And in a Louisiana prison at that. How much worse can it get?'

'So you're going to throw Helena out and let Campbell win?'

'It's not a point of letting him win. It's a point of what this is going to do to the movie. I know she's a friend of yours and I appreciate that you want to help her, but she's got to go, Kirsten.'

'She's set her heart on this, Laurence. She hasn't worked in over four years . . .'

'I'm sorry, but I can't help that.'

'But that boy's suicide happened over fifteen years ago! I know,' she sighed, 'it's in the paper today . . .'

'And it will continue to be in the paper as long as we keep her on. Is that what you want for her? Do you want people walking out of the movie because they're revolted at seeing her with teenage boys?'

'There has to be a way round it,' Kirsten said helplessly.

'Well if there is let me know and I'll consider it. You've got twenty-four hours.'

But the following morning when Kirsten arrived late in the office, having been to see Helena to explain that on this occasion there really was nothing she could do to save her, Laurence was waiting with the news that Helena was to stay on the cast.

*

'. . . and he just refuses to tell me what happened to change his mind,' Kirsten said to Helena that night. 'I mean, it doesn't make sense. He was so dead set against it and now – well, I guess we shouldn't knock it.'

'I'll tell you what happened,' Helena said staring down at her drink.

'You mean you've spoken to Laurence?'

Helena shook her head. 'No, to Dermott Campbell. He was here last night.' She gave a sad and bitter laugh. 'He came to apologize, can you believe that? He actually thought I'd forgive him.'

'What? Was he drunk?'

'Very.' Again the same dry and cheerless laugh. 'That guy has to be some kind of fruitcake to think I could ever forgive what he's done. But I can't help wondering what that makes me for going to bed with him.'

Kirsten blinked, opened her mouth to speak then closed it again. Her eyes started to hunt the shadowy room, moving over the untidy rows of paperbacks, the cheap abstract art, the old-fashioned hi-fi, the tiled grate with its gas fire. She looked back at Helena. Her head was still bowed, her hands were circled around the stem of her glass, her wiry hair sat dejectedly in a knot at the nape of her neck.

'He told me he loved me,' Helena whispered as a solitary tear splashed on to the table. 'How can he love me when he did what he did?'

'He used you to get to Laurence and me,' Kirsten answered.

'Yes. But he wanted to get to me too. He blames me for putting the idea of employing you into Laurence's head.'

'Does he really think that Laurence could be so easily influenced?'

– 263 –

'It would seem so.' The loneliness and desolation that emanated from Helena was almost unbearable. It was so rare to see her like this that it seemed all the more tragic.

'He called Laurence last night, from here,' Helena said tonelessly. 'He told Laurence that if he didn't keep me on he'd go to Dyllis Fisher with the story about how you and Laurence broke up.'

'Jesus Christ,' Kirsten murmured. 'How on earth did he find out about that?'

'I've got no idea. All I know is that Laurence told him to go to hell, but obviously Laurence has given it some more thought. My guess is Laurence wants to protect you.'

'More likely his investment,' Kirsten half-heartedly joked.

'Yeah, that too. But he can't afford for that kind of story to be spread across the papers, at least not the way Dyllis Fisher would tell it, and with this scandal of mine too . . . Don't you see, one way or another it's all to do with children. People don't take well to horror stories about children.'

'God, just what kind of man is Dermott Campbell,' Kirsten muttered. 'He calls himself a friend of Laurence's, he tells you he loves you . . .'

'He's totally fucked up, that's what he is,' Helena said. 'Like me, I guess.'

'Come on. You're not fucked up, you're just . . .'

'Kirsten, I went to bed with a guy who's just destroyed my career. Who's quite effectively seen to it that I can hardly show my face in the street again. If that's not fucked up then tell me what is?'

'What made you do it?'

'Loneliness, what do you think?'

'It must have been more than that.'

'Yeah. I fancy him. Now that's seriously fucked up, wouldn't you say?'

Kirsten was on the point of reminding her that she'd never gone for men his age before, but under the circumstances thought better of it. 'Are you seeing him again?' she asked.

'I don't know.'

'Do you want to?'

'I don't know that either.' She let go of her glass and dropped her head in her hands. 'Oh God, Kirstie, I've made such a mess of my life and nothing I do seems to change it.'

'You're still on the film,' Kirsten reminded her gently.

Helena shook her head. 'There's no way I can do it now and you know it.'

'Laurence and I have already spoken to Ruby about putting a different slant on your character. There won't be any scenes with young boys, if that's what's bothering you.'

'Isn't it what's bothering you?'

'Of course. That's why we're changing it. We want you with us, Helena.'

'You might, but Laurence is being forced to accept me. I can't work like that.'

'I'm going to call him,' Kirsten said, getting to her feet. 'I'll let him speak to you himself, because he'll put what he has to say much better than I can.'

'Oh shit, I don't think I'm up to speaking to him right now,' Helena groaned. 'No, no,' she said, as Kirsten started to dial. 'I think you'd better sit down and hear the rest of it before you do that. You might change your mind.'

'What do you mean, the rest of it?' Kirsten said, an uneasy sensation stealing over her.

'The rest of it is, that it was me who gave Dermott Campbell his information about your rise to the top.'

'You,' Kirsten said incredulously sliding back into her chair.

'I did it to stop him printing his story about me,' Helena said, her voice starting to break. 'I guess you could say he blackmailed me into it. And I asked myself which was worse, that the story about James Scott came out, or that your reputation got damaged. I thought you could weather the storm better than me, so I told Campbell what he wanted to know.'

'Including what I did when Laurence and I broke up?' Kirsten said wanting more than anything that this conversation wasn't happening.

'No. I swear I never told him that. I don't know who did either. He won't tell me. But I guess keeping that to myself isn't enough to make you forgive me for doing what I did and don't worry, I won't hold it against you if you don't.'

Kirsten sat quietly for a long time going over everything in her mind. It was almost laughable really, to think that all the time she had been trying to protect herself from being hurt by Laurence she'd had just as much to fear from Helena. In a different way, of course, but what was this thing Helena had going with Campbell?

She took a sip of wine and tried to shake off the encroaching feeling of isolation. That her own best friend should be responsible for the difficulties she was having now was hardly conceivable, and if it hadn't been Helena herself who was telling her she doubted she would ever have believed it. But she had to ask herself, if she had been in Helena's shoes with the history of James Scott hanging over her, wouldn't she have done the same thing? She honestly didn't know the answer to that, loyalty was something she put great store by, but with all that had happened to her, didn't she put even more by self-preservation?

'I guess it's too late to say I'm sorry,' Helena croaked, and as her eyes moved from Kirsten's to a distant place in her mind Kirsten sensed the same isolation wrapping itself around Helena. She too was on the point of losing her best friend, but unlike Kirsten she had no career to turn to now, neither did she have the comfort of someone doing his best to shield her the way Laurence was shielding Kirsten.

'No, it's not too late,' Kirsten said, reaching out for Helena's hand. 'We need each other, Helena. We've been through a lot together, we can weather this too.'

'Oh God,' Helena gasped, swallowing hard on the lump in her throat as her fingers tightened around Kirsten's. 'I don't deserve you, Kirstie.'

'What you don't deserve is what Campbell's done to you,' Kirsten told her. 'And you don't deserve to lose the film either. Now I'm going to call Laurence and let him tell you himself what he's done today to make it possible for you to stay.'

'No, you tell me.'

'OK. But remember, this is Laurence's doing, not mine. I know he was pushed into it, but he wants you for that part every bit as much as I do. I'm telling you that so's you know that we're both on your side. He called a conference with the publicists this afternoon and had them draw up a draft statement for the press voicing your remorse for what happened to James Scott. They've touched on your mother's involvement with voodoo, but none of us really saw that as much of a problem and it's up to you how much of it you want to reveal. My advice is to play it down. Evelyn, the chief publicist, is lining up a sympathetic journalist, probably someone from a woman's weekly magazine, to handle the story. It'll be done in the form of an interview, but most of what you say has already been written for you. I've read it myself, it's pretty moving and I imagine by the time Evelyn's finished, providing you stick to what she tells you, there won't be a dry eye in the house. Just before I left this evening she told me she'd been in touch with James' parents . . .'

'Oh God, no,' Helena groaned.

'And they told Evelyn,' Kirsten continued, 'that they've forgiven you. They said they couldn't go through their lives with so much hatred and bitterness, so they took the decision some time ago now to forgive you. They were as upset as you were that the story had come out now and they're contacting Dermott Campbell's editor to ask for a printed apology for stirring up things that were best left in the past. After that, with any luck, there'll never be any mention of it again and by the time the movie comes out hopefully most will have forgotten. But like I said, there's going to be nothing in the film now even to suggest that the character of Marie Laveau is in any way involved in procurement. Laurence is overseeing everything, he wants to see you tomorrow before you speak to Evelyn. There's only one thing left for me to say . . . I don't know how you're going to take it, but I don't really have any choice but to ask for your solemn promise that you never have anything to do with Campbell again – at least not for the duration of the film.'

'You have it,' Helena choked through her tears. Then

letting her head fall to the table and burying her face in her arms she sobbed, 'I can't believe you're doing this for me, Kirstie. I just can't believe it.'

'I'm doing it,' Kirsten said, 'because you're my friend. And because you're a great actress. A really great actress.'

– 16 –

'What did you just say?' Kirsten laughed.

'I said, you're getting too skinny,' Laurence grinned.

'And what, may I ask, does it have to do with you?'

'Nothing. Just thought I'd tell you.'

'Well if you're waiting for me to admit to being scared half out my wits because I stupidly agreed to taking on something you pushed me into . . .'

'Oh, so that's the reason you're not eating.'

'That, and the size of this ridiculous menu,' Kirsten declared. 'I mean, who's ever heard of a five-course breakfast with wine?'

'I guess the people in New Orleans have,' Laurence laughed, setting aside his menu and picking up his coffee. 'So what are you going to have?'

'I'm still undecided,' Kirsten said and returned to the menu.

They were at Brennan's on Royal Street, a New Orleans restaurant famed for its breakfasts and as Laurence was heavily into breakfast meetings this was where they were going to meet Little Joe from the Independent

Studios who had been setting up things this end for the past couple of months.

The night before Kirsten, Laurence and the rest of the recce team had checked into the Richelieu Hotel after a gruelling flight from London and gone straight to bed. So far Kirsten had only seen the town from the car in from the airport, except Laurence had walked her through the French Quarter on their way here and though she had seen instantly how wonderfully the time-worn streets and beautiful filigree balconies would add to the story, the idea that she was in charge of capturing the city on film was daunting to say the least. In fact the further into production they were going the more nervous she was becoming. There were so many people on the team now, almost two hundred at the last count, and every single one of them was depending on her, and her alone, for direction. And the fact that most of them didn't think she was up to it added an edge to her nerves that, were it not for Laurence – and Jake – could easily turn her fear to terror, or worse, panic.

Still, just so long as she remembered to delegate, to listen to other people's ideas and stand by her own when she thought she was right she'd make it through. But what she wasn't going to make it through was this absurd breakfast.

'Tea,' she said to the waiter, handing him her menu. 'And you can take that stupid look off your face,' she told Laurence who was grinning.

'I'll have the Eggs Hussarde,' Laurence said passing over his menu. 'And more coffee.'

'But what about the other four courses?' Kirsten cried. 'Don't you want a nice Southern baked apple with double cream? Or what about the bananas sauted in butter, flambé-ed in rum and served up with a nice dollop of ice-cream? And surely you're not going to miss out on the brandy milk punch?'

'I've read the menu, thank you,' Laurence responded. 'Eggs Hussarde will do me fine. And I'm hungry,' he informed her, 'so don't think you can start picking at my plate.'

'I'll just have a forkful, see what it tastes like,' Kirsten said.

'Waiter! Waiter,' Laurence called, 'make that two Eggs Hussarde, will you?'

Smiling to herself Kirsten turned to look out the window letting the burble of morning diners and clatter of crockery wash over her as she tried not to contemplate the day ahead. A few moments of relaxation was what she needed before getting started on the mammoth task of conveying her requirements for the scenes they were doing here.

'Shame it's raining,' she commented a few minutes later, 'we could have sat out there in the courtyard. Pretty, isn't it?'

'Very. We'll be seeing a lot of courtyards over the next few days, the town's full of them and you know Ruby's made good use. By the way did you – Kirsten, what are you doing?'

'Having a cigarette,' she answered, putting one in her mouth and lighting it.

'You don't smoke.'

'I do now.'

'Put it out,' he said, grabbing it from her and stubbing it in the ashtray.

'Do you mind?' she protested.

'Kirsten, you don't even know how to smoke so stop making an idiot of yourself.'

'And stop behaving like you were my father. Now, I want to talk to you about the brothel scenes.'

'What about them?'

'Well, we still haven't really decided how far we should go with the nudity and seeing as we'll be meeting the cast this afternoon I thought we should make a decision so that we can put it to them.'

'Are you asking me for the go ahead on full frontal?'

'No. I don't want full frontal.'

'Tits and ass?'

Kirsten's lips pursed at the corners. 'You're so eloquent at times.'

'I know. But my guess is what you're worried about is how far we go with the sex?'

She nodded. 'The script calls for quite graphic and unusual positions. I was taking a look at it last night and I'm afraid we might lose something of the passion – and the comedy – if we don't show a certain amount.'

'So what amount are you suggesting?'

'Well to begin with I'd like to see breasts being fondled in the parlour of the brothel. Not a great deal, but enough to tell us that this really is a place where anything goes.'

'I got no problem with that. How are you intending to shoot it?'

'On the wide, I think. I'll see when we get there. Close ups are too much of a statement and I want it to be casual. Anyway, it's the bedroom scenes that are more important. How do you feel about a naked woman on all fours?'

Laurence's hand moved to his mouth as he rubbed his fingers along his jaw trying to disguise his smile. 'Depends which angle you're shooting her from,' he answered.

'Top. Camera's on the ceiling for the wide.'

'Why the ceiling?'

'It's a point of view shot. Rochette's up there getting his kicks – and his blackmail material.'

Laurence nodded. 'I'm with you. What happens to the woman?'

'Haven't you read the script? Ruby's idea was that she was dealing with two men at the same time. And both men enter into shot rather than start in shot.'

'That'll be tricky on the wide if they're bare-assed.'

'That's what I thought, so I'll have to go in for close-ups then cut back to the wide once they're in position. That'll mean a bit extra in the script to cover the cutaways.'

'Dialogue?'

'No. In fact I don't need to bother Ruby with it, I can just put the shots in myself. All I'm saying is there'll be a slight change of emphasis.'

'OK. I'll leave it up to you. Have you thought about how you're going to handle the big love scene between Anna and Jean-Paul yet?'

Kirsten nodded. 'Total nudity. I've discussed the lighting with Jake, the music should be real lazy blues in sync with their movements to give it a surreal, kind of balletic quality. Lots of close ups and small pans. Mouths on breasts, fingers spreading across legs and buttocks, tongues in mouths, you know the sort of thing.'

'Yeah, I got the picture,' Laurence murmured, his blue eyes watching her closely.

Kirsten didn't dare look up at him. The lowering of their voices, the intimacy that was moving around them was having a disturbing effect on her. 'A lot of passion, a real closeness, eyes locked together . . .' she went on quietly. 'Her legs around his waist, her hands in his hair . . . I'd like to get the moment of penetration in big close up on her. The whole thing will be very erotic, it should have a beauty and a grace that both characters find as overwhelming as the act itself. This isn't sex now, it's love . . . Real love . . .' She glanced up to find him staring down at his coffee, his face impenetrable. 'I guess,' she said softly, 'I'm going to draw on the way we used to make love.' The instant the words were out she froze. Of course that's what she'd been thinking, but not for a second had she intended to say it. 'I'm sorry,' she said hastily. 'I didn't mean that. What I meant was . . . Well, it's just sometimes you need to draw on your own experiences . . . Please, forget I said it.'

'It's forgotten,' Laurence said, getting to his feet. 'Hi, you must be Little Joe.'

Kirsten looked up at the short, mischievous looking man who was shaking Laurence's hand.

'That's me,' Joe said cheerfully. 'And you got to be Laurence. And the lovely lady here? I guess you got to be Kirsten?'

'Hello Joe,' she said, taking the hand he was holding out to her.

'Sorry I'm late,' Joe chuckled. 'Had to drive my kid to school. Anyways, you folks ordered yet? Oh, sure you have,' he said, as the waiter set down Kirsten and Laurence's eggs. 'I'll take one of them,' Joe told the waiter. 'And some coffee. So,' he went on, rubbing his hands together. 'How you liking N'Awlins?'

'We haven't seen much of it yet,' Kirsten answered, giving Joe her whole attention. She was stinging with embarrassment at what she'd said and right now couldn't bring herself to look at Laurence. In fact she was sorely tempted to give this little man, who had been performing miracles over here on their behalf, a hearty hug for his timely arrival.

'Well, I got plenty sights lined up for you to see,' Joe told them. 'Still working on the cops for the road closures, but it won't be a problem. Your girl Alison's faxed over the designs, I got the construction guys working on 'em as of today. Do you want we go over to the studios later? No, you're seeing the actors. OK, tomorrow'll be just fine. Got plenty of office space for you. Screening room's there, costume store, we got the lot. I thought right after breakfast we could go see Marie Laveau's tomb. What do you say? You can make a wish, see if the old voodoo queen'll make your dreams come true?'

'Sounds good,' Kirsten smiled, 'but we'd better take a look at the locations we're actually shooting before we start sight-seeing. The location manager gave us a list of what you've organized. We start with the Corn Stalk, yes?'

'Yep. It's just along the street here. That's gonna be your brothel, right?'

Kirsten nodded, wishing that the day's recce had a somewhat different structure. 'Tell me, Joe, have you discussed any of the brothel scenes with the cast?'

'No, ma'am. That little pleasure can be all yours.'

'Yes, well, let's just hope I make a better job of it than I did just now,' Kirsten remarked, throwing a quick glance at Laurence.

'Did you get the costings for the locations yet?' Laurence asked Joe, his eyes fixed firmly on Joe's face.

'Sure did. They're back at the studios, but I can get my girl to fax them over to your hotel.'

'Get her to fax them to London then the accountants can give me a full picture,' Laurence said.

An hour later Kirsten and Laurence wandered out on

to the street which was by now much busier than when they had arrived. Thankfully the rain had stopped, but the air was dank and smelled of seafood, salt and horse-droppings. Kirsten watched as a horse in a flowery straw hat passed them pulling an open carriage containing a party of three tourists and a wizened old driver.

'I'll bet Tom would love to ride in one of those,' she commented.

'Yeah, I guess he would,' Laurence answered tightly.

Kirsten frowned as she turned to look up at him. 'Are you still pissed off with me for what I said?' she hissed.

'Don't create a scene in the street,' Laurence muttered under his breath.

'I'm not creating a scene. I've apologized for saying it so can we – '

'I told you, it's forgotten,' he snapped.

'Then why are you looking like you just ate a lemon?'

Laurence's eyes were steely, but as Kirsten cocked her head to one side waiting for his response, a reluctant smile started to twitch at his lips. 'OK, you hit a raw nerve in there and you know it,' he said.

'And now I've got to pay for it?'

'Look, Kirstie, this isn't easy for either of us. We know how good we were together once and we'd both be liars if we . . .'

'OK, you guys,' Joe said, putting on his coat as he came out of the restaurant. 'Where we meeting up with the rest of your crew?'

'At the Corn Stalk,' Kirsten answered still looking at Laurence. Then suddenly they both started to laugh and Joe, not knowing what the hell he was laughing at, put his arms around them and started them off down the street.

The rest of the day turned out to be impossibly hectic

and fraught with confusion. The meeting with the actors was postponed due to the location and technical problems that were constantly arising and with more than forty people, all of whom had questions that Kirsten spent half her time winging the answers to and the other half silently cursing Laurence for the way he was undermining her, she felt at times that she might scream. He was so supremely confident in all he did, handled everyone with a skill that she knew she lacked, that she could almost hate him for his arrogance as much as she detested him for making her think of him when she should be concentrating on other things. But though he might be better at hiding it than she was she knew that he was thinking about her too.

The rain came and went, the sky was dismally grey and the mood of the crew was about as cheerful as the grisly masks in the voodoo museum. They broke off around six to go back to the hotel, shower and change and get warm before going off to City Park to take a look at Scout Island where they were to shoot most of the night scenes.

Kirsten had been in her room for no more than five minutes and was on the point of stripping off her wet clothes, when she heard a barely audible knock on the door. Since she and Laurence had exchanged words on the way back to the hotel she wasn't in the best of moods. So, hoping it was David, the assistant director, or Janet Bentley the know-it-all costume designer, she yanked open the door.

'Kirstie!'

Kirsten's eyes closed as she swallowed her words and started to smile. 'Tom,' she said, stooping down to his height as her heart brimmed with affection at the beaming smile on his face. By now she had met him several times and each time she saw him she could feel herself becoming more and more attached to him. What was more, he seemed to have taken a real liking to her too. He'd even sat with her on the plane until he got tired and went to curl up on Laurence's lap. 'What on earth are you doing here?' she said.

'Jane told me this was your room,' he answered. 'I can read numbers.' He pointed up to the figures on the door and said them backwards.

'Does Daddy know you're not in your room?' Kirsten asked him.

'We went on a steamboat today,' he answered. 'I pulled the chain that made the horn go.'

'So that was you making all the noise on the river, was it?' Kirsten teased, trying not to laugh at the way he so deftly managed to avoid questions he didn't want to answer.

He nodded. 'They said it was called a whistle, but Jane said I could call it a horn because it sounded like one.'

'Tom!' Jane called from the doorway of Laurence's suite. 'You told me you were going to the bathroom.'

Tom turned his wide blue eyes back to Kirsten. 'I can go to the bathroom on my own,' he told her earnestly.

'Can you?' Kirsten laughed, hugging him to her.

'Come on young man,' Jane said, holding out her hand. 'Daddy's about to get in the bath and I thought you were getting in with him.'

Scooping Tom up in her arms Kirsten carried him the short distance to his room. 'Did you enjoy your day?' she said to Jane.

Jane nodded excitedly and Kirsten was once again struck by how child-like Jane was when dealing with adults, yet how adult when dealing with Tom. It was a shame in a way, Kirsten was thinking to herself, that Jane had become so attached to Laurence and Tom when what she so obviously needed was to find someone of her own and become a real mother. She might really begin to blossom then.

'You're going out again later, aren't you?' Jane said.

Kirsten nodded. 'In about an hour.'

'I wish I could come, but it's too late for Tom and Laurence said we've got to keep out of the way of the crew.'

'Well, not all the time,' Kirsten smiled, knowing how uncomfortable Laurence had been at bringing Tom on this recce. But she knew too that nothing would have persuaded him to leave Tom at home – having been abandoned by one parent Laurence wanted to make sure that Tom was never in any doubt that his Daddy at least would be there at the end of every day.

'The girl downstairs has given us a list of lots of things to do,' Jane said. 'And Daddy's given you some dollars, hasn't he?' she said to Tom. 'So we're going to do some shopping in the French Market tomorrow.' She turned back to Kirsten. 'Is there anything I can get for you?'

'Oh, that's kind of you,' Kirsten said, slightly taken aback. 'Um, I'll give it some thought and let you know in the morning, OK? Maybe a couple of T-shirts or . . .' she broke off as the door opened wide to reveal a lovely little indoor courtyard filled with potted plants.

'Tom,' Laurence said, avoiding Kirsten's eyes. 'Are you taking a bath with me, 'cos if you are I want you in there now.'

'Off you go!' Kirsten said, dropping a kiss on Tom's cheek as she handed him over to Jane.

'I'll see you in the morning then,' Jane said to Kirsten.

'Can I put my steamboat in the bath, Daddy?' Tom asked climbing into Laurence's arms as Jane disappeared inside.

'Sure you can.'

'It hasn't got a horn,' Tom told Kirsten solemnly.

'Never mind,' Kirsten said, 'I'm sure Daddy can find you one.'

Laurence grinned. 'Don't suppose you'd care to join us?' he said with a sardonic lift of his eyebrows.

'Oh yes!' Tom cried.

Kirsten was staring at Laurence, so amazed by what he'd said that she couldn't help wondering if he actually realized he'd said it.

'I want to have a bath with Kirsten,' Tom declared. 'Please, Daddy, can I have a bath with Kirsten?'

Laurence turned to look at him. 'No, I don't think so, soldier.'

'But you said . . .'

'I know what I said. It was a joke, Tom.'

Tom turned his eyes back to Kirsten. 'And not one of Daddy's better ones,' she remarked.

Laurence grinned.

'You don't understand,' Helena said, rocking the bed as she turned on her side to face him. 'It's not that I don't want to see you, it's just that I've given Kirsten my word.'

'So Kirsten rules your life?' Campbell said sourly.

'At the moment, yes. She and Laurence stood by me . . .'

'Because I gave them no choice.'

'Dermott, you had a choice when it came to printing that story. You needn't have done it.'

— 280 —

'I've explained that,' he said. 'I wrote it just after the last time I saw you. I was bloody furious and if I didn't get the movie then you weren't going to either. But I've made it up to you now, you're still on it, your side of the story's been printed, so let's forget it, eh?'

'OK, but I've got to stand by my word.'

Campbell laughed but his eyes darkened with lust as Helena lifted herself up and knelt over him. 'You've been here three times since you gave Kirsten your word,' he said, taking her breasts in his hands.

'I know,' she said, lowering her head to watch his hands. 'But this time has to be the last.'

'That's what you said before. So what are you doing here now?'

'Don't you like what I'm doing?' she murmured, brushing her hips tantalizingly over his.

'I like it very much, but that doesn't answer my question.'

'They're in New Orleans so they won't get to find out,' she smiled, rolling lazily on to her back and taking the sheets with her.

Campbell propped his head on one hand and as his eyes swept the long length of her body he felt his heart swell with emotion.

There were times when he only had to look at a woman, any woman, to want to screw her, Kirsten Meredith was proof of that, but anyone would want to screw the Kirstie Doll. Not everyone would want to screw Ruby Collins though, but even she had got him so worked up he'd been willing to suffer any amount of humiliation, and if he was honest with himself it wasn't only because he wanted the job. But with Helena it was different. He couldn't say why exactly, it just was. That first night they'd spent together had been something special. It wasn't that he hadn't wanted to screw her, Jesus, he'd wanted it more than anything, but at the same time he'd wanted to share an experience with her that he'd never had with any other woman. So, they'd just held each other, stroked each other, kissed and talked and slept. It was pretty weird, but he guessed it was the closest thing to making love he'd ever come across. Now of course they'd done the real thing, several times, and wild cat that she was, making love to her was just that – love. At least he assumed that was what it was because he didn't want to leave her after, neither did he want to roll over and sleep. He wanted to listen to her talk, watch her smile, feel himself sinking into those huge brown eyes that were sometimes so intense they were frightening. And only with her had he ever bared his soul, telling her things about himself he'd always thought he would rather die than have anyone know. Whatever was happening between them it was pretty good and it was something he really wanted to hang on to. But that train he'd always imagined himself on, the one that was going to hit the buffers with only him on board, it was still running out of control and it was his resentment of Kirsten Meredith that was fuelling it. Somehow he had to deal with that, but just to think of her and the way she was destroying him when it was supposed to be him destroying her just caused the train to run all the faster. But Helena was with him now, Helena the witch who was changing his life . . .

He watched his fingers as he moved them to the join of her legs and smiled at her readiness to receive him. 'I want more for us than this,' he whispered, turning to look at her.

She chuckled softly then caught her breath as his

fingers started to enter her. 'What more is there?' she groaned.

When he didn't answer she opened her eyes to look at him. He was looking down at her with an expression of uncertainty that brought a smile to her lips even as it tightened her heart. One minute so confident, the next so unsure. She knew now what power she had over him, if only she'd realized it sooner. It was as though her pain had locked into his, pulling him to her so that at times she felt she could control him completely. Yet couldn't he do the same to her? They were two of a kind, life's lost souls, so at odds with the world and the people in it that half the time they were reaching out for solace and the other half they were fighting a fate that seemed to want no part of them. She knew that he was trying to make something in his life good and he was using her to do it, but his resentment of Kirsten had reached irrational depths and Helena knew how much that frightened him. He held Kirsten responsible for the loss of his best friend, for the loss of a new beginning, for throwing him back to Dyllis Fisher. Now Kirsten was going to take her, Helena, away too, and Helena couldn't help wondering if he would want her so much were it not Kirsten who was threatening to come between them.

Her eyes searched the troubled lines of his face, a face that was handsome in its way, yet ravaged. There were times when the exceptional beauty of his smile could melt her heart, when the tenderness of his body could bring tears to her eyes. She had seen the man behind the bitterness, she had touched him and found him to be as vulnerable and as lonely as she. So long without love that maybe neither of them understood it any more. Perhaps they never had nor never would, but wasn't what they had worth building on? Should she really allow Kirsten to take it from them? Kirsten, whose fate was so wrapped up in Laurence's that there was no question they would find each other again. Why should she, Helena, remain in her world of loneliness isolated from the man whose confusion and pain ran as deep as her own, when Kirsten and Laurence were destined for a happiness she and Dermott might never otherwise find?

As Campbell's mouth closed over hers Helena wrapped her arms around him, pulling him close. He had told her so many times that he loved her. She had no idea if it was true, but knew she would never tire of hearing it. And even if it was just a pretence, what was there to stop it becoming a reality? Only Kirsten. Kirsten and the promise she had exacted. And why should they allow their lives to be governed by a woman who had everything?

For a moment Helena tensed as the jealousy flared. Kirsten had no doubts about her feelings for Laurence, she didn't know what it was like to be with a man who felt so right one minute and so wrong the next. She had no idea what it was like to be so desperate that she would accept a man's lies as truth rather than have him leave her. She wouldn't even begin to understand what it was like to be so consumed by guilt and envy and gratitude and love the way she, Helena, was for Kirsten.

Would Kirsten ever lie in Laurence's arms thinking about me the way I'm lying here thinking about her? Helena asked herself. *She has no idea what she does to people's lives, the way she takes them over and commands things they might not want to give.* Kirsten was as easy to hate as she was to love. She inspired as much envy as she did loyalty. Helena herself had been swept up in the magic of her, had been instrumental in getting Kirsten to where she was now, but what did she, Helena, stand to gain from it? OK, she had the part of Marie Laveau, but it wasn't the lead role and neither was it a role by which the success of the film hung. And if she was honest with herself what did she really care about the film now she had Dermott? He would be much longer in her life than a few minutes of screen time. So should she use what influence she had to stop him avenging himself on Kirsten? Or should she just play dumb and let him get on with it? If the movie was a failure and Kirsten fell flat on her face she'd still have Laurence. Just like the last time life had dealt her a blow she'd had Paul. There was always someone there for Kirsten, she'd never suffered alone the way Helena had, so why should she, Helena, concern herself with Kirsten now?

– 17 –

'I can't believe you just said that!' Kirsten yelled.

'Then I'll say it again,' Laurence yelled back. 'If you don't pull your finger out and give the crew proper direction then we might just as well pack up and go home now!'

'So it's all my fault!'

'You're the fucking director!'

'Oh, is that so? And there was me thinking it was you . . . I mean, you spend more time talking to my assistants than I do . . .'

'They come to me because you're not making yourself plain. They need information to do their jobs and you're not giving it to them.'

'Because they won't bloody well listen to me.'

'Then make them!' he roared. 'If you let them run circles around you now then how the hell do you think you're going to cope . . .'

'I'll cope! I'll cope just fine thank you very much, but would you like to tell me precisely how I deal with that pompous prat of a first assistant who *you* employed and who goes behind my back at every turn telling everyone how fucking useless I am?'

'Did it ever occur to you he might have a point?'

Kirsten's eyes blazed into his. 'Do you think he has a point?' she said bitingly.

'As a matter of fact I do. You're useless at handling the crew and the crew doesn't consist only of Jake Butler, though the rest of them might be forgiven for thinking so.'

'Jake is working *with* me. The others are working against me . . .'

'Then get them on your side. Stop putting up with the way they're treating you and stand up for yourself. I'm not nurse-maiding you through this, Kirsten. I've got my own problems to deal with and I expect you to deal with yours. If you're not up to it then I suggest you say so now before we go any further.'

'Do you have any argument with my approach?'

'No.'

'Do you understand what I'm trying to achieve?'

'Yes.'

'Then if you understand there doesn't seem to be any reason why everyone else doesn't, except for the fact they don't want to.'

'Then fucking well make them! How many more times do I have to say it?'

'All right! All right! I'll sit every head of department down individually and go over the script with them a page at a time and . . .'

'Are you telling me you haven't done that already?'

'Of course I've damned well done it and I'm getting results, it's just that it's like pulling teeth. They're all professionals, they'll come up with the goods in the end, but they're doing their utmost to undermine my confidence. Like coming here complaining to you that I've requested too many Walk Ons when the size of shot warrants the number I've asked for.'

'And what about costume? Janet tells me Moyna's costume is going to clash badly with the set out at the plantation house . . .'

'It's supposed to!' Kirsten almost screamed. 'I've told her that a thousand times. The lighting's going to clash with it too, but did Jake come here whingeing to you? No, he accepts what I say and if he doesn't we discuss it between us.'

'Then you'd better find a way of working your charm on the others or you and I are going to seriously fall out.'

'Well thank you for your support, Laurence. I don't suppose it's once occurred to you to tell any of them who come creeping here to you that you might just agree with what I'm doing? Or that you understand it and can't see why they don't? I don't imagine it's even entered your head to tell any of them that *you* believe in me, that you have confidence in my ability. But no, it wouldn't have, would it, because you don't? In fact you deeply regret ever asking me . . .'

'Stop putting words into my mouth!' he barked.

'Words that you don't have the guts to utter because you've got – '

'Words that are bullshit and you know it. I have every confidence in you. I know you can do this, I know you're going to make a terrific movie.'

'Then just what the hell is all this about? What's really bugging you, Laurence, because if anyone's running me round in circles right now, it's you! You criticize every damned thing I say or do. You patronize me in front of Little Joe.'

'All right! You want what's really bugging me then you got it,' he yelled. 'I don't like the way you're trying to get back with me through my son. That's what's really bugging me!'

Kirsten had already drawn breath to answer, but the shock of what he'd said for the moment rendered her speechless. 'Well,' she said, shaking her head in disbelief, 'you certainly know how to hit where it hurts.'

'Isn't that what you're trying to do, making up to Tom?' he growled, but she could see that he was already regretting his outburst.

'If you're worried about your son . . .'

'It's not Tom I'm worried about, for Christ's sake! It's you! Do you think I've forgotten what you did . . .' he stopped suddenly as Kirsten's face turned white.

'Go on say it,' she challenged. 'Finish what you . . .'

'Kirstie, I'm sorry. It wasn't what I meant. It came out wrong.'

'It was what you meant. You're afraid I'll hurt him, aren't you?'

'Of course I'm not. Jesus Christ if I thought that do you think I'd let you anywhere near him'

'Then why did you say it?'

'I told you, it came out wrong. What I meant to say

was that I know how much . . . . Oh shit!' he groaned, starting to turn away, 'this is all coming out wrong, but I don't want you kidding yourself into thinking that Tom is the child we lost.'

'You really believe I'm doing that?' Kirsten said in a voice that was as incredulous as it was quiet.

Laurence dashed a hand distractedly through his hair. She was standing so close, too close. He could feel the power of her reaching into him and right now all he wanted was to pull her into his arms. 'I don't know,' he said. 'No, I don't think that. Christ, I don't know what I am thinking half the time . . .'

'Then maybe it's time you got yourself sorted out,' Kirsten said.

As he turned back to face her the door suddenly flew open and seeing Kirsten Tom ran excitedly into her arms.

With her eyes still on Laurence's Kirsten kissed the top of Tom's head, set him down again then without another word, she turned and walked out of the room.

She didn't see Laurence again until the following afternoon when Little Joe came to drive them out to Honey Island – one of the largest of the Louisiana swamps. By then Laurence had tried several times to speak to her, to apologize for what he'd said, and though Kirsten had told him it didn't matter she refused to see him on the grounds that she had too much work to get through. It was true, she did, but she knew too that if they discussed it any more he'd only end up hurting her again.

Jake, Alison, David, the first assistant and Bob the sound man were the only ones accompanying them on the recce since it was unlikely they would use the location – it was just that Kirsten wanted to see it before making up her mind. One of the location managers had waxed lyrical about the swamp's potential as a setting for the voodoo ceremonies, but Little Joe didn't agree. Unless they had an endless amount of time and wanted to risk losing lives in the murky depths of the rivers and bayous then they'd be crazy to use it, he told them. The location manager had conceded that there might be problems, but insisted that with careful planning they were surmountable. Already Kirsten doubted it for the simple reason that travelling outside the New Orleans Parish to St. Tammany was just not feasible. It was going to eat into the schedule in a way they simply couldn't afford. Apart from which, Scout Island, Joe's find in City Park was, as far as she was concerned, a perfect location for the ritual. However, for the time being she was going to keep an open mind until she had actually seen the swamp.

It was one-thirty by the time they arrived at the Indian Village Landing where Dr Wagner, the ecologist who lived on the swamp, was waiting for them with his boat, but the darkening sky made it seem more like dusk.

As they climbed aboard, seating themselves along one of the two benches that stretched back to back down the centre of the boat, Kirsten was gazing across the water towards the dense, towering cypress trees that, to her, already seemed to resent the intrusion. There was no sign of the sun peering through the blanket of dismal grey cloud, there was no wind either. Everything was perfectly still, even the river currents seemed eerily motionless.

Dr Wagner handed out blankets to put over their knees and with Laurence at one side of her and Jake the other, Kirsten folded her hands into her lap and resolved not to think any more about Laurence or what was happening between them. The fact that they were moving towards a hiatus in their personal relationship couldn't be denied and obviously he was as aware of it as she was. Quite how or when things were going to blow up was impossible to say, but what frightened Kirsten was the lack of professionalism they were both in danger of showing. She laughed bitterly to herself at that. Laurence would never allow his feelings to get the better of him in public, it was only she who was in danger of that.

They started out down river, travelling at quite a speed to get to the bayou the location manager had set his heart on. Half a dozen or so hunters who worked with Dr Wagner and were just along for the ride, were sitting on the bench behind them, and as the boat started to slow their expert eyes began picking out the wild life secreted in the copious profusion of tupelo gum, maple and cypress trees that rose somberly and sinisterly from the stagnant water. As they pointed out great-blue herons, nutria, signs of beaver and water turkey, Kirsten's eyes were fixed on the greasy film of brilliant green duckweed half-dreading and half-hoping to see an alligator rise from the muddied depths.

Suddenly it seemed to turn very cold. Kirsten looked up at the impenetrable sky then slowly lowered her eyes to the grey Spanish moss hanging from the tress like the fraying tangled briar of old men's beards. They had turned into the bayou by now and the gnarled cypress knees protruding from the water made progress as slow as the decaying, dying gum trees that reached out towards them. They stopped for a moment to watch a racoon, high in a tree, then moved on towards the depths of the morbidly silent bayou.

Kirsten leaned forward to rest her arms on the rail.

She was aware that Laurence was watching her and had moved because she no longer wanted to feel the pressure of his body next to hers. Her lips tightened as she experienced a stinging exasperation at the way their minds and bodies were in such conflict. With the one they resisted each other with a determination and defiance that the other made a total mockery of. When at last she turned to look at him, steeling herself against him, her entire heart turned over. It was impossible to read his expression, but his dark blue eyes looked so deeply into hers she felt he might be reading her mind. Neither of them smiled, they simply looked at each other, until Kirsten returned her eyes to the grim splendour of the darkening swamp.

The constriction in her throat prevented her from answering when Jake asked her a question, but, as his hand slid into hers she turned to him and managed to smile.

'You OK,' he whispered.

Kirsten nodded.

'Pretty bloody spooky out here, isn't it?' he said.

At last they reached the spot the location manager had discovered. There was no doubt in anyone's mind that, were they able to do it, the voodoo sequence would be stupendous set on this bleak little island that seemed so remote from the world. However, though they disembarked to take a look around, both Kirsten and Laurence were agreed that to get the crew, cast, equipment and props out here at night, was not only verging on the impossible, it would be down right dangerous even to try. Apart from the risk of someone falling into the reptile infested swamp, there were any number of other hazards, like snakes falling from the cobwebbed density of Spanish moss, or wild boar making a sudden and unprovoked charge, or even, as unlikely as it was, the danger of coming face to face with a black bear.

'It's a shame,' Kirsten said as she and Laurence broke away from the group and wandered towards a tumbledown shack set in the trees, 'we could have used this for the murder sequence as well as the voodoo.'

Laurence smiled. 'Just what I was thinking,' he said.

They walked around to the back of the hut and stood for a moment looking out at the mesmerizing stillness of the crowding trees and undergrowth.

'God, it's like the end of the earth out here, isn't it?' Kirsten whispered with a shiver.

She heard Laurence laugh and turned to look up at him. His eyes were unfocused on the distance, his jaw was set in a way that suggested he might be angry. She watched him for a moment or two then was about to turn away when he said,

'I want you, Kirsten. I want you very much, you know that don't you?'

She stopped, but instead of the joy she had always imagined she would feel at hearing those words she felt only anger. 'And is that supposed to make everything all right?' she answered tightly. 'Is that supposed to excuse the way you're treating me?'

He turned to look at her. 'No,' he said. 'But I accept that it's a problem I have to deal with. But I want you to know that from now on there'll never be any question about my support and that whatever relationship you have with Tom .... Well, that's between you and Tom.'

'It isn't Tom who's the problem,' she retorted, 'it's his father.'

'I just said, I know I've got some things to sort out. But Jesus Christ, Kirstie, you're driving me crazy, can't you see that?'

'So what am I supposed to do, stop living?'

His eyes darkened. 'Why do you have to be so damned difficult about this?' he growled.

'What do you expect me to do, throw myself at your feet and say take me, Laurence? Please, Laurence, do whatever you want with me. Well don't hold your breath!'

As she made to walk away he grabbed her hand and turned her back to face him. 'We haven't finished this,' he said savagely. 'Now may not be the time, but we're going to have this out the minute we get back.'

'I've got other things to do.'

'Then cancel them,' he said through his teeth and letting her go he turned back towards the boat.

Kirsten re-seated herself between Jake and Laurence. The emotional and physical tension between her and Laurence was now moving beyond her control and she was so damned furious with him that she felt sure the others must sense it. How dare he treat her this way, as if all he had to do was crook his finger and she'd come running? Never mind that in that moment of physical contact she had felt such a desire that it had swept through her like a fire. What difference did it make that she longed to abandon herself to him and have him do anything and everything he wanted? She'd rather roast in hell than give in to him now. Just who the hell did he think he was, some kind of Lochinvar who expected a woman to drop everything just because he had the urge? Well she'd damned well show him just what she thought of that!

An hour later they were in the hotel lobby collecting their keys.

'I'd like to see you in my room. Now,' Laurence said to Kirsten and turned away as he saw the fury flicker in

– 294 –

her eyes. He knew she wouldn't argue while everyone was in earshot.

They rode up in the lift with the rest of the crew neither looking at the other, though Kirsten was aware of Jake's confusion. He mouthed something to her, but she didn't catch what it was and not wanting to encourage him she looked away. When they reached the third floor everyone got out with the exception of Kirsten and Laurence. The door closed again and they continued in silence to the fourth floor where Laurence stood back for Kirsten to walk out ahead of him.

She waited until they were in the beautifully furnished sitting room of his suite then rounded on him. 'If you think you're laying so much as one finger on me,' she yelled, 'then you can damned well think . . .'

'Jane, could you take Tom downstairs for a while please,' Laurence said calmly and Kirsten swung round to see their mystified faces staring up at her from Tom's toy corner.

Kirsten kept her head averted as Jane took Tom by the hand and led him from the room, pursing her lips to stop herself laughing.

'Try not to shout at me in front of Tom again,' Laurence said when the door closed behind them.

'I didn't know he was there,' Kirsten responded.

'Evidently.' He strolled over to the large, open brick fireplace. 'Now, you were saying, if I thought I was going to lay one finger on you . . .'

'Don't take that tone with me,' she seethed, 'it drives me nuts!'

'Then what tone would you like me to take?'

'None. I just want to get out of here.'

Laurence watched her closely, knowing that if he had any sense left in his head he'd let her go now. But she looked so goddamned beautiful standing there trying to hide the confusion she was feeling that his desire to fold her against him was too strong. If he could just touch her, just feel her for a moment. But no, that was madness, he'd never be able to stop himself...

'OK. Go,' he said.

Kirsten's surprise showed as she eyed him suspiciously. 'All right,' she said, and turning away she started across the room. When she reached the door she suddenly spun round. 'I thought we were going to have this out!' she declared.

Despite the turmoil inside him Laurence started to grin.

'Don't do that!' she cried.

'Do what?'

'Laugh like that! I'm serious, Laurence.'

'So am I. You want to go, I'm not stopping you.'

She glared at him and his smiled widened.

'You think all you've got to do is flash that damned smile of yours and I'll tear off all my clothes, don't you?' she said.

His eyebrows raised with interest. 'Is that what you're thinking every time I smile at you?' he said.

'Laurence, I'm warning you.'

'You are?'

'Yes.'

'OK. So, what are we going to do about this?'

'About what?'

'Your desire to take off all your clothes.'

'Laurence!' she almost screamed, and to her fury she very nearly laughed. 'Look, you're the one who *ordered* me to come here. You're the one who wanted to have this out. So, I'm waiting.'

Tearing his eyes away from her Laurence turned to

look out of the window. He was going to give in to this, he knew it. The strength of the desire building inside him was so demanding it was driving into his every muscle. With a fierceness he was in danger of showing he tried to push from his mind the near overwhelming need to feel his lips on hers, to take the exquisite weight of her breasts in his hands, but he couldn't. He could almost feel the confining warmth of her thighs wrapping themselves around him, the unbearably sweet join in her legs that could arouse him like nothing else ever had. Dear God, it was as though the taste of her was in his mouth already, the heat of her was closing around his genitals. How the hell was she doing this to him? She wasn't even touching him yet he was on fire for her. But it was lust, nothing more, nothing less and one way of conquering lust was to give into it. Just this one time, then he would have it out of his system. Somewhere in the depths of his mind he knew he was crazy, that as soon as he'd done it once he'd want to do it again and again, but as he turned to look at her and saw the way her hardened nipples were pushing through her blouse the unbearable sensuousness of her reached so far inside him that he knew he was beyond reasoning with it.

He moved towards her. Kirsten watched him, rooted by the sudden power that emanated from him. It pulled so hard through her body that she daren't move for fear of what she might do. Her chest was so tight she could barely breathe, the fire between her legs was becoming so intense it was as though her very soul was turning into a furnace of desire.

'You bastard,' she faltered, as he reached her. 'You bastard . . .' but the words were lost in his mouth as his lips came down hard on hers. He thrust her back against the door and as he reached out to turn the key it was as though the force of his desire suddenly blazed out of control.

For a moment Kirsten was dazed, but as his tongue found hers and he jerked her against him her hands flew to his hair. He pressed his groin to hers, grinding savagely against her, then he was tearing at her coat, pushing it down over her shoulders, ripping the buttons from her shirt and releasing her breasts.

'Laurence no,' she gasped. 'No . . .'

He tore himself away. 'You want me to stop?' he growled. 'Are you telling me you don't want this too?'

'Yes! No . . .' She looked into his stormy face. 'Oh God,' she groaned. Why couldn't she find it in her to resist him when it all felt so wrong? 'Laurence hold me,' she whispered. 'Please, just hold me.'

He drew her back into his arms, resting her head on his shoulder. The violence of his passion was still quaking in his body, frightening him almost as much as it was her. After a while he pulled back and looked down into her face. Then his hands moved back to her breasts, teasing her nipples. Her eyes closed and her head fell back against the door.

He was still watching her as he eased first her coat then her shirt down over her shoulders. Then reaching round behind her he unclasped her bra leaving her naked to the waist. At last he lowered his eyes to her breasts and as he did his desire caught him so hard that for a moment he thought he was going to lose control again. 'Look at you,' he groaned. 'Jesus Christ, just look at you,' and Kirsten's knees almost buckled as he took first one then the other nipple deep into his mouth.

Her head fell forward and as her hands moved into

his hair his mouth and his fingers tightened on her nipples.

After a while he drew himself up and looked down into her eyes. His lips were moist, his hands were moving to her waist. 'I'm going to fuck you, Kirsten,' he murmured. 'I'm going to fuck you so hard . . . Do you want me inside you, Kirstie? Do you want to feel me pushing right into you?'

'You know I do,' she whispered.

All the time he was talking he was pushing her leggings and her panties down over her hips. His mouth was touching hers, his voice was vibrating in her throat. Then he was kissing her again. His lips moulded around hers, sucking them and biting them, his tongue sought hers circling it, drawing it into his mouth and his hands came up around her face pulling her even closer. Then he was moving to his knees, sliding her clothes down over her legs, slipping off her ankle boots and pulling everything from her until she was totally naked.

'Oh my God!' she gasped as he lifted her leg to his shoulder and buried his face in her. 'Laurence! Oh God, Laurence, Laurence!'

Using his tongue and his lips he teased her and toyed with her, pulling her deep into his mouth and holding her wide with his fingers. He kept doing it, harder and faster until he felt the first contractions of her orgasm. Then suddenly he was on his feet, his mouth back on hers as he stripped away his own clothes. He was so hard now he could hardly bear it. His readiness was so exquisite it was agony. He pressed her against the door, lowered his hand to his penis and guided himself through her moistness to enter her.

Kirsten clung to him, twisting her fingers in his hair and biting his neck as she felt him filling her and filling her pushing her wider and wider joining himself to the deepest part of her. He pulled back then pushed into her again. It felt as though he was sliding into her forever. His lips were still on hers, his hands held her buttocks, pressing her to him. Then suddenly he jerked himself into her so hard she cried out. He did it again and again.

'Oh, Laurence,' she choked, lifting a leg to draw him in further. He scooped her up in his arms and carried her to the table. As he set her down he withdrew himself, turned her over then plunged into her again. His stomach was pressed hard up against her buttocks as he repeatedly pumped himself into her.

'Is this how deep you want me?' he muttered savagely in her ear. 'You want me right in you, like this?'

'Oh my God!' she sobbed as he ground himself against her while pushing a hand beneath her to rub his fingers over the most sensitive part of her. With his other hand he grabbed her hair and pulled her head back to kiss her.

'Don't come,' he growled. 'Don't come yet.'

'I can't help it,' she gasped.

He pulled away, lifted her up and folded her in his arms. Minutes later they were on the sofa. He was kneeling in front of her, her legs were on his shoulders. Then they were on the floor, he was in her mouth, between her breasts then back inside her. He rolled on to his back and gasping for breath she lowered herself on to him arching her spine, pushing her breasts to his mouth. He took them, squeezing them biting them, then suddenly his hand lashed out, slapping them hard. He slapped them again and again, watching them swing over her ribcage as she groaned and writhed in unimaginable ecstasy. Then she was riding him, pumping herself wildly up and down on him and sobbing as he circled his thumb between her legs while with his other hand he continued to slap her.

Only just did he manage to stifle her scream as the first throes of her orgasm exploded and pushing his tongue deep into her mouth he turned her onto her back and covered her with the full length of his body.

'Hold me,' he groaned. 'Kirstie, hold me!'

Her arms closed around his neck as her legs tightened about his waist. He crushed his lips brutally against hers, sucking on them and drawing her tongue deep into his mouth.

It was as though every nerve in her body was alive with flaming sensation, the ruthless thrusting of his hips pushed him to her very core. The blood rushed through her veins and she gasped as another tumultuous shudder erupted around him. It was as though every part of him was inside her. Still his lips were on hers, but she could feel them tightening as his body started to convulse. His arms pushed under her shoulders, holding her tightly to him as she met each thrust of his hips with her own. He had brought her to such a pitch she might scream if he stopped even for a moment. But he didn't, he continued to drive into her, on and on, taking them both to the brink of unparallelled frenzy. She opened her legs wider and he pressed himself down onto the part of her that only seconds later caused the full intensity of her orgasm to break around him in great juddering and relentless waves as, with a turbulent groan of agony, his seed started to spurt wildly into her.

He pushed his face into her shoulder as the spasms racked his whole body. He felt her legs slip down over his own and pushed into her again. A quick memory flickered in his mind of the time Pippa had made him think of Kirsten while he made love to her. It was the best he had ever known with Pippa, but God help him, it had been nothing like this. Nothing had ever been like this.

It was a long time later that he lifted his head to look down into her face. He smiled when he saw how dazed she still looked and took her bruised lips gently between his own. Their bodies were still joined, the dying turbulence continuing to grip them. Then Kirsten opened her eyes and as she looked up at him his heart tightened at the lazy, sensuous smile she gave him. He kissed her again and again, holding himself up on his elbows and languidly rotating his hips.

'Are you beat?' he murmured.

Kirsten looked up into his eyes, her own still clouded with the aftermath of his love-making. Again a smile crossed her full lips for they were both only too aware of the way he was beginning to harden again.

'No, but you are,' she whispered as he ran his thumb along her jaw.

He started to smile. Only with her had he ever achieved an erection twice like this, so it was only her who would have understood his question. He pushed his hands beneath her, holding her very close as he rolled onto his back. By now he was filling her again, responding to the way she was stretching herself across him so that he could take her swollen nipples into his mouth. He caressed them gently with his tongue, while curving his hands under her buttocks as he rocked himself languorously up and down.

It was a long, long time before either of them reached orgasm again, but this time, as their bodies wrapped around each others, their movements were consumed by a tenderness that was so transcending and in its way so much more powerful than the urgency that had taken them before. In the end it was Laurence who finished it for them both, by then Kirsten was too weakened by the force of so many emotions and so much sensation to do anything more than hold him.

They were still lying in each others arms, their eyes closed their breathing now steady when the door handled rattled.

'Shit! It's Tom!' Laurence cried, sitting bolt upright.

'Oh my God!' Kirsten gasped, somehow finding the energy to spring to her feet. 'Quick, where are my clothes?'

'Daddy! Daddy!' Tom called out.

'Coming,' Laurence shouted, trying to haul on his jeans at the same time as attempting to get his arms into his shirt.

Kirsten was laughing as she too frantically fought her way into her clothes.

After a delay that even Jane in her innocence would see through Laurence finally pulled open the door. 'Daddy!' Tom cried, bursting into the room. 'I'm going to float in a bubble and drive a crane.'

'You are?' Laurence said not without irony.

'Yes. And there are lots of other things to play with too, aren't there, Jane?'

'We've just been told about the Children's Museum,' Jane explained and the way her eyes were avoiding both Kirsten's and Laurence's it was clear that she knew exactly what had been happening. 'I thought I'd take Tom there tomorrow,' she said.

'That'll be nice for you, Tom,' Kirsten smiled, looking down at his upturned face.

'Yeah, well . . .' Laurence said.

Kirsten looked at him. He still had his hand on the

open door, but from the way he was nodding, almost pointing with his head, Kirsten thought he was trying to tell her something. 'Um, well,' she said, glancing behind her.

'I got you some things in the market,' Jane said to Kirsten.

Kirsten frowned her confusion, her eyes moving between Laurence and Jane.

'Do you remember I asked you if you wanted anything?' Jane said. 'I wasn't sure what you wanted . . .' She stopped, realizing that Laurence and Kirsten were trying to communicate over her head. 'Um, I'll go and get them,' she said. 'It's just a couple of New Orleans T-shirts . . .' and she disappeared into the little courtyard to go into her own room.

'What's the matter?' Kirsten said through her teeth.

'Your bag,' Laurence answered in the same way.

Kirsten looked down then hurriedly tucked her bra deeper into the files protruding from her holdall. When she looked up again Laurence was laughing. Tom was gazing up at her curiously, then Jane returned with the T-shirts.

Still trying to hide her own laughter Kirsten took the T-shirts, muttered a thank you and said, 'Well, I'd better be getting back to my room,' and giving Tom's hair a quick ruffle she added, 'See you later,' and left.

When Kirsten got back to her room amongst many other messages there was one from Alison asking her if she could go out to Little Joe's and take a look at the model that had been done of the ballroom. There was a note pushed under her door from Jake telling her that if she was going out to Joe's studios he'd like to come with her. When Kirsten called his room he answered straight away and she told him to meet her down in the lobby in fifteen minutes. She needed to take a quick shower and try to collect herself after what had happened.

In fact, by the time she went downstairs to meet Jake, she was still so dazed that were it not for the way her muscles were aching she might have thought it was all a dream. She just didn't know what to make of it. There was no doubt that the pleasure they took in each other's bodies was every bit as intense, if not even more intense, than it had ever been, but she wished she knew what had been going on in Laurence's head. Or, more to the point, what he was thinking now. They'd have to talk about it for there was no way they could carry on as though nothing had happened and she felt herself almost physically shrink from the very idea. Was this them getting started again, she wondered, or had it just been something they had to get out of their systems? Dear God, no, it couldn't be the latter for if it were it was going to be impossible for her to continue. But of course it wasn't the latter, the way they'd made love the second time made that more than plain. He'd held her in such a way it was as though he'd never wanted to let her go and she'd seen the tenderness in his eyes as he'd watched her, smiling and teasing and playing with her the way he always used to. It was as though in some ways they had never been parted for the knowledge of each other's bodies and each other's needs had come so readily they might have made love only the day before.

So why, she asked herself as she and Jake rode in a taxi through the neat grid of the French Quarter, was she feeling so uncertain and so wary?

Trying to push her misgivings from her mind she gazed out at the shadowy dusk and noticed the ominous patterns it cast over the passing streets. A strange feeling of unease crept down her spine making her skin prickle. It was odd, she reflected to herself, how she hadn't really noticed it before, but there was something, well something unusual about New Orleans. It wasn't something she could put her finger on and perhaps before she'd just been too busy to notice, but now she came to think about it she wasn't at all sure she liked this place. It was peculiar the way people dressed in curious costumes when it wasn't even Mardi Gras. And though the warmth of Southern hospitality couldn't be denied, that too, now she mulled it over in her mind, made her uncomfortable. It was as though there were deep, dark depths to the City that breathed a dissolute and immoral air into the streets. As though everyone nurtured a secret and watched you with eyes that both mocked and enticed. The decaying beauty of delicate wrought iron balconies, hidden courtyards with exotic plants and alabaster fountains, the hypnotic sounds of indolent jazz trumpets were all like a trap set to lure the innocent into an exclusive and infernal nether world.

She turned to Jake. 'Do you like it here?' she said.

'I love it,' he answered without hesitation. 'It's weird, but I love it. What about you?'

Kirsten shrugged. 'I'm not sure,' she said. 'I think it frightens me.'

Then suddenly she remembered that Helena came from New Orleans and for one horrible moment it seemed to create an unbridgeable gulf between them. But that was ridiculous, she told herself firmly. She knew Helena almost as well as she knew herself and there was very definitely nothing sinister about Helena. But nevertheless with the way Laurence had been with her that afternoon and the unsettling realization that Helena was from a culture of which she, Kirsten, knew nothing, it made her feel as though she was drifting on the outside of a world that she could see but not touch.

God, she hated feeling this way, but suddenly her head fell forward and she started to laugh. Wasn't it the way she always felt, right deep down inside? It was called paranoia. She'd hoped that her analysis had got her over these fears, but obviously it hadn't, or at least not altogether. But she'd let her maddening insecurities destroy her and Laurence once, so she just better get herself together now because there was no way she was going to let that happen again. They'd talk later, probably over dinner and she would allow the glow she felt inside to control the way she handled things, not the niggardly, persistent doubts that so expertly managed to submerge her in a vacuum of despicable, intolerable insecurity.

It was just after eight o'clock when Kirsten returned to the hotel alone. Jake, Alison and several of the others had taken themselves off to K-Paul's for a Cajun dinner, but Kirsten had declined the invitation to join them. She went straight up to her room, dropped off her bag then walked along the corridor to Laurence's suite, an impish smile twitching her lips as she envisaged the teasing intimacy in his eyes when he saw her.

'Hi,' she said when Jane opened the door. 'Is Laurence there?'

'Uh, no,' Jane said uncomfortably. 'He, um, he's gone out to a restaurant.'

'Oh,' Kirsten said. 'Do you know where?'

'Oh yes,' Jane nodded eagerly. 'I've got it written down. If you'd like to come in I'll get it for you.'

Kirsten followed Jane into the sitting room. 'Did he leave a message for me?' she said.

Jane shook her head. 'I don't think so. Well, not with me, he didn't.'

'Who did he go to the restaurant with?' Kirsten asked taking the piece of paper Jane was holding out.

'Ruby.'

Kirsten's surprise showed. 'Ruby?'

'Yes, she got here this afternoon while you were all out at the swamp.'

'I didn't know she was coming,' Kirsten said, unsure for the moment why it was bothering her. She lifted her eyes back to Jane's. 'Did Laurence know she was coming?'

'Yes, I think so. Well, he got his assistant to go and pick her up at the airport, so he must have known.'

'Then why didn't he mention it to me?'

Jane simply looked at her.

Kirsten quickly pulled herself together. 'Well,' she said, waving a hand towards the door. 'I suppose I'd better get back, I've got a lot to do.'

'Tom and I are having a midnight feast if you want to join us,' Jane offered. 'He thinks it's midnight now. He's in there waiting, probably thinking you're room service.'

'Thanks,' Kirsten smiled, 'but like I said, I've got a lot to do.'

'Do you want to say good-night to Tom? I know he'd love it if you did.'

'No, uh, not right now,' Kirsten answered starting towards the door. 'I'll see him in the morning.'

'OK. Did you like the T-shirts, by the way?'

'Yes, yes, they're great,' Kirsten assured her. 'Uh, you'd better let me know how much I owe you.'

'Oh no, that's all right. They're a present from Tom and me.'

'Well, thank you, I'll wear one tomorrow.'

Jane smiled happily. 'Are you sure you don't want to stay for the feast?' she said.

Kirsten looked at her, wanting nothing more in that moment than to get hold of her and shake her. Couldn't she see that she just wanted to get out of here? 'Quite sure, but thanks,' Kirsten said, then her heart sank as she realized from the colour that rose in Jane's cheeks that somehow Jane had detected her irritation. But the last thing she wanted was for Laurence to come back and find her cosily ensconced in his son's room looking for all the world as though she had taken that afternoon to mean that she was now a part of the family. Besides she didn't much want to eat, not when she had a horrible feeling that Laurence had pulled down the shutters again, for how else was she to read a meeting between him and the writer to which she hadn't been invited?

When the door closed behind Kirsten Jane stood at the centre of the room chewing her bottom lip. It was all very bewildering what was happening between Laurence and Kirsten – one minute they were shouting and arguing like they'd never see eye to eye and the next they were actually making love. Jane was certain that's what they had been doing when she and Tom returned to the room earlier, but now it seemed like something had gone wrong again. She couldn't even begin to work out what, but she hoped from the bottom of her heart that in the end they really would get back together. She was sure they loved each other, not that she knew very much about their kind of love, but she, or anyone, only had to look at them to see how right they were for each other. There was no doubt that Kirsten had been upset by the fact that Laurence had gone off to dinner with Ruby, but obviously she, Jane, wasn't the one to cheer her up. Probably she'd go and call Helena and Jane felt a crushing disappointment at the thought. She really wished she could be the one Kirsten turned to. But who could say, maybe one of these days Kirsten would think her special enough to confide in and then she would do everything she could to show Kirsten how very, very much she wanted her to be part of their lives.

'Sure I believe in it, Ruby,' Laurence said, digging into his smoked redfish. 'I just don't believe in all of it, is what I'm saying.'

Ruby shrugged, waving a prawn around on the end of her fork. 'I'm not saying I believe in all of it either,' she said, 'but I sure as hell wouldn't want anyone doing the whammy on me.'

Laurence laughed and picked up his wine. 'So who were these people?' he said. 'Where did you find them?'

'These people, as you call them,' Ruby answered, 'believe they're directly descended from the *loas*, at least I think that's what they were saying. I'll have to check that out.'

'*Loas*?'

'A voodoo god. Anyways, it's not easy finding someone willing to talk about the real spooky side of things,' she went on. 'I mean, what we've got so far I've taken from books, I just would like to see the real thing for myself before we start shooting.'

'Did you go to the Voodoo Museum yet?'

'Sure. Where do you think I met these guys? But like I said, they're into the touristy bit, not what we're looking for at all. I'm not saying they're not genuine, I guess they are, but it's all a bit staged. I want to find myself a real ritual where drums are beating, people are going off into trances, animals get sacrificed and,' she winked mischievously, 'unmentionable things occur.'

Again Laurence laughed then took another mouthful of the delicious fish. They were dining at Mr B's Bistro on Royal Street where the waiters were dressed in kelly green aprons and the dark wood interior with its shining brass details provided a somewhat sombre setting for the humming cheeriness of the place. Ruby was looking better than Laurence had seen her in ages and this was one occasion when he was finding himself enjoying her company.

'You reckon you'd have the courage to go to one of these rituals, do you?' he teased.

'Sure. So long as you came with me.'

'Oh no, hang on,' Laurence protested. 'You're not getting me prancing around naked in the dead of night while someone whips a goddamned python into a frenzy.'

Ruby's pencilled brows joined in a frown. 'But we got to have some kind of frenzy, wouldn't you say? It's just too flat the way it is now.'

'Sure, I'll agree with that, but we should have Kirsten with us if we're going to discuss – '

'I told you, I called her room but she was out with Jake,' Ruby interrupted. 'I'll catch up with her in the morning. Anyway, it's good us two having this time alone, I've kind of missed you since the Kirstie Doll took over.'

'Don't call her that, Ruby, you sound like Dermott Campbell.'

'I'll call her anything you want me to call her, but she sure is getting herself talked about with all that making up she's doing to Jake.'

'She needs him on her side,' Laurence said tonelessly.

'She needs us all on her side,' Ruby pointed out, 'but

– 311 –

she's not having so much success with the others, is she?'

'She'll sort it. The main thing is that you two get along.'

'Sure we do,' Ruby chuckled, her cluster of bracelets jangling as she beckoned a waiter. 'Get me a large gin and tonic, son,' she said, 'and you can take this plate away, I've finished.'

Laurence leaned back as the waiter took his plate too, then resting his elbows on the table he said, 'So tell me more about these voodoo people.'

Ruby scratched her head, then resting her cheek on her hand she said, 'They're really kind of weird. I can't seem to get inside their heads...' Suddenly her eyes opened wide. 'But hey, I'm forgetting. There's this absinthe drink you can get here and if it's mixed the way it used to be years ago it makes a person hallucinate. I was thinking about giving it a shot, I reckon I could come up with some real wild action for the ritual if I do. Maybe Kirsten should give it...'

'Don't even think about it,' Laurence said, half-laughing, half-serious. 'I need you both with your wits about you not floating somewhere in psychedelic euphoria. So when are you seeing these guys again?'

'Tomorrow. One of them's going to read my coconut.'

'Your *what*?'

'Apparently that's how she tells fortunes. I know, it sounds kind of crazy to me too, but that's what she said. I wonder if she'll get to see you there anywhere.'

Laurence eyed her for a moment and she started to laugh.

'You sure are a handsome boy,' she said, attempting to reach across the table and pinch his cheek.

'So you keep telling me,' Laurence said, jerking himself out of the way. 'Now, can we get back . . .'

'You didn't go and get yourself hooked on the Kirstie Doll again, did you?'

Laurence blinked. 'Where did that suddenly come from?' he said.

'Just wondering if it was going to pop up in my coconut. Don't want to be in for any nasty shocks, now do I?'

'I can think of plenty worse,' he laughed. 'Now mind your own business about my love life and let's – '

'Ah, so you're not denying it?'

'I'm telling you to mind your own business.'

Ruby fixed him with her watery eyes. 'She got you real screwed up once in your life, Laurence,' she said seriously.

'I'm not screwed up. I'm not hooked on Kirsten and I'm not particularly enjoying this conversation, so let's change it shall we?'

'My, my, such a touchy boy,' Ruby sighed. 'Does she know about you and me?'

'Nobody does. That's the way you wanted it, isn't it?'

'It's the way you wanted it.'

'All right, so we agreed, nobody gets to know.'

'Your old friend Dermott Campbell knows.'

'Because I told him.'

As Ruby looked at him a very real fondness came into her eyes which after a moment or two started to reflect itself in Laurence's making them both laugh. 'I sometimes wonder what the hell I'm going to do with you, Ruby,' he said. 'Now can we get back to the script and what you're going to do with these voodoo sequences?'

He grimaced as she started chuntering on about the theological and magical elements of voodoo, its origins, its blend with the Catholic Church, its spirits and divinities. He was only half listening for his mind had returned to Kirsten. He wasn't sorry about what had happened that afternoon, but then neither was he sorry that Jane and Tom had come back when they did nor that Ruby had wanted dinner. Of course Kirsten should have been here with them, but it seemed she'd already had plans. He wondered if she was actually sleeping with Jake, it seemed unlikely but it sure would help ease his conscience if she were. They'd screwed themselves senseless that afternoon and he had to admit he wouldn't mind doing it again sometime, but he knew that wasn't such a good idea. He might be able to handle it, but Kirsten couldn't. As it was he felt pretty sure that she was going to want to sit down and discuss what had happened and where they went from here. His heart sank. Were there any chance he could avoid doing that, he knew beyond a doubt that he'd grab at it for it would just complicate matters even further. The issue had seemed pretty clouded before they'd had sex, but it was crystal clear to him now – he really didn't want to get involved with Kirsten again. He'd been down that road once already in his life, he'd been married for the past four and half years and now all he wanted was to hold on to and enjoy his freedom.

Ruby was in a small dingy room at the back of a house in down-town New Orleans. The room was an *oum'phor*, a voodoo temple. She was seated at a rickety wooden table beside the *peristyle*, the rainbow-coloured post that supported the centre of the corrugated roof, and over the table was a large paper napkin. The chair she was sitting on was about as uncomfortable as the method of telling her future through a goddamned coconut was ludicrous.

The voodoo priestess who looked what she was, a scrap of a girl from the streets of Paris, was sitting at the other side of the table, her stringy blonde hair lit by the flickering flame of a candle, her sultry lips slightly parted as she concentrated on the patterns of coconut juice that had dripped onto the paper between them and the milky white flesh of the fruit which was now exposed. Ruby had broken the coconut herself, it was a part of putting her identity – on to a goddamned coconut!

Ruby was supposed to have been here a week ago for this reading, but the priestess had asked her to delay her visit. Ruby hadn't asked why, in fact she'd all but lost interest by now, but the kid had called her up this morning while the others were taking off for the airport, and since Ruby didn't have anything better to do before her own flight she'd come along.

This past week had proved a rewarding one, not that she'd managed to get to any spooky midnight rituals, in fact everyone insisted they didn't happen, but the stories she'd got out of the police, self-professed voodoo victims, street-entertainers and bar room punters had been enough to make the Kirstie Doll's hair curl. Well, it was pretty potent stuff even if she, Ruby, didn't believe half of it, and cutesy Kirstie had nearly peed her pants with excitement. Ruby grinned to herself. She kind of liked Kirsten, admired her in a way. Putting up with the surly, snobbish treatment she was getting from the high and mighty feature crew couldn't be easy, but she seemed to be handling it OK. Still, if Ruby was any judge of things they were going to get their come-uppance once they saw rushes, 'cos if Kirsten managed to pull off the approach she was taking they were going to end up with one hell of a movie on their hands. And that was why she admired Kirsten, instead of pulling rank on everyone now, she was going to let her work speak for her. Pretty neat that, Ruby thought. Yeah, the Kirstie Doll was OK, she had Ruby's vote and just so long as she stayed away from Laurence's heart they would continue to get along fine.

Ruby's heavily-ringed fingers moved to her mouth to stifle a yawn. This here voodoo girl was taking an inordinate amount of time to absorb one little old coconut and Ruby was getting bored. In fact she was feeling a bit peckish, but decided it might not be a good idea to take a chunk out of her own destiny. Her eyes started to roam the walls taking in the grisly masks of staring red eyes, protruding tongues and wolfish teeth. The sickly aroma of a sweet incense thickened the air and the strains of monotonously hypnotic pipe music drifted dreamily over the totem poles, mystical paintings and weird collection of whammy dolls. In the corner was an old iron gate with grinning skulls impaled on its spikes. More candles burned on the altar where statuettes of saints and voodoo gods stood between bunches of garlic, *gris-gris* bags and an ashtray. Ruby wasn't a religious woman by anyone's standards, but the open copy of the Bible resting incongruously on some kind of clothes horse in front of the altar wasn't something that sat too well with her. And she didn't much like the python slithering indolently about a glass tank over there either.

Her painted lips opened wide as she allowed herself a luxurious yawn. 'Oh, sorry, dear,' she said when the waif-like priestess looked up at her. 'Kind of warm in here, don't you think?'

The girl looked at her with cold, translucent eyes. Ruby stared back curiously. The girl hadn't looked that way when she'd come in here, in fact she'd looked a happy sort of soul . . . Shit, what kind of story was she reading in that darned coconut?

'You have many troubles in your life,' the priestess said in her throaty French accent.

'Tell me about it,' Ruby sighed.

'Chango, the warrior god, he speaks to me of you. Your battle is a hard one, he understands, but he does not approve of what you do.'

'Is that so?' Ruby said. 'Well how about you tell old Chango that if – ' she stopped as the priestess held up her hand.

'Deceit is not good,' she purred. 'You deceive and you will be deceived.'

Ruby didn't have much to say about that. Seemed a pretty obvious sort of statement to her, anyhow, she didn't need no spear-toting voodoo god to tell her that. And sure, she'd deceived a few people in her time, show her someone who hadn't!

'Your deception will cause you much grief. It will bring misunderstanding . . . It will hurt someone you love.' Her head came up. 'Erzulie, our goddess of love, speaks. She tells me you seek solace for your heart. The source of your love comes from your womb. I see the baby,' she said. 'Legba, our chief god, he is showing me the baby.'

Ruby's puffy cheeks paled slightly. 'Yeah?' she said. 'And which baby would that be?'

'The baby you hold in your arms.'

'I don't see no baby.'

'It is there, in your arms. Legba is showing me. It is with your memories. You nurture them, but you must let them go. Legba, he says, you must let them go.'

'I don't have no baby,' Ruby insisted.

– 317 –

The priestess blinked at her, a vaccuous look in her eyes that told Ruby she wasn't listening.

'You are surrounded by many words and many people,' the girl chanted. 'There is much creativity. You are a woman of great talent, but you are in danger from that talent. It will bring harm to those around you. There is another baby. It is very still. I see a child with that baby. I see more memories . . . They are captured in a book.'

Ruby was thinking of the photograph album that contained all the joy of her young life. She said nothing.

'There is a wish to be a mother, yet it cannot be. You are dominated by this desire, are surrounded by women who are ruled by the same desire. You have all made mistakes, done things you deeply regret, but a child is there for you all . . . I see the child and the baby . . .'

'You're not making a whole lot of sense here,' Ruby interrupted.

'I see death,' the girl continued as if Ruby hadn't spoken. 'It has already occurred, but there are three yet to come. The innocent have died and will die . . .' The girl's voice suddenly crescendoed. 'You must stop this film! You must not do it! Legba is begging you . . .' Then as though she was being possessed from within she choked, 'The first deaths will be from smoke without fire. The third is the child. The child will die.' Her eyes blazed beseechingly into Ruby's. 'Please stop this film,' she cried. 'Don't let the child die. Don't kill the child . . .'

'I'm not going to kill no child,' Ruby protested.

'But it is there. The child will die if you do this film. They will all die. You must stop protecting those who do not need it and look to those who do or you will be blamed.'

'I don't much like the way this coconut's going,' Ruby objected. 'Do you figure we could try a banana?'

The girl was by now so steeped in her prophecies it seemed she couldn't stop. 'You must try to understand what the spirits are telling you,' she demanded, seeming to speak from somewhere behind her eyes. 'There are three women, one who is very beautiful, one who is our own vodoo queen and there is you . . . Your lives are linked by this film . . . And there is a man with a child . . .'

Ruby's heart seemed to freeze over. Was she talking about Tom? Was Tom the child she reckoned was going to . . .?

'You must curb your jealousy,' the girl continued on. 'It will do you no good . . . The child needs you, she needs you all . . .'

'She?' Ruby queried with some relief.

'There is a child with a child. She lives within you . . . Look to the very heart of you and you will see the child with a child.'

Ruby's uneasiness was cracking her resolve badly. She didn't like the sound of any of this, not that she had any idea what it was about, but there were just a few too many bells ringing . . . 'Do you reckon your fella Legba there could speak plain English?' she asked.

'Memories must come from our past,' the priestess warned.

'What?'

'Do not allow her to create the memories that do not exist. You must stop her.'

'Who?'

'The child. She is a part of you.'

'I need a gin,' Ruby declared.

'The strands are so knotted it is hard to find your

– 319 –

way through. It has all begun with one woman's desire for revenge. She is to blame, not you, but you are a part of it now. The woman no longer has control, it is slipping away from her and the path is clearing. But do not let it clear for it will open the way to death. Stop this film and turn away from it.'

'Make that a large one,' Ruby grumbled.

'If you do not heed my advice you will see a castle fall. You will see the death of a woman. You will see the death of a man. Then the memories will take on reality and the baby will break into a thousand pieces . . .'

'That's it, I'm out of here,' Ruby cried, springing to her feet and almost knocking the table over.

'Then will come the death of the child . . .' the priestess's haunted voice came after her.

– 18 –

'And you're telling me he hasn't mentioned a word about it since!' Helena cried.

'Not one,' Kirsten answered, making a note next to a paragraph of stage direction.

'But you've been back here two weeks, you've got to have seen him . . .'

'Of course I've seen him. I saw him plenty of times when we were in New Orleans too. But like I said, he always makes sure someone else is around.'

'Well isn't that just typical of a man!' Helena declared.

'Always hiding behind someone's skirts when they can't face up to what they've done.'

'As a matter of fact I haven't gone out of my way to speak to him either,' Kirsten said, tucking her hair behind her ear as she flicked over a page.

'Why ever not? You can't let him get away with this, Kirstie.'

Kirsten lifted her head and rested her chin on a bunched fist. 'The way I see it he has got away with it. But it takes two, I wouldn't have done it if I didn't want to. In fact, I reckon he's having a far harder time over this than I am. I mean I know how *I* feel, but my guess is he just can't work out how he feels.'

'Shit, listen to you, Miss Cool.'

Kirsten laughed and turned back to what she was doing. 'To be honest, Helena, I've hardly had time to think about it much.'

'But aren't you just dying to know what's really going on in his head? I know I would be.'

'Well, I suppose we will have to clear the air sooner or later, so we *will* have it out and then we will continue on my terms.'

'Well, I like the sound of that,' Helena grinned. 'Going to tell me what you're planning?'

'No. But I'll let you know once I've spoken to him. Now, can we get back to this? I want to be sure you know about the visual effects that are going into the voodoo ceremony because it's going to effect your performance. Have you met up with the effects team yet?'

'Yes, last week. Can't say I really understand all those computer graphics though.'

'All right, I'll come with you next time. For now, let's go over the ritual as Ruby's written it. By the way, have you seen the designs for your costume?'

'Sure. They're terrific. I've got a first fitting next week.'

'Good. I'll check with Vicky that she's put that into my schedule, I'd like to see it before Janet goes ahead and has it made. So, tell me about your meeting with Ruby yesterday. Was she any help with the ritual?'

'Yeah, a bit. She's kind of getting herself worked up over it though. It's like . . . . Well, it's like she doesn't want me to do it. She keeps saying she's going to change it, but never does. If you ask me she's having some kind of confidence crisis.'

'Mmm, you could be right,' Kirsten said thoughtfully. She didn't add that Laurence had called the night before to say he was at Ruby's trying to sober her up and attempting yet again to persuade her not to pull out. 'Did she say anything to you about some coconut reading?' Kirsten asked.

'Some what!' Helena laughed.

Kirsten shook her head. 'It's just that she went to see some kind of fortune teller or something after the rest of us left New Orleans and it seems to have shaken her up a bit. Anyway, where were we? Ah yes, I've got a copy of a props list here so that you can see what you'll be handling during the ceremony. Try to remember that none of it's real because it's pretty revolting.'

'The goddamned python's real!' Helena reminded her.

'Yes, but you'll be trained.'

'It's not me I'm worried about,' Helena declared.

'The snake'll be trained too,' Kirsten laughed flicking through her diary which was sitting at her elbow. 'Your lessons begin while we're in Ireland,' she said. 'A Mr Peterson over in Ongar will be doing the coaching. Which reminds me, have you met the choreographer yet?'

'Yes,' Helena said. 'I've met them all, even Mr Peterslime.'

'Well I'm pleased to hear that,' Kirsten commented. 'Seems the production managers are on the ball. I've got a meeting with the stunt arrangers tomorrow otherwise I'd have come to dance rehearsals with you.'

'And who's choreographing all the Walk Ons?' Helena wanted to know.

'Someone over in New Orleans. You and your choreographer will get together with them just before we shoot. Now, at the risk of asking a silly question, how *au fait* are you with the background on voodoo? Do you want any more coaching in that than what Ruby's given you?'

Helena pursed her lips thoughtfully. 'No,' she said. 'I don't reckon so. Growing up with it's all the background I need.'

Kirsten looked up. 'Are you going to visit your mother when we're in New Orleans?' she asked.

Helena shrugged. 'I don't know. She's been in and out of that jail for a mighty long time, over twelve years now . . . I don't know what we'd have to say to each other. Well, what do you say to a person who's two toads short of a hex?'

'Does it bother you, playing this role?' Kirsten smiled. 'What with all that's happened?'

Helena shook her head. 'Nothing did happen, really. Sure she went around the place telling everyone she was putting curses and the like on them, but folks in New Orleans get used to that sort of thing. Well, some of them do. I guess the Garden District's not too clever a place to choose to go and upset people, but she seems to like it up around that way. Gets a real kick out of scaring the rich.' Her eyes were fixed on Kirsten's and after a moment her face relaxed into a smile. 'Truth is,

I am a bit antsy about going back. Someone's sure to latch on to the fact that I'm Camilla Johnson's daughter playing the part of Marie Laveau.'

'The publicists are already preparing to talk to you about it,' Kirsten said getting up to answer the phone. 'They'll handle the press, but they'll need some help from you.'

Helena nodded. 'OK,' and she turned back to her script with the heavily underscored lines that were hers. She knew them all by now, she'd learned them parrot fashion so that when Kirsten came to discuss the level of performance she, Helena, wouldn't have to return to the book. Kirsten, of course, could recite virtually the entire dialogue by now so when she read in during individual coaching she could keep her whole attention on the actor. It was pretty cool that, Helena reflected, knowing the whole script inside out. Of course she'd known other directors who'd worked that way, but being directed by Kirsten was a whole new experience. To begin with this was the first time Helena had ever been directed by a woman. She wasn't too sure she liked it, but it was something she was working on, just like the resentment she always seemed to feel when she was around Kirsten lately. She knew that it was to do with guilt. Going behind Kirsten's back with Dermott wasn't something she was proud of, but it wasn't something she was going to stop either. The thing was, it was easier to harden her heart against Kirsten when she wasn't with her, but when she was with her . . . Well, Kirsten was just about the only real friend she'd ever had, and that was what was making all this so damned difficult. However, were Laurence to get his act together and really get things going between him and Kirsten then she, Helena, might not feel quite so bad. It would be a whole lot easier to defend herself over Dermott, were Kirsten ever to find out, if Kirsten was happy with Laurence. She couldn't begrudge Helena the same sort of happiness then, if happiness was what Helena was feeling with Dermott. But yeah, she guessed it was. OK, he was a bit of an asshole, but show her a man who wasn't. And she really did think the two of them might make a go of it. She just hoped that she never got to the position where she'd have to choose between Kirsten and Dermott . . . But that would be a lot less likely to happen if Laurence stopped pissing around the way he was.

'That was Vicky doing overtime,' Kirsten said, glancing at her watch as she came back into the study. 'The production managers are having some problem with the schedule so they want me back over there. I guess I'd better go, we can continue this at the weekend.'

'Sure,' Helena said, closing up her script.

'Do you reckon you can come at me from inside Marie Laveau's skin by then?' Kirsten smiled.

'I can give it a shot,' Helena answered. 'But yeah, I reckon I've got her pretty well sussed now. Don't like her much, do you?'

'She gives me the creeps,' Kirsten laughed. 'And that's exactly what we want.' She picked up her holdall and started stuffing things into it as Helena went to get her coat.

'You can stay here the night if you like,' Kirsten said joining her in the hall. 'There's plenty to eat in the fridge.'

'No, I'd better get back. I'll drop you in Soho if you like, save you looking for a taxi.'

'OK. Got anything lined up for the evening?' she asked, pulling an anorak on over her sweater and jeans.

Helena shrugged. 'I thought I was spending it here, remember?'

'Of course, sorry. You don't mind me going off like this, do you?'

Helena shrugged. 'Just so long as I know you'd do it to Anna Sage.'

Kirsten was about to answer then stopped to give the question some thought. The last thing she wanted was to abuse her friendship with Helena, but Helena was right, she wouldn't have walked out on a meeting with Anna Sage. But there again she didn't spend what few social hours she had with Anna Sage.

'I'll make it up to you,' she said putting an arm around Helena's shoulders. 'You get my undivided attention all day Sunday. How does that sound?'

'Pretty patronizing actually,' Helena remarked. 'But I'll live with it,' she added with a grin that faded the moment Kirsten turned to open the door.

The scissors were slipping in her fingers. It had taken so long to do this and the baby just wouldn't stop crying. So many times now she had left her table and gone to the crib in the corner, lifting the tiny body into her arms and comforting it with all the love in her heart. She had held it to her breast, stroked it and changed it and whispered her dreams in its ear. The baby was sleeping now, its fair downy lashes still moist with tears, its smooth, tender cheeks flushed with warmth. The soothing tune from a musical mobile drifted over the room.

A smile curled slowly across her lips as she glued the last picture into place. She was creating the happiness for them, for her and for her baby. They were going to have a past just like they were going to have a future.

They were going to be a family – all of them. She blinked as the tears started from her eyes. This was such a beautiful photograph now. So much better than it had been before. It was right to be like this – mother, father and two children. But of course there was the baby to go in yet, and that was why she was crying. She had no pictures of her baby.

Kirsten could hardly believe how fast the time had gone. It was now the beginning of November and they were scheduled to start shooting in less than a week. Alison and her crew were already over in Ireland preparing the castle, two line-producers, two production managers, three location managers and their assistants were over there too, setting up offices in trailers, sorting the make-up and wardrobe caravans, portable dressing rooms, honey wagons, catering facilities and the hundred and one other things that needed to be done before everyone arrived. In the Soho offices last minute details of artists' contracts were being attended to, the final draft of the shooting script was going to print, Jake and his crew were doing double checks on the equipment lists and Laurence was yelling at the accountants for up to the minute costings.

Kirsten was unbelievably calm. She spent every day in a hotel conference room with the cast now, going over the script in the minutest of detail and loving every minute of it. Ruby was often at cast meetings and Kirsten frequently found her input as valuable as that of the cast themselves. Fortunately Ruby seemed to have got over whatever it was that had upset her in New Orleans, though she did appear to be drinking more heavily lately. This was something Kirsten left Laurence to handle, knowing that he was the only one who would succeed in keeping Ruby away from the cast until she was sober. Only once had she staggered in drunk and it wasn't something Kirsten wanted repeated. To start calling her own work rubbish and telling the actors they were all wasting their time and should cancel their contracts before something terrible happened to them was not particularly helpful.

Occasionally Jake popped into the meetings and to watch him work his charm on the cast was as entertaining as it was welcome. Some of them had worked with Jake before so knew him well, and he went out of his way to make himself known to those he hadn't met. There was no doubt in Kirsten's mind now that everything was going to go as smoothly as these things could. The whole unit was at last starting to mellow towards her; being in no doubt now that Kirsten knew precisely what she wanted, was rarely, if ever, indecisive and was always willing to listen had raised their confidence in her no end.

There had been a slight hiccup the week before though, when Dermott Campbell had written an article entitled *Iniquity on the Road*. In order to avoid a libel suit Campbell hadn't come right out with his accusations, but the essence of the piece was that Laurence was having to cope with a writer who was a drunk and given to manic outbursts; a Don Juan of a DP who couldn't keep his hands off the director; a director who couldn't keep her hands off anyone and whose interpretation of turn over had little to do with a camera; a cast who had no confidence in either the director or the script; and a budget that was already fast running out. Through the unit publicist Laurence had made a short statement to the press thanking his good friend

Dermott Campbell for his concern, but should he care to get his information from those in the know rather than from the mole he had planted, then he would discover that not only did he, Laurence, have a thoroughly professional team working for him, but that he had rarely had greater confidence in a director or in the success of a movie that was far from being in any financial difficulties. This was backed up by a memorandum to every member of cast and crew assuring them that the budget was in no danger of drying up and that they had his personal assurance that they would continue to be paid right up to the end of shoot. He had then, unbeknownst to Kirsten, contacted Campbell and invited him to come on to the set any time he liked to gauge for himself the inaccuracy of the information he was receiving. So far Campbell had declined. Laurence was neither surprised nor sorry. He knew he was in danger of sticking his neck out too far by issuing the invitation when they hadn't even started, but he had total confidence in Kirsten's ability and knew that any problems that might arise would not be of her making – and it was Kirsten's skin Campbell was really after.

Things had settled down again now, though not even Laurence knew about the angry words that had been exchanged between Kirsten and Helena when Kirsten had asked Helena if she was still seeing Campbell. Helena had denied it so vehemently that Kirsten believed her and apologized, but Helena was still smarting at the damned impertinence of being told who she could and couldn't see. The fact that she really wasn't giving Campbell his information any more – and hadn't been since Kirsten and Laurence stood by her over the exposé of the schoolboy's suicide – had made it easier to defend herself, but she sure would like to know which member of the crew was in his pay. Not surprisingly Campbell had refused to tell her, in fact he'd gone so far as to swear on his mother's grave that no one was, but she didn't put much store by that. Anyway, why should Kirsten worry what Campbell said when she had Laurence there to defend her all the time? Laurence, who anyone could see was as crazy about Kirsten as she was about him. He might be hiding it from himself, but seeing them together these past few weeks had left Helena in little doubt that Laurence McAllister was in love right up to his eyes.

In fact Kirsten's response to the way Laurence was behaving with her was not at all what Helena might have expected – had Helena known about it – for the way Laurence supported her, complimented her, laughed with her and perpetually flirted with her was getting on Kirsten's nerves. She hated the idea that he seemed to be handling his emotions so much better than she was, especially when for a while she'd believed that he was the one in turmoil. Well if he had been, he certainly didn't seem to be now and though Kirsten had more than enough to occupy her mind to her frustration she was becoming obsessed with getting some sort of response from Laurence before they started shooting. She'd intended all along to discuss with him what had happened in New Orleans before they got underway, she knew too what she was going to say, it was just that he wasn't giving her much of an opportunity to do it.

However, she created the opportunity the day before they flew out by closing their office door behind her, picking up the telephone and telling Sonya, Laurence's assistant and Vicky, her assistant, that she and Laurence were not to be interrupted.

Laurence looked up from what he was doing, an

expression of curious amusement in his eyes as he watched Kirsten, looking undeniably sexy in a tight black sweater and skirt, move around to the front of her desk and perch on the edge of it. 'Is something bothering you?' he asked pleasantly.

Kirsten nodded. 'Yes, as a matter of fact it is.'

Laurence put down his pen, sat back in his chair and cocked an eyebrow for her to continue.

Now that she was facing him, under the scrutiny of those annoyingly knowing eyes, Kirsten wasn't quite so sure of her ground. She gave herself a moment by turning pensively to the window and watching the drizzle etch crooked patterns through the grime. Dear God, she was thinking to herself, all I want right now is for him to get hold of me and do what he did in New Orleans. She jerked herself to her feet and went to sit behind her desk. She had it fixed in her mind what she was going to say, at least she thought she did, so now she was going to say it.

'I just want you to know,' she began looking at him as steadily as he was looking at her, 'that the incident that took place in New Orleans must not happen again.'

'And which particular incident would that be?' he asked his eyes alive with humour.

'You know perfectly well what I'm talking about,' Kirsten answered, trying not to bite out the words. 'I'm right on the point of making a breakthrough with the crew and I don't want anything you do to spoil it.'

'You can rest assured on that,' he smiled.

'I don't want any more suggestions that I got this job because I slept with the producer.'

'You didn't.'

'I know, but I don't want those accusations rearing up again once we start shooting. I'm going to have my work cut out over the next few months and I don't want you playing me any underhand tricks by trying to seduce me.'

'You got it,' he said.

Kirsten glared at him, but when his smile widened she looked away. This was all coming out wrong and she was beginning to feel extremely foolish. 'Well, just as long as we've got that straight,' she said. 'I mean, it's not that I don't want us to do it again . . .' *Jesus Christ, what was she saying?* 'It's simply that I don't need my emotions playing around with. If it was purely physical between us then it might be different, but since it goes a lot deeper than that . . . Well, I don't want to be concerning myself about you and our personal feelings when I should be concentrating on other things.'

'OK,' he said.

Kirsten's eyes darted back to his. 'OK? Is that all you've got to say?' she demanded.

He shrugged. 'What else do you want me to say?'

She took a mouthful of air then let it go without a sound. What did she want him to say? She wanted him to argue with her, that's what she wanted. She wanted him to tell her that he didn't think he could handle being around her morning, noon and night for two months without touching her. She wanted him to get up out of that chair, right now, and come over here. She wanted to hear him tell her he was as crazy for her as she was for him. All these things she could argue with, but his acceptance . . . . Well, that hadn't been a part of how she'd rehearsed this conversation at all. Why wasn't he sticking to his script, the bastard?

'So,' she said. 'I guess we've cleared the air.'

He grinned. 'Yeah, I guess we have,' he said. 'Now,

do you want to come over here, or do you want that I come over there?'

Kirsten's eyes flashed. This was better, this she was ready for. 'Didn't you hear what I just said?' she cried. 'There's to be no more sex . . .'

'I was talking about getting together over this graphic,' he interrupted, holding it up.

Kirsten felt herself colour to the roots of her hair. 'Oh,' she said. 'Um, well, I'll just tell Vicky and Sonya to start putting the calls through again,' and picking up the phone she buzzed through to her assistant.

Not until much later in the day when she was sitting alone beside the fire in her own home nursing a glass of wine did she allow herself to recall the whole insufferable conversation. Not even by the flicker of a muscle had he indicated that he was in any way bothered by her decision. If anything, he'd given her the impression that he appreciated the way she was attempting to deal with her problem.

Oh shit, she groaned inwardly. This was all she needed right on the eve of shoot, to be tormenting herself over Laurence. Their conversation that day was supposed to have prevented this, and maybe it would have if she hadn't made such a damned hash of it. Well, she just had to be tough about this. She wasn't going to let it get to her, she was going to put it right out of her mind and give everything she had to the film. She reached out to pick up the phone as it rang, knowing that right at that moment she'd have welcomed a call telling her the whole shoot was off. She gave a wry laugh. The truth was she'd be devastated. She was as excited about the next two months as she was nervous and nothing, not even some weirdo who kept playing

bloody baby chimes down the phone to her, was going
to spoil it for her now.

– 19 –

The wind was mewling like a child across the stark,
winter-torn plains of the Irish hillside. The storm gathered overhead in great mountains of purple-black cloud,
the tall, yellowy grass bent towards the gloomy castle
in the distance. The lone horseman, barely more than a
silhouette, galloped across the horizon through the driving rain, his cloak billowing furiously behind him. The
camera, perched on its tripod, held steady on the wide
shot, the operator, with small protection from an
umbrella, was being buffeted by the wind and drenched
by the rain as he panned slowly with the rider taking
him to the castle. Jake and Kirsten, huddled into the
meagre warmth of padded anoraks, moon boots and
woollen scarves, were standing together beneath their
own vast umbrella, watching the shot on a tiny black
and white screen. The rest of the crew were grouped
around them, two sound booms loomed overhead sucking the howl of the storm into their headphones. Rain
dripped from the peak of Kirsten's cap, pools of mud
swam around her feet but she was aware of nothing
more than what was being relayed from the camera to
her monitor.

At last the horseman arrived at the castle, a slight,
shadowy figure in the distance. The ominous rumbling

of thunder started to vibrate through the wind as he dismounted, handed the reins to a barely visible boy and stomped into the blackness of an open door. Kirsten's fingers crossed in her pockets as her heart seemed to fill her throat. The camera held steady, there was virtually no movement now, just the boy leading the horse away and the shuddering branches of trees straining towards the castle turrets.

After a while Kirsten's eyes flicked to the script supervisor who, checking her stop-watch, eventually raised her arm and Kirsten shouted, 'Cut! Check the gate!'

She turned to Jake to find his smile as wide as hers, then she shrieked and laughed with euphoria as he scooped her up in his arms and swung her round. The first shot, after eight takes, was in the can! There was no rain on the lens, the stunt rider hadn't slipped in the mud, no one had appeared in the castle doorway – it had been perfect . . .

'Gate's clear,' Lindon, the camera operator, shouted then joined in the round of applause as walkie-talkies crackled into life, David, the first assistant, yelled into a megaphone and Ruby took a gulp of relief from her handbag.

'Moving on!' David was shouting. 'Shot two, medium-wide from the middle of the field.'

'How long down here?' a voice came from the castle.

'Stay inside,' David answered, 'I'll let you know.'

The grips moved swiftly, rolling up cables, packing up the monitors and removing the camera from the tripod. The sound guys pulled in their booms, disconnected them from the Nagra and saluted Laurence as he walked through the milling crowd.

Kirsten and Jake, already discussing the next shot,

linked arms and started down over the hillside to the centre of the field.

'Do we want Jean-Paul for this shot?' a second assistant enquired over the walkie-talkie.

Kirsten stopped and looked back over her shoulder to David.

'No,' David answered, giving Kirsten the thumbs up as he pressed the radio to his lips. 'Get the stunt guy back on the horse. Not now, we're not ready yet. I'll give you the word. Put Jean-Paul on stand-by.'

Kirsten smiled then hugging Jake's arm they walked on. It was a heady experience knowing that all the information she'd spent the past months giving out had filtered through to the point that questions like that needn't concern her unless she decided upon a last minute change. But even more intoxicating was to watch everyone zooming around, yelling to each other, heaving equipment, rigging dollies, checking schedules, moving props, organizing the action and battling the weather all at her behest. As she watched them she was overwhelmed with emotion and knew that she had never loved Laurence more than she did in that moment for giving her this chance to fulfill a dream. She wondered if Paul could see her now and again her heart swelled. How happy he would be to see her and Laurence working together on a movie that was going to be dedicated to his memory.

The rest of the morning and the first hours into the afternoon, until the daylight had all but disappeared, were spent doing exterior shots of the castle, a tracking shot of the thundering horses hooves and a close up of Jean-Paul's face as he rode through the storm. They wrapped right on four o'clock and piled into the location buses that were taking them to the hotels, boarding houses and bed and breakfasts in the town. Laurence drove Kirsten, Jean-Paul and Ruby back in his hire car and though he'd made very few comments throughout the day Kirsten could tell from his expression that he was as delighted as she was with what they had achieved.

Billy, the chief location manager, was waiting in the lobby of the country hotel in which Kirsten, Laurence and the senior members of crew and cast were staying. He was sitting on a sofa with Jane and Tom, but when Laurence and Kirsten came in he leapt to his feet to congratulate them on how smoothly the first day had gone. As he spoke Kirsten could feel her lips twitching and steadfastly kept her eyes away from Alison, the designer, who was making lewd gestures with her hands in the background. Billy was the butt of most jokes on the unit. He was the neatest most compact little man imaginable, but it wasn't his tidily-parted hair, his flannel slacks that sat a little too high on the waist and his immaculately knotted tie that were the reason for the jokes, though they had earned him the nick-name of Ken, Barbie Doll's boyfriend – it was the mind-boggling size of his penis. No one could miss it, for he wore it pushed down the inside leg of his trousers like a truncheon.

'Don't do that,' Kirsten muttered in Alison's ear as Laurence went over to Tom and Billy followed. Billy was still wittering on and Laurence was doing his best to be polite as Alison's eyes boggled in the direction of Billy's crotch. Kirsten, Jean-Paul and Ruby were doubled up laughing as Laurence fought valiantly to keep a straight face.

As Laurence turned away to hide his laughter Billy looked round, bewildered by the hysteria. Jane, Kirsten vaguely noticed, looked extremely embarrassed and Tom was looking puzzled. Laurence scooped him quickly into his arms, shot a meaningful look at Kirsten and was about to go to the desk for his key when Anna Sage stepped out of the lift.

'Laurence, darling,' she sang out happily and walking over to him she stood on tip-toe to kiss him. 'I hear everything went perfectly today.'

'Yeah, I guess you could say that,' Laurence answered, smiling down into her girlishly pretty face. 'I see you got here all right. Was your assistant there to pick you up at the airport?'

'She certainly was. Jean-Paul,' she said, sliding a hand into her co-star's, 'how did the riding go? Ah, Kirsten, I didn't see you there. Gosh, how do you manage to look so gorgeous when you've been out in that ghastly weather all day? Still, you must be relieved to have the first day over with. Why don't we all go into the cosy little bar over there and have some champagne to celebrate? Do you have champagne?' she asked the receptionist. 'Yes, of course you do. Oh, it's all so exciting isn't it? I can't wait to get started myself.'

As she spoke her arm was snuggling its way into Laurence's and she was playfully teasing the curls away from Tom's eyes as he rested his head on Laurence's shoulder. Then suddenly breaking free she made her way to Kirsten and took her arm. 'Is there anything you would like to discuss with me this evening?' she asked, walking Kirsten towards the bar. 'I have someone coming over from the local newspaper later to interview me, is there anything particular you would like me to say?'

'You'd better discuss that with the publicist,' Kirsten smiled, gently detaching her arm. 'Now listen, please don't think me rude, but I really have to get out of these wet clothes and into a hot bath. I'll join you later, OK?'

'Of course,' Anna cried. 'Of course. Can we have dinner together?'

'Absolutely,' Kirsten said. 'I'll come and find you around seven, OK?'

As Kirsten went to pick up her key Ruby joined her. 'Do you reckon she's gonna simper her way through the next eight weeks?' Ruby hissed in Kirsten's ear.

Kirsten turned aside to hide her smile. She didn't want to encourage Ruby, but Ruby was right, as easy-going and co-operative as Anna was, she did simper.

To Kirsten and Jake's relief the weather didn't let up for the next five days causing them no continuity problems and lending its own inimical ambience to the scenes. There had, of course, been the odd hitch or two, there always were, but whatever obstacles, mysteries or misunderstandings coughed themselves up they were dealt with speedily and efficiently by a crew who was by now whole-heartedly behind Kirsten. They had all of them seen rushes, borrowing the video tape that was sent over from the labs in London for Laurence and Kirsten to view until such time as they could see the film itself in a projection theatre. Anna Sage's performance was so outstanding that even Ruby was beginning to warm towards her and Jean-Paul's indomitable charm was seeping into the camera in a way guaranteed to make any woman's heart churn.

It was on the sixth day during yet another thunderstorm which was causing all sorts of problems for the sound crew that the first major mishap occurred. It was the middle of the afternoon and Kirsten and Anna were standing together beneath the castle's bleak, bulging walls sheltering from the wind. Anna's dresser was hovering beside them, having quickly slipped a fur-lined mac over Anna's costume in order to keep her warm and holding an umbrella over them. The rest of the cast were in their trailers or snugly tucked up behind the steamy windows of the location buses, while the crew slithered about in the mud setting up for the next scene.

'I'm terribly sorry about all those takes,' Anna said to Kirsten. 'It's so hard keeping your head up in this wind.'

'I know. But it was fine in the end,' Kirsten assured her. 'It was just that your dialogue kept getting muffled. We've got it now though.'

'Was Laurence happy with it?'

'I imagine so,' Kirsten answered, watching Jake hoist himself up in the seat behind the camera to look through the view-finder. 'If he wasn't he'd have said.'

'I just wondered because I saw him talking to you just now,' Anna commented casually.

'Oh, that was about something else,' Kirsten answered, smiling to cover her irritation at Anna's persistent need to know what Laurence thought.

'Oh, I see.' Anna tilted her bloodied and dirt-smeared face towards the keep of the castle as a flash of lightning forked from the sky. 'Is he still angry about all the takes we're having to do because of rain on the lens?' she asked, watching the clouds swirl oppressively overhead.

Kirsten turned to her in surprise. 'Angry?' she repeated. 'I didn't know he was angry.'

Anna shrugged. 'Well, not angry exactly, just concerned. And I was a little worried that he'd be cross that I was adding to the number of takes by not holding my head up.'

'Don't even think about it,' Kirsten told her. 'If the take is no good we won't print it.' She refrained from adding that as the director what she thought counted every bit as much as what Laurence thought, if not more. She didn't want to show her growing irritation

with Anna for she was very much aware of the gossip
flying around the unit – Jake related it to her regularly.
Everyone was laying odds on how long it was going to
take for Anna to get Laurence into bed. For Kisten
to give way to her feelings would only add to the speculation and it was bad enough trying to deal with them
as it was. The sudden bolts of ice-cold jealousy that
lurched through her every time she saw Anna and Laurence together huddled in private conversation at the
edge of the set were already affecting her concentration
though so far, thank God, no one seemed to have
noticed.

Jake yelled out for her and she was just about to break
away from the castle wall when a second dagger of
lightning flashed down from the sky at the very instant
a thunderbolt exploded into the castle-keep.

'Good God!' Anna choked, clinging to Kirsten.
'What's happening?'

'I don't know,' Kirsten murmured, watching the
scenes guys diving for cover. Suddenly she gasped. 'Oh
my God! The whole tower's coming down. Quick!' and
dragging Anna by the arm she all but thew her out of
the way.

In the commotion that followed it was a miracle no
one got hurt. Kirsten scanned the milling crowd for a
glimpse of Jane and Tom who she was certain she'd seen
wandering towards the castle a few minutes ago. At first
she couldn't see them, but then, as Jake and his assistants
parted in their different directions she saw them standing with Laurence in the middle of the set looking down
at the ground. As Kirsten's heart relaxed she was on
the point of turning to check on everyone else when she
saw Anna Sage join the group. Immediately Laurence
put an arm around Anna and hugged her to him, as

though to comfort her, but then Kirsten realized that everyone was laughing. She couldn't imagine what there was to laugh about when half of them had almost been killed, but then she saw Alison lying flat on her back in the mud kicking her feet and pounding her hands into the stagnant puddles around her. There was something going on over on the edge of the set too, but Kirsten couldn't quite work out what it was — it wasn't until much later that she discovered that Ruby had passed out from the shock of her near miss and had been carried off to the first-aid trailer.

'I can't believe it! I can't believe it!' Alison was screaming. 'Tell me I'm dreaming. Tell me it's a nightmare.'

'What's going on?' Kirsten asked Laurence, coming to stand beside him.

'I've just told her she's got to rebuild the tower,' Laurence winked.

Kirsten started to laugh, knowing as well as Laurence did that they had all the shots of the tower they needed. She allowed Alison to continue in the horror of the massive rebuild for a while longer, then deciding to put her out of her misery she shouted, 'It's all right, we've got all the establishers we need. There's only one other wide and that'll be from over on the other hill where we wouldn't see the tower anyway.'

Alison froze in mid-tantrum and glared up at Laurence. Laurence was grinning. Alison stretched out a hand for him to haul her to her feet. Like a fool he took it and nearly found himself face down in the mud. At the last minute he managed to wrench himself out of her grasp, but nevertheless was too late to stop himself sinking to his knees.

The whole unit exploded into laughter while Laurence collected a fist full of mire and rubbed it in Alison's face.

'You bastard!' she shouted. 'I'm going to get you for this,' and sitting bolt upright, she threw her arms around him and kissed him.

Seeing the way Kirsten and Anna were laughing Laurence pulled himself to his feet and started towards them. Both shrieked and turned to run, but Anna wasn't quick enough and throwing her back in his arms Laurence kissed her full on the mouth then rubbed his cheeks against hers.

'Oh, Laurence!' the make-up girl cried. 'I'm going to have to start all over again now.'

Laurence looked down at Anna's face. 'She looks just the same to me,' he said and Kirsten winced. Not the most tactful of things to say to an artist who had spent three hours creating an effect, and make-up girls were notoriously sensitive.

'All right! That's enough!' a voice suddenly boomed behind her. 'We're already an hour behind schedule so we can't afford time out for horse-play. Everybody back in position.'

'He's a bundle of laughs, isn't he?' Anna murmured to Kirsten as David, the first assistant, lifted his walkie-talkie to yell at one of the chargehands.

'He's OK,' Kirsten answered, still laughing as Laurence went off to clean himself up. 'I know he's not much fun, but he's good at his job. Oh my goodness!' she suddenly cried. 'Tom! Tom! What are you doing? Oh, heavens, Tom, stop that . . .'

But Tom's face was already covered in mud, so were his hands, his feet, in fact everything he was wearing.

Kirsten started towards him not realizing until it was too late that he was only doing what Laurence had done, for, as she scooped him up in her arms he threw his own about her neck and kissed her.

'You little monkey!' she cried, trying to turn her face away. 'Tom, stop it!'

'I'm sorry,' Jane laughed, grabbing him. 'Come here you little rascal,' she said, pulling him into her arms.

Tom went and they all laughed as Jane got the same treatment as Kirsten.

'You know what Daddy said,' Jane chuckled, trying to hold him away from her. 'No one's supposed even to know you're here otherwise we'll have to go home.'

At that Kirsten reached out to ruffle Tom's curls. If no one was supposed to know about them then either Jane or Laurence had failed in their task, for even after just this short time Tom had become the most popular member of the crew. Particularly, she'd noticed, with the props department, for there were a myriad of things in the prop vans to keep a young mind agog for hours.

'So that's where you've got to.'

Kirsten, Jane and Anna turned as Laurence came striding back towards them. Obviously he'd got waylaid somewhere on the way to cleaning up because there was still mud on his face. In fact, as he sat Tom on his hip the two of them looked quite a picture. 'You, young man, are getting right into the shower with me and then it's off to sleep for you.'

'I don't want to sleep,' Tom declared. 'I want to stay here.'

'I expect you do, but you don't have any choice in the matter.' He looked over at Anna. 'They want you in make-up,' he said. 'They reckon you need a cleaning up too.'

'Oh, sounds like fun,' Anna said grinning at Kirsten. 'Three of us in the same shower.'

'You're beginning to sound like Alison,' Laurence frowned. 'In fact,' he added, looking at Kirsten's muddy face, 'it kind of looks to me like it should be you joining us in the shower.'

It was evident, the moment he'd said it, that both of them wished he hadn't, for at the very suggestion of such an intimacy Kirsten felt the colour rising in her cheeks and despite his wry smile Laurence couldn't have looked more uncomfortable if he'd tried.

Anna's eyebrows were raised as she looked from one to the other and it was apparent that she was wondering if she hadn't stumbled upon something here. However, for the moment, she said nothing, she merely took Laurence's arm and they walked off towards the make-up trailers.

'Where is he? I got to speak to him. I got to speak to him now!' Ruby declared, pushing her way past Jane into Laurence's room.

'He's gone out for dinner with Jake,' Jane answered, dismayed at the unmistakable whiff of alcohol that had come in with Ruby.

'Well at least he's not off somewhere with the Simpering Sage,' Ruby slurred. Her lipstick was smudged and there were dark circles under her eyes. This wasn't the first time Jane had seen her drunk, but it was the first time she was having to cope with it.

'Is there something I can do?' Jane asked. 'Can I give him a message.'

'Yeah. You can tell him from me that he's got to stop this movie now,' Ruby declared, blinking hard as though to clear her vision. 'Have you got anything to drink here?'

'Uh, no, I don't think we have,' Jane answered.

'Never mind. I've got some right here,' Ruby said delving into her bag. 'That bloody French witch told me this would happen,' she gasped, after taking a large mouthful. 'She said "you'll see a castle fall." Well it fell, didn't it? It fell and it was a goddamned miracle no one was killed. So we got to stop now before someone is.'

Jane stared at her.

'Well don't just stand there,' Ruby barked, 'get me a glass.'

Jane hurried off to the bathroom and brought one back.

'Where's Tom?' Ruby demanded.

'Asleep.'

'Well you just keep your eye on that boy. She said it was a girl, but I'm not so sure. You make sure you don't let that boy out of your sight. A child and a baby, she said, so who the hell is that would you say?'

The corner of Jane's mouth pursed uncertainly.

'Yeah, I know, you think I'm crazy,' Ruby snorted. 'Well I thought she was crazy until today . . . Coming out with all that claptrap about castles falling, people dying and babies smashing to bits . . . What's she talking about, that's what I want to know? She said it was me, inside me. But I didn't do nothing to make that tower come down . . .'

'It was a thunderbolt,' Jane said lamely.

'Yeah, but was it? Oh you can look at me anyways you like but I'm telling you that I want this movie stopped.'

'But everything's going so well,' Jane protested.

'For you, maybe. Got yourself a boyfriend I see.'

Jane's colour looked almost painful as she turned to Billy who Ruby had only just noticed sitting on the sofa.

Ruby laughed. 'Well don't let me interrupt you guys

no more, just tell Laurence I want to see him the minute he gets back,' and with that she walked from the room staggering slightly as she reached the door.

'No, no, no,' Kirsten laughed, tossing back her thick hair which was gleaming like copper in the flickering firelight, 'you've got it all wrong, Anna. There's very definitely nothing between Laurence and me these days, at least not on the personal front.'

'Are you sure?' Anna frowned, curling her delicate limbs into the deep armchair opposite the one Kirsten was sitting in. 'I mean, did you see the way he looked at you earlier?'

'I'm quite sure,' Kirsten smiled, experiencing a pleasing lift in her heart as she sipped the creamy Guinness they'd had delivered to Anna's room.

'So is what they're all saying true then? I mean about you and Jake?'

'What about me and Jake?'

'Oh come on, you know what I'm talking about. And we're girls together here, you can tell me.'

'Actually,' Kirsten said, 'people have been talking about Jake and me ever since he started on the movie and no one's yet come up with any proof.'

Anna grinned. 'Except I saw him coming out of your room very early the other morning. Don't worry, my lips are sealed.'

Kirsten was shaking her head and laughing. 'If you'd happened to come into my room,' she said, 'then you'd have seen Jake's entire crew. We all had breakfast together.'

'It's OK, it's OK,' Anna said, holding up her hands. 'If you don't want to talk about it I'll stop prying. But

I'll tell you this, if Laurence weren't around I'd give you a run for your money over Jake. He's absolutely gorgeous.'

'Mmm. I imagine his wife thinks so too.'

'He's married! Well isn't that the way of the world, someone else always manages to get in first.' She stretched and yawned. 'Tell me, is it true that I look a bit like Laurence's wife?' she asked nonchalantly.

'Mmm, yes, you do a bit,' Kirsten answered, opening her script in the hope of changing the subject.

Anna pondered this for a moment, then as her eyes came back up to Kirsten's Kirsten saw the sparkle of mischief. 'Well, since you assure me I'm not treading on your toes, darling,' she said, 'how do you reckon my chances?'

Kirsten moved restlessly, struggling to keep the smile on her face. 'Well, he's pretty wrapped up in the movie,' she said. 'And he doesn't really approve of relationships on the set . . .'

Anna laughed. 'That's what they all say until it happens to them. And to tell you the truth, Kirstie, until I saw that look he gave you today I was beginning to think he was quite keen on me.'

Kirsten started to answer but broke off as the thunder that had seconds before started rumbling through the night crescendoed ominously towards them. Suddenly, in one deafening boom, it crashed overhead and Anna jumped.

'You know,' she muttered, looking warily at the ceiling. 'I'm not going to be sorry to leave this place. I don't know whether it's all this stuff about voodoo Ruby's given me to read . . .' She spun round as suddenly the window swung open and the curtain billowed into the room. 'Good God, I'm going to have a heart attack if this keeps up,' she gasped.

Kirsten was laughing as she walked across the dimly lit room to close the window. 'Just remember this is exactly the weather we want,' she said, casting an eye over the dark flock flowers on the wallpaper and feeling slightly sorry for Anna that she was in such a sombre room.

Anna cast another lingeringly suspicious look about the room before turning back to the script resting on the arm of the chair. 'Like I said, I've been going over some of the scenes for New Orleans,' she said. 'They're amazing, brilliant, in fact, though I have to admit they've put the wind up me a bit.' She laughed. 'Heaven only knows what I'm going to be like once we come to do them. Actually, I was talking to Helena Johnson about them before I came over here . . . You know, I have to hand it to you, Kirsten, she really is amazing casting. I mean she actually looks like the original Marie Laveau with all that black hair, great big staring eyes and swarthy skin.'

'You wait until you see her in full make-up and costume,' Kirsten laughed. 'She even manages to spook me and I've known her I don't know how many years.'

'Ruby's written a great part for her,' Anna commented. 'In fact, like I said, what Ruby's done with this script is quite brilliant.'

'I'm glad you think so,' Kirsten smiled.

'She doesn't like me much though, does she? Oh, don't bother to deny it, I can tell.'

'I think you would call Ruby a man's woman,' Kirsten chuckled. 'At least, I think that's what Ruby would call Ruby. She has a bit of a problem with women.'

'You seem to get on OK with her.'

'It took a while. And you will too, once she gets used to you.'

Anna's eyes returned to the script and Kirsten watched her as after turning several pages she started to smile. 'These love scenes are really explicit, aren't they?' she said.

'Don't worry we won't be shooting them quite that way,' Kirsten laughed.

'But I'll have to do them nude?'

Kirsten nodded. 'Is that a problem? We'll close the set, of course, only essential people will be in the room.'

Anna gave Kirsten a dazzling smile. 'Will Laurence be there?' she asked.

'That depends whether you want him to be,' Kirsten answered, feeling the muscles in her face stiffen.

'I'll discuss the lighting with Jake and let you know,' Anna winked.

'Actually Jake and I have already discussed lighting,' Kirsten said. 'He's using cosmetic filters.'

'Oh. In that case then I think we'll invite Laurence, don't you?'

'Let's talk about that when the time comes, shall we?' Kirsten smiled. 'Now, getting back to what we're shooting over the next couple . . .' she broke off as the telephone beside Anna's bed jangled.

Anna got up to answer it as yet another clap of thunder boomed through the night. 'God, I hate this weather,' she mumbled, picking up the phone. 'Hello. Oh, Laurence, darling. We were just talking about you . . .' She laughed at whatever Laurence had said. 'Actually, we were discussing the love scene between Jean-Paul and I . . . No, there's no problem. Laurence, any time you want me to take my clothes off, you know you just have to ask . . .' Again she laughed. 'Did you have a good dinner?' she asked. 'Oh, I know, it's awful, isn't it? My window just flew open . . .' She turned to Kirsten and winked. 'In fact,' she went on, 'I was just saying to Kirsten that I really don't know that I can handle sleeping alone in this room . . . No, they're all booked up. Oh, it's OK, I'm sure I'll manage . . . No, really, I'm sure Kirsten's got other things to do . . .' She laughed. 'I'm sure she'd agree – at least sleeping with this particular star might be going beyond the call of duty. Oh, Laurence, I'd love to join you . . . I've got a very early call though. OK, breakfast at six-thirty,' she added and Kirsten relaxed. 'Yes, sure, I'll pass you over.'

'Thanks,' Kirsten said, taking the receiver.

'Ruby's back on her coconut trip,' Laurence said. 'I think we'd better get over there.'

'Of course,' Kirsten answered. 'Just don't suggest I sleep with her as well, will you?'

Laurence laughed. 'See you in five,' he said and rang off.

When Laurence and Kirsten got to Ruby's room it was to find Ruby virtually incoherent. A near empty bottle of gin was resting precariously against the lamp beside her bed and as they walked in the door she struggled to reach it. Laurence whisked it out of the way while Kirsten pulled back the eiderdown and resettled it over Ruby. Then, as Ruby mumbled on about Legba and Erzulie and Damballah, and all the other voodoo gods she could think of, Kirsten picked up the phone and called the unit nurse to ask her to come and sit with Ruby for a while.

When the nurse arrived Kirsten and Laurence left the room and made their way along the narrow shadowy landing, their footsteps muted by the shabby rugs. 'I can't make head nor tail of what she's talking about these days,' Laurence grumbled.

'Me neither.'

'She crashed into my room earlier and amongst other things warned Jane never to let Tom out of her sight.'

'She what!' Kirsten cried. 'Oh, she's going too far now, we've got to do something to make her stop.'

'Got any suggestions?'

They had reached Kirsten's room by now and Kirsten turned to lean against the wall pushing her hands into the pockets of her skirt. Laurence stood in front of her, his hands too were in his pockets.

'Not off the top of my head,' Kirsten said. 'But there is someone who might be able to help. Helena. She knows a bit about voodoo, not that I am in the least convinced that a blinking coconut reading is anything to do with voodoo ... It might be that Helena can talk some sense into her though ...'

'OK. It's worth a shot. We'll see how Ruby shapes up over the next couple of days and if things look like they're getting any worse we'll fly Helena over.'

'I'll call her and warn her,' Kirsten chuckled. 'So, did you and Jake have a good dinner?'

'It was OK. You should have come.'

'I wasn't hungry.' She laughed again, this time a little uncomfortably. 'It seems that Anna is making quite a play for you.'

Laurence cocked an eyebrow as he looked deep into her eyes. 'Yeah, it would seem that way,' he said. 'You don't like her much, do you?'

'I think she's turning in a terrific performance.'

'That's not what I said.'

'I know.'

'Don't worry, no one else would know it, it's just that I know you pretty well . . .'

'Are you trying to suggest I might be jealous?' Kirsten said, lifting her chin defiantly at the same time suddenly realizing that he was standing much closer than he needed.

'Are you?'

'No, of course I'm not.'

'That's good.' There was a teasing, almost seductive tone to his voice and his eyes had taken on that sleepy quality that could turn her knees weak.

'Laurence,' she said quietly, 'I told you before we started, I don't want you playing with me like this . . .'

'You don't?'

'Laurence, stop it.'

He lifted a hand from his pocket and as he brushed it lightly over her breasts the desire that clenched her was so painful her breath caught in her throat.

'Laurence,' she whispered, but as his fingers swept sensuously over the front of her sweater her hands remained rooted in her pockets, just as her eyes remained fixed on his.

Neither of them could have been in any doubt where it would have ended had Jake and Lindon not stepped out of the lift at that moment. But, by the time Kirsten was tucked up in bed, she was glad that it hadn't gone any further. She'd recognized the signs and it wasn't his lust she wanted, it was his love.

As their days in Ireland progressed the storms, which still showed little sign of letting up, began to take their toll on morale. Anna had suddenly taken it upon herself to acquire a nervous disposition which was as false as it was pathetic. Everyone could see through it, even Laurence, whose task it was to comfort her when she claimed that the storms or Ruby's ramblings were putting her on edge. It was Anna's way of getting Laurence to herself and since she was the star there was little Laurence could do but appease her. However, he didn't seem to object, in fact it looked to Kirsten like he rather enjoyed his role as the great protector. And when he wasn't with Anna he was with Ruby, mollifying her and trying to keep her off the bottle.

Fortunately, he made relatively few visits to the set and Kirsten couldn't have been in any doubt during that time how vital her own morale was to the rest of the crew. She had to contain her jealousy for their sakes even more than her own, she realized, she owed it to them for they were as loyal to her now as they were dependent on her. It was only Jake who seemed to sense the cracks, and always he was there to help smooth them over. He could make her laugh when it was the last thing she felt like doing and get her enthused at a time when the wind was painfully stinging her ears and the rain was dripping down her neck.

Still, there were moments in the day when their laughter rang over the hillside, particularly when Alison started to come up with cartoon sketches of Jane and Billy, the location manager, and what they might look like were they ever to get it together. Even Laurence had to choke back his laughter when he saw them. Whether Billy and Jane ever knew what amusement they were causing was impossible to tell, except Vicky, Kirsten's assistant, did whisper to Kirsten one day that Jane had got hold of one of the sketches.

'Oh shit! How did she take it?' Kirsten asked and she

and Vicky promptly burst into laughter at the inappropriateness of the question.

'Sssh, she's in there with Tom,' Vicky murmured, nodding towards a connecting door in the production trailer. 'I don't think she much liked how big Alison made her teeth. But there again, I don't suppose it was the size of her *teeth* that brought her eyes out on stalks . . .'

'Stop it,' Kirsten laughed. 'Now tell me, did you manage to get on to the labs?'

'Lindon did. Everything's OK. It wasn't our rushes they had a problem with.'

'Thank God for that. Does Laurence know yet?'

'Yes. I told him earlier. There's something else I'd better warn you about though. Ruby's got it into her head to really spook the Simpering Sage. You know what she's like with any woman around Laurence, well she's been feeding the Sage all sorts of rubbish about voodoo, I mean more than we realized and . . .'

'Does Laurence know?' Kirsten said soberly.

'If he doesn't he's certainly going to. Ruby says if the Sage wants to be nervous then she can have something to be nervous about.'

'I'd better speak to him,' Kirsten said. 'We can't have Ruby doing that sort of thing, not when she takes it seriously herself. She really could frighten Anna and quite frankly that's the last thing we need.'

But Kirsten was too late. When she went to Laurence's trailer Anna was already there, weeping in his arms. Quite how successful Ruby had been was anyone's guess for Anna was as capable as any actress of turning on a performance, but whatever the real effect on her was she was certainly making a meal out of her distress. And she continued to do so for the next two days, by which time Kirsten was viewing her departure from the set with unmitigated relief. It wasn't that anyone was taking either her or Ruby's ramblings seriously, it was just that they were becoming extremely tedious by now. And the fact that Laurence had spoken sharply to her, Kirsten, about it, telling her that she should be a little more tolerant of the weaknesses in others had made Kirsten want to scream.

They had added a further two days to the shoot which were going to be spent doing pick-ups and Jean Rochette's solitary amblings through the bleak Irish downs. Laurence was going on ahead to New Orleans with Ruby, Alison, Anna and several other members of the production team.

On the day of their departure Kirsten woke up feeling particularly depressed. She tried hard all morning to shake it but she couldn't help feeling angry with herself for being so damned obsessed with the fact that Laurence and Anna were going off to New Orleans together.

It was just after lunch as Laurence, assisted by Tom, was clearing out his trailer, that Jane came to stand beside Kirsten at the edge of the set. It was one of the rare occasions when Kirsten wasn't surrounded by people or shouting instructions, receiving information, blocking the cast or being shown a prop or a costume.

For several minutes she and Jane stood in the drizzling rain watching the stunt co-ordinator round up the stunt riders and horses in front of the castle.

Eventually Kirsten looked down at Jane and smiled. 'Laurence not ready yet?' she said.

Jane shook her head. 'A few more minutes he said. It all seems to be going pretty well, doesn't it?' she added nodding towards the set.

'I think so,' Kirsten answered cheerily. 'At least I hope

so. Anyway, what about you? How are you getting along? I don't see much of you these days.'

'Oh, I'm fine. Tom and I have really enjoyed ourselves here.'

'That's good. It seems that both of you have scored quite a hit, one way or another.'

Jane's blush looked painful. 'Are you talking about Billy?' she said shyly.

Kirsten's smile widened. 'Keen on him, are you?' she said.

'I think so,' Jane confessed. 'Well, he's a bit old for me, but . . . Well, I was wondering if I might be able to talk to you about it. I mean, I don't really have any experience of boyfriends . . .'

'Oh Jane,' Kirsten laughed. 'You're talking to the wrong person. You know what a mess I've made of my life and the way Laurence and I are with each other right now is hardly an advert . . .'

'Sssh,' Jane said seeing Alison come swooping out of a trailer behind them carrying one of her set decorators on her back.

Kirsten turned to watch them, laughing as they tumbled to the ground then looking down at Jane again she said, 'Have you been out on a date with him yet?'

'Oh no,' Jane said. 'He comes and keeps me company when I'm looking after Tom in the evenings, but . . .'

'Kirstie!' Jake yelled.

'Oh, Jane, I'm sorry, we'll have to continue this another time,' Kirsten said. 'We'll get together in New Orleans, OK? Laurence can look after Tom . . .' She laughed at Jane's wide-eyed delight, patted her cheek then was on the point of running over to Jake when he shouted that it didn't matter.

'Seems I'm all yours again,' Kirsten said. 'So, where were we?'

'Oh, it can wait till you've got more time,' Jane answered. 'By the way, Helena called this morning. She wanted to know how things were going over here and if . . . If the . . .'

'Come on, spit it out,' Kirsten encouraged her.

'She wanted to know if the . . . If the rumours about Laurence and Anna were true,' Jane said.

Immediately Kirsten's smile faded. 'Helena's heard about that, back in London?'

Jane nodded sheepishly. 'It would seem so. She told me to tell you that she's making a voodoo doll of Anna Sage that you can stick pins in . . .'

'For God's sake!' Kirsten snapped. 'I'm relying on Helena to sort Ruby out not to spread even more of this nonsense about the place. If Anna Sage ever got wind of that . . .' She shuddered. 'It doesn't bear thinking about. Anyway, sorry, I didn't mean to snap at you and it looks like Laurence is ready so I'll wish you *bon voyage*.'

'Thank you,' Jane murmured, then turning her eager young face up to Kirsten's she said, 'Thank you for being so nice to me.'

'Oh, Jane!' Kirsten cried, hugging her. 'I've neglected you horribly these past few months, but I'll make up for it once we get to New Orleans. And by the way, thank you for the hand and foot warmers. I really needed them.'

'That's all right,' Jane said happily. 'I'll see you in New Orleans then.'

As she walked away Laurence came to join Kirsten. 'You OK?' he said as they watched what was going on on the set.

'I'm fine. How about you?'

Laurence turned to face her. His jet black hair, wet from the rain, was slicked back from his forehead and his face, burned by the wind, somehow made his eyes seem bluer than ever. 'I'm worried about you,' he said softly.

Kirsten's surprise showed. 'About me, why?'

He shrugged. 'I guess leaving you here to cope with all this,' he said throwing out an arm towards the set.

Kirsten's expression turned to one of irony. 'You're taking the problems with you,' she reminded him.

He nodded and as his smile disappeared he looked past her towards the gloomy castle perched on the hillside.

'What're you thinking?' Kirsten asked after a while.

He didn't answer for some time and as the minutes passed his frown deepened. Then, as he looked down at her again, Kirsten had the startling and overwhelming feeling that he was about to kiss her.

She waited, meeting his gaze and silently daring him to give in to the urge she could almost feel him fighting. God, how she wanted to discard her principles and feel the hardness of him at that moment. They were so close, their lips only inches apart, their eyes locked in wordless combat, each challenging the other to give in. Kirsten shivered as the surface of her skin tingled with awareness, her hands were like lead weights yearning to be lifted yet were too heavy, too awkward to move. For those timeless moments it was as though they were alone on the hillside, oblivious to the commotion of the set only feet away, unaffected by the mewling cry of the wind as it wrapped itself around them as though to push them closer together.

'You look lovely,' Laurence murmured, then suddenly

his eyes closed and he groaned as though in anguish, but the groan rapidly turned to laughter which made Kirsten laugh too.

'You're doing just great, you know that?' he told her.

'Thank you,' she said.

'I reckon we're gonna have our work cut out over there in New Orleans,' Laurence remarked, and from the way he was looking straight into her eyes Kirsten knew he wasn't just referring to the film.

'Yeah, I reckon we are,' she said quietly. 'But I think I can handle it. What about you?'

Laurence's bottom lip came out as his eyes danced with humour. 'Yeah,' he nodded. 'I reckon I can. But, hey, no hanging around here in Ireland. Get finished and get out there smartish 'cos I can handle it a whole lot better when you're around.'

'You can?' Kirsten teased.

Laurence laughed, then winking at her he turned towards Alison who was heading in their direction. Shit, this was hard, he was thinking to himself. Much harder even than he'd expected. He badly wanted to make love to her again, but how the hell was he going to do that without getting himself involved more deeply than he'd be comfortable with. If it were any other woman he wouldn't be thinking twice, he'd just go right ahead and screw her, but Kirsten was going to read a whole lot more into it than he wanted her to. But, hell, keeping himself in check was proving so goddamned difficult when these past few days he'd only had to look at her to feel himself start to get an erection. He knew her resolve that they didn't sleep together during the shoot would be as easy to shatter as it would be for him to give in to his desire, but he didn't want her thinking that they were going to be an item again when he had every intention of hanging on to his freedom.

Kirsten had wandered over to the stunt co-ordinator who was lining up the horsemen for the next shot. Jake was with him and as usual he greeted Kirsten with a resounding kiss, and as usual Kirsten chided him for his lack of respect. She listened as he explained what was happening, they changed several positions, pulled in three more horses then after blocking the scene through David yelled out for everyone to start setting up for a take.

Kirsten was on her way to the location caterers to get herself a coffee when Laurence pulled his car to a halt on the dirt track leading to the main road and waved her over. By the time she got there Tom was hanging out of the back window, holding out his arms for a kiss. Laughing, Kirsten gave him as big a hug as she could then after uttering a few encouraging words to Anna she turned to Laurence. But before she could speak he said so that only she could hear,

'Have a word with your friend Helena before you get to New Orleans. I want this voodoo rubbish knocked on the head.'

'I intend to,' Kirsten told him, hiding her exasperation at his ever-changing moods. His expression was as black as the thunderous clouds and his irritation was equally as evident. Still, with Ruby Collins in the back seat and Anna Sage in the front she didn't suppose she'd be any too happy herself. 'Anything else before you go, oh lord and master?' she quipped.

A flicker of amusement sparked in his eyes and Kirsten knew that he was thinking of the private games they had once played. She pursed her lips in a smile. The chemistry leapt between them so strongly at times it took only one word, one movement, for it to spring into life, but on this occasion Laurence turned abruptly away. 'No, nothing else,' he said. His eyes returned briefly to hers. 'Nothing at all,' he added and as Kirsten looked down at him curiously he pressed hard on the accelerator and the car sped off.

— 20 —

'Oh come on, can't we drop it now?' Helena grumbled, adjusting her seat to lie more comfortably. 'I told you it was a joke, how the hell do I know how to make a goddamned whammy doll?'

'I'm not saying you do,' Kirsten said. 'I'm just asking you not even to mention it in front of Anna. Or Ruby. Laurence is relying on you to try and calm them both down. Though if you ask me Anna's faking her fear. In fact everyone thinks she is. She just likes playing the damsel in distress and having big strong Laurence take care of her.'

'Yuk!' Helena muttered. 'Anyway,' she said, yawning and settling deeper into her seat, 'I take it there's no truth to the rumours? They're not having an affair?'

'I don't think so,' Kirsten answered. And she didn't. How could they be when Laurence was behaving the way he was with her?

'So, how are things doing between you two?' Helena asked. 'Any progress?'

Kirsten smiled. 'Yes and no,' she said. Then she

groaned, 'I have to tell you, Helena, seeing him every day and feeling the way I do is a living hell. I told you what happened outside my hotel room, didn't I? Yes, of course I did. Well, since then I've kind of come to a decision.'

'Which is?' Helena prompted.

'I'm going back on all I said before and if he makes one more approach to me I'm not going to do anything to stop him. No, I know what you're going to say, I never have stopped him, and believe you me I despise myself for being so weak. But I have to accept the fact that I can't resist him so the next time anything looks like it's going to happen I'm going to come right out with it and tell him exactly how I feel about him.'

'You are?' Helena said, evidently impressed.

'I am. I'm almost positive he feels the same way, at least sometimes I am and I thought that maybe if I came clean about my feelings it might encourage him to come clean about his and that way I can get on with things without tying myself up in knots about what might or might not be going on in his head.'

'Sounds reasonable,' Helena commented.

'I just hope I'm right,' Kirsten went on a little less confidently. 'I mean, I know there's no problem with regard to the sexual side of things, but as to whether or not he's in love with me . . .'

'Of course he is,' Helena interrupted. 'Any jackass can see that.'

Kirsten laughed and squeezed Helena's hand. It was exactly what she'd wanted to hear.

She rested her head against the back of the seat and closed her eyes. As happy as she felt the ambiguity of his parting words had been preying on her mind ever since he'd left and they were in danger of taking on a meaning that she longed to escape. But she couldn't, and by now she'd lost count of the times she'd asked herself if perhaps she hadn't got it all wrong. Maybe the chemistry between them lived only in her mind. Was the certainty that they would get together in the end merely wishful thinking on her part? The way he sometimes looked at her, was she only seeing what she wanted to see and blinding herself to the reality? Perhaps he was simply stringing her along, playing with her, teasing her . . .

Suddenly she sat forward in her chair and pulled her script from her bag. She was aware of how easy it was for her to fall victim to her insecurities and she just wasn't going to let that happen. It was a shame that she couldn't handle her feelings as well as she was handling the film, but that was no reason to dwell on them.

After changing planes in New York, then again in Atlanta, they were at last approaching New Orleans. Kirsten was just about all in, but was nevertheless looking over the storyboard Alison had left with her. Jesus Christ, she was thinking to herself, they had one hell of a lot to get through in New Orleans. The cast was going to multiply and the technical requirements would be sure to stretch the budget to its limits, if not beyond. Right now she didn't want to think too much about that, but it was something she and Laurence were going to have to take a long hard look at once she arrived. She turned to Helena and found her watching her with a curious expression in her eyes.

'Why are you looking at me like that?' she asked.

Helena shrugged. 'Just wondering how you manage to keep going.'

Kirsten smiled and put aside the storyboard. 'To tell you the truth, I love it. As difficult as it sometimes is to control my emotions I wouldn't change things for the world. Honestly, when I saw the rough cut in London . . . Well, I can hardly describe how I felt. Laurence had already seen it, he called me right after . . . He doesn't enthuse about things as much as I do, but I knew he was pleased, more than pleased.' She laughed softly. 'I'm really glad you're here. I missed you when I was in Ireland.'

'That's good to know,' Helena smiled. 'I missed you too. I can't tell you how much I've been looking forward to getting started myself. We're going to have a lot of fun over here.' Her smile was so mischievous that Kirsten's eyes started to dance.

'I'm warning you, Helena,' she said, 'if you do anything to give me the heebie-jeebies . . . No, don't look at me like that, I know you, I've worked with you before, remember? One iota of encouragement from the crew and you'll come up with something to put my hair on end while we're doing those night shoots, but if you do, I'm warning you, I'll be making a voodoo doll of my own.'

Helena squeezed her hand. 'That's something I hope you'll never feel the need to do,' she murmured.

An hour or so later they were checking into the Richelieu Hotel. The welcome Kirsten received from the receptionists who remembered her from the recce was so warm it was almost embarrassing. She looked fondly around the faded splendour of the baroque lobby and felt her heart contract as she remembered the day Laurence had virtually ordered her to his room. Suddenly the nerves she felt at seeing him were affecting her badly.

Jake and the crew came in behind them and despite

how tired they all were after the long flight he insisted that they have a quick drink before going to their rooms. The dark, long bar just behind the reception was, as usual, half filled with locals who were engrossed in the TV screen where the Saints were playing. The conservatory adjoining the bar was dark, but the swimming pool beyond was lit up. Everything was just the same – not that she'd expected anything to have changed, it was simply that as they'd driven in from the airport she'd started once again to get that uneasy feeling about New Orleans.

After downing a glass of cold beer and refusing Jake's offer of dinner, Kirsten and Helena took themselves off to the lift. 'You know, I might change my mind about dinner,' Helena remarked, patting her hair in the mirror as they began the journey up to the fourth floor. 'Where did they say they were going?'

'Brigstens.' Kirsten started to laugh. 'You know sometimes, Helena, you're so transparent . . .'

Helena grinned. 'Well come on, even you have got to admit that Jake Butler is pretty damned gorgeous. All that baby blond hair and those sexy brown eyes . . .'

'Make him the heart-throb of the entire unit,' Kirsten finished for her. 'But as far as I know he's happily married.'

'Shame,' Helena grimaced, standing aside to let Kirsten walk out ahead of her. 'What number are you, by the way?'

'Four-oh-four. About three doors from you.'

'Kirsten! Is that you?'

Both Helena and Kirsten turned to see Alison bearing down on them in a blaze of luminous pink plastic.

'Where on earth did you get that outfit?' Kirsten cried, holding up a hand to shield her eyes.

'Great, isn't it?' Alison laughed, giving them a twirl, 'and look, it's all held together with velcro,' and with that she tore the upper-part away to reveal a matching bra with tassles swinging from the points of the cups.

'Wow! That's fantastic!' Helena gasped. 'I've just got to have myself one.'

'Down in the French market. Forty dollars,' Alison told her. 'It's driving everyone wild.'

'You don't say,' Kirsten remarked dryly.

'I do, but anyway, have I got news for you! Gossip! Gossip!' She gave a shudder of glee and pulling Kirsten and Helena around the corner and away from the lifts she said, 'The Simpering Sage has cracked it! She and Laurence have been at it morning, noon and night ever since they got here. I'm telling you they're screwing themselves brainless. Laurence can hardly keep his eyes open during our meetings and Ruby . . . Shit, the fireworks!'

Helena was already looking at Kirsten and it was all she could do to stop herself slipping an arm around her shoulders when she saw the strain in Kirsten's face.

'How do you know?' Kirsten faltered.

'Christ, it's hard not to know!' Alison cried. 'Oh God! Look! See what I mean?' And she nodded excitedly for Kirsten to look behind her. Half way down the corridor Laurence was coming out of one of the rooms. Anna was with him, but ventured only to the threshold where she gave him a lingering kiss on the mouth before he took her arms from around his neck and walked off in the opposite direction.

Without giving herself time to think Kirsten called out after him. He turned, and when he saw her standing there in the dimly-lit corridor, so obviously having seen what had happened, his discomfort was evident.

'There are things I need to go over with you,' Kirsten said, biting out the words, '*if* you can find the time.'

'I have the time,' he bit back.

'Good. Perhaps we can meet in an hour.'

'I'll be in my room,' he barked and abruptly turned to walk on.

'Ooops, seems like more fireworks on the way,' Alison giggled. 'Anyway, better rush. See you later,' and she was gone.

'Kirstie?' Helena said carefully.

'Please, don't say anything,' Kirsten muttered.

'Come on, let's get you to your room.'

'I'm not a fucking invalid,' Kirsten snapped, when Helena made to take her arm.

'OK, OK, I'm sorry,' Helena said, drawing away. 'I reckon you'd better have yourself a stiff drink.'

But when they reached Kirsten's room after unlocking the door Kirsten turned to Helena saying, 'I know you mean well, and don't think I don't appreciate your concern, but really, right now, I'd like to be alone if you don't mind.'

Helena studied her face, searching for the tears she felt sure wouldn't be far away, but to her surprise there was no sign of them. 'OK,' she said, hesitantly, 'but you know where I am if you need me.'

Kirsten closed the door behind her and leaned against it, closing her eyes in the darkness and pushing her head back into the solid wood. This couldn't be happening, she was telling herself, it couldn't be true. But it was, she'd seen it with her own eyes. He was sleeping with that stupid bitch of an actress and he was flaunting it in the face of the entire crew. Which could only mean that her recent misgivings had been correct. Everything she had felt growing between them had been in her

imagination. He had been playing with her, leading
her on to believe that something would happen between
them and all the time he'd known what effect he was
having on her.

'What a fool!' she seethed, tears squeezing their way
through her tightly closed eyes. 'What a damned fool
I've made of myself!'

Reaching out a hand she fumbled in the darkness for
the light-switch. When she found it she immediately
hunted around for the mini-bar. But no! The hell she
was going to be drunk when she confronted him. She
wanted her faculties intact, and he'd just better come
up with some damned good talking to get himself out
of this one. For a moment the pain and jealousy was so
intense it was all she could do to stop herself screaming.
She wanted and needed him so badly that the very
thought of him even so much as touching Anna was too
much to bear. But she couldn't cry, she couldn't go to
him with eyes that betrayed her hurt, even though in
that moment she didn't know that she could face him
at all.

And in the end she couldn't. It wasn't only that she
was afraid to, it was that she really didn't see what
purpose it would serve to confront him. He'd made his
choice and she was just going to have to live with it.
But how she was going to get through the next four
weeks dealing with Anna Sage on a day to day, almost
minute to minute, basis she just didn't know.

It was eleven o'clock when Laurence called. 'I thought
you wanted to see me,' he said.

'No. It's late and I'm tired,' Kirsten answered, her
heart so weighted by pain and betrayal her voice was
thick with it.

'I see. Well, if there's nothing . . .'

'There's nothing, Laurence,' she said, 'nothing at all,' and she replaced the receiver.

'OK, let's take it from the drive up,' Kirsten shouted, clapping her hands to try and break through the noise around her.

'*Stand by for another rehearsal!*' David boomed into the loud-hailer. 'Reset the carriage! Main cast in first positions!'

'Am I delivering my first line as I get out of the carriage or do I wait until I'm on the sidewalk?' Helena asked.

'Start speaking as your foot hits the ground,' Kirsten answered. 'We'll go in with your turn for a close up on Anna. But play the scene through to the end.'

'Got it,' Helena said and lifting her long, drab skirts she hoisted herself back into the landau.

As the carriage was turned and led back down Decatur Street Kirsten walked over to Jake. 'That sky is bothering me,' she said looking up at the way the sun was threatening to burst through the cloud.

'It's bothering me too. We'll have to be quick about this or nothing's going to match.'

'Did you take a look inside the carriage? Are we seeing them all right, or shall we take the roof down?'

'Which would you prefer?'

'That the roof is up.'

'Then we'll make it work. Phil!' he shouted to the gaffer and leaving Kirsten he went off to organize the lights.

'Make-up!' Kirsten called.

'Right here,' an assistant answered.

'Take another look at Anna before we go for a take.

– 370 –

Her hair's too tidy. No, don't do it now, we'll do the rehearsal first. Have you got any more of that lip salve?'

The make up assistant handed it over, Kirsten ran it quickly over her wind-chapped lips then moved off to talk to the sound guys.

'There's no dialogue until the carriage stops,' she told them, 'so we can wild track the horse's hooves.'

'Danny's already over there rigging up the mike,' Bob told her.

'Great. Did you get the steamboat whistles earlier?'

'Not really. Too much other noise.'

'OK, we'll get it set up for another time.' She swung round as a trumpet suddenly blasted from across the street.

'David!' she yelled. 'David!'

'I'm on it,' he called back and Kirsten watched him briefly as he headed off towards the busker who had somehow broken through the police cordons. 'How are we doing up there, Russell?' David shouted into his walkie-talkie.

'A few more minutes,' Russell answered. 'The carriage is almost here.'

Kirsten stood with her hands on her hips absently watching the riggers as they greased the tracks on the pavement and checked the dolly for progress. Her mind was already leaping ahead to the scenes they would shoot that afternoon. It could be, if the sun did come out, that they would have to change the schedule and do some interiors.

'Vicky!' she shouted.

Vicky came running down the street.

'Get on to the production managers and find out what's set up over at Little Joe's studios,' Kirsten said.

'Once you know dig me out the scenes that correspond to the set.'

'OK. Laurence called just now, by the way. He said do you want to join him and Joe for lunch?'

'Not unless it's important.' She took off her cap, ran her fingers through her hair and made off towards the chair. 'How are we doing?' she shouted to anyone within earshot.

'Nearly there,' someone called back.

Kirsten perched on the edge of her canvas chair beside the script supervisor. 'Remind me what we're coming off of here,' she said, peering over Nicola's shoulder.

'Off the steamboat wheel,' Nicola answered, moving her script so that Kirsten could get a better look.

'That's right. A mix. Steamboat wheel to carriage wheel. Great. Did you get the dialogue changes for the ballroom scenes from Ruby?'

'Yes. The cast have them too.'

Kirsten nodded, put her hands behind her head and relaxed back in her chair. Seconds later she was out of the chair again, sitting at the camera, one eye pressed to the view finder as it tracked down the street. Then she was running up to the carriage pulling open the door and talking to Anna.

'. . . I know, it's terrific,' she was saying. 'Just make sure you keep your face as much in the light as you can. You look wonderful. Remember, you're going to be dignified about this . . . You don't care what anyone else thinks . . . But don't forget the touch of uncertainty, especially when Marie Laveau . . .'

'It's all right,' Anna laughed, 'don't worry, I've got it. Helena is going to turn to me on her line. I thought I'd give just a split-second of hesitation before I get out . . .'

'Great. That should do it. Keep your eyes down until you get right into close up. Do you need a mark?'

'I don't think so. We'll see after the rehearsal.'

'All right!' Kirsten shouted, closing the carriage door. 'Clear the street . . . Lindon! Lindon!' she was heading towards the camera operator. 'I want you to take them through the gate up to the house, tracking back along the pavement and holding those railings foreground.'

'Yeah, Kirstie,' he laughed, 'we already discussed it.'

'Did we? So we did. OK, everyone!' she shouted. 'Let's go.'

Fifteen minutes later the shot was in the can, the clouds had smothered the sun and they were setting up for another street scene.

By now they were ten days into the shoot and Kirsten was as amazed by how well it was going – mainly thanks to Little Joe and his faultless organization – and she was delighted. Every night after rushes Laurence went out of his way to tell her how great it was all looking, the crew hung on her every word of praise and the cast were constantly begging her to dine with them so that they could either boast about their performances or discuss their roles. Kirsten was happy to listen, encouraged them as much as she could and was hardly able to believe the thrill she was getting from it all. It was as though she had developed a totally separate personality. Kirsten the director had now eclipsed Kirsten the woman and were it not for the odd moment in the day when she saw Anna looking so blissfully happy as she caught sight of Laurence coming on to the set Kirsten might have persuaded herself to believe that she didn't care about their affair at all. The fact that her heart seemed to clench at her chest when she saw them disappear into Anna's trailer together, or when she saw them laughing at some private joke while everyone raced about the set, was something she would admit to no one, with the exception of Helena, and not even for a moment did the pain show through the mask of total happiness and absorption she wore. And the fact that she consistently refused Laurence's invitations to lunch or dinner was because she just couldn't stand the way he looked so damned guilty every time he set eyes on her. It was as though he felt sorry for her and though the temptation to tell him just what he could do with his pity was almost overwhelming, she had so far managed to refrain.

On every other level she and Laurence were getting along fine. They spoke civilly to each other, even made each other laugh, but should Laurence ever look like he might be about to broach something of a more personal nature Kirsten would always make some excuse to get away.

By the beginning of the third week they were into the brothel scenes. Several of them were already in the can and had caused a great deal of ribald laughter as well as a quickening of pulses during the shooting and at the viewing of rushes. It was in the largest of the upstairs rooms in the brothel that Anna and Jean-Paul were playing out their big love scene. At that moment Anna was in a two hour make-up call having any tiny blemish the camera might pick up covered and all the relevant parts of her body high-lighted. In the meantime they were setting up for a scene between Jean-Paul and one of the prostitutes.

As Kirsten and Laurence walked through the languid ambience of the amber and carmine lit room out on to the cable strewn landing Helena was watching them. She had plenty more to worry about than Kirsten right now, but a brief feeling of sympathy coasted through her as she thought of the way Kirsten was trying so very hard to keep her feelings under control. Helena was still in no doubt though that it would all come right for Kirsten in the end, so why waste the pity when she had her own problems to deal with? The local press were hounding her for an interview, wanting to know what it felt like to be playing a voodoo priestess in light of her mother's involvement with the cult. The publicists were handling them for the moment, but Laurence was of the opinion that she should make some sort of statement herself. He'd asked to see her later in the day to discuss it, which meant that Helena had had to postpone her date with Campbell who had flown in the night before and was staying in a hotel on Bourbon Street. She wasn't going to mention anything about his arrival to Laurence, Dermott could do that himself, but boy was she going to have something to say to Laurence when she saw him! In fact she was crazy to have held back this long because with Campbell's arrival on the scene she was running out of time.

Out on the landing Kirsten and Laurence were leaning against the banister, talking quietly to each other.

'You sure you should be here?' Laurence said. 'You still look pretty peeky to me.'

'I'm fine, and that's the fourth time you've asked so can we just drop it now,' Kirsten answered. 'It was a touch of food poisoning, nothing more. Now, I want to talk about these extra rehearsals the choreographer's requested. I know we can't afford to take the time out, but neither can we afford not to. They just have to have the whole cast together for at least one more day.'

'I thought you were asking for two,' Laurence said.

'I was. But I've talked to the choreographers and they

think they can manage with one, but it's barely enough, Laurence.'

'Do you have a day in mind?'

'The production managers are looking at the schedule.'

Laurence nodded. 'OK. I'll see what they come up with. By the way I've just given the go ahead for a local news crew to come in and interview later today,' he said. 'They want you, Anna and Jean-Paul.'

'OK for the other too, not me though.'

Laurence grinned. 'Now how did I know you were gonna say that?'

'I don't know, how did you know I was going to say that?' Kirsten sighed.

'I guess,' he said, his eyes narrowing as he looked down at her, 'that I know pretty well most things about you, Kirsten Meredith.'

'Well if that's true, Laurence McAllister, then how come you don't know that I'd like to slap your arrogant face for a remark like that?'

'But I do know it,' he laughed. 'And I also know that you're not going to do it in front of the crew.'

'No?'

He shook his head.

'Then perhaps you do know me well,' she said and crunching her heel down on his toe she turned and walked away.

That might have been an end to it, but for the fact that Laurence reappeared later in the day with an extremely large bandage around his foot. Seeing him hobbling into the room Kirsten rolled her eyes, but Anna, who was blocking through her love scene with Jean-Paul, immediately drew herself up from the bed and, clad only in a thin sheet, went to kneel at Laurence's feet. Kirsten watched her as she stroked the bandage like some Grecian nymph paying obeisance to a greater god. The whole crew was watching her, slightly stunned by such an open display of intimacy that was turning them all in to unwilling voyeurs. A couple of them sniggered and turned away, but not even the fact that Laurence's embarrassment showed how deeply he regretted the stunt could bring a smile to Kirsten's face. Inside she was feeling murderous. As if her own imagination wasn't hard enough to deal with, she was now being forced to face the reality of what the two of them looked like together. And when Laurence stooped down to pull Anna to her feet and Anna slipped her arms around him Kirsten felt such a surge of jealousy as his hands brushed lightly over Anna's back that it was only Jake, who shoved the console operator aside and deftly switched the lighting to a garish, unflattering mauve, that saved her.

'Are you going to stay for the rest of the scene?' she heard Anna whisper to Laurence.

Laurence's eyes were on Anna's. From where she was standing Kirsten couldn't read his expression but she heard him say, 'Do you want me to?'

Anna nodded and smiled and for one terrifying moment Kirsten thought they were going to kiss.

She turned away as Jake came up behind her. 'Sit down, don't say a word,' he muttered in her ear.

Kirsten lifted her eyes to his. They had never once discussed her relationship with Laurence, but this wasn't the first time Jake had indicated that he knew how she felt. 'I want to kill her,' Kirsten said through clenched teeth as Lindon and the other assistants started to mount the camera on its tracks and Anna remained at

Laurence's side, the sheet barely covering her nudity. 'Why is she doing this?' Kirsten seethed.

'To make you jealous, why do you think?'

'But she's the one who's got him?'

Jake's eyebrows arched. 'Is she?'

Kirsten turned away irritably. She wasn't getting into that. 'Anna!' she snapped. 'Can we have you back on the bed, please. Flissy, could you bring something to cover Anna up while we get settled.' She waited for Anna to prise herself from Laurence's side then walked over to him. 'A word, please,' she said, pulling open the door.

She walked ahead of him down the stairs and into a deserted room off the main hall. 'I'm sorry you've forced me to do this,' she said, as he closed the door behind them. 'But as the director of this film I am requesting that you do not come on to the set during scenes that Anna is playing nude. That little display up there just now . . .'

'I apologize,' he interrupted. 'I only came back to show you this goddamned stupid bandage. It was a joke that back-fired. I forgot you were doing that scene . . .'

'I don't care whether you forgot or not. Just please keep away from the set while we do this. Now, if you'll excuse me . . .' and sweeping past him she walked out of the room and straight into Helena.

'I just heard,' Helena said. 'What the hell got into him . . .'

'Not now,' Kirsten said abruptly and ran off up the stairs.

'OK,' Helena said, tapping her fingers on the arm of the sofa in Laurence's hotel suite, 'you want me to come clean and make a statement, then why don't you do the same thing?'

'It's not my mother who's in jail,' Laurence answered, none too tactfully.

'Well maybe she should be, just for having a goddamned son like you,' Helena snapped.

Laurence's head came up in surprise. 'I think we're getting off the topic here,' he said. 'I'm talking about . . .'

'I know what you're talking about,' Helena interrupted. 'And OK, I'll do the interview. So what about you coming clean about what's going on around here? What the hell is this farce of an affair with the Simperer all about?'

Laurence's dark eyes flashed. 'What the hell gives you the right – ' He collected himself quickly. 'My private life is my own affair, Helena, so don't come here thinking you can speak up for Kirsten.'

'Well someone's got to, it's just a shame you don't have anyone to speak up for you. And even more of a shame you don't have the guts to speak up for yourself. What's going on with you, Laurence? We both know you're crazy about Kirsten, so what the hell is all this about?'

'Jesus Christ!' Laurence raged. 'Just where does everyone get off telling me what I do and don't feel. You sound like my goddamned wife and God knows I won't tolerate it from her. From you . . .'

'You can shout and bully other people around as much as you like, Laurence,' Helena declared, 'but it doesn't do anything for me. You wanted Kirsten on this movie, you wanted her to direct it and you were the one who wanted the partnership. Are you so fucking goddamned stupid that you can't see why you did that? So why the hell are you doing this to her now?'

'Apart from the fact that it's none of your fucking business what I do, I don't know what you're getting so worked up about when Kirsten's hardly starved of company herself. It can't have escaped your notice the way she is with Jake Butler. Now do I come running to you asking you to tell her to back off?'

'Do me a favour,' Helena sneered. 'There's nothing going on between Jake and Kirsten and you know it!'

'Do I?'

'Yes, you do. You just want to think there is to appease that conscience of yours. Well it's not going to work. She's not having an affair with Jake any more than I am. But I'll tell you this. I wouldn't say no, and if pushed I don't reckon Kirsten would either. And you sure are doing a lot of pushing, Laurence. Shit!' Her hand suddenly crashed down on the arm of the sofa. 'I can't believe you guys!'

'And I can't believe you've got the fucking audacity to sit there saying those things to me. Just tell me, what is it to you what we do, Helena?'

'I'll tell you what it is to me,' Helena cried, springing to her feet. 'She's my friend and I care about what this is doing to her. Open your eyes, Laurence. Look at her. She's right on the edge and she can't take much more. Oh sure, she hides it well, I don't reckon even she knows how close she is, but take it from me if you want this movie finished then you give it up with the Simperer and give it up soon or you're going to live to regret it. Now I'm out of here before you get me really mad.'

21

'Oh come on, Ruby, don't cry,' Kirsten said, going to
sit beside her on the bed and putting an arm around
her shoulders. 'We'll work it out together.'

'Sure,' Ruby sniffed into her handkerchief, 'I know
we will, we always do.'

'Then why are you getting so upset?'

Ruby shook her head and gazed absently down at the
cluster of cheap bangles on her wrist. Her fingers were
stained with fountain-pen ink, her nail polish, normally
so immaculately applied, was chipped at the edges.

'Come on, what is it?' Kirsten prompted gently.

'You're gonna think I'm crazy,' Ruby said. She gave
a dry laugh as her head fell back. 'I guess you already
do, the way I've been carrying on . . .' She paused for a
moment and closed her eyes tightly. 'I don't like what's
happening to me lately,' she said. 'I can't seem to stay
off the juice for more than a couple of hours at a time.
It's like the world frightens me . . . I can't handle it or
something.'

'But you've done a great job with the script,' Kirsten
reminded her. 'And we're only talking about minor dialogue changes. Laurence and I will do them if you like.'

Ruby shook her head, then, as the tears welled in her
eyes again, her chin dropped on to her chest and she
bunched her fists to her eyes. 'I hate this goddamned
place, Kirstie,' she sobbed. 'Don't ask me why. I mean,
I don't believe in all that voodoo rubbish any more than

you do, but that darned French kid, the one who calls herself a priestess, she really got to me. You know I tried to get to see her again, to get her to explain what she was talking about, but she's gone. No one knows where she is and it feels like she's left me with some goddamned curse hanging round my neck.

'Ssh, ssh,' Kirsten soothed. 'Come on now, that's not true and you know it.'

'Do I? I don't know what to think any more.'

Kirsten gazed at Ruby's forlorn, wrinkled face and felt her heart go out to her. 'Maybe we should try to think of something to stop this getting to you the way it is,' she said. 'Gin isn't going to help, we both know that. Perhaps if you spoke to Helena . . . She knows about voodoo and she laughed when I said you'd had your future told through a coconut. She'd never heard of it.'

'I know, I already talked to her. And I got to tell you, Kirstie, I feel pretty damned stupid going on like this. But it's keeping me awake at night. You know, I even thought about going to see a priest, I mean a real, Roman Catholic priest, to see if I was possessed or something . . .'

'Oh Ruby!' Kirsten laughed, hugging her. 'The only demon that ever possesses you is drink, and I've got to admit you can get a bit out of hand then, but if you did as Laurence said and got some help . . .'

'Yeah, I know what Laurence said, but I don't reckon it's the drink making me do things. I reckon there's something going on inside me making me do things and I don't even know I'm doing them. That kid, the French one, she said there was a child in me . . . Well we all got a child in us, don't we? But what if mine's some kind of monster? What if it's taking me over and I don't

know it . . .' She wiped a hand across her mouth and
gave a watery laugh. 'Jesus Christ, listen to me . . . I'm
turning into some kind of fucking fruitcake. You know
what I was thinking yesterday? I was thinking that Anna
Sage was going to get pregnant with Laurence's kid and
do to it what you did . . . That's what I was thinking . . .
The French girl, she said something about a baby . . .'
She stopped as she felt Kirsten's arms stiffen.

It was a while before Kirsten spoke. The idea that
Anna might get pregnant by Laurence had never
occurred to her before now and the very thought of it
was so unbearably painful it made her feel faint. Then
she realized what else Ruby had said, about her own
baby, and turned to look at her. 'I didn't know you knew
about that, Ruby,' she said in a hollow voice.

Ruby's face creased in hopeless confusion. 'Shit, there
I go,' she said, 'saying things and I don't even know
what I'm saying . . .'

'But you do know about . . . about my baby?'

Ruby nodded. 'Sure, I know,' she sighed.

'But how? Laurence would never have told you.'

'No. Thea told me. His mother. But I know how badly
screwed up he got over it, it was why he married that
silly bitch, Pippa. He got himself two kids within the
space of two years after what you did.'

'Two?' Kirsten said.

'Tom and Pippa. Now he's getting himself another in
the Sage. That woman's no good for him, she's as wrong
for him as Pippa ever was, but he's as likely to make the
same mistake again, men do . . . They're not like women,
they don't see these things . . . He'll get her pregnant,
she'll have a kid and then something terrible will happen
to it.'

'Ruby! You've got to stop this,' Kirsten declared,

shaking her. 'You've got no way of knowing that and you're making yourself ill. And you have to stop worrying about Laurence this way. I know he means a lot to you, but he can take care of himself.'

'No, he can't. Men never can. They need the right woman . . .'

The way Ruby's pale eyes were staring into hers looked to Kirsten uncomfortably like a challenge. 'Are you . . .? Are you saying you think you're the right woman for him?' Kirsten breathed, hardly able to believe she was even voicing the question when the idea of Laurence and Ruby together defied imagination.

'No, that's not what I'm saying,' Ruby sighed, blinking back a fresh flow of tears. 'But I can't stop worrying about him and there are things I could do for him, things a mother should do, like try to protect him . . .'

Kirsten felt herself start to laugh, but caught herself sharply. Ruby *was* insane, she had to be if she was deluding herself that she was Laurence's mother. Christ, she was talking about Thea not two minutes ago. Kirsten had never met Thea, but he knew how devoted Laurence was to her and to his father.

'I know it's kind of hard to believe, someone like me, Laurence McAllister's mother,' Ruby said sadly, 'but it's true. Why do you think he puts up with me the way he does? Anyone else would have fired me long before now . . .'

Kirsten's head was starting to spin. 'But how?' She took a breath. 'I don't understand . . .'

Ruby smiled and looked down at her hands. 'I guess it's hard for me sometimes too,' she said. 'He's such a fine, handsome boy. Thea did well, he's always going to think of her as his mother, I know that. She brought him up since he was two. Don's his father, I mean his real father. He married me when I was a kid of sixteen. I had Laurence a couple of years later, just when my career was getting going. I didn't want no kid then, I didn't want no husband either. I walked out on them and two years after that Don met Thea. After we got divorced he married her and that was that, until I took it into my head that I wanted to meet Laurence. He was at University by then and my career had long wrapped up. I'd done a bit of writing, but nothing any good, I was just a drunk really, I was the way Dermott Campbell was before Dyllis Fisher hiked him out of the gutter and aimed him at you. But then Don let me meet Laurence. 'Course he didn't realize what I'd do . . . Neither did I at the time, but it was a real shock when I saw Laurence. He was such a good looking boy and he wanted to get to know me. I couldn't get myself to believe that – this handsome young boy wanted to know *me*. It had been so long since anyone was interested in me or what I thought, what I had to say. And I couldn't handle it . . . Having such a grown up son . . . But he didn't feel like my son. So I flirted with him. I mean I came on to him pretty strong, frightened the hell out of him . . . I won't go into what he said, I guess you can work that out for yourself, and, well, you can't blame him now, can you? I deserved it right enough, a mother coming on to her own son that way. See, I was kooky even then. But like I said it had been a long time since a man was interested in me and Laurence, well you know, he's got that way with him that can make a woman feel real special when he wants to – and I just couldn't think of him as my own flesh and blood. 'Course, he walked out on me, said he never wanted to see me again – that I disgusted him. I wrote to him after, all the time, trying to say I was sorry, but he wouldn't have no more to do with me. And he didn't, not until little Tom was born. I don't know what made him change his mind then, but I think it was Thea. God knows what she said to him, but he gave me another chance. It was because he gave me that chance that I started to get myself together again and then, when I came up with this screenplay he said he'd do it. Oh, I'm not kidding myself here, he didn't do it out of no sentimental reasons, if he hadn't liked it he'd have turned me down just like anyone else. But I'd worked real hard on it before I took it to him . . . He could see that and well . . . the rest is history.'

Kirsten was very still. In the street outside she could hear the clatter of horses' hooves and the distant roar of traffic. A steamboat whistle blasted into the dusk and someone along the hall slammed a door. On Ruby's bedside table there was a half full bottle of gin, a phial of pills and an overflowing ashtray. It was strange how her conscious mind was taking in all these mundane things while her subconscious tried to work out why this mind-numbing revelation of Ruby's should be so important. 'Why are you telling me all this?' she asked softly.

Ruby shook her head. 'Because, that goddamned slip of a French kid came up with all sorts of stuff that meant things to me. She said the child was going to die. I keep asking myself does she mean Laurence? Does she mean Tom? It's driving me crazy, Kirstie. I know I shouldn't listen to her, but it all just keeps going round in my head and I wish to God I could forget it.'

'I think that somehow you're going to have to,' Kirsten said gently. She attempted a smile and gave Ruby a quick hug. 'Come on, I've even heard *you* laugh at the fact that this was all done through a coconut. And the way you're interpreting it, well it's all pretty abstract, you have to admit.'

'That's because what she said was abstract,' Ruby said miserably.

'So you're just making things apply. I know, I know, you're thinking about the castle tower coming down. Well, I have to admit that was a bit of a coincidence, but people dying, children dying . . . It's all a bit far-fetched, wouldn't you say?'

'Sure, the whole goddamned thing is far-fetched. It's just like I said, I feel that something kind of weird is happening to me. Shit! I can hardly believe I'm going to say this, but *you* don't reckon that kid has put some kind of curse on me, do you?'

Kirsten laughed. 'No, of course I don't. But I'll tell you what, if you're really worried about it then I think you should talk some more to Helena and perhaps go along to see someone who you know for sure doesn't practice the blacker elements of voodoo. They'll get you sorted out, because remember, when you started this research it was you telling me how much good voodoo can do for people . . .'

Ruby was shaking her head, but as her hand reached out for Kirsten's she gave a tired laugh. 'You're a good kid, Kirstie,' she said. 'I reckon there're a whole lot of people who have been wrong about you, but you have got to be as big a nutso as me if you think I'm having any more to do with those people. Leave well alone now, is what I reckon. I'll get over this, talking helps. I guess if I didn't get so stuck into the gin we could have talked sooner . . . But just listening to myself makes me see that I've been kind of stupid not to have put all this out of my mind right after it happened. I mean, come on, I'm a grown woman, I might have my problems, but I sure as hell ain't no bubblehead. So, what do you say, how's about you and me hang on to the little secret I told you and make a pact?'

'What's that?' Kirsten smiled.

'That we see this movie right through to the end and make it a winner.'

'We've got a pact,' Kirsten said, squeezing her hand.

'And I'll make you a promise. I'm gonna try specially hard to stay off the gin. I mean, I know that's not really a promise, but it's a good intention, right?'

'Right,' Kirsten laughed. 'So what are you going to do now?'

'Me, I'm gonna rewrite those bits of dialogue, and you, you're going to go off and enjoy yourself the way I did when I was your age. Well, I guess you'd be wiser to be a bit more circumspect these days, but that Jake seems like a decent boy to me.'

When Kirsten left Ruby's room a thousand and one thoughts were chasing through her mind. That wasn't so unusual, it had been like that since she'd started the movie and it was almost impossible, unless engaged in something palpable, for her mind to alight on one topic for more than a few seconds at a time. As she walked along the corridor what Ruby had told her was already being eclipsed by the angle at which she had taken a particular shot that day and how it was going to cut into the shots before and after – should she mix through and if so how many frames? Then she was thinking about lighting and how stupendously it had affected Jean-Paul's performance. The soundtrack played itself through her head, adding effects that were as yet only in her imagination. She thought of the composer and wondered if he should come out here. She'd speak to

Laurence. Thinking of Laurence she felt a strange sort of vacuum open up inside her which was quickly filled by the re-emergence of what Ruby had said. But again her mind was racing on to other things. She must contact Little Joe – Vicky would remind her what about. What time was she meeting with the choreographers tomorrow? How long would it take to rig the set at Scout Island? Was she happy with the costume parade she'd seen the night before? She thought so – yes, she was. There was so much to think about and it was all going round so fast in her mind.

When she reached her room she checked for messages, then went downstairs to find the others. They'd wrapped early that day, had viewed rushes by six-thirty and probably most would have taken themselves off to a jazz club or some other exotic night spot on Bourbon Street, taking advantage of the lie in they would have the next day before the night-shoots began. Helena, Kirsten thought, seemed particularly edgy about the night-shoots, but that was understandable as they were her biggest scenes. Anna fortunately had much less to do, just one scene in total, which was a godsend for Kirsten was feeling so exhausted lately that she wasn't too sure how much longer she could carry on on this relentless emotional see-saw.

It was over a week now since they'd shot the big love scene between Anna and Jean-Paul and still the vision of Anna standing semi-naked in Laurence's arms was playing cruelly on her mind. But she wasn't going to let it get the better of her, she needed her wits about her for what was coming up and Helena obviously needed a great deal of support. The trouble was it seemed as though Helena didn't want the support, she was drawing away from Kirsten in a way that confused and upset

Kirsten. She'd tried to talk to Helena, but Helena had denied that there was anything wrong.

Still, at least she'd managed to make some headway with Ruby tonight, Kirsten thought, feeling herself start to reel all over again at the amazing revelation that Ruby was Laurence's mother. In fact she still wasn't too sure whether or not to believe it, Ruby was as capable of making up a story as any actress was of turning on a performance. The trouble was Ruby had seemed to believe it, and come to think of it, it was exactly how she behaved towards Laurence, as though she were his mother. Kirsten wondered if perhaps she should talk to Laurence about it, but as she avoided all personal conversations with him these days she decided not to.

She was wandering over to the reception desk, humming along to Fats Domino singing 'Walking Through New Orleans' which was wafting out of the juke-box in the bar when she heard a burst of laughter coming from the same direction. There was no need to ask the receptionist where Helena was, she'd recognize that laugh anywhere and turning back she walked into the darkened, smoke filled atmosphere of the bar. It was populated by locals and a couple of the hotel staff, but there was no sign of Helena. It wasn't until Kirsten had gone deeper into the bar that she spotted her, sitting out in the conservatory, the rippling glow of pool lights reflected on the window behind her casting her in an almost dreamlike radiance.

Smiling, Kirsten started towards her then suddenly, seeing who Helena was with, she froze. For a moment she couldn't believe her eyes, felt it surely must be some trick of the light. Though she didn't move she could feel herself recoiling at what she was seeing. It wasn't so much that Helena was sitting at the table with Laurence and Anna, or the way that Laurence had his arm draped across the back of Anna's chair, though that was bad enough – it was that Dermott Campbell was at the table too and the four of them looked so cosy, so at ease and so wrapped up in each other that they hadn't even seen her come into the bar.

Still laughing, Helena disappeared beneath the table to get something from her bag and at that moment Laurence happened to glance up. The instant he saw Kirsten the smile faded from his lips. He turned to follow the direction of her eyes and saw Campbell, slouched in his chair, a glass cupped in one hand, a fat cigar in the other and a grin of unmistakable triumph curving lazily across his mouth. Quickly Laurence turned back to Kirsten, but before he could speak Kirsten had turned and walked out of the bar.

So many thoughts, so many words, so much charging through her mind. Fear and panic, hurt and betrayal. A craziness that was permeating the very pores of her skin. She had to get away from them, get out of here, run, scream, do anything to stop the truth of what she had seen. As she rode up in the lift she took deep breaths, holding on to the rail in order to steady herself. Dear God, please don't let me have an attack how, she prayed silently. Please don't let this be happening at all. She jerked her face up to the mirror beside her, glared at herself and willed herself to remain calm. There was no explanation in the world that could either excuse or lessen the pain of what she had seen, but she must not even look for one. She had just to get a hold of herself, remind herself of the way everyone was relying on her now to finish what she had started. She couldn't back away from it, she couldn't let them down. She wasn't going to think about what she'd seen, she wasn't even going to try to analyze what was behind it because if Helena really was still having an affair with Campbell, if Laurence knew about it and accepted it; if he'd decided now to go public about his affair with Anna and if they were going to throw all this in her face Kirsten just knew that she wouldn't be able to handle it.

She was fumbling her key into the door when she heard Jake calling to her from the end of the corridor.

'I've been looking all over for you,' he said. 'Didn't you get my message?'

'Hi!' Kirsten said, brightly, swinging round to face him. 'No. Nothing's wrong is it?'

He laughed. 'Why should anything be wrong? I was trying to get hold of you to see if you wanted to go to a jazz club.'

'Oh, that sounds nice,' Kirsten said. 'Why not? Would you like to come in while I get myself ready? It won't take long.'

Once they were inside the room Kirsten suddenly felt emotion swelling in her like a storm. She was so close to breaking she could hardly bear to look at Jake. He was always there for her, turned up just when she needed him. He never questioned her, he simply gave her his support. There was nothing devious about him, he was kind and caring and honest and straightforward. So often people took those they loved for granted. Kirsten didn't ever want to take Jake for granted. She wanted him to know how much she appreciated all he did for her, she wanted him to understand that there was nothing she wouldn't do for him in return. She wanted him to hold her and embrace her with the kindness and warmth that came so naturally to him. She wanted to feel the strength of his arms around her, holding her physically the way his support held her mentally.

She turned to face him. Distantly she was aware of the nervousness quaking inside her, the fear that he would say no. That he was happy to flirt with her, to be there for her when she needed him, but that he was married and he loved his wife. But then he looked up from the *Lagniappe* he was flicking through and when he saw the look in Kirsten's eyes he dropped the magazine and went to her.

'Christ, Kirstie,' he murmured as he folded her in his arms. 'What is it?'

'I want you, Jake,' she whispered. 'I want you very much.'

She looked up into his deep, brown eyes. His thick blond hair fell over his brow briefly touching the jet black curves of his eyebrows. His mouth looked hard, yet inviting, the dark shadow around his jaw leant it a strength to which she could feel herself responding. As he lowered his lips to hers Kirsten's hands moved into his hair, twisting it around her fingers as she pressed herself against him.

'Are you sure about this?' he whispered.

'I'm sure,' she answered, pulling his mouth back to hers.

As his hands touched her breasts the memory of Laurence touching her that way flickered through her mind. She pushed it away and lowering her hands to the buttons at the neck of her dress she started to undo them. Jake took a step back, watching her with eyes that were his, then Laurence's, then his again. Slowly she peeled off her dress until she was standing before him in her bra, her panties and gartered stockings. Jake groaned and closed his eyes as his arms went round her again, pulling her to him as he unfastened her bra. He ran his hands over her back, stroking it, caressing it and losing his fingers in her hair as his tongue found hers and he kissed her with a tenderness that seemed to turn her heart to liquid. This was what she had longed for from Laurence, the tenderness that would take the edge from the lust. Again she forced down the shutters in her mind and made herself think of Jake. Gently she pushed him away and pulled the straps of her bra down over her arms allowing her breasts to fall free.

'Oh, sweet Jesus,' Jake murmured looking down at the most beautiful breasts he had ever seen. He reached out a hand and ran a thumb lightly over her achingly hard nipples, then suddenly he jerked her against him and buried his tongue deep into her mouth. She could feel his erection pressing against her, was aware of deep and bitter sensations pouring through her veins. As he struggled to remove his shirt Kirsten's fingers were fumbling with his zip. He lifted her hands, lowered the zip himself and as he pulled his jeans to his knees Kirsten removed her panties.

Taking her by the waist he turned her around and laid her back on the bed. As he knelt between her legs she lifted her knees and moaned softly as he ran his hands over her inner-thighs. Her eyes were closed, her head was rolling from side to side and in her mind she was seeing Laurence, feeling his fingers stroke her, tease her and torment her. She forced her eyes open, looked up at Jake then held her arms out to him.

'Please,' she whispered, 'I want you now.'

He lowered his body to hers, taking her lips between his and gently rotating his hips seeking the point of penetration. It was at that moment that the telephone rang,

'Fucking hell,' Jake muttered. 'Just leave it,' he growled as Kirsten reached out to answer it.

'I can't,' she said, then groaned as he started to push his way inside her.

The telephone kept on ringing until Kirsten reluctantly pulled herself away and turned to lift the receiver. 'Hello,' she murmured.

'Hi. You OK? You sound kind of sleepy.'

At the sound of Laurence's voice Kirsten's heart twisted so painfully it took her breath away. Her eyes moved to Jake who had sulkily flung himself down on the bed beside her. She looked in dismay at his erection, straining towards his navel, then suddenly she turned away.

'No, I'm fine,' she said into the receiver.

'That's good.' She could hear the smile in Laurence's voice and suddenly the need for him was so strong she could feel it filling her as though it might suffocate her. 'What can I do for you?' she whispered, wondering what had happened to her anger and confusion and why it was she could still want him so much after what he had done, after what she had seen.

'I'm calling to apologize for not telling you Campbell was here. I didn't know until a few minutes ago that Helena hadn't told you either.'

'What's he doing here?' Kirsten mumbled, then swung her legs to the floor as Jake reached out for her breasts.

'Well, to tell you the truth,' Laurence began, 'I got this crazy notion in my head when we were back in England to invite him on to the set so's he could see for himself how well you were doing. I thought maybe then he'd let up on you. He turned me down at the time, but he called me a couple of days ago and said he wanted to take me up on the offer. He was already here in New Orleans, so I agreed to meet up with him tonight to discuss it.'

'Don't you think you should have consulted me first?' Kirsten said.

'Yeah, I guess I should have . . . But Kirstie, you've been so damned unapproachable lately . . .'

'No one else seems to be having that problem with me, Laurence,' she interrupted. 'But you do what you want. You're the producer, you make the decisions.'

'Kirsten, don't take it that way. Don't you see – '

'I've seen all I needed to see,' Kirsten said.

'Look, for Christ's sake, I can't do anything about him being here. It's a free world, he can go wherever he wants. But I can stop him going to the set . . .'

'Don't bother. I've got nothing to hide.'

'Look, Kirstie, can we talk about this? Let me come over there.'

'No! I don't want to discuss this any more, Laurence. You know how I feel about that man, you know Dyllis Fisher won't rest until she's got me where she wants me, so you go right ahead and help them. I can't stop you.'

'Kirsten! Listen to me. I'm on your side, goddammit! Maybe it's your friend Helena you should be speaking to, it was her who invited him over here.'

'I'd already guessed that. I didn't know that you had as well, though, until now. I don't know what you're all playing at Laurence, but whatever it is I just hope you're getting some kind of kick out of it.'

'Kirstie, we got to get this sorted. We've got to talk, you and me . . .'

'Good night, Laurence,' she said.

As she replaced the receiver Kirsten leaned forward against the bedside table, pressing a hand to her mouth.

'Hey, remember me?' Jake said taking her shoulder and trying to pull her back on to the bed.

Kirsten turned away. 'Can you go, please?' she said her voice strangled by tears. 'I need to be . . .'

'Go? What, are you crazy?' Jake laughed.

Kirsten turned to look at him, her chest starting to heave. 'Jake, I'm sorry,' she whispered. 'I just can't go through with it. I thought I could, but . . .'

'Hey come on,' he said. 'You're not pulling that one on me. You wanted it five minutes ago, you got me all fired up . . .'

'No, Jake!' she cried as he pulled her down on to the bed. 'Jake, for God's sake! I made a mistake. I'm sorry, I didn't mean to lead you on . . . No!' she screamed as he pushed his legs between hers.

'Listen,' he growled, 'you wanted my cock, now you're going to get it!'

For a moment Kirsten was so dazed she couldn't move. This couldn't be the same man as the one who'd been making love to her just a few minutes ago. The man who stood at her side throughout the day . . . The man she thought was her friend . . .

With a strength she hardly knew she possessed she threw him off her and leapt up from the bed. 'Just go!' she shouted. 'Please, just get out of here!' and before he could say any more she ran into the bathroom and turned the key in the lock.

Seconds later she jumped as the door slammed behind him, then wrapping herself in a towelling robe she sank down on to the edge of the bath and leaned her head against the wash basin.

She was shaking so hard that when she reached out for the taps she could barely make her fingers turn them. It was her own fault, she shouldn't have done that to Jake, but she was so confused, so disoriented by all that was happening she barely knew what she was doing.

As the basin filled with icy water she splashed it over her face, taking deep breaths in an effort to calm herself. But everything was crowding in on her. The betrayal was like a stone in her heart, obstructing her breath, expanding the pain.

God, she hated this place. She wanted to leave, to get as far away from it as she could. Nothing was normal here, people behaved in strange, uncharacteristic ways . . . Everyone around her was changing . . . She could feel herself being sucked into a void of interminable confusion. She didn't have it in her to cope with this . . . She'd tried to make herself believe she did, but she didn't.

Dry, racking sobs convulsed her body as she thought of Helena and Campbell. The deceit was almost as hard to bear as Laurence's love for Anna.

She squeezed her eyes tightly and pressed her hands to her face as though to block out the gathering faces that seemed to be closing in on her. Ruby, with her fears of insanity. Jake, whose gentleness had suddenly turned to violence. Helena, whose friendship was as false as her word, and Laurence . . . Dear God, Laurence . . . How maliciously the memory of his hands touching Anna's body tortured her mind. Yet how desperately she yearned to feel his arms around her now, soothing the pain, trying to take it from her. She needed him so much, yet she could feel herself reaching into darkness. He wasn't there. None of them were there. She was alone, so terrifyingly, bewilderingly alone . . .

22

Kirsten rose early the next morning, showered, dressed, had coffee sent to her room and sat down with the scenes she was shooting that night. She hadn't slept well, her eyes were gritty and slightly swollen, but her mind was centred totally on the task ahead. Later in the day the construction team would be going off to Scout Island to complete the set, the crew would join them a couple of hours later and start rigging. Costume and make-up trailers, personal trailers, location caterers, props trucks, generators, the whole fleet of transport was already there, parked just inside the gates of City Park. The make-up call for the cast was at ten that evening, on set at midnight. Extra make-up artists and dressers had been drafted in to deal with the support cast, two more film crews had been employed to man the other cameras. Tonight was the most expensive night of shoot so naturally everyone was going to be on edge and Kirsten wanted to see to it that everything went as smoothly as possible.

Alison's plans and storyboard were spread out across the desk beneath the script as Kirsten checked over every shot, every movement, every lighting change, every sound source and every line of the French dialogue to be chanted by Helena throughout the ritual.

She had a diversion on her telephone, relaying all internal calls to reception, who were also taking messages from all external calls. Every hour or so she rang down to see if there was anything urgent, but there was nothing that couldn't wait. In fact most of the messages were from either Helena or Laurence. Kirsten got Vicky to contact them to find out whether the calls were anything to do with the movie and as they weren't she didn't reply. Both had tried knocking on her door, but Kirsten had informed them that she had a lot to get through and didn't want to be disturbed.

As the day progressed she was aware of the nervousness building up inside her. The idea of staging a voodoo ritual in the dead of night while she was surrounded by people she felt she didn't know any more was disturbing her more than she wanted to admit. She might have been able to get a better grip on it though were it not for the strange telephone calls she had been receiving ever since she'd arrived in New Orleans. Whether or not they were connected to the baby chimes she had heard in London was impossible to say, but somehow she felt they were. Though there was no way of being certain about that, since whoever the caller was she only ever uttered Kirsten's name in a breathy, halting sort of way that suggested she could be crying. And a crying woman, in the dead of night, whispering no more than her name, was as chilling as Kirsten suspected Dyllis Fisher intended it to be.

She hadn't mentioned the calls to anyone and she was sure she wouldn't have been giving them any thought now were it not for the fear that somehow Dyllis had managed to get to Laurence and to Helena in the same way she had to Campbell and that they were all now in some kind of conspiracy against her. But that was absurd, she was allowing her paranoia to get out of hand, because Laurence would never do anything to jeopardize the movie even if Helena and Campbell would – though still, even now, she couldn't quite bring herself to believe that Helena would.

She knew, deep down inside, that she felt very frightened, very alone, but she had to keep it suppressed. She wished with all her heart that she hadn't made that stupid mistake with Jake for he would have been the sole comforting presence on the unit that night, but it was too late now, she had allowed herself to act irresponsibly and she had no choice but to face the consequences. She couldn't imagine that Jake would behave unprofessionally, but she dreaded seeing him and feeling the rift she knew there would be between them.

It was around the middle of the afternoon when Kirsten tensed as someone knocked on her door for the first time in over an hour. She turned to look at it, willing whoever it was to go away. As the director, she had the right to shut herself away without being questioned and as a crew they must respect that. It was only when she heard Jane's timid voice calling out to her that Kirsten relaxed. Jane was someone she would see, even wanted to see, because Jane was as innocent and as guileless as she, Kirsten, was paranoid. It would do her good to take her mind off things for a while and discuss Jane's budding romance.

'Hi,' Kirsten said, pulling the door open.

'Hello,' Jane smiled, almost pulling back as though she was expecting to be sent away. 'I thought . . . Well, I wondered, if perhaps you'd like some company. I mean, I expect you're too busy, but I just . . .'

'Come in,' Kirsten smiled. 'Unless of course Laurence has sent you.'

'Laurence has gone out to location,' Jane said. 'He's taken Tom with him so I've got a bit of time on my hands.'

'Billy out at location too, is he?' Kirsten asked, closing the door and waving Jane towards a round based armchair.

Jane nodded.

'So how are things there?' Kirsten asked.

'Oh, they're OK. I mean, I don't suppose we're setting the world on fire, but we seem to be making everyone laugh.'

Kirsten's eyes narrowed as she studied Jane's face. 'I imagine you find that pretty hurtful,' she said.

Jane's answering smile was one of resignation. 'It doesn't really matter,' she said. 'Actually, I didn't come here to talk about him. Well, I did, at least I wanted to, but . . .' A fierce blush started to seep into her cheeks. 'I know this is none of my business,' she went on, 'but . . . well, I can't help being aware of what's going on . . . You know, with Laurence and with Helena and Dermott Campbell, and I thought, well, I wondered if you might need a friend.'

'Oh Jane!' Kirsten laughed, wanting to hug her.

'I expect I'm just being silly, really,' Jane rushed on. 'I mean, you're the director and everything and you've probably got so much to think about that you're not a bit bothered by what's happening.'

'Jane,' Kirsten stopped her, 'I might be the director, but I'm still a person and I am bothered about what's going on. I know I shouldn't be, but I can't help it.'

Jane's face was imbued with happiness at receiving such a confidence. 'I don't expect there's anything I can do,' she said, 'except listen, if you want to talk, that is.'

'I do want to talk, but not about that. Let's talk about you and Billy, eh?'

Jane seemed uncertain. 'Well, if you want to,' she said. 'But, I thought it might be a good idea if you . . .'

'If I what?' Kirsten prompted.

'Nothing,' Jane said, looking away.

'Come on, out with it,' Kirsten smiled.

'Well,' Jane began hesitantly, 'if you realized that I can be quite a good listener and I'm only guessing, but I thought you might be feeling a bit let down by Helena . . . well, and by Laurence I suppose and I didn't want you to think you had no one.'

This time Kirsten didn't resist the urge to hug her. 'Well now I know that's not true, don't I?' she said, squeezing her. 'So where do you want me to begin?'

'Oh, wherever you like,' Jane said.

Kirsten sat herself down on the bed and drew her legs in under her. Then she started to laugh. 'Are you sure about this?' she said.

'Absolutely sure!'

'Then let me see. Why don't we start with what's really bothering me today?'

Jane nodded.

Kirsten had just drawn breath when there was an urgent knocking on the door.

'Kirstie! Kirstie!' Vicky called out. 'The choreographer's downstairs, says he's got to see you now.'

Kirsten looked at Jane and rolled her eyes. 'It'll be about the dance routines for tonight,' she explained. 'He's a bit of a panicker, I'm afraid, but I'll have to see him.'

'Oh that's all right,' Jane insisted. 'We can talk later if you like. Or any time. Just as long as you know that I'm there and that if there is ever anything I can do for you you only have to say.'

'Thank you,' Kirsten smiled fondly. 'I'll keep that in mind.'

Laurence and Dermott Campbell were strolling towards the dark cavern in the trees of Scout Island which was being made ready for that night's shoot. Tom was on Laurence's shoulders and as they reached the clearing he started to grab at the overhanging branches, jerking Laurence backwards and laughing at the way Laurence scolded and shook him. The sun was dappling through the leaves casting strange patterns over the disorderly mass of equipment and the dank smell of sodden earth rose from the ground. All around them the scenes and props guys were assisting in the construction of the set, which for the main ritual consisted of not much more than the altar, but the couple of scenes leading up to the ritual entailed the building of a voodoo temple and its various sections of worship. Those scenes would be shot after the main ritual which called for a vaulted arbor just like the one Laurence and Campbell were walking through, and, providing everything went to schedule, there was one further scene to be done at dawn which called for the construction of a tumbledown shack on the banks of the *bayou*.

'I couldn't help overhearing you and Helena talking just now, Dermott,' Laurence said, as they wandered towards a partially constructed camera platform. 'And I'm afraid I've got to ask what it was all about.'

He wasn't looking at Campbell so missed the sudden twitch that crossed Campbell's face. Campbell stopped, waiting for Laurence to turn back. When Laurence did Campbell's momentary unease had vanished and his shoulders started to vibrate as a deep chuckle resonated through his frame. 'I don't think you want to know, mate,' he said.

'But I do,' Laurence corrected him. 'Or more to the point I want to know if it had anything to do with Kirsten.'

Campbell's eyebrows shot up. 'Now why would you think that?' he said, hastily trying to recall exactly what he and Helena had been saying to each other when Laurence had come upon them outside one of the wardrobe trailers.

Laurence eyed him meaningfully, then swinging Tom down from his shoulders he kissed him, cried out in pain as Tom clutched at his face making Tom squeal with laughter, then handed him over to the props guy who had promised to show him the masks.

' "I'm trying, Dermott!" ' Laurence said, quoting Helena as he watched Tom disappear into a props van. ' "But it's not easy. You'll just have to give me more time." ' He turned to face Campbell. 'So, what was it all about, Dermott?' he said.

Campbell's narrowed eyes looked uncomfortably about the clearing as a faint colour started to rise from under his collar. 'It's personal,' he said. 'Can we leave it at that?'

Laurence stared at him hard. 'Sure,' he said stonily, 'just so long as I have your word it has nothing to do with Kirsten.'

Campbell lifted a hand. 'Scout's honour,' he grinned.

Laurence shot him a look that didn't in any way fail to reveal how unamused he was by the pun or how much store he put by Campbell's word and as he turned to walk on he said, 'One step out of line, Dermott, and you're out of here. Got it?'

'Got it. Would I be right in thinking this is where

you'll get the top shot from?' he asked, relieved at an opportunity to change the subject.

'No, we've got the crane for that. This is for the master shot. Over there, where the smaller platform is being put up is where the camera with the zoom lens will be. What's the big joke?' he called out to Lindon whose legs were dangling from the main camera platform as he held his sides laughing.

Don, the focus-puller, who was on the ground beside Jake looked up at Lindon and the two of them burst out laughing again.

'Seems Jake here got kicked out of bed last night,' Don said, clapping a hand on Jake's shoulder.

Laurence's smile instantly vanished. 'Is that right?' he said tightly. 'Bad luck, Jake,' and taking Campbell's arm he started to usher him away.

'She's a fucking prick-teaser, that's what she is,' Jake called after them.

Campbell turned back.

'You want the dirt?' Jake snarled. 'Well you got it. The bitch is a prick-teaser.'

'I take it we're talking about the Kirstie Doll,' Campbell smirked, hardly able to stop himself taking out his notebook.

'Oh yeah, that's who we're talking about all right,' Jake confirmed. 'Flaunts herself around this set like some bloody whore, gives the biggest come on since Salome, then won't deliver.'

'Maybe,' Campbell suggested, 'you're just not big enough in the um . . . finance department.'

'Yeah, maybe you're right there,' Jake sneered, then catching sight of Laurence's thunderous face he turned away to continue what he'd been doing.

Before Laurence left the set he sent a runner over to

Jake to tell him to report to the hotel production office at seven o'clock sharp.

'I have two reasons for not firing you over what you did today,' Laurence said replacing the phone to Kirsten as Jake closed the door behind him. 'The first is we need the continuity. The second is that I've managed to persuade Campbell to forget what he heard.'

Jake's boyish face had turned crimson. 'You want to fire me, go right ahead and do it,' he said sulkily. 'The woman comes . . .'

'Call her by her name!' Laurence roared. 'She is your director and you'll show her some damned respect.'

'Don't take that tone with me Laurence or I'll walk out of here now,' Jake said testily. 'I'm not a school kid.'

'Then quit behaving like one. What the hell did you think you were doing talking to Campbell that way? You know the history, Kirsten's up to her eyes in problems right now, and she doesn't need you adding to her load. So get off her case, Jake, and don't go near Campbell again.'

Jake's anger was simmering very close to the surface. 'OK, I'll stay out of his way if that's what you want, because you're right, I was out of order. But what about you, Laurence? What the hell do you think you're doing to her? You've got her so tied up in knots . . .'

'What goes on between Kirsten and me is none of your damned business,' Laurence said tightly. 'Now get the hell out of here before I really lose my temper.'

As the door closed behind Jake Laurence dropped his head in his hands. His whole body was tensed with rage and frustration. Jesus Christ, what was he doing? Jake was far too senior a member of the team to be spoken to in that way, but the truth was he'd wanted to get hold of Jake and tear him limb from limb for what he'd done.

Shit, what am I doing here, he groaned inwardly. He was making such a fucking mess of everything and he just didn't know how to get himself out of it. What the hell was he doing sleeping with Anna Sage? He didn't even like the woman much, but he couldn't even consider breaking it off now, not half way through the shoot. He felt a surge of bitter self-loathing as he recalled the first time they'd slept together. He'd done it because he'd been trying to kid himself that what he wanted was to play the field. Just what kind of a jerk did that make him? Not only for blinding himself to the truth, but for picking on the goddamned star of the movie to do it? Just how many problems did he want? With a sickening shame he recalled the day Anna had stood almost naked in his arms right in front of Kirsten. God only knew how Kirsten felt about that, but if it was anything like the way he felt when he'd heard Kirsten had been in bed with Jake . . . Jesus Christ, how the hell could he have convinced himself that he wanted her to sleep with another man?

His fists tightened as the throbbing in his temples increased. He was so goddamned confused and Pippa didn't help, the way she asked about Kirsten every goddamned time he spoke to her. And Anna was plaguing him night and day to compare her favourably with Kirsten. Did he think she was as beautiful? Was she as good in bed? Did he prefer smaller breasts? Was blonde hair more feminine? Christ, the questions she asked, they were driving him crazy. But he didn't see he had much choice but to put up with them now, he was the fool who'd allowed pride and cowardice to smother his feelings and now was definitely not the time to try dealing with them. He just had to stay away from Kirsten as much as he could, because the last thing he wanted was to hurt her any more than he already had and were he to give in to his feelings then what the hell kind of situation would he be facing with Anna?

He looked up as someone opened the door. Jesus Christ Almighty, he seethed inwardly when he saw Anna's anxious face, someone please tell him what he had to do to get this woman off his back before he ended up doing something he wouldn't want to be held responsible for.

Kirsten was on the point of leaving her room to go downstairs when the telephone rang. She'd had the diversion taken off a couple of hours ago – so close to call-time she'd had no choice but to make herself available.

'Hello?' she said propping the receiver under her chin as she juggled with the plans and script.

'Kirstie, it's Laurence. I have something to ask you.'

'Yes?'

'It's Anna. She's not feeling too good.'

'What's the matter with her?' Kirsten asked tersely.

'She's kind of nauseous, got a headache, you know the sort of thing. Anyway, she's asking can we bring her scene forward. Shoot it before we get round . . .'

'You've got to be joking!' Kirsten cried. 'Everyone's already called for the ritual, they'll be in make-up by now . . .'

'I know, I know. All I'm saying is as we just want her for a couple of cutaways for the ritual, can we do them first?'

'Yes. But we can't do the other scene until dawn.'

'But you could do the interiors. It's only the exterior you need the dawn for and she's not in those shots.'

He was right, Anna wasn't in those shots, but Kirsten, just like everyone else, was already working herself up for the ritual and she didn't see why they all had to be thrown off course because Anna Sage had a headache. 'I don't suppose,' Kirsten remarked, 'that this headache of hers has anything to do with the fact that she's got the next three days off and just happens to be going up to Washington and might want to get an early start, does it?'

'Have you ever known her to pull a stunt like that before?' Laurence retorted and something in his tone told her that Anna was right there with him.

'No. But there's always a first time. And why isn't she speaking to me about this herself?'

'Does it matter which one of us she speaks to?'

'In this instance, yes.'

'I don't see why.'

Kirsten didn't bother to explain. 'The ritual is going to take a long time to shoot, Laurence,' she said. 'I don't want to still be doing it when the sun comes up and if we don't get started as near to midnight as we can then that's going to happen.'

'We're only talking two or three shots here, and they're not complicated ones. They won't hold us up long.'

'OK, Laurence, you're the producer. You know how much tonight is costing, so you're the one who'll have to take the consequences if we run into dawn. And believe you me, I'll be wanting another night-shoot scheduled if we do. Have you talked to David, or the production managers?'

'Of course not. I wanted to clear it with you first.'

Everything inside Kirsten was still screaming out to say no, but right at that moment she couldn't think of a good enough reason. 'Where are you now?' she snapped.

'Out at the set.'

'Then tell David to meet me in my trailer as soon as I get there. In the meantime you can speak to the cast and crew yourself to explain what's going on. But I'm not having Helena messed around. She's going to do her master shot when it's scheduled and I'm afraid, headache or not, Anna will have to wait,' and with that Kirsten replaced the receiver and walked out of the door.

A few minutes later she slipped into the warmth of the chauffeur driven car waiting outside in Chartres Street. There was someone else in the car, but not until she spoke did Kirsten realize it was Helena.

Kirsten turned to look at her.

'Now don't fly off the handle,' Helena said quickly, taking Kirsten's hand.

Kirsten gave a humourless laugh. It was strange how throughout the day confusion and refusal to analyze or even speculate much had blunted her pain, yet now she was setting out, or maybe it was because she was facing Helena, there was a burning, raw ache in her that far surpassed the nervousness she was still unable to shake.

'I've been trying to talk to you all day,' Helena said, 'but you haven't been too receptive. Not that I blame you,' she added hastily. 'I mean it can't look too good from where you're sitting, can it?'

Kirsten turned away and gazed out at the black night. 'Then how should it look?' she said tonelessly.

Helena sighed. 'Pretty pathetic, actually,' she answered wearily. 'Ageing, overweight actress with rented apartment, limited finance and terror of spending the rest of her life alone takes the only thing left on offer.'

Kirsten's face was a stony mask of scepticism as she turned back. 'I'm not swallowing it, Helena,' she said.

'No, well I don't guess I would either if I were you,' Helena conceded. 'But I'm afraid it's true.'

'So what's he been asking you to fix over here for him?'

Helena's surprise was apparent. 'What do you mean?' she said warily.

'I'm talking about what Laurence overheard today – he's told me.'

'It wasn't about you, Kirstie, I swear it,' but as she said it her heart was turning over, the passion in her voice rang so false.

Kirsten could feel the betrayal burying deep into her chest. It was almost too much to bear, but it was easier to handle this than what was happening with Laurence. 'I'm not going to ask you to choose between me and Campbell,' she said. 'You know what he and Dyllis are trying to do to me so from now on Helena, I am your director and you are a member of the cast. Our relationship will not go beyond that.'

'Oh, Kirsten, please, don't do this. Honestly, it's not . . .'

'The subject's closed, Helena.' Kirsten's face looked pale in the flickering, vivid lights that undulated the car as they sped towards City Park. 'Now, if there's anything you wish to discuss about your performance tonight I'll be glad to do so. I imagine – '

'Kirsten, just listen to me . . .'

'No, Helena, not unless it's about – '

'All right! For God's sake, I'll tell you what Dermott

and I were talking about! He wants me to marry him. He's practically begging me to and I just don't know what to do. It's hard to imagine us being happy together, but how happy am I gonna be spending the rest of my life on my own?' She stopped abruptly and Kirsten almost felt her agitation deflate. 'But knowing how he feels about you,' Helena went on, 'what he and Dyllis are doing to you . . . Don't you see, it's making it all so much more difficult. You mean a lot to me, Kirstie, a hell of a lot, but I'm lonely. I want a man and he's all I can get.'

The desperation and desolation in Helena's voice swept through Kirsten with such an intensity that her head fell forward. 'Oh God,' she groaned, covering her eyes with her hand. 'Helena, what's happening to us? What the hell is going on with our lives?'

'Don't ask me,' Helena said. 'All I know is that as long as we're there for each other we'll survive. And I'll always be there for you, Kirstie. I swear it. But just like you need Laurence I need a man too.' At the mention of Laurence she saw Kirsten flinch. 'Kirstie, look at me, please,' she said. She took Kirsten's chin and lifted her face into the light. 'Talk to me,' she pleaded. 'Don't bottle things up for God's sake. We both know what happened the last time, you can't go through it again.'

'I won't,' Kirsten said, pushing Helena's hand away. 'Now, we've got a heavy night ahead of us – we're going to be shooting past dawn . . .'

'Kirstie, listen to me,' Helena persisted, taking Kirsten's shoulders. 'Don't ask me to explain what he's doing, or what the hell is going on in that beautiful, idiotic head of his, but take it from me the Sage is on her way out. It's you he wants.'

Helena's words were like a soothing balm on the

searing heat of her pain, but as the desperate hope flared in her, Kirsten said, 'I'd like nothing more than to believe you, Helena, but . . .' She lifted a hand to her head. 'Jesus Christ, I don't know what to believe anymore.'

'Believe me, Kirstie. Please! I'm telling you the truth about Dermott. I've even tried to make Laurence face up to his feelings for you, but he won't. OK, I tried for selfish reasons, I thought if you were happy with him then you'd be more understanding about Dermott and me. But don't you see, it's because what you think matters to me . . .'

'We're here,' Kirsten interrupted, as the car bumped onto the track leading to Scout Island. 'Let's drop this now. We've got a busy night.'

'Just tell me,' Helena said holding Kirsten back as she made to get out of the car. 'Do you understand about Dermott? I mean, is there anyway I can persuade you?'

'I understand,' Kirsten said, but what she didn't add was that she simply didn't know if she should either believe or trust. But, she reminded herself glumly as she weaved through the pitch darkness between the trailers, Helena wasn't the only one who could turn on a performance when it was necessary, she, Kirsten, could do it too and tonight, without any question, called for it.

It was as she stopped to open the door of her own trailer that she happened to glance over at Laurence's. And there he was, silhouetted in the window, his arms around Anna as he gazed down into her upturned face. If only, Kirsten was thinking to herself as her whole insides seemed to open up to the pain, they were shooting the real death of Anna Sage and not the make-believe one of Moyna O'Malley. It might not bring Laurence back, but it would at least help to control the dreadful feelings of hatred she felt every time she looked at Anna.

As Kirsten walked through the darkness towards the cavernous opening in the trees of Scout Island she was looking at the curving sweep of the branches that reached across the top of the clearing. Shafts of bright light were shooting upwards through the entwining foliage, a chill wind was swaying the shadows. 'Have enough branches been chopped away for the camera to see through?' Kirsten was asking David.

'Yep. The crane is already rigged. You can go up and take a look as soon as you're ready.'

'OK. What about the other cameras?'

'They're being set up now. The operators seem to know their stuff, I'll introduce you.'

'All right,' Kirsten said, wincing as Ruby tightened the grip on her arm.

'Shit, just take a look at all this,' Ruby said, her eyes steeped in awe as they entered the clearing where electricians, props men, sound guys, cameramen and their myriad assistants were busily setting up for the big scene. The atmosphere was electric, excitement reverberated through every voice that yelled out, exhilaration and exuberance flowed like a magnetic force through the misty night air. In the flooding beam of working lights everyone hefted and carried, threw and caught, climbed and jumped, spun cables, laid tracks, mounted cameras and rigged booms. Alison and her two art directors were at the altar which towered magnificently towards the roof of knotted branches. They were supervising the last minute decoration, but already the altar was so impressive as to arrest Kirsten in her tracks. As she gazed up at the gargoyle faces, the fiercely protruding tongues, wolfishly bared teeth and chillingly obscene emblems of *loa* worship she felt a tingling inside that seemed to spread to every part of her body. She could feel herself smiling as her heart thudded with profound admiration at the effect Alison had created, yet at the same time she was aware of her bitter resentment that all this energy would have to be put on hold while they moved to the other set for Anna's scene. The chief electrician was talking to Alison now and Kirsten knew they'd be discussing the intricacy and texture of the mystical light to be directed on to the sacrificial shrine.

'Is the other set being got ready?' she asked David, biting hard on her irritation.

'Yes. But the camera boys are waiting to hear from you where you want them to do this shot on Helena before we go over there.'

'OK. Get them to put it there, slightly off centre,' she said pointing to where the graphics team were carving cabalistic signs in the thick ashes strewn over the ground in front of the altar.

As David disappeared into the crowd Ruby said, 'I'm going to get me a coffee. Want one?'

'No thanks,' Kirsten answered, wondering where, in all this mayhem, she might find Jake. She experienced a quick pang of nerves at the prospect of seeing him, but knew the quicker she got it over with the better. A sound assistant raced up to her, hooked a set of headphones around her neck and clipped a battery to her belt.

'Monitors over on the left side,' he told her waving an arm in the general direction of where some of the cast were already beginning to gather.

Kirsten thanked him and made her way towards Jean-Paul, stepping to one side as a handful of scenes men carried a massive, grisly looking totem pole towards the altar. In the distance Kirsten could see the working lights of the other set. The solitary house with its grey stone walls, narrow windows and decrepit roof was, as far as she could see, just perfect and Alison was right, they'd achieve a much more sinister effect by putting it in the midst of the looming shadows of this mist-shrouded island. But damn it, it needed the dawn!

She turned back at the general gasp of wonder that went up as simultaneously the working lights went off and the thickly-coloured hue of vermilion and ochre lamps beamed shafts of eddying light on to the altar.

'The man is a genius, no?' Jean-Paul whispered in Kirsten's ear as Jake waved a hand for the electricians to revert back to working lights.

Kirsten turned to Jean-Paul and gave a startled scream as she came face to face with the glittering red eyes of a demon's mask.

Jean-Paul laughed and lowering the mask he planted a kiss on each of Kirsten's cheeks. 'So, how are you feeling?' he said. 'Please tell me you are as nervous as I – it might make me feel a little better.'

'As nervous as hell,' Kirsten laughed.

They talked quietly together for a while, going over the notes she had given Jean-Paul during their discussions, until David came running over to tell her that Helena was ready and should he ask her to come on to the set?

'Just give me a moment,' she said, catching Jake by the arm as he passed.

'It's looking fantastic,' she told him.

'You ain't seen nothing yet,' he smiled, looking down into her eyes. 'I owe you an apology,' he said softly.

'I owe you one.'

Jake's head tilted to one side as his eyes creased in a smile. 'What do you say we put it down to a moment of madness and go back to the way we were?' he said.

Kirsten lifted a hand and touched his arm. 'Let's do that,' she whispered, ashamed at the weakness in her that was once again making her want to press herself into the comfort of his arms. She felt so shut out by everyone she cared for, but at least the situation with Jake seemed to be over.

'Hey,' he said, lifting her troubled face to the light. 'It's going to be great. We're all rooting for you, you know.'

'Thanks,' Kirsten smiled.

'So how about we get this show on the road?'

'OK,' she laughed. 'You know about the change in schedule?'

'I do. I imagine you're pretty pissed off about it.'

'That's an understatement,' Kirsten remarked. 'Anyway, how far are you off here?'

'We're about ready for a rehearsal.'

'All right, David,' she said, turning back to where he was still hovering. 'Bring Helena on. Who's giving her an eyeline?'

'I think Anna's doing it herself,' David answered, 'but I'll check. Do we want any of the extras?'

'No.'

A frantic string of messages started up over the walkie-talkies then, calling for Helena, for Anna, for make-up, continuity and costume.

Kirsten looked around for Jean-Paul again, but he was gone and suddenly her heart tightened as she saw Laurence at the other side of the set. He was standing beside Ruby who was hanging on to his arm as he talked to the choreographer. Kirsten averted her eyes. How was he feeling right now, she wondered. Was he nervous, like everyone else, or was he, as she suspected, quietly confident that all would go to plan? Well it just damned well better, she seethed to herself, because if it didn't . . . But she didn't want to think about that, she had somehow to control her anger and make this debacle of a revised schedule work.

She started across the clearing as Helena, in the full costume of a high priestess of voodoo, stalked majestically on to the set to a round of applause. Kirsten smiled fondly. No matter what was going on between them personally, tonight was Helena's night and Kirsten was going to do all she could to make it special for her. This, of all the scenes, was the one in which Helena was the absolute star, for Marie Laveau, as the great mambo of the idolatrous ritual, was to conduct the pagan ceremony of sacrilege and sacrifice.

'OK, let's have first positions,' Kirsten called out to David, as she reached Helena's side. 'We'll start blocking through. You look amazing,' she told Helena.

Helena grinned and Kirsten gave a gasp of laughter as her heart almost skipped a beat. Helena's own teeth were covered by another larger set which was cracked, blackened and blood-stained. And whatever the make-up artist had used to bring out the colour of Helena's eyes was equally chilling. As Helena moved into the light they sparked and flashed like flames. For the moment there was no expression in them, except perhaps a touch of anxiety as Helena began psyching herself up for the performance. The darkened skin of her face was painted with jagged red scars, her eyes were thickly rimmed with white grease. Her hair was combed viciously back from her face, heightening the harsh bones of her cheeks. Her lips were blood red, so too were her fingernails. Beneath the sombre black cape whose collar sat high and stiff behind her head, was a glittering gold and silver robe, cut so low that the dark circles of her nipples were almost visible.

She stepped in behind the altar. Anna Sage appeared and though she cooed her appreciation of the way Helena looked, Kirsten could see it was an effort. Maybe the headache wasn't a sham after all, she looked dreadfully pale.

'I'm sorry about this change,' Anna said to Kirsten. 'I hope I'm not being too much of a nuisance. It's not often I get these migraines, but I do from time to time. I suppose it's the pressure of . . .'

'It's all right,' Kirsten said cutting her off. 'I understand. And you don't have to be here for the eyeline, you know, your stand-in can do it.'

'No, it's OK. I'd rather do it myself. It wouldn't be fair on Helena otherwise.'

Kirsten looked at her. Anna always did her own eyelines and was extremely grateful when the others did theirs. It was much easier, she maintained, to get the level of performance right when you were playing to the real person. 'Jean-Paul's around somewhere,' Kirsten said. 'If you find David he'll take you to your positions.

There's no hurry though, we'll be a while blocking this through.'

As Anna went off Kirsten turned back and watched Helena going over her moves with the choreographer. All around them people were starting to gather, as fascinated by the set as they were by Helena.

At last, having watched an entire rehearsal through the viewfinder while the focus-puller rehearsed his own performance, and having decided to use the camera on the crane for the end of the sequence, Kirsten jumped down from the camera seat and walked over to Laurence who was standing at his monitor, his hands resting on the back of Ruby's chair.

'What do you think?' she said, failing to disguise her irritation.

He nodded. 'I think it's going to be great.'

'Any notes?'

'None.'

'OK, set up for a take!' Kirsten shouted.

'You still mad about this change of schedule?' Laurence said, though Kirsten barely heard him above the noise that had started up.

'Laurence!' she answered, raising her voice to be heard. 'I want to shoot the whole scene now, complete with zombies, nude dancers, sacrifices and offerings, the way it was planned.' This veering away from the climax was getting her angrier by the minute and she knew that even Helena's single performance, which was going to be stunning, wouldn't get her worked up to the pitch of excitement she and everyone else had been heading towards. 'So yes, I'm still mad,' she went on. 'And I'm standing by what I said. If we haven't finished by the time the sun comes up then I want another night-shoot and that's going to double the cost of what we've already laid out.' In other words that was the price they would have to pay for his pandering to Anna's headaches. She didn't say that of course, but the words lay there unspoken between them.

A few minutes later she was back at the altar with Helena. 'How are you feeling?' she asked, shielding her eyes from the dazzling lights.

'OK,' Helena answered. 'Happy with what you've seen?'

'Happy. I know you're holding back for the rehearsal, but when it comes to the take I want you to go for it. I mean really go for it.'

'Don't worry, I will.'

'OK. Why don't you go and sit down for a while?' Kirsten said, as the set decorators hovered around lighting candles and incense and adding the finishing touches to the props.

'No, I'll stay here,' Helena said, looking down at the python as it was laid out in front of her. 'Hi there little Dermott,' she said, running her fingers down its back.

Kirsten burst out laughing.

'For God's sake don't tell him,' Helena grinned. 'Anyway, you'll have to excuse us, 'cos little Dermott and me have got to have a bit of a chat before we go for a take.'

Leaving Helena to it Kirsten strolled to the edge of the set, wincing when she passed David as he yelled, 'Let's have a bit of quiet, please!'

She was leaning against a tree just a couple of feet from the set watching the chaos taking shape when she heard a rustling behind her. She turned to see who it was, but there was nobody there except those who were working on the tumbledown house, but that was too far distant to have accounted for the noise she'd heard.

Suddenly all her senses were alert as she peered into the darkness and listened. Somebody was there, she could hear them breathing and she was about to yell to one of the burly electricians when to her amazement she saw Tom totter out from behind some bushes and into the light.

'Tom!' she gasped, running forward. 'What on earth are you doing here?' Quickly she hoisted him up in her arms, wrapping her coat around him to cover his pyjamas. 'Does Daddy know you're here?' she said.

'Daddy's up there,' he said, pointing to where Laurence was leaning on a balustrade of the camera platform looking down at the set.

'Yes, but does he know you're down here?'

Tom shook his head solemnly, then to Kirsten's dismay a single tear rolled from the corner of his eye.

'Oh, what is it, honey?' she said, hugging him to her. 'Did something frighten you?'

She felt him shake his head and held him more tightly as his tiny arms gripped her neck.

'Then what is it, sweetheart? Do you want to see Daddy?'

'Yes,' Tom said, his little voice choked with tears. 'I want to see Daddy.'

'Oh, come on then, let's go and see if we can get him to come down.'

As she walked towards the camera platform Kirsten lifted her walkie-talkie in order to speak to Laurence, but she got no further than pressing the button when Jane suddenly came racing out of the darkness.

'Oh, thank God,' she gasped. 'I've been looking all over for him. I just popped out to get myself a coffee and when I got back he was gone. He was fast asleep when I left.' She was breathless and shaking so hard that Kirsten didn't immediately hand Tom over.

'Honestly, it gave me the fright of my life,' Jane went on. 'God, if anything had happened to him – he might have wandered off anywhere, fallen into the river . . .'

'But he didn't,' Kirsten said soothingly. 'He's right here and quite safe, aren't you, soldier?'

'Jane,' he whimpered and letting go of Kirsten he held his arms out for Jane. 'I want my Daddy,' he said, trying very hard not to cry.

Jane looked anxiously at Kirsten. Obviously Laurence would be furious if he discovered Tom had been out here while all this was going on, though what Kirsten wanted to know was why Jane and Tom weren't back at the hotel.

'Tom wanted to sleep in the trailer tonight,' Jane explained. 'Laurence said he could providing he didn't set foot outside.'

'Then you'd better get him back there pretty quick,' Kirsten told her, 'before Laurence sees either of you.'

'Yes, yes, you're right,' Jane said, glancing nervously towards the stretch of forbidding darkness between the set and the trailers.

Kirsten called out to the third assistant and told him to escort Jane and Tom back to their trailer. 'And whatever you do, Jane,' she cautioned, 'make sure you lock the door next time you want a coffee.'

'Oh, I will, I will,' Jane assured her. 'I'm sorry, really. Oh gosh, I wish we could go back to the hotel, I don't like it out here at all.'

For some reason Jane's nervousness seemed to incite Kirsten's and suddenly Kirsten remembered Ruby's fear that the child in her reading was Tom. It wasn't that Kirsten believed it, but there was no harm in being extra careful while they were out here in the dead of night. 'If I were you,' she said to Jane, 'I'd lock yourselves in when you get back.' Then to the third assistant she added, 'Ask the security guards to keep an eye on the trailers.'

She watched until the three of them had disappeared into the shadows, then turning back to the set she called out to David. 'How are we doing over there?'

'Couple more minutes,' Jake shouted back as he watched the console operator making final adjustments to the lighting.

At last the cameras started to roll. A feverish silence descended over the set as a harsh red light beamed down on the altar.

Everyone was still.

'Shot five hundred, take one,' the clapper-loader announced, slamming the board together.

Kirsten waited for him to settle. David moved quietly across the front of the crowd that had gathered. Kirsten looked at Jake and as Jake touched the console operator's shoulder fluid motions of warmly glowing lights began rippling over the altar. Helena's face was a study of unholy, transcendent rapture.

Kirsten raised a hand. The sound man hit the playback machine and a tattoo of dense, sonorous beats throbbed into the night. A few seconds later slowly, rhythmically, Helena's body started to sway as she lifted her face towards the canopy of gnarled and mist-shrouded foliage overhead. Undulating streams of light touched her, painting her with a sleazy saturation of lurid colour, as the leafy shadows cast strange and ungodly images over her writhing body.

'*Papa Legba, Ouvrir barrière pour nous passer,*' she chanted, the turbulent emotion of her husky voice blending with the hypnotic monotony of the drums. *'Papa Legba, Ouvrir barrière pour nous passer,'* she repeated. Her head fell back, her arms spread her cloak like wings and before her on the altar the slithering blood python moved sluggishly over the objects of tribute. At last her hands closed around the creature's succulent flesh, her fingers fanning the circles of its body as her thumbs lifted the pointed face to her own. 'Damballah, Damballah,' she intoned. Suddenly she jerked the snake upwards as her head dipped and the drums thundered into a terrible rhythm. She coiled the snake over her shoulders and began a blood-curdling liturgy to the ancestors. And as her body writhed, jerked and vibrated to the diabolical rhythm and the python curled itself lovingly about her so the gathering before her watched, spellbound.

The power emanating from her was mesmerizing. Kirsten had seen Helena rehearse this dance on countless occasions and always she had felt the strength of her performance but that was nothing compared to what was happening to her now. It was as though the mounting frenzy of Helena's writhings was becoming a force of its own, moving with the mist throughout the set and invading the very soul of all those present. Kirsten could feel the pummelling rhythm of the drums as though their every beat was being thrummed upon her heart.

Then suddenly the drums stopped, cutting the air with silence.

Kirsten tensed as sparks of yellowy-green light exploded from the portals of the altar. Helena was lying across it, the snake grasped between her legs its head poised over her face, its flickering tongue lashing towards her. Then suddenly she was upright and as her eyes blazed across the set towards the spot where Anna was secreted a piercing and spine-chillingly demented scream flew through the night. A tremor of unease coasted through Kirsten's stomach at the evil that seemed to seep from the frozen expression on Helena's face even as her heart swelled at the extraordinary power of the performance.

'Hold it! Hold it!' Kirsten shouted. 'Nobody move!'

The crane, which had been holding a close up of Helena's face, swooped down to the altar like a ravenous vulture, taking fast-moving pans of the grisly objects, until finally it rose back into the darkness and Kirsten yelled, 'Cut! Check the gates.'

Breathless, Helena turned to Kirsten. Kirsten looked back. With the exception of those checking cameras no one moved. Not until both assistants had given the all clear did Kirsten allow herself to smile. As she did the relief that came into Helena's eyes turned Kirsten's smile to laughter.

'It was brilliant!' she cried waving her fists in the air. 'Absolutely, fucking brilliant!' and running over to Helena she threw her arms around her and the two of them danced around the altar, as everyone else started to applaud.

Kirsten broke free when she saw Laurence coming towards her.

'Do you want to do another for cover?' he said.

What Kirsten wanted was to go right ahead with the full drama of the scene, but there was no point in arguing with him now. 'Yes, I suppose we ought,' she said, 'but that was perfect for me.'

Laurence nodded then turned as they heard someone running up behind them.

'Laurence, Kirsten,' Kelly, one of the design assistants gasped. 'I think one of you'd better come. Anna Sage is having hysterics over there. Ruby's gone off her head or something and Jean-Paul's threatening to do them both an injury if they don't shut up!'

Kirsten and Laurence went after the designer, around the edge of the set where the technicians were getting ready for another take, past the animal handlers who were already being organized for the cutaways, to the clump of trees where Anna, as Moyna O'Malley, had positioned herself to give Helena the eyeline.

The moment she saw Laurence Anna ran towards him, her arms outstretched her whole body racked with sobs. 'Get that woman away from me!' she choked. 'She's mad! She's insane! Get her away from me!'

'What the hell is going on?' Laurence demanded as he wrapped Anna in his arms, wincing as Ruby cackled with laughter. 'For Christ's sake, pull yourself together, Ruby!' he shouted.

But Ruby just gripped her sides and let out another wail of mirth.

Kirsten went to her, took her by the shoulders and shook her. She started to cough, so hard it was making her retch.

'She's done it again,' Anna sobbed into Laurence's shoulder. 'She's trying to frighten me with all that witch-craft stuff. She's off her head, I know she is, but . . .'

'It's not me doing the scary bits,' Ruby wheezed. 'It's her!' She was pointing at Helena. 'She's the one that did it. That look – you saw that look she gave her at the end . . . Stupid bitch thought it was for real. Thought an evil spell was being cast on her . . .'

'Stop it!' Kirsten shouted, so appalled at the way Ruby was speaking to Anna she wanted to slap her as much for that as she did for the fact that she was drunk on the set. She turned her angry eyes to Laurence. 'Get

Anna to her trailer, someone!' she snapped still glaring at Laurence. 'David! David! Where are you?'

'Right behind you,' he answered.

'Get someone to take care of Ruby,' Kirsten muttered under her breath. 'Lock her in my trailer if you have to, and don't let her out until she's sobered up.'

'I'm sorry,' Anna was wailing, 'I'm so sorry. I didn't mean to cause a fuss.'

'Laurence,' Kirsten interrupted. 'Could I have a word, please?'

The two of them walked further into the woods out of earshot. 'Please do whatever you have to do to calm her down,' she said, 'then get her into make-up. We'll do her scene now.'

'What? Are you saying you're going to de-rig the camera before . . .'

'That's precisely what I'm saying. I don't need another take on Helena, we'll have her well covered on the wider shots and I want Anna's scene done and her out of here before I do something one of us might regret.'

An hour later everyone was over at the other set on the banks of the bayou. The frayed tempers of earlier had abated though Kirsten was fully aware that the tension and excitement Helena had created was ebbing too. She should have had this scene put back to another day when it could have been done the way she wanted it, and had Anna not gone to Laurence with her request then that was precisely what Kirsten would have done. As it was she'd allowed her feelings to cloud her judgement. It was the first time she'd done it, and it couldn't have happened over a more critical situation.

As the crew milled around setting props, dry-ice machines, lamps and cables, Kirsten watched the riggers haul the dolly into the house. The air was dank, there was a strong smell of mildew mingling with the chemical solution of the dry-ice and the bitter aroma rising from the brackish water of the bayou. Moisture dripped from the trees, night creatures rustled, scurried, squawked and chirped, but could barely be heard over the din of the crew. Kirsten looked up at the impenetrable sky where a thin sliver of the moon emerged from a bank of cloud and inwardly vented her frustration on a god who probably wasn't even listening.

After what seemed an interminable amount of time they were ready to shoot. The rehearsals had coughed up all kinds of problems, though Anna seemed remarkably well recovered which, perversely, irritated Kirsten even more. Still, at least the technical hitches had been dealt with and now it just remained for Kirsten to return to her chair while make-up did their finishing touches. However, she continued to stand over Anna who was sitting on the makeshift bed baring her neck to the make-up artist, going over some last minute notes. The room which was lit with a hot, purplish-red light, was horribly claustrophobic with its low ceiling and stone walls coated in moss and there was barely enough space for the bed and the camera mounted on the dolly. The floor was strewn with straw, the single window was boarded up and a small cannister of dry-ice in the corner puffed thin wisps of mist around the ragged blankets on the bed.

Having gone over what was to happen Kirsten went out into the swirling mist to look for Laurence.

Tucked in behind the monitors, unnoticed so far by anyone except Helena, Ruby sat swaying around on a canvas chair, so drunk she wasn't any too sure where she was. How she'd managed to get herself there was a mystery Helena wasn't interested in solving as she moved alongside Ruby, planting herself in such a way that Kirsten probably wouldn't notice her. Then she beckoned to one of the riggers to come and fill out the blockade. They were so close to a take now that the last thing either Anna or Kirsten needed was Ruby throwing a tantrum as she was escorted from the set.

Helena could see Kirsten and Laurence exchanging what looked like heated words at the door of the house, then both of them went inside. A few seconds later the make-up girl came out, then the camera operator squeezed in, checking the connections on the cables for he was doing this scene by remote control since once the camera started to move there would be no room for him.

The whole atmosphere had a strange surreal quality about it, Helena was thinking to herself. It was as though they were all taking part in some kind of silent movie. Lips were moving, but it was as though no sound was coming out. But there was sound. It just seemed, oddly, to be coming from a long way off.

She shivered, drew her cloak tighter around her and continued to watch as everyone moved about the set. After a while Kirsten and Laurence came out of the house, parted at the door and went to their monitors.

Kirsten looked around, found the actor whose hands and back were to be featured in the scene, walked him to the house then gave a nod to the props man.

'OK,' she said, rubbing her hands together as she returned to her monitor. 'Let's do it.'

As everyone moved into position she squeezed Helena's arm as it linked through hers. 'This isn't going to work,' she muttered. 'The light's all wrong, I want the door to open and close in shot, for Christ's sake we have to see the guy come in. Shit!' she suddenly seethed. 'If it had been anyone else but Anna I'd have thought this through better. But now look what's happening. We've got two hundred or more extras lined up for the ritual, we've got all the animals on stand-by, the make-up artists have slogged their guts out . . . I know it's childish, Helena, but I want to cry. I've been looking forward to that ritual – it's the biggest challenge of the entire film – and now that spoiled, pampered little cow has ruined it. Isn't it enough that she has Laurence? Why does she have to fuck this up for me too?'

'She hasn't fucked it up,' Helena said comfortingly. 'We'll do it. And it'll be great, you'll see.'

'No!' Kirsten suddenly cried, hearing the continuity girl give the wrong instructions to the props guy. 'All we want for now is the end of the struggle – the hands leaving the throat, the retreating figure and a few second hold on Anna's face. Ask Jake, can we do it with the door open to get the guy out?'

'Sure we can,' Jake answered, having heard the question. 'Just give me a minute and I'll sort it.'

Kirsten nodded. 'God, this is taking forever,' she said to Helena and as she glanced at her watch her heart sank. 'Just look at the time! We'll never . . .'

'Kirsten! Kirsten!' Anna's voice came from inside the house.

'What is it?' Kirsten said, pushing her way inside.

'Could we just go over this again, please? If John here is going out of the door . . .'

Kirsten turned to John. 'You pause at the door – we'll give you a mark. Give the camera time to pan back to Anna then go out of the door. It'll already be open and as you come out it'll be the cue for props to activate the mist. Then close the door behind you.'

– 432 –

'Thank you,' Anna smiled.

It was another ten minutes before the clapper-loader ran into position raising a thumb as the script supervisor called out the shot number; David had a final few words with the actors and Laurence went to stand beside Jake at the monitor positioned just in front of Kirsten's.

'OK, turn over,' Kirsten said, as David cleared shot and came out of the house.

'Camera's rolling.'

'Shot five hundred and one, take one.'

Kirsten peered down at her monitor. After a moment or two she looked up, and was just drawing breath to call action when Ruby keeled over and landed with a thud on the grass.

Despite herself Kirsten giggled. So too did Helena, but as one of the runners made to help Ruby up Kirsten said, 'Leave her!' Then turning back to her monitor she looked at it again for several moments before saying, 'OK, and . . . Action!'

Her eyes were fixed on the tiny screen as the frantic buzz of swamp life came over her headphones together with the muted sounds of the struggle going on inside the house. Immediately she made a mental note that the sound perspective was wrong. A dark figure was looming over Anna, his hands gripping her throat, his knee pressing hard into her chest. Anna's eyes were twin pools of panicked terror as she tried to fight him off, but slowly, and alarmingly convincingly, as his fingers dug deeper into her delicate flesh, she began to relinquish the life from her body. The camera pulled back as the figure turned towards it, cloaking the screen in an unsteady movement of black. The camera moved with him to the door, still nothing more definable on the monitors than the sharp glint of a buckle. Just before the door the figure turned to look at the body on the bed. The camera panned with his gaze, registering the purple swellings on the neck, the blackened lips and faintly fluttering eyelids. A thick cloud of morning mist billowed in the draught from the closing door. Then, at the last minute Anna remembered that her eyes should be open, bulging, still steeped in terror and as her eyelids flew open Kirsten groaned.

'Cut!' she yelled, striding out from behind the monitor. 'Set up for another. Make-up!'

'On my way,' Trudie called, already heading towards the house.

'Too heavy on the mist,' Kirsten shouted to the props man as she went to speak to sound while the make-up girl sorted out Anna. Behind her Helena was prodding Ruby with her foot, but the only response she got was a depleted groan. Laurence was wandering off the set, deep in conversation with one of the production managers. Everyone else was re-setting.

Suddenly a scream came from inside the house. For a moment everyone froze. Then spinning round Kirsten started towards the house, Jake close on her heels. They burst in through the door to find the make-up girl backing towards them her hand clamped over her mouth. Kirsten's eyes shot to Anna as the make-up girl stumbled into her. Kirsten shoved her aside and ran to the bed.

'What is it? What's happening?' Jake cried, kneeling beside Kirsten.

Kirsten lifted Anna's shoulders and began shaking her. Jake got to work wrenching open the neck of her shirt.

'Anna! Anna!' Kirsten cried, slapping her face.

'Get the nurse!' Jake yelled.

Two props guys hefted the bed away from the wall and one of them threw himself into the narrow gap to start the kiss of life.

'Laurence! Somebody get Laurence!' Kirsten shouted.

'I'm right here,' he answered, coming in through the door.

He pushed his way to the bed and took over the mouth to mouth, keeping frantically at it until the nurse arrived. Immediately she pushed Laurence aside and laid her ear on Anna's chest.

Kirsten stood beside Laurence looking down at the determined ministrations of the nurse. Inside Kirsten was screaming with fury and frustration. Nobody spoke, there was no room to move, the only activity was the astonishing performance being played out on the narrow bed.

'Get an ambulance,' Kirsten muttered to anyone who was listening as the nurse pushed violently at Anna's heart. 'Get it now!'

There was a scuffle at the door as someone ran off. A few seconds later the nurse turned to look up at Kirsten. The blood drained from Kirsten's face as she turned to Laurence, her eyes wide with confusion and shock. Then they both looked back at the nurse whose slender face was pinched with distress.

Within twenty-four hours the New Orleans Police Department had set up an investigation headquarters on the first floor of the hotel. Anna's body had been taken to the Coroner's office, but as yet no one knew when the results of the post-mortem would be made known. Which, as Laurence remarked to Kirsten, made it odd that the police were so keen to begin interviewing. Laurence had been in touch with the Chief of Police, but all he had been told was that the day-record from the Coroner's office had stated that the cause of death at this stage was unknown. Now the forensic pathologist was awaiting a toxicology report from the State laboratory.

For a while it was as though the entire crew had gone into shock, no one spoke other than in hushed tones, and their faces were ashen masks of confusion, stupefied disbelief or, in some cases, distinct discomfort. The support actor who had taken part in the strangulation scene was under sedation, the shock had been too much for him to handle and his protestations of innocence, until quieted, had served perhaps more than anything else to fan the flames of morbid speculation. So far no one had actually voiced the suspicion that Anna's death was unnatural, instead they were tentatively suggesting that perhaps the tension had affected her brain and a blood vessel had burst. Or that maybe she had had a heart attack, but it wasn't long before some started to wonder if the rumour that she had overdosed just before the scene because Laurence had ended their relationship was true. And quite soon another kind of post-mortem was taking place behind the closed doors of the hotel bedrooms where many were asking, even conjecturing, as to who might have the strongest motive for killing Anna Sage.

A copy of the rushes had been sent to the police and out at Little Joe's Kirsten and Laurence played and replayed the scene to try and work out what might have happened. There was no doubt in either of their minds, mainly because of the way Anna had opened her eyes, that until the moment the door had closed she was still alive. And in the thirty or so seconds that had followed no one had entered the house. So, as far as they could see there was no question of foul-play.

As the days passed and still no news of the cause of death was forthcoming the tension began building to such a pitch that it was as though a ticking bomb had been flung into their midst.

It was in the middle of the morning, three days after Anna's death, that Jane came to Kirsten's room looking even paler than usual to tell Kirsten about the interrogation she had just undergone.

'They didn't actually come right out and say it,' she said wringing her hands as she gazed down at the floor, 'but they gave me the impression that they think Anna was murdered.'

'But for God's sake, how could she have been?' Kirsten snapped. 'We were all there, we were watching the monitors – the only one who had a chance to do anything was the actor, and since Anna didn't die of strangulation . . .'

'But how do you know she didn't?' Alison, who was sitting on the bed, interrupted.

'OK, I'm assuming. But if she had they'd have established that by now and there'd be no question as to what kind of enquiry this is. Anyway, what kind of things were they asking you, Jane?'

Jane's agitation seemed to increase and Kirsten turned away so that she wouldn't see her irritation.

'Well,' Jane began hesitantly, 'they were asking me about Laurence mainly and what his relationship was with Anna. No, first of all they wanted to know if I had any idea who might hate Anna enough to want to ... um, how did they put it? Um, I think they said "harm her in any way". That was when I thought that there might be more to it than they were saying.'

'What did you tell them?' Kirsten asked, feeling the muscles in her face starting to numb.

'I said that I didn't think anyone hated her that much. Then they wanted to know if I knew anything about how she got the part.'

'What!' Kirsten cried. 'Why on earth were they asking *you* that question?'

Jane shrugged, her pale grey eyes moving from Kirsten to Alison and back again.

'What else did they say?' Alison prompted.

Apprehension leapt into Jane's eyes as her gaze flickered uncertainly towards Alison before she said, 'They asked me what I knew about Laurence's relationship with you, Kirsten.'

'But what the hell's that got to do with anything?' Kirsten cried.

'I don't know,' Jane answered miserably.

'So what did you say?'

'I said that you had been his girlfriend once, a long

time ago, but that now you were just friends – and colleagues.'

Suddenly there was a frantic knocking on the door. Kirsten yanked it open to find Helena in as bad a state as Jane.

'They've just had me in there again,' Helena cried, stalking into the room. 'They were asking me about my fucking voodoo doll! Can you believe it? Someone told them that I'd made an effigy of Anna and they wanted to know if I'd used it!'

'You can't be serious,' Kirsten laughed uneasily.

'I'm deadly serious. They wanted to know why I made one.'

'But you didn't make one,' Kirsten interrupted. 'It was a joke . . .'

'I know that, you know that, but try telling them that.'

The initial stirrings of dread were beginning to gnaw at Kirsten. 'So did you tell them why you had made one – I mean joked about making one?'

'Not really, no,' Helena answered. 'I just said that she was a pain in the ass and I'd talked about doing it . . .'

'But they can't seriously believe that Anna was killed by some kind of voodoo?' Kirsten declared, then quickly moved to Helena as Helena covered her face with her hands.

'If you ask me they still don't know how she did die,' Helena choked. 'But they're throwing up everything about my mother. Asking me when I last saw her; did I take lessons from her; all sorts of rubbish like you wouldn't believe. Shit! This is some kind of nightmare. I mean we were all sitting there watching so it can't be murder. It's impossible! We'd have seen it happen.'

'Unless it *was* something to do with voodoo,' Jane said in a tremulous whisper.

Kirsten shot a daggered look at her, but they all fell silent as they looked at each other in appalled disbelief. It was clear that none of them wanted to believe it, but if the police had introduced the subject into their enquiries then they obviously weren't ruling out the possibility.

'Have they spoken to Ruby?' Kirsten asked hoarsely.

'She went in just after I came out,' Helena answered. 'She's in a terrible state. Well, you've seen her. She can't even speak she's so horrified. She just keeps mumbling about that fucking coconut.'

Kirsten's hand suddenly slammed down on the table. 'This is ridiculous!' she shouted. She started towards the door. 'I'm going to see Laurence.'

'He's down in the production office with the accountants,' Jane told her.

Kirsten pulled a face. 'Yes, I'll bet he is. Jesus Christ, this is going to finish us . . .'

An hour later Laurence, Kirsten and the production managers were in Laurence's room when Jane opened the door and ushered Ruby in. She was badly shaken, her fleshy face so pinched with distress that Laurence set her down and poured her a stiff drink as the production managers left.

'They think I did it,' Ruby mumbled. 'They think I killed the stupid bitch.'

Kirsten and Laurence looked at each other. 'Nobody killed her,' Laurence said going to sit with Ruby. 'OK, we don't know how she died, but that doesn't mean someone killed her.' Again he glanced at Kirsten, then putting an arm about Ruby he said, 'Start at the beginning. Exactly what did they say to you?'

'They reckon I killed her,' Ruby mumbled again. 'They reckon I did it. I know they do.' It was evident from the dazed look in her eyes that she could barely think.

'Oh, God,' Kirsten sighed. 'Until we know how Anna died this is just going to get worse. Haven't they told you anything, Laurence?'

He shook his head as the telephone started to ring. 'They haven't spoken to me at all today. Get that, will you?' he said to Jane.

'Kirsten, it's for you,' Jane said, holding out the receiver.

It was Helena, could Kirsten come to her room quick?

'What is it?' Kirsten asked as she closed Helena's door behind her.

'I've got to warn you about this,' Helena said. 'The crew are gossiping . . .' She put a hand to her head. 'Oh shit, Kirstie, I hardly know how to tell you this. Dermott's with the police now, he told everyone what he was going to say before he went in.'

'What do you mean?' Kirsten said, the colour draining from her face.

'He's going to tell them everything he knows about you and Laurence.'

'Oh God!' Kirsten cried, clasping her hands to her head. She started to pace the room, so caught in the rapid tangling of her thoughts that not one of them seemed to make sense. 'You don't suppose,' she began, then groaned as she covered her face with her hands. 'Campbell couldn't have fixed this to make it look like it was me, could he?' she said. 'You don't think . . .'

'I don't know,' Helena said, going to put an arm around her. 'He was out at the set . . .'

'I didn't see him,' Kirsten snapped.

'Neither did I. But he was there, apparently. At least for some of the time. But look, we don't know it was murder yet, and besides how the hell could he have done it?'

'God knows, but it's one hell of a coincidence, isn't it, that Anna should die while he's here? And it's well and truly fucked up the film, hasn't it? That's what Dyllis Fisher wanted.' Her eyes came up to Helena's and suddenly she couldn't believe how dense she was being. 'Helena,' she said softly. 'Helena, please tell me that you had nothing to do with this. Tell me that this isn't what he asked you to fix . . .'

'No! I swear it!' Helena cried. 'I told you what he was talking about and it was the truth, Kirsten. Please, believe me, it was the truth. I know it doesn't look too good, and I understand you thinking the way you are, but I swear on my mother's life he never once even mentioned anything like this. Jesus Christ, if he had I'd have told you straight away.'

'But let's face it, Helena, I've got as good a motive as anyone to want to be rid of Anna and he knows it.'

'Yes,' Helena muttered. 'And if Dermott's telling the police what he said he was going to then I'm afraid they'll know that by now.' She bowed her head and Kirsten saw her nails dig painful weals into her palms.

'There's more, isn't there?' Kirsten whispered.

Helena nodded. 'They had me back in there, just before Dermott went in. I had to tell them exactly why I was joking around about the voodoo doll. I'm sorry, Kirstie, but I had to tell them that it was because of you. And then . . .' she faltered. 'Then they asked me if I knew that you had once threatened to kill Laurence's wife?'

Panic suddenly flared in Kirsten's chest. But no, she wouldn't give into it. She'd done nothing. She had no reason to be afraid. She just had to remain calm. She hadn't liked Anna it was true, and yes she was in love with Laurence, but neither of those facts was enough to prove that she had killed anyone. For God's sake, how could anyone prove it when she hadn't? 'I have to speak to Laurence,' she said and getting up from the chair she all but ran out into the corridor.

However, when she reached Laurence's room it was to discover that the police had sent for him ten minutes before.

Kirsten was waiting outside when Laurence finally left the investigation room. She'd received a telephone call only minutes before to ask her to report to the police officer stationed outside.

'How did it go?' she whispered as Laurence closed the door behind him.

Laurence's face was drawn with tension. 'They still won't admit this is a murder investigation,' he said, 'but it sure as hell seems like one to me. The strange thing is though they still seem to be considering suicide as an option. They wanted to know everything about my relationship with Anna – and was it true that I'd ended it the evening she died.'

'And did you?' Kirsten asked.

'Miss Meredith?'

Kirsten looked up to see a policewoman standing at the open door.

'Could you come in now, please?' she said.

Feeling as though she were moving through some kind of nightmare Kirsten walked into the dingy room. Seated behind the file- and ash-strewn desk were the two homicide detectives, Greengage and Kowski, who had interviewed her the night Anna died. The police-woman who had come to the door held out a chair for her to sit down then went to position herself on the window ledge.

The balding, long-faced man, Kowski, who Kirsten knew to be the more senior of the detectives, was engrossed in whatever it was he was reading, the other offered Kirsten a cigarette.

She shook her head and inwardly willed herself to contain her fear and not be intimidated by the air of antagonism she could already feel closing in around her.

'OK,' Kowski drawled in his pronounced Kentucky accent. He lifted his head and bared his yellow teeth in a grin that was so carnivorous Kirsten almost shuddered. 'I just been going over your statement here, ma'am,' he said. 'It's all pretty straightforward, but our further enquiries mean that there are a couple more things we need to ask y'all. They're kind of personal, but I'm sure you're keen to tell us all we need to know.'

Kirsten watched him, saying nothing.

His eyes flicked towards the other detective, then leaning back in his chair he stuffed his hands into his trouser pockets. 'Is it true that you once threatened to kill Mr McAllister's wife, ma'am?'

Kirsten felt almost dizzied by the smooth matter-of-factness of the question. 'Not quite,' she answered sounding far steadier than she felt. 'They weren't married at the time, so it was his girlfriend I threatened to kill.'

'And why was that?'

'Because I was in love with Mr McAllister.'

'Did you ever do anything about this here threat? I mean, did you try to carry it out'n'all? Before you answer that, ma'am, I gotta tell you these things are real easy to check out.'

'Please go right ahead and check,' Kirsten said tightly.

'I did nothing to endanger Pippa's life and nor would I.'

'But you did threaten her life?'

'I was mentally unstable at the time,' Kirsten said bluntly and knew immediately she shouldn't have. However, it was too late now, and, she kept reminding herself, she had nothing to hide.

'Would you be considering yourself mentally stable now?' Kowski enquired.

'Yes, I would.'

'Even though Mr McAllister has recently been engaged in an affair with the deceased?'

Kirsten merely looked at him, her insides churning with fear and resentment.

'You did know about Mr McAllister's relationship with the deceased, didn't you, ma'am?'

'Yes, I knew about it.'

'Were you jealous, ma'am? Jealous enough to want her dead?'

Kirsten flinched as the words hit her.

'Would I be right in thinking that you didn't want Miss Sage on your movie?' Kowski said. 'That you opposed her casting because of her resemblance to Mr McAllister's wife?'

'It had nothing to do with her looking like Pippa,' Kirsten said. 'I just didn't think she was old enough for the part, but I was wrong. She's worked out very well.'

Kowski pursed his lips and let his chin fall onto his chest. 'I would be right in thinking, ma'am, wouldn't I, that you still have feelings for Mr McAllister?' he said eventually.

'You would,' Kirsten answered.

'And would Mr McAllister be returning those feelings?'

'I'm afraid you'll have to ask him that question.'

'But in your opinion . . .'

'Not any more, no. I thought he might, but it seems I was wrong.'

'Mmm. I guess it's kind of difficult to swallow that, him dumping on you twice the way he did.'

'Yes, it is difficult, but not so difficult I'd kill because of it,' Kirsten almost shouted as Kowski made to interrupt her.

Kowski's head tilted to one side as he smirked, then getting up he walked around the desk and came to perch in front of her. Kirsten could smell the musky odour of his stale cologne and the tobacco on his breath. 'Did you ask Miss Johnson to make an effigy of Miss Sage, ma'am?' Kowski smiled benignly.

'No.'

He nodded thoughtfully, but as his eyes met Greengage's Kirsten could sense the malicious humour passing between the two men. 'Do you know anything about poison, Miss Meredith?' Kowski asked. 'I mean in the context of your job you've got to have come across a lot of things the average person don't ever see. Would poison be one of them?'

Kirsten felt her skin starting to prickle. 'No,' she answered. Then lifting her head to look him right in the face, she said, 'Are you saying that Anna was poisoned?'

Kowski turned to look at the policewoman. 'Was the deceased poisoned?' he repeated, as though mulling the question over to himself. His strangely elongated face came round to look at Kirsten again. 'Is there any reason you can think of as to why Miss Sage might have taken her own life, ma'am?' he asked.

Kirsten shook her head. 'None that I know of.'

'Do you recall where Mr McAllister was at the moment of death?'

'I'm not sure at what moment Anna died,' Kirsten answered. 'But during the scene Laurence was at his monitor, just in front of me, and afterwards we were both in the house.'

'Was Miss Collins with you?'

'In body, yes. She passed out drunk just as we were going for a take.'

Kowski's bottom lip jutted forward. 'Is Miss Collins usually as drunk as all that?' he wondered.

'Sometimes, yes.'

'You know that Miss Collins believes there is some kind of curse on her?' his voice was so imbued with sarcasm Kirsten almost felt herself blush.

She nodded. 'Yes, I know, but I've never taken it seriously.'

'Why?'

'Because I don't believe in that sort of thing.'

'No,' Kowski sighed, getting to his feet, 'neither do we. But someone around here sure wants us to believe it. And you got to admit, ma'am, there's something of a mystery here.'

'Yes, there is. But I don't believe that anyone killed Anna. I have no idea how she died, I assume you don't either or you'd have told us by now.'

'She didn't die from no voodoo curse, Miss Meredith,' Kowski said.

'Then how did she die?'

'Now that's what we're still trying to find out. But me, I reckon there was some kind of poison at work here . . .'

'Then it would have been self-inflicted,' Kirsten said hotly.

Kowski's eyebrows lazily arched his surprise. 'Yet you said earlier that you knew of no reason why she would kill herself.'

'I don't. But she might have.'

'There's no suicide note.'

'Is there any poison?'

Kowski laughed, lifted a foot on to the corner of her chair and rested an elbow on his knee. 'Let's go back to the beginning, shall we? Just how did you come to be working on this movie?'

The interrogation went on, hour after hour, so many questions, so many suppositions and so many oblique accusations that Kirsten's head was spinning so hard she was losing the ability to think straight. They gave her water, offered her cigarettes, shouted at her, consoled her, threatened her, sympathized with her, did everything they could to wear her down. It was as though their mocking Southern accents were tangible things wrapping themselves around her hauling in every word, then twisting it, bending it, stretching it, enmeshing her in so much doubt that she could barely even be sure of her own name. Over and over she reminded herself that she just had to keep to the truth, but Kowski was running her round in such circles she finally started to lose track of even that.

At last one clear thought erupted through the chaos in her mind. 'I want a lawyer,' she cried. 'You shouldn't be questioning me like this without a lawyer present.'

'Do you need a lawyer, Miss Meredith?'

Kirsten was so exhausted she could feel herself brinking on frightened tears. 'Yes, when you're accusing me of murder, I do.'

'But no one's accused you.'

'Not directly, but you're insinuating it.'

'Was there a murder?'

'No! I don't know.'

'Is there anything you want to tell us?'

'I've told you everything. You know my movements from the very start of the shoot, you know I was there when she died . . .'

'In fact you watched her die.'

'I didn't know she was dying!'

'Someone must have. *If* it was murder.'

'That's it, you don't know! So why are you putting me through this? I haven't done anything. I don't know what happened, all I know is what I've told you. And if it is murder then I've been set up . . .'

'Set up!' Kowski pounced on it.

Kirsten recoiled sharply. 'Yes, set up,' she cried. 'There's a vendetta . . . A woman in England, she wants to ruin me . . .'

Kowski looked at Greengage and grinned. 'Dermott Campbell's employer?' he said.

'Yes,' Kirsten answered, her eyes darting between them. 'Dyllis Fisher hates me, she wants to destroy me . . .'

Kowski waved a dismissive hand. 'We've heard the background from Mr Campbell, but I gotta tell you Miss Meredith neither Mrs Fisher nor Mr Campbell are possible suspects here . . .'

'Why not? She'd like nothing more than to see me in prison.'

Kowski's lips pursed thoughtfully as once again he turned to Greengage.

'I want a lawyer,' Kirsten repeated.

'Yeah, I reckon you could need one,' Kowski remarked, looking up as the door opened. He took an envelope from the uniformed officer who'd come in and

– 449 –

nodded towards the police woman who walked to the telephone and started to dial.

Kirsten watched as Kowski read, dreadful images of a future in a Louisiana State prison for something she hadn't even done racing so fast through her mind she was almost choking on her panic. Then, just as the policewoman was making contact with someone on the other end of the line Kowski's hand came up. Immediately the policewoman cut the connection.

'OK, Miss Meredith,' he said, 'y'all can go.'

Kirsten's eyes flew open. 'You mean . . .? Are you saying . . .?'

'I'm telling you you can go.'

'So you don't think I killed her?'

'Not unless you want to tell me different.'

Dumbly Kirsten shook her head. She was already half way to the door before it occurred to her that what Kowski had read could have been the toxicologist's report. She turned back.

'Yeah,' Kowski answered, 'that's what it is right enough. It would appear, Miss Meredith, that your star died a natural death.'

Kirsten's confusion was evident. 'What do you mean? Did she have a heart attack or something?'

He looked down at the report in his hand. 'It says right here that she died of natural causes.'

'Natural causes?' Kirsten echoed.

'That's what it says. So either you got some genius at work here or we all got to start believing in voodoo curses.'

Kirsten stiffened. 'So you still think it was murder?'

He grinned. 'I think she died a natural death, is what I think. But what your crew are gonna think and how much convincing they're gonna take is another matter

Helena was shaking her head. 'We can't go on like this, Dermott,' she said. 'I mean, if we can suspect each other of murder, *murder* for Christ's sake, then what the hell chance do we stand?'

'We'd stand a much better one if we got Kirsten Meredith out of our lives,' he answered.

'See! There you go again! Saying things like that just makes me more suspicious than ever.'

'Why are you so quick to suspect me and not Kirsten?' Campbell said sourly. 'Like I said, she's got the best motive.'

'And why are you so quick to suspect Kirsten when Ruby's given a full confession?'

Campbell gave a snort of laughter. 'Ruby's off her head and you know it. Not even the police took her seriously. Possessed by a demon child, my ass! She's been watching too many movies.'

Helena was staring down at her hands. 'She told Kirsten that Laurence is her son,' she said absently.

'He is.'

Helena lifted her head.

'Laurence told me himself. A long time ago.'

Once again an oppressive incredulity throbbed through Helena's mind. 'I can't take any more of this,' she said. 'I'm going with the Coroner's verdict and I don't want ever to discuss any of it again.'

'Helena,' Campbell said as she reached the door.

She turned back.

'What about us?'

She looked at him for a long time. 'I don't know,' she sighed. 'I was always afraid that one day I might have to choose between you and Kirsten. I got round it once, but this time, Dermott . . .'

'Don't let her do this!' Campbell protested, an edge of panic in his voice.

'It's not her who's doing it, it's you! Don't you see, whatever it is you feel about Kirsten it's of your own making? She had you fired because of what you'd already done. You got your comeuppance and you deserved it. But now you can't leave her alone. You're more bent on destroying her than Dyllis Fisher is and I don't even think you know why.'

'Because she's coming between us,' Campbell cried.

Helena looked at him sadly then turning to the door she opened it, walked out into the hall and closed it quietly behind her.

Kirsten had just returned from Laurence's room where Jane and Tom were packing up their belongings and carrying them out into the little courtyard. She had left Laurence still sitting at the dining table, endless accounts and unpaid bills spread out in front of him. He'd looked just about all in, but he'd wanted to pay whatever they owed in New Orleans before they left. She knew he was worried about Ruby too, that he felt he should have flown back to England with her the day before, but there had been too many things here still to be sorted. Kirsten had never spoken to him about what Ruby had told her, but seeing his concern over these past few days she was beginning to wonder if Ruby really had been telling the truth. Poor Ruby, she'd taken all this so hard, she was so convinced she was responsible that even the priest Laurence had asked to come and see her hadn't been able to get through to her.

Now, as Kirsten walked into her room where her suitcase was lying open on the bed, she looked down at the day-old British newspaper that contained the damning insinuations that she was behind what had happened. For a moment it felt as though the ground was shifting beneath her feet. It was so hard to take in that anyone would believe her capable of murder . . .

A sudden cold chill curled through her. Was that what Laurence was thinking? Was that why he wouldn't speak to her about it? Did he think that she'd managed to delude even the police by using some extraordinary means to kill Anna in order to get him back?

Kirsten turned to the door knowing that she had to speak to him now, to find out what he was thinking. She just couldn't leave it the way it was, with so much unsaid and so much still to get through.

She was on the point of opening the door when she saw a note on the floor. As she stopped to pick it up her heart, for no apparent reason, was starting to pound. Her fingers were unsteady as she tore open the envelope, and as she read the words, cut from a newspaper and glued on to a single blank sheet, it was as though the world was caving in beneath her.

— 25 —

Her fingers frantically turned the pages of the album, revealing the faces of all the people she had made a part of her life. Her eyes were feverish, tremors of passion rippled through her heart. The baby was screaming, but it didn't matter. She'd let the baby scream because she had to look at her pictures.

There was Laurence as a child. Or was it Tom? They were so alike. But it had to be Laurence because the picture was old and in black and white. How she loved Laurence. How she had longed for him. But she had him now, he was hers, or he would be soon and he would be everything to her she wanted him to be. They would be so happy together, all of them. No one was going to stand in the way now. The memories were almost complete, she had all the pictures . . .

Her eyes misted over, a smile trembled her lips as she gazed down at the photo of the wedding. Laurence was so tall and handsome . . . Pippa wasn't there any more, she should never have been there, so using her scissors she'd got rid of Pippa.

She smoothed her fingers lovingly over the sharp edges of the picture, then turning the page her body began to quake with excitement as she saw the most exquisite portrait of them all. She had made such a good job of this one . . . There she was as a baby in the arms of her mother while her father looked dotingly down on them both. There was such a thing as a happy family; she knew it because she had it – at least, soon she would have it.

A spasm of fear suddenly clutched at her mind, jerking her head upwards. Dermott Campbell was going to spoil it. He was writing things that weren't true. But how was he going to prove there had been a murder when even the police said there hadn't been? A brittle laugh burst from her lips. Dermott Campbell hadn't even managed to bring the film to its knees, though he probably thought he had. But she knew differently. She knew that they'd be shooting again right after Christmas, because, of course, Anna's death had been due to natural causes so the insurance company were going to pay out . . .

Anna's death! The two words clashed together inside her head. Frenzied colours exploded before her eyes. She'd done it. She'd taken a human life and now it was as though she had stepped from her skin into a world of endless chaos and terror. Her heart thudded a strident beat, pumping cowardly dread to her veins, discord and violence to her thoughts. She had killed once and knew if she had to she'd do it again. A muscle in her cheek began to twitch. She crushed it with her hand. Her fingers were rigid, crooked like claws. She was gasping for breath, so afraid of herself she could feel it lapping at the shores of her sanity. She pushed the album away, pressed her hands to her ears. The baby was screaming, screaming, screaming . . . The tide was drawing closer, she was drowning in the screams . . .

Ten days had gone by since they'd returned from New Orleans and the planning of the reshoot was already underway in earnest. As far as Kirsten could see they were all going to be working right up to the last minute on Christmas Eve, after which Laurence had declared that everyone should take a week off and begin again in the New Year, preparing to film by the middle of January. The part of Moyna O'Malley had already been recast. Elizabeth Bradley, an actress with whom Kirsten had worked before, was taking over the role, though not until she had been given all the details of Anna's death did Elizabeth agree to take it on. Kirsten understood completely, with all that was still being bandied about in the press it was only natural that Elizabeth would want to hear first-hand what had happened. So, Kirsten and

Laurence had taken Elizabeth to dinner and told her all she wanted to know. Just like everyone else Elizabeth was fascinated by the mystery of Anna's death, though, knowing Kirsten she didn't consider, even for a moment, that there was an iota of truth in the oblique accusations that Kirsten was responsible.

It was becoming extremely difficult now for Kirsten to show her face in public. How Cambell managed to get so many pictures of her laughing Kirsten didn't know, but he did and seeing her so happy less than a year after Paul Fisher's death, six months after Laurence's wife had left him and a mere couple of weeks after the mysterious demise of her rival made it – at least the way Campbell told it – seem as though she was so ruthless and dangerous in her schemings that nothing, least of all the sanctity of human life, was going to stand in the way of whatever Kirsten Meredith wanted.

For Kirsten it was like reading about a stranger, someone who had stolen her identity and was using it with such malicious and harmful intent she was as frightened by it as she was bewildered. She just couldn't come to terms with the fact that anyone could believe she was the monster being portrayed in the press, and neither could she understand what route her life was taking to have made her the victim of such injustice and prejudice. Her lawyers had applied for an injunction against Campbell's newspaper now, but it wasn't likely to be granted until after Christmas. In the meantime, the libellous allegations continued and so too did the serving of writs. In fact getting into a legal battle with Dermott Campbell and Dyllis Fisher was just about the last thing Kirsten wanted for it was earning her even more publicity, but Laurence had insisted that she had no alternative.

She had told no one about the note she'd received just before leaving New Orleans. She was certain now that Campbell had sent it, though if, as the note had said, he could prove that she'd killed Anna, then why was he holding back? To torment her further? It could be, but what greater torment could there be than to find herself charged with murder? So it would seem that despite what the note claimed, he wasn't able to prove it at all and Kirsten was only sorry that she hadn't kept the note so that she could hand it over to her lawyers.

Right now she and Laurence were in the festively decorated production office going over the revised schedule with the production managers. All around them phones were ringing, computers were printing out, faxes were coming in and people were yelling at each other for information. A number of the scenes from the original shoot were still usable, so too were shots within scenes, so this time round the planning of the schedule was a good deal more complicated than the last. Plus the fact that they were faced with almost insurmountable problems over the weather.

'So what you're suggesting,' Kirsten said to Melvin, the chief production manager, 'is that when we return to New Orleans we go straight out to the Plantation House and do those scenes first?'

Melvin nodded. 'If we don't,' he told her, 'then we're going to run smack bang into the middle of Mardi Gras.'

'Yes, of course,' Kirsten said, casting an eye over the polaroid photographs of Oak Alley, the Plantation House they had selected for the shoot. She felt a pleasing lift in her heart at the prospect of filming there, it was such a magnificent house and was – at least so far as the shoot was concerned – still virgin territory. 'What do you think, Laurence?' she said turning to him.

'Sounds sensible to me,' he answered, taking the polaroids from her.

'Have you discussed this with Little Joe?' Kirsten asked Melvin, perching on the edge of his desk and stretching her legs out to rest them on his chair. 'Can he get us the equipment and crew we need during Mardi Gras?'

'He thinks so,' Melvin answered. 'He's getting back to me sometime later this week. I can't see Joe letting us down though. My guess is if he can't get what we want locally he'll hire in from Hollywood.'

'Don't let him do that until you've spoken to me,' Laurence interjected. 'In fact don't book anything over there yet, just put a provisional hold on it. The same goes for the flights.'

'I think, taking Mardi Gras into consideration,' Melvin said, 'that we'll have to be more positive than that.'

'Just speak to me first,' Laurence repeated, trying not to show his discomfort at how closely Kirsten was watching him. He handed back the photographs staring sightlessly down at her legs in their long black boots and skin tight jodphurs. Then, avoiding her eyes, he turned towards their office.

'If you ask me he's having an enthusiasm failure,' Melvin remarked to Kirsten. 'You don't think he's going to pull the plugs, do you?'

'No,' Kirsten answered, sounding more confident than she felt. 'He's just being cautious.'

'Well he's making everyone pretty edgy lately. I mean, if he is going to pull out we need to know, because some of us are turning down other work.'

'He's not going to pull out,' Kirsten assured him. 'He's just got a lot on his mind. Now, where were we?'

For the next hour or so they went over the schedule in minute detail until Melvin complained he was starving and went to join the others for lunch.

When he'd gone Kirsten wandered towards her own office, trying to decide whether or not she really wanted to go in. She knew Ruby was there and she wasn't too comfortable in Ruby's company lately – not since Ruby had got God. Actually, there were times when it was quite amusing, but being told constantly to repent of her sins was becoming a little wearing, particularly when Kirsten wasn't too sure whether or not it was some kind of accusation. Still, at least Ruby's counselling with a priest seemed to have cured her of her coconut ravings and, to a certain extent, her dependence on gin.

She opened the door to her office and found Ruby there alone, studying her Bible. She looked up as Kirsten came in and immediately made the sign of the cross.

'I wish you wouldn't do that,' Kirsten complained.

' "Seek ye the Lord while He may be found, call ye upon Him while He is near",' Ruby advised her.

'OK,' Kirsten said, sitting down at her desk. 'Where's Laurence?'

'In the screening room,' Ruby answered, then putting her hands together she bowed her head and started to mumble.

'Ruby, aren't you taking this just a bit too far?' Kirsten groaned.

'You can't ever go too far down the road to our Lord,' Ruby told her. 'And I'm saying a prayer for you here, Kirsten.'

'Well that's very kind of you,' Kirsten said, 'but it's a bit distracting.'

Neither of them spoke for some time then, as Kirsten began checking through her script to make sure there were no shots missing from the schedule and Ruby returned to her Bible. In the end, aware of the way Ruby kept glancing over at her, Kirsten looked up.

'Do you have something on your mind?' she said.

'As a matter of fact, I do,' Ruby answered, popping a Nicorette gum into her mouth. She sat back in Laurence's chair, resting her elbows on the arms and knitting her fingers across her chest. ' "Forgetting those things which are behind, and reaching forth unto those which are before, I press towards the mark",' she said sombrely.

Kirsten sighed and waited.

Ruby nodded. ' "Learn to be silent. Let your quiet mind listen and absorb",' she counselled. 'Pythagorus said that,' she added informatively.

'Did he?' Kirsten said. 'Well, I'm listening.'

For a moment Ruby gazed mournfully across at her, then summoning a smile brimming with heartfelt compassion, she said, 'The Lord has counselled me to speak. There are things Laurence don't want to say, so I'm gonna do it for him. Hell, someone's got to. But Kirstie, my child, if you'd had the good sense to pull out of this movie the minute we left New Orleans I wouldn't have to be saying this at all.'

Kirsten watched her, tight-lipped.

'Look, honey,' Ruby said, her voice sugary sweet. 'Laurence and I, we were working on this movie long before you came on the scene. You know that. It means a lot to us . . .'

'And it doesn't to me?'

'Ah, ah,' Ruby admonished, raising a hand. 'Remember, "listen and absorb". But sure, I guess the movie does mean something to you too, but for the wrong reasons. You put your dough in to get Laurence, the whole world knows that. Well you gotta know by now that that ain't gonna happen. Not even with poor Anna out of the way are you gonna get him.'

'Was that some kind of accusation?' Kirsten snapped.

Ruby looked blank. Then, 'Oh, I see what you're getting at. No, I know there are those who reckon you were behind that terrible event,' she said, crossing herself, 'but not me.' She shrugged. 'But you've read all that stuff in the press and what I'm asking here is that you think about Laurence. This is his movie. He wants to shoot it but he can't get the insurance cover this time round. Now why do you suppose that is?'

'Why don't you tell me, Ruby?'

'OK. Something real weird happened that day on the set, we all know that, and you were there. Now I'm not saying you did it, I'm not saying that at all, but remember Kirsten, one day you will have to answer to the Lord. But He is a merciful Lord . . . Anyways, even if you didn't kill the woman yourself someone's done it and made it look like you. That don't bode well for going out into the field with you on board again, now does it?'

'Nobody killed Anna, she died of natural causes,' Kirsten reminded her, trying to ignore the horrible unease that was gripping her.

'Of course, God rest her soul. All's I'm saying is what other people think. Now Laurence, he don't want to fire you, he's afraid you'll pull out your dough if he does, but, well,' she shrugged, 'I guess you're getting my drift.'

Kirsten was, only too well. And in truth, didn't she already know it herself, it was just that she hadn't wanted to face it. But of course they couldn't go on with her, not when the press were doing what they were, for who in their right mind was going to be prepared to take a risk on something like that happening again?

Kirsten left the office early saying she wanted to work from home. As she left her smiles and encouragement were as bright as always and no one would have guessed what was going on in her heart. She was trying very hard not to think of how fond she had become of them all, of how she had started to look upon them as her family for she couldn't bear to think of how much she was going to miss them, how empty her days were going to be without their laughter and support.

By the time she arrived home she was so choked with tears that the door was barely shut behind her before she broke down completely. It seemed that every time she felt she was at last getting somewhere a cruel twist in fate was waiting round the corner to snatch it all away. She was misjudged, maligned and made to feel an outcast no matter what she did. She had never claimed to be perfect, but never had she set out to hurt someone the way Dyllis Fisher was hurting her. Dyllis Fisher, the woman who hid behind her empire, never showing her face, but making sure that the power she wielded lanced to the very core.

Still wearing her coat Kirsten went into the sitting room and picked up a photograph of Paul. As she gazed down at his smiling face so full of kindness and humour, she knew that, no matter what, she could never regret the years she had spent with him. She just wished he was there now to help her through what she knew already was going to be another crisis in her life. Resentment swelled within her. A few months ago if someone had told her that she'd have to deal with all that she had, the rejection and hostility of a production team, the perversity of Laurence's behaviour, seeing him with another woman, the horrible suspicion that she had contrived to murder that woman, she'd never have believed she could do it. But somehow she had. Somewhere, deep down inside she had found a strength she hadn't known she possessed and in her own way she had been pulling through. But she could feel that strength ebbing away from her now, disappearing into a terrible gulf that was swallowing everything that mattered in her life. Her career, her friends and all that she felt for Laurence.

She desperately needed to speak to someone now. She wished, more than anything, that it could be Laurence, but how could it be when he must bitterly regret ever having asked her to work with him. His last film hadn't done well at the box office and he couldn't afford another failure. They were crazy, both of them, ever to have thought they could stand up to Dyllis Fisher, but was it that that was really bothering Laurence now, or was it that he just couldn't be sure whether or not she had had anything to do with Anna's death? As the frustration and anger surged through her Kirsten pressed her hands to her head. It seemed insane that anyone should suspect her of being responsible for what happened, but that Laurence could was so horrible she just couldn't bear it.

She thought of calling Helena, but since returning from New Orleans they had hardly seen each other. As she thought about that, Kirsten could feel her heart contracting. She had been so busy she hadn't made any time for Helena even though she had known that Helena was having a rough time over Dermott. Despising the man as much as she did Kirsten had found it difficult to sympathise, so how could she expect Helena to be there for her now?

Covering her face with her hands she turned to the

wall and cried as though her heart would break. She was so afraid of the loneliness, so tired of the battle, but knew that both were closing in on her again and there was nothing she could do to stop it.

Then suddenly, for no reason, she thought of Jane. Shy, nervous, little Jane who had told her that if ever there was anything she could do for her she only had to say. A welter of emotion flowed through her as Kirsten remembered those words, yet she knew that she couldn't burden Jane with her problems, especially not when Jane was so close to Laurence. Besides, what could Jane do? What could any of them do? She had to let go, to take stock of her life again and sort out for herself where she went now. But first she had to speak to Laurence. There was a partnership to dissolve, finance to rearrange as well as a handover to another director. And as the enormity of it all started to sink in she could feel the dread consuming her.

'What you're doing is unjustifiable, unreasonable and so goddamned pitiful, Dermott, that I don't even want to discuss it,' Helena said lifting the phone and carrying it over to the sofa.

'OK, so we'll talk about something else,' he said, 'just let me come over.'

'I keep telling you, no, I don't want to see you.'

'You're not still thinking I had anything to do with what happened in New Orleans, are you?' he asked uncertainly.

'Frankly, Dermott, I don't know what I'm thinking these days, except that to do what you're doing to Kirsten's reputation, never mind her life, is so disgusting, so pathetic . . .'

'Helena! I've told you, I'm not writing it myself. Dyllis Fisher is doing it and using my name.'

'And you're letting her! For Christ's sake, Dermott, haven't you got the guts to stand up to her?'

'If it were over anyone else I would,' Campbell cried. 'But how can you expect me to feel sorry for Kirsten Meredith when she's got all she's got – you included. And answer me this, do you honestly think she's going to want to know about you once she finally hooks Laurence and rises to the top? She'll forget about you, she probably won't even bother to remember your name, then where will you be?'

'God, you don't know her at all, do you?' Helena said, reaching for a cigarette. 'She's not like that, Dermott, in fact she's so not like that that it makes me want to scream just to hear you say it. And let me tell you, once this libel case goes into court you're the one who's going to lose everything, you and Dyllis Fisher, not me. Not Kirsten either, because she didn't kill anyone any more than I did.'

'Well Dyllis Fisher is convinced she did. In fact she even claims she can prove it . . .'

'Oh, do me a favour!' Helena cried scornfully. 'How the hell is she going to do that when even the New Orleans police department couldn't find any evidence of murder?'

'I don't know,' Campbell answered. 'All she says is she's going to prove it. Now when Dyllis tells me something like that you can be sure she's pretty damned confident and she wouldn't be going for it in the paper the way she is if she wasn't, would she? And Kirsten's played right into her hands by throwing those lawsuits at us because it's a sure-fire way of getting that case reopened.'

'Then why don't you let Dyllis get on with it and get the hell out of it?'

'Are you mad? I've got everything to lose if I do that and everything to gain if I don't.'

'Are you sure about that? I mean, have you thought about how you're going to stand if Dyllis is wrong?'

'Women like Dyllis are never wrong,' Campbell declared. 'Like I said, there's no way she'd be putting herself out on a limb like this if she thought there was any chance of losing.'

'Well as long as you're fighting on her side, Dermott, you and I are through, 'cos I'm not standing by and watching you do this to my best friend and looking like I'm a goddamned part of it.'

'Helena, this attitude isn't helping to soften me up any, you know. I mean, how do you expect me to feel about the woman when it's because of her you won't see me.'

Helena's head fell back against the sofa as she took a long, thoughtful draw on her cigarette. 'But from what you're saying, Dermott,' she said steadily, 'even if I did start seeing you again all that stuff in the papers is going to continue.'

'I've got no control over what Dyllis does, you know that.'

'And you say she can prove that Kirsten did it?'

'So she says.'

Helena was shaking her head. 'I'm not buying it, Dermott, because I just know Kirsten didn't do it. But I'll tell you what, I'll see you on one condition. That you try to find out for me just how Dyllis is going to prove Anna was murdered.'

It took some time, longer even than Helena had expected, but at last Campbell agreed to give it a shot and with a smile of satisfaction Helena rang off as pleased with her subterfuge as she was with the fact that she was no longer facing Christmas alone.

A few minutes later she picked up the phone to call Kirsten. There was no answer from Kirsten's home and she wasn't at the production office either. Oh well, there was no particular urgency, they'd be sure to catch up with each other sooner or later and besides, when was the last time Kirsten had called her?

A yellowy warm light from the fringed lamps filled the cluttered family room with a seasonal glow. Multi-coloured fairy-lights lit up the gaily decorated Christmas tree in the corner and from somewhere else in the house came the distant sound of Tom's little tape-recorder playing 'Away in a Manger'. In the old stone hearth a log fire crackled and hissed adding an old-fashioned feeling to the sleepy mood of the dark winter's night.

At that moment Laurence had his back turned so Kirsten couldn't see his face. He was setting out cups on a tray while the coffee percolated in the corner of the kitchen. Kirsten was sitting at the table swallowing hard on the emotions rising in her heart. Despite the languor of the atmosphere there was a restlessness inside her that was making her want to run, to get as far from him as she could, yet she knew that the moment she walked out of the door all the pain she had locked inside would be released.

She averted her eyes and gazed up at the gently swaying Christmas trimmings. Knowing that this was probably the last time she would see him was like feeling a part of herself die. Outwardly she remained calm, fully prepared to stand by what she'd said five minutes ago and though she longed to hear him say he didn't want her to go she knew, from his silence, that he wasn't going to.

She turned to watch him as he came towards her with the tray and felt her heart turn over at the way his dark, handsome face was so taut with concentration. Catching her watching him and seeing her expression his eyebrows gave a sardonic lift.

'You warm enough?' he said, his voice low as though not wanting to disturb the restful ambience of the room.

She nodded. 'Yes, thanks,' she answered, the tone of her voice matching his.

He didn't speak again until he had poured the coffee, not asking how she took hers because of course he knew. Then at last, holding his cup in both hands, his elbows resting on the table, he said, 'I'm not accepting your resignation . . .'

'Laurence, be sensible,' she interrupted, her voice still quiet yet mercifully steady. Dear God, was he really going to stand by her? But even if he was she couldn't let him. 'You and I both know,' she went on, 'that my involvement is what's preventing you getting cover.'

'Bullshit,' he said softly.

'Laurence, please listen . . .'

'No, you listen. I'm not letting you walk out on me now. I don't give a fuck about Dyllis Fisher and her vendetta. You're the one who's made this movie work. It's as much a part of you now as it is of either me or Ruby – and if you listen to that woman again . . .'

'She told you she'd spoken to me?'

'She told me. And I told her what I'm telling you now. That I make the decisions around here as to who's hired and fired. And I am not firing you, neither am I accepting your resignation.'

'I'm not pulling out my investment,' Kirsten said, lifting her cup then replacing it without drinking. 'So you don't have to worry about that.'

'I'm not. I know you won't pull out, because I know you won't let me down. And neither am I going to let you down. I'll get the insurance and we'll start over.'

Kirsten was shaking her head. 'For your own sake, and for mine too, I have to leave. It's the only way to stop this press speculation, it'll give Dyllis Fisher what she wants and like I said, the insurance companies . . .' For a moment her voice faltered, but swallowing hard she made herself go on. 'I'll wind things up as neatly as I can so that there won't be too much of a problem for whoever takes over and after that – other than a return on my investment,' she smiled, 'I want no further involvement. Now, that's my final word on the subject, so please, don't let's argue.'

As she lifted her coffee to her lips she was aware of how searching his eyes were as they swept over her face. She didn't know how much longer she could hold on, but inside she was willing herself not to break down in front of him. She had no idea what he was thinking, or of what he was going to say next, but she knew that whatever it was her resolve was absolute. She wasn't going to change her mind and right now that was all that mattered.

Laurence continued to look at her, silently, almost wonderingly. In the shimmering soft light she looked so unbelievably lovely and so heartrendingly vulnerable. He knew her so well it was easy for him to see through her bravado. He knew too that she believed in it, that she thought her inner strength would support her, and maybe, at least for a while, it would. But he wasn't going to let her go through this alone. This time he was going to be there for her. He wanted so much to tell her he loved her. How he had never stopped loving her. But how was he going to explain all that he had done when he hardly understood it himself? Why was it that he had fought so hard to keep her out of his life when she was all he had ever wanted? Why had he married Pippa knowing that it would break Kirsten's heart? How could he have allowed anger to have governed his life that way? He knew what pain he had caused her, he knew it so well because it had been there for him too. It had all but destroyed Kirsten, and who could say, perhaps in a way it had destroyed him too.

What a lie he had lived these past six years, and how many people he had hurt. And he'd gone on and on hurting, Pippa, Kirsten, Anna until it was almost as though he couldn't stop. Yet Kirsten was the only one who mattered. All he had ever cared about was her and she, because of his shameful inability to face up to his mistakes and his feelings, had been the one he had hurt the most. Making love to her that day in New Orleans had been like re-awakening his soul and if he'd been honest with himself then he'd have admitted that a part of her lived inside him just as a part of him lived inside her. Perhaps if Pippa hadn't called him right after and mocked him, taunting him with his inability to face his own emotions, he wouldn't have done what he had. Goddammit, why had he been so desparate to prove Pippa wrong? What the hell did it matter what she thought? Kirsten was all that mattered and the love they shared that neither of them would ever be able to defeat.

He didn't want to defeat it now, he wanted to give in to it, to take her in his arms and feel her against him, moving into him as though their very souls were joined. He wanted to feel the luxuriant softness of her hair sliding through his fingers, to feel her lips moving beneath his. He wanted to feel the beat of her heart, the warmth of her skin, the unbelievable depth of her love.

He watched the gentle rise and fall of her breasts as she breathed and felt an overpowering need to touch her. He was afraid, he knew that, afraid of the resolve still glittering in her eyes. Her life was being torn apart by one woman's rabid jealousy and so far she had struggled with it alone, but now he was going to help her. He had to make her go on with this film, she had to have a sense of purpose and a chance to succeed in the face of all that was being pitched against her. He owed her that, but how in God's name was he going to do it, when she was right, he couldn't get the cover they needed because of her?

His heart turned over as she lowered her head, trying to escape his scrutiny.

'Kirsten,' he said softly and as his hand covered hers Kirsten's eyes closed.

'No, Laurence,' she said, her voice strangled by the tears in her throat.

'Kirstie, look at me, please.'

'I can't,' she murmured pulling her hand free.

'I love you,' he whispered.

'Oh God, don't say that!' she cried covering her face with her hands. 'Please don't say it! No, Laurence,' she choked as he took her by the shoulders.

'Kirsten, listen to me, please,' he said. 'About Anna. Let me tell you about Anna.'

'No! I don't want to hear it. Laurence, please,' she sobbed as he tried to take her hand again. 'Can't you see how hard this is for me? I just can't let you go on hurting me . . .'

'Darling, I'm not going to hurt you. I love you . . .'

'But for how long, Laurence? For tonight, while you're feeling lonely? For the next week, the next month, until you find someone else? No! It's over between us, Laurence. It was over six years ago. I've never really been able to make myself believe that, but I do now. So I'm leaving. I'm saying goodbye, because I can't keep pretending that one day you'll be there for me when in my heart I know I can't trust you anymore.'

'Kirsten, come back!' he cried, leaping to his feet as she ran to the door, but as she dashed down the front step he stayed where he was, letting her go because he knew that right now he had to. Nothing he said tonight was going to get through to her, she had set herself against him and after the way he had treated her who could blame her for that? But there had to be something he could do, there had to be an answer for them somewhere.

– 26 –

Despite her resolve of that night over the next few days Kirsten found herself hoping beyond hope that Laurence would call. She wanted more than anything in the world to hear him persuade her to believe he loved her, to know that she meant so much to him he was prepared to do anything to get her back. But as the days passed and still he didn't call, she knew that she had finally to admit that he wasn't going to. Jane called her often, but every time Kirsten heard her voice she made some excuse as to why she couldn't talk and rang off. In truth she longed to speak to Jane, but keeping contact with her was only going to prolong the pain over Laurence.

She'd spoken briefly on the phone to Helena just before Helena took herself off to spend Christmas in Scotland where she and Dermott were going to give it another go. Kirsten knew, because Helena had told her before leaving New Orleans, that Helena felt horribly torn between her and Dermott Campbell, but it seemed now that Helena had made her choice. Kirsten guessed that was why Helena hadn't made much of an effort to be in touch with her lately, and she couldn't help wondering if Helena's decision might have been different if she knew what was going on in Kirsten's life right now. But Kirsten wasn't into emotional blackmail, which was why she hadn't told her. In the end they had wished each other a Happy Christmas and made a tentative arrangement to meet up in the New Year.

On Christmas morning Kirsten got out of bed early and went downstairs to light the fire. She already knew how she was going to spend the day and in a perverse sort of way was almost looking forward to it. She flicked on the TV, hummed gently along with the Christmas carols as she padded about the place in her dressing-gown and slippers knowing that come what may she wasn't going to let herself get down. It didn't matter that she was alone, self-pity was no companion for a Christmas day, especially when her sitting room was by now filled with glittering cards, all from the cast and crew of Moyna O'Malley. Alison had gone so far as to enclose a note telling her what a dream she was to work for even though she was as stubborn as a mule, and how much everyone was looking forward to starting afresh in the New Year. Obviously Laurence hadn't told any of them yet and Kirsten wondered if maybe that task shouldn't actually fall to her. Whether it should or shouldn't she wasn't going to think about it today.

After tidying up the magazines and newspapers she had left strewn across the coffee table she went into the kitchen and gave a wry laugh when she saw the turkey through the glass door of the oven. It was huge. But she hadn't wanted anyone in the supermarket to know that she was spending Christmas alone so she had stuffed her trolley full to the brim with the things she'd watched other people buy.

Still humming along tunelessly she turned on the oven, poured herself a glass of champagne and went back to the sitting room to open the three gifts tucked neatly under the tree. One had come through the post from Helena and Jane had put two more into her bag the night she was at Laurence's.

When she opened the first she felt a lump rising in her throat. It was a beautifully framed photograph of her and Helena looking so happy on the set in New Orleans. She turned the tag over to read the message. 'For a very special friend, all my love, Helena'.

The second gift was a book from Jane. It was all about Hollywood and the inscription inside read: 'May all your dreams come true'. Kirsten smiled as she recalled a conversation she'd had with Laurence after their first week of shoot when they were so excited they'd talked about taking over Hollywood. Jane had been there at the time and had obviously remembered.

Her third gift was from Tom and when she saw the little *gris-gris* bag to ward off bad luck that he had obviously made himself her emotions rose so close to the surface that she got briskly to her feet, stoked up the fire and went to check on the turkey.

Around midday, having showered and changed into a pair of silk pyjamas and matching robe, she found herself standing at the window watching a family party in the house opposite sit down to their turkey dinner. They were all wearing paper hats and looked so happy that Kirsten wandered over to the Christmas tree, tugged on each end of a cracker and took out a hat for herself. Then catching sight of herself in the mirror, with her bright yellow hat, chaotic hair and mascara smudged eyes she knew that she wasn't going to be able to ward off the terrible, agonizing loneliness much longer. Quickly she poured herself another glass of champagne and went to baste the turkey.

Quite what time it was when she drifted off to sleep Kirsten couldn't say, but before she did she had managed to eat part of her lunch and finish the entire bottle of champagne. Vaguely she remembered holding an imaginary conversation with Paul over the dining table, but she had no idea now what it had been about. Obviously she had cried herself to sleep. Her eyes hurt, hardly wanted to be prised open and her whole body ached. However, that could be because she'd fallen asleep in the chair.

She looked around the room. What time was it? It was dark outside, the fire had gone out and the routine action-adventure film was on the TV. Oh God, isn't Christmas over yet, she groaned? It was hard work entertaining herself when all she really wanted to do was howl like a baby and give in to her self-pity.

It was only when the doorbell sounded again that she realized what it was that had woken her. Wearily she pulled herself up and went to find the packet of cigarettes she always kept for the old lady next door who was continually running out.

Raking her hands through her hair and tightening the belt of her dressing gown she went to the door, wondering whether or not to invite the old lady in. Deciding she would, she put on a welcoming smile and pulled open the door.

Almost instantly her smile froze. She had to blink several times before she could actually register who was standing there, his face almost lost in shadow, the shoulders of his black overcoat spattered with rain.

'Laurence?' she said, uncertainly.

'Were you expecting someone else?' he said, his eyes narrowing with irony.

'Uh, no.' Her hand flew to her hair. 'Oh God, I look like a nightmare.'

'Yeah, I've seen you better,' he grinned. He looked past her down the hall. 'Do I get to come in?'

Still somewhat dazed she stood back for him to pass her then followed him into the sitting room.

'Where's Tom?' she asked, feeling her heart starting to pound as he turned to look at her.

'With Pippa.'

'In Italy?'

He shook his head. 'With Pippa's parents. I would have come earlier, but he kicked up a bit. He didn't want to go . . .'

For a moment or two Kirsten was at a loss and glanced nervously about the room. 'Uh, can I get you a drink?' she offered.

'Mm. Sounds good. Have you got any more of that?'

Kirsten followed his eyes to the empty bottle of cham-

– 478 –

pagne. 'I expect I can find another,' she said, pursing her lips in a smile.

'You do that.'

As soon as she left the room Kirsten ran upstairs to freshen up and change. When she came back with a new bottle and two glasses on a tray Laurence was still standing where she had left him, his hands in his trouser pockets, his coat bunched behind him as he gazed thoughtfully down at the TV.

'I'll do that,' he said, as she picked up the bottle of champagne.

Kirsten handed it to him and for a brief moment their eyes met. He winked and Kirsten looked away, a reluctant smile curving her lips.

'OK,' he said when both glasses were full.

Kirsten took one, then felt herself turn weak as he put a finger under her chin lifting her face so that she was looking at him and said, 'Merry Christmas.'

'Merry Christmas,' she whispered.

They drank, then Laurence turned to look at the dead fire. 'I reckon we could do with that going again,' he said.

Kirsten watched him as he started to pile on the kindling. His movements were deft and quick despite the heavy bulk of his coat. Should she ask him to take it off, she wondered. 'Laurence?' she said.

'Mmm?'

'Laurence, I don't understand . . . Why are you here?'

'To give you a Christmas present, of course,' he said, as though she should already have known that. He continued with the fire until the flames were roaring up the chimney then standing up again he put a hand inside his overcoat and pulled out an envelope.

Kirsten took it watching him closely and wondering

why his eyes were dancing the way they were. As she tore it open he took off his coat and threw it across a chair. All the time he was watching her as she read what she'd taken from the envelope, waiting for her reaction.

Finally Kirsten looked up. Her smile was a little shaky but she managed to say, 'Congratulations. I'm really pleased for you. I told you you'd get it if I was out of the way.'

'I got it,' Laurence said, taking the insurance documents from her and throwing them on to the table, 'without telling them that you'd resigned. So now, would you like to make my Christmas by withdrawing the resignation?'

Kirsten looked at him for a long time before lowering her eyes and searching through the flickering fire-lit shadows as though to find the words she needed to say. He waited, but in the end, when she continued to say nothing, he reached for her hand.

Before she could stop herself Kirsten snatched it away. 'No,' she said. 'I can't. You don't understand, Laurence. I can't go on with it . . .'

'Darling . . .'

She closed her eyes tightly. 'Laurence, don't call me that. We said, at the beginning, that ours was to be a professional relationship. Well we both know that we've failed at that, but don't you see, I can't go back into it the way things are. You frighten me, Laurence. It's so easy for you to hurt me and as much as I want to do the film . . .'

He made to take her in his arms but she backed away.

'No, Laurence. I know what you're going to say, but you'll walk out on me again, I know it, and I just can't bear for that to happen.'

'Kirstie, listen to me for a moment . . .'

Her eyes were flashing as they came up to meet his. 'I love you, Laurence, I want you so much you've got no idea what it's doing to me. But I told you, I can't trust you any more – no, Laurence, don't touch me! Laurence, don't!' she cried as he pulled her into his arms.

'At least give me the chance to explain,' he said. 'Then if you tell me to go I'll walk out of here and never try to see you again.'

She despised herself for being so helpless in his arms, but the feel of him was crushing her resolve, and the temptation to give in was overpowering. Nevertheless, she managed to push him away and moved to the other side of the sofa. 'I'll listen,' she said, 'but I don't want you to touch me. I want you to stay right where you are . . . Laurence!' she cried as he started towards her.

Laughing, he threw up his hands. 'OK, OK,' he said. 'I'm rooted to the spot. Now, are you going to turn off the TV?'

For a second or two she eyed him suspiciously, then reaching behind her she fumbled around on the mantelpiece to find the remote control. The room fell into silence and suddenly realizing how cosy and intimate it was with just the soft glow of a reading lamp and the fire-light Kirsten moved to the door and switched on the overhead light.

Laurence was still smiling, but then, as she turned back to him, the challenge clear in her eyes, his smile melted away and he wiped a hand over the dark stubble on his chin.

Kirsten waited, staying right where she was at the door. How desperately she wanted to return to his arms, but too much had happened, too many times in the past he had let her down, she couldn't take that risk again.

'Hell, I hardly know where to begin,' he said, lifting his head to look at her.

Kirsten said nothing.

He sighed. 'Damn it, Kirstie, can we at least sit down?'

She waved an arm towards the sofa, but remained where she was.

'I guess I should tell you about Anna,' he said, sinking into the feather-filled cushions.

Still Kirsten was silent as his eyes returned to hers as though asking her if he should go on.

'I wasn't in love with her,' he said. 'Christ, I can't even say I liked her very much, but she came on to me so strong, and . . . Hell, I slept with her to try and prove to myself that it was just a woman I wanted. Any woman. That it wasn't you I was getting so screwed up over, it was just the need for sex. I guess I knew I was still in love with you, but goddammit I didn't want to admit it. If I did then I'd have to admit to all the other mistakes I'd made and I just didn't have the guts to face up to them.'

'When was the first time you slept with her?' Kirsten asked after a pause.

'The first night we were in New Orleans. There I was back in the room where we'd made love. Jesus Christ, I couldn't get you out of my mind. It was driving me insane seeing you day after day and wanting you so badly . . .'

'Don't lie!' she cried.

'I'm not lying, for God's sake! And you can't tell me you didn't sense it, Kirstie, you must have known what it was doing to me seeing you all the time, I could hardly keep my hands off you. Like I said I tried to persuade myself it was just sex, but it was you, Kirstie, I was going

– 482 –

goddamned crazy for you. It was like I was possessed by you. You've got to remember the way we always used to talk about being a part of each other. For me that's never changed. When I was making love to Anna I was with you. Every time I made love to Pippa I was with you. You were there, in my head, you never went away. I wanted to get over you, Kirsten. I convinced myself I was. Hell, I couldn't handle the fact that you could have so much damned power over me. I hated you for that. It drove me so crazy I hardly knew what was happening to me. My whole fucking life has been a mess since we broke up. My marriage failed, my career . . .'

'But you walked out on me, Laurence!' Kirsten cried. 'You had a choice, you could have stayed but you left. You turned your back on me . . .'

'And you'll never know how much I've hated myself for that. I know you're not responsible for what you did to the baby, it's me who's responsible. I screwed you up so bad you just didn't know what you were doing. I realize that now, but I had so much goddamned pride I couldn't admit it was my fault. I started seeing you as my nemesis, someone who would stalk me for the rest of my life. But it's not you who's my nemesis, it's me. It's all the guilt I've got inside for what I did to you. Shit, it's taken me a long time to understand it, to realize that I'm still punishing myself for letting you down the way I did. All this time, ever since you came back, I've been telling myself that I just don't feel anything for you any more. I've lived a lie for five years, I've lived a fucking nightmare this past year. What I never allowed myself to think about was how much I was hurting you. I couldn't. But then I looked at you one day and I could see it. You'll never know what that did to me, to see the pain there so clear in your eyes and to know that I was to blame. After, I couldn't think about anything else except how badly I wanted you, to try and make up for all I had done to you – and I guess it was then that I admitted, accepted, how much I still loved you.

'By then I'd already made the mistake with Anna. I knew, even before I did it, that I'd end up regretting it. But it was like I was on fire. I had to have the release. Every time I thought about you . . .' He was shaking his head. 'You know what you do to me, Kirsten. There's never been anyone like you and there never will be, at least not for me, but I just couldn't accept it. And Anna was there. She wanted to, she made it so goddamned easy and I . . .' He lifted his head and looked long into her eyes. 'I despise myself for my weakness almost as much as I do for my mistakes. I know I've hurt you real bad, Kirsten, but I've got to ask if you can forgive me. I know I don't deserve it, and I wouldn't blame you if you told me to get the hell out of your life and never come back. But if you love me as much as you say you do, if you want me the way I want you . . .'

'Why did you go on sleeping with her if you felt the way you did about me?' Kirsten said.

'I didn't see I had any choice. She was the star, for Christ's sake. If I upset her I'd upset the entire movie. And she was as jealous as hell of you. She must have sensed the way I felt about you and besides, at the time, at least at first, I thought it was what I wanted. I thought if I kept on sleeping with her I'd get over you. Jesus, I was a mess. Then there was Pippa . . .'

'Pippa?'

'Yes, Pippa. She called me that night, right after we'd made love. She went on and on about how weak I was for not facing up to the way I felt about you. She told me that I'd prove her right though, that she knew how I'd been lying to myself all the time I was married to her. She got me so mad . . .'

'Pippa knew how you felt about me?' Kirsten said incredulously.

'Sure, she knew. And she's been at me about it ever since she left. I wanted to prove her wrong. I wanted to make her suffer for the way she'd walked out on Tom. I wanted . . . Oh God, how the hell do I know what I wanted when I've fucked everything up the way I have.' He smiled wryly, but Kirsten could see the pain in his eyes. 'I remember you asking me once, a long time ago, if I'd give you another chance. Well it looks like the tables have turned, 'cos it's me asking you now if you'll give me another chance. If you'll let me at least try to make up for all I've done. I love you so goddamned much . . .'

But Kirsten was shaking her head. 'No, Laurence,' she said, only a very slight tremor in her voice. 'I can't do it. I want to believe you, I want to so much, but . . . No, don't touch me, please!' she cried pressing herself to the wall as he got up.

'You're going to deny us both something we want more than anything else?' he said.

Kirsten looked at him, feeling as though she might choke on the turmoil inside her. In her heart she knew she couldn't resist him, that all she'd ever wanted in the world was standing right here in front of her, but tearing her eyes from his she pushed herself away from the wall and walking over to the window she pulled the curtains. It was a long time before she turned back and even longer before she spoke again. 'What time do you have to leave?' she said softly.

'I don't. Unless you want me to.'

Endless minutes ticked by. Her eyes moved to the fire as it shifted and sighed. 'If you stay,' she said still staring into the flames, 'I want you just to hold me. I don't want any more than that – at least not yet.'

As he folded her into his arms he didn't even attempt to kiss her, he just pulled her close, stroking her hair and gently rocking her from side to side. After a while Kirsten drew back her head and looked up into his eyes. He smiled and ran his fingers over her cheek. She turned to kiss his hand. It all felt so right, so perfect and so natural, but still the fear wouldn't go away.

'How's about we just sit here and talk?' he said, taking her hands and pulling her down beside him on the sofa. For a while they did, until, almost without thinking, Kirsten leaned towards him resting her head on his shoulder. His arms came up to hold her, one hand found its way beneath her hair and gently caressed her neck. After a while Kirsten lifted her face and as he looked down, his mouth barely an inch from hers she lifted a hand to his cheek and pulled his lips to hers.

As he turned her to hold her tighter against him her arms circled his neck and her fingers moved into his hair. She felt his tongue push gently into her mouth and the smell of him, the feel of him, the very taste of him was curling deep into her body. She groaned and clung to him even tighter as his hands found her breasts, but then, as though suddenly realizing what he was doing, he pulled abruptly away.

'I'm sorry,' he mumbled. 'Shit, I didn't mean to do that. I got carried away.' His eyes came to hers and he smiled. 'This is kind of hard for me, Kirstie,' he said, 'when I feel the way I do about you, but it won't happen again, I swear it, not until you're ready.'

Kirsten was gazing up at him, taking in every line

and every shade of his hypnotic blue eyes. She lifted a hand and ran her thumb gently over his lips, then pulling herself from his arms she got up from the sofa and went to turn off the light.

When she returned she stood in front of him. He looked up at her and she smiled at the confusion in his eyes. She held them with her own as her fingers untied the knot in her dressing gown. She saw him look down at what she was doing, then raise his eyes questioningly back to hers. She shrugged the dressing gown over her shoulders, letting it pool at her feet, then one by one she unfastened the buttons of her pyjama jacket. A tiny murmur escaped his lips as she bared her breasts to him and let the jacket fall to the floor. Then hooking her thumbs under the waistband of the flimsy silk trousers she eased them down over her hips and stepped out of them.

Her skin glowed like burnt amber in the firelight, her coppery hair curled tantalizingly about her shoulders.

'Dear God, have you got any idea just how beautiful you are?' he murmured softly, taking her by the hand.

'Make love to me, Laurence,' she said, her voice catching on her desire as she looked down at him.

As their fingers entwined he circled his other hand around her hips and scooped her towards him burying his face in the musky scent of her. Then both his hands were on her buttocks, massaging them gently as he pulled her closer. He felt her shudder as he pushed his tongue into the tender, sensitive flesh and was aware of the way he too was responding.

His fingers grazed lightly over her thighs, barely touching her, yet it was as though he was igniting a thousand tiny sparks inside her. She pushed her fingers into his thick, dark hair then her head fell back as he took her as far into his mouth as he could. His hands moved to the backs of her legs and he pulled her forward so that she fell on to her knees over him. His mouth was on a level with her breasts now, but after softly kissing each swollen nipple he looked up into her eyes.

'Are you sure?' he whispered, circling her waist with his hands. 'Is this what you really want?'

Kirsten laughed huskily. 'You have to ask?' she said.

There was no answering smile, his eyes were too clouded with love, his lips too bound by the sheer intensity of emotion welling inside him. He lifted her off him, sitting her on the sofa beside him. Then dropping to his knees in front of her he raised her legs up on to the luxuriant patterned silk cushions. With one hand he gently pushed her back so that she was lying down and her entire body was laid bare to his lips. All the time he kissed her, moving his mouth from the velvety smoothness of her naval, down to her thighs, to her toes and back to the delicious succulence of her nipples, he held on to her hand, squeezing it, caressing it and curling his fingers around hers. It was as though this joining of their hands was every bit as intimate as the one they were moving inexorably towards.

Then he was sitting at her feet, easing her legs apart. Their eyes were locked and they remained that way as he lifted her knees and ran his hands along the insides of her thighs. When he reached her and felt the heat of her burn through his fingertips Kirsten's eyes fluttered closed. She could feel the probing hardness of his fingers as slowly, agonizingly, he pushed them into her; then came the warmth of his breath as he moved closer and closer to her. Then his tongue was there, once again moving languorously across that most sensitive part of her. As though from a great distance she heard herself whimper as his lips closed around her, sucking her gently and drawing every sensation of her body into the very depths of his mouth.

Again he reached out for her hand, lacing their fingers as with his tongue he teased and tormented her. The faint contractions deep inside her were beginning to mount, her feet came to rest on his shoulders, her head was moving from side to side. Her fingers tightened around his, squeezing them and twisting them as he drew her ever closer to the edge. His own desire was a solid, pounding force, the depth of his love was like a liquid heat flowing through his veins.

'Laurence,' she murmured. She struggled to sit up, but as the pressure of his tongue increased she fell back again. 'Laurence,' she whispered. 'Laurence, I want you.' She groaned and sobbed as his mouth moved through her dark thatch of hair. Her legs fell from his shoulders, her breasts rose to meet the descent of his lips. 'Laurence,' she said, taking his face between her hands. 'I want to see you.'

He pulled her up into his arms and covered her mouth with his in a kiss so tender, so intimate and so filled with the immensity of his feelings that Kirsten felt as though her heart was swimming in an entire ocean of love.

'Take off your clothes,' she murmured, when finally he pulled back to look into her eyes.

A glimmer of humour leapt into his eyes as, letting her go, he hauled his sweater and T-shirt over his head.

Kirsten lifted her hands to caress the hardened muscles of his shoulders. 'Laurence, tell me you love me, please.'

'I love you, honey,' he whispered, running a finger over her lips. 'I love you more than I know how to say.'

He stood up and resting one arm on the back of the sofa and the other on the arm behind her he stooped to kiss her. As he did her fingers moved to his belt, tugging it free of its loops, before starting on the zip below it. In the end, because he was already so very hard, he removed his jeans himself. And as he stood over her, showing her the full extent of his physical need for her, Kirsten drew herself up to her knees and took first one, then the other testicle into her mouth, massaging them gently with her tongue. But, as she circled her fingers around the stem of his penis and made to draw him towards her, he took her wrists in his hands and pulled her to her feet.

'Honey, I can't hold out much longer,' he murmured, draping his arms about her waist and pulling her against his straining erection. 'I wanna be with you, right there inside you.'

Feeling a surge of near delirious joy Kirsten brushed her lips gently over his, before taking his arms from her waist and drawing him down with her to the floor.

The burning embers of the fire cast dark golden shadows over the splendid nakedness of their entwining bodies, and as Laurence filled her with the whole of his desire Kirsten felt herself being submerged. He moved slowly, tenderly, holding his entire body against hers, keeping their lips together, rolling and pushing his hips, feeling her hands exploring the taut muscles of his back and buttocks while yielding herself up completely and unconditionally to wave after wave after wave of the most exquisite, most profound sensations either of them had ever known.

A long time later they were still lying in front of the fire. Laurence was stretched out on his back, one hand behind his head, the other idly toying with a glass of champagne. Kirsten was on her side, her head propped up on one arm as she gazed laughingly down at him.

'I don't see what's so funny,' he remarked, raising his head to take a sip of the champagne. 'It was hell, I'm telling you . . .'

'Oh, poor Laurence,' Kirsten mocked. 'Got all confused about his emotions and now he's looking for sympathy.'

'Damned right I am,' he said, 'but it sure doesn't look like I'm going to get it around here.'

'No, you could be right there,' Kirsten nodded, leaning forward to take a sip from the glass he was holding out for her. At the last minute he swung it away and as a look of indignance widened her eyes he pulled her into his arms.

'It was hell,' he said softly, 'but I guess it was a whole lot worse for you. But I'm gonna make it up to you, Kirstie, you know that, don't you? I'm here for good now unless you tell me no.'

'Do you think I'm going to do that?' she said, teasing him with her eyes.

'I hope to God not.' He looked at her. 'No, I guess you know as well as I do that we're a hell of a lot better together than we ever could be apart.' He rolled over on to his side, cushioning his head on his elbow and running a hand lazily over her arm. 'You sure about this now?' he said. 'No doubts?'

'No doubts,' Kirsten assured him, knowing that in that moment it was true.

'And if there are any, if you feel afraid, if you ever get scared about anything, you'll tell me?'

She nodded. 'I'll tell you.'

He smiled. 'Just make sure you do. And from now on no more pretence. I don't care who knows about us . . .'

Kirsten put a finger over his lips. 'I don't want anyone to know,' she said. 'At least not yet. Let's get the movie done. That's what's important now. I don't want the press saying that I've managed to lure you back into my web, or doing whatever they can to come between us, so let's keep it as our secret for now, mm?'

'We'll do it whichever way you say,' he answered. 'Just so long as you know that I love you is all that matters to me.'

– 27 –

The oppressive, grey-stoned sixteenth-century mansion was set high on the cliffs in one of the bleakest parts of Cornwall. Far below its foundations a turbulent, treacherous sea hurled itself savagely against the rocks and crashed purposefully into every cove and secret cave along the barren, almost sinister, coastline. The sounds of laughter and music and excitable children carried incongruously on the raging wind that swept the stark landscape and brightly flickering Christmas lights reflected their warmth on to windows that were blackened by night and drenched by driving rain.

As he pulled his car to a halt outside the towering iron-studded front door he felt a shiver of unease run down his spine. He knew already what would happen – he would be taken straight through to the study where she would be waiting for him. He wouldn't meet her family, it was doubtful he would even see them. Her grandchildren were as precious to her as her power, her sons and daughters as cherished as any could be and during this festive season she wouldn't want her family disturbed by the intrusion of a stranger.

Some five minutes later, having been relieved of his coat and led discreetly through a number of gloomy passageways in a circuitous route to the study, he was standing at the threshold of the large, comfortably furnished room watching Dyllis Fisher stooping to stoke up the fire.

The silent, liveried footman who had brought him here closed the door quietly and as his footsteps receded into the distance Dyllis straightened and turned around. She was a tall, painfully thin woman with neat grey hair and a sharp-boned face that aged her beyond her seventy-two years. She was dressed in an expensive, formal beige suit that matched the colour of her piercing, hawk-like eyes. Deeply ingrained frown lines creased her forehead and indented the corners of her thin-lipped mouth, and he knew that beneath the exquisite, sapphire broach pinned to her jacket beat a heart of pure malice.

As she walked towards him, holding out a bony hand to shake his, he struggled to keep his eyes from the magnificent portrait hanging over the hearth. He'd been here before so it wasn't the first time he'd seen the painting of her husband and he knew how much it could move him. He, like so many others, had adored Paul Fisher and could only wonder why a man like that had ever married a woman like Dyllis Fisher. That was how he felt now, but six years ago when Fisher had deserted his wife and gone off to France with Kirsten Meredith, he had felt sorry for Dyllis. He hadn't known Dyllis then and neither had he known what it was to be in the presence of someone who was as vengeful as she was powerful. Now he knew both. But as much as her malevolence disturbed, even frightened him, it exhilarated him too.

'I was surprised to receive your call,' she remarked in a clipped, disdainful voice as she removed her hand from his. 'Can I get you some refreshment after your long drive? Tea? Coffee? Something a little stronger?'

'Scotch?' he said.

She nodded then turned to the drinks cabinet secreted in one of the bookcases. As he watched her, studying her efficient movements and the harsh outline of her fleshless figure he could feel the biting heat of lust stinging deliciously at his groin. All that power could turn him on like nothing else he'd ever known.

'So,' she said, handing him a glass and waving him to a black leather Chesterfield, 'Laurence McAllister has been at my husband's Chelsea home for two days.'

He nodded. 'He arrived on Christmas Day and as far as I know he hasn't left yet.'

'I see.' Her lips had compressed so tightly they'd turned white. 'I imagine we must therefore assume that they are reconciled. The only thing that surprises me about that is how long it's taken.'

He sipped his Scotch and waited for her to continue, aware of how the venom was starting its vicious trail through her body, like molten lava preparing to gush its deadly heat over those who dared trespass its path. Of all the enemies he might ever make in his life he hoped to God Dyllis Fisher was never one of them.

'We will destroy the relationship, of course,' she said.

'That should be easy enough,' he responded.

Her flinty eyes darted to his then a slow, malicious smile twisted itself across her mouth. 'Maybe,' she said, 'if I had full confidence in what you've told me . . .'

'I can assure you, Dyllis,' he said mildly, 'that everything happened exactly the way I reported it. I saw it with my own eyes. Anna Sage was murdered, I know how it was done and my guess is we can get her to do it again.'

'And how would we do that?'

'We would use her obsession with Laurence, of course.'

Dyllis was shaking her head incredulously. 'It was so damned ingenious, how did she ever think of it?'

'Does it matter? The fact is, she did.'

'And gave us exactly what we wanted.' She laughed, but it was a horrible crackling sound, like branches breaking under a violent, dry wind. 'She gave us so much more than we wanted and who would ever have dreamed her capable? Does Kirsten suspect her?'

He shook his head.

Dyllis was still for a moment and he could almost see the hatred of Kirsten flowing beneath her papery skin alongside the sheer elation she felt at the way fate had played so providently into her hands. He knew how she worshipped at the altar of her own power, equated herself with no living soul and saw the murder of Anna Sage as nothing less than Divine justification of her vengeance.

'Dermott Campbell's been trying to find out what I know,' she said suddenly peering at him through narrowed eyes.

'What have you told him?'

'That I can prove Anna Sage was murdered.'

He nodded. 'But he wants to know more.'

'Of course he wants to know more,' she said irritably. 'Wouldn't you if you were Helena Johnson?'

'Are you going to tell him what you know?'

'Don't be a fool!'

'Then what are you going to do with it?'

'I'm going to see Kirsten Meredith behind bars, that's what I'm going to do,' she said smoothly.

'They have the death penalty in Louisiana,' he reminded her.

'I'm going to show that whore just what it means to take something that belongs to me,' Dyllis went on as though he hadn't spoken. 'And while I'm at it I shall make sure that film never gets finished.'

'I thought Campbell was doing that for you.'

'Campbell!' she scoffed. 'He's gone soft in the head over the Johnson woman. He's willing enough to see the whore fall flat on her face, but not so McAllister. And if McAllister is back with the whore then there's every chance he'll persuade Campbell to ease off on her. But I'm telling you this, I'll see them all in hell before I allow that movie with its dedication to my husband on any screen. She humiliated me publicly once, she'll never do it again. Now, I shall have to hand your report to my lawyers, but it's going to need some work on it before I do that. And I need to be wholly convinced that you are going to stand up as a witness to say that it was Kirsten Meredith who committed the murder.'

'You have my word on it. Are you going for just the one murder or shall I try to see if we can get our friend to commit another?' He smiled, almost jovially.

Unimpressed by his humour Dyllis tore her eyes from his and took some time to think about that. 'I'll let you know,' she said eventually. 'I think for now you're going to have to watch carefully to see if things start to settle down the way you suspect they will. She's going to have everything she wants so why should she commit another murder?'

'Why should either of them?' he smirked. 'But a reason could always be found – or planted.'

It was incredible, almost mind-blowing, he was thinking to himself, how matter of factly the two of them could sit here discussing murder as though they were exchanging seasonal civilities when her grandchildren were playing so close by and when, over the next few days, any number of high-ranking government ministers, captains of industry, high court judges, peers of the realm, even royalty would be populating the house for the New Year celebrations. But, to his mind, even more disturbing was the mesmerizing portrait of her husband whose gentle eyes followed her about the room as though he too were listening to all that was being said. But nothing, it seemed, fazed this woman. Kirsten Meredith had taken her husband and for that Kirsten Meredith was going to pay with everything she had, maybe even her life. And the tragedy of it was, at least so far as Kirsten was concerned, that it wasn't really Dyllis Fisher she had to fear at all, it was someone much closer to home.

'I want this sealed up so tightly that not even a shred of doubt can escape,' Dyllis said getting to her feet. She opened a drawer in her desk, pulled out an envelope and handed it to him. 'But if in the end we can't prove it then I shall see to it that she is driven to suicide – and that, my friend, given her precarious state of mind, is going to be a lot easier to manage than you might think.'

'So what's stopping you going ahead with it now?' he enquired, pocketing the envelope.

She started to answer then stopped, suddenly. He waited, watching her closely as she slowly raised her hard, impenetrable eyes to his face. 'Sit down,' she said, quietly. 'Sit down, I don't think we've quite finished . . .'

Half an hour later Dyllis was standing at the window watching the tail lights of her guest's Montego disappear down the drive. Her cruel brown eyes were glittering with triumph, though in her heart was a tempest of frustration. Her hands clenched at her sides. She was so close now to seeing the end of Kirsten Meredith, to witnessing the public disgrace of the whore who had destroyed her marriage, that she mustn't allow her impatience to run away with her. It was going to happen, of that there was no doubt, it was just going to take a little more time.

She waited until the car had disappeared then turned back to her desk. As she lifted the receiver she looked up at her husband, a vicious smile twisting her lips. What a fool the man was never to have realized what she would do to his precious whore once he was gone. And what an even bigger fool to have made such a will. He'd have done better to have left out his children altogether, but as it was he'd left the money in trust for the whore to live on for the rest of her life! And even more absurdly, he'd provided for any offspring his whore might have in the future. Dyllis's smile widened. He was the only one who could have protected Kirsten Meredith, but dolt that he was he hadn't seen it. Instead he'd left her wide open to the mercy of someone who knew no mercy when it came to dealing with the theft of that which belonged to her. And not even Laurence McAllister was going to stand in the way, for as besotted with the whore as McAllister might be, Dyllis would stake her life on the fact that he'd never put her before his son.

'Hello, Lucy?' she said as she made the connection

to her secretary's Battersea home. 'Yes, Merry Christmas to you too. Get me Thea McAllister's number will you and call me back . . .'

Discovering each other again after all this time, after all the pretence and struggles of the past six years, was in its way as calming as it was exciting. They talked endlessly, about Paul, about Pippa, about Ruby and the fact that she was Laurence's mother, about Helena and Dermott, about Jane and Tom, about so many things, but mainly they talked about themselves. They were so alive, so ridiculously happy that Laurence could hardly bring himself to leave her to go and collect more clothes. When he returned they fell into each others arms, kissing frantically as though they had been parted for a month rather than an hour. Kirsten could be in no doubt as to how much he loved her, neither could she mistake the way he was still suffering for all he had done. So often he would wake in the night and pull her into his arms, holding her tightly and whispering,

'I can't believe you're here. Hold me, Kirstie, hold me and tell me you love me.'

He brought her breakfast in bed each morning, fed her, made love to her, showered her and made love to her again. His teasing humour fuelled her laughter, his wry confessions swelled her heart. They were like children chasing each other about the house, rolling around the floor and laughing till passion stole their smiles and desire took them over. Just like in the past erotic games started to spice their love-making and Laurence wondered how he had managed to live without her for so long. Her imagination was as mind-blowing as her exploits, her appetite for sex as insatiable as his own.

Once or twice they went out to the cinema where they dived into cartons of popcorn, held hands and kissed throughout the film. Occasionally they would sit down to discuss their own movie, but it was never long before one of them would reach out for the other, maybe just to touch, or to kiss, but the need to reassure each other of their feelings was constant. They never fought and only rarely did they discuss the final days of their break up. It was part of the past now and why look back when they had so much to look forward to?

From time to time a treacherous doubt would flare inside Kirsten, but Laurence was always there to comfort her, to tell her how very much he loved her. His patience during those times was endless, his tenderness so moving and so absurdly poetic that Kirsten would find herself laughing through her tears. He accused her of faking her insecurity just so's he'd make a clown of himself and in truth Kirsten couldn't always deny it.

The only truly difficult moments over that time came on New Year's Eve when Laurence insisted that Kirsten join him and Tom at his parent's house for dinner. At first Kirsten refused. She couldn't quite say why she was so reluctant, but she was. Perhaps it had something to do with leaving their fantasy world and confronting reality, but it was more likely that she remembered Jane telling her how Pippa and Laurence's mother had never got along. Kirsten had no idea whose fault that was, but she had an uncanny feeling that Thea McAllister wasn't going to be an easy woman. However, in the end, Laurence managed to have his way by putting Tom to work on the persuasion. Faced with two pairs of those shamelessly beseeching blue eyes Kirsten found herself unable to say no.

For the main part the evening went well. Thea McAllister was the perfect hostess, though Kirsten wondered if she ever let down her veneer of regal politeness when she was alone with her family. She was such a formal woman, so courteous and considerate yet when she looked at someone her gaze stopped just short of them, as though not quite wanting to touch them. That was unless she was looking at Laurence or Tom. It was then that Kirsten felt that it might be possible to warm to the impeccably dressed, perfectly mannered American woman, for there could be no mistaking how much she doted on her stepson and grandson. And her husband too, Kirsten thought, seeing the way their hands touched as Don McAllister got up from the table to go and fetch more wine. One look at Laurence's father was enough to see exactly where Laurence and Tom had got their looks, not to mention their mischievous humour; the three generations were, despite the varying ages, virtually identical.

Tom struggled his way through the meal, looking adorable perched on his cushions on the grand high-backed dining chair. He tried hard to keep abreast of the conversation which was mainly about Laurence and Kirsten's film and hotly denied that he was tired even though his curly black head kept lolling towards his plate. He was determined he was going to make it through to midnight, but half an hour before he was curled up in Laurence's lap, fast asleep.

Laurence took him off to bed leaving Kirsten in the drawing room with Thea. Don was in the kitchen sorting out champagne for the toast.

The instant they were left alone together Kirsten was overcome by the feeling that she wanted to be anywhere but where she was. Thea's perfect smile and serenely benevolent manner was making her so uncomfortable it was all she could do to stop herself squirming. And the fact that, at Laurence's insistence, she was wearing no underwear was turning her hot with embarrassment. She watched as Thea plumped up the shimmering raw-silk cushions of the sofa opposite Kirsten's, then smiled awkwardly as Thea turned to face her.

'I'm glad to have this chance to speak to you, Kirsten,' she said smoothly, leaning back on the sofa and crossing her silk-stockinged legs.

Kirsten smiled in return.

Thea bowed her head, as though in acknowledgement of Kirsten's permission to continue. 'Laurence means a great deal to his father and me,' she said, still smiling, but though there was a hint of her perfect white teeth, her dark eyes were glinting like ice. 'He's been through a lot this past year, what with Pippa leaving him and that dreadful mishap on the film. It's to be expected that he should act out of character for a while, and naturally if he wants to have a – how shall we put it? a liaison? – then Don and I wouldn't dream of standing in his way.'

Kirsten could feel her cheeks starting to burn, but still she said nothing.

Thea's smile widened, somehow turning it even more glacial. 'I will be blunt, Kirsten,' she said. 'I could have wished that Laurence had chosen someone else to . . . shall we say, help him over this bad time. But I guess we should have expected it to be you.' She sighed. 'It is my hope that this affair between you will burn itself out much more quickly than it did the last time, after all we don't want a repeat of what you did then, do we? It took Laurence a long time to come to terms with that abortion and the way you went about it, it hurt him much more deeply than I think you realize. And since we're talking frankly I think you should be aware that

– 502 –

Laurence's inheritance will come from me – not his father.' Her eyebrows were raised questioningly, as though asking Kirsten if she understood what she was saying.

Kirsten did, only too well, but Thea McAllister decided to spell it out.

'Mine is one fortune you will not get your hands on, Kirsten, even if it does mean cutting Laurence out of my will.'

Kirsten's throat was so constricted she could barely speak. 'I love Laurence, Mrs McAllister,' she began.

'Oh, I don't think so,' Thea interrupted, flicking invisible cotton from her lapel. 'I've come across your type many times in my life, and even without the corroboration of the press, I know a fortune-seeker when I see one. I think, Kirsten, that you have . . .' Her eyes suddenly darted to the door as it opened and Laurence came back into the room. Thea's expression was instantly transformed to one of motherly affection. 'Ah, there you are, darling. Tom settled is he?'

'Settled and snoring,' Laurence answered going to sit beside Kirsten and draping an arm around her. 'Where's Dad?'

'Getting the champagne, I hope,' Thea said glancing up at the French ormolu mantel clock. 'Only a few minutes to go.'

On the stroke of midnight they all stood to drink a toast, then pulling Kirsten into his arms Laurence whispered, 'Happy New Year,' and brushed his lips lightly against hers.

'Happy New Year,' Kirsten smiled, but feeling Thea's eyes boring into her she looked away.

Laurence lifted her mouth back to his. 'What is it?' he said softly. 'You've gone quiet all of a sudden.'

'Oh nothing,' Kirsten said, 'just a bit of a headache. In fact, I think perhaps I should be going.'

'Are you serious? Already?'

'Yes,' and turning back to the sofa she picked up her bag. 'It's been a lovely evening,' she said to Thea and Don. 'Thank you so much for letting me share it.'

'But there's all this champagne to be got through,' Don protested. 'You can't run out on us now.'

'I'm sorry,' Kirsten said. Then looking at Thea. 'Maybe I could call a taxi.'

'By all means, my dear.'

'Don't be ridiculous. I'll take you,' Laurence snapped, dragging his eyes from Thea.

'No, no really. I'll be fine in a taxi.'

'The hell you will.'

They drove home in silence. Kirsten could sense Laurence's smouldering anger, but kept her face turned to the window, wishing to God that she could do something to stem the tears that were threatening to spill from her eyes.

'OK,' Laurence said tightly, as they pulled up outside Kirsten's house. 'What did she say?'

'Who?'

'You know who. So come on, let's have it.'

'Honestly, Laurence, it doesn't matter.'

'It does matter,' he barked, pulling her back as she made to get out of the car. 'She told you to back off, didn't she?'

'Laurence, please . . .' Kirsten said, trying to twist her arm free.

'I should have known it,' he seethed. 'What'd she say? That she'd cut me off if I continued to see you?'

Kirsten looked away.

'Yeah, that's what she said all right. For God's sake,

Kirstie, can't you see that you just played straight into her hands by walking out of there? She tells you there's going to be no money and you leave. She was testing you, for Christ's sake! She doesn't want to believe all she's read about you, but she loves Tom and me and this is her way of trying to protect us.'

'From me?' Kirsten suddenly flared. 'Yes, the whole world needs protecting from me! And maybe she's right! Maybe I am just after your money! And far be it from me to stand between you and your inheritance,' and throwing the door open she jumped out of the car and ran towards the house.

Laurence caught her as she fumbled in her bag for her keys. 'Don't ever demean yourself to me like that again,' he thundered, spinning her round to face him. 'I know the way you feel about me and goddammit I'm not going to let anyone, least of all you, deny it. Now listen to me! Listen to me!' he shouted shaking her and making her look at him. 'I love you, Kirsten. I love you, do you hear me?'

'Why?' she cried. 'Why me, when there are so many *suitable* girls your mother – '

Her words were cut off as his mouth came crushing down on hers. 'You want the reasons,' he said savagely when he broke off, 'then you got them. I love you because you're the only woman in the world I can ever love. I love you because you make me so damned mad. I love you because you're a bloody fool.' He snatched the keys from her and threw open the door. 'I love you because you make my life worth living.' He pushed her inside. 'I love you because you love me.' He slammed the door and pushed her hard up against the wall. 'I love you because you're so damned insecure,' and he kissed her again. 'I love you because you need to be loved,' he groaned pushing her skirt to her waist. 'I love you because you do things to me no other woman ever has,' he said, fumbling with his fly. 'And I love you,' he added, pushing himself inside her, 'because of this.'

Kirsten was panting for breath. Her legs were turning weak, but as he hammered into her he kept her against the wall.

'They're not coming between us, Kirsten, do you hear me?' he growled. 'No one is every going to come between us again. Not even you.'

— 28 —

It took only a few hours of being back in the office to show both Kirsten and Laurence how crazy they were to think they could keep their relationship a secret. They had only to look at each other for the entire team to realize that the romance they had all known was inevitable was at last back on the rails. The way they made each other laugh infected everyone especially when Laurence would unthinkingly put an arm around Kirsten and Kirsten would stare at him as if he was mad. But the humour in her eyes always gave her away and no one ever walked into their office without knocking now.

'You have to try and control yourself a bit better,' she told him at the end of the first week.

'How the hell can I do that when just looking at you

gives me a hard on,' he groaned, running his hands down over her buttocks.

'Don't exaggerate,' she said, wriggling out of the way. 'And we've got plenty of time for that in the evenings, so will you at least try to behave like a responsible producer while we're here?'

'I'd be a whole lot better at that if you didn't wear those tight clothes,' he answered, putting his hands over her breasts.

'I wore them before but you didn't lose control like this then,' she reminded him, sliding her hands into her skirt pockets as he caressed her through her sweater.

'You don't know how close I came,' he told her, his eyes dancing with amusement as he squeezed her nipples and watched the effect it was having on her.

'Laurence, at this rate we'll be going home for an early lunch again,' she said huskily, 'and it's embarrassing having everyone know what we're doing.'

He laughed. 'They reckon we're doing it right here,' he said.

'Only because you won't let them come in without knocking.'

'You want them to catch me feeling your tits?'

She rolled her eyes and laughed. 'You're so coarse at times,' she remarked.

'How about I remind you of the things you were saying last night?' he offered.

'No thank you. Now, will you answer that phone.'

Turning to his desk he picked up the receiver, listened to what his assistant was telling him then, looking at his watch, he rang off. 'I've got an appointment at the bank,' he said. 'Wanna come along?'

Kirsten shook her head. 'No, that's your territory. I've got more than enough to do here. Elizabeth and

Jean-Paul are coming in to look at the rushes and rough-cut – again! Still, it's not every director who gets the opportunity to put right the things they weren't happy with first time around so I guess I should think myself lucky. Oh God,' she groaned, 'don't ever let anyone else hear me say that. It'll just add more fuel to the suspicion that I was behind Anna's death. Which is another reason,' she went on as he pulled her into his arms, 'why we shouldn't flaunt ourselves this way.'

'I told you before, I love you, Kirsten, and I don't care who the hell knows it.'

'But I don't want people to start suspecting me again – for all I know they haven't even stopped.'

'They will, and just so long as you've got rid of that crazy notion that I suspected you . . .'

'You sure you didn't?' she whispered her lips touching his.

'Hell, Kirstie, I can't even believe you thought I did. I know you had nothing to do with it, and remember, it wasn't murder. Why does everyone keep forgetting that? Oh Christ,' he groaned as at last he managed to pull her skirt up to her waist.

Taking his face between her hands she pushed her tongue deep into his mouth as he squeezed her naked buttocks and pressed himself against her. All she was wearing was a pair of gartered stockings. He walked her backwards to her desk, sat her on the edge and as her legs opened he lowered his hand and started to rub his fingers back and forth. She supported herself with her hands as he leaned over her, kissed her lingeringly and erotically while slowly inserting his fingers. Then, quite suddenly, he pulled away.

Kirsten's eyes flew open. 'Laurence!' she cried as he started towards the door.

'Sorry,' he grinned, 'we got plenty of time for that in the evenings. Gotta go,' and he started to open the door. 'Uh, better make yourself decent,' he said, 'we don't want everyone knowing how you throw yourself across the desk at me.'

As the door closed behind him he laughed as he heard a book crash against it and was tempted to go back, but if he did he knew he'd be late for his meeting at the bank. So, helping himself to the morning paper from Vicky's desk, he went outside to hail himself a taxi.

Just like everyone else he and Kirsten were still waiting to see what the press would have to say about their relationship, but so far there had been an almost deafening silence. The only person who seemed upset by the relationship was Ruby. It wasn't that she ever passed comment, she simply studied them with her watery blue eyes then lowered her head and started to pray. Fortunately she didn't come to the office often, though she was repeatedly asking Laurence for private meetings, but knowing that she would use the opportunity to talk about Kirsten Laurence always claimed that he was too busy to go all the way out to Richmond. The fact that both his mother and step-mother disapproved of Kirsten was causing a rift between them all, but he was not going to be manipulated by two women whose love and concern he appreciated but whose reluctance to give Kirsten a chance was as intolerable as it was unjust. They would just have to come to terms with the fact that his loyalty was to Kirsten now, his future was with her and if Thea and Ruby wanted to remain a part of his life they would have to accept that Kirsten was here to stay. Happily he had no such problem with Tom who adored Kirsten as much as she did him, and just to watch them together, chattering and playing games, filled

Laurence with such emotion that he could only wonder at what kind of fool he was to have denied himself this for so long. And Jane's evident delight that Kirsten was spending so much time at the house in Kensington was so touching that neither he nor Kirsten even attempted to hide the way they felt in front of her. Their love seemed to give Jane almost as much pleasure as it did them and Tom got so excited when they kissed that they were starting to feign weariness at having to indulge him so often. However, when it came to sleeping with them Laurence put his foot down. Tom could try to kiss Kirsten the way Daddy did, he could take a bath with them, he could even on the odd occasion go into the office with them, but he was not getting into bed with them. Tom sulked, Kirsten tried to persuade Laurence to relent, but Laurence was unmoved as he reminded her that she too had to start showing Tom some discipline and stop spoiling him.

Over the next couple of weeks everything went so smoothly on all counts that they should have known it wouldn't last, and sure enough, only days before they were about to depart for Ireland they learned that County Westmeath was under at least a foot of snow.

Laurence went into immediate action, calling in the heads of all departments and telling them to turn everything around and get themselves ready to shoot in New Orleans the following week. The Irish scenes, he said, would be better in March anyway.

'It seems to me,' Kirsten remarked to Helena a week later when they met up in a wine bar on the eve of their departure for New Orleans, 'that the entire team have been performing miracles. I can hardly believe how they've got this going so fast. It almost makes me dizzy to think of it.'

'It's amazing what you can do when you put your mind to it,' Helena smiled. 'Anyway, it's real good to see you at last, it's not the same on the phone.'

'I know,' Kirsten groaned. 'And I've really missed you.'

'I missed you too. You look terrific. I guess that's what love does.'

Kirsten laughed. 'Sometimes I feel like I'm about to explode with the sheer joy of it,' she said. 'He's getting fed up with the way I keep pinching him to make sure he's really there and it's not all a dream.'

'So what happened to putting the career first and never letting anything or anyone touch you again?' Helena teased.

'Oh, don't remind me,' Kirsten grimaced. 'The resolutions we make . . . Still, I suppose self-preservation calls for them at times. But you and I both know that no amount of success can ever take the place of love.'

'It's pretty good to have both though, isn't it?' Helena commented. 'So tell me, how do you feel about going back to New Orleans after all that's happened?'

'I don't know really,' Kirsten said, gazing thoughtfully around the wine bar. 'I mean, being back with Laurence changes a lot of things, but going over old ground for the reasons we are feels, well it feels pretty awful actually. I know brooding over Anna's death wouldn't help, but it's horrible to think she can be replaced so easily.'

'Only in the context of a movie,' Helena said. 'You have to think of it that way. It's not real, any of this, and she's not forgotten.'

'No, she's certainly not forgotten,' Kirsten said, pouring more wine into their glasses, 'it's just that sometimes it feels like she is.'

'Does Laurence ever talk about her?'

'Not really. After all, what is there to say that hasn't already been said?'

'Nothing I guess, except that we're all sorry it ever happened. Of course, if it hadn't you and Laurence would have taken a bit longer to get back together, but you would have eventually, everyone knows that.'

'I wish I'd had your confidence,' Kirsten smiled. 'Still, like I said, there's no point in brooding on what's past, God knows I've got enough to think about for the next few weeks. I'm glad we're starting in the Plantation House though, it's the nearest thing we're going to get to a fresh start. Talking of which, and changing the subject neatly, how are things going with Dermott?'

Helena took a deep breath and stared down at her wine. 'Hard to say really,' she answered. 'We're still seeing each other, but I just don't know if I can bring myself to make a real commitment to him. I want to, but something's holding me back.'

'Probably the fact that you don't love him,' Kirsten suggested.

'Probably. But I might grow to. I guess it's whether or not I take that chance. Well I'm gonna have to if I want kids, 'cos time's ticking on and I don't hold out much hope of meeting anyone else before the child-bearing years run out – if they haven't already.'

'Is it really that important to you that you have children?' Kirsten asked softly.

Helena nodded. 'Yeah. Now I know I might not be able to I want them more than anything.' She gave a wistful laugh. 'Isn't that the way of the world? Always want what you can't have.'

'But you don't know for sure you can't have them, not yet. Are you taking any precautions?'

'No.'

'Does Dermott know that?'

'Yep. He's real happy about it.'

'But you just don't know if it's him you want as the father?'

'Sometimes I do, sometimes I don't. To tell the truth I reckon he'd be a good dad. Sure, he's pretty screwed up, gets himself in a twist about things so's he can't even see straight at times, but if he got himself sorted out ... I think I told you I persuaded him to go get some counselling.'

'How's that going?'

'OK, I think. Well, he's only been twice and I reckon he's going for me rather than himself. But he needs it all right. That year he spent drinking himself to oblivion left him pretty scarred. And working for Dyllis Fisher doesn't help. I can't make out too much of what goes on between those two, but she sure as hell gets to him at times. He's scared of her, that's for sure, but then he knows better than most what she's capable of. Well, I guess you can't be in much doubt of that either.'

'Not really,' Kirsten commented.

Helena lifted her eyes from her glass and turned them to Kirsten. Ever since she and Dermott had returned from Scotland she had been trying to decide whether or not to tell Kirsten that Dyllis Fisher was claiming she could prove that Kirsten had killed Anna. Dermott still hadn't been able to find out what proof Dyllis had, which made Helena doubt its existence, for if Dyllis was confident she could carry it off she'd surely have done so by now. 'Tell me,' she said, 'in your heart of hearts, do you reckon Dyllis might have had something to do with Anna's death?'

Kirsten's lips pursed as she slowly shook her head. 'I don't know,' she answered eventually. 'Obviously it's crossed my mind, but if she did then that means Dermott might have had something to do with it too.'

'I know,' Helena said despondently. 'That's what worries me.' Then for no apparent reason she smiled and reached out for Kirsten's hand.

'What was that for?' Kirsten asked in surprise.

'For being you, I guess. For finding the time to talk about my problems when you're such a big-time director now.'

'I'm hardly that,' Kirsten laughed.

'But you will be,' Helena assured her with a sigh. 'I just wish my life was as cut and dried as yours. I mean, you got no doubts about Laurence and thank God he's come to his senses and realized he doesn't have any about you. And my guess is you two'll be adding to that family before too much longer. Shit, I wish I was still your age. I don't suppose I'd be having all these doubts about Dermott if I was, don't guess I'd be seeing him at all come to that. Now why can't I find myself someone like Laurence, is what I want to know?'

'He's not so perfect,' Kirsten smiled, her heart tightening with love. 'Even Ruby seems to be having her doubts on that score since we got back together. But she's another matter altogether. She *is* his mother, by the way.'

'Yes, Dermott told me. Pretty bizarre that, don't you think?'

'A bit, but as crazy as she's getting lately, I think I'd rather deal with her than Thea. That woman absolutely terrifies me. She's so cold and well, I don't know, I can't quite put my finger on it, but I think she resents me a whole lot more than Ruby does. God save us from mothers, eh?'

'Amen. Dermott's has been so obliging as to depart

this world, thank God. He never knew who his father was . . . Well, I always knew he was a bastard,' she laughed. 'But at least he's not trying to damage your relationship with Laurence. In fact I don't think a word's been printed has it?'

'Not that I know of. And if you're responsible for getting him to back off then I'm deeply in your debt.'

'Would that I had that kind of influence, but I've done my best. The truth is though that on the whole Dyllis is the one who's been writing his columns where you're concerned, or so he claims. So she's the one who seems to have backed off.'

'Maybe she knows when she's beaten,' Kirsten said hopefully. 'And if she doesn't she's going to find out, because this time round nothing is going to come between Laurence and me and nothing is going to stop us finishing that film. Dermott's banned from the set I'm afraid. That was Laurence's decision, not mine.'

'Yeah, I guessed as much. But that's no bad thing, I can take this time away to think things through, as if I haven't done enough of that already. I reckon seeing you and Laurence together is going to help me come to a decision. I don't hold out much hope of ever finding what you two have, but it might make me come to terms with what I can have. Are Jane and Tom coming along by the way?'

'Of course. Laurence wouldn't leave Tom behind even if he wanted to be left, which he doesn't.'

'That's good. Seeing you all as a family might push me in the right direction. I'll bet Jane's cock-a-hoop at having you around all the time.'

Kirsten laughed. 'She does seem quite pleased about it, yes. And she's getting a bit more time off now which

Laurence and I are thinking up ways of helping her to fill. It might be easier if she weren't quite so shy.'

'Is she still seeing the Ken doll?'

'On and off. Between you and me I think he wanted to go to bed with her and it frightened her a bit.'

'A bit!' Helena cried. 'With that thing he carries between his legs I should think it scared her half out of her wits. I know it would me. The man's a walking tripod.'

Kirsten laughed. 'Laurence says I should sit down and discuss things with her, see how she really feels about it all. What do you think?'

Helena nodded. 'Sounds like a good idea. It'll embarrass the hell out of her, of course, but she needs someone to help her out. Mind you, with the size of Billy the Ken it might take surgery. Where is she tonight, by the way? I thought she was coming too.'

'She was, but they're all spending the night at Laurence's parents before we go off tomorrow and I didn't want her to have to tell Thea that she was with me. It would only put her in an awkward position and it's not fair that she has to deal with problems that aren't really hers.'

'So you and Laurence are spending the night apart?'

'For the first time since Christmas,' Kirsten grinned. 'But he's threatening to turn up in the middle of the night, so we'll see. And what about Dermott? Aren't you seeing him before you go?'

'I'm going over to his place straight from here. As usual he was pretty pissed off that I was seeing you when I'm going to be spending the next few weeks with you anyway. I don't suppose I helped much by telling him to grow up, but I wish the hell he'd stop putting me in a position where I feel I have to choose between you.'

'I'm afraid I've been guilty of that too,' Kirsten said. 'With justification. But sure, I was pissed off about that too. Still, the main thing is that we know we're there for each other now.'

It was Kirsten's turn to take Helena's hand. 'And that will never change,' she smiled.

It was around one in the morning that Kirsten came awake with a jarring suddenness. All her senses were alert, prickling beneath the surface of her skin as her heart thumped heavily in her chest. She lay very still in the darkness, wondering what it was that had woken her.

Her eyes moved over the shadowy silhouettes in the room, half expecting them to move. There was no noise, even the wind had dropped. Her body was rigid as she pulled herself up. A strange, yet muted panic was rising through her.

'Is anyone there?' she said softly. 'Laurence, is that you?'

There was no reply, yet to her horror she realized she could hear someone breathing. Her own breath froze and instantly the gentle rasping sound stopped. Closing her eyes with relief, she gingerly pulled aside the duvet and swung her feet to the floor. Then, lifting her hand she reached out for the lamp and a gentle light filtered into the room. It was exactly as she had left it, her half-packed suitcase on the floor, her dressing gown draped over the armchair, her make-up bottles standing innocently on the dressing table.

Slowly she made her way to the door, feeling the silence as though it were a living presence. Her heartbeats were pounding in her ears as she took hold of the door handle and twisted it downwards. It opened without a sound.

The landing was lit by the soft, greyish glow from a street-light. Everything was still.

'Hello?' she called, then suddenly she screamed as the telephone shrilled.

She turned to look at it. Not since she was in New Orleans had she had one of the calls with the woman crying nor had there been a repeat of the chilling tinkle of baby chimes she had heard before.

Her eyes were wide as she moved towards the bed. Something was telling her not to answer, yet already her hand was reaching out for the receiver. As she lifted it she turned to look at the door, terrified someone might come in behind her.

She put the receiver to her ear and listened. There was nothing, the line was dead.

'Oh my God,' she sobbed, dashing a hand through her hair, then quickly pressing the connectors she started to dial. She didn't care if Thea answered, she had to speak to Laurence.

'I'll go wake him for you,' Don told her sleepily.

Kirsten waited, still glancing nervously around the room.

'Hi, sweetheart,' Laurence's voice came over the line a few minutes later. 'I just tried to call you.'

'That was you!' Kirsten cried, sinking onto the bed.

'Sure, who else calls you in the early hours?'

'But why did you ring off?'

'You were taking such a long time to answer I thought you'd switched off the phone.'

'Oh,' she said, a sob of laughter breaking through her relief.

'Are you OK? You sound kind of edgy.'

'Yes, I was a bit.'

'You want me to come over? It was why I was calling.'

'Yes,' she said. 'Yes, come over. I miss you.'

'I'll be right there,' he said. 'And Kirstie, don't let's do this again, huh?'

'What? Do what again?'

'Spend the night apart.'

'No,' she laughed. 'No, don't ever let's do it again.'

— 29 —

Being back in New Orleans, Kirsten quickly discovered, was nothing like she had expected it to be. Gone were the sinister feelings of before, though she realized that the fact she was so warming to the city had a great deal to do with seeing it through the eyes of a woman who was in love. And as she, Laurence and Tom took the first couple of days to explore she became so entranced by the sheer magic of the place that she could almost have wished that there was no movie to shoot and that they could just go on and on the way they were.

While the sets were being made ready, the equipment was checked and actors were refitted for their costumes, the three of them roamed the French Market buying up spices and cookbooks, fancy knick-knacks and painted masks and gorging themselves on po'boys, jambalaya and gumbo soup. Tom was enthralled by the street entertainers on Jackson Square and even joined in one of their stunts. Kirsten clicked away with her camera while Laurence protested loudly at being dragged into the stunt himself. They took a horse and carriage ride through the cobbled streets, revisited the captain of the steamboat who remembered Tom from the last time and joined in the impromptu dancing to a lively saxophonist outside the Café du Monde. At least Kirsten and Tom did, Laurence decided to sit that one out and joined Jane at a table for *café au lait* and a *beignet*. This was the first time they had managed to persuade Jane to come along with them and it was only as she and Laurence were talking now that he learned the reason for her reluctance. She had believed that Laurence, Kirsten and Tom needed some time for themselves and hadn't wanted to intrude.

'But how can you think that?' Laurence cried, amazed she was thinking that way. 'You're a part of the family, Jane. You know that.'

Jane smiled and for the first time Laurence noticed that she wasn't shrugging quite so much lately. 'I hoped I was,' she said. 'But I didn't want to presume.'

'Presumptuousness is just about the last thing you could be accused of,' he laughed. 'And this little holiday's going to be over at the end of today so I'm glad you changed your mind and came along. There won't be another one till Kirsten and I honeymoon, I reckon, and you definitely won't be invited along on that.'

'That's good,' Jane laughed. 'So when are you planning to get married?'

'First things first,' Laurence answered. 'I've got to get divorced and she's got to finish the movie. I won't ask her till it's over, she's got enough to think about. My guess is that there's some kind of conspiracy going on right now to give us this break,' he went on, 'because no one seems to have any problems they want to discuss with us.'

Jane's smile widened. 'You guessed right,' she told him. 'There is a conspiracy. Helena told me. In fact I think she was the one who came up with the idea.' The music suddenly crescendoed and she had to raise her voice to be heard above it. 'It was partly why I didn't come with you before,' she shouted. 'Helena didn't exactly tell me not to, but I thought if everyone else was keeping out of your way then maybe I should too.'

'I can't hear a goddamned word you're saying,' Laurence shouted back. 'We'll talk about it later . . .'

'Talk about what later?' Kirsten cried, flopping down beside Laurence as Tom, made-up like a clown, climbed into Jane's lap.

'You got to take more exercise,' Laurence told her, seeing how breathless she was.

Kirsten threw him a look which made him laugh and taking her hand he turned to watch Jane and Tom who were trying to work out how a toy on a stick worked.

It was nearing the end of the day when Laurence flagged down a taxi to take Jane and Tom back to the hotel. Tom was so sleepy by then he didn't even protest at not being able to go with Mummy and Daddy. It was only over the past couple of days that he had taken to calling Kirsten that and neither Kirsten nor Laurence were too sure what to do about it. On the one hand they were delighted that he could think of Kirsten that way when to all intents and purposes that was exactly what she was going to be, but on the other neither of them wanted him to shut Pippa out.

'I guess,' Laurence said as they strolled hand in hand along Moon Walk, 'that I'll have to talk to Pippa about it.'

'Then I'd make it soon,' Kirsten said, watching the fiery sunset ripple dreamily over the Mississippi, 'we don't want him referring to me as Mummy when he's speaking to her on the phone.'

'No, you're right,' Laurence sighed, then as a lone busker started to play 'Walking Through New Orleans' he let go of her hand and pulled her into the circle of his arm. 'You ready to go look at the sets tomorrow?' he said after a while.

'Yes. I wouldn't have swapped this time for the world, but I'm looking forward to getting started again now.'

He nodded. 'Me too. You know we have your friend Helena to thank for the break?'

'Really?' Kirsten said, looking up at him in surprise.

'Apparently, so Jane tells me. It seems she's been going round telling everyone not to bother us unless they have to.'

'Well that's what I call a friend,' Kirsten smiled, resting her head on his shoulder.

'Mmm,' he murmured stopping to take her in his arms. 'You know what?' he said, smiling into her eyes. 'I love you so much I don't want this day to end.'

'It's a perfect end though,' Kirsten smiled back. 'We've even got the sunset.'

'I know,' he said, touching his lips lightly to hers, then turning her in his arms and circling her waist they stood quietly on the banks of the river watching the blazing sun until it disappeared over the horizon.

The next morning everyone set off early to go and view the new location for the strangulation scene. Both Kirsten and Laurence had felt it wiser, given the circumstances, to relocate the setting and now, seeing what Alison and her crew had done to a derelict shack which had once been a part of the slave quarters of a tragically neglected plantation house, all were agreed that the new location was even better than before. The shack itself was almost hidden by reeds and brambles and the bayou running alongside it, with its viscous coating of duck-weed and shimmering glints of winter sunlight, twisted its way towards the solid mass of swamp trees barely more than half a mile away, where Tom insisted that Jane took him to watch the diamond-backed water snakes slithering into the marshy depths.

They wouldn't be shooting the scene until the end of the week, but already Kirsten could sense an unease creeping into the unit. Not surprisingly it was Elizabeth Bradley who was feeling it the most so Kirsten went out of her way over the next few days to try and calm the nerves Elizabeth wouldn't actually admit to. That was until Ruby took it into her head to join Elizabeth one morning on the brink of the hill where Elizabeth was gazing thoughtfully down at the slave quarters.

For a while they stood together in silence, two solitary figures in an endless landscape of wind-blown fields. It was several minutes before Elizabeth realized that Ruby was muttering something under her breath and leaning towards her she tried to make out what Ruby was saying.

'. . . "humbly commend the soul of this thy servant, our dear sister, into thy hands, as into the hands of a faithful Creator . . ."' Ruby chanted.

Elizabeth gaped at her in horror. This was such bad taste and so ill-timed it defied words and only just managing to stop herself slapping Ruby's puffy face, she turned and marched back to her chauffeur driven car which took her straight to Oak Alley, the Plantation

House a mile or so along the road, where Kirsten was shooting.

'That's it!' she said to Kirsten as Kirsten left the set to come and find out what was wrong. 'I can't stand any more of that woman! She's got to go, Kirstie. I'm sorry, but it's her or me. She's mad! Stark raving mad!'

'Would I be right in thinking we're talking about Ruby?' Kirsten said, taking Elizabeth's arm and starting to walk her through the magnificent archway of live oaks that formed the avenue to the house.

'You would. What in God's name is she trying to do? I mean, does she get some kind of kick out of scaring people or something?'

'What did she do?' Kirsten asked.

It was a moment or two before Elizabeth answered, but when she did there was the ghost of a smile crossing her handsome face. 'She only started gabbling the last rites to me while I was looking at the set over by the bayou,' Elizabeth said. 'OK, I know it might sound funny, but honestly, after what happened to Anna, that was just about the last thing I needed.'

Elizabeth was right, it did sound funny, but Kirsten wasn't in any way ignorant to the seriousness of it. 'I'll speak to Laurence,' she said. 'He has more influence over her than most. And please, Elizabeth, don't worry about the scene. It's going to be all right, I promise you. Anna died of natural causes, remember? There was nothing underhand, no plot to do away with her . . .'

'Yes, I know all that, but honestly, Kirstie, there's a part of me that's starting to regret taking this on. It's got me really spooked, at least Ruby Collins has. Or I don't know, maybe it's something about this place. Even with the size of the cast and crew, with all the people running around and making so much noise, there are still times when I could feel like I was at the end of the earth out here. I don't think I've ever been anywhere that makes me feel quite so desolate. Do you know what I mean?'

Kirsten did, for she could remember thinking precisely that the last time she was there. 'It can be pretty bleak on a day like today,' she smiled, looking up at the colourless sky, 'and I can imagine how Ruby's religious chunterings are getting you down. They don't do much for me either. But like I said, I'll speak to Laurence. In fact I don't think it would be a bad idea to send her back to London.'

'Neither do I,' Elizabeth agreed. 'That woman needs help if you ask me. I mean apart from everything else, you have to have noticed the way she keeps slurping at that gin bottle she's got stashed in her bag. And a bible bashing alcoholic isn't exactly conducive to calming the nerves.'

Kirsten was silent for a moment as she wondered if Laurence had noticed that Ruby was drinking again. She certainly hadn't and surely if Laurence had he'd have mentioned it as soon as he realized. It was a sad reflection on how engrossed they had become in each other not to have noticed Ruby slipping off the rails and it made her wonder how many other things they might have missed.

'Hey, you two!'

Both Elizabeth and Kirsten turned to see Jake standing in the open doorway of the splendid Greek Revival house.

'Everyone's yelling for you in here, Kirsten,' he called out. 'We're about ready for a take.'

'Join Laurence and me for dinner after rushes tonight,' Kirsten said to Elizabeth and giving her arm a quick squeeze she ran back towards the house where she was about to do the first shot in a scene that was going to take all day to shoot.

By the time the three of them sat down at a window table in the Court of the Two Sisters around nine thirty that night, Elizabeth was in a far better frame of mind and told them that she just didn't want to discuss the strangulation scene any more. She was already in danger of getting it out of proportion and to dwell on it would only make matters worse.

'Just let's get it over with and get things back to normal around here,' she said, tucking into her seafood. 'I just wish we didn't have to wait until Saturday, that's all. And as for Ruby, well she's obviously waiting for Kingdom come and making a stop-off in oblivion along the way, and as far as I'm concerned she can get on with it. But like I said, I'll be glad when all this waiting's over.'

It wasn't until they were back in their suite at the Richelieu and taking a nightcap before going to bed that Kirsten said to Laurence, 'I'm going to see about getting some of Elizabeth's scenes pulled forward. She shouldn't have to be waiting around like this, not considering the circumstances. I know we can't do the strangulation scene until Saturday, but we can slot in some of her Plantation House scenes a bit earlier than scheduled. If nothing else it'll keep her mind occupied – and it'll keep her away from Ruby.'

'Sure,' Laurence sighed, lifting his feet on to the coffee table. 'Good idea. I guess I'd better speak to Ruby though. If she's really back on the gin she'll be better off in London where she can't go about the place upsetting the cast.'

'Do you think she'll go?' Kirsten said, settling Tom's head a little more comfortably in her lap.

'Not without a fight. I'll try and speak to her some time tomorrow or the next day, so stay out of her way if you can because she's almost certainly going to blame you for being sent back.'

'Has she been talking to you about me?'

'No. I don't give her the chance. But I can see the way she looks at you. That's something we'll have to work on at a later date, I don't want you worrying yourself now about anything other than the movie.'

Kirsten smiled and looking down smoothed the hair from Tom's face. 'I suppose I'd better put this young man back into bed,' she said, leaning forward to set her glass on the table.

'Go on, I'll do it, you look just about all in.'

As Laurence took Tom from her Kirsten gave him a gentle kiss on the cheek then felt her heart swell at the way his head flopped on to Laurence's shoulder as he put an arm around Laurence's neck. Even in sleep it seemed he knew when he was with his father and seeing the way Laurence's strong arms wrapped around him so protectively Kirsten could only wonder how Pippa had ever been able to leave them.

'Have you managed to speak to Pippa yet?' Kirsten asked as Laurence came back into the room.

'No. It seems she and Zaccheo are over in London. Jane said she rang here earlier though, but Tom was asleep so Pippa told her to leave him. Which reminds me, I've been meaning to talk to you about Jane.'

'Mm?' Kirsten said, getting to her feet. 'What about her?'

'Well it seems she's got some notion into her head that she might be intruding . . .'

'Intruding? In what way?'

'On us. I told her, she's part of the family, but I think she'd like to hear it from you too.'

'Of course,' Kirsten said. 'God, we can't have her feeling like that. Although,' she went on, resting her head on Laurence's shoulder as they walked towards the bedroom, 'I've told you before that I think she should have more of a life of her own. In fact, now don't take this the wrong way, but it's something I've been thinking about for a while now . . .'

'What's that?' he said.

'Well, sometimes it feels like I've just slipped into Pippa's shoes. I have her husband, her son and I have her nanny too. Well obviously I couldn't, or wouldn't, change you and Tom, but Jane . . . No, hear me out,' she said as he closed the door. 'I'm not suggesting we fire her, God forbid. All I'm saying is, if we can help her build something of a life for herself, you know with Billy or Ken or whatever he's called, or with someone else come to that . . . Well, don't you think it would be better for her?'

'I don't know, maybe you're right,' Laurence said thoughtfully. 'But Tom's got so attached to her now.'

'That's what I mean. She needs to have children of her own.'

'So do we,' he said, sitting on the edge of the bed and taking hold of her hands.

Kirsten smiled as her heart overflowed. 'I know,' she said, 'and we will – but we can't be selfish about this Laurence. Jane gives us far too much of herself as it is, we should do something for her in return. But we don't need to discuss this now, we can do it when we get back to London. When the movie's edited and on the screen even. There's no rush, it was just a thought and to be perfectly honest I don't want to let her go at all. In fact, I can't even begin to imagine what we'd do without her. I just want to be fair to her, that's all.'

'Sure. And you're right, you need to make your own stamp on our lives. I'm just not convinced that getting rid of Jane is the right way to go.'

'We're not getting rid of her, darling. We're keeping her with us until we know for certain that she's found somewhere she'll be happy. And if it turns out that she's only going to be happy with us, then that's where she'll stay. But for her sake, let's at least give her a chance of finding out.'

'OK, you got it,' he yawned. 'Now get into this bed and get yourself some sleep will you?'

'Sleep? But I thought we were going to make babies?'

'Sure, we're gonna do that too.'

But by the time Kirsten came back from the bathroom he was fast asleep right where she'd left him.

Over the next couple of days a barely submerged hilarity started creeping into the shoot. Elizabeth was now on the set and her repartee with Jake and Jean-Paul and the stunts the three of them were pulling to make Kirsten and Laurence laugh, was turning the off-camera moments into nothing short of a pantomime.

The high spirits continued all Friday morning by which time Kirsten was aching she had laughed so much, particularly at Jake who was professing to have fallen for Frank DeCarter's on-screen character and kept mincing around him, goosing him and pursing his lips for a kiss. In the end Frank got hold of him, pressed his firmly closed mouth right over Jake's and wildly wiggled his head. Jake roared his protest which all but brought the house down at which point David called lunch and someone outside obligingly rang the plantation bell summoning all slaves to the location caterers.

It was early afternoon before Kirsten saw Laurence again when he came to join her in a small room at the back of the house which had been transformed into a library. She was watching the stunt and effects co-ordinators who were setting up for the outbreak of the fire. She smiled when she saw Laurence come in, but the smile disappeared when he came to stand so close behind her that she could feel the desire gathering like a storm in her lower body.

'How long do you reckon we've got before they go for the next scene?' he whispered.

Kirsten glanced over to where a dry-ice machine and stacks of books were being carried in through the back door of the house. 'An hour? Maybe more,' she answered.

Laurence nodded. 'That's about what I reckon,' he said, and turning away he started back out of the room.

'Cold?' he said, as Kirsten fell into step beside him and drew her fur-lined coat tighter around her.

'A bit,' she answered, glancing at him from the corner of her eye.

'I just took Elizabeth over to the slave quarters,' he said as they strolled out into the garden heading towards Kirsten's trailer. 'She seems pretty OK about it all now.'

'Good. I hoped it would work, bringing her scenes forward. How do you feel about it?'

'I'll be glad when it's done,' he answered with an ironic smile.

'You and me both,' Kirsten laughed, waving to Jane and Helena who were sitting on the steps of Laurence's trailer. 'Fortunately we haven't had any voodoo scenes leading up to it this time. I think that freaked everyone last time, don't you?'

'Mmm, a bit. By the way, did you get a chance to look over the latest budget report yet?'

'Yes,' Kirsten nodded. 'It didn't look too bad at first glance, but on a second look . . . We're overspending badly, aren't we?'

'It's serious, but not critical.'

'We'll go over it now, shall we? I've made some notes, in fact, there are some other things I want you to take a look at too,' she added as they reached her trailer. 'The publicity people dropped off some artwork earlier and the stills guy wants us to look at some contacts of Elizabeth and Jean-Paul, I think I've got them with me. Oh, and Carrie rang earlier to say that the video of Helena's dance routine has arrived.'

'Good,' he said, pulling open the door. 'But don't show it until we come to pick up the scene again.'

'OK.'

Laurence followed her inside and closed the door behind him. 'So where's this budget report,' he said, his eyes starting to widen as Kirsten removed her coat. She was wearing a much shorter skirt than normal, a black bustier that barely contained her breasts and a pair of thigh-high black boots. She most certainly hadn't been wearing that this morning so obviously she'd changed some time over lunch.

Kirsten was still talking as though there was nothing untoward in her attire and as she hung her coat on the back of the door and started across the trailer, Laurence ignored the stirrings in his groin and barely disguising his smile went along with the charade.

'Here are the contacts,' she said, picking up a large brown envelope and sliding them out. 'I took a brief

look through earlier and have circled some already – I
think these here,' she said, handing him one sheet,
'portray the right degree of passion,' she flicked through
the others. 'Ah, and here, take a look at these, the
humour in Jean-Paul's eyes is terrific.'

As he took them she perched herself on the edge of
the desk and rested one foot on the corner of his chair.
Her firm, smooth thighs were bare and as she leaned
forward to watch him leafing through the contacts he
was acutely aware of the way her breasts were spilling
from the flimsy lace cups.

'I'm not too keen on Elizabeth's costume here,' Laurence remarked. 'It doesn't have enough colour. Did the
stills guy blow any up?'

'Only half a dozen,' Kirsten answered, straightening
up. Her dark nipples were now showing in half moons
and Laurence could feel himself hardening. Then, as
she turned to pick up the ten by eights, her legs parted
and he saw instantly that she wasn't wearing any panties.

His eyes were alive with laughter, but his voice was
perfectly grave as he took the blow-ups from her, saying,
'Sure, you're right about the expressions here, but
there's going to have to be some touching up. See the
lines here around her eyes? And the neck. Get him to
sort that and we'll take a look again.'

Kirsten took the photographs back and put them on
the desk behind her, at the same time picking up a wad
of colour photocopies of the artwork. 'The originals are
out at the production office,' she said, passing them to
him, 'together with the lettering.'

'Mmm,' Laurence said, looking through them.
'They're a bit yellow, don't you think? Or is that just
the photocopier?'

'No, they're yellow. Grant's going to do something

about that, but he gave me these just to show the general idea.' At that moment her telephone rang and as she leaned across to answer it her left breast broke free of the basque.

'Yes, he's right here,' she said, passing the phone to Laurence. 'It's Sonya for you.'

Laurence stood up to take the phone, as he did he drew Kirsten's nipple deep into his mouth and sucked hard. Kirsten's eyes fluttered closed, then suddenly he let her go and started to speak to Sonya who was relaying the messages that had come in from the UK overnight.

As he listened Laurence turned to sit beside Kirsten on the edge of the desk. Kirsten got up and falling to her knees in front of him started to unbutton his jeans. By now Laurence's erection was pounding, but as she licked and kissed him, then took him right into her mouth, he continued to give Sonya instructions as to how she should deal with his messages.

Eventually he rang off and as he replaced the receiver Kirsten got back to her feet and continued as though nothing had happened. 'OK,' she said, 'I think we should leave any further decisions over artwork and stills until we've talked to Grant and Alison. Shall we take a look at the budget now?'

'Sure.'

Laurence moved back to his chair, making no attempt to cover his penis and Kirsten sat on the desk, this time lifting both feet onto his chair and displaying herself totally.

'I see here that you're still waiting for Alison's latest figures,' she said, picking up the computer printout and starting to unfold it, 'but she's already warned us of the overspend. Have we had the figures from the effects guys yet?' she said looking up.

'Tomorrow,' he said, taking her knees and pulling her legs even wider apart.

'But at the moment it looks like they're under? They don't know it of course, because you told them they had less to spend than we'd allocated. I think we should pour more into Jake's budget, if there's anything . . .' her voice faltered as Laurence leaned forward to look at the print out and at the same time pushed his fingers deep inside her. 'going begging,' she added weakly.

She managed to keep going for some time, suggesting reallocations, proposing tighter measures, until he started to circle her clitoris with his thumb.

'Oh God, don't ever stop doing that,' she murmured letting the printout fall to the floor and lifting her feet to the arms of his chair. Supporting her arched back by resting her hands on the desk behind her, she moaned softly as he removed his hand and put his tongue where his fingers had been.

It was as the first waves of orgasm started to coast through her that the door was suddenly wrenched open.

'I knew it!' Ruby screamed, as both Kirsten and Laurence swung round. 'I knew I'd find something like this going on here. You filthy bitch, getting my son to lick your cunt!'

Laurence was on his feet. 'Get out of here!' he yelled. 'Get out now!' and pushing her back through the door he slammed it in her face and locked it.

'Jesus Christ!' he muttered breathlessly. 'Sometimes that woman just goes too far . . .'

He turned to find Kirsten hunched over her knees, her body shaking convulsively. He moved quickly back to her, half afraid she was crying. 'Jesus, don't let her get to you,' he said, lifting her into his arms. 'She had no goddamned right coming in here like that . . . Kirsten? Kirsten, are you laughing?'

She lifted her head and Laurence's mouth curved in a wry grin when he saw that she was almost beside herself. 'That'll teach us to lock the door,' she gasped. 'Of all the positions to catch us in. Her precious boy with his head between the enemy's legs.'

'Well I'm sure glad you can see the funny side,' he grunted.

'Even funnier is the fact that you're still on display, my darling.'

Laurence looked down at his semi-erect penis, then back up to Kirsten. 'Oh shit, who the hell cares?' he grinned.

Kirsten slipped off the desk and went to put her arms around his neck. 'Do we get to finish this scene?' she murmured as his hands moved beneath her skirt and started to caress her buttocks. She didn't wait for an answer, but dropped down to her knees and sucked him until he was rigid.

It was some time before he eased himself gently out of her mouth, then pulling her back to her feet he kissed her tenderly, lifted her breasts right out of their cups and turned her so that she was facing away from him.

'I hope you're ready for this,' he said, standing so close behind her that his penis was brushing against her buttocks, "cos I'm gonna fuck you so hard, Kirsten Meredith, you're not gonna know what day of the week it is,' and putting a hand at the back of her neck he pushed her forward across the desk.

'Oh God, Laurence,' she groaned as she felt him start to enter her.

'Open your legs,' he murmured, pulling back and pushing into her again. 'Wider.'

Kirsten did, then gripped the edge of the desk as he slammed the full length of himself right into her. 'Oh God, Laurence, Laurence,' she cried, as he held onto her hips and started jerking himself savagely in and out of her. Kirsten's arms spread across the desk, she opened her legs even wider and Laurence pounded so hard into her that in a matter of seconds her orgasm started to break around him. She shuddered and convulsed, tears burned in her eyes as great surging sensations swelled and eddied and coursed through the depths of her body. The feel of him, so hard and so unyielding inside her was unbelievable. But he wasn't going to let her go, and the blatant carnality of his fiercely pounding hips was already firing her to renewed heights of ecstasy. 'Oh yes, yes,' she moaned. 'Fuck me, Laurence. Fuck me hard . . .'

Suddenly he pulled himself out of her, spun her on to her back, lifted her legs and plunged into her again. 'Now tell me to fuck you,' he growled.

She looked up at him, still dazed from her orgasm and the dizzying power of so many sensations raging inside her. 'Fuck me, Laurence,' she gasped. 'Push your cock right up inside . . . Oooh, Laurence,' she groaned, as he ground himself viciously against her.

Again and again his hand cracked against the quivering soft flesh of her breasts. Her nipples were so distended they felt they might explode, and it was as he stooped to take one in his mouth that her second orgasm began to erupt in pulsating, searing, tumultuous currents. And still he was there, harder than ever before, thrusting deeper and deeper into the burning heat of her, squeezing and tugging her breasts, until he knew he couldn't hold out any longer. As he fell across her her arms and legs closed around him. His mouth sought hers and as their tongues entwined so his seed started its rapid, fervent ascent into her body.

'Jesus Christ,' he seethed into her open mouth as his body was seized by the shuddering release. 'Christ, Kirstie!' he choked, as her fingers found his testicles and gently kneaded and squeezed them. He pushed his arms under her and held her tightly against him as again and again he rammed himself into her, driving every last seed from his body into hers.

A few minutes later they were still lying across the desk, breathing heavily and holding each other close though Kirsten's legs had fallen from his waist. Laurence's eyes were closed, but as Kirsten turned her head to look at him, he opened them and she could see all the love he felt for her reflected in their clouded depths.

'How did life ever get to be this good?' he said softly.

Kirsten smiled. 'I love you,' she whispered, then felt as though her heart was expanding throughout her chest as he raised himself up, looked long into her eyes, then kissed her so tenderly, so lovingly that though they were vaguely aware of the commotion on the set, could hear people running around and yelling to each other, it was as though they were enclosed in a world entirely their own.

'So what do you reckon?' Kirsten murmured after a while. 'Is Ruby going to tell everyone what she's just seen in here? Incidentally, you do realize she called you her son when she burst in, don't you? Anyone might have heard.'

Laurence nodded. 'Yeah, but I don't see what difference it makes, people knowing.' Again he kissed her, sucking her bottom lip between his own. He groaned softly as her inner-muscles clenched him. 'I don't have the energy to do it again,' he said ruefully.

Kirsten shook her head, resignedly. 'Just my luck to find myself an old man,' she said as the plantation bell started to ring. 'I suppose that's their subtle way of summoning us,' she laughed, 'so we'd better get back out there, they should be about ready for a rehearsal by now.'

Laurence withdrew himself carefully, nevertheless Kirsten, still lying across the desk, groaned her disappointment as he left her. He laughed and was idly fondling her breasts when they heard someone racing towards the trailer.

'Laurence! Kirsten! Are you in there?' Alison cried, banging frantically on the door.

'Be right there,' Laurence shouted as both he and Kirsten hurriedly made themselves decent.

'Oh Christ!' Alison gasped, when Laurence threw open the door, her agitation making her green frizzy hair seem even more outlandish. 'You better come quick, both of you. There's been an accident . . .'

'What kind of accident?' Laurence demanded, starting down the steps as Kirsten grabbed for her coat.

'God knows,' Alison answered. 'It was really weird . . .'

'Who is it?' Kirsten wanted to know. 'Are they badly hurt?'

'It's Jake and Elizabeth . . . They've – oh God, you'd better come and see for yourselves.'

'What's happened to them?' Kirsten persisted.

'I'm not sure. They were on the set alone, everyone was having coffee. It seems like Jake was on a ladder doing something or another with a light and he fell. Elizabeth ran to get help and she fell too. Oh God, I don't know . . . She seems pretty badly hurt though. But at least she's conscious.'

'You mean Jake's not!' Laurence cried.

'He wasn't when I left. There was blood on his forehead so he must have hit it as he went down.'

'Where is he now?' Laurence said, breaking into a run through the gardens.

'Still in the library. Elizabeth's in the pantry place outside. The nurse is there ....'

When they reached the house it was to find the entire unit crowded into the hall outside the library. Immediately a path opened for Kirsten and Laurence to push their way through. The first thing Kirsten saw when they entered the room was the small pool of blood beside Jake's inert body. Then, as she moved her eyes to watch the nurse she felt a sickening paralysis grip her insides. The nurse lifted her head then lowered it again to resume the kiss of life. Laurence and Kirsten exchanged a quick look, both horribly struck by the fact that they had witnessed this scene before.

'An ambulance is on its way,' the stunt-coordinator told them. 'Seems like Elizabeth has broken her leg.'

'Where is she?' Kirsten demanded.

'I think one of the sparks carried her into the drawing room.'

Kirsten and Laurence pushed their way out again, both trying very hard to remain calm. Elizabeth was stretched out on a sofa, Helena and some of the other cast and dressers were with her, she looked to be in a great deal of pain.

'It's all right,' Kirsten assured her, 'the ambulance is coming. What happened?'

'I don't know,' Elizabeth said, wincing as she tried to move. 'One minute we were chatting while he was climbing the ladder, the next he was on the floor in front of me. I could see he'd hit his head so I went to get help.

On the way out I tripped over one of those damned prop machines and before I knew what was happening I was on the floor myself. I tried to get up, couldn't, fell back against the door, which was why they carried me over here so's they could get in to see to Jake. How is he?'

'The nurse is with him,' Kirsten answered, glancing at Laurence. Inside she was screaming. This couldn't be happening, it just couldn't. It was a nightmare and any minute now she would wake up. Jake had merely bumped his head and Elizabeth had twisted her ankle. That was all. It would be all right. They could go on with the film . . .

'Laurence!'

Kirsten and Laurence turned to see Jane standing at the door holding Tom by the hand.

'Laurence, it's Ruby,' Jane said softly.

'What about her?' he snapped.

Jane's normally pallid face turned puce at the way everyone was looking at her. 'She's . . . Well, she's run away,' Jane said.

'What do mean, run away?' Laurence demanded, going to her.

'She came running out of here and went off in the direction of the other set. She – she was screaming.'

'What the hell is going on around here?' Laurence cried, dashing a hand through his hair. 'Has everyone gone crazy? Billy! Billy, get a few of the guys together and go after Ruby. *Don't* bring her back here. Take her to the hotel and shut her in her room and keep her there until I get there. Jane, get Tom out of here, will you? No, son,' he said as Tom started to protest. 'You gotta go with Jane. How's Jake doing?' he said as Lindon came into the room.

Lindon's face was horribly pale. 'It's not looking good,' he said. 'The ambulance is here.'

Pushing past him Laurence ran back to the library arriving just in time to see a blanket being drawn over Jake's face.

'Oh my God!' Kirsten gasped.

Numbed by disbelief and horror Laurence pulled her into his arms, burying her face in his shoulder. Then, along with everyone else, he watched in terrible silence as the ambulancemen lifted up the stretcher and carried it out of the room. It was only when they had gone that Laurence spotted Detectives Kowski and Greengage watching from the back of the crowd.

'Jesus Christ Almighty,' he muttered. 'Just what the hell is going on?'

– 30 –

'You've got my word on it, Dyllis,' he said, speaking into the phone as he straightened his collar in the mirror, 'I had nothing to do with it. She just went off at the deep end. I don't know what set her off. I had no idea it was going to happen. She's crazier than I thought . . .'

'Well there's no point worrying about it now,' Dyllis's taut voice came down the line. 'We're just going to have to see how we can use this to our advantage. Did she use the same method as last time?'

'Yes.' He watched his own eyes round with amusement and incredulity at the way Dyllis discussed murder as though it were some piquancy she was adding to a stew.

'Where was the whore at the time?' she demanded.

'Whoring, apparently. In her trailer with Laurence.'

'Don't they ever think about anything else?' Dyllis said waspishly. 'How are the police dealing with it? Are they treating it as murder?'

'Don't think so. They're still waiting for the Coroner's verdict and they're making a few enquiries, but everyone reckons it's going to be accidental death.'

'But you're telling me it wasn't.'

'Not as such.'

'What do you mean, not as such? Either it was or it wasn't.'

'I reckon it could have been an accident.'

'But you said . . .'

'An accident in that she got the wrong person. Either that or she had something going with the Director of Photography that I didn't know about. Poor bastard. He's married, apparently, got a couple of kids too.'

'So how do we make it look like the whore did it if she was screwing around in her trailer?' Dyllis enquired, sparing no time for sympathy.

'Same way as last time. She doesn't have to be right there when it happens. No one does – except the victim of course. I told you before, it's the perfect murder.'

'So what motive would she have for killing this DP?'

'Who?'

'Either of them. Kirsten.'

'Search me.'

'Then you'd better think of one, my friend.'

'I'll do my best, but you're going to have a hard time proving this one, Dyllis,' he warned. 'There's no accounting for what the real killer might take it into her head to do. I mean, what if she goes and confesses?'

'Just make sure she doesn't,' Dyllis snapped.

'And how am I supposed to do that? She doesn't even know I know she did it. And I don't want her to know or I might find myself next on her list.'

'That's your problem, you work it out. And don't plant any suspicion anywhere until you get back here. Then I'm going to sit back and watch that whore's life crumble. Have you still got the keys to her house?'

'Yes.'

'Then hang on to them, you might need them again.'

'No way. The last time I went in there she came back. I stayed shut up in that bloody cupboard for over nine hours before they went off to the airport.'

'But you planted the formula, that's what matters.'

'It's with her script.'

'Are you mad?' Dyllis cried. 'If she's carrying it around with her script it won't be in the house anymore. In fact she's probably thrown it away by now not knowing what the hell it was. You'll have to go back in there. Anyway, we'll discuss that when you come back to London. When's that likely to be?'

'In the next few days I should think. I can't see how we can go on over here. The lighting guy could have been replaced, but the star can't. Her leg's broken in two places. She's going to be laid up for months. Of course, the insurance will cover it.'

'Not when they find out foul play was involved,' Dyllis sneered. 'This is going to bankrupt them.'

'Well, it'll bankrupt Laurence, that's for sure. He's got his house up for this.'

'Shame. Well, he's got a few more surprises coming his way, did he but know it. In fact he's going to end up rueing the day he ever laid eyes on that woman. And she is going to find out just what it's like to have him walk out on her a second time. I wonder if she's pregnant yet,' she mused.

He felt himself shiver as Dyllis started to laugh. Then, quite suddenly, the line went dead.

The Coroner's verdict of accidental death was delivered less than twenty-four hours after Jake had been carried from the house. By then both Kirsten and Laurence had been interviewed by the police and neither of them were left in any doubt that Kowski was deeply unimpressed by what had happened.

Kirsten could hardly come to grips with the fact that she was once again face to face with this man. She had thought never to see Kowski again in her life, but his wolfish teeth, elongated cheeks and predator's eyes were right there, swimming before her as he asked her about a death she still couldn't believe had happened. His presence, just like his questions, was as nightmarish as the newspaper headlines that had been faxed over from the UK.

'Kirsten's DP Falls to his Death' one of them said. 'New Orleans Police Question Kirsten.' 'What's it all about, Kirstie?' another asked. 'Star breaks leg, DP dies, Kirsten questioned.' There were so many of them and most all of them were linking her to what had happened in a way that was as terrifying as it was unjust.

When the British press started swarming into New Orleans Laurence refused to make any comment on what had happened and no one got even close to seeing Kirsten. She remained in their suite where the police came first to interview her then to tell her the verdict on Jake's death. It seemed to her that Kowski no more believed it was innocent this time around than he did the last. The blow to the head, he told her, wasn't normally enough to kill a man, but in this instance it seemed it had ...

'Seemed,' Kirsten said to Laurence as soon as the door closed behind Kowski. 'He doesn't believe it was an accident, does he?'

'I don't know,' Laurence sighed. 'It's hard to tell with the cops. They're a real cynical bunch. He was probably just saying it that way 'cos it gives him some kind of kick to do that to people.'

'Do you believe it was an accident?' she said, her lovely face pale and anguished.

'I sure as hell wish I knew what to believe,' he sighed, shaking his head. 'This is just too much of a coincidence, having two deaths on the same movie. Just thank God we were together when it happened and that Ruby and Alison saw us.'

'That's not stopping the press though is it? They're trying to make out I had something to do with it.'

'I know.' His hand suddenly crashed against the wall. 'Shit! What is going on here?' he seethed. 'Why can't that fucking woman just leave you alone?'

'Maybe she will once the verdict is made public,' Kirsten suggested, though there wasn't much hope in her voice. 'I suppose what's important is that we know I didn't do it and no one can prove otherwise.'

'Dermott's flying in later today,' he said after a pause. 'Did Helena tell you?'

Kirsten nodded. 'I wish we could just get out of here and go home,' she said.

'There's nothing stopping us doing that,' he said, pulling her into his arms.

'But I thought . . . Aren't we going to recast Moyna and carry on?'

He shook his head. 'No. We can't do that. I know we only shot a few scenes with Elizabeth and the insurance will cover, but the cast, at least most of them, are saying that unless their fees are doubled – trebled in some cases – they don't want to continue. Two deaths on the same movie they reckon is a jinx and they don't want to run the risk of any more unless they're well compensated for it. And we just can't afford what they're asking. So I'm calling the whole thing to a halt.'

'But Laurence, what about the completion bond?'

'We'll just have to sort it out once we get back to London,' he said.

Kirsten put a hand to her head as it started to spin. 'Oh God, I'm sorry,' she whispered.

'Hey, hey,' he said, pulling her back. 'Will you stop that? It's not your fault.'

'But I just know this wouldn't be happening if I wasn't here. It's got something to do with me, I know it has.'

'Kirstie, we've got to go with what the police tell us and ignore what's going on in the press or we're going to end up as crazy as Ruby.'

'How is she?' Kirsten asked.

'Not good. The nurse is flying home with her later today. The whole thing's terrified her out of her mind. She's back on her coconut trip, I'm afraid. Said all this was foretold. First the castle, then a woman, then a man. Well, you know how she goes on, you heard it all before. She tried to tell Kowski that some kid inside her pushed Jake off the ladder, but Elizabeth says Ruby wasn't even in the room. No one was except those two.'

'What's going to happen to Ruby once she gets to London?'

'Thea's sorting that out. I spoke to her while you were with Kowski.'

Had Kirsten not been so numbed by everything else that was going on she might have been surprised to hear that, but as it was her mind was refusing to function much beyond what was happening right now. But then as she recalled the ludicrously funny image of Frank kissing Jake and Jake's comical outrage she felt the tears sting her eyes.

'God, who would have thought,' she said, shaking her head in bewilderment, 'while we were all messing around on the set yesterday that in less than three hours he would be dead. It's so frightening. He was so full of life. So kind and uncomplicated. Everyone loved him. No one, just no one would have done this to him so it had to be an accident.'

'Sure it was,' Laurence said, stroking her hair. 'That's exactly what it was and don't you forget it.'

'Honest to God, Helena,' Campbell said, 'I don't know what's going on. I tried speaking to Dyllis again but she's as tight as a horse's ass. She still reckons she can prove Kirsten killed Anna, I know that, but what she's making out of this one is anyone's guess.'

'Thanks,' Helena said as a stewardess put a gin and tonic in front of her. 'Well she's sure having a damned good go at trying to pin it on Kirsten,' she remarked to Campbell. 'Either that or she enjoys libel suits. Anyway, you've got to find out somehow what's going on, if you don't I'm going to the police myself.'

'What?' he laughed. 'To tell them what?'

'That Dyllis Fisher has got evidence on those two deaths – or at least on one of them – that she's withholding.'

'I wouldn't mess with her if I were you,' Campbell warned.

'She doesn't scare me,' Helena said savagely. 'And either you find out what she's up to or . . .'

'Don't you start threatening me, I've had enough of that this past twenty-four hours with Laurence.'

'What do you mean? What's he been saying?'

'He's protecting the Kirstie Doll, what do you think? And if you ask me he's overdoing it. In fact, it wouldn't surprise me if he knew a bit more about what was going on around here than he's letting on. His mother's gone off her head, his girlfriend's under suspicion and he won't let anyone near either of them. So what's he trying to cover up, that's what I want to know?'

'Oh get real, Dermott. You're not seriously trying to tell me that Laurence had something to do with it all.'

'The thought has crossed my mind. Either that or Kirsten did and he knows it.'

'Oh yeah? And just where does Ruby fit into this little scenario?'

'How the fuck do I know? All I'm saying is that Laurence is acting just a bit too heavy. Or with me he is.'

'Because, you fuckwit, you work for Dyllis Fisher. And you've got to have seen the headlines in your own paper these past few days.'

'Of course I have. And that's why I suspect the whole damned lot of them. Dyllis would never be so stupid as to stick her neck out like this if she wasn't sure of her ground.'

'Yeah, well you better find out what she does know, Dermott, or you and I are through.'

'Oh, and I suppose that's your way of telling me that for the moment we're not.'

'For the moment I'm thinking about it. I'll let you know my decision when you give me the information Dyllis has on those deaths.'

'What are you so keen to know for? It's not your head on the chopping block. Or is it?'

'Don't start that again. Just because you weren't even in the country when it happened this time doesn't mean you're in the clear. At least not so far as I'm concerned.'

Campbell grinned. 'Ever thought about joining the mile-high club?' he murmured as the lights went down.

'Fuck off, will you,' she grumbled, turning away. 'I'm not in the mood.'

'NICE TRY, KIRSTEN, SHAME YOU GOT THE WRONG PERSON. BEING WHERE YOU WERE ISN'T GOING TO SAVE YOU THOUGH, IS IT? NOT WHEN I KNOW HOW YOU DID IT. START COUNTING THE DAYS, KIRSTEN.'

As Kirsten stared down at the note great waves of fear were tearing through her. They were back in England now and both she and Laurence had been with Ruby on and off these past forty-eight hours, sitting beside her hospital bed waiting for her to come out of the blinding stupor she had drunk herself into. Kirsten had just returned home to pick up the mail and get some sleep before joining Laurence at the bank later.

She was still jet-lagged and hardly able to think straight and as she turned and walked into the sitting room, her mind reeling with thoughts so chaotic and terrifying, she felt she might be losing her sanity. She couldn't even begin to understand what was going on, or how anyone could possibly prove that she had anything to do with the deaths when she hadn't even been near Anna or Jake when they'd died. But obviously someone believed they could. Either that or they were just doing this to frighten her. She looked down at the note again, a nauseous horror tightening her stomach as she read the words again. But that was it, she decided, someone was trying to frighten her. After all, how many times did she have to tell herself, she couldn't be charged with murders she hadn't committed – that hadn't been murders at all.

Nevertheless, she knew in her heart that she hadn't heard the end of this yet. That the intent behind these notes was every bit as menacing as the words themselves, and this time she was going to speak to Laurence about it, show him the note and ask him to go with her to the police.

Having dropped Kirsten off first Laurence had then gone to his parents to pick up Jane and Tom where they'd been staying since Ruby had been taken to hospital.

Now, as Jane set about making some lunch for Tom and Laurence gathered up their bags to take them upstairs, he was wondering if he could manage to grab half an hour's sleep when the telephone started to ring.

Putting the bags back on the floor he went into the study to answer it. To his annoyance it was Pippa, just about the last person he needed to speak to right now.

'I've been trying to get you all morning,' she said peevishly. 'Did you get my messages?'

Laurence looked down at the blinking light on the answerphone. 'I haven't got round to playing them back yet,' he said, struggling to keep the irritation out of his voice. 'We just got in ten minutes ago.'

'I take it Tom's with you?'

'Of course.'

'Good. I'm at my mother's now, I can be there in fifteen minutes,' and before Laurence had a chance to object she hung up.

Replacing the receiver Laurence carried the bags upstairs then wandered back down to the kitchen where Jane was trying to coax Tom to eat. 'Is everything all right?' she asked, when she saw Laurence standing in the doorway watching them.

'Everything's fine,' he answered, 'that is if you discount the unholy mess we're in. Mommy's on her way over,' he added to Tom.

But Tom didn't appear to be listening, he was too excited about being back amongst his own toys.

Laurence watched him for a while, feeling an absurdly strong need to see Kirsten right now. Then Tom looked up and gave him such a beaming smile that Laurence's heart turned over. 'Got a kiss there for Daddy?' he said.

'Can we play with the trains?' Tom asked, as he leapt up into Laurence's arms.

'Sure we can,' Laurence smiled. 'Let's just eat some of this lunch first, shall we?'

'But I'm not hungry. I want to play with the trains.'

'Come on now, Tom, be a good boy, huh?'

'I'll bet my train will go faster than yours,' Tom challenged.

Laurence looked helplessly at Jane and knowing that he was about to give in anyway, Jane said, 'It's OK, I'll give him something later. But,' she added, as Laurence put him down and Tom started for the door, 'you've got some unpacking to do before you can play with those trains.'

Tom looked back at Laurence. 'Do I have to, Dad?'

'Yes, you do. I'll be up in a minute so get to it.'

'I didn't realize Pippa was in London,' Jane said once Tom had left the kitchen.

'No, neither did I,' Laurence sighed. 'I hope to God she's not coming round here expecting to take Tom off for the weekend – with all that's been happening he doesn't need any more disruption. Still, I can hardly stop her seeing him, can I?'

'Not really, no,' Jane mumbled. Then her eyes came shyly up to his. 'Would you though, I mean if you could?'

Laurence sighed heavily. 'It'd be a whole lot easier if Tom wanted to see her. But who knows, maybe this time he will.'

Tom didn't though, for as soon as he heard his mother's voice downstairs talking to Jane he shut his bedroom door and stood with his back pressed against it. Laurence was in there with him and felt a lump rising in his throat when he saw the anguish in Tom's eyes.

'Let's hide, Daddy,' he pleaded. 'Let's pretend we're not here.'

'We can't do that, soldier,' Laurence smiled sadly. 'Mommy's come a long way to see you.'

'She's not my mommy. Kirstie's my mommy now.'

'Hey, hey. You know that's not true. Kirsten loves you very much, but you've already got a mommy, Tom. And she loves you very much too. You got to at least say hello to her.'

'I don't want to,' Tom declared, his bottom lip starting to quiver.

'It's only polite, son,' Laurence said, stooping down to Tom's height. 'And she wants to see what a big boy you've got to be since she saw you.'

Two fat tears rolled from Tom's eyes. 'She'll make me go to Granny and Grandpa Smith's and I don't want to go there, Daddy. I want to stay here with you.'

'But you like it at Granny and Grandpa Smith's,' Laurence said, pulling him into his arms.

'No, I don't. I hate it there. I want to be here with you. You're my best friend, you said so.'

'Sure I am, and you going to Granny and Grandpa's with Mommy isn't going to change that.'

'You wouldn't make me go if I was really your best friend,' Tom sobbed.

For a while, as Laurence held him, he was at a loss what to do. In the end he held Tom back so that he could see his face and said gently, 'How about I go downstairs and talk to Mommy?'

'No,' Tom cried, clinging on to him. 'I don't want you to speak to her. I want you to stay here with me. Please, Daddy, stay here with me.'

It was a long hard battle and one that eventually got Laurence so choked he was finding it difficult to speak, but eventually he managed to persuade Tom to let him go just for five minutes.

Pippa was in the sitting room with Jane, but as soon as Laurence walked in Jane got up and left them alone.

'How are you?' Laurence said as Pippa walked over to the drinks cabinet and helped herself.

'Fine,' she answered.

'And Zaccheo?'

'Yes, he's fine too. Thank you.'

There was an awkward silence as Pippa stared down at her drink, unable to meet Laurence's eyes. She'd noticed the instant he walked in the room how very tired he looked, which was hardly surprising considering what he'd been through lately. She was about to ask how Ruby was but stopped herself, her only reason for asking would be to stall for time and there was nothing to be gained from that. So, mustering her courage, she lifted her head and looked him straight in the eyes. 'I'm sorry, but there's no point beating about the bush here, Laurence,' she said. 'I've come to take Tom away with me. I want him to leave right – '

'Hold it! Hold it!' Laurence said. 'What do you mean, take Tom away with you?'

'I'm taking him to Italy.'

'Like hell you are.'

'Laurence, please don't fight me on this,' Pippa pleaded, putting her drink down. 'It's for Tom's own good.'

'I'll be the judge of what's for Tom's own good,' Laurence raged. 'You forfeited that right the day you walked out of here.'

'I haven't forfeited any rights,' Pippa cried angrily. 'He's my son. He should be with his mother, especially in light of what's been happening these past months.'

'Would you like to make yourself a little clearer on that, Pippa?' Laurence said tightly.

'Two people have died on that movie,' she shouted. 'How much clearer do you want it? Do you think I want my son around that sort of thing? And if you were any kind of a father you'd see that it was in Tom's interests to be away from you right now.'

'Tom's place is right here with me,' Laurence yelled. 'And if you're trying to accuse me of something here . . .'

'I'm not accusing you of anything! I'm just telling you that I don't want him around – '

'What you want doesn't feature here, Pippa.'

'I'm his mother, for Christ's sake! I only want what's best for him. A home . . .'

'He's got a home!'

'But for how much longer? What are you going to do, Laurence, when the banks start calling in their loans? What home will you have for him then?'

'I'll find us a home, you don't need to worry about that.'

'But I do worry. And so should you. You're already in debt up to your ears thanks to that bloody film and don't think Thea is going to bail you out, not while you're sleeping with Kirsten Meredith. And that's another reason for taking Tom away with me. I don't want that woman anywhere near my son.'

'I don't fucking believe this!' Laurence roared. 'You knew she was going to be a part of my life again – Christ, you practically pushed us together yourself. You weren't quite so concerned then though were you, when you wanted to run off with Zaccheo. No, all that mattered then was you, and what you wanted. Well I've got what I want now and I don't mind admitting you were right all along about Kirsten. I do love her, I never stopped loving her, and let me tell you this, Pippa, she's already a better goddamned mother to Tom than you ever were.'

'You bastard!' Pippa cried knocking him back as she slapped him hard across the face. 'You fucking bastard!'

Laurence lifted a hand to his cheek, his eyes still blazing with anger. For a while they were breathlessly silent, glaring at each other with seething resentment. In the end it was Laurence who backed down first.

'I'm sorry,' he said, dashing a hand through his hair. 'That was below the belt. You always tried to be a good mother to him – until the day you walked out that door. He hasn't forgiven you for that, Pippa.'

'Maybe you won't let him.'

'You know me better than that. I've never stopped you seeing him, even when he didn't want to go, but here is where I draw the line.'

'I'm sorry, Laurence, but I'm taking him.' As she made to push past him Laurence grabbed her. She gasped. For a moment Laurence thought he had hurt her, but then following her eyes he saw that Tom was standing at the door. 'Oh Christ,' he groaned.

'Come on, Tom, come to Mummy, darling,' Pippa said holding out her arms to him.

Tom just stared at her.

'Come on,' she coaxed. 'We're going on a nice trip, in an aeroplane.'

Tom's eyes shot to Laurence's and Laurence's heart contracted at the look of betrayal. 'Daddy, please don't make me go,' he begged.

'But you'll like it where we're going,' Pippa insisted.

'No, no, I want my Daddy,' and Tom dashed across the room and threw himself against Laurence's legs.

Laurence swept him up in his arms. 'It's OK, soldier, you don't have to go anywhere you don't want to.'

'Laurence!' Pippa cried.

Laurence ignored her as he tried to comfort Tom.

'Look Tom,' Pippa said, walking behind Laurence so she could see Tom's face. Tom immediately turned his head. 'Tom,' she pleaded. 'Aren't you even going to give Mummy a hug? Please.' She was trying to prise his arms from Laurence's neck.

'Pippa, don't put him through this,' Laurence muttered under his breath.

'Can't Mummy just have one kiss?' she persisted.

'No!' Tom shouted. 'I hate you. I hate you. I hate you.'

Pippa's face was stricken and despite everything Laurence felt his heart go out to her. He was even tempted to try persuading Tom himself to give his mother a hug, but he knew that it was only a ploy on Pippa's part to get hold of him. And the last thing Laurence wanted was Tom in the middle of a physical tussle between them. As it was Tom could barely catch his breath he was sobbing so hard.

'I think it would be better if you left now,' Laurence said.

Very close to tears herself Pippa nodded and turned to pick up her bag. 'I have to warn you though Laurence,' she said, 'I shall be fighting you for custody. I've already spoken to my solicitor and you must know that your chances of keeping him aren't good.'

Laurence didn't answer. Tom had heard too much already.

Five days later, after a marathon session with his lawyers Laurence turned up at Kirsten's looking so exhausted he might fall asleep on his feet.

'How did it go?' she asked, taking his coat and going to pour him a drink.

'Are we talking about the movie or about Tom?' he answered flopping down on the sofa. He smiled grimly. 'Either way, about as bad as it could.'

'Has she petitioned for custody yet?'

He nodded.

'What does your lawyer say?'

'That it doesn't look good. We're still going to fight it, naturally, but, well, with everything that's happened . . .' He sighed heavily. 'The house goes on the market tomorrow.'

Immediately Kirsten put down his drink and going to sit on his lap put her arms around him and held him tightly.

'Oh, Kirstie,' he murmured into her hair, 'you don't know how good it feels to hold you. I love you, do you know that? I love you so much, but if I lose him . . .'

Kirsten pulled her head back to look at him. 'You won't lose him,' she said firmly. 'No one's going to take him from you.'

'I wish I could be so certain.'

'You could be if you'd just do as I say.'

'No, Kirstie,' he said breaking away from her. 'We've been over this and over it and I'm not going to let you do it. Paul left you this house . . .'

'But Laurence, I don't need a great big house like this. If I sell it I can give you the money and you can pay off the outstanding . . .'

'No!'

'Tom needs a home,' she argued. 'Just think of how much greater your chances will be of keeping him if you didn't have to worry about selling . . .'

'Kirsten, no!'

'OK, then look at it this way,' she said. 'How on earth are you going to buy somewhere else? You're not going to have anything left once they've finished.'

'We'll go live with my parents,' Laurence answered. 'I talked it over with Dad last night, it's what they want . . .' He laughed, mirthlessly. 'Did I tell you, Ruby is after me to go live with her? Can you imagine?'

Kirsten winced. 'I'd rather not,' she said, reaching out to pick up his drink. 'You know you could always . . .'

'I could always what?' he asked, taking the glass from her and putting it to his mouth.

Kirsten shrugged self-consciously. 'Well, you could always move in here with me.'

Laurence laughed. 'You've been talking to Tom.'

'He wants to come,' Kirsten smiled.

'And don't I know it.'

'I want you to come too,' she said quietly. 'Both of you. If *you* want to, that is.'

Laurence looked at her, searching her eyes with his and despite all the reassurance he had given her these past months he could see that, deep down inside, she was still afraid to believe that he truly did love her just as much as she loved him. He lifted a hand to her face and ran his thumb along her jaw. 'Yeah, I want to come,' he said softly and as the relief and joy flooded into her eyes he drew her lips to his.

She still hadn't told him yet about the anonymous notes, how could she when he had so many other problems to face? And what did they matter anyway compared to what he was going through? They were obviously from someone with a sick mind, someone who'd get fed up sooner or later, and meanwhile she had to be there for Laurence and Tom and put her own petty problems to one side.

'You've got to be out of your tiny mind,' Ruby snarled.

'You're in the way,' Laurence retorted as the removal men struggled towards them with a heavy dresser.

Ruby, still pale from her stay in hospital and several pounds lighter, squashed herself against the wall then headed off down the hall after him. 'How the hell do you think you're going to hold on to your son, living with a woman like that!' she shrieked. 'They'll laugh you out of court. They'll . . .'

'Excuse me, guv,' a removal man interrupted. 'This one here for store or for moving?'

Laurence threw Ruby a vicious look and went to check the box. 'For moving,' he said.

'That woman is a goddamned jinx on your life,' Ruby shouted, the moment the removal man had disappeared. 'Ever since she's been back on the scene you've had nothing but trouble. Your wife walked out on you, the movie fell about your ears, you're losing your house and now thanks to her you're gonna lose your son.'

'To begin with,' Laurence shouted back, 'Pippa walked out on me for another man. You won't have forgotten that, I'm sure. Neither, I hope, will you have forgotten that of all of us Kirsten stands to lose the most by that movie going down . . .'

'How can you say that when you're right in the middle of moving out of your own house?'

'Her investment was still more than any of ours. Besides which, she was trying to build a new life for herself. She's lost that now, and I'm going to do all I can to help her get it back.'

'And what about your son? Or has he ceased to feature in all this?'

'Don't ask stupid questions, Ruby. Now either help or go.'

'I'm not going anywhere till I've made you see sense,' she cried. 'Why you've got to go and live there when I got a perfectly good home . . .'

'I love her, Ruby,' he yelled in exasperation. 'Have you got that? I love her and I want to be with her. Tom does too. End of story.'

– 560 –

'What is it, you gone soft on whores all of a sudden?' she sneered.

She gasped as Laurence rounded on her savagely. 'So help me, Ruby, if you were a man I'd lay you out for that,' he seethed. 'Now get out of here! Go now before I do something we'll both be sorry for.'

Had he not actually manhandled her out of the door Ruby might have stayed the entire day getting under his skin, but even when she'd gone Laurence's temper didn't diminish any. The fact was that a part of what Ruby had said was true. He could be putting his custody of Tom into jeopardy by going to live with Kirsten. But for Christ's sake, it was where Tom wanted to be, it was where he wanted to be too. The trouble was though he knew already that the press were going to have a field day over this custody battle and it wouldn't be his worthiness as a father that would be on trial, it would be Kirsten's motives and morals. But perhaps there was something he could do about that. It was a long shot, a real long shot, but what choice did he have?

'Shit, Laurence,' Campbell groaned, 'are you aiming to get me fired, or what?'

'Dermott, you and that rag of yours have all but ruined her life, and you're going to ruin mine too if you don't do this. So come on, man, I've given you the scoop that we're living together now ...'

'For five days?' Campbell said incredulously. 'Now how come no one's picked up on that yet?'

'I don't know and I don't care. Now come on, Dermott, let me hear you say that you're going to do the decent thing for once in your life.'

Campbell regarded him for some time, absently breaking bread over his plate as he considered the situation.

He wasn't in much of a mind to do anything to help the Kirstie Doll, why should he, she'd never done anything for him? But on the other hand as resentful as he'd felt towards Laurence these past months he couldn't deny that he had a strong affection for the man. And neither could he forget how Laurence had once helped him out when times were hard. If the truth be told he wasn't entirely averse to doing what Laurence was suggesting since it might be a way out of Dyllis Fisher's clutches and Laurence would very likely feel obligated enough to give him a job once Dyllis fired him. The real hitch though was that Dyllis couldn't be relied upon just to fire him, she'd find some other way of repaying him for his disloyalty and he didn't even want to think about what it might be.

'Look,' Campbell said as a waiter poured more wine into their glasses. 'I'm going to be straight with you, Laurence, Dyllis Fisher is aiming to blow Kirsten right out of the water any day now. I don't know how, exactly, but she's saying she can prove that Kirsten was behind Anna Sage's death.'

Laurence's face turned pale, his mouth was a tight line of fear and frustration. 'Then you've got to stop her, Dermott,' he said.

'I can't. She's a law unto herself, you know that. No, no, hear me out,' he said as Laurence started to interrupt. 'I don't know what she's making of what happened to Jake Butler, but you've only got to read the papers to see that she's trying her damnedest to pin that one on Kirsten too. Now I don't know if there are things you aren't telling me here, Laurence, but if you do know anything about what went on on those two sets then . . .'

'Dermott, I know as much as you do. As much as Kirsten does, or any of us. The police are satisfied that there are no suspicious circumstances surrounding the deaths.'

'But are they? Are you sure those files are closed?'

'If they weren't we wouldn't have been able to leave New Orleans.'

'OK, then Dyllis is aiming to open them up again. She's going to get Kirsten, Laurence, and nothing you or I do is going to stop her.'

'For Christ's sake, Dermott, you can't seriously believe Kirsten had anything to do with those deaths?'

'It's not what I think that counts.'

'Dermott!' Laurence seethed through gritted teeth. 'I'm right on the verge of losing my son here, and that sure as hell is going to happen if you don't do something to stop Dyllis Fisher. I'm going to lose them both, Dermott . . .'

'You might well hang on to Tom if you weren't involved with Kirsten.'

What little appetite Laurence had was obliterated by Campbell's words, for in his heart he knew Campbell was right. But how could he even consider leaving Kirsten now if Dyllis Fisher was about to do what Campbell had said. Not for a minute did he believe that Kirsten was guilty, but the battle to prove her innocence was going to be vicious, drawn out and very public. And what judge in the land was going to award him custody of Tom with all that going on? Campbell really was his only hope and somehow he had to persuade him at least to try to do what he could to bring this lethal vendetta to an end.

'Look,' he said, 'I know I'm asking you to lay yourself on the line here. I know that Dyllis Fisher will do everything she can to stop you ever working in Fleet Street again, but . . .'

'Yeah, you're right about all of that, but Dyllis Fisher aside, Laurence, I'm gonna look pretty stupid retracting everything I've said about Kirsten in the past. Who's ever going to believe a word I write after that, if, as you say, I get to write again?'

'It could make you look pretty big going to print admitting you've misjudged someone and want to set the record straight. Jesus Christ, it'll be a first.'

'It doesn't work like that.'

'Why?'

'It just doesn't.'

'Then how does it work, Dermott? Tell me, because I need to know. For the sake of the two people I love most in this world, I've got to know.'

'Well,' Campbell said after long moments of deliberation, 'there might be a way. I'm only saying *might*, mind you. And a lot of it will depend on the Kirstie Doll herself. And before you knock my head off, OK I'll never call her that again.'

'Dermott, if you can help us out over this then Kirsten herself 'll be the first to tell you you can call her what the hell you damned well like.'

Dyllis Fisher was sitting alone in her penthouse office overlooking the Thames. She had just learned of Dermott Campbell's meeting with Laurence McAllister and what Campbell was intending to do. He had to be stopped, of course, which he would be, for he knew far too much about her persecution of Kirsten to be allowed to go to print. The trouble was he wasn't intending to do it in her newspaper, he was going to use another by-line and do it for someone else. Well the man was a fool if he thought he stood any chance of getting away with it. He had to know already that she'd fire him, so clearly that wasn't bothering him quite so much as it used to. What she had to do now was find a quick and efficient way of silencing him . . .

Her eyes slowly opened wide. Her laughter started quietly then died as she concentrated. Didn't she, thanks to the deaths of Anna Sage and Jake Butler, now know of the most perfect way of silencing Campbell? And didn't Kirsten Meredith have just the most perfect motive for wanting to do away with him?

Everything was falling into place so neatly that even she, who was rarely surprised by the way the twists and turns of fate often played so deftly into her hands, could hardly believe it. She would get rid of Campbell and at the same time she'd eliminate all possibilities of the real killer getting in the way by doing something so foolhardy as confessing. In other words she'd kill two birds with one stone and lay the whole thing at Kirsten Meredith's door.

Of course it was all going to take time to set up, to manoeuvre everyone into the right place at the right time which meant that she might just not be able to stop Campbell going to print. But did that matter? She could always pre-empt his story with one of her own. One that was as true as it was damning. Her teeth clenched behind the curve of her smile. She'd waited a long time to go to print with this, she'd been right to wait.

'Put me through to the news desk,' she said into the phone a few minutes later.

'Your car is waiting downstairs to take you to the Lord Mayor's dinner,' her secretary answered.

'Good. Now put me through to Phillip Mackintyre.'

31

The pram was moving fast down the street. Her hands were gripping it so tightly her knuckles were white. Her eyes were glazed, the baby was screaming. Cars sped by, puddles showered her legs, people leapt out of her way. She crashed into a bus stop, dented the pram, jolted the baby and her album spilled on to the pavement.

Hurriedly she bent to retrieve it, pushing the photos back inside and rushing on. She didn't know where she was going, she couldn't think, the baby was crying so hard she couldn't hear.

Images were dancing before her eyes. Laurence and Kirsten laughing. Laurence and Kirsten loving. Laurence and Kirsten succeeding. The future yawned like a cavern before her, swallowing her into its blackened depths. Fear and resentment burned her heart, desperation whipped her mind. The echoing, sinister sounds of the baby chimes rang in her ears, drowning the screams, twisting the sobs in her throat.

She reached the park, wheeled the pram inside and sat down on a bench. The drizzling rain soaked her, curious stares incensed her. She was so afraid she was choking on it. She'd killed two people, she was going to kill more. Kirsten, she had to kill Kirsten. She snatched the album from the pram. A frenzied panic blazed in her eyes as she stared down at the mud-spattered pictures of Kirsten. Of Kirsten and Laurence. Of Kirsten and Tom. Of Kirsten and Jane. Of Kirsten's family . . . But it wasn't Kirsten's family, it was her family. Laurence and Tom belonged to her . . .

She got abruptly to her feet throwing the album into the pram. It hit the baby's head. She didn't care. Let the baby scream. Let it bleed, let it know pain the way she was knowing pain. She wasn't going to comfort it. No one ever comforted her . . .

It was past eleven o'clock by the time Kirsten returned home, fighting her way through the torrents of wind and rain. It had been a long and tiring week, fraught with tension and fear as the legal processes of winding up the film and preparing for the custody battle ground mercilessly on. Jane especially had started showing signs of strain which was why Kirsten had taken her off to a movie, just to get her out of the house for a while and perhaps take her mind off things. A few minutes ago Jane had caught the last bus to go off and spend the night with her parents. Tom was with Thea and Don and Kirsten was trying not to mind about how much she was going to miss him just for this one night. But maybe Laurence had picked him up on his way home and already in her mind's eye she could see the two of them stretched out on the sofa in front of the fire waiting for her – and very likely fast asleep.

But, as she ran around the corner into Elm Park Gardens she saw that the house was in darkness. She hurried to the door, her umbrella being buffeted by the wind, her feet drenched by the rain. After what seemed an endless search she managed to dig her keys from her handbag and all but fell in through the door. As she poked her umbrella into the stand she reached out to flick on the light.

'Damn!' she muttered when nothing happened, trying to remember where she'd put the spare bulbs, and picking her way carefully through to the sitting room she attempted to turn on that light. Still nothing.

She'd never been particularly afraid of the dark, power cuts had been so frequent in France she'd got used to them a long time ago, but for some reason, the mysterious loss of power in her own house, right here in the middle of London, when the street-lights outside were working, was unsettling.

She turned towards the kitchen, trying to remember where she'd put the candles when suddenly she turned rigid. At first she wasn't too sure what the sound was, but as her ears strained into the silence she was aware of a gentle whirring sound.

Then suddenly a deep, resonant voice echoed out of the darkness, floating around her and settling over her heart in a paralyzing layer of fear.

'Who is it?' she cried. 'Who's there?'

'*Kirrrr-sten.*'

'Laurence!' she called, a horrible buzz starting in her ears. 'Laurence is that you?'

'*Kirrrr-sten.*'

'Oh my God,' she choked. 'Who is it? Who's there?'

She was backing across the room, stumbling into furniture her heart thudding violently through a gale of terror.

'*Kirrrr-sten.*'

The wind and rain beat against the windows, hammered against the door, howled wantonly down the chimney. It was as though she was drowning in a maelstrom of baleful sound . . .

She clasped her hands to her ears at the very moment that her foot caught on the corner of the sofa. In her panicked state she thought someone had tripped her and screamed as she crashed awkwardly on to the cushions.

She waited, breathlessly, her heart crashing against her ribs, her stomach heaving with sickening dread. Swaying tree shadows careened across the room, a sudden crack of thunder punctured the appalling silence.

She heard a noise at the front door and threw herself wildly across the room. 'Laurence!' she gasped hoarsely, 'Laurence!'

'Kirsten! Kirsten, are you all right?'

'Helena! Oh my God! Helena, is that you?'

'Of course it's me. Where are you? What's happened to the lights?'

'They're not working. Oh, Helena! Helena!' she cried, throwing herself into Helena's arms.

'My God, what's the matter?' Helena demanded. 'You're shaking like a leaf. Where's Laurence?'

'I don't know,' Kirsten whispered, trying to pull herself together. 'Helena, we've got to get out of here. There's someone . . . .'

'*Kirrrr-sten.*'

Kirsten stifled a scream as Helena almost jumped out of her skin. 'Fucking hell!' Helena hissed. 'What's going on here?'

'I don't know. Come on, let's go.'

'Not on your life,' Helena declared. 'Where do you keep the candles?'

'Don't be a fool,' Kirsten said, reaching out for the door. 'Let's just get out of here.'

'But there are two of us and only one of him,' Helena whispered. 'Come on, follow me.'

Steadily they inched their way through to the kitchen where Helena stood guard at the door as Kirsten rummaged in a drawer.

'Oh thank God,' Kirsten gasped the moment she saw Helena's face in the candlelight. Then suddenly a bolt of fear shot through her chest. The drooping black shadows were contorting Helena's features, the eerie, flickering light gleamed in her eyes. For one blinding second the night of the voodoo ritual flashed vividly before Kirsten's eyes.

'*Kirrrr-sten.*'

'Maybe you're right,' Helena breathed, 'we ought to get out of . . .' her voice was choked by a strangled scream as they heard the front door open then close. Footsteps started down the hall. Kirsten's eyes were twin pools of petrified disbelief. Helena reached out for her hand. Kirsten took it, but with the other she started to fumble in the drawer for a knife. Then they heard Laurence swear as he tried to turn on a light.

'Laurence!' Kirsten cried. 'Oh Laurence!' and dashing into the hall she almost knocked him over in the dark.

'What's the matter? What's happened to the lights?' he said.

'*Kirrrr-sten.*'

'What the hell was that?'

'Sssh,' Kirsten whispered. 'There's someone in here. There's . . .'

'*Kirrrr-sten.*'

Helena loomed out of the darkness, her face lit by candlelight and for one ghastly moment, as the point of the knife's shadow plunged into the curling shadow of Kirsten's hair, Laurence half expected Kirsten to slump against him. 'Give me that,' he growled and grabbing both the knife and the candle from Helena he turned into the sitting room.

'*Kirst . . .*'

This time the name was cut off half-way through, and Kirsten heard Laurence ejecting a cassette.

'What's been going on here?' he demanded as Helena and Kirsten followed him into the room.

'Oh God,' Kirsten gasped, seeing him holding up the cassette. 'What a fool! I should have realized. I thought someone was in here.'

'Well obviously someone has been,' Laurence stated. 'How else did that get on the tape deck?'

Kirsten turned to Helena, a nightmarish suspicion suddenly gathering horror to her heart. 'How did you get in?' she asked.

'I've got a set of keys, remember?' Helena answered. 'I only used them because I thought no one was in. I was round the corner in the Arts Club and thought I'd beg a bed for . . .' she trailed off as Kirsten started to back away from her.

Suddenly everything was crowding in on Kirsten. So many things that just didn't add up, that had never added up, that she had blinded herself to because she just hadn't wanted to believe it.

'It's you, isn't it?' Kirsten cried, backing up against Laurence. 'It's you who sent me those notes?'

Helena stared at her dumbfounded. 'What notes?'

'Why?' Kirsten shouted. 'For God's sake why are you doing this to me?'

'Doing what?'

'The stories in the papers!' Kirsten cried. 'All those evil, vicious things that have been written about me! Oh my God! Anna! And Jake! What did you do to them?'

'What the fuck are you talking about?' Helena yelled. 'What's she talking about?' she shouted to Laurence.

Laurence was holding Kirsten tightly, aware of how badly she was shaking, that she was nearing hysteria.

'Ssh, ssh,' he soothed her. 'Take it steady now. Just tell us . . .'

'How could you do it, Helena?' Kirsten screamed. 'What did I ever do to you? I thought you were my friend . . .'

'Come on,' Laurence soothed her. 'Get a grip, honey . . .'

'You don't understand, Laurence. You don't know what she's been doing. You were trying to frighten me, weren't you,' she shot at Helena. 'With those notes! With this tape! Well it worked. I was terrified. Does that satisfy you? Is that what you wanted, or is there more?'

'You're crazy,' Helena whispered incredulously. 'I didn't send you any fucking notes.'

'She's lying,' Kirsten sobbed, turning her face into Laurence's chest. 'Get her out of here, Laurence. Make her go! Please, make her go.'

'It's all right, I'm going,' Helena retorted. 'I'm not staying around here to be abused by a sick mind.'

'Leave those keys!' Kirsten screamed after her.

Helena turned back, threw them furiously across the room and stormed out of the house.

Laurence held Kirsten for a long time, stroking her hair and waiting for her to calm down. 'Now what is it, honey?' he said at last. 'Just what was all that about?'

'I'm not sure,' Kirsten said, blowing her nose. 'It's all so . . . Oh Laurence, I should have told you when it started, but . . . you had so much else to think about. I mean no one can prove that I killed Anna and Jake, they *can't* because I didn't do it . . .'

'I think you'd better start at the beginning,' Laurence said, his heart churning as he recalled Dermott's warning that Dyllis Fisher was claiming that she could prove it.

After several false starts Kirsten managed to get out the whole story. She told him about the strange telephone calls, the notes that had arrived after Anna's and Jake's deaths, the fact that she had thought there was someone in the house the night before they went to New Orleans and how, all along, she had tried to tell herself that all that had happened to her was nothing to do with Helena, but when she looked back over the past year she could see now that everything had been moving towards this. 'From the time she took me to your party just after I got back to England right up until now everything's been pointing to her,' she said. 'Her relationship with Campbell, the broken promises, the stories in the press giving details only she would know . . . Then tonight,' she shuddered, 'that voice on the tape . . . I forgot she had the keys, I didn't even know she had any keys, but don't you see, she was probably already in here when I came in. She started the tape, I couldn't see anything . . . Then she *pretended* to let herself in . . .'

'But honey, it was a man's voice.'

'What difference does that make? Just think how many actors she knows. How many technicians who could set it up for her.'

'That still doesn't explain why, though.'

'Oh Laurence, all my life people have resented and hated me.'

'Hey, come on,' he said, hugging her to him and trying to dismiss the horrifying image of Helena standing behind Kirsten with a knife. 'No more tears. I'm here, aren't I? And nothing's going to happen to you while I'm around. And this is one guy who loves you, remember?'

'Do you swear it, Laurence? Do you swear that you'll always love me?'

'I swear it,' he said, smiling at the uncertainty in her eyes. If only he could wipe away this insecurity altogether, make her more sure of herself and of him so that she'd never doubt, not even for a moment, that this time he really wasn't going to let her down. Or was he? Jesus Christ, he didn't know what the hell he was going to do, they were in Campbell's hands now and after what had just happened with Helena he didn't even want to consider what the next few days might hold. 'How's about I see if we can get some light back on the scene,' he said, 'that candle's just about had it.'

'OK.'

'You going to be all right in the dark? I'm just going down to the cellar and look at the fuse box. Do you want to come with me?'

'No,' Kirsten laughed through her tears. 'I'll wait here.'

He'd only been gone a few minutes when the room flooded with light.

'What do you think we should do about Helena?' Kirsten asked when he came back. 'I mean, what if she did kill Anna and Jake? Or if she knows who did . . .'

'Do you still have the notes?'

'One of them, yes.'

'Then we'd better give it to the police and let them take over.'

Kirsten nodded.

'Shall we do it now?'

'OK.'

'Kiss?'

After a long and tender embrace Laurence pulled away and turned on the sofa to look at her. He didn't want to voice the doubts he now had about the interview she had given Campbell the day before when the three of them had sat together in this very room going over the details of Kirsten's past and Campbell, as though he had undergone some kind of metamorphosis, had gently probed and coaxed, reassured and comforted, while the tape recorder had whirred softly on the table between them. The story was written now, Campbell had faxed it over to them early that afternoon and Kirsten, stunned not only by the sensitivity and discretion Campbell had shown when writing about her early years, but by the frankness of his own involvement in her persecution and the regret he now felt, had given it her approval. It was scheduled to be run in the *Express* the following morning, but though he had read the article himself, had shown it to his lawyers before allowing Kirsten to give the go ahead, Laurence was still uneasy. He wanted more than anything to believe that Campbell would be true to his word, that he really was doing all he could to help Laurence hang on to both Kirsten and Tom, but even with the watertight contract they had drawn up, Laurence was very much afraid that he was going to learn how foolish he'd been to put Kirsten at Campbell's mercy. He'd been nervous about it from the start but now that Helena had shown up here tonight he was terrified that in some way she and Campbell were planning something that was going to blow their entire lives apart.

He pulled Kirsten back into his arms and rested her head on his shoulder. Dear God, if this backfired in any way he'd never forgive himself. She hadn't wanted to go through with it at all, she'd only agreed for him and for Tom and Laurence was horribly aware of how he had played on her feelings for them to get her to agree.

She'd seemed more relaxed about it once she'd read the article, was prepared to believe that Campbell really might be working for them, but he doubted very much that she felt as confident now. And as if to confirm his suspicions she pulled herself upright and said,

'Laurence, do you think there's any way we can put a stop on that story now? I mean, do you think we should?'

'I don't know,' he sighed. 'Campbell's going to be in a lot of hot water if he doesn't run the story we read. The lawyers have checked it out and . . . Oh, hell, Kirstie, I think we've just got to trust him.'

Kirsten lowered her eyes. 'I'm frightened, Laurence,' she whispered. 'I don't know who to believe or who to trust any more. Nothing seems to make sense.'

Inside Laurence was trying hard to keep calm. If they didn't take this chance then he might just as well hand Tom over to Pippa now. Either that or he was going to have to get up and walk out of here, leaving her alone to deal with all that was happening. He knew he would never do that, but if only, he thought savagely to himself, he could believe that Tom would be happy with Pippa and Zaccheo there might not be such a problem. But that wasn't true. It would break his heart to let his son go and as he gazed down into Kirsten's anxious face he had never felt so bitterly torn in his life.

'I'll do anything to keep him, Kirstie,' he said. 'Anything. And this is the only thing I can think of that will help us. It's only Campbell who can set the record straight about you and give it the impact we need. Sure, we could ask someone else to do it, but he's already written about the way Dyllis Fisher has been persecuting you and if it does go to print then it could be that this whole damned vendetta will be at an end.'

Kirsten looked long into his eyes then slowly, shakily she started to smile. 'OK,' she said. 'We'll just wait and see what tomorrow brings.'

The relief that rushed through Laurence was indescribable and as he pulled her into his arms he said, 'It'll be all right, Kirstie, I swear it. No matter what happens somehow we'll get through this. And remember?' he smiled, tilting her face up to look at her, 'Nothing in the world's ever going to come between us, not even you.'

Kirsten touched her fingers lightly to his lips. She wanted so desperately to believe him, to ignore what had happened with Helena and pretend it was all just a bad dream, but a horrible sixth sense was telling her that something was going to happen to break them up and it was something that was going to be beyond either his or her control.

'Jane, what on earth are you doing down here in the middle of the night?' Jane's mother said, turning on the light as she came into the kitchen.

'I couldn't sleep,' Jane answered dully, staring down at the dregs of her cocoa.

Amy Cottle eyed her daughter with a mixture of hostility and exasperation, then taking the few steps to the table where Jane was sitting she hoisted Jane's chin up to look into her face. 'What have you been crying for?' she demanded.

'Just leave me alone,' Jane said, pushing her mother's hand away.

'It's about that child, isn't it?' Amy sneered. 'I heard you talking to your father earlier. You think they're going to get rid of you, don't you? If his mother wins custody, you reckon you're going to be out on your ear.'

'Just shut up,' Jane sobbed. 'Shut up and mind your own business.'

'Well, I can't say I'd blame them if they did,' Amy remarked. 'I don't know how that Laurence has put up with having your sullen face around him for so long.'

'It's not sullen when I'm with them,' Jane countered. 'It's only you who makes me like this.'

'Oh, I see, it's my fault, is it?'

When Jane didn't answer Amy turned to the stove and poured boiling water on to a spoonful of cocoa. 'Do you want some more?' she barked over her shoulder at Jane.

Jane shook her head.

Amy turned back to what she was doing. 'So what's happening over there now then?' she asked.

'They're getting ready for the custody battle,' Jane answered.

'His mother'll get custody,' Amy stated. 'Mothers always do.'

'Why don't you just go back to bed,' Jane said, fresh tears starting in her eyes.

Amy's eyebrows shot up in surprise. 'If you ask me you're too wrapped up in that family and their affairs.'

'No one's asking you.'

'All right, but if you're going to sit here worrying yourself sick over whether or not they're going to get rid of you then have it out with them. Ask them straight.'

'That's not what I'm worrying about,' Jane cried, burying her face in her hands.

Amy's glassy eyes gleamed her cynicism. 'Who are you trying to convince here? Me or yourself?' She watched Jane steadily for a moment or two. 'You've done something to get up their noses, haven't you?' she said. 'That's what this is all about. You manage to get up everyone's nose in the end.'

'That's not true!' Jane cried, looking up at her mother. 'I know you'd like me to think it is, but it isn't. And if you must know, the reason I'm sitting here, the reason I can't sleep, is because I'm trying to work out what I can do to make everything all right.'

'*You!*' Amy scoffed. 'You don't have it in you to do anything that takes any guts. You never have. Turn out the light before you go to bed and wash that cup up.'

As Amy retreated down the hall Jane was watching her, such sadness in her heart it seemed to weight her to the chair. Amy never had had any time for her, had mocked and ridiculed everything she did throughout her life. But this time Jane was going to show her! She was going to find out soon enough just what kind of courage Jane had. She'd change her tune then. Oh yes, she'd do that all right, in fact she'd regret every scathing attack, every belittling remark, every derogatory word she'd ever uttered about a daughter who wasn't even hers to criticize.

She just needed some more time to think this through then she would know what to do . . .

It had taken Helena over half an hour in the pouring rain to find a taxi after leaving Kirsten's. When she finally had, by then soaked to the skin, she'd taken it straight to Dermott Campbell's.

By now she had been in his top-floor apartment for almost twenty minutes, and though she was a lot calmer than when she'd arrived as Campbell finally grasped what she was telling him he could feel his own nerves starting to clench.

'You mean – you're saying she actually came right out and accused you of those murders?' he said.

'More or less. The bitch! How could she think that *I*, her own best friend, would do something like that? I mean, suspecting me of feeding you the odd bit of information about what was going on in her life was one thing, and OK, I did, but that was ages ago now and she knows why I did it. But why the fuck would I kill Anna Sage and Jake Butler is what I want to know! *Jesus*!' she seethed. 'I can't believe she said it. And she accused me right out of sending some fucking note and setting up that tape. What, does she think I'm sick in the head or something? Well if you ask me it's her who's sick – Dyllis Fisher might be after her skin, but that doesn't mean the whole fucking world is – God damn you, don't just stand there, say something!'

Campbell was nonplussed. He didn't know what to say. If Kirsten suspected Helena did that mean Laurence did too? If Laurence did then for some reason it was throwing everything into a whole different light. 'Uh, well, what were you doing there?' he mumbled. 'I mean at Kirsten's?'

'I told you, I was round the corner, in the Arts Club, I'd had a bit to drink and didn't fancy trekking all the way home in the rain.'

As Campbell looked at her his stomach was knotting with fear. He'd been at the Arts Club himself all evening so he knew she was lying. 'What did Laurence say when Kirsten started accusing you?' he asked dully.

'He was as shocked as I was, what do you think? The

woman's out of her mind, I'm telling you, and he knows it too. Christ, it wouldn't even surprise me if she did kill Anna and Jake.'

'Oh, come on,' Campbell said, distractedly, 'no one killed them . . .'

'Well you've sure changed your tune!' Helena spat. 'What is it, did she work the Meredith charm on you too? Got you eating out of her hand after she gave you her sob story, did she?'

'She's had a bad time, Helena, you know that better than most, so just cool it with the jealousy will you and give her a break.'

Helena's eyes were smouldering with rage. 'It's you who's giving her the goddamned break and why, is what I want to know? What suddenly happened to change your mind about her? Don't you care about what she's doing to me? What I'll have to go through if she goes to the police and tells them some crazy story about what she thinks I'm doing to her.'

Campbell wasn't used to playing devil's advocate and the unfamiliarity of it was putting him in danger of saying things he didn't mean. Not until Laurence had asked him to step in had he considered what it would be like to be in the role of Mr Nice Guy and he still wasn't too sure how he felt about it. What he did know though was that the repercussions of his story, once it hit the newstands, were scaring the hell out of him. Dyllis Fisher wasn't going to take this sitting down and if Laurence and Kirsten suspected Helena of being involved in Dyllis's persecution then were they asking themselves now if he too was planning to double-cross them? If they had any doubts about him he knew that as flimsy as it was his safety net would be hauled away.

He would be on his own and heading straight back to the gutter – or worse. But, he reminded himself, once the story was in print any doubts they might have would be erased. They would see that they could trust him and that he was doing what he could to make amends for the past.

But what about Helena? Where did she fit into all this? What if she was working in some kind of conspiracy with Dyllis Fisher? As the horrible thought clenched at his conscience he turned abruptly away from her, not wanting her to see his face. Jesus Christ! He'd never seriously believed she'd had anything to do with it but now . . .

Helena was talking. She was standing behind him but he didn't want to listen, he didn't want to touch her. And yet he longed to. He wanted her in his arms.

He turned to face her and she stopped.

'Dermott,' she whispered. 'Dermott, don't look at me that way.'

But he kept on looking at her, searching her troubled eyes for something, anything, that would tell him he was wrong. She looked so tired, so distraught, so confused, angry and afraid . . . She looked so many things and his heart tightened cruelly as he reminded himself again that she was an actress. She could look anything she wanted to look. If only she hadn't lied about where she'd been tonight it would have been so much easier to take her in his arms now and comfort her. But she had lied and still he was afraid to know why.

'Dermott,' she said, 'please tell me you're not thinking what I think you are. Please don't do to me what Kirsten's done, I couldn't bear it.'

As she moved towards him his arms went round her, but as she wept into his shoulder and he absently stroked her hair he was staring at the leaflet poking out of her bag. He recognized it because he had one himself. They'd been giving them out that night at the Arts Club. So maybe she had been there, maybe he just hadn't seen her. He knew that was possible, there had been a lot of people in that night, but even as his arms tightened around her he had the sense that he was clutching at straws.

'Can I stay here with you tonight?' she whispered, sounding so vulnerable and afraid it wrenched at his heart. 'Just us two, safe from the world,' she said.

'Yes, yes,' he said hoarsely. 'But I have to call Laurence.'

'What for?' she said, pulling her head back to look at him.

'I just have to,' he answered. 'The story I did on Kirsten is going to print tomorrow.'

'So?'

'So . . .' His head fell forward against hers as the words knotted in his throat. Why did he have to call Laurence? To reassure him that he had had nothing to do with Helena's visit to Kirsten's that night? What difference did it make? Laurence would read the papers tomorrow just like everyone else, then Laurence would see for himself that he, Campbell, was being true to his word.

Nevertheless, an hour or so later, when he was sure Helena was sleeping, he crept quietly from the bedroom and picked up the phone. As much as he dreaded hearing it, he wanted Laurence to tell him what had gone on over there that night. But though he let the phone ring and ring there was no answer from Kirsten's house so in the end he went back to bed and pulled Helena into his arms. His own innocence would be proved when the story, that had had every word and every nuance checked and double-checked, came out tomorrow. He just wished it was going to be so easy to prove – to believe – in Helena's innocence.

32

Laurence stared down at the newspaper, rigid with shock. The words swam before his eyes, all his senses were recoiling from the bitter distortions and slanderous allegations of the article that bore no resemblance at all to the one they had gone over with lawyers and was as damning as it was possible to get. *Child-killer Battles for Custody*, the headline in Dyllis's rag screamed, and as the real horror of the story that followed began to register with him Laurence knew that he would never feel such anger, such hopelessness or such violence again in his life. Campbell, in leading them to believe he would tell Kirsten's story under a by-line for the *Express* had not only betrayed them by going to Dyllis, but had done it in the worst possible way.

Six years ago, Campbell had written, Kirsten Meredith had cold-bloodedly slaughtered – *slaughtered!* – her own child as an act of revenge on the lover who had jilted her – the lover she had now so ingeniously lured back into her life and who was preparing to do battle with his wife for custody of his four-year-old son, a custody he intended to share with the woman who had so callously killed his first child. All the details were there as to how Kirsten had gone about her abortion, making it sound like the pre-meditated, calculated act of a psychopath. Laurence's stomach churned. He could hardly bring himself to believe that Campbell was capable of doing something like this.

The article went on to say that this wasn't the first time Kirsten had 'murdered an innocent child', there was at least one other occasion that was known of, so was she or could she ever be a fit parent? She had denied two fathers their right to their children, she had used her bountiful charms to beguile Paul Fisher into turning his back on his children, so what would she do if Tom McAllister ever threatened her in any way?

And it got worse. According to unnamed yet reliable sources Kirsten didn't actually want Laurence to win custody of his son. She didn't want another woman's child – in fact history proved that she didn't want a child at all. All she wanted, now that she had Paul Fisher's fortune, was Laurence McAllister. Pippa McAllister had stood in the way, luckily for Pippa she had escaped to Italy. Anna Sage had threatened to come between them, but as everyone knew, Anna – who had borne a striking resemblance to Pippa and whom Kirsten had never wanted on the film – had conveniently departed this world in an incident that was still surrounded by mystery. Jake Butler, the same reliable sources claimed, had threatened to reveal what he knew about Kirsten and now Jake Butler was no longer around to tell the story. Where, Campbell demanded, was it all going to end?

Laurence's fist closed around the paper. Fury throbbed in his temples. What the hell had ever induced him to trust a man like Campbell? What in God's name was he going to say to Kirsten when she saw what Campbell had done? A burning pain closed around his heart as he thought of Tom – he would never win custody now, he was going to lose his son as surely as he was going to finish Campbell for this mindless act of treachery. The pain suddenly intensified, so bitterly and so cruelly that Laurence pushed himself away from the table and moved restlessly about the kitchen. For a wild moment he considered going upstairs, waking Kirsten and Tom and taking them away somewhere where no one would ever find them. He didn't want Kirsten to go through this, she'd suffered enough and he had to do something to stop her suffering any more. She needed him now like she had never needed him before, but Jesus Christ what was he going to do? The allegations that she had been involved in Anna's and Jake's deaths were now so blatant that the police would have to investigate. He banged a fist into one of the oak-panelled cupboards then dropped his forehead against it. There was a frame-up going on here the like of which he couldn't even begin to comprehend and the result of it was going to be that he would lose his son and Kirsten would lose her liberty.

He snatched the telephone from the wall and dialled Campbell's number. There was no reply. He tried the newspaper offices, Campbell wasn't there either. He dialled Helena's number and got the answerphone. He slammed the receiver down just as Jane let herself in through the front door.

From the look on Jane's face it was plain that she had already read the article. In fact she was carrying the newspaper under her arm and as she regarded Laurence with fearful eyes Laurence felt a bolt of panic rush through him. Even now he was unable to fully gauge what the repercussions of all this were going to be.

'Where's Kirsten?' Jane asked softly.

'Still in bed,' he answered, running a hand over his unshaven chin. They'd been at the police station until the early hours – Jesus, what were the cops going to make of all this now? Laurence hadn't slept well at all, neither had Kirsten, they'd been uptight after the interview and nervous about this story. He'd left Kirsten in bed to go out and get the paper and thank God she'd been asleep by the time he got back. But she would have to know sooner or later, there was no way of shielding her from it, though Campbell could consider himself fortunate that Laurence didn't know where he was right now or both Laurence and Kirsten would be up on murder charges.

Murder charges! Fucking murder charges! This was insane. The whole goddamned world was crazy.

He turned away from Jane and clamped his fists on the edge of the sink, taking a deep breath to try and steady himself. Their whole lives were being blown apart and there was nothing he could do to stop it. Nothing, except get the hell out of here now and take Tom with him. Tom, the innocent victim in a raging battle that had nothing to do with him.

'Shall I make some coffee?' Jane offered.

Laurence nodded. The muscles in his arms were like rock, the frustration in his heart was overwhelming. He wasn't going to walk out on Kirsten, it was what Dyllis wanted and the hell was he going to give her the satisfaction. The depth of his love for Kirsten was something Dyllis hadn't reckoned on, but she was going to find out that this was one thing she couldn't destroy. His eyes closed as the muscles in his jaw stiffened. But what about Tom? What the hell was he going to do about his son? Already he could feel his heart breaking apart as he saw Tom's face when he realized that his daddy, his best friend, was sending him away. His daddy had made a choice between him and Kirsten and Daddy hadn't chosen him. Laurence stopped breathing as emotion lodged in his throat. He couldn't do it to Tom, he just couldn't.

'Here,' Jane said, putting a cup on the draining-board beside him.

Laurence turned his head to look at her and when he saw the concern and fear in her upturned face he smiled wearily and lifted a hand to stroke her cheek. 'It's OK,' he said, 'it's going to be all right. We'll get through this, all of us, we just have to take it one step at a time.'

Jane nodded and smiled uncertainly.

'I'm going upstairs to see Kirsten now,' he said. 'See to Tom will you. Try to stop him coming into the bedroom for a while.'

'Yes, of course,' Jane whispered. 'And Laurence, if there's anything . . . Well, anything else I can do . . .'

Laurence smiled. 'I know,' he said.

Half an hour later Laurence was sitting on the bed with Kirsten cradling her in his arms. She had cried for a while, but the tears were gone now, she was trying to be strong and practical, but no matter what she said he was still refusing to leave, in fact he wouldn't even discuss it.

'I need to speak to Campbell again and see if I can find out exactly what's going on,' he said, kissing the top of her head and stroking her hair. 'God only knows where he is but I'm going to find out.'

'That won't be easy,' Kirsten said. 'He'll know how angry you are . . .'

'Angry! I want to kill the bastard! Just what the hell does he think he's doing? He signed the goddamned contract, he's got to know there are no loopholes there that are going to save him.'

'I think,' Kirsten said, 'that we're going to have to decide what *we* do next. I mean, it's unlikely you'll be able to get hold of Campbell and libel suits aside, there's the custody hearing coming up and . . .' she stopped as the telephone shrilled into the room and turned to pick it up.

Before she could speak Campbell's panicked voice came down the line. 'Laurence! Laurence, is that you?'

Kirsten handed Laurence the receiver.

'Campbell?' Laurence raged. 'Where the hell are you? Just what – '

'Listen to me, Laurence. Just listen! I've only just seen the papers. Helena and I have been with the police since seven o'clock. We just got back . . . Laurence, I had nothing to do with that article, I swear it. Dyllis went to print using my name.'

'Do you think I'm buying that, you bastard! I don't know what you and Helena are playing at . . .'

'We're not playing at anything, I swear it, Laurence. The police have questioned Helena after you saw them last night, she's pretty cut up about it. She's got nothing to do with what's going on, I'd stake my life on it. She doesn't know any more than you do.'

'Then tell me, Dermott, what the hell was all that about round here last night? And where the hell is the story you wrote about Kirsten? Why isn't that in the papers this morning?'

'I don't know, but you can bet your life that Dyllis is behind it somewhere. But listen, I'll tell you what I'm going to do. I'm going to try and get myself a TV interview, If I can I'll say publicly that Dyllis has gone to print under my name. I'll talk about the article I've written and do whatever I can to get it into print. And while I'm at it I'll try again to find out what I can about what's behind Dyllis's allegations. I know her secretary pretty well, she might know something. You've got to face it though, Laurence, she's going to believe herself pretty watertight by now to have gone this far.'

'And just how did she think she was going to shut you up? If, as you claim, you had nothing to do with that story?'

'I don't know and I don't think I want to know. I hope I'm over-reacting here, but I'm moving out of my apartment. I'll call you again later to let you know where you can reach me,' and the line went dead.

'Would you care for something to drink, Ruby?' Thea asked, rolling her eyes at Ruby's bent head.

' " . . . Come hither; I will shew unto thee the judgement of the great whore that sitteth upon many waters: With whom the kings of the earth have committed fornication and the inhabitants of the earth have been made drunk with the wine of her fornication".' Ruby lifted her pale eyes from the Book of Revelations and fixed them on Thea.

'Coffee?' Thea said, not wanting to get into a debate on theological allusion, though she understood perfectly why Ruby had chosen to read her those particular verses.

'Gin,' Ruby said, closing the Bible.

'It's a bit early in the day to be drinking gin, don't you think?' Thea remarked putting the coffee pot down and going to the mahogany and brass cabinet.

'Let's forget my habits and discuss what's really the issue here, shall we?' Ruby retorted. 'Did you speak to Laurence yet?'

'No.' Thea handed her a glass then went to sit on the sofa carefully crossing her legs.

'Well did you try?'

'Of course I've tried. He won't speak to me.'

The muscles in Ruby's tired face seemed to collapse. 'No, me neither,' she sighed. 'So what do we do, go round there?'

Thea's brows arched. 'If you want to make a spectacle of yourself Ruby, go right ahead, but don't expect me to join you.'

Ruby's glass hit the table. 'What is it with you?' she demanded. 'I know you don't approve of me, but for Christ's sake, you brought the boy up. Don't you care what damage this is doing him?'

'Of course I care,' Thea answered through gritted teeth. 'But he's a grown man now, Ruby. I've done everything I can to get him away from Kirsten Meredith and it hasn't worked.'

'So what, you're going to give up, is that it?'

'I don't see any alternative right now and I suggest, for your own peace of mind, that you consider doing the same.'

'Yeah, well he's my son, my flesh and blood, and I guess that's why I don't give up so easy. I know you all laugh at what that kooky kid told me out there in New Orleans, but even the Good Lord couldn't convince me that everything she said didn't come true, 'cos it did. Everything that is, except about the child. Well I reckon that child's Tom and that's why I'm going to do something about what's going on here.'

'But Ruby you don't have the first idea what's going on here,' Thea retorted, still stung by Ruby's accusation that she didn't care as much for Laurence as Ruby did.

'Don't I?' Ruby said. 'Well maybe that's just where

you're wrong. Maybe I've been approaching this from the wrong angle, maybe there's something I didn't see that was staring me right in the face . . .' As she trailed off thoughtfully, gazing into the transparent stripes of winter sunlight, Thea reached forward for her coffee.

'Maybe,' Thea said after a moment or two, 'you should take a few more sessions with the counsellor I found for you, perhaps he could help.'

Ruby blinked herself back from her reverie taking a few seconds to register what Thea had said. When she did her smudged upper lip curled. '*You!*' she snorted. 'Laurence found that counsellor . . .'

Thea was shaking her head. '*I* found that counsellor, Laurence was busy trying to sort out his own problems at the time. You, I'm sorry to say, were adding to them, which was why I agreed to help out.'

Ruby's watery eyes narrowed as a glimmer of triumph shone in Thea's. '*I*,' Ruby said, pulling herself to her feet, 'am going to rescue my son and grandson from the clutches of that whore who, just like the kook with the coconut told me, is trying to create a family that ain't her own. And if you want to stand by and watch some baby getting blown to bits then you do that . . .'

'Ruby, what are you talking about now?' Thea said with a note of exasperation.

'I told you before, the coconut kid told me a baby was going to get smashed. Well you and I know which baby that is, don't we? It'll be the one the whore of Babylon is carrying right now . . .'

'Kirsten's pregnant?' Thea said unable to hide her surprise.

'. . . and like it says in the paper,' Ruby went on, 'she's not backward in killing kids she don't want and she's got a pretty unique way of going about it. Well she can do what she wants with the one in her belly, but she sure as hell ain't getting away with nothing where my son and grandson are concerned. I came here to see if you would lend me your support, but I can see that between the manicurist and the cocktails you just don't have the time.'

'Whereas between the gin and the counselling you do,' Thea remarked, replacing her cup on the table.

'I got any amount of time for Laurence,' Ruby seethed.

'Then allow him to sort this out for himself,' Thea advised. 'A pair of interfering mothers is the last thing he needs right now. He loves that woman . . .'

'He just thinks he loves her. He don't know what's good for him, he never did.'

Thea sighed. 'Ruby, you're forcing me to say things I'd rather not,' she said. 'But you haven't been around Laurence's life long enough to make a statement like that. Sure, he's made his mistakes . . .'

'And you could have stopped him.'

'Ruby,' Thea said in a long-suffering voice. 'He's not a child. I've tried to do what I thought was best for him, but he has to live his own life. I didn't like the idea of him going back to Kirsten any more than you do, but we've both got to face the fact that he loves her. He loves her more than either of us and what he's doing right now proves it.'

'No, what it proves is that he's not thinking right. Like it says in the Bible, he's drunk with the wine of her fornication. Well we got to sober him up otherwise he's going to lose that boy and you can't tell me he loves that woman more than he loves his own son.'

'I'm not trying to tell you that. All I'm saying is that he has to make his own choices and you and I Ruby have to stand by whatever his decisions may be. His aim right now is to keep both Kirsten and Tom – he might not succeed, but whichever one he loses he's going to need us to help him over what will be one of the worst times of his life. So don't interfere now, Ruby. Don't judge, don't smother and for heaven's sake don't go round there ranting about that ridiculous coconut episode or getting on your soapbox when you've got no more idea than I have if Kirsten's pregnant. Just put your prejudices and your needs to one side and think of Laurence.'

'Yeah, well as I see it that's just what I am doing,' Ruby retorted and downing the last of her gin she gathered up her bag, lit a cigarette and walked unsteadily out of the door.

When she had gone Thea crossed the room to pick up the newspaper she had left behind. She had read the story many times already that day, but something inside her was forcing her to read it again. She wished she could stop, that she could pretend that none of it was happening, for it hurt so much to see those cruel words, to wonder and not know for sure what it was doing to Laurence. If only she hadn't set herself so vehemently against Kirsten, if only she hadn't done what she had, then maybe she could help them now. As it was she understood completely why Laurence wouldn't speak to her, he was trying to protect Kirsten from suffering any further at the hands of those who were so prejudiced against her. But dear God, what was he going to do to get them out of this mess? As Campbell himself had asked, where was it all going to end? Suddenly Ruby's quote from Revelations surfaced in her mind. Equating Kirsten with the whore of Babylon was ludicrous, but Thea couldn't stop herself wondering what had happened to the whore. Hadn't she died by fire? Thea's heart contracted and for a moment she was tempted to go and seek out the Bible to check. But she didn't – it would make her as crazy as Ruby if she pursued that line.

'Hey, come on,' Don said, coming into the room and finding Thea with her head in her hands over the newspaper. 'Put it away now. You're punishing yourself needlessly. What's done is done and there's nothing you can do to change it.'

'Isn't there?' Thea said in a strangled voice. 'If it weren't for me then none of this would be happening.'

'You don't know that for sure, and you only did what you thought was best at the time,' Don comforted her.

'You and I know that, but what on earth is Laurence going to say when he finds out?'

'Did you talk to him yet?'

'No. Jane's answering the phone, poor thing. God only knows what it must be like in that house today. I wish Laurence would let Tom come here.'

'I'll tell you what, I'll give it a go, see if he'll talk to me,' Don said. But when he tried the number it was busy and remained that way for the rest of the day.

It wasn't that Kirsten and Laurence had taken the phone from the hook, it was simply that it just didn't stop ringing. First their lawyers, then reporters, then Jane's parents demanding she come home, then Ruby threatening to come over. Laurence dealt with Ruby, telling her they were going out so she'd be wasting her time and before she could say any more he banged down the phone. Kirsten talked to Jane, tried to coax her into doing what her parents wanted, but Jane refused to go.

They needed her right now, she declared with a rare show of defiance, so she was going to stay. All Jane ever seemed to want was to feel needed and knowing that to shut her out now would hurt her immeasurably both Kirsten and Laurence agreed to let her make up her own mind. Pippa had called several times, but hers were amongst the calls Laurence was refusing to take. Sensing the atmosphere Tom stuck close to Laurence except while Laurence was speaking to Campbell when Kirsten took him upstairs to his own room to play.

So far Kirsten hadn't allowed herself to give into the fear and panic that had threatened to overwhelm her when she'd first read the article that had gone out under Campbell's name. It helped that she had to be strong for Laurence and Tom, but every now and again as the reality of what was happening washed over her she could feel her control slipping. She was going to lose them, she knew that, it was simply a matter of time now. She was sure Laurence felt the same way which was why he was holding on and fighting so hard. He, no more than she, wanted to accept that Dyllis, together with Campbell or Helena or both, was going to succeed in breaking them up, but when Campbell had called earlier to tell them that the police had gone to Dyllis's office to interview her they had both known that time was fast running out.

Laurence's lawyers had come just before lunch, fighting their way through the clutch of reporters camped outside, and hadn't left until three. They were fully appraised of the situation, were preparing the libel suits, but until they knew what the police were intending to do with whatever information Dyllis gave them they, like Kirsten and Laurence, were forced to play the waiting game.

Kirsten knew that Laurence was in half a mind to start trusting Campbell, but though she wanted more than anything to believe that Campbell was doing all he could to help them, she couldn't. As yet the TV interview hadn't materialized and there was still no commitment by another paper to run his story. It was true that he was calling regularly, giving them details of what little information he was managing to glean and he had checked into a hotel somewhere in Bloomsbury, but it could all still be a ploy. Kirsten had no idea where Helena was, all she knew was that she longed to hear something to confirm that she had been wrong about Helena, but during the brief calls he had made to Laurence Campbell hadn't mentioned her.

She was going to lose everyone in the end, Kirsten just knew it, everyone and everything including her freedom. She hated herself for being so pessimistic but it was hard not to be when she knew so little of what was really going on.

She was sitting on the end of Tom's bed reading him a story when Jane came in.

'Laurence has finished on the phone now,' Jane told her solemnly.

Kirsten nodded. 'OK, I'll go down,' she said.

Laurence was waiting for her in the sitting room. He looked exhausted, but there was a light in his eyes that hadn't been there earlier.

'What's happened?' she asked, going to sit beside him.

'Campbell's got his interview. Sky News are broadcasting it on their *Live at Five* programme.'

Kirsten glanced at the clock. Fifteen minutes to go. This was going to be one of the worst fifteen minutes of their lives as they waited to see if Campbell would be true to his word.

He was. And as Laurence's hand tightened over Kirsten's they listened to Campbell repeating, almost word for word, what he had written in the article he had faxed them.

'I regret bitterly,' he was saying, 'all that I have written about Kirsten Meredith in the past and I am fully prepared to admit that I am as guilty as Paul Fisher's wife of pursuing a vendetta that is as unjustified as it is vindictive. There is no doubt in my mind, despite what Mrs Fisher has printed under my name in her paper today, that Kirsten had nothing to do with the deaths of either Anna Sage or Jake Butler. And I challenge Mrs Fisher to come up with her proof or prepare herself for one of the most costly libel suits anyone in her position has ever faced.'

'Are you saying,' the interviewer asked, 'that Mrs Fisher has manufactured evidence to suggest that there was foul play regarding the, er, accidents?'

'I don't know what Mrs Fisher has done,' Campbell answered, 'but I do know that just over a year ago, at the time Kirsten returned to London, Mrs Fisher swore that she would destroy Kirsten's life no matter what. As I said, I deeply regret ever getting involved. I was having personal problems of my own at the time, Mrs Fisher exploited them, but nothing will excuse what I have done to a woman whom I now wholeheartedly believe to be innocent of all charges being levelled against her. And with regard to Kirsten not wanting children I would suggest that you read the Express tomorrow to find out the real truth of that.'

'Which is?' the interviewer prompted.

'Kirsten has an excellent relationship with Tom McAllister,' Campbell answered. 'Tom adores her and Kirsten, in my opinion, will make – already makes – an excellent mother. And just like her and Laurence I hope that one of these days they get to add to their family. No child could ever wish for more loving parents.'

'I don't believe it,' Kirsten whispered. 'I never dreamed he'd ever do anything like this.'

Some ten minutes later Campbell was back on the phone. 'Did you see it?' he said to Laurence.

'We saw,' Laurence answered. 'And Dermott, I'll never be able to thank you enough.'

'Yeah, well, hold your horses,' Campbell said. 'We're not out of the woods yet. A long way from it, in fact. I've just heard what Dyllis is planning to print in tomorrow's papers. She going to suggest that it was Kirsten herself who told her about the abortion.'

'What! But that's crazy! No one's ever going to believe that.'

'Hear me out,' Campbell said. 'She's going to say that Kirsten went behind your back and let it be known to someone who would be sure to tell Dyllis that she had that abortion just so's Dyllis would run the story when the time came for Tom's custody battle. In other words, by the most devious means imaginable, Kirsten is seeing to it that you don't get custody, that she won't have to share you, that she won't be saddled with another woman's child, but all the time she's making sure to look like she wants exactly the opposite.'

Kirsten's eyes widened with alarm as she saw Laurence's face pale. 'Who did tell her, Dermott?' he whispered. 'Do you know that?'

There was a pause at the other end and Laurence's heart turned over. 'You do know, don't you?' he said.

'Yeah, yes I do,' Campbell answered. 'I found out a while ago – it was the same person who told me . . . You're not going to like it, I'm afraid . . .'

'Just get on with it,' Laurence snapped.

'It was your mother who told her,' Campbell said flatly.

Laurence frowned. 'My mother?' he repeated. 'You mean, Ruby?'

'No, I mean Thea.'

'What!' Laurence hissed.

'I'd speak to her if I were you,' Campbell said. 'See if she'll do something to stop Dyllis.'

'I'll get right on to it. Where are you?'

'At the Sky studios. I've got a few more calls to make then I'm going back to my hotel. But listen, Laurence, I know I don't have to spell this out to you, but I'm going to. No matter what I said in that interview, nor what your mother decides to do about sorting things out her end, we still don't any of us know what evidence Dyllis has got against Kirsten – and believe you me whatever it is it's not going to be as easy to blow out of the water as the rest of it's been.'

'I know,' Laurence said. 'But we will. Somehow.'

Helena looked up as an oblong of flowered wallpaper opened in the wall and Campbell walked into the room. She was sitting with her back against the headboard of the bed, her legs stretched out in front of her, a remote control in her hands. 'So,' she said, as he took off his coat and hung it on the back of the door, 'you've just earned yourself two friends for life.'

'I did what I had to do,' he answered.

'Even though she's trying to accuse me of murder?'

'Look, what are you so worried about? The police have cleared you . . .'

'That's not the point, Dermott, and how do you know

they've cleared me? They didn't say that. In fact what they said was to let them know if I was planning any trips out of the country.'

'They have to do that. You were on the set both times, once their enquiries really get under way, *if* they get under way, they'll want to interview everyone who was there.'

'Yeah, well,' Helena said, throwing the remote control on the bed. 'You try having your best friend do something like this to you and see how you feel.'

'You try having someone you love lie to you about where she was the night Kirsten found that tape and see how you feel,' he retorted, going to help himself from the mini-bar.

'Well, you know where I was now,' she said sulkily.

'I know where you said you were. I just hope you're not lying, Helena, 'cos if you are the police will find out.'

'Jesus Christ!' she cried. 'What is it with you? Suddenly Kirsten can't do any wrong, whereas *me*, the woman you profess to love, I'm a liar and a murderer.'

'I don't think so,' he smiled, going to join her on the bed and handing her a beer. 'It would help though if you could remember the kid's name.'

'He never told me. It was just a quick screw. I wanted to see if I still preferred young boys, or whether what I had with you was better.'

'And is it?' he asked, running a hand along her thigh.

'Don't ask me that now,' she said, swinging her legs to the floor. 'I don't want to think about it. I've got too much else on my mind.'

— 33 —

The next day Campbell's article was published. The other papers did follow-up stories on what had happened the day before, but from Dyllis's papers there was a resounding and unnerving silence. Neither was there anything the next day, nor the day after that. Each morning Laurence scanned the tabloids and broadsheets that were part of Dyllis's empire, hardly daring to hope that she might be backing down. She sure seemed to be and he wondered if it had anything to do with Thea's threat to contradict Dyllis's claim about where she had got her information regarding the abortion. He had no idea what his mother had said to Dyllis when the two women had spoken, he was still in no frame of mind to forgive Thea for what she had done. He hadn't communicated with her since he'd called to demand that she tell the truth, though he had allowed Jane to take Tom round there a couple of times.

There had been no calls nor visits from the police either and Laurence was beginning to consider exactly what might happen to Dyllis if the libel suits went against her. In this instance the defamation of character was so serious he wondered if her fall from grace might actually include a jail sentence. She sure as hell should be locked up; a woman who exploited her power the way she did, harboured grudges and went about wrecking people's lives as if she was some latter day Fury made her as dangerous as any psychopath and, for all he knew, that was just what she was.

For Kirsten the time passed in a daze. She was wholly aware of all that was going on around her, the sound of the telephone ringing; the echo of hope in Laurence's voice; Jane's amazement at the quantity of letters that started to pour in as a result of Campbell's story; Tom's glee as he skidded into the pile of multi-coloured envelopes; the cautious optimism of the lawyers; Laurence's refusal to speak to Thea; Pippa's calls that were filled with concern, though she was still adamant that she was going to win the custody battle; Ruby's drunkenly deranged predictions for the future yelled from the street outside; there was so much going on it was as if a whirlwind had hit the house. Yet to Kirsten it seemed unreal, intangible, as though she were standing apart from it unable to reach it, unable to stop the storm that would eventually sweep them all from her life.

Outwardly she was responding; her skin absorbed the feel of Laurence's arms around her, her lips smiled at his confidence and words of reassurance, her eyes watched as he played with Tom, tumbling him and tickling him, she listened to them laugh, heard them calling her name, she went to them, played with them and laughed too, but inside her heart was numb with fear.

Laurence, Jane, Campbell, even the lawyers, were all saying that the worst was over. A week had gone by since Dyllis Fisher's article and though the writs had been served there had been no response. Campbell was no longer sure where Dyllis was, the lawyers hadn't been able to learn anything from the police and everyone, with the exception of Kirsten, took this to mean that in the end Dyllis had been unable to make her accusations stand up. Kirsten wished she could share in their optimism, wanted so much to believe that at last Dyllis was going to leave her alone, but as the date for the custody hearing grew closer the silence was, to her, so ominous it was making her ill.

So far she had managed to hide this from Laurence, shutting herself in the bathroom and running the taps while she leaned over the lavatory and vomited. Afterwards, when she finally found the energy to lift her head she felt exhausted. Her stomach felt as though it had been pulled from its roots, her breath fluttered and panted in her lungs as her heart hammered the blood back into her veins. She longed to cry, to release at least some of the tension, but she was afraid to. Her eyes looked bruised from lack of sleep, her skin was pale from lack of nourishment. Blinding spells of dizziness descended upon her pushing her towards a blackness she fought hard to resist. Once she had fallen, sinking slowly, slowly to the floor, watching the walls rear up around her as vivid pinpoints of light flashed before her eyes, but somehow she'd managed to pull herself back before she'd lost consciousness.

That morning, despite her insistence that she was fine, Laurence had called in the doctor. Jane had now gone off to the chemist to get the sleeping pills that had been prescribed, though Kirsten knew she wouldn't take them. She hadn't been totally honest with the doctor about her symptoms – had she been she knew he'd never have prescribed Tamezepam.

Now, as she walked down the stairs, her dark amber hair shining and clean, her eyes feverishly bright and her pale face flushed with colour, Laurence looked up at her and felt his throat tighten at how very lovely, yet how fragile she looked. The anxiety in his eyes tore at

Kirsten's heart. As she reached him she lifted a hand to his face and touched him lightly.

'I love you,' she whispered.

'I love you too,' he said thickly, drawing her to him. His hands moved into her silky hair, the hardness of his limbs pressed against her bones. She was losing so much weight it was as though she was wasting away before his eyes. He clung to her, afraid that somehow she would slip away from him.

'Kirstie, please stop shutting me out like this,' he murmured. 'Tell me what's going on in your mind.'

Kirsten smiled. 'All I think about, Laurence, is how very much you mean to me.'

'Then why are you so sad? We're together, we're going to keep Tom, we're getting through this . . .'

'I know,' she said, but inside she felt as though she was dying. She longed to tell him that she was pregnant, to see the joy light up his beautiful blue eyes, to feel his arms squeezing her tightly and laugh at the tears of happiness as they rolled on to his cheeks. But she couldn't do it. Soon, very soon now, it would all come to a head and he would have to leave her. He would have to do what was best for Tom and she couldn't use her own child to hold him when she knew already how difficult it was going to be for him to go. As it was she could hardly bring herself to think about the baby, not knowing what future she would have, where she would end up or what would become of them was too painful, too frightening to consider. She knew she was behaving like a guilty woman, was losing faith in the justice that would work for her, but unlike everyone else she didn't underestimate Dyllis Fisher. She knew that something terrible was going to happen to her and as the silence stretched on the more powerless to control the fear she was becoming.

Yet oddly, right now, as she stood there in Laurence's arms, she felt a gentle buoyancy ripple through her. They could be happy for now, they didn't need to think about the future, not yet, and she just couldn't bear to see him hurting the way he was when he was trying so hard to give her hope.

'How about we take a look at some of those letters?' she smiled up at him. 'Have you read any yet?'

'Well,' he shrugged, 'I guess I did read a couple.'

She laughed. He'd opened her mail without her permission and he was so like Tom when he was guilty.

They went into the study and Laurence sat down in the big leather armchair while Kirsten curled up at his feet to make a start on the hundreds of letters that were waiting for her. Outside rain was beating against the windows, footsteps hurried past, cars made a soft swishing sound on the wet roads. A fire flickered and crackled in the hearth beside them, on the mantelpiece above a photograph of Paul smiled down on them as they read.

Kirsten was deeply moved by the letters. After reading Dermott's story women from all over the country had written to express their sympathy and understanding of what she had done and what she was going through now. Some told of their own sufferings, how they had come through them and how they had at last found happiness. A lot offered encouragement, advice, help and even friendship. Many wanted her to know that they had never believed the terrible things printed about her and said how happy for her they were that she had at last been able to set the record straight. Several old men wrote telling her about the younger women they had married and how their lives had changed because of it, and she could sense their pride in being able to identify with the great Paul Fisher. It was as though by him doing it they had received the seal of approval they'd never had from their families, and the proof that it was possible for someone so much younger to genuinely love a person nearing the end of their days. Even if they didn't say it in so many words it seemed to Kirsten that every one of them in their own way was telling her to believe in the future, to believe that things would come good in the end and as she set one letter on top of the other she was beginning to ask herself if she dared to do that.

After a while she stopped reading and laid her cheek against Laurence's leg. Maybe things would work out, maybe they could fulfil their dreams of Hollywood and a family and a life of togetherness and success. Laurence seemed so sure of it, so why couldn't she be? Maybe it was the old paranoia come back to haunt her, stealing into her confidence and overwhelming it with doubt. It could be, as one woman had suggested, that she had more to fear from the power of her negative thoughts than she did from Dyllis Fisher.

She inhaled deeply, feeling her senses flood with the intoxicating scent of Laurence's masculinity. She slipped a hand under his jeans and stroked the solid muscle of his calf. The room was so warm, the air so sleepy. They hadn't made love for almost a week, she'd pushed him away, afraid to let him come any closer than he already was.

She turned her head to look up at him and found he was watching her. His lazy blue eyes were so steeped in love it caused her breath to catch in her throat. His hair looked so unbelievably black in the shadowy light, his thick brows were drawn in question, his full mouth was half smiling. She looked at his hands, lean and powerful, at the broadness of his shoulders, the strength of his jaw. In some ways it was as though she was seeing him for the first time, unable to believe how incredibly handsome he was. It was so hard not to tell him about the baby, so very, very hard, but despite how desperately she wanted to make herself believe in the future, she knew she couldn't tell him – at least not yet. Maybe in another week, maybe by then, with the custody battle behind them, she would have overcome her fears.

'What are you thinking?' he whispered.

Her eyes began to sparkle as she smiled into his and with an ironic lift of his eyebrows Laurence set aside the letter he was holding. He moved from the chair and sat beside her on the floor, holding her against him and stroking her as they stared into the fire. His love for her was expanding across his chest, throughout his body. For a while he had been afraid he was losing her. He'd always sworn that he would never let her come between them, but faced with it he hadn't known what to do. She had closed herself off from him and there was no way in. He knew that no matter how long it took he would have kept on trying, but she was here now, returned to him and loving him as much as he loved her.

She moved in his arms, lying her head back on his shoulder and lifting her mouth to his. He kissed her tenderly, lingeringly, savouring the taste of her lips, inhaling the scent of her and feeling it spread a stirring heat through his loins. Her hair was luxuriant in his hands as he bunched it around her face pulling her closer. She unbuttoned his shirt and pushed her hands inside, spreading her fingers through the coarse black hair. He felt the gentle moan of desire vibrate in her throat as he caressed her neck and circled her lips with his tongue.

Kirsten opened her eyes and looked up at him. He looked back. Neither of them smiled, it was as though the depth of their feelings was merging, binding their souls together, filling their hearts with a love that surpassed all they had known before.

Very gently, never taking his eyes from hers, Laurence removed her clothes. Their need to join physically knew no urgency, yet it transcended all other needs. Her skin held a longing to be covered by his, as his did to feel hers so smooth and satiny beneath him. Only when he was naked did Kirsten reach out to touch him, running her hands over the solid muscles of his shoulders, his arms, his chest, his abdomen. She caught her lip between her teeth as he brushed his fingers lightly over her nipples. Her eyes fluttered closed, then she felt his mouth come crushing down on hers.

'I love you,' he breathed. 'Oh God, I love you.'

She gazed up at him again and watched the strain of passion cross his face as she took him in her hand and squeezed him.

He laid over her, covering her legs with his, pushing his arms beneath her and feeling all of her against him. She kept her legs together, loving the way he pushed himself into the moist, soft flesh, yet not entering her. After a while she lifted her legs over his and he guided himself into her.

'Sometimes,' Kirsten whispered, 'I wish I could take all of you inside me.'

He smiled. 'You already have all of me,' he answered, gently circling his hips as he smoothed the hair from her face.

Kirsten's eyes moved to his mouth and as their lips

met she felt her heart rising to her throat. *Don't ever leave me*, she was crying inside. *Please, don't ever go.* But then she smiled, laughing to herself at how gloomy she could be. It was going to be all right, really it was, and she must keep telling herself that.

'She looks lovely, doesn't she?' Jane said to Laurence as they waved Kirsten off in a taxi which was taking her to a lunch with an editor from Crowthers Publishing.

'Doesn't she?' Laurence answered, experiencing a pang of anxiety as he wondered how Kirsten would cope with the meeting. But she'd be fine, he told himself. He was worrying too much, after all she'd been much more herself this past twenty-four hours, even the dark shadows beneath her eyes were starting to fade. And the idea of writing a book had quite excited her when he'd read the letter out to her, it seemed that now she was allowing herself to think about the future again.

Closing the door he turned round and laughed when he saw Tom sulking at the end of the hall. 'Come on, soldier,' he said, 'she'll be back before you know it.'

'I wanted to go,' Tom pouted.

'I know you did, but she couldn't take you this time,' and shaking his head he said to Jane. 'He's like her shadow these days.'

'Kirsten says he's like yours,' Jane laughed. 'Want to play spacemen?' she asked Tom.

Tom rolled his eyes. 'That's a silly game.'

Jane looked at Laurence and grinning Laurence said, 'What do you want to do then? And don't say go with Kirstie.'

'I'm going to mow the lawn,' he said defiantly and stomped off down the hall to find his new lawnmower.

'He's settled in real well here,' Laurence remarked following Jane into the kitchen.

'Mmm, I know,' Jane said, picking up a tea towel and watching Tom through the window as he bumped his toy lawnmower up and down the garden. 'My life would be pretty empty without him,' she said softly. 'I can't bear to think of Pippa taking him away.'

'It won't come to that,' Laurence told her, feeling a dark shadow moving over his heart. 'He needs a brother or sister,' he said, half to himself, then glancing at Jane from the corner of his eye, 'What do you think? It would keep you pretty busy, that's for sure.'

Jane turned her eyes to Laurence's and to his surprise he saw that they were filling with tears.

'What is it?' he asked.

She shook her head. 'Nothing.'

Laurence's eyes closed as he belatedly realized that with so much going on around them they hadn't given much thought to Jane and how she must be feeling about what was happening. Obviously she was as terrified as he and Kirsten were that they were going to lose Tom. He wished there was something he could say to reassure her. Instead he put an arm around her and hugged her. 'I don't know how we'd have coped throughout all this without you,' he smiled, then almost laughed at the way those few words made her glow with pleasure. She was so easy to take for granted, seemed almost to encourage it, but just like anyone else she needed to know she was appreciated.

'I wish there was more I could do,' she said, dabbing at her eyes with the tea towel. 'I wish I could turn back the clocks and make it so that none of this was happening.'

– 611 –

She was starting to shake so sitting her down at the table he turned to the percolator and poured her a coffee.

'I'll tell you what,' he said, drawing up a chair to sit beside her, 'once this is all over we'll take a nice long holiday, mm? The four of us? How does that sound?'

Jane's answering smile made her mouth twitch. Her breathing was becoming laboured and tears were rolling down her cheeks. 'I'm sorry,' she gasped. 'I'm just so frightened.'

'There's nothing to be afraid of,' he soothed, taking the tea towel and wiping away the tears. 'Whatever happens no one's going to hurt him.'

'No,' she said, 'no one's going to hurt Tom.'

An hour and a half later Laurence was on the phone to his lawyer. Jane was in the garden with Tom picking up dead leaves and making sure that he didn't overhear the conversation.

'Things are looking up,' his lawyer was telling him. 'I don't want to get your hopes too high, but we could be in with a chance. It was a good move getting public sympathy behind Kirsten and the judge won't be too keen on a mother who just upped and walked out on her own son.'

'Do you know when Pippa's coming over?'

'Tomorrow, I believe. I've had a request through her lawyer for her to speak to you before going into court.'

'Through her lawyer?' Laurence said surprised. 'Why didn't she just call me herself?'

'Search me. My guess is she's going to try and persuade you to hand him over without going through all this.'

'She can try, but she won't succeed.'

'That's what I thought you'd say. I'll call you again when I know more.'

As Laurence was replacing the receiver Kirsten came in through the front door. He knew immediately from the way her eyes were sparkling that the lunch had gone well and he felt a lift in his heart to see her looking so happy. 'You'll never guess how much they've offered me!' she cried flinging her bag onto a chair.

'How much?'

'A hundred thousand pounds! Can you believe it?'

Laurence gaped at her in amazement, then laughing he swept her into his arms. God, did that publisher have any idea what he had done? This was exactly what Kirsten needed to help focus her mind on something other than what was happening now. 'I guess this calls for a celebration,' he said. 'Hang on, you did accept, didn't you?'

'Of course I did. At least I said I'd write the book, but I told them my agent would be in touch to discuss details.'

'Agent?'

'You, you idiot. You can do the negotiating for me and take the ten per cent. So come on, out with the champagne!'

'I've got some more good news,' Laurence said as he popped the cork. 'I've just spoken to my lawyer, he reckons our chances of keeping Tom have improved this past week.'

'Oh Laurence!' Kirsten cried, throwing her arms around him. 'That's fantastic news. Oh we'll win, we will, I just know it.'

34 –

The next morning Laurence, Kirsten, Jane and Tom were having a noisy breakfast in the kitchen when there was a knock on the door.

'I'll get it,' Kirsten said, taking a mouthful of coffee as she got up. 'It's probably the postman with another parcel of letters. And yes, OK, I could start the book at the point you suggested, but I think my idea's better.'

'You always think your ideas are better,' Laurence declared.

'Because they are.'

'Go get the door,' he laughed pouring Tom more orange juice, 'we'll talk about it later.'

Kirsten skipped off down the hall in her trainers and jogging suit, for one morning mercifully free of the nausea.

'Hi,' she said cheerfully to the two men standing in the drizzling rain. She looked from one to the other then suddenly it was as though everything was slipping from focus. The world was tilting, the menacing sky was swooping down on her, the wet pavements were rearing up at her.

'Good morning, Miss Meredith,' Detective Kowski grinned.

Nausea rose in her stomach. Blood roared in her ears.

'This is Detective Sergeant Fulmer of New Scotland Yard,' Kowski said as Fulmer pulled his badge from his pocket. 'He kinda knows your territory better than me so he's come along to advise.'

'On what?' Her broken voice seemed to come from a long way away.

'We got a number of questions we'd like to ask you, ma'am,' he answered. 'It'll be easier to speak over at the Yard.'

'Oh my God!' Kirsten muttered. 'Laurence! Laurence!'

'What is it?' Laurence said, coming out of the kitchen. Then seeing Kirsten's face he turned sharply to the two men. 'What's going on?' he demanded. 'Who are you? Kowski! What the hell are you doing here?'

'Pursuing enquiries,' Kowski answered, then turning back to Kirsten. 'You'll be needing your coat, ma'am,' he said, hunching himself into his collar.

'What kind of enquiries?' Laurence demanded.

'Enquiries concerning two cases of homicide in the Parish of New Orleans . . .'

'Homicide?' Kirsten repeated. She turned to Laurence, her luminous green eyes simmering with terror.

'This is crazy!' Laurence shouted. 'The New Orleans Coroner . . .'

'Certain evidence has now come to light,' Fulmer interrupted, 'that shows the Coroner's findings were . . . uh, incomplete. So, miss,' he went on, turning back to Kirsten, 'like Mr Kowski said, if you would get your coat and accompany us . . .'

'Are you arresting me?' Kirsten whispered, putting a hand to her head as though she could stop it spinning.

'We would like your help with our enquiries,' he responded tonelessly.

Again Kirsten looked up at Laurence. 'Isn't that the

same thing?' she said, trembling at the onslaught of panic.

Laurence looked to Kowski for the answer. 'It would be in your own interests to come.'

'But Kirsten wasn't even there when Jake died, so how can you -?'

'It will be easier if you'd come without a fuss,' Fulmer interrupted, looking at Kirsten.

Kirsten turned back inside.

'I'm coming with you,' Laurence said.

'I don't think that would serve any purpose at this time, sir,' Fulmer interceded.

'I don't want her questioned without a lawyer present,' Laurence snapped. 'I take it she does have that right.'

'Naturally.'

'Then where are you taking her?'

'New Scotland Yard,' Fulmer answered. 'For the time being.'

Laurence's eyes were blazing. 'And what's that supposed to mean?' he demanded.

Fulmer just looked at him, then stood aside for Kirsten to lead the way out to the car.

As Kowski opened the back door for her to get in Kirsten stumbled. Laurence rushed forward, but Kowski held her.

'It's OK,' Laurence heard her mumble. 'I'm OK.'

Her head was lowered, she didn't turn to look at Laurence, all she knew was the fear tearing at her heart and the painful throbbing in her head. She'd been a fool to dare to hope when she'd known all along that it would come to this. A muted voice was crying out inside her, telling her not to give up, but the feeling of resignation was overpowering. She couldn't even begin to imagine how they were going to prove she had killed Anna and Jake when she didn't even know how they'd died, but what she did know was that whoever had done it was clever enough to have deceived a State Coroner.

She jumped as Fulmer slammed his door and started up the engine. Would they allow her to keep her baby, she wondered, hugging herself as bitter tears stung her eyes. *You're innocent for God's sake!* the voice inside her screamed. She took a deep breath. Vaguely she was aware of Kowski talking beside her. He was saying something to Fulmer about a search warrant. They must be talking about her house, but they'd find nothing there. Suddenly she turned rigid and it was then that the final seal of resignation locked around her heart as she recalled the night she had thought someone was in the house. Something had been planted. Then there was the night she had come home to the tape – and Helena. Had something been planted then too?

Before the police car had even left the street Laurence was on the phone to his lawyer.

'Shit, I don't believe it,' Hellerman groaned. 'It couldn't have come at a worse time. Your chances of keeping Tom are right out the window now.'

'But she didn't do it, for Christ's sake!'

'Maybe not, but clearing her name before Friday's hearing is going to be just about impossible, you've got to face that, Laurence. And even if we could, the fact that she's been taken in . . . does anyone know? Were there any press hanging about?'

'Not that I know of.'

'Good. Keep it under wraps for as long as you can. Now, where have they taken her?'

'New Scotland Yard.'

'OK. I'm on my way. Meet me there.'

Twenty minutes later, as Laurence fought his way through the dense traffic of Victoria any hope he or Hellerman had of keeping things from the press were dashed the moment he turned on the radio. It had already made the ten o'clock news.

For over three hours Laurence paced a featureless room in New Scotland Yard waiting for Hellerman who had joined Kirsten and the two detectives in an interview room. Eventually Hellerman came out and one look at his face was enough to turn Laurence's stomach inside out.

'What's happening?' he asked, feeling as though his voice was being dredged from a bottomless pit.

'Good and bad,' Hellerman sighed, shaking his silvery head. 'Anna Sage and Jake Butler were definitely murdered. Don't ask me how – I'm not sure I understand it myself. Something to do with the mix of liquid nitrogen and oxygen in the dry-ice you use for fog. It kills in a matter of seconds and leaves no trace.'

'So how do they know now what it was?'

'They've received information, they're not saying who from yet . . .'

'It's got to be Dyllis Fisher,' Laurence stated. 'She told Campbell she could prove it was Kirsten.'

'You could be right,' Hellerman said. 'But remember she wasn't there when it was done. So there's someone else involved here.'

'Helena Johnson.'

Hellerman shook his head. 'I don't know. They're going to have to tell me eventually, but I'm going to recommend that Ernie Shore takes the case from here.

It's not my field and he's one of the best criminal lawyers . . .'

Laurence winced. 'What about bail?' he asked.

Hellerman was taking a mobile phone from his brief-case. 'You don't need to worry about that unless she's charged. But if she is, can you raise it?'

'I'll get it,' Laurence declared rashly.

Hellerman eyed him sceptically. 'If they don't charge her then there's a chance we can have her out of here before the end of the day,' he said. 'But if I were you, Laurence, I'd go back home and get Tom out of that house pretty sharpish.'

'Can't I see her?'

'Not yet, no. And to be frank, mate, the best thing you can do now is distance yourself as far from her as you can.'

'Are you serious? You think I'm going to run out on her at a time . . .'

'Be sensible, Laurence. You want to keep your son, don't you? Well you've really got your work cut out now. You heard the news I take it?'

'Yes.'

'Then do as I say. Go home, get Tom and take him to your parent's place.'

But for the moment Laurence couldn't see beyond what was happening there. 'The dry-ice?' he said. 'You say it was tampered with?'

Hellerman nodded. 'Put me on to Ernie Shore,' he said into the phone. He raised a hand as Laurence started to speak again. 'OK, have him call me on this number the minute he gets there. A matter of urgency, tell him.'

'But the forensic team checked those machines right

after Anna died,' Laurence said. 'They found nothing wrong with them.'

'No. They wouldn't. Apparently once out of a confined space the gas rebalances itself.'

Laurence was shaking his head. 'But how the hell would Kirsten know about something like that?'

'She probably doesn't, but how's she going to prove she doesn't?'

'I thought a person was innocent until proven guilty,' Laurence remarked savagely.

'So they tell me. But as far as the police are seeing it right now, Kirsten had a motive for killing Anna Sage. She also had a motive for getting rid of Jake Butler, or so they claim.'

'This can't be happening,' Laurence cried, dashing a hand through his already dishevelled hair. 'It's a fucking nightmare. It has to be. How's she taking it?'

'Pretty well, considering. Still a bit dazed though.'

'When will I be able to see her?'

'Laurence, think of Tom, will you? He's got to come first right now.'

It cut hard with Laurence to know that Hellerman was right and that there really was no more he could do for Kirsten at the moment, but in the end he had to accept it and telling Hellerman to call him the minute he heard anything Laurence returned to his car.

As he drove through the rain-soaked London streets the whole nightmare was running through his mind with a cruelty that made him want to lash out for the sheer madness of it. Who the hell could hate Kirsten so much to want to do this to her? Dyllis Fisher was the obvious answer, but like Hellerman said, Dyllis wasn't there when it happened. So had Dyllis paid someone to do it? Helena Johnson? Had Dyllis given Helena money to kill two people and make it look like Kirsten had done it? But Jesus Christ why? What reason could Helena have to hate Kirsten that much?

Almost missing a red light on Sloane Square he screeched to a halt then snatched up the car phone. A few seconds later he had Campbell on the line.

'Laurence, is that you?' Campbell cried through the interference. 'Where the hell are you? I've been trying to reach you!'

'I'm in the car on my way home,' Laurence shouted. 'Where's Helena?'

'The police have just taken her in.'

'Did she do it, Dermott? Tell me, I've got to know.'

'The honest answer? I don't know. I don't think she did, but, shit, Laurence . . .'

'What did she tell you about that tape?'

'She said she had nothing to do with it.'

'Yeah, well she isn't going to admit to it, is she? Not when she's trying to put Kirsten in the frame. Have you been able to find out anything more about what Dyllis knows?'

'Not really. Her secretary says she's never seen Helena anywhere near Dyllis's office. Do you know yet how they died?'

'Yeah. Something to do with the mix of dry-ice. Ring any bells?'

'No. All I know is that Helena told me Elizabeth Bradley tripped over one of those things when she was going to get help for Jake. It was how she broke her leg.'

'That's right,' Laurence said, 'she did. It set it off.' He was racking his brains to remember what else had happened that afternoon. Elizabeth had fallen, the dry-ice machine had tipped over . . . Hadn't Elizabeth said something about falling against the door? Yes, she had, that was why they had carried her to the drawing room, to get her out of the way so they could get inside to Jake. Christ, this could mean that Jake's death really was an accident. He'd been shut inside that room, already unconscious, with a lethal mix of chemicals . . . But why was the dry-ice there at that moment? Who was going to be playing that scene? Elizabeth, Frank . . . The camera boys would have been in there, sound, effects, Jesus, it would have killed the whole damned lot of them. Unless . . .

'Laurence, are you still there?' Campbell shouted through the static.

'Yeah, I'm here. Look Dermott, do me a favour,' he said, digging into his pocket for his address book. 'I'm going to give you the number of the chief location manager on the movie. Get in touch with him and ask him who was in charge of props the day Jake died. He'll have it there on the schedule. And ask him how many dry-ice machines were prepared for use that afternoon.'

'Got it,' Campbell said. 'Are you going to tell me what you're thinking?'

'That Jake's death was an accident. That someone took that machine from the store in all innocence and put it on the set for rehearsals. In other words, whoever tampered with it probably wasn't expecting it to leave the store when it did.'

'Shit,' Campbell muttered. 'Are you saying that it had been got ready for someone else?'

'That's what I'm saying. That's why I want to know how many machines were primed for use that day. If it was more than one, which it would have been because we were staging a fire, then I'll stake my life on the fact that someone had other plans for that particular cannister. It could well be that it was never intended for use on the set at all.'

'Meaning that someone, not Jake Butler, was scheduled for the Stygian ferry that day?'

'Maybe,' Laurence answered. 'But I don't want to get into that right now. I'll call you back in an hour.'

By now he had arrived home, but he continued to sit in the car, thoughts galloping through his head as randomly and anarchically as the rain beating against the windscreen. He was so tense that every muscle in his body jarred. He was so afraid that no reason could break through the disjointed maelstrom of his mind. He had to calm down, he knew that, but how the hell he was going to manage it was beyond him. But something wasn't adding up, he knew that, both he and Kirsten had missed something somewhere, but for the life of him he couldn't figure out what. Everything pointed so conclusively to Dyllis but, he had to ask himself, would a woman in Dyllis Fisher's position really go so far as to plot two murders in order to revenge herself on Kirsten? Sure, it took one hell of a brain to pull off something that could defy even a coroner, and doubtless Dyllis had that kind of brain. What was more she had Kirsten's neck in a noose now, which was where she'd always wanted it. But he couldn't believe that she'd put her own neck on the line by trying to frame up something like this. It was too risky, she'd stand to lose everything if she was found out, and she'd have to know that there was every chance she would be. And there it was again, that niggardly suspicion flickering elusively in his mind, that he was missing something somewhere, something so obvious and so vital that it was going to change the face of everything.

He got out of the car and walked to the front door.

His head was pounding, his hand barely steady as he inserted the key in the lock.

He closed the door behind him, saw a pile of mail on the table and next to it a well-thumbed copy of the Moyna O'Malley script. And it was then that it hit him – so forcefully, so blindingly and so repellently that his head jerked back as though the horrendous realization had struck him a physical blow. Ruby!

Ruby, with her stifling protectiveness . . . Her unnatural hatred of every woman he got close to . . . Her incessant struggle to make him her own . . . The changes in the script just before those two crucial scenes . . . The number of times dry-ice was referred to in the stage directions . . . .

'Jesus Holy Christ,' he muttered falling back against the door.

'Are you all right?'

He looked up to see Jane standing in the doorway of the kitchen.

'I thought I heard you come in,' she said in a tremulous voice. 'What's happening?'

What was happening? Jesus Christ, just that the world was ending, nothing more than that. That his own mother could do this to the woman he loved . . . That she could wreck his chances of keeping his son in the hope of having him all to herself. Jesus Christ! Ruby had even confessed to both murders but no one had taken her seriously!

'I'll explain later,' he said. 'Where's Tom?'

'Asleep.'

'Go and wake him, we're taking him to my parents.' Dear God, how was he going to deal with this? How was he going to face Thea when her animosity towards Kirsten was already something he could barely tolerate?

As Jane went upstairs the telephone rang. Laurence snatched it up.

'Laurence, hello there, it's Frank, Frank Cottle.'

'Oh yes, hello. She's right here.' Calling Jane, 'It's your father. Don't worry, I'll get Tom. And if your Dad's ringing because he's heard the news, if he's telling you to get the hell out of this mess then if I were you I'd do as he says.'

Laurence dragged himself upstairs to Tom's room. Though panic was driving shots of adrenalin through his body he made himself stop in the doorway and for a long time he simply stood looking down at his son's sleeping face. Of all the emotions that had run through his heart that day he knew that nothing, just nothing in the world could be as powerful as what he felt for that little scrap of humanity. But he wouldn't think beyond that, he couldn't. For the likelihood that he was going to lose him had already become a raw, open wound in his heart.

After taking Tom to his parents' Laurence returned to Kirsten's to let in the uniformed officers who had come to search the house. He was surprised that the police hadn't asked to interview him yet, but knew that it couldn't be long in coming. He'd tried several times over the past couple of hours to get hold of Hellerman again but so far he hadn't succeeded. There was no reply from Ruby's either. In fact it was as if the whole goddamned world had gone walkabout, because even Campbell hadn't got back to him yet.

While the police went systematically through all Kirsten's possessions Laurence sat in the study, going over and over in his mind all the details he could remember of what had happened just prior to Anna's and Jake's deaths. In Anna's case Ruby had been right there – she had keeled over drunk just as they were going for a take. Had it been an act? Was everything, her dementia, her drunkenness, her religion and all the other crazy stuff she got involved with, just a performance designed to mislead them? It was hard to tell. And even harder, given where he'd been himself just before Jake's death, to know where Ruby was. She was around the set, that was for sure because she'd barged into Kirsten's trailer, but he had no idea where she'd gone from there. However he did know that she'd gone running off somewhere screaming like a banshee right after Jake had been declared dead. Had she done that because she thought that goddamned coconut junk was coming true again, or was it because she'd killed the wrong person?

He slumped forward across the desk, burying his face in his hands. He felt so tired suddenly, so drained of energy and emotion. He didn't want to believe that Ruby was guilty but it sure was looking that way. Except the tape ... Why would she have arranged something like that? And how the hell had Dyllis Fisher got to find out so much? Surely to God Ruby wouldn't have told her. As far as he was aware the two women didn't even know one another.

He looked up as a police officer popped his head round the door to tell him they were finished. He went to show them out wondering what they had found to take away with them. He didn't bother to ask, he knew they wouldn't tell him.

After trying Ruby's number again and still getting no reply he drove back to his parents. On the way Campbell called him. He hadn't managed to get hold of the location manager yet, it could be though that he was down at the Yard being questioned along with everyone else.

So why wasn't he himself, Laurence wondered. As the producer he'd have thought he'd be one of the first they'd pull in. Still, he guessed they'd get round to it when they were ready.

Half an hour later when Jane had taken Tom into the garden, Laurence's father was going pedantically over everything that had happened that morning. Laurence was barely listening. He was watching Thea's face wondering what she was thinking, and why as yet, she hadn't said a word. In the end he couldn't take her silence any longer and cutting his father off mid-sentence he shouted,

'Mother, if you've got something to say then damn well say it!'

Thea's eyes widened with surprise, but before she could speak Laurence said, 'I guess you're over the moon that this is happening, that you're hoping I'll turn my back on Kirsten and leave her to rot in some goddamned cell for something she didn't even do. Well, let me tell you – '

'That's enough, Laurence!' his father barked.

'Believe it or not, Laurence, I'm as upset as you are,' Thea told him, cutting short his next tirade, 'and not only because of what it could mean to you and Tom, but because I'm fully prepared to admit when I've made a mistake about someone. Kirsten needs help right now and this family is going to give it. If it comes to it I will put up the bail money myself. I will also cover all the legal expenses. If there's anything else, financial or otherwise, then you have only to ask.'

Laurence turned away, still too angry to confront his shame or the emotion his mother's words had engendered, but when she came to sit beside him and slipped her hand into his he clung on to it so tightly that Thea turned his face into her shoulder and held him.

At last, around five in the evening, the telephone rang. Laurence jumped on it.

'It's like a bloody circus over here,' Hellerman grumbled. 'Dyllis Fisher's been in, half the cast and crew from that movie of yours . . .'

'Never mind that, how's Kirsten?'

Hellerman paused and Laurence's heart stopped.

'The news isn't good, I'm afraid,' Hellerman said gravely. 'They're about to charge her.'

'But they can't!' Laurence cried. 'She didn't do it! It was Ruby. Listen to me.' He was aware of the exchange of glances between his parents, almost felt the ripple of shock as it went through them.

'Ruby's just left,' Hellerman interrupted. 'She's been here all day.'

'What! Oh my God, what the hell's she been telling them?'

'I can't answer that, but what I can tell you is that they found the formula for mixing the dry-ice in Kirsten's house. And they've got a witness here who says he saw Kirsten tampering with the canisters on both occasions.'

'He?' Laurence repeated. 'Who is it?'

'I don't know his name. I haven't seen him either. Hang on, just a second.'

Laurence could hear Hellerman's muted voice at the other end as he spoke to someone, then he came back on the line. 'I'm sorry, Laurence,' he said. 'They've just charged her. First degree murder on both counts.'

It was just after seven o'clock when Hellerman called again to say that Kirsten was to appear in front of the magistrate at ten-thirty the next morning. 'We'll apply for bail,' he said. 'I don't know if we'll get it, but I should warn you, the seriousness of the charges make it doubtful.'

'They've got the wrong person,' Laurence said, his voice strangled with emotion. 'I'm telling you, it was Ruby.'

'Can you prove it?'

'No.'

Hellerman sighed. 'You do realize that even if you're right, Laurence, it won't change the situation as far as Tom's concerned? Even if we could get the charges dropped against Kirsten we wouldn't be able to do it in time for the hearing now.'

'I know,' Laurence said, unable to keep the defeat from his voice. 'How's she bearing up?' he asked.

'Quite well,' Hellerman answered, knowing that it would serve no purpose to tell Laurence the truth. Kirsten was sick, even the police were agreed on that which was why a doctor had been called in just after the charges had been read out.

'If you get the chance, James, tell her I love her.'

'Of course,' Hellerman answered.

When Laurence rang off he took himself upstairs and lay down on the bed with Tom. His feelings were so near the surface that only with superhuman effort did he manage to stop himself crushing Tom in his arms, as if by doing so he could join their two bodies in such a way that no one could ever tear them apart. Instead, he simply lay there beside him, gazing at his heartrendingly handsome little face and wondering how in the hell he was going to cope with losing him.

After a while Thea came into the darkened room and sat with them. 'We've given Jane the night off,' she said softly. 'Apparently her father called her today and wanted to know what was going on. I thought it was best she go see them so Dad's just driven her home.'

'Thanks,' Laurence whispered. 'I should have done it myself.'

'Are you going to speak to Ruby?' Thea asked after a while.

'Yeah. I'll go see her in the morning before I see Pippa.'

'Pippa's here, darling. She arrived about ten minutes ago.'

It was only then, when Laurence turned to look at her, that Thea saw the tears on his cheeks and reached out for his hand.

'I'm going to tell her to take him,' Laurence said, his voice catching in his throat as he turned back to Tom.

'Yes, I guessed as much,' Thea said.

'I can't put him through it when I know already that I'm going to lose. You understand that, don't you?'

'Yes, darling, I understand. So does your father.'

'The question is though, will Tom?' Laurence said, closing his eyes at the desperate sense of loss that swept through him.

— **35** —

She sat alone at an upstairs window staring out into the dawn. Her face was ashen. Her heart was lead. Beside her the baby lay silently in its cradle. It didn't cry anymore. It hadn't cried for some time. Its skin, once so warm and soft, was now cold and cracked. The downy lashes were brittle and matted.

She had no idea what she was going to do now. She couldn't think, her mind was as motionless as the photographs she held in her lap. She didn't look at them. Her neck was rigid, her head wouldn't move.

Somewhere, not too far from here, fates were being sealed and hearts were breaking. A chasm of devastation cleaved open inside her. It was as though it was squeezing away her soul, emptying her body and making her a void. Soon she wouldn't exist any more. Even the shell of her skin would disappear.

Her head fell forward as burning sobs tore at her throat. The calmness in her mind was so brutal, more brutal even than the torment. It forced her to see the eroded edges of her sanity, the danger of her desperation.

She lifted a hand to the window, as though to reach out to the rising sun. Her fingers stabbed against the transparent wall between her and life. Her wide eyes stared out at the distant trees. The bare branches stood like arteries against the bloody sky. They were like the veins of her mind, brittle and jagged, forlorn and devoid of everything beautiful. She felt their urgency for nature's loving hand – for them it would come, but for her there was nothing now, nothing at all . . .

The next morning, just after nine thirty, Kirsten was ushered out of a back door of Scotland Yard, bundled into a waiting car and driven to the magistrates court. James Hellerman and Ernie Shore, the criminal barrister, were waiting for her. An hour later, after bail had been set for a less staggering sum than expected, Hellerman drove her home.

When they arrived he went in with her. She looked pale and tired almost to the point of exhaustion, but on the whole she seemed better than she had the night before. It was the surprising turn in events that had come just after nine o'clock that morning that had given her this temporary revival in spirits and an unthought for freedom. The voice on the tape had been identified – it belonged to the very man who was giving evidence against her. In light of that it had taken Ernie Shore very little time to convince the magistrate that Kirsten could be precisely what she was claiming to be – the victim of an unscrupulous conspiracy. In fact, as they'd left the court, Shore had been laughing, so confident was he that they would soon get all charges against Kirsten dismissed.

How much Kirsten had taken in of what was being said was hard to tell, but a little colour had returned to her cheeks and unless Hellerman was greatly mistaken there was the tiniest flicker of hope in her eyes. As yet, none of them knew who the man giving evidence was, but Kowski himself had gone along with the other officers to escort him back to Scotland Yard immediately the results of the voice test were known.

Now, as Kirsten went through the mechanical process of lighting a fire, Hellerman offered to fix her something to eat. She smiled, told him she wasn't hungry and continued with the fire until the flames were roaring spiritedly up the chimney.

At last she sat down. Hellerman waited for her to speak, but when it was apparent she wasn't going to, he said, 'I think we can safely assume that whoever the man is he's the one who's been giving Dyllis Fisher her information. Whether or not he committed the murders though is another matter. We'll probably know more later today. But to have bungled over something like that tape suggests an ineptitude that is not in keeping with the brilliant execution of the killings. Nevertheless, it is a carelessness for which he is going to pay dearly.'

'Do you think,' Kirsten said hoarsely, 'is there any chance that I might be cleared before the custody hearing tomorrow?'

Hellerman's sun-weathered face showed the compassion and admiration he felt for this woman whose prime concern, despite all she was facing herself, was for the man she loved. 'It's doubtful,' he said. 'But even if by some miracle you were, there's an added complication I'm afraid.'

Kirsten turned to look at him.

'Laurence thinks, is convinced, that Ruby is in some way involved in what's been going on. He hasn't spoken to the police yet, but as soon as he does she will be questioned and as Laurence's mother . . . Well, I'm sure you don't need me to spell it out . . .

As he was speaking he was watching what little colour there was in Kirsten's face drain away. Suddenly her hand went to her mouth and excusing herself she ran to the bathroom.

She was gone for some time during which Hellerman wondered if he should go to check on her. But as a father he knew there was really nothing anyone could do for a woman in the early stages of pregnancy. His heart went out to her, having to cope with all that was going on while her body was responding so treacherously to its hormonal change, it was no wonder she had virtually passed out when the police had charged her. He couldn't even begin to imagine the fear she must have felt for herself and her child at that moment. Hellerman was convinced that Laurence didn't know about the pregnancy, if he did he would have certainly mentioned it by now. Hellerman himself wouldn't have known unless the police had told him after the doctor had examined her. For now he would keep the knowledge to himself, it wasn't his place to interfere in matters of that nature.

When finally Kirsten came back looking haggard and drawn and smelling of toothpaste Hellerman smiled at her kindly.

'How's Laurence?' she asked.

'I haven't spoken to him yet today,' Hellerman answered, 'but he was pretty shaken up last night. He's worried about the custody hearing tomorrow, naturally, though his main concern right now is that you're all right.'

'Tell him I am, won't you? Tell him not to worry about me at all. I'll be fine.'

Not long after that Hellerman left and Kirsten huddled into a blanket trying to stop herself shivering. If only she could speak to Laurence, just to hear his voice might calm her a little, but the lawyer had told her she shouldn't. It helped to know that the police were now starting to believe that she had had nothing to do with the murders, that they were, perhaps, getting close now to who had actually done it. She wondered if Laurence was right about Ruby, but her mind shied away from what it would mean if he was ... So much had happened within the past twenty-four hours that emotionally it was hard to feel anything now. But what a relief it had been to receive Laurence's message last night, when he'd asked Hellerman to tell her he loved her. She had been terrified that he was blaming her for what this would do to his custody case for Tom.

But she had to face the fact, just as Laurence would have to, that Pippa was going to take Tom away. Were Tom her own child Kirsten couldn't have loved him more and the thought of losing him was tearing her apart. But God only knew what it was doing to Laurence. Nothing could ever make up for the gap he would leave in Laurence's life, not even the baby she was carrying.

As Laurence drove through the streets of South London his mind was concentrated rigidly on the task ahead. He wouldn't allow himself to think about the meeting with Pippa last night, that was something he'd have to deal with later. For now he had to sort out in his mind exactly what he was going to say to Ruby and how, if he was right about her, he was going to hold himself back from smashing her whole goddamned life to pieces the way she was doing with his.

The car phone rang. It was Hellerman telling him that Kirsten was home. Straight away Laurence dialled Kirsten's number. 'I was just starting to panic,' he said when her voice finally came on the line.

'I was in the shower,' she said. 'How are you?'

'I'm doing just fine. How about you?'

'Better now. How's Tom?'

As a lump rose in Laurence's throat he found himself unable to answer.

'Laurence? Are you still there?'

'Sure. Tom's OK.'

'Where are you now?'

'On my way to Ruby's.

'Hellerman told me what you told him. Laurence, are you sure about this? I mean . . .'

'No, I'm not sure,' he interrupted. 'That's why I want to speak to her before I speak to the cops. Did they tell you exactly how it was done?'

'Not really. I imagine you already know that it was to do with the dry-ice, but as Kowski put it, "what we have here is tantamount to the perfect murder", so I don't expect they'll ever tell us exactly how it was done. What they did tell me though was what it does to you.'

'Which is?'

'Apparently, when you inhale it it hits the muscle that controls the larynx first, so you can't shout. It happens in seconds. The next muscles to go are the leg muscles so you can't move, and within less than a minute you're dead. It can only happen in a confined space and as soon as you let more oxygen into the room it ceases to be lethal. Kowski says it would take a physicist to work out something like that.'

'Or an effects guy, a props guy, a scene hand, anyone who works with the stuff. Or a writer who makes it her business to research what she does to the point of actually carrying it out. Anyway, I guess we're going to find out soon enough and all that matters to me is that you're where you are. You sure you're OK?'

'Sure. Still a bit numb, I suppose, but better now I've spoken to you.'

'Go see if you can get some sleep,' he said, wondering if he should tell her what was in his mind. In the end he decided he had to. 'Sweetheart, I want you to lock all the doors. I don't want to scare you and I'm pretty sure there's nothing to be scared of, but don't let's take any chances.'

'What do you mean?'

'I mean that I think Jake's death was an accident. That there was every chance that particular canister of dry-ice had been made up for someone else . . .'

'Laurence, you're frightening me. Are you saying that someone might come here to try to . . .? Maybe I shouldn't be here. Maybe I should go out.'

'Yeah, maybe you should. Go over to my parents. Call yourself a cab right now and get yourself over there. My father's right here with me, but Thea's there with Tom.'

'But . . .'

'Please, Kirstie, do as I say. We're almost at Ruby's now so I'm going to ring off. I'll call you again later.'

'OK. I miss you.'

'I miss you, too.'

As Laurence pulled the car to a halt outside the mansion block he gazed up at the dirty windows of Ruby's apartment. His father was silent beside him, neither one of them was relishing what they had to do. If they were wrong there was no calculating the hurt they were going to cause her, but if they were right . . .

'I guess we should start by finding out if she's still at home,' Don said.

Laurence turned to look at him.

'It's been over half an hour since you called to tell her you were coming,' Don explained. 'Kirsten's release has been on the news since then.'

Helena was at the wheel of her rusty 2CV. Her progress through the dense traffic of central London was slow, but her mood was cheerful. In fact she was humming along to the radio. Since Dermott had gone off to Scotland Yard for further questioning and Dyllis, according to the news, had been pulled in again too, Helena had checked out of the Bloomsbury Hotel where she and Campbell had been staying and returned to her apartment. It was just as she was pouring herself a coffee that the news had come on announcing that Kirsten had been granted bail. Immediately Helena had gathered up a few things, taken them down to the car and headed off towards Kirsten's.

So, Kirsten was free, she was thinking to herself, and she, Helena, was off the hook. At least she assumed she was, if she wasn't then surely the police would have called her in again too.

She checked her mirror, half expecting to see a cop car behind. Maybe there was, but who could tell in this kind of traffic? In fact, now she came to think about it this snarl-up was beginning to get on her nerves. She could always come out of it by heading down to the Embankment, not that the traffic would be any lighter there, she guessed, but by then she might have a better idea as to whether or not she was being followed and then she could come to a decision as to whether or not she should continue on to Kirsten's or take a circuitous route back home. She imagined going home might be the best idea because it wasn't very likely Kirsten was going to let her in, but still she'd see . . . Maybe she would give it a shot – after all, with the way things stood right now, what did she have to lose?

'I, like the Lord our Saviour, ask the Lord our God to forgive you, for you know not what you doeth,' Ruby declared solemnly. 'Deliver unto me a cross and I shall bear it through the streets of London whereupon you may crucify me for sins I have not committed.'

Laurence glanced at his father. Don was staring at

the woman to whom he had been so briefly married, who had borne him a son whom he loved and who had, over the years, changed beyond recognition so that for the moment it was as though he had forgotten the purpose of their visit as he gazed in sadness at this stranger. How beautiful she had once been, how proud and defiant – and how she had broken his heart when she had chosen her career over him and Laurence. There was barely a vestige of her beauty now and there was no pride in the crumpled, stained silk suit she wore, nor in the faded furnishings that seemed to reflect the dearth of love in her life. There was however a hint of defiance in the way she tilted her glass of gin and emptied it between her painted lips. It almost made him smile.

'Laurence, my son,' she sighed, 'if you'd come here before, if you'd spoken to me when I called I could have told you who was doing this to you. But no one wants to listen to me, I am as ignored as the child within you.'

'Ruby,' Laurence said tightly. 'Let's just quit talking in riddles, shall we? If you know who killed Anna and Jake then for God's sake tell us.'

'I'm telling you,' she said. 'It's just like the coconut kid said, it's the child within us all. The one who goes unnoticed, the one we all take for granted, the one you have allowed to mother and smother your son . . .'

Laurence's face was starting to freeze. His father started to speak, but Laurence put out a hand to stop him. What Ruby was saying was insane, crazy, it was so goddamned ludicrous . . . but shock and disbelief gave way to fear as he remembered a telephone call he had taken just the day before when he'd returned from Scotland Yard. 'Jesus Christ Almighty!' he murmured, then pushing his way past Ruby he snatched up the phone and started to dial.

'What is it?' his father cried. 'What – who are you talking about, Ruby?'

'Mary fucking Poppins,' Ruby answered. 'Who else?'

– 36 –

It hadn't been Kirsten's intention to fall asleep right after she'd spoken to Laurence, it was simply that the moment she'd put the phone down she'd felt suddenly so weary that she hadn't had the energy to stand up. Deciding to give herself a moment or two to gather her resources she'd sunk back on the bed and the next thing she knew almost half an hour had gone by.

Now, as she struggled to her feet, she was hoping that the rest of her pregnancy wasn't going to be as taxing as these early weeks for even though it seemed she was no longer destined to spend them in prison, she didn't much relish the idea of spending them flat on her back either.

Smiling to herself, she went into the bathroom to freshen up. The truth was she'd happily endure anything that meant she'd hold Laurence's baby in her arms at the end of it. Even as she grimaced at her mawkishness her heart seemed to trip over the flood of joy that rushed into it. She laughed and pressed her hands to her cheeks. It was so hard to believe that everything really was going to be all right now, that they were close to finding out who really had killed Anna and Jake, that she could tell Laurence about the baby, that they could work towards fulfilling their dreams . . . Oh, please, please, please, God, she prayed, clasping her hands together, let us be able to keep Tom. Let us stay together.

Suddenly the warmth drained from her smile and she turned to look out of the bathroom, across the bedroom to the open door leading to the landing. In the same instant that she heard the noise again she recalled Laurence warning her either to lock the doors or go to his mother's.

'Oh my God,' she breathed, praying that she was mistaken, that the noise had come from outside. But no, there was definitely someone moving about downstairs and whoever it was didn't seem to care that they might be heard.

Maybe, she thought, they didn't realize she was in here. If that was the case then perhaps she could close her bedroom door and call the police without them knowing she'd done it.

She started towards the phone then jumped back as it suddenly shrilled into the room. To her amazement after two rings it stopped then she heard Jane's voice downstairs saying hello.

Immediately Kirsten relaxed and only then did she realize how furiously her heart was beating, that her entire body had broken out in a sweat. She waited a moment, then hearing Jane replace the receiver, she went back into the bathroom to brush out her wet hair.

A few minutes later, still wearing her towelling robe, she tripped lightly down the stairs feeling stronger than she had done in days. By now though, she was getting used to the fact that her energy only came in short bursts so she was glad to think Jane was there, if only to help a pregnant old lady out to the taxi when it came.

'Hi,' she said, seeing Jane standing in the doorway of the kitchen. 'You gave me quite a fright just now, I didn't hear you come in. How did you know I was home?'

'I heard it on the news,' Jane answered.

'Of course. Who was that on the phone?'

'Just my dad ringing to see if I'd got here all right.'

Kirsten nodded and wondered why Jane continued to stand in the doorway as though . . . Kirsten's head went to one side, curious . . . as though she was barring the way. 'Are you all right?' she asked.

'Yes, yes, I'm fine,' Jane said, her teeth baring in the nervous giggle Kirsten hadn't seen in weeks. 'How are you?'

'Right at this moment it's hard to put into words. Are you sure you're OK?' Kirsten said, looking at Jane closely.

'Yes. Yes, I'm fine,' Jane repeated.

Kirsten shrugged then turned into the sitting room. As she picked up the bellows to liven up the fire she was wondering if Jane was reacting to the belief that she might have killed someone. Kirsten sighed, watching a fountain of sparks fly up the chimney. What was she going to say to put Jane at her ease?

She had already drawn breath to call out to Jane when she turned to look over her shoulder and found Jane standing so close to her that the air was expelled from her lungs in a breath of surprised laughter. 'There you are,' she said. 'I thought you'd gone into the kitchen.'

Jane looked at her, her pinched, pale face as motionless as her staring eyes. 'Why did they let you go?' she said.

Kirsten blinked. Then suddenly her stomach heaved. 'Oh Christ,' she muttered and clasping a hand to her mouth she ran past Jane and into the downstairs bathroom.

'Sorry about that,' she said, coming out a few minutes later still watery-eyed and slightly breathless. 'It must be the food they gave me yesterday.'

Jane was standing in the hall, watching her with that same deadened expression.

Kirsten smiled awkwardly. 'Shall we have a cup of tea?' she said, waving an arm towards the kitchen.

'Why did they let you go?' Jane repeated.

'Well,' Kirsten said, eyeing her curiously, 'mainly because I didn't do it. And because they've identified the voice on the tape.'

'Whose voice was it?'

'I'm still not sure yet. Jane, at the risk of repeating myself, are you sure you're all right?'

Jane turned away, walked into the sitting room and picked up a bundle of blankets.

'What have you got there?' Kirsten asked, going in after her.

Jane cradled the bundle to her meagre chest, lowering her head so that Kirsten could no longer see her face. Kirsten was on the point of repeating the question when she heard footsteps on the stairs and turned round.

'Tom!' she cried, seeing his little face peeping over the banister.

'Granny bought me a new train,' he said. 'I've been playing with it.'

'Have you?' Kirsten said, feeling a strangeness in the air she couldn't quite comprehend.

'Want to play too?' Tom offered.

'Um, uh, yes,' Kirsten answered.

'No,' Jane said as Kirsten started towards him. Her voice was muffled by the blankets, strangled by tears.

Kirsten paused.

'Don't, Kirsten, please,' Jane begged, lifting her head to look at Kirsten. Kirsten looked back, perplexed and oddly unnerved by the intensity of feeling that was making Jane's normally bland face almost unrecognizable. After a moment she turned to Tom. His wide blue eyes moved anxiously between Kirsten and Jane.

'Jane, you're frightening him,' Kirsten said softly.

'Tom, go upstairs and play with your trains.' Jane's thin, choked voice held an unexpected note of command.

Tom looked at Kirsten.

'Go on, sweetheart,' Kirsten said. 'I'll be up in a minute.'

Obediently Tom turned round and climbed back up the stairs.

'Jane, what is going on?' Kirsten demanded. 'What's happened to you? I've never seen you like this before.'

Jane looked at her for a long time, then suddenly something in her seemed to fracture and to Kirsten's amazement she could see an unsteady emotion beginning to surface. 'You don't care what's happened to me,' Jane sobbed. 'You don't care about anything except yourself and Laurence.'

'But that's not true. Of course I care about you,' Kirsten insisted.

Jane was shaking her head, jerking it backwards and forwards almost as though she didn't know what she was doing. 'No, no you don't. You want to get rid of me. I heard you telling Laurence.'

Kirsten's head was starting to spin. 'You must have misunderstood . . .'

'No, I understood,' Jane interrupted. 'I heard what you said. I was there in the room when you said you felt as though you'd stepped into Pippa's shoes. You didn't mind taking Laurence and Tom, but you didn't want me.'

'Oh God,' Kirsten groaned. 'You did misunderstand.'

'No! You never had any time for me, you never held me the way you hold Tom . . .'

'But Jane, he's just a child.'

A hot colour was flooding Jane's cheeks, her teeth were bared in a quivering grimace of heightening emotion. Tears flowed from her eyes as mucus seeped from her nose. 'He's not your child though is he?'

'No, he's not mine, but . . .'

'It was me who told him to call you Mummy. I did that for you . . .' To Kirsten's amazement Jane raised a hand as though to strike her. Kirsten caught it, squeezing the frail bones in her grip.

For a moment, Jane's eyes bored into hers, then, quite suddenly, the fight seemed to leave her and pulling her hand free she sat down on the sofa with her bundle of blankets. 'Sssh, sssh,' she soothed, 'there's no need to cry. Mummy's here.'

A curl of unease twisted through Kirsten's gut. 'Jane,' she said, moving tentatively towards her.

Jane raised her head and Kirsten stopped, arrested by the inexplicable sadness that was now suffusing the pale, grey eyes. 'Do you want to hold him?' Jane said.

Kirsten stared down at the bundle Jane was offering. Jane's delicate fingers pulled open the blankets. The instant Kirsten saw the tiny face a hand flew to her mouth to stifle the scream as she recoiled in horror. 'Jane, for God's sake what is this?' she gasped.

'He's just a baby,' Jane answered.

Kirsten's heart was pounding. She lowered her eyes again to the huge staring blue eyes, the cupid-bow mouth and the hideous black cracks that were fracturing the lifeless white face.

'Sometimes I used to pretend he was yours,' Jane said. 'I pretended that you'd lied to Laurence about the abortion and that I was looking after him for you.'

A sob of disgust and fear erupted in Kirsten's throat. How could Jane have harboured this kind of madness and no one ever have noticed?

'Here, take him,' Jane offered again. 'He's a very good baby.'

Kirsten started to back away. 'I don't want to hold him,' she said. 'He's not . . .'

A feral rage contorted Jane's face, so suddenly and so terrifyingly that Kirsten reeled back as though she'd been struck. Jane ripped away the blankets, swung the baby into the air and hurled it savagely against the wall. 'Then I don't want him either,' she screamed.

Kirsten watched in horrified disbelief as the fragile body smashed in a thousand pieces and tiny fingers and toes scattered over the floor.

As the final remnant of porcelain came to rest Kirsten lifted her eyes back to Jane. Jane's grief stricken eyes were fixed sightlessly ahead, her hands were pushed together in her lap.

Long minutes ticked by before Jane's head suddenly jerked towards Kirsten. 'I know you got rid of the baby, I know you did it to punish Laurence for leaving you,' she cried, 'but I didn't want you to be like that. I wanted you to be kind and care about him.'

Kirsten's head was throbbing. So many horrifying thoughts were looming from the corners of her mind that she couldn't make herself think straight. The baby chimes on the phone, the female voice sobbing her name . . . What the hell was it all about? Why was Jane so tormented by an abortion that had happened so long ago, that had been nothing to do with her?

'He had the most beautiful mother in the world,' Jane cried beating her fists on her lap, 'but you didn't want him. You didn't care about him . . .'

'If he'd lived I would have,' Kirsten said, so stunned she hardly knew what she was saying.

'No. No you wouldn't,' Jane cried, shaking her head vehemently. 'You never wanted him. You never wanted any children, it was why you got rid of me too. I was prepared to forgive you, in the beginning . . . I did forgive you. And I loved you . . . but you never loved me.'

'Jane,' Kirsten breathed, 'I don't understand what – '

Jane's grey eyes were glittering, her lips were a tight line of resentment. 'Why did you tell everyone you got rid of me!' she said. 'Why did you tell them I was aborted when you knew it wasn't true?'

Kirsten looked at her, so shocked that nothing in her could respond.

'Well say something!' Jane cried, saliva collecting at the corners of her mouth as her cheeks quivered with frustration.

'I don't know what to say,' Kirsten answered. 'I don't know what you're talking about.'

'Liar! *Liar! Liar! Liar!* You know who you are. You know who I am and what I am to you, so stop all these lies, Kirsten – '

'Jane . . .'

'Jane? Is that the name you chose for me? Or did you let someone else choose it? How well did you know me when you let me go, Kirsten – when you gave me to strangers? Well enough to name me? Did you ever feed me?'

'In God's name, Jane, what are you talking about?'

'Stop pretending!' Jane screamed, leaping to her feet. 'You're my mother! You know you are, so stop lying!'

Kirsten's eyes darted towards the stairs. She was so stunned that for the moment the only coherent thought in her head was that Tom shouldn't hear any of this.

'Why did you tell everyone you'd got rid of me?' Jane raged on, her face strained with bitterness. 'Why did you tell them you had an abortion when the truth was you gave me away? Your own child, a defenceless baby not even a year old and you gave me away. Why, Kirsten? Why did you give me away?'

'Jane,' Kirsten whispered, 'I'm not your mother . . . .'

'*You are*! You are, you are! Was it because my father left you?'

'Jane, please listen to me. I'm not your mother . . .'

'Stop lying! You're my mother. Look at me, can't you see the resemblance? I look like you . . .'

'Jane, you're nothing like me and even if you were, it's just not possible.'

'It is! You're my mother and Laurence is my father! We're a family!'

'Oh God,' Kirsten groaned, burying her face in her hands. 'Jane, please believe me. I'm not your mother. I can't be your mother because I never had a child. Never, do you hear me? And even if I had that child still couldn't be you.'

'Why?' Jane cried, her brilliant eyes gleaming the challenge. 'Why couldn't it be me? Because I'm not pretty enough?'

'Oh God, Jane, what do I have to say to convince you?'

'You can admit to the truth, that's what you can do. You can admit that I'm a part of you, that you carried me in your womb.'

'Jane!' I've never carried a child beyond three months, but even if I had it could never have been you. You're too young. I was fifteen when I was pregnant, I'm thirty-seven now and you're only twenty-two.'

'You see, it adds up.'

'No, it doesn't! You're not allowing for the other six months I'd have had to carry you. I'd have been sixteen by then, well and truly sixteen. But even so, Jane, I had an abortion.'

'No, it's not true,' Jane said, banging her fists together. 'It can't be true. You're my mother, I know you are. And Laurence is my father.'

'Jane, I didn't even know Laurence then.'

Jane's nostrils were flared, her teeth were clamped together and her eyes glittered as she stared sightlessly into the fire. 'Laurence is my father,' she whispered. 'I know he is. And you are my mother.' Her eyes came up to Kirsten's. 'Please say it's true,' she begged.

Kirsten merely looked at her.

'I can prove it,' Jane said.

Kirsten took a breath as she pushed her fingers through her hair.

'I've got the pictures,' Jane declared, tears of desperation spilling down her cheeks. 'I can show you. I've got them here,' and before Kirsten could stop her she had run into the kitchen and picked up her album.

'Here,' she said, offering it to Kirsten. 'Here are all the pictures of when you and Laurence got married. When you had me . . .'

Not knowing what else to do Kirsten took the album. Jane came to stand beside her and Kirsten could feel the trembling of her slight body. 'See here,' Jane said triumphantly as Kirsten turned to the first page. 'There you are on your wedding day.'

Kirsten's heart contracted as she looked down at the photograph that had had Pippa's face cut from it and her own glued on beside Laurence's.

Excitedly, Jane turned to the next page. 'See here,' she said, 'this was when I was born.' And there was a picture of Kirsten, one that Laurence had taken six years ago, with a tiny black and white snapshot of a baby stuck to it. Fleetingly she remembered Jane once telling her that Laurence had kept the photographs in the attic of his Kensington home. Obviously this was where Jane had got them.

On the next page was another photograph from the same era, this time of Kirsten and Laurence together and added to it was a picture of the baby Kirsten now recognized to be Jane. Around the picture of Jane were the same scissored edges as before. There were more, many more, and as Kirsten went through them, despite the fear mounting inside her, she felt as though her heart was breaking. It seemed that the only pictures Jane had been able to find of herself were those of when she was less than a year old and those that Kirsten and Laurence had taken when they were in New Orleans. There was nothing in between.

'So you see, it's all there,' Jane said, tearing her eyes from a photograph of Kirsten, Laurence, Tom and herself that a waiter had taken for them at the Café du Monde and gazing beseechingly into Kirsten's face. 'We're a family. I know you don't want me, I know you're trying to get rid of me again, but Laurence won't let you.'

Silently Kirsten closed the album, put it down on the coffee table and turned to take Jane in her arms. As she held her she felt Jane's fragile body start to convulse.

'That's it,' Kirsten soothed, stroking Jane's hair as

the sobs tore painfully through Jane's chest and her scalding tears soaked Kirsten's shoulder. 'Let it all out. Come on now, no one's going to hurt you.'

Jane's grip tightened, but after a while she pulled away. 'Will you let me call you Mummy?' she asked, her eyes still glistening with tears.

'Oh Jane, Jane . . .' Kirsten groaned, putting a hand to her head.

'Just once, please!' Jane whispered.

When Kirsten didn't answer Jane turned to the sofa and sat down hugging her spindly knees to her chest. 'I just had that doll,' she said softly. 'That was all I ever had. I pretended it was a baby, a real, live baby that loved me. I could even hear him crying sometimes. I mean I know he didn't cry really, but I could hear it. I used to talk to him because I had no one else to talk to. You always said you would talk to me, but you never did. I used to call you up so I could hear your voice, but then I was too afraid to speak. Sometimes I said your name, but whenever I did you hung up on me.' Tears were flowing freely down her cheeks, her tiny body was shaking. 'I just wanted you to love me, Kirsten,' she sobbed. 'I wanted you to be a part of our family, just me, you, Laurence and Tom. I even killed Anna so that she wouldn't come between us all.'

Kirsten watched her, feeling so impotent and so torn apart with shock that she just didn't know what to say.

'Mummy,' Jane whispered, holding a hand out towards Kirsten.

Kirsten looked at it, not knowing whether or not she should take it, in the end she left it.

Jane continued to cry. Kirsten stared down at her hardly able to think. It wasn't credible, Jane could never have done something like that, yet Kowski's voice was ringing in her ears. 'It would take a physicist to work something like that out . . .' Kowski had said, and Jane's father was a physicist, had tried to encourage Jane to become one too, had taught her chemical formulas . . . Kirsten's head fell forward as she thought of Anna, saw her body being carried from the set – the innocent victim of a madness that had been festered by an unimaginable loneliness and need to be loved. A madness that was at last surfacing through the layers of buried emotion and destroying the poor, tortured mind that harboured it.

'What about Jake?' she whispered.

For a moment or two Jane didn't answer, then her voice came, almost as an echo, from the depths of a bottomless pain. 'I didn't mean to kill him,' she croaked. 'I liked Jake, I didn't want him to die.' She raised her head, blinked as though clearing her vision. Her pale skin was mottled, huge tears still rolled down her cheeks. 'It was supposed to be you,' she said staring absently into the fire.

Kirsten looked at her.

'You were going to shut me out,' Jane said.

Still Kirsten could only look at her.

'You were going to take Laurence away from me. I tried everything I could to get close to you, to show you that I loved you, but Laurence was the only one who cared. You never cared. You were nice enough to me when it suited you, but you laughed at me, Kirsten, and mocked me, just like all the others. Then you told Laurence you wanted me to go.'

'Oh Jane, why did you never speak to one of us about the way you were feeling?' Kirsten groaned.

But Jane wasn't listening. 'I didn't want to go. I wanted to stay. I'd never had a family before, the people you gave me to, they didn't want me. They hated me. You didn't want me either, but Laurence did. He wanted me to stay, but you were going to make him push me out. I loved you, Kirsten. I loved you so much, why didn't you want me?'

'Oh Jane, I did,' Kirsten said, going to kneel in front of her. 'I was trying to think of what was best for you.'

'No. You didn't care about me. You just wanted me to go. No one ever wants me. No one's ever cared about me . . .'

'I care about you, Jane.'

Jane's desperate eyes searched Kirsten's face. 'Do you?' she said.

Kirsten smiled and nodded, but though her heart was churning with pity all she wanted was to get Jane out of the house. It made no sense to be so afraid of a tiny scrap of a girl, but she was.

Jane looked down at their joined hands. 'They'll be coming for me soon, won't they?' she said brokenly. 'They'll take me away and lock me up and I'll never see any of you again.' She lifted her head and gazed at Kirsten with wide, desolate eyes. 'I don't want to go to prison,' she said. 'But I'll have to, won't I?'

'I don't know,' Kirsten answered.

'Do they have the electric chair in New Orleans?' Jane whispered.

'Oh God,' Kirsten groaned. 'I don't know, Jane. I . . .'

Suddenly Jane started to giggle, then jamming her hands and legs out in front of her she started to vibrate as though being electrocuted.

'Jane stop it! Please!' Kirsten cried, gripping her shoulders and holding her steady, but suddenly Jane was on her feet. She moved so fast that Kirsten didn't even know what was happening until the blinding pain exploded in her head. She staggered back against the chair.

'Jane, stop, please,' she cried, holding out her hands to defend herself.

'Liar! Liar! Liar!' Jane screamed, slamming the poker relentlessly down on Kirsten's hands, cracking her fingers, bruising her arms. 'You don't care about me! No one cares about me!'

'Jane! Jane!' Kirsten cried.

Jane backed towards the fire, her eyes fixed on Kirsten. She picked up the shovel, stuffed it into the hot coals then brought it out again, overflowing.

Kirsten watched, dumbfounded. It was as though it was all happening in slow motion as Jane's arm started to glide through an endless arc and the shimmering red and black coals flew through the air.

It was the pain of the fire searing into her flesh that brought Kirsten to her senses. Leaping to her feet she made a dive for Jane and brought her to the floor. Jane made no attempt to struggle, she simply lay there, panting for breath and staring up at the ceiling.

After a while Kirsten pulled herself up, lifting Jane with her and leaned her back against the fireside chair. 'I want to help you,' she said softly. 'I'm not going to desert you, but please, Jane . . . .'

'Why didn't you love me?' Jane mumbled. 'Why didn't you want me?'

'Jane, please listen to me – '

'They hated me, the people you gave me to. They never loved me like Laurence did. He is my father, isn't he?' he said, turning pleading eyes to Kirsten.

Kirsten didn't answer. She knew that somehow she had to get Tom away from here or at the very least get help, but using the phone while Jane was there was out of the question. She wondered if she could contrive a reason for going upstairs, she could use the phone in the bedroom.

She looked down at Jane's colourless face. For the moment she seemed calm. Carefully Kirsten edged herself out of their embrace and got to her feet.

'Don't leave me,' Jane whispered as Kirsten reached the door. 'Please, don't leave me.'

Kirsten turned back to see Jane's crumpled, forlorn little body huddled on the floor. She was a stranger, yet that peculiar little face was so familiar. And seeing the helplessness and bewilderment in Jane's eyes Kirsten was almost tempted to go back. 'I won't be long,' she said gently.

Jane's gaze returned to the fire. Kirsten walked to the bottom of the stairs. She was on the point of going up when she heard Jane move. She turned round, saw Jane coming and put out her arms. Suddenly Jane's hand whipped out from behind her back and the poker crashed brutally down on Kirsten's wrists.

Kirsten cried out, snatched her hands back, gasping at the excruciating pain. Jane lifted the poker again. Kirsten ducked, the poker slammed against her skull and she staggered to her knees.

'He's my father!' Jane cried. 'You're trying to take him away, but I won't let you.'

'Jane, please,' Kirsten choked, clutching the stair rail and trying to pull herself up. It was strange how, despite the reality of the pain, she still couldn't make herself believe this was happening.

'He loves me! He cares for me! Why don't you? You're my mother! Why don't you love me?'

Kirsten started to speak, but suddenly her head snapped back as the poker crashed into her face. Blood spurted from her lips and nose. She choked, spluttered and groaned in agony. Somehow she managed to push past Jane and stagger into the kitchen where she fell against the sink, turned on the tap and almost screamed as she brought the cold water to her injuries. But the pain was nothing compared to the fear.

'Laurence won't want you if you're not beautiful,' Jane said, coming in after her, and to Kirsten's horror she snatched a knife from the wall.

'Jane, for God's sake, please stop this,' Kirsten choked, backing up against the sink, but there was an inhuman energy in Jane's eyes and Kirsten could see there was no reaching her. As Jane lunged Kirsten twisted herself away, but Jane grabbed her hair and dragged her head back so far that Kirsten clutched the sink to keep herself up.

As the knife plunged towards her face Kirsten let go of the sink and dropped to the floor. The knife cut through the air, but already Jane was lifting it again. Kirsten rolled away, throwing herself under the table, so panicked and shaking so hard it was as though every part of her was bound in paralyzing knots of terror.

She watched helplessly as Jane flung the chairs across the kitchen. Then everything went silent. She could see Jane's legs, standing at one end of the table, unmoving. Briefly she turned her head to see if the way was clear to the door, but when she turned back she saw Jane start across the kitchen as though sensing her intention. It was then that Kirsten saw the canister of dry-ice leaking tendrils of smoke in the corner.

'Oh God help me,' she mumbled.

Jane was standing at the door now. With an energy that defied her injuries Kirsten pulled herself up at the other end of the table. Jane was watching her, her grey eyes glittering with fear, sobs of terrified laughter spluttering through her lips.

'Jane, please, put the knife down,' Kirsten implored. 'Put it down and then we can talk.'

'But there's nothing to talk about any more. It's too late. I know you don't want me, I know you're never going to love me . . .'

Kirsten was about to speak when a sudden wave of dizziness swept over her and she clutched the table to hold herself up.

'Kirstie, why is your face bleeding?'

At the sound of Tom's voice Kirsten's head came up. 'Oh my God,' she muttered, starting across the room. 'Tom! Go! Go back upstairs!' but Jane already had hold of him.

'Jane, he's just a baby, for God's sake let him go!' Kirsten cried, her heart freezing with terror.

'It's all right, Tom,' Jane was saying, as she dragged him into the sitting room. 'No one's going to hurt you. You just be a good boy now.'

'Kirstie!' Tom wailed, trying to look back over his shoulder.

'Jane! Let him go!' Kirsten shouted, but as she came up behind her Jane spun round, lashing out with the knife.

Kirsten gasped as it sliced into her hand. Tom struggled to break free, screaming Kirsten's name, but Jane wrenched his arms behind him and held the blade to his throat.

'This is the baby you want!' she sobbed. 'But he's not yours. You can't have him. He's mine and Laurence's. He's not yours!'

'Jane, don't do this to him,' Kirsten begged. 'You love

him, you can't . . . _Jane_!' she screamed as the point of the blade sunk into Tom's tender flesh.

The whole of Tom's body was shuddering with sobs as he gulped Kirsten's name.

Jane's tormented eyes held Kirsten's. 'You're all going to be together,' she said. 'You're going to have everything you've ever wanted and I'll be alone. No one will care about me. But why should you have everything? Why should Tom have so much love when I never had any?'

'Jane,' Kirsten pleaded, her voice shrill with panic, 'can't you see that if you do anything to Tom you'll break Laurence's heart. If you love him, Jane . . .'

'Daddy!' Tom whimpered.

Jane looked down. Kirsten seized her chance and slammed bunched fists into the side of Jane's head. The knife flew across the room as Jane crashed against the back of the sofa and grabbing Tom's hand Kirsten fled to the front door.

'I want my Daddy! I want my Daddy!' Tom gulped.

The front door was locked. There were no keys. 'It's all right, darling,' Kirsten panted and hitching Tom under her arm she ran as fast as she could up to her bedroom.

She slammed the door behind her and heaving Tom on to her hip dashed to the phone. The line was dead.

'Oh no,' she muttered under her breath, realizing that Jane must have disconnected it.

'I don't want Jane to be frightening any more,' Tom sobbed.

'No, sweetheart, neither do I,' Kirsten mumbled looking frantically around the room and wondering what to do next. Then realizing there was no lock on the door she ran into the bathroom and locked the door behind her.

Still holding Tom she turned on the tap and put a facecloth under the running water. Then putting his head back she dabbed at the cut on Tom's neck. To her relief it was no more than a scratch. Not so the one on her hand and as she stared down at the gaping flesh she felt a terrible, nauseating fear rush through her. What the hell was she going to do now?

She lowered the lid of the lavatory seat and sat down, holding Tom tight. She must make herself think. There was a way out of this, there had to be, but dear God how much easier it would be if Tom weren't there.

Suddenly she stiffened. The creak of a floorboard, the soft tread of footsteps. Jane was coming up the stairs.

Kirsten's head was pounding. Even after all that had happened she still couldn't accept that it was Jane, the Jane they had known – at least thought they'd known – and loved who was doing this.

'Kirsten! Kirsten!' Jane called.

Tom buried his face in Kirsten's neck and clutched her tightly.

'Tom? Where are you, Tom?' Jane's voice was as normal as if they were playing hide-and-seek.

'I think you must be in here,' Jane said and Kirsten knew she was at the bedroom door.

She listened, every nerve in her body clenching with fear as Jane's footsteps drew closer.

'Yes, I think you're in here,' Jane said, and both Kirsten and Tom jumped as Jane rattled the door.

Kirsten tried to look down at Tom, but his face was still pressed against her neck. 'It's all right, sweetheart,' she whispered, smoothing his hair. 'It's going to be all right.'

She could hear Jane moving about in the bedroom and closed her eyes tightly. How in God's name had this happened? How could a person have changed so much, or hidden so much for so long? Never in a million years would she have thought Jane capable of anything like this. What the hell had her parents done to her to have forced her into imagining herself the daughter of someone else? What kind of cruelty had they inflicted? Just what had happened to her to have devastated her so completely?

'You see, you're shutting me out again, Kirsten,' Jane said. 'But it doesn't matter any more. I know Laurence loves you and Tom, but he loves me too. He'll still have me.'

Tom's fingers tightened on Kirsten's dressing-gown and Kirsten, her eyes glued to the door, nervously kissed the top of his head.

'Bye bye, Tom,' Jane said. 'You stay there with Mummy.'

'I want my Daddy,' Tom whispered, pulling his head back to look up at Kirsten.

'I know, darling. He'll be here soon,' Kirsten answered, wishing to God it were true. She didn't even want to think about how Laurence was going to take it, knowing that he had trusted his precious son to the care of someone so profoundly disturbed. But nothing had happened to him, at least not yet.

She listened as Jane's footsteps retreated across the bedroom. The bedroom door closed and dimly she heard Jane walking down the stairs. For a while she heard nothing, then it was as though furniture was being dragged across the hall. Oh please God, Kirsten prayed, don't let her be barricading us in . . . Suddenly she froze. The dry-ice! And at the very instant the thought occurred to her she saw the smoke curling its way in under the bathroom door.

'Jesus Christ!' she gasped springing to her feet. Fear

was battering her mind so hard she couldn't remember what Kowski had said. 'Can't shout . . . Can't move . . . Kills within seconds . . .' Nearing hysteria she glanced about the bathroom. Jesus, of all the rooms to have chosen, there was no window!

She looked down, the smoke was already getting thicker, she could smell it now . . . *It was entering their bodies!*

Hardly knowing what she was doing she pushed Tom's face inside her dressing gown, snatched up a towel and tore open the door. A cloud of lethal gas billowed in her face. She pressed the towel to her mouth and nose and started across the bedroom, already feeling her limbs beginning to drag. As she reached the window Tom's weight was starting to pull her down. She dropped the towel, reached out for the catch, fumbling and holding tightly to her breath. She staggered, tears blinded her. Her head hit the window as she started to fall. She pressed a hand to the sill, trying to hold herself up. She lifted a hand again, clung on to the catch and as she sank to her knees she pulled it down with her. A gust of wind caught the window and flung it open. Kirsten leaned towards the fresh air, gulped at it, then feeling a small strength returning to her limbs she turned back, grabbed the smoking cannister and hurled it into the garden below.

Shuddering and panting she let her head fall against the window-frame, closing her eyes and thanking God for their escape. She jumped as suddenly the front door slammed.

'It's Daddy!' Tom cried wriggling to get down.

'No!' Kirsten said, snatching him back. 'No, you can't go down. Not until we know for sure if it's Daddy.'

She walked unsteadily to the door, opened it a fraction

and listened. The house, the street outside, the whole world, it seemed, had been plunged into sudden and total silence. Her ears were straining for any kind of noise that might tell her Jane was still in the house, but as the minutes ticked by there was still only silence. Nevertheless, she wasn't going to run the risk of taking Tom down with her, so returning to the bathroom she set him down on the lavatory and crouching in front of him said, 'I want you to be a brave boy now, darling. I want you to stay here while I go downstairs and I want you to promise me you'll bolt the door behind me. OK?'

Tom stared at her, wide-eyed with terror.

Kirsten's heart turned over. 'OK?' she repeated huskily, struggling to fight back the tears.

'I want to stay with you,' Tom said, his bottom lip starting to tremble.

'I know, sweetheart,' she said hugging him. 'But I promise you, I'll be right back. And nothing's going to happen to you because I won't let it. Now, will you do as I say and bolt the door? Daddy'll be so proud of you when he hears how brave you've been.'

At last Tom let her go and waiting only until she heard the bolt slide across, Kirsten started gingerly down over the stairs. The hall was in chaos. The table had been overturned, books dragged from the shelves, coats and umbrellas were strewn across the floor and the coatstand was teetering precariously against the sitting-room door.

Kirsten picked her way through the mayhem, her eyes darting from side to side, her heart crashing in her ears. Carefully, she lifted the coatstand away from the door and stood it upright. Then, her mind feeling as though it was about to explode with tension, she pressed down on the handle and slowly pushed the door open. For several seconds she stood where she was, scanning the room with her eyes, then leaning towards the door jamb she peered through to see if Jane was behind the door. There was nobody there.

She turned away and stole quietly towards the kitchen. The door was open, she could already see inside. The kitchen was empty, but then her eye was caught by the cupboard door under the stairs. Too afraid to open it she pressed an ear to it and listened. Instantly she froze, but then realized that it was her own breathing she could hear. She put her hand on the door knob, squeezed it hard as she turned, then abruptly threw it open and jumped back towards the kitchen.

Nothing moved. Everything was still. Silent. Kirsten turned round. Her throat was parched and still burning from the chemicals. She walked over to the sink and turned on the tap. She drank, long and deep, then putting the glass on the draining board she leaned heavily against the unit, shaking uncontrollably as the tension ebbed from her limbs. All she had to do now was get Tom out of here and go straight to a phone. She had no idea where to tell them to start looking for Jane, but right now that didn't matter.

Drawing a hand through her dishevelled hair she turned round and as she looked back down the hall her heart dissolved in terror.

'Jane,' Kirsten mumbled. 'Jane, please stop this.'

Jane's face was ravaged with grief, saliva and mucus leaked from her mouth and nose, her matted hair was plastered to her cheeks. Her hands were behind her back, but Kirsten was in no doubt that she was once again holding the knife.

She knew she was insane to go near her, yet knew too that she had no choice. Where Jane stood she was between Kirsten and the stairs, she could get to Tom and there was no way of being sure that Tom would keep the door locked.

Jane's face twitched. Her bottom lip shuddered against her teeth as she giggled and watching Kirsten come steadily towards her, her frightened, bewildered eyes continued to glitter. Then suddenly she was wielding the knife.

Kirsten's heart catapulted against her ribs. 'Jane, I just want to hold you,' she breathed. 'You're my baby . . .'

'No! Get away from *me*,' Jane yelled, but as Kirsten's hand closed around her wrist, she let the knife fall to the floor and collapsed sobbing to her knees.

'It's all right,' Kirsten said, kneeling beside her and putting her arms around her. 'It's going to be all right.'

'I'm sorry,' Jane sobbed, hardly able to draw breath. 'I didn't mean to do it. I don't want to go to prison. Don't let them take me, Kirsten, please don't let them take me.'

'Ssh, ssh,' Kirsten soothed burying her face in the back of Jane's neck and pulling her closer. She didn't see Jane's arm snake out, neither did she see Jane's fingers closing around the handle of the knife . . .

— **37** —

Laurence sped up over the Hammersmith flyover his foot jammed flat on the accelerator as he careered perilously from one lane to the other. He was aware of the police sirens behind him and glancing in the mirror saw the blue flashing light weaving furiously through the traffic. He changed down to give himself more power. The car screeched in protest, another driver bumped his car on to the pavement to clear the way. The lights ahead were turning green and pressing his hand on the horn Laurence blasted his way through the sluggish traffic.

Of all the times for his goddamned car to have broken down this couldn't have been a worse one. He'd have been at Kirsten's by now if he hadn't had to go through the rigmarole of borrowing a car from Ruby's neighbour and having to explain the urgency. He'd tried calling Kirsten from Ruby's, to his horror Jane had answered. She'd said no more than hello before hearing his voice then ringing off and disconnecting the line. He'd left his father at Ruby's to contact the police and keep trying Kirsten's number until he got a reply.

He wasn't even trying to understand why Jane had done what she had, couldn't even begin to grasp the horror that someone as docile as her, as close to his family as she was, had killed two people, for right now none of that mattered. All that mattered was that he got there before anything happened to Kirsten.

As he attempted to force his way through red lights, ignoring the hoots and fury of other drivers, he saw the police car bump up on to the pavement, swerve around the filtering traffic and screech to a halt in front of him. He didn't even wait for them to get out of their car, instead he leapt from his own, ran to meet them and explained who he was and what he was doing, thanking God for the publicity surrounding Kirsten's arrest, which meant that one of the officers recognized him.

Within minutes they were once again speeding

through the streets of London, this time with the police car in the lead, and one of the officers shouting frantically into his radio.

Blood was still streaming from the wound in Kirsten's shoulder, the pain was stiffening her arm and as she drifted in and out of consciousness her only thought was for her baby.

Dimly she was aware of Jane sitting beside her, of thin fingers stroking her face and depleted sobs gently convulsing the frail shoulders that hovered through her clouded vision.

'Jane,' she whispered, trying to lift herself up. 'Jane, you have to get help. Please!'

'I'm sorry,' Jane murmured, her hands moving gently through Kirsten's hair. 'I'm sorry. I didn't mean to do it.'

'Jane,' Kirsten's voice was so frail it was barely audible. 'Jane, I'm going to have a baby, please help the baby . . .'

'I'm sorry,' Jane whispered. 'I didn't mean to do it.'

Kirsten's head fell back as another wave of dizziness overcame her.

'You're so beautiful,' Jane choked, touching Kirsten's face with her blood-stained fingers. 'So beautiful.'

Kirsten's eyes fluttered open. For a moment her vision was clear. Jane was looking into her face, intently, yet Kirsten knew she wasn't seeing her. Then Jane's other hand came up. The knife was still dripping blood.

'Laurence is my Daddy,' she said, and as the knife moved towards Kirsten's stomach Kirsten suddenly found an energy that was beyond human power.

'No, not my baby,' she gasped, grabbing Jane's hand. 'Not my baby.'

'Why do you protect it and not me!' Jane sobbed. 'Why don't I matter to you?'

'You do, Jane. You do,' Kirsten breathed, keeping hold of Jane's hands as somehow she pulled herself up. The pain in her shoulder was lessening as that side of her body turned numb.

Jane hunched her shoulders, drawing her hands and the knife between her knees.

Grabbing hold of a stair rail Kirsten prayed silently to God as she heaved herself to her feet. She staggered forwards as dizziness swelled through her again. But she was stronger now, she was almost up . . . She could get help . . .

But as she started down the hall she felt Jane's hand close around her ankle. 'No, please, no,' she sobbed, clinging to the stair rail to keep herself up.

'I don't want to hurt you,' Jane sobbed, wiping a hand over her tear-stained face. 'I don't want to do it . . . Not to you. But no one cares about me . . .'

'Oh God, Jane, no!' Kirsten choked, starting to reach for her.

But Jane only giggled, that pathetic, lonely little sound she so often made and with the knife clenched in both hands she fixed her sorrowful eyes on Kirsten's and drove the blade deep into her gut.

'Jane! Jane!' Kirsten cried, throwing herself against her.

Jane fell awkwardly to one side, her hands still holding the knife. Blood was oozing from the wound as tears of pain and torment poured from her eyes. 'I love you, Kirsten,' she whispered.

'Oh Jane! Jane, please . . .' Kirsten wept, cradling her head. 'Jane, you've got to hold on . . .'

Suddenly the front door crashed open.

'Kirsten!' Laurence cried running towards her. 'Oh my God! What happened?'

'You've got to get help,' Kirsten gasped.

'It's right here. The police are with me. Dear God, Jane,' he said, seeing the blood running over her hands.

Jane's eyes were barely focused as she looked up, but seeing the dark shadows of police uniforms start to surround them she croaked, 'I want to stay with my Mummy. Please let me . . . stay with . . .'

'It's all right, I'm here,' Kirsten said hugging her.

'Sssh,' Laurence soothed, pulling Kirsten up into his arms as the ambulancemen began filing into the hall. 'Oh, Jesus Christ, look at you,' he said, seeing the blood seeping from Kirsten's shoulder.

Kirsten turned back to look at Jane, but as she made to reach out for her Laurence held her more tightly. 'Let them take her, sweetheart,' he said.

'She's my Mummy,' Kirsten heard Jane whisper brokenly to the men who stooped over her. 'She's my real Mummy.'

'Oh God,' Kirsten groaned, turning her face into Laurence's shoulder. 'We can't let her go like this, we have to go with her.'

'It's all right,' Laurence said, holding her close and over her head he nodded at an ambulanceman who was preparing to take her. 'It's OK,' he said softly, 'I'll bring her out.'

'Oh God, Laurence,' Kirsten said, lifting her head. 'Tom. We have to get Tom.'

Laurence's face turned white. 'What do you mean?' he said.

'He's upstairs.'

'What's happened to him!' Laurence shouted starting up over the stairs. 'Where is he?'

'He's upstairs. In the bathroom.'

'What the hell's he doing here?' Laurence demanded panic blazing in his eyes.

'Jane brought him.'

As Laurence vanished Kirsten turned to look on helplessly as Jane was carried from the house.

'I think we'd better get you to hospital, miss,' a policewoman who had come to stand beside her said. 'That wound looks pretty nasty to me.'

Kirsten looked up as Laurence appeared at the top of the stairs holding Tom tightly in his arms. 'I'm sorry, Laurence,' she said. 'I'm so sorry. I had to get him to lock himself in, it was all I could think of.'

'Ssh, ssh,' he said, drawing her into the circle of his arm as he reached the bottom of the stairs. 'You did right. He's fine, just a bit shaken, isn't that right, soldier?'

'Excuse me, miss, but I really think you should come along with us now,' an ambulanceman said.

Laurence looked down at the wound in Kirsten's shoulder. 'Go on,' he said gently. 'I'll take Tom home and meet you there. Which hospital are you taking her to?' he added to the ambulanceman.

'Charing Cross.'

'OK, I'll come as soon as I can.' He looked down at Kirsten. 'Will you be all right?'

'Of course. Just see to Tom.'

'What was it all about?'

'I'll tell you later,' Kirsten whispered, tears welling in her eyes.

'Don't think about it now,' Laurence said, kissing the top of her head. 'Just get yourself to the hospital, I'll follow on as quick as I can.'

As Kirsten, escorted by the ambulanceman, reached

the door she turned back. 'Did you see Pippa?' she asked, feeling as though she was asking about something that belonged to another world.

Laurence nodded.

'And?'

'Later,' Laurence said, looking away. 'We'll talk about it later.'

It had been dark for several hours by the time Laurence and Kirsten arrived back at the house. The doctor had wanted to keep Kirsten in overnight, but Kirsten had refused. She wanted only to be with Laurence now, for him to be there as she tried to come to terms with all that had happened. During the afternoon they had both given statements to the police while Jane underwent emergency surgery. She was in intensive care now, her condition reported to be stable though serious. Kowski had been at the hospital too, though neither Kirsten nor Laurence had ventured to ask what would happen to Jane once she was in a position to leave the hospital.

By the time Kirsten and Laurence left there had still been no sign of Jane's parents, though Laurence himself had called to tell them their daughter was undergoing surgery.

'It makes you wonder just what kind of people they are, doesn't it?' Kirsten said, going to sit beside Laurence on the sofa and relaxing carefully into his arms. Her shoulder was heavily bandaged, her arm was in a sling, the cut on her lip had two stitches, the one on her hand had four.

'Bad enough for her to fantasize that we were her parents,' Laurence said, rubbing a hand over his tired eyes.

'Did you ever have any idea?' Kirsten asked. She was

staring down at the scorch marks on the rug, hardly able to believe that it had all happened that morning when already it felt like a lifetime ago.

Laurence shook his head solemnly. 'Not one. I mean I knew it was important to her to feel she was a part of the family, but it seems none of us understood just how important.'

'God, what she must have been going through all these years . . . It doesn't bear thinking about.'

They sat quietly for a moment. 'I know it's too late for this now,' Kirsten sighed, 'but I keep thinking of all the times I told her I'd spend time with her and never did. Of all the things she did to please me and I never really showed any gratitude. I suppose the trouble was I didn't notice her half the time. She sort of blended into the background and we all just took her for granted.'

'You know what intrigues me,' Laurence said, 'is how Dyllis Fisher got to find out so much. Did Kowski tell you, by any chance?'

Kirsten shook her head, then moved to one side to let him stand up as the telephone rang. While he want to answer it Kirsten switched on the TV to listen to the news. And that was how she discovered all that had been going on during the afternoon while they were at the hospital. Dyllis Fisher, it was reported, had been charged with perverting the course of justice and conspiracy to murder. Billy Fields, the chief location manager – and Jane's boyfriend – had also been charged. Not surprisingly, though nonetheless pleasingly, all charges against Kirsten had been dropped. She couldn't help a wry smile as she watched an interview with Dermott Campbell who was delightedly announcing his intention to sue Dyllis for fraudulently using his name. Then a reporter did a piece to camera from outside Charing Cross Hospital where 'Jane Cottle is under police guard, but has still not yet regained consciousness after her operation.'

Laurence came back in time to catch the end of the report, Kirsten filled him in on what had been said while he was out of the room.

'It's so awful to think that the little romance Jane had in her life was just a sham,' Kirsten said. 'Dear God, Dyllis Fisher's got a lot to answer for. What do you think will happen to her now?'

'It's hard to say, but I'd stake my life on the fact that she'll try to buy her way out of this.'

'Then I shall make damned sure she doesn't. And what's more I'll ask Dermott Campbell to help me.' She grinned. 'Now there's poetic justice if ever there was any,' she remarked. Her smile quickly faded. 'Actually what happens to Dyllis isn't important really is it? She's just a bitter and twisted old lady who's getting her comeuppance with all the terrible publicity she's receiving and who, if there is any justice in the world, is going to find herself behind bars for what she's done. It's what happens to Jane that matters. I feel so responsible, so . . . Oh, I don't know. I just want to make sure she gets all the help she needs. If I can I want to try and stop her being extradited and put somewhere here where she'll receive the counselling she should have and where we can visit her.'

'Mmm,' Laurence said.

Kirsten turned to look at him. 'What's the matter?' she said. 'Don't you want to help her?'

'Yeah, sure I do,' he said, shifting his position slightly. 'It's just . . .'

'Just what?' Kirsten prompted.

'I don't know. I guess I've just got other things on my mind right now.'

'Oh God,' Kirsten groaned, 'How could I have forgotten? It's the hearing tomorrow. Who was that on the phone? Hellerman?'

'No, my mother. Tom won't settle.'

'Then maybe you should go over there and be with him. It was quite an ordeal for him.'

'He'll be OK,' Laurence said, kissing her forehead. 'What matters right now is you.'

'I'm fine, at least I think I am. Maybe I'm still in shock, I don't know. But Laurence, you have to think of Tom. If Pippa wins tomorrow this could be your last night with him.'

'It won't be,' Laurence said.

Kirsten drew herself up looking at him curiously. 'What do you mean?' she said. 'Has something happened?'

'Yes, but it can wait.'

'I'd rather you told me now,' she said, an uneasy sensation starting to gather at the pit of her stomach. Oh, dear God, no. She couldn't take any more. Not today. Please let her be reading this wrong. 'Laurence?' she said, as he got to his feet. 'Laurence, what is it?'

'I told you, it can wait.'

'No,' she said shaking her head. 'I want to know now.'

He turned round and when Kirsten saw the look on his face a debilitating numbness started to creep into her heart. 'Laurence, tell me, please.'

'There's nothing to tell,' he said.

'Laurence! Don't lie to me. Something's happened and I want to know what it is.'

'Kirstie, you've been through enough for one day. We'll talk about it tomorrow.'

'No! How the hell do you think I'm going to sleep knowing that you're holding something back from me. I want to know now – whatever it is.'

'Kirstie, don't make me do this. For your own sake . . .'

'Oh God, Laurence, you're frightening me. What's happening to Tom? You said you saw Pippa? Did she say something?'

'Yes, she said something.'

'Then what!'

'She's decided that Tom should stay here in England,' he said, unable to meet her eyes.

'But that's fantastic, isn't it?' Kirsten said uncertainly. 'Aren't you pleased?'

'Yes, of course I am. It was what I wanted. Well, you know that . . .'

'But?' she said.

At last he turned to look at her and reaching out to take her hand he pulled her gently to her feet. 'Kirstie, you know how much I love you, don't you?' he said.

'I thought I did,' she breathed her eyes darting between his.

'I do. I love you, Kirsten, and I don't ever want you to doubt that.'

'Then why am I starting to?'

His head fell back. 'Oh God, I don't know how to tell you this,' he groaned. 'Not now, not ever.'

'Laurence, please,' Kirsten whispered, feeling the numbness in her heart turning to ice.

'Pippa's agreed to let me have custody . . .' he said. 'But not quite the way we wanted.'

'Then in what way?'

'She wants to come back. She wants us to be a family again.'

For a long time Kirsten just stared at him. She knew that the pain was there, struggling its way through, but for the moment all she knew was the incapacitating shock that now, after all they had come through, she was going to lose him anyway. In the end she gently extracted her hands and said, 'Then that's what you have to do.'

'Oh God,' he murmured. 'I shouldn't have told you, not tonight.'

'It's all right,' Kirsten said calmly, but deep down inside she knew it wasn't. 'If that's how you get to keep Tom, then that's what you must do.'

'I love you, Kirstie. I'll always love you.'

She smiled shakily. 'I think you should go now,' she said.

'I'm not leaving you tonight . . .'

'Laurence, please. I . . .' her voice faltered, but mustering her courage she tried again. 'I think it would be best if you did. Please, don't argue. There's no point dragging this out, it'll only be more painful for us both. Laurence *please*,' she said as he started to argue again. 'You've made your decision, I understand the decision, but I want you to go.'

She turned away, so desperate to cling to him, to beg him to stay and so filled with pain at the knowledge that for the second time in her life she was losing him while carrying his baby that she couldn't look at him any more. For one fleeting moment she almost told him, the words were there on her tongue crying out to be spoken, but she stopped herself. She couldn't do that to him. She loved him too much to want to see him so torn apart by the agonizing choice she would force on him.

A few minutes later she heard the door close behind him and at the sound of it she knew that her whole life was breaking irreparably apart.

— 38 —

'I can't work out what's going on,' Campbell grumbled, throwing his coat down on a chair as he came in through the door.

'Did you speak to Laurence?' Helena asked, removing her feet from the table, putting down the paper and handing him his coat back.

'No. He wasn't there,' he answered taking his coat and hanging it up.

'But surely his mother told him you were coming,' Helena cried. 'Where was he?'

'God knows. No one was in, not even his parents. Did you call Kirsten?'

'Yes. I left a message on her answerphone, but she hasn't called back.'

'So where the fuck is everyone?' Campbell complained.

'I can tell you where Kirsten is,' Helena said, going to sit down again. 'Or at least where she was this afternoon.'

'I can tell you where she was this afternoon,' Campbell stated looking at the untidy shelves of paperbacks. 'She was at the hospital with Jane Cottle, where she's been every day this past week. I listen to the news, too.'

'OK, don't get antsy with me,' Helena said.

Campbell turned round. 'Why don't you go round there?' he said.

Helena's luminous eyes regarded him for a moment, then shaking her head she picked up the paper again.

'But why, for God's sake? If it's true she and Laurence have split up then she could probably use a friend right now.'

'If she wants me she knows where I am,' Helena answered.

'Shit, you and that pride of yours!' Campbell seethed. 'You can't still hold a grudge against her for thinking you were trying to set her up, not after all she's been through.'

'I'm not holding a grudge,' Helena responded tartly. 'I'm just saying, if she needs me she can call. And I for one don't believe that she and Laurence have split up.'

'Then why is he at his parents' house and she's still there in Chelsea? And why is Pippa over here when she should be in Tuscany with Marigliano?'

'And why has Dyllis Fisher been remanded in custody when Billy Fields got bail? I don't know, Dermott. I'm as much in the dark as you are. Now quit hassling me will you? I've tried calling her because you asked me to and she hasn't bothered to call back. So why don't we just let them get on with their lives, God knows they've had enough interference.'

'Mmm,' Campbell grunted. 'You were prepared to go and see her the day you found out she was bailed,' he reminded her.

'And I changed my mind.'

'Why?'

'I don't know, I just did. Look, if we're going to get into another fight about this then I'm out of here. I've about had it with your obsession over what's happening between those two. If they have split up then they'll get back together, you can bet your life on that. So, can we talk about something else?'

'Yeah, you can tell me how Jane's doing. I only caught the last part of the news, did they say anything about her condition? Is she getting any better?'

'Stable, is all they said. And I don't call that changing the subject.'

Campbell was shaking his head. 'You've got to be just about the only person in this country who's not interested in what's happening with that family. Why?'

'I don't see what difference it's going to make to my life what the hell is happening to them. You've got a new career to start over, I've got to find myself another job. Life goes on, Dermott. Now tell me about your meeting with Phillip Lowe today. Is he going to give you a column?'

'Yep. I turned it down.'

'What! Why did you do that?'

'Because I've decided to freelance, that's why. I'm tired of doing assassination jobs on people, which is what he wants. What I want is to earn a decent living for once in my life. I want to be one of the good guys,' he grinned. 'Do you have a problem with that?'

'In believing it, yes,' Helena answered with an ironic smile. 'But you do what you want, it's none of my business.'

'Then you'd better start making it your business,' he retorted, 'because I don't want a wife who's not interested in what I do.'

'Then you'd better go find yourself someone else,' she said.

Campbell rolled his eyes. 'This hard to get act of yours

isn't washing with me,' he said. 'I've already booked the register office, we're getting married a week on Monday.'

'Then you just better go and unbook it, hadn't you?' Helena said, smiling sweetly.

But Campbell wasn't listening. 'I wish to God I could get hold of Laurence,' he said. 'I want him to be my best man.'

'Hah!' Helena cried. 'If you think I can't see through that then you're an even bigger dickhead that I thought you were.'

Campbell looked at her mystified.

'You, Dermott Campbell,' she said, walking towards him and poking him in the chest, 'are just using me and this farce of a wedding as an excuse to get to Laurence without seeming the nosy, interfering, scandal merchant you are. "Hello, Laurence. How you doing, Laurence? Want to be my best man, Laurence? Oh and by the way Laurence, is that right you and Kirsten aren't an item any more?" You, you double-crossing, underhanded, transparent little jerk, are looking for a scoop to start off your new career. And what better scoop is there right now than the inside story on Kirsten and Laurence? So, if you think I'm going to marry you just so's you can set the ball rolling by asking Laurence to be your best man, then think again, buddy.'

'Shit, you've got one convoluted mind, Helena,' Campbell said incredulously. 'It didn't even occur to me to do anything like that. But now you come to mention it, it's not such a bad idea.' He nodded thoughtfully. 'Mmm, it's not a bad idea at all. Yeah, I can see we're going to work pretty well as a team you and me.'

'Forget it. I just told you, I'm not marrying you. And I sure as hell am not encouraging you to use our friends

– 679 –

and whatever traumas and tragedies they might be going through to further your sordid little ends.'

'As a matter of fact,' Campbell said seriously, 'I happen to care a great deal about what's going on between Kirsten and Laurence. I even care about that kid lying there in hospital and what she's going to go through once she comes out. And you can tell me different until you're blue in the face, but I happen to know that you care too.'

Helena turned away, but not before he'd seen the tell-tale anguish darken her eyes.

'Come on, what is it?' he said gently, putting a hand on her shoulder. 'What's the real reason you won't go to see Kirsten?'

'If I tell you, you'll end up despising me,' she answered. 'Not that I care about that. You can despise me all you want . . .'

'Helena, let's just get to the bottom of this, shall we?'

She took a deep breath, shrugged his hand from her shoulder then walked back to the table and sat down. 'The truth is,' she said, running her finger around the rim of her wine glass, 'that I reckon Kirsten and Laurence have split up. He's gone back to Pippa and I just know what that will have done to Kirsten. Right now she's doing all she can for Jane, but sooner or later she'll have to face up to the fact that it's over for her and Laurence and . . . and if she cracks up, the way she did last time, if she goes under the way I reckon she will . . . well, I'm not the one to handle it. Don't get me wrong, I want to. God knows I want to, but I'm afraid. I'm afraid that one day I'll walk into that house and find her . . . find her so pumped full of pills or floating in a bath filled with blood or . . . Oh, I don't know, but if she did something like that I just don't know what I'd do. I'm not a good enough friend to her, I never have been and . . .' She looked up and her eyes were pleading with him to understand a deficiency in herself she was finding it impossible to justify. 'Dermott, it's not me she wants, it's Laurence. It's always been him and nothing I do is going to change that. I can't watch her fall apart, I just can't. I'm no Paul Fisher. I can't hold her together the way he did, I can't bring her through it and I don't want her to think I can when I know I don't have it in me to do it. So please, don't ask me to call her any more, don't ask me to go round there and don't let's talk any more about getting married. I'm a selfish bitch, I know, but I can't help her and I can't help the way I am either. She's got to face it alone. I don't want to be there to see it and have to deal with the fact that it's all my fault.'

'How is it your fault?' Campbell challenged.

'You, of all people, need to ask that question,' she cried. 'You were the one, Dermott, just over a year ago now, who gave me her phone number just after she'd got back from France. And I was the one who went round there, who pretended to be her friend, who persuaded her into going to that goddamned party at Laurence's. I was the one who didn't have the guts to say no to your blackmail and I was the one who sold her down the river to save my own skin. OK, I know all that changed later, but I was the one who set it all rolling. And look what's happened. Two people are dead, there's a kid lying there in hospital in God alone knows what state and despite the way you and I both know they feel about each other Laurence and Kirsten haven't made it through. No, I'm not getting involved in her life again, Dermott, she's better off without me and it's hard enough handling the guilt without having it stare me right in the face.'

'And if she does end up killing herself? How are you going to feel then?'

'Fucking awful. But she won't. Something will happen to save her at the last minute, it always does with Kirsten.'

'That's what you always say, but one of these days, Helena, you might just find out you're wrong.'

Kirsten was sitting beside Jane's bed in the private ward she'd had her moved to as soon as the doctor had declared her out of danger. It had been almost two weeks now since the day Jane had attacked her and Laurence had left, two weeks in which Kirsten had tried hard to accept that the nightmare was reality, but it was as though her mind could only hover over the truth, occasionally grazing it, then pulling back sharply as it found the pain. She knew that sooner or later she would have to let it in, to face it and deal with it and already there were times when it came, unbidden and unprepared for, closing around her like a vice as though to crush her. But mainly she was able to hold herself away from it and think only about the hour she was living, to take herself steadily through each day and not think about the future.

She gazed down at Jane's hand lying limply on the stark white sheet and covered it with her own. It was hard to say what her feelings towards Jane were now, all she knew was that being here and doing all she could to see Jane through was giving her a sense of purpose she badly needed.

There was a tube inserted into Jane's wrist another

into her nose. Her face was deathly pale, her lips were cracked and dry, her feathery lashes were fluttering gently as she struggled out of a deep and dreamless sleep.

Kirsten knew it would take some time, it always did, but she would come round eventually and they would talk some more. Not for long though, Jane tired so easily. The doctor had confided to Kirsten the day before that by now he'd hoped to be seeing more signs of recovery. But she was a little stronger than when she'd first regained consciousness, he'd said, and that she was talking now was a good sign.

Kirsten was her only visitor, if one discounted the detective who had taken over the case since Kowski had returned to New Orleans. He was a kind man, but a busy one. He only ever stayed long enough to listen to Kirsten's reports on what she and Jane had talked about then he went, leaving a uniformed officer on duty outside.

There had still been no sign of Frank and Amy Cottle, the people who had adopted Jane at a year old and had never cared enough even to take a photograph of her childhood. There were flowers though, from Kirsten, from Ruby, from Thea and Don – and from Laurence and Pippa. The ones from Laurence and Pippa had arrived three days ago and even now Kirsten could still feel the terrible ache in her heart that she'd felt when she'd seen their names together on the card.

She'd spoken to Laurence that morning. He'd called to find out how Jane was and to ask if he could come over and pick up his and Tom's belongings.

Kirsten glanced at her watch. He'd probably be there now and as the pain raked itself through her she silently prayed that he understood why she'd asked him to come when she wasn't there. It would have been hard enough facing him, but watching him take everything of himself from the house would have been too much to bear. As it was just hearing his voice on the phone, hearing the dark intimacy of his tone that told her he was suffering just as much as she was had caused her such indescribable pain that she had made him promise never to call her again. Staying in touch was only going to make it worse for them both. Laurence had argued, had reminded her that there was still a great deal to do to clear up the film, but Kirsten had told him she was putting it all into the hands of her lawyers. When at last he had given his promise Kirsten had felt as though a part of her was dying, but she knew it was for the best.

She started to smile as at last Jane's eyes came open. 'Hello,' she whispered. 'How are you feeling?'

Jane's fingers tightened slightly on hers and gently Kirsten returned the pressure as Jane tried to smile. 'Is Laurence here?' she croaked.

'No,' Kirsten answered. 'It's just me.'

Jane's eyes drifted closed as the disappointment she felt showed in a tiny spasm across her brow. 'Can I have some water?' she whispered.

Kirsten stood up, poured some into a glass then raised Jane to hold the drink to her lips. She didn't take much, most of it dribbled from her mouth and dripped on to the pillow. Kirsten took a tissue and wiped her face. 'Better?' she said.

Jane nodded. 'I was thinking,' she said after a while, her voice so frail Kirsten had to lean forward to hear. 'After you left yesterday, I was thinking. All those things Billy told me, when he said that you and Laurence didn't want me . . . None of it was true, was it?'

'No,' Kirsten said, brushing the wispy hair from her

– 684 –

forehead. 'None of what Billy told you was true. And I explained what you heard me say to Laurence was only a part of it. We were never going to let you go unless you wanted to.'

Kirsten knew now, because Billy had made a full confession to the police, how cruelly he had fuelled Jane's fears that she and Laurence were going to dismiss her. How he had worked Jane to such a pitch of desperation that she had lost her precarious grip on what little sanity she had until she'd thought the only way to save herself was to do the same to Kirsten as she'd done to Anna.

'So Billy didn't care about me either,' Jane said softly a single tear sliding from the corner of her eye and running down into her hair. 'I knew he didn't. He said that if you did get rid of me I could always go to him, but he didn't mean it.'

'We weren't going to get rid of you,' Kirsten said. 'We love you and care for you very much, Jane.'

Slowly Jane shook her head and closed her eyes. 'You can't. Not after what I did to you. I know I hurt you, but I don't remember much about it now. I was frightened. I could hear the baby crying, but I'd killed it. I remember doing that. I threw him against the wall. But it wasn't a baby, was it? It was a doll. My doll. I'd had it since I was a baby. Did you give him to me, before you gave me away?'

Kirsten didn't know what to say, so clasping Jane's hand in both of hers she lifted it to her mouth and kissed it.

'Mummy?' Jane said after a while.

'Mmm?' Kirsten answered.

Jane opened her eyes. 'Can I call you Mummy?' she asked.

Kirsten smiled. 'If you like.'

'I know you're not my mother really,' Jane said. 'But I wish you were.' She turned her head slightly. 'When I get better, when they let me leave here, can I come and live with you again?'

'Of course.' Now was not the time to be telling Jane about the ordeal she would have to face when she was released.

'And can I pretend that you and Laurence are my parents? I don't know who my real ones are, but they can't be as nice as you.'

'You'll always be a part of our family,' Kirsten said.

Jane sighed and closed her eyes again for a while. 'You know what Laurence told me?' she whispered.

'What did he tell you?'

Jane's lips parted and there was a distant echo of the nervous giggle that was so much a part of her. 'It was a secret,' she said. 'Laurence told me a secret.'

'Did he?' Kirsten smiled at the pride in her voice.

'Do you want to know what it was?' Her eyes opened. 'I expect he's told you by now, but he told me first. He is going to ask you to marry him.'

As Kirsten's heart turned over a sob rose in her throat. 'Is he?' she said.

Jane nodded. 'It was our secret. Don't tell him I told you, will you?'

'No, I won't tell him,' Kirsten said, swallowing hard.

'You should be married if you're going to have a baby,' Jane said.

Kirsten looked at her.

'You are going to have a baby, aren't you?'

Kirsten smiled. 'Yes,' she said. 'Yes, I am.'

Jane's grey eyes widened slightly. 'You mean you're already pregnant?' she said.

For a moment Kirsten looked confused, then realizing that Jane must have forgotten she'd already told her and that her questions were about the future rather than the present she laughed softly. 'Yes, I'm already pregnant,' she said.

To her surprise Jane's eyes filled with tears. 'Laurence said he wanted a little brother or sister for Tom and now he's going to have one.' She started to cry, tiny sobs hiccoughing from the fragile depths of her. 'You're all going to be a family and I . . . I . . . What's going to happen to me, Kirsten? What are they going to do to me?'

'They're not going to do anything,' Kirsten soothed, taking her in her arms as best she could. 'No one's going to hurt you, we're all going to do everything we can to help you.'

'But I killed two people. I've got to be punished for that. I know I have. And I know that Laurence won't let me see Tom any more and he won't let me see the new baby either. He'll be afraid of what I might do. But I didn't mean to do those things . . . Honestly, Kirsten, I didn't mean it.'

'I know you didn't,' Kirsten said, hugging her. 'And Laurence isn't going to stop you seeing the new baby, I promise you. And we're not going to be a family without you, Jane. We're going to be a family together. You me and the baby. Would you like that? Just us three?'

'But what about Laurence and Tom?'

'Laurence and Tom are with Pippa, where they belong. And you're going to be with me, where you belong.'

'But Laurence and Tom don't belong with Pippa, they belong with you,' Jane argued.

'No, sweetheart. Pippa's Tom's mother and he should be with her.'

'And I should be with you because you're my mother?'

'If that's the way you want it, yes.'

Jane was quiet for so long after that that Kirsten thought she had fallen asleep again. But in the end she spoke. 'Kirsten,' she said. 'If Laurence has left you, if he's gone back to Pippa and you're . . . You won't . . . You won't do what you did last time to the baby, will you?'

'No,' Kirsten assured her. 'No, I'll never do that again.'

'That's good, because I want to have a little brother or sister. Pippa will give Tom one, and you will give me one.'

'That's right,' Kirsten said knowing that Jane didn't realize how much those words had hurt.

Jane did sleep then and it was two or more hours before she woke up again. When she did she seemed dazed and disoriented, kept asking Kirsten to tell the baby to stop crying and calling out for Laurence. 'I want my Daddy,' she said when Kirsten tried to calm her. 'I don't want you, I want my Daddy. He loves me, he won't let you get rid of me.'

She started to shiver, her skin broke out in a sweat, her eyes were dilating and her mouth kept opening and closing in silent screams. Kirsten fetched the doctor and a few minutes later she left knowing there was nothing more she could do that day. It wasn't unusual for Jane to wake up that way, Kirsten had seen it several times before, though the fever had seemed slightly worse today. She'd call the hospital later to find out how Jane was and then she'd set about finding out just who would be the right psychiatrist to treat her.

The moment she arrived home she knew that Laurence had been. Little things were missing, like the shoes at the bottom of the stairs, the books from the shelves, the old jeans he'd left in the downstairs bathroom to dry. She hunted around to see if there was a note and it was only when she didn't find one that she realized how desperately she'd wanted one. But maybe there would be one beside the bed. Except right now she just couldn't bring herself to go upstairs, to find his side of the wardrobe empty, his shaving things gone, his loose change scooped off the dressing table. It would be too painful to look at the bed they had shared and know he wouldn't lie there any more, to wander into Tom's room and find all the trains and pictures and other toys gone. Suddenly her heart contracted, so painfully she almost cried out. And she knew then, as she looked at the keys he'd left beside the phone, that this really was the end now. He wouldn't be coming back, there was no reason to. Of course she could always give him a reason, but she was still resolved never to tell him about the baby.

She thought of Jane then and wondered if she had done the right thing in telling her. It was hard to know, but tomorrow she would ask Jane to keep it as their secret just in case Laurence did go to see her.

Should she, she asked herself, call Laurence and ask him to go? Jane had said several times now that she wanted to see him. Kirsten knew he'd go if she asked him to, but feeling the way she did right now she knew she wasn't up to speaking to him. If she did she was sure she'd break down. The house seemed so empty, it was as though he had taken its very soul and all she wanted right now was to beg him to come back. To beg him not to make her face the fact that they would never sleep together again, never eat together, bath together, work together, laugh together or grow old together. For now there was little she could do about the great gulfs of longing that threatened constantly to overwhelm her, nor the panic that suddenly flared as though to consume her. But they would ease in time. Though she must stop those foolish moments when she tried to guess what he might be doing now. Or worse when she pictured him making love to Pippa the way he had with her. It was such torture, such unnecessary torment that she knew she had somehow to control it.

Maybe, she was thinking as she took off her coat and hung it up, she would call Laurence in the morning. By then she might not be feeling so close to the edge. With any luck Thea or Don would answer then she wouldn't have to speak to Laurence at all. She could just leave a message telling him that Jane wanted to see him. But what if he turned up at the hospital while she was there? What if Pippa answered the phone? Oh dear God, what if Tom did?

No, she wouldn't call, she'd send a note through the post. In it she'd ask him to let her know when he intended to go and she would stay away that day. She would use the time to go and see her lawyers to find out how things stood with Jane and with the film. Perhaps she would go and clear out her office as well – the lease was due to run out at the end of the month and Vicky had left several messages asking her if she was intending to go in. She'd bring home some cassettes of the rushes, a memento of a career that nearly was. She had no thoughts of a career now. All that mattered now was the baby. And Jane. She swallowed hard on the guilt she felt at being so grateful to Jane for needing her. What had happened to Jane was a tragedy, yet it was Jane's helplessness that was giving Kirsten the strength to get herself over these first terrible weeks of loss. Poor Jane. She had never known what it was to be loved, to matter as much to someone as she and Laurence mattered to each other, as Tom mattered to them all. But Kirsten was going to make that up to her, she was going to care for her and make sure she was there during all the dreadful times to come. It was ironic really to think that now, at last, Jane was so needed. It was what she had always wanted and Kirsten hoped that one day Jane would be well enough to understand just how much she had been needed.

'Where is everyone?' Laurence asked, walking into the sitting room and finding only Pippa.

'Your parents have gone to some function at the American Embassy,' Pippa answered, putting aside the manuscript she was working on.

'And Tom?'

'Upstairs. Sulking.'

Instantly Laurence's face darkened. 'Why?'

'Why do you think?'

'Did you smack him again, Pippa?'

'As a matter of fact, yes. He deserved it. He was so bloody rude to me . . . Where are you going?' she cried, getting to her feet as Laurence turned to leave the room.

'To see to Tom, where do you think?'

'Laurence! We've got to present a united front on this. He's getting out of hand and you know it.'

'What he's getting is smacked,' Laurence said tightly, 'and I'm not siding with you on that, Pippa. You can't expect to walk back into his life and have him behave as though nothing has happened. He doesn't trust you. He's afraid you're going to leave him again.'

'Bullshit! He's afraid he's never going to see Kirsten Meredith again, that's what he's afraid of.'

'Of course he is. He loved her, Pippa, and he's going to need some time to deal with it . . .'

'He's had over a month now, how much longer does he need?' she snapped angrily.

'How much longer do you need?' Laurence countered.

Pippa turned away.

'Look,' Laurence sighed, letting go of the door and coming back into the room. 'This hasn't been an easy time for any of us, but I thought we agreed that Tom should come first.'

'He does,' Pippa said miserably. 'It's just that I get so hurt when he talks about Kirsten and what she would and wouldn't let him do.'

'I know,' Laurence said, putting a hand on her shoulder. 'But you've got to be patient, Pip. He's just a child and all he can see right now is a mother who's always angry with him.'

'Always?' Pippa said turning to look up at him.

Laurence nodded. 'Pretty much.'

'I do love him, you know that, Laurence, don't you?'

'Sure I do. You just got to convince him of that. And smacking him isn't the way.'

'But what am I supposed to do when he's so defiant and throws those godawful tantrums the way he does? Do I just let him get away with it?'

'No. But don't hit him. Try to reason it out with him and *tell* him you love him.'

Pippa tilted her head to one side and brushed her cheek against his hand. 'You still miss her too, don't you?' she said softly.

Laurence swallowed hard. 'Yeah,' he said. 'I miss her.'

'Are we doing the right thing here, Laurence?' Pippa

asked, her eyes shining up at him the same way Tom's did whenever he was unsure of something.

'I don't know,' he answered, dropping his forehead on to hers. 'I wish to God I did.'

'I want it to work,' Pippa whispered. 'And I know you're doing everything you can, so I guess it's for me to try a bit harder, mm?'

'I guess so,' Laurence said, folding her into his arms. As he gazed up at the ceiling he was trying hard to suppress the resentment that was flooding through him. If only she would admit it wasn't going to work, if only she would give up and go back to Zaccheo where she really belonged. Neither of them were happy and neither of them truly believed they could be, but until Pippa was ready to give up there was nothing he could do. Perhaps if Tom was willing to go with his mother it might make things easier, but as it stood, there was no way in the world Tom was going to let go of his father – he felt safe and secure in Laurence's love and Laurence couldn't even begin to contemplate doing anything to shatter that.

But, dear Christ, he missed Kirsten. Not a minute of the day went by when he didn't think about her and long to pick up the phone and speak to her. He'd stuck by his promise not to call because he'd known it was her way of handling things, but it was tearing him apart. He was so afraid of what might be happening to her, how she was dealing with the blow of Jane's death so soon after everything else. He knew she'd do everything she could to pull herself through, but what he didn't know was whether, ultimately, she had the strength. She'd suffered too much in her life, was too vulnerable, too dependent on the love she had for him – as he was on the love he had for her. They shouldn't be apart this way, they needed each other in a way that he and Pippa never had nor never would.

Lately, his sleeplessness had become constant and his inability to make love to Pippa was, he was sure, soon going to become permanent. He wanted only Kirsten, his entire body and soul ached for her in every way imaginable.

He was due to start work on a new project the following week, but his heart wasn't in it. With Kirsten he could have gone to Hollywood and with Kirsten he guessed he could make just about anything work. But all the dreams they had shared of a great future together had turned to ashes the day Pippa had asked to come back. And now the fear that Kirsten's life was falling irreparably apart haunted him night and day. He didn't want to break his promise, but he knew that sooner or later he was going to pick up that phone because he just had to know if she was all right.

Hearing the front door close and his parents' voices in the hall Laurence let Pippa go. 'I'd best go see to Tom,' he said.

Pippa smiled sadly. 'I'll come with you,' she said. 'And then, Laurence, I think we'd better talk. We've got to sort something out here, something that's going to work for us all – but I think you already know what the answer is.'

'Do I?' Laurence said.

'Yes. You want her back. You can't stop thinking about her . . . Neither can Tom. And if she can make you both happier than I can then perhaps I should go back to Zaccheo and leave you two to get on with your lives.'

For long moments Laurence looked down at her, then putting an arm around her shoulders as they turned to walk from the room and trying to hold back on the euphoria, he said, 'At least we tried.' Dear God, how he wanted to go to the phone right now and call her, to tell her he loved her and ask her to take him back. But Pippa was right, they had to talk first and sort out just what her relationship with Tom was going to be.

Smiling distantly to herself Kirsten looked down at the letter she was holding and read it again. It had arrived that morning along with a letter from her lawyer telling her that Dyllis Fisher had once again been refused bail and that there was every likelihood now that she would not only serve a prison sentence for conspiring to commit a murder, but would be forced to hand over the reins of her power to someone of a more stable disposition. Kirsten had thrown that particular letter away. She wanted to hear no more of Dyllis Fisher. The law would take its course and as far as Kirsten was concerned the bitter need for revenge that had driven Dyllis was not going to be what drove her. That was all a part of the past now and the only pleasure Kirsten could feel in Dyllis's downfall was relief to be free of her.

The other letter however, Kirsten had kept and had read several times already that day. Each time she did she could only marvel at the cruel way life played these little tricks, reminding her of all she'd once dreamed of and letting her know that now it would never be. She wondered if Laurence had received the same letter, but reminding herself that it did no good to think that way, she put the letter down and ran upstairs to continue her packing.

Since she'd made the decision to leave, to take herself back to France and bring her baby up in the depths of Provence, she had felt much better. They would be happy there, the two of them, safe and secure and as unlikely to cause Laurence any more pain as they were to be discovered by the press. Paul had left her well enough provided for so that she need never work again, but she would fulfill the contract she had with the publisher and write her book. That wasn't going to be easy, she knew, but she'd take her time over it and only write when she felt up to it. And maybe, one day, she would feel the need to go out into the world again and take on the challenge of getting her ideas on the screen. But for now that ambition had left her. Whether it had gone with Laurence or whether it was because she wanted her baby to come first she didn't know and what did it matter? She was getting her life sorted out, she was coming through and though she missed him every hour, every minute of the day, she reminded herself constantly that in time the pain would ease. In time she would hold his baby in her arms and could give it all the love in her heart.

For a moment she stopped what she was doing and sat down on the bed. She knew she was going to cry, was willing to let the tears come. The doctor had told her that bottling up her emotions the way she had been was no good for either her or the baby. It hadn't been easy at first, but now she sometimes wondered if she would ever stop. And as the terrible voice of denial started to cry out inside her, trying to turn her back from a future without Laurence, she took the picture of him from beside the bed and hugged it to her.

Eventually she dried her eyes, got up and went into the bathroom to splash cold water on her face. It was all right, it really was, it was just that sometimes the memories stole over her and made it hard to be strong. She loved this house, had known such happiness here that she was dreading leaving it. But she could always come back, she reminded herself. There was nothing in the world that was making her do anything she didn't want to do and right now she really did want to leave. She needed to sever the bonds that still tied her to Laurence, to remove herself from the temptation to call him and tell him how much she still loved him. In her heart she knew that his suffering was as great as hers and to do that to him would only make it worse.

Walking back into the bedroom she continued with her packing. She wished desperately that she had someone to talk to, someone with whom she could share all that was in her heart, maybe then the burden wouldn't seem quite so great. Jane's death, strangely, hadn't come as such a surprise, but filling the void she had left was hard. She knew it was madness to blame herself for all that had happened, that in coming back she had brought only pain and misery to those she loved, but it was difficult not to. In her bleaker moments she saw herself as someone who carried bad luck with her, who was in some way tainted by the hand of misfortune and passed it on into the lives that touched hers. But thinking that way served no purpose and besides gloomy thoughts would make for a gloomy baby – or so she told herself.

As she snapped one suitcase shut and opened another she was wondering whether or not to call Helena before she left. It would be so good to hear her voice, to see her even and be able to apologize for all the hurt she must have caused her. Whether or not Helena would forgive her was hard to say. It had been over three weeks now since Helena had left a message on the answerphone. Had she not been pregnant Kirsten would have called her long before now, but she didn't trust herself to see Helena and not tell her about the baby. If she did that then there was no doubt in her mind that Helena would go straight to Laurence.

However, now that the flight was booked for the following morning, her packing was all but complete and it was too late in the evening to ask Helena to come over, there was little chance she'd do more than say how sorry she was and wish Helena good luck for the future.

She looked across at the telephone and almost laughed at the bolt of nerves that began agitating her stomach. Maybe she should call Laurence, too. They should say goodbye, that way the break would be cleaner. In fact, now she came to think about it, to disappear without a word the way she was planning would hurt him immeasurably. So yes, maybe she should call him; she didn't have to tell him where she was going, but she could at least let him know that she was all right.

The bedroom was in such chaos that she decided to go downstairs and use the phone. When she reached the landing she stopped. Was this really such a wise thing to do? They'd made a pact not to contact each other and though she longed every day for him to break his promise . . .

She started as the telephone rang. Instantly she wondered if it was him even though she knew it wouldn't be. But it might be. This time it might just be him and allowing the hope to gather in her heart she ran down the stairs.

She didn't even see the little toy train that she stepped on, neither did she see the packing case at the bottom of the stairs. It all happened so fast that all she knew was the blinding dagger of pain that shot through her head just before the ringing stopped and she was swallowed into the swirling realms of darkness.

Thea let herself quietly into the room and closed the door behind her. Helena looked up from where she was sitting beside the hospital bed, her fingers curled around Kirsten's.

'How is she?' Thea whispered.

'Still sleeping.'

Thea walked to the bed, leaned over and brushed a loose strand of hair from Kirsten's face. 'Thanks for letting me know,' she said.

'Have you told Laurence?'

'No. Not yet.'

'Will you?'

Thea smiled down at Kirsten's pale face. 'He tried to call her last night,' she said. 'There was no answer . . . Well, we know why now. Thank God you got to her in time.'

'Helena?' Kirsten croaked.

'Yes, I'm right here,' Helena said turning back to her. 'How are you feeling now?'

Kirsten was blinking, trying to clear her vision. 'I'm not sure. My head hurts . . . Where am I?'

Helena smiled. Obviously Kirsten had still been too dazed when she'd regained consciousness earlier to register anything Helena had told her. 'In the hospital,' she answered.

'Why? What happ . . .' Kirsten stopped and as she

squeezed her eyes tightly closed Thea left the room to go and find the nurse.

'Lie still,' Helena admonished gently as Kirsten tried to lift herself up.

'Who was in here?' Kirsten asked.

'It was . . .' Helena stopped herself, any reference to Laurence might not be wise right now. 'Just a nurse,' she said.

'How did I get here?'

'By ambulance. I came round, last night. I thought it was time we patched things up.' She laughed shakily. 'Talk about leaving it until the eleventh hour. Anyway, I knocked and knocked. I could see the lights were on so I knew you were in. I was terrified you might have . . . Well, you know . . . So I ran next door to use their phone. The police broke the door down and the ambulance brought you here.'

Kirsten was shaking her head and smiling, as though silently chiding herself for having caused so much fuss. 'Thank you,' she said, tightening her hold on Helena's hand. 'I don't deserve you as a friend after the way I treated you.'

'It's me who doesn't deserve you,' Helena whispered. 'But we'll leave that for another time.'

Kirsten looked down at their joined hands then lifted her head and smiled. 'It wasn't deliberate,' she said. 'I know you think it was . . .' She swallowed hard on the lump rising in her throat. 'I would never have done anything like that not when . . . not when . . .'

'It's all right,' Helena soothed as Kirsten's eyes filled with tears.

'Helena, tell me, please . . . The baby . . . Is it all right?'

'Baby?' Helena repeated.

'Oh God,' Kirsten said, closing her eyes as fear pushed her heart into her throat. Surely that would have been the first thing they'd do, check if the baby was still alive and if they hadn't mentioned it to Helena . . .

'Helena, please, you have to find out for me.'

'Find out what?' Helena asked.

'Whether or not I . . . I lost the baby when I fell.'

'Oh Christ,' Helena groaned. 'You mean you're pregnant. Oh God, Kirstie . . . I'll go and fetch the doctor right away. You just stay right there. Don't worry, it'll be all right. I promise you, everything will be all right.'

When the door opened a few minutes later the doctor came in alone. Kirsten took one look at his expression and covered her face with her hands.

Later in the day, Helena brought Kirsten fresh clothes to travel home in. She wasn't at all sure that the doctor would release Kirsten, but after he had checked her over earlier Kirsten had been so insistent that she was all right to leave that Helena had thought it wise to bring the clothes, if only to humour her.

When she walked into the room she found Kirsten sitting on the side of her bed looking . . . Helena blinked. She looked almost radiant. Of course her cheeks were still pale, so too were her lips and the edge of the cut where she'd hit her head on the packing case showed vividly just beneath her hairline, but her eyes were shining so brightly they were very nearly dazzling.

'For someone who's just tried to top herself you look like you just won the pools,' Helena remarked.

'I didn't try to top myself,' Kirsten retorted. 'And maybe I have won the pools. At least, in a manner of speaking.'

Helena eyed her sceptically.

'Oh, Helena, you should see your face,' Kirsten laughed. 'I'm all right now, honestly. They wouldn't be letting me go home if I weren't.'

'But I've never seen such a quick recovery. And are you sure the doctor said you could leave, because I'm warning you, I'm not being an accomplice to anything he hasn't agreed to.'

'If you don't believe me then go right ahead and ask him yourself. We had a long chat this afternoon,' she pulled a face, 'I have to spend the next couple of weeks taking it easy, but on the whole he thinks we'll both be all right. Oh Helena,' she said as an unsuppressible emotion flooded from her heart. 'I just can't believe it . . .'

'Hey,' Helena laughed, taking Kirsten in her arms as tears started in her own eyes. 'Come on now, that baby's sure to be all right. After all he's come through and he's still hanging on.'

'He?'

'OK, she. What does it matter just so long as it's all right?'

'It doesn't matter one bit,' Kirsten laughed, using her fingers to wipe away the tears.

'Why the hell didn't you ring me?' Helena said.

'Why didn't you ring me?' Kirsten challenged.

Helena gave a wry smile. 'Now that,' she said, 'is a long story and one I'm not particularly proud of. But we'll save it, shall we, until you're out of here and back on your feet.'

'OK. But tell me what's been happening to you?' Kirsten smiled. 'How are things working out with Dermott?'

Helena's eyebrows arched comically as she pulled up the corners of her mouth. 'We got married,' she said.

'Two weeks ago. He bulldozed me into it, but I'm kind of glad he did.'

'Oh, Helena, congratulations,' Kirsten laughed, putting her arms around her again.

'I guess we're destined for the divorce courts, at least that's what I keep telling him, but I reckon we might rub along all right together. He's not a bad sort of jerk as jerks go.'

Kirsten was laughing. 'Did you have a honeymoon?'

'Not yet and to tell you the truth I don't want one. At least I don't fancy what he wants very much.'

'Why? What does he want?'

'Brace yourself. He wants to take a nice slow train ride from anywhere to anywhere just so long as it's slow and just so long as he can get off whenever he wants. Me, if I had to suffer that, I'd push him off just for being a dickhead, but I don't guess we'll be going anywhere until we get some money together. He's hoping for a real bundle out of Dyllis for using his name the way she did, but in the meantime he's as broke as I am.'

'But haven't the lawyers paid you for the movie yet?' Kirsten said.

'Sure they have, but we've got to live on something till Dermott gets what he's calling his inheritance.'

'I'll tell you what,' Kirsten laughed. 'I've rented a cottage in Provence. I should have been going this morning. Well, I can't now, at least not for another week or so, so why don't you and Dermott go there?'

Helena was shaking her head. 'You think I'm running off and leaving you now?' she said. 'Someone's got to look after you and make sure you rest up and that's just what I'm going to do. I've already told Dermott I'm leaving him for a fortnight. He's threatening to come too, but don't worry . . . .'

They both looked round as someone knocked on the door, and the smile faded from Kirsten's lips as Thea put her head in.

'Thea?' she said, feeling a painful lurch in her heart.

'How are you feeling?' Thea smiled.

Kirsten's eyes darted to Helena. 'Better,' she said. 'Yes, much better, thank you,' but Helena could see the haunted look that had come into her eyes. Obviously Kirsten was thinking that she, Helena, might have told Thea about the baby.

'It's all right,' Helena whispered, 'No one knows. I haven't breathed a word.'

'Are you well enough to receive a little visitor?' Thea asked.

Kirsten's eyes widened with uncertain delight.

'He's right outside,' Thea said. 'Shall I get him?'

'Yes,' Kirsten said, starting to laugh. 'Oh, please yes.'

Thea opened the door, popped her head out and said, 'OK, put that back and then you can come in.'

Kirsten was already crying by the time Tom flung himself into her arms. 'Kirstie!' he shouted. 'I've just had a go in a wheelchair!'

'Have you?' she laughed through her tears. 'And what was it like?'

'Brilliant. You ought to give it a go.'

'I will,' she said, holding him so that she could look at him and kiss him some more.

'I've got a present for you,' he declared.

'You have?'

'Yep, I did a painting of you. I put it up on my wall at home, but Granny said you might like to have it. So I brought it with me.'

'Then where is it?' Kirsten laughed.

Tom looked up at Thea, suddenly confused. 'I forget the next bit,' he said.

It was Kirsten's turn to look at Thea in confusion. 'I think he must have left it in the car,' Thea laughed. 'I'll go and get it.' At the door she turned back, and catching Helena's eye signalled for her to come too.

'So,' Kirsten said to Tom when they were alone. 'What have you been up to?'

'Oh lots of things. But I missed you, Kirstie. I even cried because I missed you. Mummy got angry with me, but Daddy said it was all right to cry. He told me a secret. He said that he cried too because he missed you.'

'Did he?' Kirsten whispered shakily, 'I miss him, too.'

'Didn't you learn yet how to keep a secret, Tom?'

Just the sound of his voice was enough to make Kirsten's heart tighten so painfully that as she turned to see him standing at the door she felt an uncontrollable rush of tears lodge in her throat.

'Hello,' she said, swallowing hard as she tried to smile.

'Hello.' His eyes were dancing mischievously, but Kirsten could see the concern and instantly felt her cheeks colour. Did he too think she had tried to kill herself?

'Did you bring in my painting, Daddy?' Tom asked chirpily.

'It's right here,' Laurence said, putting it on the end of the bed. 'A pretty good likeness, huh?'

Kirsten felt a bubble of laughter rising from the very core of her heart as she looked down at the awkward spindly limbs, the fiery bush of hair and smiley face. 'You're so clever,' she said to Tom, shaking him and squeezing him.

Laurence came to sit on the bed beside them and lifted a hand to run it over Kirsten's hair. 'I love you,' he whispered. 'If anything had happened to . . .'

'It's not what you think,' Kirsten said. 'It was an accident, I promise you.'

His eyes were looking deep into hers.

'I swear it,' Kirsten said, and at last he started to smile.

'I tried to call you . . .' he said. 'Last night . . .'

'You mean that was you?'

'Yeah. Or I should say it was us,' he added, chucking Tom under the chin.

'I dialled the number,' Tom said proudly. 'I know it off by heart now.'

'And what were you calling about?' Kirsten asked, looking at Tom.

'We were ringing to ask if we could come home,' Laurence answered.

Kirsten's heart stood still. She hadn't heard him right, she couldn't have . . .

'Can we, Kirstie, please? Can we?' Tom begged.

Kirsten turned her eyes to Laurence. 'I don't understand,' she said. 'What about . . .?'

'We're getting a d-i-v-o-r-c-e.'

'And c-u-s-t-o-d-y?'

'Mine. She's not going to fight it now. I'll explain later, when old big ears here is out of the way. So what do you say, can these two guys who love you come home?'

'Why are you crying, Kirstie?' Tom said, his own chin starting to wobble. 'Don't you want us to come?'

'Of course I want you to come, silly,' she said, hugging him.

Laurence waited until she let Tom go, then turned her mouth to his and kissed her softly. 'There's something else I want to ask you,' he murmured.

'You mean about the letter? Did you get one too?'

Laurence looked baffled. 'What letter?'

'Never mind. I'll tell you about it later. What were you going to ask?'

'As a matter of fact I was going to ask you to marry me.'

'Oh yes!' Tom cried triumphantly. 'Oh please, Kirstie, say you'll marry us. Please.'

Both Kirsten and Laurence burst out laughing. 'How can I possibly refuse,' she said, ruffling his hair and feeling a deep sadness that Jane wasn't there to share in this moment.

'Oh yuk! Not more of them, Daddy,' Tom cried, pushing Laurence away. 'Come on, let's go home.'

Laurence looked at Kirsten. 'Are you sure you're well enough?'

'I'm well enough,' she smiled. 'In fact I've never felt better in my life.'

'So,' Kirsten said, looking up as Laurence came back into the bedroom after the third attempt at putting Tom to bed, 'what happened with you and Pippa?'

'With me and Pippa not very much,' Laurence said, taking his brandy from her and putting it down. 'With Pippa and Tom, plenty.'

'Meaning?'

'Meaning that they just couldn't get along,' he said, sitting down beside her and pulling her into his arms. 'She never was cut out for motherhood, she'll admit as much herself. Oh, she loves him all right, but she just doesn't know how to handle him. In so many ways she's like a child herself, she wants all the attention, all the praise . . . Not that she isn't prepared to give it, she's just better at taking it. She came back because she thought it was the right thing to do, and because she truly did want us to work as a family, but it didn't take long for us to see that it was going nowhere. She's still in love with Zaccheo and with him she can be a free spirit, never have to take on any responsibility she doesn't want to and never have to play second fiddle to a child. She missed Zaccheo more than she'd admit . . . Then Tom started getting on her nerves because he was missing you. They started to fight, there were tears every night . . . It was pretty bad all round.'

'Poor Tom,' Kirsten smiled. 'Anyway, he seems happy enough now and what I want to talk about is us . . .'

'You want to set a date for the wedding?'

'Get your divorce first,' she laughed.

'That's not going to take too long,' he said, lifting her chin and kissing her softly on the lips. 'God, it's been a rough road, Kirstie, but having you here at the end of it . . . Did you ever wonder, sometimes, if love was measured against pain?'

'Yes, I've wondered. Maybe that's why it's been so hard for us.'

He smiled. 'The deeper the pain, the harder the struggle, the greater the love?'

She nodded and her eyes closed as he leaned forward to kiss her.

'OK,' he said, before reaching her, 'what was all that about a letter?'

'It's right here,' Kirsten laughed, reaching across to the bedside table. But unable to contain her excitement she decided to tell him herself what was inside. 'It's an offer from Columbia to talk to us about Moyna O'Malley or any other ideas we might have for movies. They want us to go out there as soon as we can to meet with them.'

'I don't believe it,' Laurence said, scanning the letter. 'It's what we always talked about.'

'Well now you've got it.'

'We've got it,' he corrected her.

'Uh, uh,' she shook her head. 'You'll have to find someone else to boss around, I'm afraid. You see, I'm not going to be available.'

'Well I'm sure as hell not going without you,' he declared.

'Too right you're not. We're all going.' She grinned. 'All four of us.'

Laurence's smile started to fade as he looked from her eyes to her mouth and back again.

Kirsten nodded. 'We're going to have a baby.'

Still Laurence just looked at her. 'Oh Christ, I don't know what to say,' he murmured. 'Kirsten, oh God, Kirstie, are you sure?'

'Of course I'm sure.'

'Then just thank God it turned out this way. I'd never have been able to live with it, you having my baby and me not with you. But it would never have come to that, I'd have been there. I wouldn't have let you down, not a second time.'

'I know.'

Once again his eyes were studying hers and she could almost read his thoughts before he spoke them. 'How long have you known?' he whispered.

'I just found out today,' Kirsten lied, knowing that it would only hurt him to think she'd known all along and had tried to spare him. 'So,' she went on, 'I thought I could write my book and look after Tom while you're talking big ideas and big bucks with the big guys.'

He was still gazing at her, looking as though he wanted to say something but wasn't too sure what. 'I'm going to find a way of telling you how much I love you,' he said hoarsely, 'I just got to figure out the words without making you laugh.'

'Who needs words?' she smiled, 'when we've got so many other ways.'

'You sure you're up to that?' he said.

'Oh, I'm sure,' she said.

It was in the middle of the night, when they were making love for the second time, that the bedroom door opened and Tom walked sleepily into the room to find Kirsten sitting astride Laurence.

'Can I play Humpty Dumpty too, Daddy?' he said rubbing his eyes.

Kirsten looked down at Laurence who groaned when he saw the laughter spring to her eyes. And sure enough, wrapping a sheet around her, Kirsten rolled onto her back and swept Tom into the bed with them. Still, Laurence decided, he was man enough to concede defeat on this occasion, when there were going to be plenty of other chances for them to play their version of Humpty Dumpty. And, he guessed wrapping them both in his arms, tonight was a night when the three of them – four of them – really should be together.